B+T
P9-DNV-006

Alexander Pushkin:
Complete Prose Fiction

ALEXANDER PUSHKIN

COMPLETE PROSE FICTION

Translated, with an Introduction and Notes, by

PAUL DEBRECZENY

Verse Passages Translated by Walter Arndt

STANFORD UNIVERSITY PRESS
Stanford, California

RICHARD R. DRY MEMORIAL
LIBRARY
ERIE COMMUNITY COLLEGE
NORTH CAMPUS
BUFFALO, NEW YORK 14221

Title-page drawing by Alexander Pushkin, 1823

Stanford University Press
Stanford, California
© 1983 by the Board of Trustees of the
Leland Stanford Junior University
Printed in the United States of America
Cloth ISBN 0-8047-1142-9
Paper ISBN 0-8047-1800-8
Original printing 1983
Last figure below indicates year of this printing:
08   07   06

Published with the assistance of
the National Endowment for the Humanities

RICHARD R. DRY MEMORIAL
LIBRARY
ERIE COMMUNITY COLLEGE
NORTH CAMPUS
BUFFALO, NEW YORK 14221

PG
3347
.A15
1983

Acknowledgments

THE PREPARATION of this volume was made possible by a grant from the Translations Program of the National Endowment for the Humanities (an independent federal agency). A visiting fellowship at the Kennan Institute for Advanced Russian Studies enabled me subsequently to clear up a number of problems accumulated in the course of translation.

I would like to thank Madeline G. Levine for her helpful reading of some of the text, and Walter Arndt for contributing verse translations of both the poems or poetic fragments by Pushkin occurring in the prose works and the epigraphs culled by him from other poets. A few folk songs of irregular metrics, which do not lend themselves to verse translation, have been rendered by prose paraphrases in the text and footnoted accordingly.

The two maps that accompany *A History of Pugachev*, which are based primarily on the one Pushkin published with the first edition of his study, have been augmented from a variety of more recent sources to show most of the place names mentioned in the text. Smaller places, not found on commonly available maps, have been located on survey maps prepared by the Defense Mapping Agency, Topographic and Hydrographic Center (Washington, D.C.: various dates), Series N 501, 1: 250,000 (Eastern Europe) and Series N 502, 1: 250,000 (Western Siberia). I am grateful to Elena Elms and Meg Kays for their help in drafting the maps, which was made possible by a grant from the University of North Carolina, Chapel Hill.

Finally, let me thank JoAnn Van Tuyl for her excellent typing.

Chapel Hill, N.C.   P.D.
June 1981

Contents

PART TWO: A HISTORY OF PUGACHEV

Translator's Note

THE WORKS CONTAINED in this volume have been translated from the Russian texts as given in the Soviet Academy's ten-volume collected edition of Pushkin (B. V. Tomashevskii, ed., *Polnoe sobranie sochinenii*; Moscow: Akademiia Nauk SSSR, 1962–66), collated with the large, seventeen-volume edition (V. D. Bonch-Bruevich et al., eds., *Polnoe sobranie sochinenii*; Moscow: Akademiia Nauk SSSR, 1937–59).

In one respect—in the arrangement of the texts—the translation more closely follows the large Academy edition than the ten-volume one because the large edition makes less of a purely quantitative distinction between fragment and unfinished work. The ten-volume edition, arbitrarily it seems to me, places *A Novel in Letters* among the larger works while relegating to "Fragments" other important incomplete pieces, such as "The Guests Were Arriving at the Dacha" and "In the Corner of a Small Square"—two attempts at a psychological novel that were to inspire Tolstoi in writing *Anna Karenina*. Pushkin's development as a prose writer, in my view, can be observed most clearly if all his fictional pieces, except for tiny fragments and minor outlines, are placed together in reasonably close chronological sequence. Following this principle, I have moved even "We Were Spending the Evening at Princess D.'s Dacha"—a fragment very important to the understanding of *Egyptian Nights*—into the main body of the volume.

Further departures from the arrangement of the large Academy edition are that "In the Corner of a Small Square" has been moved next to "The Guests Were Arriving at the Dacha" in order to emphasize the two pieces' thematic closeness; "A Tale of Roman Life" has been put in front of "We Were Spending the Evening at Princess D.'s Dacha" for the same reason; and *The Captain's Daughter* has been placed as the last fictional piece for the sake of a more accurate chronology.

Only the omitted chapter of *The Captain's Daughter*, minor fragments, undeveloped outlines, and the apocryphal "A Lonely Cottage on Vasilev Island" have been relegated to the Appendixes. From *A History of Pugachev*, the narrative text of the first volume alone has been included under the assumption that the lengthy notes to Volume One and the source materials collected in Volume Two are of interest only to specialists.

A History of Pugachev, "A Lonely Cottage" (which was orally narrated by Pushkin and written down by a contemporary), and most of the fictional fragments (including the two pieces that were to influence Tolstoi) are given here for the first time in English translation.

The transliteration follows the modified Library of Congress system; soft and hard signs are indicated in the notes but not in the text. Russian common terms used in the translation (e.g., *guberniia*) are italicized, as are the foreign words and phrases Pushkin used. (Full or nearly full sentences in foreign languages, however, usually French, are not italicized.) In all other instances, except where noted, italicized passages show Pushkin's own emphasis.

Alexander Pushkin: Complete Prose Fiction

Introduction

ALEXANDER SERGEEVICH PUSHKIN, widely acknowledged the progenitor of modern Russian literature, was born in 1799 and died of a wound received in a duel in 1837. His greatest achievement was in poetry—lyrical, epic, dramatic—and he did not turn to prose in a serious way until the end of the 1820's, but the fiction he wrote in the last decade of his life was to have a tremendous impact on the subsequent development of Russian prose.

The art of prose writing in Russia could not boast of great accomplishments at the time Pushkin entered on the scene. Its healthiest tradition—an earthy realism in the adventure story of the seventeenth century—had left only faint traces on later picaresque novels, such as V. T. Narezhnyi's *Russian Gil Blas* (1814). The age of neoclassicism produced some works of fiction—most notably *Ernest's Letters to Doravra* (1766) by F. A. Emin and *The Fair Cook* (1770) by M. D. Chulkov—but on the whole treated fiction as an inferior genre. The prose narrative as a serious kind of literature did not come into its own until the advent of sentimentalism in the late eighteenth century. The most widely renowned cultivator of the new sensibility, N. M. Karamzin, was to be acknowledged by Pushkin in 1822 as the best Russian prose writer up to that time. Indeed some of Karamzin's stories—especially "Poor Liza" and "Natalia the Boyar's Daughter" (both dated 1792)—were to evoke echoes in Pushkin's own prose works.

The 1820's saw sentimentalism grow into romanticism. This trend was most clearly manifested in the stories of A. A. Bestuzhev-Marlinskii, among which "An Evening on Bivouac" (1823) and "An Evening at a Caucasian Watering Place in 1824" (1830) were to provoke the strongest reaction from Pushkin. E. T. A. Hoffmann's influence was reflected, above all, in the tales of Antonii Pogorelskii (A. A. Perovskii), collected in the volume *The Double* (1828). Walter Scott found his most ardent Russian follower in M. N. Zagoskin, whose *Iurii Miloslavskii* (1829) and *Roslavlev* (1831) bore the distinction of being the first Russian historical novels. The picaresque tradition, on the other hand, spawned such satirical-didactic novels of manners as the most popular work of the late 1820's, *Ivan Vyzhigin* (1829) by F. V. Bulgarin.

With the appearance of new writers and trends and with the growth of readership in the 1820's and early 1830's, prose fiction became increasingly popular. The royalties Bulgarin received from *Vyzhigin* were impressive. But the quality of this fiction, in a style that ranged from the romantics' florid rhetoric to Bulgarin's trivial verbosity parading as wit, was generally low. At least some of Pushkin's work in prose was a response to the banal trends of the time.

The few fictional fragments and outlines Pushkin jotted down before 1827 represented only occasional spurts of inspiration. There is some evidence, however, that between 1821 and 1825 he filled several copybooks with nonfictional sketches of his life and times. Since these sketches contained politically incriminating details about him and his friends, he destroyed most of them after the December 1825 uprising. But the few that survived, salvaged either by friends or by Pushkin himself, are important to the historian because they demonstrate that Pushkin's fiction—as it eventually emerged in the last decade of his life—had developed primarily from nonfictional prose.

This circumstance had a bearing on Pushkin's understanding of prose in the 1820's. At that time prose appeared to him as an antithesis to poetry, a mode of writing shorn of embellishments and deprived of histrionic gestures. Whereas poetry was all ornament and pleasant form, he wrote, prose represented pure content, tolerating no decorative frills and demanding "thoughts and thoughts, without which magniloquent phrases serve no purpose" (from the sketch "On Russian Prose"). Prose was "humble," compared with contentious, turbulent poetry, but there was also something flat-footed about it, something unimaginative, to which one "stooped," like Belkin of *A History of the Village of Goriukhino*, when poetic inspiration was lacking.

Most of Pushkin's statements characterizing prose in this way were made in the 1820's, either before he had seriously tried his hand at fiction writing or when he was just beginning to. In these statements no clear line was drawn between the prose of fiction and expository prose. At the end of the decade, however, as he became a practitioner of the trade, he came to differentiate between fiction and other kinds of prose, and increasingly appreciated prose's potential for varied applications. His realization of this rich potential was a gradual and painful one, achieved through several failures and false starts. And though he modified his original concept of prose over the years, the idea of a mode of writing that eschewed all poetic gestures remained attractive to him. His development as a fiction writer was largely the result of the tension between his original concept of prose and its later modifications.

Pushkin's first serious attempt at writing fiction—*The Blackamoor of Peter the Great*—reflects the view of prose he held in the 1820's. It is narrated in a detached, omniscient manner, most unusual for the period. Jane Austen had developed a similar authorial stance in the preceding decades, but Pushkin was probably not familiar with her works. Balzac and Stendhal had not yet published the novels that were to make their fame. In the fiction popular at the time—most notably in the works of Walter Scott and Washington Irving—authors played elaborate games in order to disguise or reveal their identity, and narrators emerged as distinct personalities. Given these conventions of the period, it was a bold undertaking on the part of Pushkin to begin his career as a prose writer with an impersonal narrative—of a kind that anticipated the development of fiction writing in the second half of the nineteenth century.

What mattered most, as Pushkin sought a new manner of writing, was not just the question of whether the author was hidden from the reader or revealed to him, whether he spoke in the first person or the third, but the question of whether he would be courageous enough to write as an intelligent chronicler whose attitudes would be subtle and implicit, without clownish masks and false assumptions. In *The Blackamoor* he projects the image of an author who does not have to pretend—for the sake of a joke with the reader or for any other reason—that he possesses only half the truth about his characters. Unencumbered by a play-acting narrator's jocular or sentimental postures, he can reveal his characters' feelings in their full complexity. His narrator knows that human affairs are beset with both passion and compromise, and he does not feel obliged to apologize for this knowledge.

Such a mode of narration, however, presented enormous technical difficulties, with which Pushkin was as yet unable to cope. Several successful scenes notwithstanding, *The Blackamoor* demonstrates that Pushkin the prose writer had not yet mastered dialogue (Ibrahim, the central hero, hardly speaks at all), or point of view (which shifts from one character to another in a kaleidoscopic fashion), or atmosphere (which at times changes too rapidly from pathetic to comic).

These technical difficulties—arising precisely from the pioneering nature of Pushkin's venture—were probably the reason why he abandoned his project.

Still, far from being discouraged by his experience with *The Blackamoor*, in the following years Pushkin endeavored to apply an omniscient mode of narration to the psychological novel—an even more formidable task. The two fragments remaining of his efforts—"The Guests Were Arriving at the Dacha" and "In the Corner of a Small Square"—were promising indeed: so much so that they subsequently influenced Lev Tolstoi in writing his *Anna Karenina* (1877). Once more, however, the technical difficulties—especially the task of expanding rapid synopsis into vivid scene—were so enormous that the two fragments remained fragments.

Pushkin's difficulty in all these early unfinished works—including an experiment with the epistolary form entitled *A Novel in Letters*—was that he insisted on treating complex material, though he had not found the right key, the right narrative point of view, the right technique for the new genres he was experimenting with. In order to find a solution, he had to lower his sights.

The Tales of the Late Ivan Petrovich Belkin signaled a retreat toward simpler subject matter, to be presented by simpler narrators, much more in keeping with the conventions of the time. Ascribing his stories to fictitious narrators, Pushkin was openly following the example of Walter Scott's *Tales of My Landlord* (1816–19) and such collections by Washington Irving as *Tales of a Traveller* (1824). Pushkin's Belkin is an essentially uneducated man, who has heard the tales he is presenting from people of his own kind; and his biography is given by an uncultured neighbor and introduced by a pompous, self-important "Publisher." The resulting volume amounts to a parodic anthology of early-nineteenth-century prose writing, both Russian and Western. The themes carry with them a range of style, from the Karamzinite early sentimental through the Byronic to the Hoffmann-esque. On the other hand, writing in this satirical vein was not merely Pushkin's vengeance on contemporary prose writing, whose standards he had tried but had not succeeded in surpassing. Parodying contemporary trends, he provided himself with an opportunity for stylistic exercise, and the deeper he delved into his exercises the more interest he developed in them.

At least two of the stories included in the volume—"The Blizzard" and "The Squire's Daughter"—are entirely comic, verging on the absurd. "The Undertaker," with its gleeful treatment of the macabre, has a touch of the grotesque to it. "The Shot"—still a parody, in this instance of the monomaniacal Byronic hero—represents a great technical achievement with its skillful manipulation of three different narrators' respective points of view. The crowning achievement of the volume, however, is "The Stationmaster," in which symbolic images —the pictures depicting the parable of the Prodigal Son—play an important role, far more important than Pushkin had originally thought poetic devices should play in a prose tale. In this instance Pushkin transcended parody to create an original masterpiece.

In *The Tales* Belkin appears only as collector and recorder of stories; but in *A History of the Village of Goriukhino* he is the actual narrator. Ludicrous as he may appear, writing the history of a mere village in the officious tones of an empire's historian, what he tells us is not altogether funny: his naïve, laughable presentation of events turns into a moving description of the plight of the Russian feudal peasant.

A fictitious narrator is employed in *Roslavlev*, too, but this time with less success. Perhaps the reason Pushkin left this projected novel unfinished is that its narrator, who starts out as a "lady" author intent on defending the "shade" of her late friend, soon loses her identity and instead of whitewashing her friend's memory, provides a fascinating, but at the same time unflattering, portrait of a complex woman—a portrait that a detached omniscient narrator might just as well have drawn.

Having written several pieces in compliance with the conventions of his time—or in mockery of those conventions—Pushkin once more attempted to create a detached third-person narrator in *Dubrovskii*. What initially drew him to the subject was an interest in the causes of social unrest—much pressed on his mind by the turbulent times in which he lived. The account of the two landowners' litigation and of the subsequent riot of Dubrovskii's peasants does indeed add up to a narrative of social significance. The characters of Troekurov and Andrei Dubrovskii, as well as of their servants and hirelings, are skillfully drawn, with the aid of vivid scenes and dialogues. But Pushkin, evidently hoping to combine a serious study of social processes with popular appeal, added to his narrative a conventional love intrigue, using timeworn clichés and stereotypes. The incongruity between the original social theme and the traditional love-plot might have contributed to his decision not to complete the work.

A triumph of detached narration, "The Queen of Spades" stands at the peak of Pushkin's achievement as a prose writer. Its three main characters—all negative—are surrounded by an intricate system of images, signifying winter and night, doom and madness, chaos and destruction. In this story Pushkin succeeds in drawing the kind of complex characters that eluded his firm grasp in the early fragments. "The Queen of Spades" also demonstrates how far he had revised his earlier concept of prose writing: instead of presenting bare thoughts with no decorative frills, here he conveys the meaning through a system of symbols worthy of epic poetry.

Although the narrative mode used in "The Queen of Spades" proved fully successful, Pushkin was not about to limit his range to it. For one thing, he remained attracted to the spare, unadorned quality of expository prose, even though he had changed his tactics in fiction. The result of this attraction is *A History of Pugachev*—a historical study outstanding not only by the standards of Pushkin's own time, but also by those of modern scholarship. But it is far more than a serious scholarly work, based strictly on evidence and drawing far-reaching conclusions: it is a triumph for the prose stylist as well. Its chief stylistic characteristic is that Pushkin not only quotes from sources directly, but allows the language of witnesses and documents to inform the narrator's own diction, with emphasis on carefully selected vivid expressions. It represents Pushkin's ideal of objectivity. The narrator's tone, to be sure, is consistent enough to bring coherence to the diverse sources, but his personality is so inconspicuous that his function is reduced simply to conveying "thoughts and thoughts" as befits "stern prose."

Nor did the success of "The Queen of Spades" lead Pushkin to relinquish the device of the imaginary narrator altogether. Turning history into fiction in *The Captain's Daughter*, he pretended to present a first-person account of the Pugachev Rebellion by one of its survivors. This technique enabled him, on the one hand, to eliminate some details of Pugachev's cruelty and lack of personal loyalty, which were objectively described in the *History*. Seen through the eyes of an impressionable young man, Pugachev acquires a romantic halo in the novel—which is one aspect of the fascinating process we are allowed to watch of Pushkin's turning a factual account into a vivid fictional representation. The naïve narrator's presence, on the other hand, allowed Pushkin to suffuse the narrative with a gentle irony, undercutting the two warring camps' conflicting fanaticisms. The tone of the novel, it would seem, oscillates between the mildly comic and the mildly sentimental; but one jarring event—the execution of Captain Mironov, his wife, and his comrade-in-arms, Ivan Ignatich—disturbs the general atmosphere. The critic's judgment of the novel's aesthetic qualities depends largely on whether he considers that scene of unmitigated cruelty properly integrated into the general texture of the work.

A History of Pugachev fulfilled Pushkin's expectations of objective, unadorned prose writing, and *The Captain's Daughter* followed the tradition of *The Tales of Belkin.* But the tradition of the early fragments, continued in "The Queen of Spades," was not abandoned either. Several of the unfinished works of Pushkin's last years indicate that he was deeply involved in an attempt to create psychological fiction, narrated by an all-seeing, detached, intelligent observer. *Egyptian Nights*, considered along with "We Were Spending the Evening at Princess D.'s Dacha," is the most promising of these late fragments. Not only does it pick up the theme begun in "The Guests Were Arriving" and "In the Corner," of the psychological complexities of a certain social type contemporary to Pushkin, but it also introduces the question of the artist's relation to society. The Italian improvisatore, humiliatingly dependent on his audience's whims, and the aristocratic poet Charskii, torn between his social position and his vocation as a poet, both seem to be equally close to Pushkin's heart. Exploring his dual theme, Pushkin goes beyond the kind of poetic representation he made full use of in "The Queen of Spades," to introduce verse into the very texture of prose.

Although many of Pushkin's prose projects remained unfinished, the extant fragments displayed such depth and variety that few of his successors in Russian fiction were able to escape their influence. And his completed masterpieces rank among the best not only in Russian, but in world literature of the nineteenth century.

PART ONE
Prose Fiction

The Blackamoor of Peter the Great
(1827–28)[1]

Russia
Transformed by Peter's iron will.
IAZYKOV[2]

I

I am in Paris;
I have begun to live, not just to breathe.
DMITRIEV, "DIARY OF A TRAVELER"[3]

Among the young people whom Peter the Great sent to foreign
lands to acquire knowledge needed in the transformed Russian state,
there was a blackamoor called Ibrahim, a godson of the Emperor.[4] He
received his training at the Military Academy of Paris,[5] graduated
with the rank of captain of artillery, distinguished himself in the
Spanish War,[6] and returned to Paris severely wounded. The Emperor,
engrossed though he was in his vast undertakings, never neglected to
inquire after his favorite, and always received laudatory reports about
his progress and conduct. Highly satisfied with him, Peter urged him
several times to return to Russia, but Ibrahim was in no hurry to do
so. He kept excusing himself under various pretexts, such as his
wound, his desire to complete his education, and his lack of money.
Peter, for his part, acceded to the young man's wishes with indulgence, told him to take care of his health, and expressed his appreciation for his industry, and—though always extremely careful about his
own expenses—he liberally provided for his godson from the Treasury, adding fatherly advice and cautionary exhortation to the gold
coins.

All historical records show that the frivolity, folly, and luxury of the
French of that time was unprecedented. No trace was left by then of
the last years of Louis XIV's reign, which had been characterized by
fastidious piety at Court and by a grave tone and decorum. The Duke
of Orleans, whose brilliant qualities were combined with faults of all
kinds, did not possess, unfortunately, one modicum of hypocrisy.[7]
The orgies at the Palais Royal were no secret in Paris, and the example
was contagious. Just then Law made his appearance on the scene;[8]
greed for money was united with thirst for amusement and dissipation; fortunes went to ruin; morality perished; and the French

laughed and calculated, while the state was falling apart to the playful tunes of satirical vaudevilles.

Society provided an entertaining spectacle. Education and the demand for amusement drew the different estates together. Wealth, good manners, fame, talent, even eccentricity—all attributes that excited curiosity or promised enjoyment—were accepted with equal indulgence. Literature, scholarship, and philosophy emerged from quiet study rooms to appear in the midst of high society, both bowing to fashion and governing it. Women ruled, but no longer demanded adoration. Superficial courtesy took the place of profound respect. The pranks of the duc de Richelieu—of this Alcibiades of a latter-day Athens—are a matter of historical record, providing an insight into the mores of the period.[9]

> Temps fortuné, marqué par la licence,
> Où la folie, agitant son grelot,
> D'un pied léger parcourt toute la France,
> Où nul mortel ne daigne être dévot,
> Où l'on fait tout excepté pénitence.[10]

As soon as Ibrahim arrived in Paris, his outward appearance, his education and native intelligence, caught everyone's attention. All the ladies, wishing to see le Nègre du czar in their drawing rooms, vied with each other in trying to captivate him; the Regent invited him to his merry soirées more than once; he was present at dinner parties enlivened by the youth of Arouet, by the old age of Chaulieu, and by the conversation of Montesquieu and Fontenelle;[11] he did not miss one ball, one festivity, one premiere; in general, he threw himself into the whirl of social life with all the ardor of his youth and race. What daunted Ibrahim, however, was not just the thought of exchanging this libertinage, all these splendid amusements, for the austere simplicity of the Petersburg Court. Other, more powerful bonds tied him to Paris. The young African was in love.

The Countess D., though not in the first bloom of youth, was still renowned for her beauty. At the age of seventeen, right after leaving the convent school, she was married to a man to whom she had not had time to grow attached, a fact that had not particularly worried him, then or later. Rumor ascribed lovers to her, but thanks to the lenient code of high society, she enjoyed a good name simply because she could never be accused of any ridiculous or scandalous escapades. Her house was among the most fashionable, attracting the best Parisian society. Ibrahim was introduced to her by the youthful Merville, generally regarded as her latest lover—a rumor that the young man made every effort to make people believe.

The Countess greeted Ibrahim politely but without fanfare, which flattered him. As a rule, people looked at the young black man as if he were some strange phenomenon—they surrounded him and showered him with salutations and questions. Their curiosity, though disguised as courtesy, offended his pride. The sweet attention of women, almost the sole aim of our efforts, not only did not gladden his heart, but filled it with downright bitterness and indignation. He felt that in their eyes he was a kind of rare animal, a peculiar and alien creature who had been accidentally brought into a world that had nothing in common with it. He even envied people who attracted no one's attention, regarding their insignificance as a happy state.

The thought that, by nature, he was destined not to have his affections reciprocated saved him from presumptuousness and vanity, and this lent a rare charm to his conduct with women. His conversation was simple and demure, and it attracted the Countess D., who had grown tired of the endless jests and subtle insinuations of French wit. He became a frequent guest at her house. Little by little she grew accustomed to the young Black's appearance and even began finding something attractive in that curly head, standing out with its blackness among the powdered wigs in her drawing room. (Ibrahim had been wounded in the head and was wearing a bandage instead of a wig.) He was twenty-seven years old, tall and well built; and quite a few beautiful young women glanced at him with feelings more flattering than mere curiosity, though he in his prejudice either did not notice anything or fancied only flirtation. When, however, his eyes met those of the Countess, his distrustfulness vanished. Her glance conveyed such good nature, her conduct with him was so simple and unaffected, that it was impossible to suspect in her even a shade of coquetry or mockery.

The idea of love had not crossed his mind, but to see the Countess daily was becoming a necessity for him. He sought her out everywhere, and meeting her seemed to him an unexpected favor from heaven each time. The Countess recognized his feelings before he himself did. Whatever you say, love without aspirations and demands touches the feminine heart more surely than all the wiles of seduction. When she was with Ibrahim, the Countess followed every movement he made and listened carefully to every word he said; in his absence she grew thoughtful and sank into her habitual distractedness. Merville was the first to notice this mutual inclination, and he congratulated Ibrahim. Nothing inflames love so much as the encouraging remark of an outsider. Love is blind, and distrustful of itself, eagerly grasps any support. Merville's words awakened Ibrahim. Until then the idea that he might possess the woman he loved had not even occurred to him; now hope suddenly lit up his soul; he fell madly in love. The Countess, frightened of the violence of his passion, tried to counter with friendly exhortations and prudent admonitions, but all in vain; she herself was weakening. Incautiously granted favors followed one another in quick succession. And at last, carried away by the force of the passion she had herself inspired, overpowered by its moment, she gave herself to the ecstatic Ibrahim...

Nothing can be hidden from society's watchful eyes. The Countess's new liaison soon became common knowledge. Some ladies were surprised by her choice, but many found it perfectly natural. Some laughed; others thought she had committed an unforgivable indiscretion. In the first transports of passion, Ibrahim and the Countess did not notice anything, but the double entendres of the men and the caustic remarks of the women soon began to catch their attention. Ibrahim's demure, cold manner had previously protected him from all offensive behavior; now he suffered the attacks with impatience and did not know how to ward them off. The Countess, accustomed to the respect of society, could not resign herself to being the butt of gossip and jests. She would now complain to Ibrahim in tears, now reproach him bitterly, now beg him not to take up her defense lest some useless row bring about her complete ruin.

A new circumstance confounded her situation even further. The consequence of her imprudent love had become apparent. All consolations, counsel, suggestions, were considered, and all rejected. The Countess saw that her ruin was inevitable, and waited for it in despair.

As soon as the Countess's condition became known, common talk started up with renewed vigor. Ladies of sensibility moaned with horror; men took bets on whether the Countess would give birth to a white or black baby. Epigrams proliferated at the expense of her husband—the only person in Paris who knew nothing and suspected nothing.

The fateful moment was approaching. The Countess's situation was terrible. Ibrahim came to see her every day. He watched her spiritual and physical strength gradually wane. Her tears and horror burst forth every minute. At last she felt the first pains. Measures were taken quickly. A pretext was found for sending the Count away. The physician arrived. A couple of days before, a destitute woman had been persuaded to give up her newborn son; now a trusted agent was sent to fetch him. Ibrahim waited in a study right next door to the bedroom where the unfortunate Countess lay. Hardly daring to breathe, he heard her muted groans, the whisperings of the maid, and the doctor's commands. She was in labor for a long time. Every groan rent his heart, every silent interval submerged him in horror... Suddenly he heard the feeble cry of a child; unable to contain his joy, he rushed into the Countess's room. A black baby lay on the bed at her feet. Ibrahim went up to it. His heart throbbed violently. He blessed his son with a shaking hand. The Countess gave a faint smile and stretched her weary hand toward him, but the doctor, anxious to protect the invalid from too much excitement, drew Ibrahim away from her bed. The newborn was placed in a covered basket and taken out of the house by a secret staircase. The other child was brought in, and its cradle placed in the young mother's bedroom. Ibrahim left somewhat reassured. The Count was expected. He returned late, learned about his wife's successful delivery, and was satisfied. Thus the public, which had anticipated an uproarious scandal, was frustrated in its expectations and had to content itself with mere vilifications.

Everything returned to normal, but Ibrahim felt that the course of his life would have to change, since his love affair might sooner or later come to the Count D.'s knowledge. In such a case, whatever the circumstances might be, the ruin of the Countess would be inevitable. Ibrahim was passionately in love, and was loved with an equal passion, but the Countess was capricious and careless. It was not the first time she had been in love. Revulsion and hatred might replace the most tender feelings in her heart. Ibrahim imagined the moment she would grow cold toward him. He had not experienced the feeling of jealousy before, but now he had a terrifying presentiment of it, and he fancied that the torments of separation would probably be less painful. He contemplated breaking up his ill-fated liaison, leaving Paris, and returning to Russia, where he was being summoned both by Peter and by his own vague sense of duty.

2

No more does beauty lull me so,
No more does joy's enchantment linger,
Nor is my fancy quite so free,
My spirit so serenely pleased...
By honor's fever I am seized:
The sound of glory calls on me!

DERZHAVIN[12]

Days, months went by, but the enamored Ibrahim could not bring himself to leave the woman he had seduced. The Countess became each day more and more attached to him. Their son was being brought up in a remote province. The gossip began to abate, and the lovers enjoyed greater peace, silently remembering the storm that had passed and trying not to think of the future.

One day Ibrahim attended the levee of the Duke of Orleans. Passing by him, the Duke stopped and gave Ibrahim a letter, telling him to read it at leisure. It was a letter from Peter I. The Emperor, guessing the real reason for Ibrahim's extended stay abroad, wrote to the Duke that he did not wish to coerce his foster son in any way, leaving it to him to decide whether he wanted to return to Russia or not, but that he, the Emperor, would in no case leave him without support. This letter touched the very heartstrings of Ibrahim. From that moment his fate was sealed. The next day he informed the Regent of his intention to leave for Russia immediately.

"Think what you're doing," the Duke said to him. "Russia is not your native land; I doubt whether you'll ever have an opportunity to see your own sultry fatherland again, but your long sojourn in France has made you unfit for both the climate and the way of life of semibarbarous Russia. You were not born a subject of Peter's. Listen to me: take advantage of his generous permission. Stay in France, for which you have already shed your blood, and you can rest assured that here, too, your services and talents will earn their just rewards."

Ibrahim sincerely thanked the Duke but remained firm in his decision.

"I'm sorry to see you go," said the Duke, "but, actually, you are right." He promised to release Ibrahim from the service, and reported the whole matter to the Russian Tsar.

Ibrahim was soon ready to leave. He spent the eve of his departure, as he would most evenings, at the house of the Countess D. She was not aware of anything: Ibrahim had not had the heart to reveal his plans to her. She was calm and cheerful. She called him to her side several times and teased him about his pensive mood. After supper all the guests left. Only the Countess, her husband, and Ibrahim remained in the drawing room. The unfortunate Ibrahim would have given anything in the world to be left alone with her, but the Count D. seemed to be so serenely settled by the fireplace that there was no hope of getting rid of him. All three were silent.

"*Bonne nuit*," said the Countess at last.

Ibrahim's heart sank as he suddenly apprehended the full horror of parting. He stood motionless.

"*Bonne nuit, messieurs*," repeated the Countess.

He still did not move... At last his vision became blurred, his head began swimming, and he could just barely walk out of the room. Having reached home, he wrote the following letter in an almost unconscious state:

I am leaving, my dear Léonore, abandoning you forever. I am writing to you because I have not the strength to explain myself to you otherwise.

My happiness could not last. I have enjoyed it in defiance of fate and nature. You were bound to cease loving me: the enchantment was bound to vanish. This thought always haunted me, even at those moments when it seemed I was oblivious to everything, when I lay at your feet intoxicated with your fervent self-sacrifice, with your boundless tenderness... Society, with its fickle ways, ruthlessly persecutes in practice what it permits in theory: its cold mockery would have sooner or later overpowered you, it would have humbled your soaring spirit, and you would in the end have grown ashamed of your passion... What would then have become of me? No! I'd sooner die, I'd sooner leave you, than wait for that terrible moment...

Your tranquility is dearest of all to me, and you could not enjoy it while the gaze of society was fixed on us. Remember everything you have suffered through, all the humiliations, all the torments of fear; remember the terrifying birth of our son. Just think: should I subject you to the same worries and dangers even longer? Why struggle to unite the fate of such a tender and graceful creature with the unlucky lot of a Negro, a pitiful being, scarcely granted the title of man?

Farewell, Léonore, farewell my cherished, my only friend. Abandoning you, I abandon the first and last happy moments of my life. I have neither fatherland nor family. I am leaving for gloomy Russia, where my only comfort will be my complete solitude. Hard work, to which I am going to devote myself from now on, will, if not stifle, at least divert agonizing recollections of those days of rapture and bliss... Farewell, Léonore—I am tearing myself away from this letter as if from your arms; farewell, be happy—and think sometimes of the poor Negro, of your faithful Ibrahim.

The same night he left for Russia.

The journey did not turn out to be quite as grim as he had expected. His imagination prevailed over reality. The farther behind he left Paris, the more vividly, the more immediately, he could recall the forms he had abandoned forever.

He was on the Russian border before he knew it. Autumn was setting in, but the drivers, despite the bad roads, drove him along with the speed of the wind, and on the morning of the seventeenth day of his journey he arrived in Krasnoe Selo, through which the main highway led in those days.

Only twenty-eight versts were left from here to Petersburg. While the horses were being harnessed Ibrahim went into the post station. In the corner a tall man, in a green caftan and with a clay pipe in his mouth, was leaning with his elbows on the table, reading the Hamburg newspapers. Hearing somebody enter, he raised his head.

"Ha! Ibrahim?" he exclaimed, getting up from the bench. "Welcome, godson."

Ibrahim, recognizing Peter, was about to rush up to him with joy, but stopped respectfully. The Emperor came up to him, embraced him, and kissed him on the head.

"I was informed you'd soon be arriving," said Peter, "and I came out to meet you. I've been here waiting for you since yesterday." Ibrahim could not find words to express his gratitude. "Let your carriage follow behind us," continued the Emperor, "while you sit with me. Let's set out for home."

The Emperor's carriage was driven up; he and Ibrahim got in, and they galloped off. They arrived in Petersburg in an hour and a half. Ibrahim looked with curiosity at the newborn capital that had risen from the swamp at the bidding of autocracy. Open dikes, canals without embankments, and wooden bridges testified everywhere to the recent victory of human will over the resistance of the elements. The houses, it seemed, had been erected hastily. There was nothing impressive in the whole city except for the Neva, not yet adorned by a granite frame but already strewn with warships and merchantmen. The Emperor's carriage stopped by the palace in the so-called Tsaritsyn Garden. A woman, aged about thirty-five, attractive and dressed according to the latest Parisian fashion, met Peter on the portico. He kissed her on the lips and, taking Ibrahim by the hand, said:

"Have you recognized my godson, Katenka? Please welcome him and be kind to him as in the old days."

Ekaterina turned her dark, penetrating eyes on Ibrahim and amiably gave him her hand. Two beautiful young girls, tall, graceful, and fresh as roses, stood behind her and respectfully approached Peter.

"Liza," he said to one of them, "do you remember the little black boy who used to steal apples for you from my garden in Oranienbaum? Here he is: I present him to you."

The Grand Duchess laughed and blushed. They entered the dining room. The table had been laid in anticipation of the Emperor's arrival. Peter sat down to dinner with his family, inviting Ibrahim to join them. Over dinner he talked with Ibrahim about various topics, questioning him about the Spanish War, the internal affairs of France, and the Regent, whom he loved though in many ways disapproved of. Ibrahim had a remarkably precise and perceptive mind; Peter was highly satisfied with his answers; on his part he remembered some details of Ibrahim's childhood and related them with such warmth and gaiety that nobody would have suspected this cordial, gracious host of having been the hero of Poltava, the mighty, dreaded reformer of Russia.

After dinner the Emperor, in keeping with Russian custom, retired to rest. Ibrahim was left with the Empress and the duchesses. He did his best to satisfy their curiosity, describing the Parisian way of life, the festivities held in the French capital and its capricious fashions. In the meanwhile some persons of the Emperor's immediate circle were gathering at the palace. Ibrahim recognized the illustrious Prince Menshikov, who, seeing the black man conversing with Ekaterina, cast a haughty glance at him; Prince Iakov Dolgorukii, Peter's stern counselor; the learned Bruce, who had the reputation of a Russian Faust among the people; the young Raguzinskii, Ibrahim's onetime friend; and others who were either bringing reports to the Emperor or awaiting his instructions.[13]

The Emperor reappeared in about two hours.

"Let's see whether you still remember how to carry out your former duty," he said to Ibrahim. "Take a slate and follow me." Peter locked the door of the turnery on the two of them and busied himself with state affairs. One by one he called in Bruce, Prince Dolgorukii, and the chief of police, de Vière; and he dictated several decrees and resolutions to Ibrahim.[14] The latter was astounded by his quick and firm grasp of problems, the power and versatility of his concentration, and the diversity of his activities. When the work was done, Peter pulled out a pocket notebook to check if everything planned for the day had been accomplished. Then, as he was leaving the turnery, he said to Ibrahim:

"It's getting late; you're tired I suppose. Spend the night here as you used to. I'll wake you up in the morning."

Ibrahim, left by himself, could scarcely collect his thoughts. He was in Petersburg; he had once again met the great man in whose company, not yet comprehending his worth, he had spent his childhood. He had to confess to himself, almost with a sense of guilt, that for the first time since their separation the Countess D. had not been the sole preoccupation of his day. He could see that the new way of life that was awaiting him—the work and constant activity—would be able to revive his soul, fatigued by passions, idleness, and an unacknowledged despondency. The thought of being closely associated with a great man and of shaping, together with him, the destiny of a great nation awoke in his heart, for the first time in his life, a noble sentiment of ambition. It was in this state of mind that he lay down on the camp bed prepared for him. His wonted dreams soon carried him to faraway Paris, into the arms of the dear Countess.

3

> Like clouds in summer skies,
> Thus thoughts within us change their
>   fleeting shapes,
> And what we love today, tomorrow we detest.
>   V. KIUKHELBEKER[15]

The next day Peter woke up Ibrahim as he had promised, and congratulated him on his appointment as first lieutenant in the Preobrazhenskii Regiment's artillery platoon, of which he himself was the captain. The courtiers surrounded Ibrahim, each trying in his own way to show esteem for the new favorite. The haughty Prince Menshikov shook his hand cordially. Sheremetev inquired after his Parisian acquaintances, and Golovin invited Ibrahim to dinner.[16] Others followed Golovin's example, so much so that Ibrahim received enough invitations to last him at least a month.

Ibrahim's days were unvaried but busy; consequently, he felt no boredom. With every day he became more and more attached to the Emperor, more able to comprehend his lofty mind. To follow the thoughts of a great man is a most engrossing intellectual occupation. Ibrahim saw Peter in the Senate, where Buturlin and Dolgorukii were disputing with him and where he grappled with important legislative matters; watched him in the Admiralty, where he was building Russia's naval might; observed him in the company of Feofan, Gavriil Buzhinskii, and Kopievich, and in his hours of leisure as he examined translations of foreign political writers or visited merchants' warehouses, craftsmen's workshops, scholars' studies.[17] Russia seemed to Ibrahim like an enormous manufacturing plant, where only machines were in motion and where each worker, subject to an established order, was busy with his assignment. He, too, felt obliged to work at his bench, trying to think of the amusements of Parisian life with as little regret as he possibly could. It was more difficult to dismiss from his mind another, dear recollection: he often thought of the Countess D., imagined her just indignation, tears, and despair... At times a dreadful thought took his breath away: the distractions of high society, a new liaison, another lucky man—he shuddered. Jealousy began to seethe in his African blood, and burning tears were ready to course down his black face.

One morning he was sitting surrounded by official papers in his study when he heard a loud greeting in French; turning around in excitement, he found himself in the embrace, accompanied by joyous exclamations, of the young Korsakov, whom he had left behind in Paris, in the whirl of society life.[18]

"I've only just arrived," said Korsakov, "and come directly to see you. All our Parisian acquaintances are missing you and send their regards; the Countess D. enjoined me to summon you to return without fail. Here is a letter from her."

Ibrahim grabbed the letter with a trembling hand and looked at the familiar handwriting on the envelope, not daring to believe his own eyes.

"I'm glad to see that you have not yet died of boredom in this barbarous Petersburg," Korsakov continued. "What do people do here, how do they pass their time? Who is your tailor? Has at least an opera house been established?"

Ibrahim, lost in thought, answered that the Emperor was probably at work in the shipyard. Korsakov burst out laughing.

"I can see that your mind is elsewhere at the moment," he said. "We'll have a good talk later; right now I'll go and present myself to the Emperor." Having said this, he spun around on one heel and ran out of the room.

Left by himself, Ibrahim hastened to open the letter. The Countess tenderly complained, reproaching him for his dissemblance and distrust. "You say," she wrote, "that my tranquility is dearest of all to you. Ibrahim! If that were true, could you have subjected me to the predicament to which the unexpected news of your departure reduced me? You were afraid that I would hold you back, but I assure you that though I love you, I could have sacrificed my love for your well-being and for what you consider your obligation." She concluded the letter with passionate assurances of love and implored him at least to write to her occasionally, even if there was no hope for them ever to meet again.

Ibrahim reread this letter twenty times, kissing the precious lines in ecstasy. He burned with impatience to hear more about the Countess, and was just about ready to go to the Admiralty in the hope of finding Korsakov still there, when the door opened and Korsakov himself reappeared: he had already presented himself to the Emperor and, as usual, seemed to be very satisfied with himself.

"*Entre nous*," he said to Ibrahim, "the Emperor is a peculiar man: just imagine, when I found him he was wearing some sort of sackcloth vest and was perched on the mast of a new ship, where I had to clamber after him with my dispatches. Standing on a rope ladder, I did not have enough room even to bow properly and became all confused, which had never happened to me before. But the Emperor, having read the papers I had brought, looked me over from head to foot and was, to all appearances, pleasantly surprised by the taste and refinement of my attire: at least he smiled and invited me to tonight's assembly. But I am a total stranger in Petersburg: during my six-year absence I have completely forgotten the local customs, and I'd like to ask you to please be my mentor, come with me and introduce me."

Ibrahim agreed and hastened to steer the conversation to a topic more interesting to him. "Well, how is the Countess D.?"

"The Countess? As you might expect, she was at first very much upset by your departure; but then, as you might expect, she gradually regained her equanimity and took a new lover. Do you know whom? That lanky Marquis of R. But what are you staring at me for with those Negro eyeballs of yours? Or does all this seem strange to you? Don't you know that lasting grief is not in the nature of the human being, especially of a woman? Think this over thoroughly while I go to take a rest after my journey, and don't forget to come and fetch me."

What sensations filled Ibrahim's heart? Jealousy? Rage? Despair? No; rather a deep, benumbed feeling of depression. He kept repeating to himself: I foresaw this; this had to happen. Then he opened the Countess's letter, read it once more, hung his head, and burst into bitter tears. He wept for a long time. The tears eased his sorrow. Then, looking at his watch, he realized it was time to go. He would have been glad to excuse himself, but the assembly was an official function, and the Emperor rigidly insisted on the attendance of the members of his close circle. Ibrahim got dressed and set out to fetch Korsakov.

Korsakov was sitting in his dressing gown, reading a French book. "So early?" he asked seeing Ibrahim.

"Mercy," the latter responded; "it's already half past five. We'll be late; get dressed quickly and let's go."

This threw Korsakov into a flurry, and he started ringing with all his might; his servants rushed in; he began dressing hastily. His French valet brought in his red-heeled shoes, his blue velvet breeches, and his pink caftan embroidered with spangles; his wig, quickly powdered in the anteroom, was brought in, and he thrust his close-cropped small head into it; he asked for his sword and gloves, turned around before the mirror about ten times, and declared himself ready. The footman helped him and Ibrahim into their bearskin coats, and the two young men set out for the Winter Palace.

Korsakov showered Ibrahim with questions. Who was the most beautiful woman in Petersburg? Who had the reputation of being the best dancer? What dance was currently in vogue? Ibrahim satisfied his friend's curiosity grudgingly. In the meanwhile they had arrived at the palace. A large number of long sleds, old coaches, and gilded barouches stood in the field already. By the portico there was a large crowd of liveried and mustachioed coachmen, of mace-bearing footmen resplendent in tawdry finery and plumes, of hussars, pages, and awkward-looking haiduks, loaded down with their masters' fur coats and muffs—an indispensable retinue in the opinion of the boyars of that time. Ibrahim's arrival provoked a general murmur among them: "The blackamoor, the blackamoor, the Tsar's blackamoor!" He led Korsakov through this motley crowd of servants as fast as he could. A palace servant opened the doors wide for them, and they entered the hall. Korsakov was dumbfounded... In the large room, lit by tallow candles that burned dimly in the clouds of tobacco smoke, droves of dignitaries with blue sashes across their shoulders, ambassadors, foreign merchants, officers of the Guards in green coats, and shipmasters wearing short jackets with striped trousers were moving up and down to the incessant sound of a brass band. The ladies sat along the walls, the young ones glittering with all the finery of fashion. Gold and silver glistened on their robes; their slim waists rose from their luxuriant hooped skirts like flower stems; diamonds twinkled in their ears, in their long tresses, and around their necks. They cheerfully glanced left and right, waiting for cavaliers and for the dance to begin. The elderly ladies' outfits represented shrewd attempts to combine the new mode of dress with the old styles frowned upon: their headdresses were very like the Tsaritsa Natalia Kirilovna's sable hat, and their gowns and mantles resembled sarafans and wadded jackets.[19] They attended these newfangled spectacles with more bewilderment, it seemed, than pleasure, and looked askance at the wives and daughters of Dutch skippers who sat in their calico skirts and red blouses, knitting socks, laughing, and chatting among themselves, as if they were at home. Korsakov could not regain his presence of mind. Noticing the newly arrived guests, a servant came up with beer and glasses on a tray.

"Que diable est-ce que tout cela?" said Korsakov to Ibrahim under his breath.[20] Ibrahim could not suppress a smile. The Empress and the grand duchesses, glittering with beauty and elegance, walked through the rows of guests, amicably conversing with them. The Emperor was in another room. Korsakov, wishing to show himself to him, had a hard time pushing his way there through the constantly moving crowd. In that room sat mostly foreigners, solemnly smoking their clay pipes and emptying their earthenware mugs. Bottles of beer and wine, leather pouches with tobacco, glasses of rum punch, and chessboards were placed on the tables. Peter sat at one of them, playing checkers with a broad-shouldered English skipper. The two of them kept zealously saluting each other with salvos of tobacco smoke, and the Emperor was so preoccupied with an unexpected move of his partner's that he did not notice Korsakov, much as he twisted and turned around them. At this moment a massive gentleman with a massive nosegay on his chest came bustling into the room, to announce in a thunderous voice that the dancing had commenced; then he was gone again, and many of the guests, among them Korsakov, followed after him.

Korsakov was struck by an unexpected sight. Along the whole length of the ballroom, resounding with peals of the most pitiful music, ladies and cavaliers were ranged in two rows, facing one another; the cavaliers bowed low and the ladies curtsied, bending even lower, first straight ahead, then to the right, then to the left, then straight ahead again, to the right again, and so forth. Korsakov stared at this intriguing sport wide-eyed and bit his lips. The bowing and curtsying continued for about half an hour; when it stopped at last, the massive gentleman with the nosegay announced that the ceremonial dance was over, and ordered the musicians to play a minuet. Korsakov rejoiced and prepared to shine. One of the young ladies present attracted him particularly. She was about sixteen, dressed expensively but tastefully; she sat by an elderly man of dignified and stern appearance. Korsakov scampered up to her and asked her to do him the honor of dancing with him. The young beauty looked at him with embarrassment, not knowing, it seemed, what to say to him. The man sitting next to her knitted his brows, looking even more stern. Korsakov stood waiting for her answer, but the gentleman with the nosegay came up to him, led him into the center of the ballroom, and said gravely: "My dear sir, you have committed a breach of etiquette: first, you went up to this young person without the required triple obeisance; secondly, you took it on yourself to select her, though in the minuet the right of choice belongs to the lady, not to the cavalier; for which reasons you are to be severely punished, namely you must drain the *goblet of the Great Eagle*."

Korsakov grew more and more astonished. The guests instantly surrounded him, loudly demanding the immediate execution of the sentence. Peter, hearing the laughter and shouts, and very fond of personally participating in such punishments, came out of the adjacent room. The crowd made way for him, and he entered the circle where the marshal of the assembly stood facing the culprit with an enormous goblet filled with malmsey. He was vainly trying to persuade the condemned to submit to the law voluntarily.

"Aha!" said the Emperor, seeing Korsakov, "you've been caught, brother! Please be so good as to quaff it down, *monsieur*, and don't let me see you wince."

There was no way to escape. The poor fop drained the whole goblet in one gulp and handed it back to the marshal.

"Listen, Korsakov," Peter said to him, "the breeches you're wearing are made of velvet, of a kind even I don't wear, though I am much richer than you. This is extravagance; watch out that I don't fall out with you."

Having listened to this censure, Korsakov wanted to leave the circle, but he lost his balance and almost fell down, to the indescribable joy of the Emperor and the whole merry company. This episode not only did not spoil the unity and interest of the main action, but enlivened it even further. The cavaliers began scraping and bowing, and the ladies curtsying and tapping their heels, with even greater zeal, no longer paying any attention to the rhythm of the music. Korsakov was unable to participate in the general merriment. The lady he had chosen went up to Ibrahim under orders from her father, Gavrila Afanasevich, and casting her blue eyes down, timidly gave him her hand. He danced a minuet with her and led her back to her seat; then he went to look for Korsakov, led him out of the ballroom, put him in a carriage, and took him home. On the way home Korsakov began muttering inaudibly, "Accursed assembly! Accursed goblet of the Great Eagle!," but he soon fell into a deep slumber, unaware of how he

arrived home, how he was undressed and put to bed; the next morning he woke up with a headache and could only vaguely remember the
scraping and curtsying, the tobacco smoke, the gentleman with the
nosegay, and the goblet of the Great Eagle.

4

> Our forebears were no hasty eaters,
> Not speedily, you would have found,
> Did jars and silver pledging-beakers
> Of wine and ale go foaming round.
> *Ruslan and Liudmila* [21]

I must now acquaint my gracious reader with Gavrila Afanasevich
Rzhevskii. A descendant of an ancient lineage of boyars, he possessed
an enormous estate, was a generous host, loved falconry, and had numerous servants. In other words, he was a true gentleman of the Russian soil; as he himself was fond of saying, he could not endure the
German spirit, and in his household he made every effort to preserve
the cherished customs of olden times.

His daughter, Natalia Gavrilovna, was seventeen years old. She had
been brought up in the old way, that is, surrounded by nurses and nannies, companions and maidservants; she knew how to do gold embroidery, but she was illiterate. On the other hand her father, despite
his aversion to everything foreign, gave in to her desire to learn German dances from a captive Swedish officer who lived in their house.
This worthy dance teacher was about fifty years old; his right leg had
been shot through at Narva and was therefore not quite up to minuets
and courants, but with his left one he could execute even the most
difficult *pas* with amazing skill and lightness. [22] His pupil did honor to
his efforts. She was renowned as the best dancer at the assemblies,
which had indeed been one of the things that led Korsakov to his *faux
pas*. The latter came to Gavrila Afanasevich to offer his apologies the
next day, but the easy manner and dandyish appearance of this young
fop did not please the haughty boyar, who subsequently gave him the
witty nickname of French monkey.

One festive day Gavrila Afanasevich was expecting several relatives
and friends. A long table was being laid in the ancient hall. The guests
arrived, accompanied by their wives and daughters, who had at last
been freed from their domestic seclusion by the Emperor's decrees
and personal example. Natalia Gavrilovna went up to each guest with
a silver tray laden with gold cups, and the men emptied their cups,
regretting that the kiss that used to accompany such occasions was

no longer a custom. They sat down to table. In the place of honor, next to the master of the house, sat his father-in-law, Prince Boris Alekseevich Lykov, a seventy-year-old boyar; the other guests sat according to the rank of their families, thereby evoking the happy old days of the order of precedence.[23] The men were seated on one side, the women on the other. At the end of the table were placed, as usual, the housekeeper in her old-fashioned headgear and bodice, a midget— a prim and wrinkled little darling of thirty—and the captive Swede in his timeworn blue uniform. The table, laden with a great number of dishes, was attended by numerous bustling domestics, among whom the butler was clearly distinguishable by his stern expression, large stomach, and majestic immobility. During the first minutes of the dinner, attention was devoted exclusively to the products of our old-fashioned cuisine; only the clatter of the plates and assiduously laboring spoons disturbed the prevailing silence. At last the host, judging that it was time to divert his guests with pleasant conversation, turned around and asked, "And where is Ekimovna? Call her here."

Several servants were ready to dash off in different directions, but just at that moment an old woman with a powdered and rouged face, bedizened with flowers and trinkets and wearing a damask robe with deep décolletage, danced into the room humming a tune. Her appearance evoked general delight.

"Good day, Ekimovna," said Prince Lykov. "How are you doing?"

"Never felt better, my good friend: singing and dancing, bridegrooms enticing."

"What have you been up to, old goose?" asked the host.

"I've decked myself out, friend, for your dear guests, for the holy day, by the Tsar's command, by the boyars' demand, to give the world a laughing fit with my German outfit."

These words were greeted with loud laughter, and the jester took up her position behind the master's chair.

"A fool may sometimes speak to purpose,"[24] said Tatiana Afanasevna, the master's elder sister, whom he sincerely respected. "Today's fashions really make the whole world laugh. Now that even you men have shaved off your beards and put on cut-off caftans, there is little to be said about women's rags; yet, I'll vow, one can't help missing the sarafan, the maiden's ribbon, and the married woman's headdress. Look at today's beauties—you have to laugh and weep at once. The poor things' hair is all fluffed up like tow, greased and bespattered with French flour; their tummies are laced in so tight it's a wonder they don't break into two; and with their petticoats hitched on hoops, they have to get into carriages sideways, and tilt over going through a door. No way to stand, sit, or breathe. Veritable martyrs, the poor darlings."

"My dear Tatiana Afanasevna," said Kirila Petrovich T., a former administrative official of Riazan, who had in that capacity acquired, by hook or crook, three thousand serfs and a young wife, "in my opinion, let the wife dress as she will; I don't mind if she looks like a scarecrow or a Chinese Emperor as long as she doesn't order new dresses every month, throwing away old ones that are still perfectly good. It used to be that the granddaughter was given her grandmother's sarafan in her trousseau, but look at the latest robes: you see them on the lady today, on her serving girl tomorrow. What can you do? It's simply ruining the Russian gentry. A disaster, no two ways about it." As he spoke these words, he looked with a sigh at his Maria Ilinichna, who did not seem to be pleased either by his praise of the olden days or by his railing against the latest customs. The other beauties present shared her discontent but kept silent, because in those days modesty was considered an indispensable attribute of a young woman.

"And who is to blame?" asked Gavrila Afanasevich, filling up his mug with frothy sour kvass. "Aren't we to blame ourselves? The young wenches are playing the fool, and we let them have their way."

"But what can we do if it's not our choice?" rejoined Kirila Petrovich. "There's many a husband would be glad to lock his wife in the tower chamber, but she's summoned to the assembly by drums and clarion. The husband grabs after the whip, the wife grabs after her frippery. Oh, these assemblies! The Lord has inflicted them on us as a punishment for our sins."

Maria Ilinichna was on tenterhooks: she was itching to speak. Finally she could not bear it any longer, and turning to her husband, she asked him with an acid smile just what it was that he found wrong with the assemblies.

"I'll tell you what's wrong with them," answered her husband, flushed. "Since they've begun, husbands have been unable to cope with their wives. Wives have forgotten the Apostle's words, 'Wives, submit yourselves unto your own husbands';[25] their minds are on new dresses, not on the household; what they care about is catching the eyes of featherbrained officers, not pleasing their husbands. And is it becoming, my dear lady, for a Russian noblewoman to consort with German snuffers and their maidservants? Whoever heard of dancing into the night and parleying with young men? Not with relatives, mind you, but with strangers who haven't even been introduced."

"I'd add a word or two of my own, but even the walls have ears,"[26] said Gavrila Afanasevich, frowning. "I must confess the assembly is not to my taste either: it doesn't take long before you run into a drunkard or find yourself forced to drink till you become a public laughingstock. If you don't watch out, some scamp will start playing pranks at the expense of your daughter. Today's young generation's been so utterly spoilt it's beyond belief. Look at the son of the late Evgraf Sergeevich Korsakov, for instance: he created such a scandal with Natasha at the last assembly that it made me blush. The next day, I suddenly notice, somebody's driving straight into my courtyard. Who in the name of heaven could this be, I say to myself; it isn't Prince Aleksandr Danilovich, is it?[27] And who do you think it was? Ivan Evgrafovich! Do you think he could have stopped at the gate and troubled himself to come up to the porch on foot? No, not he! And then? You should have seen how he flew into the house, bowed and scraped, and gibble-gabbled. The fool Ekimovna can imitate him capitally; which reminds me: come, old goose, show us how the overseas monkey carries himself."

Ekimovna the jester seized the lid of a dish, put it under her arm as if holding a hat, and began making grimaces, bowing and scraping to all sides, and muttering words that resembled *monsieur, mamselle, assemblée, pardon.* Once more, general and prolonged laughter testified to the guests' delight.

"The spitting image of Korsakov, as like as two peas," said old Prince Lykov, wiping away the tears of laughter, as calm was gradually restored. "There's no concealing the fact: he's not the first, nor will he be the last, to come back a clown from those German lands to holy Russia. What do our children learn out there? To scrape with their feet and prattle in God knows what tongue, to treat their elders with disrespect, and to dangle after other men's wives. Of all the young people educated abroad (God forgive me), the Tsar's blackamoor's the one that most resembles a man."[28]

"Indeed so," remarked Gavrila Afanasevich; "he is a solid, respectable man; you can't compare him with that good-for-nothing... But who is this now driving through the gate into the courtyard? It isn't that overseas monkey again, is it? What are you gawking here for, idiots?" he continued, addressing his servants. "Run and turn him away, and tell him that in the future, too..."

"Are you raving, graybeard?" the jester Ekimovna interrupted him. "Are you blind? It's the Imperial sled, the Tsar has come."

Gavrila Afanasevich hastily rose from the table; everyone dashed to the windows and indeed beheld the Emperor, who was ascending the steps, leaning on his orderly's shoulder. There was a great commotion. The master of the house rushed to meet the Emperor; the servants ran in all directions as if bereft of reason; the guests were terrified, some of them even wondering how to slip away at the earliest opportunity. Then suddenly Peter's thunderous voice could be heard from the entrance hall; all fell silent; and the Tsar came in, accompanied by the master of the house, who was struck dumb with joy.

"Good day, ladies and gentlemen," said Peter with a cheerful expression on his face. They all bowed low. The Tsar glanced over the crowd quickly, seeking out the host's young daughter; he called her to him. She approached him quite boldly, though she blushed, not only to the ears but down to the shoulders.

"You're becoming prettier by the day," the Emperor said to her, kissing her, as was his habit, on the head. Then he turned to the guests: "Have I disturbed you, ladies and gentlemen? You were eating your dinner; please sit down again, and as for me, Gavrila Afanasevich, would you offer me some aniseed vodka?"

The host dashed to the majestic-looking butler, snatched the tray from his hands, filled a gold goblet himself, and proffered it to the Emperor with a bow. Peter, having downed his liquor, ate a pretzel and asked the guests once more to continue their dinner. All resumed their former places, except for the midget and the housekeeper, who did not dare remain at a table honored by the Tsar's presence. Peter sat down by the master of the house and asked for some cabbage soup. His orderly handed him a wooden spoon inlaid with ivory and a small knife and fork with green bone handles, for he never used anybody's cutlery except his own. The dinner party, which had been noisy and lively with good cheer and conversation only a minute before, now continued in silence and constraint. The host, overawed and overjoyed, ate nothing, and the guests were all stiff, reverentially listening as the Emperor spoke in German with the captive Swede about the campaign of 1701. The jester Ekimovna, to whom the Emperor put several questions, answered with a kind of timid coldness, which (I might say in passing) did not at all testify to innate stupidity. At last the dinner was over. The Emperor, and after him all the guests, rose to their feet.

"Gavrila Afanasevich," he said, "I would like to have a private word with you." And, taking his host by the arm, Peter led him into the drawing room, locking the door behind them. The guests remained in the dining room, discussing the unexpected visit in a whisper; then, not wishing to appear immodest, they soon began to leave one by one, without thanking their host for his hospitality. His father-in-law, daughter, and sister saw the guests off quietly, and finally remained by themselves in the dining room, waiting for the Emperor to emerge.

5

I shall find a wife for thee,
Or a miller I won't be.
FROM ABLESIMOV'S OPERA
The Miller[29]

In half an hour the door opened and Peter came out. He acknowledged the threefold bow of Prince Lykov, Tatiana Afanasevna, and
Natasha with a solemn inclination of the head and went straight
through to the entrance hall. The host helped him on with his red fur
coat, accompanied him to his sled, and on the porch thanked him
once more for the honor. Peter left.

As he returned to the dining room, Gavrila Afanasevich looked
very worried. He curtly ordered the servants to clear the table fast,
sent Natasha to her room, and informing his sister and father-in-law
that he needed to talk to them, led them to the bedroom where he
usually rested after dinner. The old Prince lay down on the oak bed;
and Tatiana Afanasevna sat in an ancient damask-upholstered armchair, putting a little footstool under her feet. Gavrila Afanasevich
locked all the doors, sat on the bed at Prince Lykov's feet, and in a low
tone began the conversation with the following words:

"It was not for nothing that the Emperor came to see me: guess
what it was his pleasure to speak to me about?"

"How could we know, dear brother?" said Tatiana Afanasevna.

"Did the Tsar command you to govern a province?" asked the father-in-law. "It was high time. Or did he offer you an ambassadorship?
Why not? After all, men of nobility, not only scribes, can sometimes
be sent to foreign monarchs."

"No," answered the son-in-law, knitting his brow. "I am a man of
the old school; our services are not needed these days, though it is
quite reasonable to think that an Orthodox Russian nobleman is
worth today's upstarts, pancake peddlers,[30] and infidels—but that's
another story."

"Then what did he please to talk to you about for such a long time,
brother?" asked Tatiana Afanasevna. "You haven't come upon some
adversity, have you? The Lord preserve us and have mercy on us!"

"Adversity or no adversity, I must confess it gave me a start."

"But what is it, brother? What is the matter?"

"It concerns Natasha: the Tsar came to arrange a marriage for her."

"Thank God," said Tatiana Afanasevna, making the sign of the
cross. "The girl is marriageable, and if the matchmaker is anything to
judge by, the bridegroom cannot be unworthy either. God grant them
love and good counsel; the honor is great. And for whom does the
Tsar seek her hand?"

"Hum," grunted Gavrila Afanasevich, "for whom? That's just it, for whom."

"Who is it then?" repeated Prince Lykov, who had been on the point of nodding off.

"Try to guess," said Gavrila Afanasevich.

"My dear brother," responded the old lady, "how could we guess? There are many eligible men at court; any of them would be glad to take your Natasha. It's not Dolgorukii, is it?"

"No, not Dolgorukii."

"It's just as well; he's so terribly arrogant. Is it Shein then, or Troekurov?"

"No, neither the one nor the other."

"I'm not keen on them either: frivolous young men, too much imbued with the German spirit. Well, is it Miloslavskii?"

"No, not he, either."

"Let him be: rich but stupid. Who then? Eletskii? Lvov? Neither? It's not Raguzinskii, is it? For heaven's sake, I'm at my wit's end. Who is it that the Tsar is asking Natasha's hand for?"

"The blackamoor Ibrahim."

The old lady gasped and clasped her hands. Prince Lykov lifted his head from the pillows and repeated with amazement, "The blackamoor Ibrahim!"

"Brother, my dearest," said the old lady in a tearful voice, "don't destroy the issue of your own flesh and blood, don't throw Natashenka into the clutches of that black devil."

"But how can I refuse the Emperor," objected Gavrila Afanasevich, "when he is promising to reward me with his favor, both me and my whole family?"

"How now," exclaimed the old Prince, whose drowsiness had entirely disappeared, "to give Natasha, my granddaughter, in marriage to a bought Negro!"

"He is not of common birth," said Gavrila Afanasevich. "He is the son of a black sultan. The Moslems captured him and sold him in Constantinople; our ambassador paid a ransom for him and gave him to the Tsar. His elder brother has been to Russia with a sizable ransom and..."

"Gavrila Afanasevich, dear brother," the old lady interrupted him, "we have heard the tales of Bova Korolevich and Eruslan Lazarevich.[31] Tell us rather what you answered to the Emperor's proposal."

"I said that he ruled over us, and it was our duty as his vassals to obey in all things."

At this moment a noise could be heard behind the door. Gavrila

Afanasevich went to open it but felt something obstructing it; he gave it a strong push, and when the door opened, they saw Natasha lying prostrate in a swoon on the blood-spattered floor.

When the Emperor had locked himself in with her father, her heart sank. Some premonition whispered to her that the matter concerned her. When Gavrila Afanasevich sent her off, declaring that he had to speak with her aunt and grandfather, she could not resist the promptings of feminine curiosity and quietly stole through the inner apartments to the door of the bedroom. She did not miss one word of the whole horrifying conversation; when she heard her father's last words, the poor thing lost consciousness, and as she fell, she hit her head against the iron-plated chest in which her trousseau was kept.

The servants came running; they lifted Natasha up, carried her to her room, and put her on the bed. After a while she came to and opened her eyes, but she could not recognize either her father or her aunt. A high fever developed. In her delirious state she kept talking about the Tsar's blackamoor and a wedding, and suddenly let out a piercing wail: "Valerian, dear Valerian, my treasure! Save me, here they come, here they come!" Tatiana Afanasevna anxiously glanced at her brother, who blanched, bit his lip, and left the room without a word. He returned to the old Prince, who, unable to climb the stairs, had remained below.

"How is Natasha?" he asked.

"Unwell," answered the distressed father. "Worse than I thought: in her unconscious state she is raving about Valerian."

"Who is this Valerian?" asked the grandfather, alarmed. "Could it be that orphan, the son of a Strelets, whom you took into your house?"[32]

"The very same one," answered Gavrila Afanasevich. "To my misfortune, his father saved my life at the time of the rebellion, and the devil made me take the accursed wolf cub into my house.[33] Two years ago, when he voluntarily enlisted in a regiment, Natasha, saying good-bye to him, burst into tears, and he stood as if petrified. This seemed suspicious to me, and I discussed it with my sister. But since that time Natasha has not mentioned him, and nothing whatever has been heard of him. I thought she had forgotten him, but evidently she hasn't. This decides the matter: she's to marry the blackamoor."

Prince Lykov did not contradict him: it would have been in vain. The Prince returned home; Tatiana Afanasevna remained at Natasha's bedside; Gavrila Afanasevich, having sent for the physician, locked himself in his room, and the house grew silent and gloomy.

The unexpected marriage proposal surprised Ibrahim at least as much as it had Gavrila Afanasevich. This is how it had happened. One time, as Peter was working with Ibrahim, he said to him, "I notice, brother, that you've grown a little listless. Tell me frankly, is there anything you want?"

Ibrahim assured the Emperor that he was happy with his situation and wished for nothing better.

"All right," said the Emperor, "if you feel spiritless for no reason, then I know how to cheer you up."

When they finished their work, he asked Ibrahim, "Did you like the girl with whom you danced the minuet at the last assembly?"

"She is a charming girl, Your Majesty; and she struck me as a modest and good-natured one, too."

"In that case I'll see to it that you get to know her better. Would you like to marry her?"

"I, Your Majesty?"

"Listen, Ibrahim, you are a solitary man, without kith or kin, a stranger to everyone except me. If I should die today, what would become of you tomorrow, my poor blackamoor? You must get settled down while there is still time; you must find support in new connections, entering into alliance with the Russian gentry."

"Your Majesty, I am blessed with Your Highest protection and favor. God grant me that I may not survive my Tsar and benefactor: I ask for no more. But even if I were inclined to marry, would the young lady and her relatives consent? My appearance..."

"Your appearance! What nonsense! You're a fine young man in every way. A young girl must obey the wishes of her parents, and we'll see what old Gavrila Rzhevskii says when I come as your matchmaker." With these words, the Emperor sent for his sleigh and left Ibrahim plunged in profound thought.

"To marry!" mused the African. "And why not? Or am I destined to spend my life in solitude, never experiencing the greatest joys and most sacred obligations of a man, just because I was born below the fifteenth parallel?[34] I cannot hope to be loved, but that is a childish objection. Can one trust love in any case? Does it exist at all in the fickle heart of woman? Having given up sweet libertinage forever, I have succumbed to other allurements, more significant ones. The Emperor is right: I must ensure my future. Marriage with the young Rzhevskaia will affiliate me with the proud Russian gentry, and I will no longer be a newcomer in my adopted fatherland. I will not demand love from my wife: I shall be content with her fidelity. As for her friendship, I will win it by unfailing tenderness, trust, and indulgence."

Ibrahim wanted to get down to work as usual, but his mind wandered. He abandoned his papers and went for a stroll along the embankment of the Neva. Suddenly he heard Peter's voice; turning around he saw the Emperor, who had dismissed his sleigh and was coming after Ibrahim with a cheerful expression on his face.

"It's all accomplished, brother," he said taking Ibrahim by the arm. "I've asked for her hand on your behalf. Tomorrow pay a visit to your father-in-law, but make sure to honor his boyar pride: leave your sleigh at his gate, go across his courtyard on foot, speak about the services he has rendered his country and about the prominence of his family, and he'll become devoted to you. And now," he continued, shaking his cudgel, "walk with me to that scoundrel Danilych's house; I must talk to him about his latest pranks."

Ibrahim, having sincerely thanked Peter for his fatherly solicitude, saw him to the gate of Prince Menshikov's magnificent palace, and returned home.

6

A sanctuary lamp burned quietly before the glass case holding the family's ancient icons in their glittering gold and silver frames. The lamp's flickering flame cast a faint light on the curtained bed and on the little table covered with labeled medicine bottles. A maidservant sat at a spinning wheel close to the stove; the light whir of her spindle was the only sound that disturbed the silence of the bedroom.

"Who is here?" said a weak voice. The maid rose immediately, went to the bed, and gently raised the curtain. "Will it soon be daylight?" asked Natalia.

"It's already noon," answered the maid.

"My God, why is it so dark then?"

"The windows are shuttered, miss."

"Bring me my clothes quickly."

"I can't, miss; it's against the doctor's orders."

"Am I sick then? Since when?"

"It's been two weeks already."

"Has it? To me it seems as if I'd gone to bed only yesterday."

Natasha grew silent, trying to collect her scattered thoughts. Something had happened to her, but exactly what it was she could not remember. The maid still stood in front of her, waiting for her orders. At that moment an indistinct rumble could be heard from downstairs.

"What's that?" asked the sick girl.

"Their Honors have finished dinner," answered the maid. "They're getting up from the table. Tatiana Afanasevna will come up here now."

Natasha, it seemed, was pleased; she feebly moved her hand. The maid pulled the curtain to and sat down at her spinning wheel again.

In a few minutes a head wearing a broad white cap with dark ribbons appeared in the doorway and a subdued voice asked, "How's Natasha?"

"Hello, auntie," said the invalid softly, and Tatiana Afanasevna hastened to her.

"The young mistress has revived," said the maid, cautiously drawing an armchair up to the bed.

The old lady, with tears in her eyes, kissed her niece's pale, languid face and sat down by her. Soon after, the German physician in his black coat and scholar's wig entered the room, felt Natasha's pulse, and announced, first in Latin and then in Russian, that the danger had passed. He asked for paper and ink, wrote out a new prescription, and left. The old lady got up, kissed Natalia once more, and went downstairs to tell Gavrila Afanasevich about the good news.

In the drawing room sat the Tsar's blackamoor, in uniform, with sword by his side and hat in hand, respectfully conversing with Gavrila Afanasevich. Korsakov, stretched out on a soft divan, was listening to them absentmindedly while teasing a good old gray hound; when he had grown tired of that occupation, he went up to a mirror—his usual refuge from boredom—and in the mirror caught sight of Tatiana Afanasevna, who was vainly trying to signal to her brother from the doorway.

"You're wanted, Gavrila Afanasevich," said Korsakov, turning to his host and interrupting Ibrahim. Gavrila Afanasevich promptly went to his sister and closed the door behind him.

"I marvel at your patience," said Korsakov to Ibrahim. "Not only do you listen a whole blessed hour to these ravings about the Rzevskiis' and Lykovs' ancient lineage, but you even add your own virtuous commentary! If I were you, *j'aurais planté là*[35] the old prattler and his whole tribe, including Natalia Gavrilovna, who is putting on airs, pretending to be sick, *une petite santé...*[36] Tell me honestly, can you be in love with this little *mijaurée*?[37] Listen, Ibrahim, take my advice just this once: honestly, I am wiser than I seem. Give up this freakish idea. Don't marry. It seems to me that your fiancée has no particular liking for you. Anything can happen in this world. For instance, it goes without saying that I cannot complain about my looks; but I have had occasion to deceive husbands who were, I swear, no worse than I. And you yourself... Don't you remember our Parisian friend, Count D.? One cannot rely on woman's fidelity; lucky the man who can contemplate the matter with indifference. But you? Should you, with your passionate, brooding, and suspicious nature, with your flat nose and thick lips, and with that kinky wool on your head, throw yourself into all the dangers of matrimony?"

"I thank you for the friendly advice," Ibrahim interrupted him coldly, "but you know the saying: it's not your duty to rock other people's babies."

"Take care, Ibrahim," answered Korsakov, laughing, "take care not to let it happen that you should illustrate this proverb in a literal sense."

Meanwhile, the conversation going on in the adjacent room was becoming heated.

"You're going to kill her," the old lady was saying. "She will not survive the sight of him."

"But think of it yourself," argued the obstinate brother. "He's been coming here as her bridegroom for two weeks, yet hasn't seen his bride once. He may think at last that her illness is a mere fabrication, that we're only stalling for time in order to find some way to get rid of him. And what will the Tsar say? He has already sent inquiries about Natalia's health three times. Say what you like, I've no intention of quarreling with him."

"The Lord be merciful," said Tatiana Afanasevna, "what will the poor thing come to? Let me at least prepare her for the visit." To this Gavrila Afanasevich agreed, and he returned to the drawing room.

"Thank God," he said to Ibrahim, "the danger has passed. Natalia is much better; if I weren't embarrassed to leave my dear guest, Ivan Evgrafovich, all by himself, I would take you upstairs for a glimpse of your bride."

Korsakov rejoiced over the news and, assuring Gavrila Afanasevich that he had to leave, asked him not to worry about him. He ran out into the entrance hall, giving his host no chance to see him off.

In the meanwhile Tatiana Afanasevna hastened to prepare the invalid for the frightening guest's arrival. Entering the bedroom, she sat down, out of breath, by the bed and took Natasha's hand; but before she was able to utter a word, the door opened. Natasha asked who it was. The old lady, horror-stricken, lost her faculty of speech. Gavrila Afanasevich drew the curtain aside, looked at the patient coldly, and asked how she was. She tried to smile at him, but she could not. Struck by her father's stern glance, she felt apprehensive. Presently it seemed to her that somebody was standing at the head of her bed. She raised her head with an effort and suddenly recognized the Tsar's blackamoor. This brought everything back to her mind, and all the horror of the future presented itself to her imagination. But her exhausted body did not register a visible shock. She let her head fall back on the pillow and closed her eyes... Her heart beat feebly. Tatiana Afanasevna signaled to her brother that the patient wished to go to sleep, and everybody left the room quietly, except for the maidservant, who set to work again at her spinning wheel.

The unlucky beauty opened her eyes and, no longer seeing anyone by her bed, called the maid to her and sent her to fetch the midget. At that same moment, however, the rotund little old elf was already rolling toward her bed like a ball. Lastochka (as the midget was called)[38] had run up the stairs behind Gavrila Afanasevich and Ibrahim as fast as her short legs could carry her, and she hid behind the door, in keeping with the inquisitive nature of her sex. As soon as Natasha saw her, she sent the maid away, and the midget sat down on a little stool by the bed.

Never has such a small body contained such a lively spirit. She meddled in everything, knew everything, fussed about everything. Her shrewd mind and ingratiating manner earned her the love of her masters and the hatred of the rest of the household, over which she ruled despotically. Gavrila Afanasevich listened to her denunciations, complaints, and petty requests; Tatiana Afanasevna perpetually asked for her opinion and took her advice; and Natasha had a boundless attachment to her, entrusting her with all her thoughts and all the stirrings of her sixteen-year-old heart.

"You know, Lastochka," said Natalia, "father is going to marry me to the blackamoor."

The midget sighed deeply and wrinkled up all the more her already wrinkled face.

"Is there no hope?" continued Natasha. "Is father not going to take pity on me?"

The midget shook her little cap.

"Isn't grandpapa or auntie going to intercede for me?"

"No, miss. While you've been sick the blackamoor has succeeded in charming them all. The master is devoted to him, the Prince raves about him, and Tatiana Afanasevna says, 'What a pity he's black; otherwise we couldn't wish for a better bridegroom.'"

"Oh my God, oh my God," groaned poor Natasha.

"Don't grieve, my beauty," said the midget, kissing Natalia's weak hand. "Even if you have to marry the blackamoor, you will have your freedom. Today it's not as it used to be: husbands don't lock up their wives. The blackamoor, they say, is rich; your house will be like a cup brimming over; you'll live in clover..."

"Poor Valerian," said Natasha so softly that the midget could guess more than hear her words.

"That's just it, miss," she said, confidentially lowering her voice. "If the Strelets's orphan weren't quite so much on your mind, you wouldn't rave about him in a fever, and your father wouldn't be angry."

"What?" said the frightened Natasha. "I raved about Valerian, father heard me, father is angry?"

"That's exactly the trouble," answered the midget. "After this, if you start asking him not to marry you to the blackamoor, he will think that the reason is Valerian. There is nothing to be done: you must submit to his paternal will and accept what fate brings you."

Natasha did not utter a single word in protest. The thought that her secret love was known to her father produced a powerful effect on her mind. Only one hope remained for her: to die before the hateful marriage came to pass. This idea comforted her. She submitted to her fate with a faint, sorrowful heart.

7

At the entrance to Gavrila Afanasevich's house, to the right of the passageway, there was a tiny cubicle with one small window. In it stood a simple bed covered with a flannel blanket, and in front of the bed a little deal table, on which a tallow candle burned and some sheets of music lay open. A soldier's old blue coat and a three-cornered hat of the same age hung on the wall; above the hat, a print showing a mounted Charles XII was fastened to the wall with three nails. Notes from a flute resounded through the humble dwelling. Its solitary inhabitant, the captive dance teacher in his nightcap and nankeen dressing gown, was enlivening the monotony of the winter evening by playing old Swedish marches, which reminded him of the gay time of his youth. Having devoted two hours to this exercise, he took his flute apart, put it away in a box, and started undressing.

Just then the latch on his door was lifted, and a tall handsome young man in a uniform entered the room.

The Swede rose to his feet, surprised, before the unexpected visitor.

"You don't recognize me, Gustav Adamych," said the young visitor with feeling. "You don't remember the boy whom you drilled in Swedish musketry and with whom you almost started a fire in this same little room, shooting off a toy cannon."

Gustav Adamych looked at his visitor intently.

"Ah!" he cried at last, embracing him, "god dag to you, so are du here now? Sitt down, your old scamp, so shall ve speak."[39]

The Guests Were Arriving at the Dacha
(1828, 1830)[1]

I

The guests were arriving at the dacha of X. The drawing room was filling up with ladies and men, all driving over at the same time from the theater, where they had just seen a new Italian opera. Order was gradually established: the ladies settled on the sofas, with the men forming circles around them; parties of whist were set up; only a few young people remained standing. A perusal of Parisian lithographs replaced the general conversation.

Two men sat on the balcony. One of them, a Spanish traveler, seemed to be greatly charmed by the northern night. He looked with admiration at the clear pale sky, at the majestic Neva, illuminated by mysterious light, and at the neighboring dachas, whose silhouettes showed in the transparent twilight.

"How splendid is your northern night," he said at last. "I shall miss its charms even under the skies of my own country."

"One of our poets," answered the other man, "has compared it with a towheaded Russian beauty.[2] I must confess that a swarthy, black-eyed Italian or Spanish woman, full of liveliness and southern sensuality, captures my imagination far more. But of course the old controversy between *la brune et la blonde* has not been settled. Incidentally, do you know what explanation a foreign lady offered me for the strictness and purity of Petersburg morals? She declared that our winter nights were too cold and our summer nights too bright for amorous adventures."

The Spaniard smiled.

"So it is owing to the climate," he said, "that Petersburg is the promised land of beauty, amicability, and purity."

"Beauty is a matter of taste," answered the Russian, "but as far as amicability is concerned, we have little to boast about. It's not in vogue: nobody has the least inclination to be amicable. The women would be afraid that they would acquire the reputation of flirts, the men that they would lose their dignity. All aim to be nonentities with decorum and propriety. As for the purity of morals, one should not take advantage of a foreigner's trustfulness, so let me tell you an anecdote..."

With this the conversation took a most decidedly satirical turn.

Just then the door of the drawing room opened, and Volskaia came in. She was in the first bloom of youth. Her regular features, her large black eyes, her lively movements, even her eccentric dress—everything compelled attention. The men greeted her with a certain jocular affability, and the women with marked hostility. Volskaia herself noticed none of this; while giving haphazard answers to the customary questions, she absently looked about her on every side. Her face, changeable as a cloud, expressed vexation. She sat down next to the lofty Princess G. and, as the expression goes, *se mit à bouder.*[3]

Suddenly she shuddered and turned toward the balcony. She got up, passed by the armchairs and tables, stopped for a moment behind the chair of old General R., and without acknowledging his subtle compliment, slipped out on the balcony.

The Spaniard and the Russian rose to their feet. She walked up to them and said a few words in Russian with embarrassment. The Spaniard, assuming he was superfluous, left them and returned to the drawing room.

The lofty Princess G. followed Volskaia with her eyes and said to her neighbor in a low tone, "This sort of thing is just not done."

"She's terribly frivolous," answered he.

"Frivolous? More than that. Her behavior is inexcusable. She's free to have as little self-respect as she wishes, but society ought not to be treated with such disdain. Minskii should give her a hint."

"Il n'en fera rien, trop heureux de pouvoir le compromettre.[4] With all that, I bet you their conversation is perfectly innocent."

"I'm convinced of that... But since when have you become so charitable?"

"I must confess I take an interest in the fate of that young woman.[5] There's much more good and much less bad in her than people think. But passion will ruin her."

"Passion! What a big word! What is passion? You don't really imagine, do you, that she has an ardent heart and a romantic disposition? She's simply had a bad upbringing... What lithograph is that? Is it a portrait of Hussein Pasha?[6] Would you pass it to me?"

The guests were leaving; there was not one lady left in the drawing room. The hostess alone, with unconcealed displeasure, stood by the table at which two diplomats were finishing their last game of *écarté.*

Volskaia, suddenly noticing that it was getting light, hastened to leave the balcony, where she had spent some three uninterrupted hours alone with Minskii. The hostess said good-bye to her coldly and did not so much as deign to look at Minskii. Several guests were waiting for their carriages at the entrance; Minskii helped Volskaia into hers.

"It looks like it's your turn," said a young officer to him.

"Not at all," he answered. "She is otherwise engaged; I'm simply her confidant or call it what you like. But I love her sincerely: she's excruciatingly funny."

Zinaida Volskaia had lost her mother before she was six. Her father, a busy and dissipated person, entrusted her to the care of a French governess, hired tutors of all kinds for her, and paid no further attention to her. By age fourteen she had grown beautiful and was writing love letters to her dance teacher. Her father learned of this, dismissed the dance teacher, and considering her education completed, brought her out in society. Her appearance on the social scene created a great sensation. Volskii, a wealthy young man who usually let his feelings be governed by the opinions of others, fell head over heels in love with her[7] because the Sovereign had once met her on the English Embankment and talked with her a full hour. Volskii sought her hand. Her father was glad to get the fashionable debutante off his hands. Zinaida burned with impatience to marry in order to be able to see the whole of Petersburg in her drawing room. Besides, Volskii was not repugnant to her, and thus her fate was soon sealed.

At first her sincerity, unexpected pranks, and childish frivolity made a favorable impression: even high society was grateful to her for breaking the decorous monotony of its aristocratic circles. They laughed at her antics and kept talking about her strange sallies. But years went by, and Zinaida still remained a fourteen-year-old at heart. People began to grumble. It was decided that Volskaia did not possess the sense of decency appropriate to her sex. The women began to avoid her, while the men drew closer to her. Zinaida comforted herself with the thought that she was none the worse off for it.

Rumor began to ascribe lovers to her. Calumny, even without proof, leaves almost indelible marks. According to the code of high society, plausibility equals verity, and to be the target of slander lowers us in our own estimation. Volskaia, shedding tears of indignation, resolved to rebel against the authority of unjust society. An opportunity soon presented itself.

Among the young men of her circle Zinaida singled out Minskii.

Evidently a certain similarity in character and circumstances must have drawn them to each other. In his early youth Minskii, too, had incurred society's disapprobation and was punished by slander. He left society, pretending to be indifferent. For a while passions muted the anguish of his wounded pride, but eventually, humbled by experience, he reappeared on the social scene, this time bringing with him, not the ardency of his incautious youth, but the concessions and outward decorum of egoism. He did not like society, yet did not scorn it, knowing how important it was to secure its approbation. With all this said, it must be remarked that though he respected society in general, he did not spare it in particular instances, and was ready to make any of its members victims of his rancorous vanity. He liked Volskaia for daring to despise certain conventions that he hated. He goaded her on with encouragement and advice, assumed the role of her confidant, and soon became indispensable to her.

B. had appealed to her imagination for some time.

"He's too shallow for you," Minskii said to her. "All his ideas derive from *Les Liaisons dangereuses*,[8] and all his genius amounts to a plagiarism of Jomini.[9] When you get to know him better, you'll grow to despise his oppressive immorality, just as military men despise his trivial pronouncements."

"I'd like to fall in love with R.," said Zinaida.

"Nonsense!" he answered. "What makes you want to get involved with a man who dyes his hair and repeats with rapture every five minutes, '*Quand j'étais à Florence.*' They say his insufferable wife is in love with him. Leave them alone; they're made for each other."

"And how about the Baron W.?"

"That's a little girl in an officer's uniform. What do you see in him? But you know what? Fall in love with L. He'll appeal to your imagination: he's just as exceptionally clever as he's exceptionally ugly. *Et puis c'est un homme à grands sentiments.*[10] He'll be jealous and passionate; he'll torment you and amuse you: what more would you wish?"

But Volskaia did not take his advice. Minskii guessed in which direction her heart was inclining, and his vanity was flattered. Not suspecting that frivolity could be joined with strong passions, he foresaw a liaison without any significant consequences, an augmentation by one more name of the list of his flighty mistresses; and he coolly contemplated his impending conquest. It is likely that if he had anticipated the storms awaiting him, he would have declined his victory, because a man of high society readily sacrifices his pleasures—and even his vanity—for convenience and seemliness.

2

Minskii was still in bed when a letter was brought to him. He broke the seal with a yawn and, shrugging his shoulders, unfolded two sheets covered to the last square inch with the minutest feminine handwriting. The letter began in the following way:

> I wasn't able to express to you everything that was on my mind: in your presence I couldn't give form to the ideas that are now so vividly haunting me. Your sophisms don't allay my suspicions,[11] but they silence me, which proves that you're invariably superior to me, but that is not enough for happiness, for the tranquility of my heart...

Volskaia reproached him for his coldness, his distrust, and the like; she complained and entreated, not knowing herself what about; showered on him a profusion of tender, affectionate assurances—and made an assignation to meet him in her box at the theater that evening. Minskii answered her in a couple of lines, excusing his tersity on the plea of tedious but unavoidable business, and promising to come to the theater without fail.

3

"You are so open and kind," said the Spaniard, "that I feel encouraged to ask you to solve a riddle for me. I have wandered all around the world, have been introduced at all the European Courts and frequented high society everywhere; but nowhere have I felt as constrained and awkward as I do in your accursed aristocratic circles. Every time I enter Princess V.'s drawing room and see these speechless and motionless mummies, which bring to mind Egyptian burial grounds, I feel frozen to the bones. I am not aware of anyone with spiritual authority among them, nor has fame impressed anyone's name on my memory—why then do I feel so timid?"

"Because of an air of malice," answered the Russian. "It is a trait of our mores. Among the simple people it finds expression in a jeering disposition; among the higher circles, in coldness and inattention. Besides, our ladies receive a very superficial education, and nothing European ever captivates their minds. The men need not even be mentioned: politics and literature do not exist for them, and wit has been banned as a sign of levity. What can they all talk about? About themselves? No, they are too well-bred for that. What remains for them is a kind of domestic, petty, private conversation, comprehensible only to a few—to the select. And the person who does not belong to this small herd is received as an alien—not only if he is a foreigner, but even if he is Russian."

"Forgive me for all these questions," said the foreigner, "but I shall hardly find another opportunity to obtain satisfactory answers, and therefore I hasten to take advantage of you. You have mentioned your aristocracy: what does Russian aristocracy mean? Studying your laws, I see that in your country there is no hereditary aristocracy founded on the indivisibility of landed property. There exists, it seems, a civil equality among your nobility, and access to its ranks is not limited. What, then, is your so-called aristocracy founded on? On ancient lineage alone?"

The Russian laughed.

"You are mistaken," he answered. "The ancient Russian nobility, precisely because of the reasons you have mentioned, has fallen into obscurity and has formed a kind of third estate. This noble plebs of ours, to which I myself belong, considers Riurik and Monomakh its forefathers.[12] I can tell you, for instance," continued the Russian with an air of self-satisfied unconcern, "that the roots of my family reach back into the dark, distant past; you come across the names of my forefathers on every page of our history. Yet if it entered my head to call myself an aristocrat, many people would probably laugh. As for our actual aristocrats, they can scarcely name their grandfathers. The ancient families among them trace their lineage back to the reigns of Peter and Elizabeth. Orderlies, choristers, Ukrainians—those are the kind of forefathers they have. I am not saying this with disapproval: merit, after all, will always remain merit, and the interests of the state demand that it be rewarded. Only it is ridiculous to see in the insignificant grandsons of pastry vendors, orderlies, choristers, and sextons a haughtiness befitting the Duke of Montmorency, the first Christian baron, or Clermont-Tonnerre.[13] We are so practical-minded that we stand on our knees before the accident of the moment, before success, and before... well, in any case, no fascination with antiquity, no gratitude for past accomplishments, no respect for moral virtues, exists among us. Karamzin has recently narrated our history for us,[14] but we hardly listened. We pride ourselves, not on the glory of our forefathers, but on the rank of some uncle or other, or on the balls our cousin gives. A lack of respect for one's forefathers, mark my word, is a fundamental indication of barbarity and immorality."[15]

In the Corner of a Small Square

(1830 or 1831)[1]

I

Votre coeur est l'éponge imbibée
de fiel et de vinaigre.
CORRESPONDANCE INÉDITE[2]

In the corner of a small square, in front of a little wooden house, there stood a carriage—an unusual phenomenon in this remote area of the city. The driver lay asleep on the coach box, while the postilion played snowballs with some serving boys.

A pale lady, no longer in the first bloom of youth but still beautiful, dressed with great refinement, lay on a sofa strewn with cushions, in a room appointed with taste and luxury. A young man of about twenty-six sat in front of the fireplace, leafing through an English novel.

The pale lady's black eyes, deep-set and blue-shadowed, were fixed on the young man. It was getting dark and the fire was going out, but he continued his reading. At last she said:

"Has anything happened, Valerian? You're angry today."

"I am," he answered, without raising his eyes from the page.

"With whom?"

"With Prince Goretskii. He's giving a ball today to which I'm not invited."

"Did you very much want to attend his ball?"

"Not in the least. The devil take him with his ball. But if he invites the whole town, he must invite me too."

"Which Goretskii is this? Prince Iakov?"

"Not at all. Prince Iakov's been dead for a long time. It's his brother, Prince Grigorii, the well-known jackass."[3]

"Who's his wife?"

"She's the daughter of that chorister, what's his name?"

"I haven't gone out for so long that I'm beginning to forget who's who in your high society. In any case, do you so highly value whatever attention Prince Grigorii, a well-known scoundrel, pays to you, and whatever favor his wife, the daughter of a chorister, bestows upon you?"

"Of course I do," answered the young man heatedly, tossing his book on the table. "I'm a man of aristocratic society and don't want to be slighted by any one of its members. What their lineage or morality may be is none of my business."

"Whom do you call aristocrats?"

"Those with whom the Countess Fuflygina shakes hands."

"And who's this Countess Fuflygina?"

"A stupid and insolent woman."[4]

"Are you saying that being slighted by people whom you despise can upset you so much?" she asked after a brief silence. "Do confess, there must be some other reason."[5]

"So that's what you're driving at: suspicions and jealousy, all over again! God be my witness, this is intolerable."

With these words he rose and picked up his hat.

"Are you leaving already?" the lady asked anxiously. "Don't you want to have dinner with me?"

"No, I promised to eat with someone."

"Do have dinner with me," she resumed in an affectionate and timid voice. "I've had some champagne bought for the occasion."

"And what did you do that for? Do you think I'm some kind of Moscow gambler who can't do without champagne?"

"Last time you found fault with my wine and were cross because women don't know anything about wines. There's no way to please you."

"I'm not asking anybody to please me."

She made no answer. The young man immediately regretted the rudeness of his last words. He stepped up to her, took her hand, and said with tenderness:

"Zinaida, forgive me: I'm just not myself today; I'm angry with everybody for everything. At such times I should sit at home. Forgive me: don't be angry with me."

"I'm not angry, Valerian. But it hurts me to see how much you've changed lately. You come to visit me as if out of duty, not because your heart draws you here. You're bored with me. You don't talk, you don't know what to do, you just leaf through books, and find fault with everything in order to quarrel with me and be able to go away. I'm not reproaching you: our feelings are not in our power, but I..."

Valerian was no longer listening to her. He was pulling at his glove, which he had put on long before, and was impatiently looking out into the street. She fell silent with an air of restrained irritation. He squeezed her hand, uttered some meaningless words, and ran out of the room like a restless schoolboy from a classroom. Zinaida went to the window and watched him waiting for his carriage, then climbing in and leaving. She stayed at the window for a long time, pressing her burning forehead against the icy pane. At length she said aloud:

"No, he doesn't love me!"

She rang for her maid, told her to light the lamp, and sat down at her desk.

2

Vous écrivez vos lettres de 4 pages plus vite que je ne puis les lire.[6]

X. soon found out that his wife was unfaithful. It threw him into great perplexity. He did not know what to do: it seemed to him that to pretend not to notice anything would be stupid; to laugh at this so very common misfortune would be despicable; to get angry in earnest would be too scandalous; and to complain with an air of deeply offended feeling would be too ridiculous. Fortunately, his wife came to his aid.

Having fallen in love with Volodskii, she conceived the kind of aversion to her spouse that is characteristic only of women and is understandable only to them. One day she walked into his study, locked the door behind her, and declared that she loved Volodskii, that she did not want to deceive and secretly dishonor her husband, and that she was resolved to divorce him. X. was alarmed by such candor and precipitousness. Giving him no time to collect himself, she removed herself from the English Embankment to Kolomna that same day,[7] and sent a brief note about it all to Volodskii, who had expected nothing of the kind...

He was thrown into despair. He had never meant to tie himself down with such bonds. He hated boredom, feared every obligation, and valued his egotistical independence above all else. But it was a *fait accompli*. Zinaida remained on his hands. He pretended to be grateful, but in fact he faced the pains of his liaison as if performing an official duty or getting down to the tedious task of checking his butler's monthly accounts...[8]

A Novel in Letters
(1829)[1]

1. Liza to Sasha

Dear Sashenka, you must have been surprised by my unexpected departure for the country. I hasten to explain it all candidly. My dependent position has always been painful to me. It goes without saying that Avdotia Andreevna brought me up as an equal with her niece. Yet in her house I always remained a ward: you cannot imagine how many petty grievances are attached to that title. I had to put up with a great deal, to yield in many things and close my eyes to others; while my vanity assiduously took note of the remotest hint of a slight. My very equality with the Princess was a burden to me. When we appeared at a ball in identical dresses, it annoyed me that she wore no pearls. I felt that the only reason why she had not put them on was that she didn't want to be different from me, and this very tactfulness offended me. Does she presume envy or any such childish meanness of spirit in me, I asked myself. The way men treated me, however polite they might have been, wounded my vanity every minute. The coldness of some and the affability of others both suggested a lack of respect for me. In short, I was an extremely unhappy creature, and my heart, though tender by nature, was becoming more and more hardened. Have you not noticed that all young girls who have the status of wards, distant relatives, *demoiselles de compagnie*, and the like, are usually either base sycophants or insufferable eccentrics? The latter I respect and exonerate with all my heart.

Exactly three weeks ago I received a letter from my poor grandmother. She complained of her lonely life and urged me to come and live with her in the country. I decided to take this opportunity. I could just barely persuade Avdotia Andreevna to let me go, and I had to promise to return to Petersburg for the winter; but I have no intention of keeping my word. Grandmama was overwhelmed with joy: she had not really thought I would come. I cannot tell you how much I was moved by her tears. I have grown to love her with all my heart. At one time she belonged to the best society, and she has retained much of the courtesy of those days.

Now that I am living *at home*, I am the mistress of the house, and you will not believe what a heartfelt pleasure this is to me. I grew used to country life in next to no time, and the lack of luxury doesn't seem strange to me at all. Our property is truly charming. An ancient house on a hill, a garden, a lake, and pine forests all around—all this is somewhat melancholy in the fall and winter, but must seem like paradise on earth in the spring and summer. We have few neighbors, and so far I haven't seen anyone. I love solitude—just as it is sung in the elegies of your Lamartine.[2]

Write to me, my angel; your letters will bring great comfort to me. How are your social gatherings and our common acquaintances? Although I have become a recluse, I have not given up all the vanities of the world: news about it will be entertaining to me.

The Village of Pavlovskoe[3]

2. Sasha's Reply

My dear Liza,

Just imagine how astonished I was when I heard about your removal to the country. Seeing Princess Olga by herself, I thought you were unwell, and I couldn't believe what she told me. Then, the next day, I get your letter. Congratulations, my angel, on your new way of life. I'm glad you like it. Your complaint about your previous situation moved me to tears, though it sounded unduly harsh. How can you compare yourself with wards and *demoiselles de compagnie*! Everybody knows that Olga's father was obligated to yours for everything he had, and that their friendship was as sacred as the closest family tie. It seemed that you were content with your lot. I would never have guessed that you were so oversensitive. Confess: isn't there another, secret reason for your hurried departure? I suspect... But you're being terribly discreet with me and I don't want to anger you with my conjectures from a distance.

What can I tell you about Petersburg? We are still at our dacha, but almost everybody else is already gone. The balls will start in a couple of weeks. The weather is wonderful. I walk a great deal. The other day we had some guests for dinner: one of them asked me if I had any news of you. He said that your absence is as noticeable at the balls as a broken string in a piano—and I completely agreed with him. I keep hoping that this fit of misanthropy will not last long. Come back, my angel: otherwise I'll have nobody this winter with whom to share my simplehearted observations and the epigrams born in my heart. Farewell, dear—give it some thought and change your mind.

Krestovskii Island[4]

3. Liza to Sasha

Your letter cheered me up no end. It reminded me of Petersburg so much; it seemed as if I were hearing your voice. How ridiculous are your perpetual speculations! You suspect in me some deep, arcane feelings, some unhappy love, don't you? Calm down, my dear, you're wrong: I resemble a heroine only in that I live in a remote village and pour cups of tea, like Clarissa Harlowe.[5]

You say you won't have anybody this winter with whom to share your satirical observations. But what is our correspondence for? Write to me about anything that attracts your attention: I repeat I have not at all given up society, and everything connected with it interests me. As proof, let me ask you who the person was that found my absence so noticeable. Was it our warmhearted chatterbox, Aleksei R.? I am sure I've guessed right... My ears were always at his service, which was all he wanted.

I have become acquainted with the X. family. The father is a buffoon and a great host, the mother a fat, well-humored matron, very fond of playing whist, and the daughter a slender melancholy girl of seventeen, brought up on novels in the fresh air. She is in the garden or in the fields with book in hand all day, surrounded by dogs from the farmyard; she speaks about the weather in a singsong and offers you jam with affection.[6] I found a whole bookcase full of old-fashioned novels in her room. I intend to read them all, and I have already begun with Richardson. Only if you live in the country do you get the opportunity to read the vaunted *Clarissa*. Crossing myself, I began with the translator's preface and, finding in it an assurance that though the first six parts were a bit on the dull side the last six would fully reward the reader's patience, I bravely set about the task. I read the first, the second, the third volumes... at last I reach the sixth one: dull beyond endurance. Well, thought I, now I shall be rewarded for my pains. And what happened? I read about the deaths of Clarissa and Lovelace, and that was the end of it. Each volume contained two parts, and I did not notice the transition from the six boring to the six entertaining ones.[7]

Reading Richardson led me to some reflections. What a frightful difference between the ideals of the grandmothers and those of the granddaughters! What is there in common between Lovelace and Adolphe?[8] Yet at the same time the role of women has not changed. Clarissa, except for some ceremonious curtsyings, is very like heroines in the latest novels. Is this because man's attractiveness depends on fashion, on attitudes of the moment, while that of women is based on an emotional makeup and nature that are enduring?

You see, I'm chattering on with you as usual. Please don't be any less generous in your epistolary conversations with me. Write to me as often as possible and as much as possible: you cannot imagine how much one looks forward in the country to the day the post comes. Looking forward to a ball cannot be compared with it.

4. Sasha's Reply

You are mistaken, my dear Liza. I declare, in order to humble your pride, that R. does not notice your absence at all. He has attached himself to Lady Pelham, an Englishwoman recently come for a visit.[9] He never leaves her side. She responds to his remarks with a look of ingenuous surprise and with the little exclamation: "Oho!" He is in raptures. Let me tell you: the person who has been inquiring after you and is missing you with all sincerity is your faithful Vladimir Y. Are you satisfied? I imagine you are, and let me presume, in my usual way, that you didn't need my help to guess who it was. Joking aside, Y. is very much preoccupied with you. If I were you I'd draw him out as much as I could. Why not? He is a highly eligible young man... There is no reason why you shouldn't marry him: you would live on the English Embankment, throw parties on Saturday nights, and drive by to pick me up every morning. Stop being silly, my angel: come back and marry Y.

K. gave a ball the other day. There were swarms of people. The dancing went on until five in the morning. K. V. was dressed very simply: a white crepe dress, without even any lace trim, but on her head and around her neck half a million's worth of diamonds—that's all! Z. as usual was dressed in an excruciating fashion. Wherever does she get her outfits? She had, instead of flowers, some sort of dried mushrooms sewn on her dress. Did you, by any chance, send them to her from the country, my angel? Vladimir Y. did not dance. He is going on leave. The C.s came (probably the very first), sat through the night without dancing, and were the last to leave. The oldest of the girls, I fancied, had put on some rouge—it is high time, too... The ball was a great success. The men were not satisfied with the supper, but then men always have to be dissatisfied with something. I had a very good time, even though I danced the cotillion with that insufferable diplomat, St., whose innate stupidity is reinforced by a blasé manner, imported from Madrid.

Thank you, sweetheart, for your report on Richardson. Now I have some notion about him. With my impatience I have little hope of ever reading him: I find superfluous pages even in Walter Scott.

That reminds me: Elena N.'s romance with Count L. seems to be drawing to a conclusion; at least he looks so crestfallen and she is giving herself such airs that a wedding date appears to have been fixed. Farewell, my precious one, are you satisfied with my chatter today?

5. Liza to Sasha

No, my dear matchmaker, I am not about to leave the country and come back to attend my wedding. I admit frankly that I did like Vladimir Y., but it never entered my mind to marry him. He is an aristocrat, and I am a humble democrat. I hasten to explain and proudly remark, like a true heroine of a novel, that by lineage I belong to the most ancient Russian nobility, while my cavalier is the grandson of an unshorn millionaire. But you know what aristocracy means with us. Be that as it may, Y. is certainly a man of good society and he may even like me, but he will never forgo a rich bride and an advantageous connection for my sake. If I ever marry, I'll choose a forty-year-old landowner right here. He will get involved in his sugar-refining plant, I in my household—and I'll be happy, even though I will not be dancing at the house of Count K. and will not be giving Saturday-evening parties on the English Embankment.

Winter has arrived: in the country *c'est un événement*. It radically changes one's way of life. Solitary walks come to an end; bells are tinkling; hunters ride out with their dogs—everything becomes brighter and gayer with the first snow. I never expected it to be this way. Winter in the country used to frighten me. But every cloud has a silver lining.

I have become better acquainted with Mashenka X. and have grown fond of her; she has many good qualities and much originality. I've learned quite by accident that Y. is a close relation of theirs. Mashenka has not seen him for seven years but is enchanted with him. He once spent a summer with them, and Mashenka still cannot stop talking about all the details of what he did then. As I read her novels I come across his faintly penciled marginalia: it is obvious that he was still a child back then. At this time he was struck by ideas and sentiments that he would of course laugh at now; but at least his remarks show a fresh, impressionable mind. I read a great deal. You can't imagine how strange it is to read in 1829 a novel that was written in 1775. It seems as if you suddenly stepped out of your drawing room into an ancient, damask-wainscoted hall, sat down in a soft atlas-upholstered armchair, and saw around you old-fashioned costume yet familiar faces, in which you recognized your uncles and grandmothers, grown young. Most of these novels have no other merit. The action is entertaining, and the plot skillfully tangled, but Bellecour stammers and Charlotte stutters.[10] A clever man could adopt these ready-made plots and characters, amend the style, eliminate the absurdities, supply the missing links—and the result would be a splendid original novel. Pass this on to that ungrateful R. from me. It is time he stopped wasting his wits on conversations with Englishwomen. Embroidering new designs on an old canvas, he should present us, in a small frame, with a picture of our society and people, which he knows so well.

Masha is well versed in Russian literature—generally, belles lettres occupy people here more than in Petersburg. They receive the journals, take a lively interest in the squabbles therein, trust each side in turns, and become indignant on behalf of their favorite author if the critics tear him to pieces. Now I understand why Viazemskii and Pushkin are so fond of provincial misses: they are their true reading public.[11] I myself thought I'd take a look at some journals, and started reading critical reviews in the *European Herald*, but the banality and boorish tone of these writings struck me as repulsive: it is ludicrous when a work of literature that we have all read—we, the touch-me-nots of St. Petersburg!—is being pompously accused of immorality and indecency by a former seminary student.[12]

6. Liza to Sasha

My dear, I cannot pretend any more; I need the help and advice of a friend. He from whom I have fled, whom I fear as the plague, Vladimir Y., is here. What am I to do? My head is swimming; I am at a loss; for heaven's sake decide for me what I should do. Let me tell you all about it.

You noticed last winter how he would never leave my side. He did not visit us at home, but he and I saw each other everywhere. I armed myself with coldness, even with scornful looks, but all in vain: there was no way for me to get rid of him. At balls he always managed to find a place next to me; on our walks we always ran into him; and at the theater his lorgnette was always directed at our box.

At first this appealed to my vanity. It is possible that I made that all too obvious to him. At least he fancied he had acquired new rights over me and kept speaking to me about his feelings, now voicing jealousy, now complaining... I asked myself with alarm what all this was leading to, and acknowledged with a sense of despair that he had power over my heart. I left Petersburg in order to prevent calamity while it was not too late. The decisive step I had taken and the conviction that I had done the right thing were beginning to calm my heart; I was already thinking of him with greater equanimity and less grief. Then, I suddenly see him.

This was how I saw him. Yesterday there was a name-day party at the X.'s house. I arrived just before dinner: as I come into the drawing room I find a whole crowd of guests; I see uhlan officers' uniforms; the ladies surround me; I exchange kisses with them all. Noticing nothing, I sit down next to the hostess and lift my eyes: Y. is right in front of me. I was stunned... He said a few words to me with such a look of tender, genuine joy that I could not gather enough strength to hide either my confusion or my pleasure.

We went to the dining room. He sat just across the table from me; I did not dare look at him but noticed that everybody else's eyes were fixed on him. He was silent and distracted. At another time it would have very much amused me to see such a general desire to attract the attention of a newcomer—an officer of the Guards—such unease on the part of the young ladies and such awkwardness in the men, roaring with laughter over their own jokes while their guest showed cool politeness and total indifference... After dinner he came up to me. Feeling obliged to say something, I asked him rather unfelicitously whether some business had brought him to our part of the world.

"I've come on a business on which the happiness of my life depends," answered he in an undertone, moving away from me immediately. He sat down to play Boston with three old ladies (grandmama among them); as for me, I went upstairs to Mashenka's room and lay on her bed until evening on the pretext of a headache. Indeed I felt worse than ill. Mashenka did not leave my side. She is enraptured with Y. He is going to stay with them a month or more. She will be spending all day with him. The truth of the matter is that she is in love with him—may heaven grant that he, too, fall in love with her. She is slender and enigmatic—just the two traits men want.

What am I to do, my dear? I shall not be able to avoid his relentless attentions here. He has already succeeded in charming grandmama.

He will be coming to see us—and the confessions, laments, vows will pour forth anew: *but to what end?* He will obtain my love, my confession; then he will consider the disadvantages of marrying me, will go away under some pretext, abandon me, and I... What a terrible prospect! For heaven's sake, hold your hand out to me! I am sinking.

7. Sasha's Reply

Isn't it much better to have unburdened yourself with a full confession? You should have done it a long time ago, my angel! Why on earth did you not admit to me, what I had already known, that Y. and you are in love? And what's the great misfortune about that? Enjoy it. You have a knack for looking at things from God knows what angle. You're asking for misfortune: take care not to bring it on yourself. Why not marry Y.? Where do you see insurmountable obstacles? He's rich and you're poor—that's immaterial. He's rich enough for two: what else do you want? He is an aristocrat; but aren't you one also by both name and upbringing?

Some time ago I heard a discussion concerning ladies of the best society. R., as I learned during the discussion, had once declared himself on the side of the aristocrats because they wore nicer shoes. Isn't it clear, if we follow his logic, that you are an aristocrat from top to toe?

Forgive me, my angel, but your pathetic letter made me laugh. Y. had arrived in the country in order to see you. What horror! You're going to ruin, you're asking for my advice. I fear you've really become a provincial heroine. My advice is this: hold the wedding at your wooden church as soon as possible, and move to Petersburg in order to take the part of Fornarina in the tableaux vivants that are just being organized at S.'s house.[13] Your cavalier's gesture has touched me, I'm not joking. Of course, in the old days a lover went to fight in the Holy Land for three years in order to win a charitable smile, but in our day and age, if a man travels five hundred versts from Petersburg in order to see the one who rules his heart, it truly means a great deal. Y. deserves his rewards.

8. Vladimir Y. to a Friend

Do me a favor, spread the rumor that I am on my deathbed; I intend to extend my leave, but I want to do it observing propriety in every possible way. I've already been here in the country for two weeks, but

I've scarcely noticed how time flies. I am taking a rest from Petersburg life, which had really gotten on my nerves. Only the pupil of a convent school, just freed from her cell, or an eighteen-year-old gentleman of the Emperor's bedchamber can be forgiven for not loving the countryside. Petersburg is the entrance hall, Moscow is the maidservants' quarters, the village is our study room. A man of good breeding goes through the entrance hall by necessity and drops by the maids' quarters on occasion, but he sits in his study. And that's what I'll end up doing. I am going to retire from the service, get married, and settle in my village near Saratov. The occupation of a landowner is also a service. To manage three thousand serfs, whose welfare depends entirely on us, is more important than to command a platoon or to copy diplomatic dispatches...

The state of neglect in which we leave our peasants is inexcusable. The more rights we have over them, the greater our obligations toward them. Yet we leave them to the mercy of some scoundrel of a steward, who oppresses them and robs us. We use up our future income in payment of debts; we ravage our property; old age catches us in need and worry.

This is the reason for the rapid decline of our nobility: the grandfather was rich, the son lives in want, the grandson goes a-begging. Ancient families come to insignificance; new ones rise, but in the third generation disappear again. Estates merge, and not one family is conscious of its ancestry. What does such political materialism lead to? I don't know. But it is time to put some obstacles in its path.

I have never been able to contemplate the degradation of our historic families without sorrow: nobody cherishes them in our country, not even those who belong to them. Indeed what pride of the past can you expect from a people whose national monument is inscribed with the words: "In memory of Citizen Minin and Prince Pozharskii"? Which Prince Pozharskii? What does Citizen Minin signify? There was a privy councillor called Prince Dmitrii Mikhailovich Pozharskii, and a citizen named Kozma Minich Sukhorukii, elected representative of the state.[14] But the fatherland has forgotten even the correct names of its liberators. The past does not exist for us. A wretched people!

No service aristocracy can replace a hereditary aristocracy. The gentry's family traditions should be the nation's historical heritage. But what family traditions are there for the children of a collegiate assessor?

When I speak out in favor of the aristocracy, I'm not trying—like

A Novel in Letters   59

the diplomat Severin, grandson of a tailor and a cook[15]—to pose as an English lord; my origin, though it is nothing to be ashamed of, gives me no right to do that. But I agree with La Bruyère's statement: "Affecter le mépris de la naissance est un ridicule dans le parvenu et une lâcheté dans le gentilhomme."[16]

I've arrived at all this wisdom by living in someone else's village and watching petty landowners manage their estates. These gentlemen are not in the service, and they do manage their small villages, but I confess I wish they would go to ruin just like you and me. What barbarity! As far as they are concerned, Fonvizin's times have not yet passed. Prostakovs and Skotinins are still flourishing among them.[17]

This, by the way, does not refer to the relative I'm staying with. He is a very kind man, his wife a very kind woman, and their daughter a very kind little girl. You can see I've become very kind myself. In truth, since I've been living in the country I've grown exceedingly benign and forbearing—the effect of a patriarchal way of life and of the presence of Liza Z. I had truly been missing her.[18] I came to persuade her to return to Petersburg. Our first meeting was splendid. It was at my aunt's name-day party. The whole neighborhood had assembled. Liza came too, and could hardly believe her eyes when she saw me... She couldn't in all honesty not realize that I had come here solely for her sake. At least I did my best to let her perceive it. My success here has surpassed all my expectations (which means a lot). The old ladies are enraptured with me, and the young ones run after me "because they're patriots."[19] The men are distinctly annoyed with my *fatuité indolente*,[20] which is still a novelty in these parts. They're all the more furious because I am exceedingly polite and proper: although they sense that I am insolent, they cannot quite say what that insolence consists of. Good-bye. What are our friends doing? *Servitor di tutti quanti.*[21] Write to me at the village of X.

9. The Friend's Reply

I have carried out your commission. Last night I announced at the theater that you had succumbed to a nervous fever and in all likelihood had already given up the ghost; ergo, enjoy life until resurrected.

Your ethical reflections on the management of estates make me rejoice on your behalf. They are long overdue.

> Un homme sans peur et sans reproche.
> Qui n'est ni roi, ni duc, ni comte aussi.[22]

The position of the Russian landowner, in my opinion, is most enviable.

Ranks in Russia are a necessity, if only for the sake of post stations where you cannot get a horse unless you have rank.[23]

Indulging in these weighty considerations I quite forgot that your mind is not on them just now: you are busy with your Liza. Whatever makes you imitate M. Faublas and get entangled with women all the time?[24] It's not worthy of you. In this respect you are behind your times, behaving like a *ci-devant* chesty officer of the Guard, dated 1807. Right now this is only a shortcoming, but soon you'll become even more ridiculous than General G. Wouldn't you do better if you got used to the austerity of mature age in good time and gave up your withering youth voluntarily? I realize I am preaching in the wind, but that is my destiny.

All your friends send their greetings and are deeply upset by your untimely demise. Count among them your former mistress, too, just back from Rome and in love with the Pope. How very like her, and how very thrilled you must be to hear it! Won't you return in order to compete *cum servo servorum dei*?[25] That would be very like you. I am going to expect your arrival any day.

10. Vladimir Y. to His Friend

Your censures are totally unjust. Not I, but you have fallen behind your times, by a whole decade. Your grave metaphysical musings belong to the year 1818. At that time an austere code of behavior and political economy were in vogue. We made our appearance at balls without taking our swords off; we were ashamed to dance, and had no time to devote to the ladies. I have the honor to report to you that all this has now changed. The French quadrille has replaced Adam Smith; all flirt and make merry as best they can.[26] I adapt to the spirit of the time; it is you who are hidebound, *ci-devant*, *un homme sté-réotype*. Aren't you tired of sitting all by yourself, glued to the bench of the opposition? I hope Z. will guide you in the right direction: I hereby entrust you to her Vatican-style coquetry. As for me, I have entirely abandoned myself to a patriarchal way of life: I go to bed at ten o'clock in the evening, ride out with local landowners, tracking down the game in the fresh snow, play Boston for kopeck stakes with old ladies, and get upset if I lose. I see Liza every day, falling deeper and deeper in love with her. She's captivating in many ways. Her mien has something quiet, dignified, harmonious, about it, showing the grace of the best Petersburg society, and yet there is in her a spontaneity, a capacity for tolerance, and (as her grandmother puts it) a constitutional good humor. You never notice anything sharp or uncharitable in her judgments, and she doesn't scowl when faced with a new impression, like a child before taking rhubarb. She listens and understands—a rare virtue among our women. I have often been struck by a dullness of intellect or by an impurity of imagination in otherwise perfectly well-bred ladies. Frequently they will take the most subtle joke, the most poetic compliment, either for an impertinent epigram or for an indecent banality. On such occasions the frigid countenance they affect is so atrociously repulsive that even the most ardent love cannot survive it undamaged.

I experienced just this with Elena N., with whom I was madly in love. When I addressed a tender phrase to her, she took it for an insult and complained to a girl friend about me. That incident dashed all my illusions about her. In addition to Liza, I have Mashenka X. here to amuse myself with. She is sweet. These girls, brought up by nannies and nature among apple trees and haystacks, are much more appealing than our stereotyped beauties, who cling to their mothers' opinions until their weddings and to those of their husbands ever after.

Farewell, my dear friend; what's new in society? Tell everybody that I have at last plunged into poetry. The other day I composed an inscription for Princess Olga's portrait (for which Liza scolded me very charmingly):

As stupid as the truth, as boring as perfection.

Or would this be better:

As boring as the truth, as stupid as perfection.

Both versions look as if there was some thought in them. Ask V. to furnish a rhyme for the next line and to consider me a poet from now on.

The Tales of the Late Ivan Petrovich Belkin

(1829–30)[1]

Mme. Prostakova: Aye, truly, my
sir, he's been fond of histories
ever since he was little.
Skotinin: Mitrofan takes after me.
The Young Hopeful[2]

From the Publisher

Having undertaken the task of publishing I. P. Belkin's *Tales*, herewith offered to the public, we wished to append to them a biography, however brief, of their late author and thus at least partially to satisfy the legitimate curiosity of lovers of our native literature. With this purpose in mind we approached Maria Alekseevna Trafilina, Ivan Petrovich Belkin's nearest of kin and heir, but unfortunately she was unable to provide any information due to the circumstance that she had never met the deceased. She advised us to address ourselves on the subject to a certain estimable gentleman who had been a friend of Ivan Petrovich's. We acted on her advice and received the desired response, as follows below. We print it without any change or annotations, as a precious document testifying to a noble frame of mind and to a touching bond of friendship, and, at the same time, as a perfectly adequate biographical sketch.

My dear sir,

On the twenty-third of this month I had the honor of receiving your esteemed letter of the fifteenth in which you express your wish to obtain detailed information concerning the dates of birth and death, army service, family circumstances, and occupations, as well as the moral character, of the late Ivan Petrovich Belkin, my erstwhile sincere friend and owner of an estate neighboring mine. It is a great pleasure for me to comply with your request, and I herewith convey to you, my dear sir, everything from his conversations as well as from my own observations that I can recall.

Ivan Petrovich Belkin was born of honest and noble parents in the village of Goriukhino in the year 1798. His late father, Second Major Petr Ivanovich Belkin, had been joined in matrimony to the maiden Pelageia Gavrilovna of the Trafilin family. He was not a rich man, but he was frugal and quite clever at managing his estate. Their son received his elementary instruction from the parish sexton. It was to this honorable man that he owed, it seems, his fondness for reading and for exercising his pen in the realm of Russian letters. In the year 1815 he enlisted in a chasseur infantry regiment (whose number I do not recall), in which he remained until 1823. The death of his parents, occurring almost simultaneously, compelled him to retire from the service and to return to the village of Goriukhino, his patrimony.

Having assumed the management of his affairs, Ivan Petrovich, who lacked experience and possessed a soft heart, soon let his estate fall into disarray by relaxing the strict discipline established by his late father. He dismissed the reliable and efficient village elder with whom the peasants (as usual) were dissatisfied, and he handed over the management of the village to his old housekeeper, who had won his confidence by her art of telling stories. This stupid woman could never tell a twenty-ruble note from a fifty-ruble one; the peasants, who were all her bosom friends, did not fear her in the least; the new elder they elected indulged them so much, cheating along with them, that Ivan Petrovich had to abolish corvée and introduce a very moderate quitrent;[3] but even then they took advantage of his weakness—persuading him to give them a considerable reduction in the first year, paying over two-thirds of the rent in nuts, bilberries, and such in the following years, and still remaining in arrears.

As a friend of Ivan Petrovich's late father, I considered it my duty to offer my advice to the son as well, repeatedly volunteering to restore the earlier order that he had allowed to deteriorate. Once I came to his house with this purpose in mind, demanded to be shown the ledgers, summoned that crook of an elder, and started examining said ledgers in the presence of Ivan Petrovich. The young landowner at first followed my investigations with the greatest possible attention and assiduity; but as soon as it became evident from the accounts that in the last two years the number of peasants had increased while that of the poultry and cattle belonging to the estate had noticeably decreased, Ivan Petrovich contented himself with these preliminary reckonings and would not listen to me any more; and at the very moment when I had thrown that rogue of an elder into utter confusion by my investigation and stern questioning and had reduced him to total silence, I caught, to my great irritation, the sound of Ivan Petrovich vigorously snoring in his chair. From that time on, I ceased interfering with his business arrangements, and entrusted his affairs (as did he) to the care of the Almighty.

This incident, by the way, did not in the least disturb our friendly relations, since though I regretted his weakness and his disastrous negligence—a trait common to all our young noblemen—I nevertheless loved him sincerely; indeed it would have been impossible not to love such a meek and honest young man. On his part, Ivan Petrovich showed respect for my years and was deeply attached to me. Until his very end he met me almost every day, cherishing my simple conversation, even though in habits, way of thinking, and character we were hardly alike.

Ivan Petrovich led a most temperate existence, avoiding all manner of excess; I never once saw him tipsy (which can be regarded as an unheard-of miracle in these parts); he had a great fondness for the fair sex, but he was truly as bashful as a maiden.*

In addition to the tales that you were pleased to mention in your letter, Ivan Petrovich left behind quite a number of manuscripts. I have some of them, but others have been used by his housekeeper for various domestic purposes. As a case in point, last winter all the windows in her wing of the house were sealed up with the first part of a novel that he had left unfinished. The above-mentioned tales, if I am not mistaken, represent his first experiments. They are, as Ivan Petrovich said several times, mostly true stories that he had heard from different people.** The proper names used in the stories, however, are almost all fictitious, invented by himself; as for the names of towns and villages, they are taken from our neighborhood, which is the reason why my village is also mentioned somewhere. This happened not because of any malicious intentions, but solely because of a lack of imagination.

In the fall of 1828 Ivan Petrovich fell ill with a febrile cold, which turned into a high fever; he passed away in spite of the unremitting efforts of our district doctor, an exceptionally skillful man, espe-

---

*Here follows an anecdote, which we will not print believing it to be superfluous; we wish to assure the reader, however, that it contains nothing injurious to the memory of Ivan Petrovich Belkin.

**Indeed in Mr. Belkin's manuscript there is a note above each tale in the author's hand: "heard by me from such and such a person." (There follow the person's rank or title and initials.) We will copy them out for inquisitive researchers: "The Stationmaster" was related by Titular Councillor A.G.N.; "The Shot" by Lieutenant Colonel I.L.P.; "The Undertaker" by the steward B.V.; and finally both "The Blizzard" and "The Squire's Daughter" by the maiden K.I.T.

cially in the cure of such deep-rooted ailments as corns and the like. Ivan Petrovich died in my arms in the thirtieth year of his life and was buried near his deceased parents in the churchyard of the village of Goriukhino.

Ivan Petrovich was a man of medium height, with gray eyes, light brown hair, and a straight nose; his complexion was fair and his face thin.

This, my dear sir, is all that I can remember with regard to the way of life, occupation, moral character, and appearance of my late neighbor and friend. I ask you humbly, however, under no circumstances to mention my name even if you deem it fit to make some use of my letter: although I much respect and like authors, I would think it unnecessary and at my age improper to take up their vocation.

Yours very sincerely, etc.
November 16, 1830[4]
The village of Nenaradovo

We think it is our duty to respect the wish of the honorable friend of our author, and therefore we will merely express our deepest gratitude for the information he has provided and hope that the reading public will appreciate its sincerity and kind intention.

A.P.

The Shot

> We exchanged shots.
> BARATYNSKII

> I swore I'd shoot him by the rules of
> dueling (I still had my turn coming).
> "AN EVENING ON BIVOUAC"[5]

I

We were stationed at the small village of N. Everybody knows what the life of an infantry officer is like. Drills and riding exercises in the morning; dinner at the house of the regimental commander or at a Jewish tavern; rum punch and cards in the evening. In N. there was not one house open to us, not one marriageable girl; we gathered at each other's lodgings, where we encountered nothing but each other's uniforms.

There was only one person belonging to our circle who was not in the military service. He was about thirty-five and therefore we considered him an old man. His store of experience made him superior to us in many ways; besides, his habitual sullenness, acrimonious temper, and sharp tongue made a strong impression on our young minds. There was something mysterious about him; he seemed to be Russian, yet had a foreign name. At one time he had served in a hussar regiment, and had even served with distinction; nobody knew what had made him retire and settle in a poor little village, where he led an existence at once frugal and prodigal: he always went around on foot, in a worn black coat, yet all the officers of our regiment were always welcome at his table. It is true that his dinner consisted of only two or three dishes, prepared by a retired soldier, but his champagne flowed like a river. Nobody knew what his circumstances were or what income he received, and nobody dared question him about these matters. There were books lying about his apartment, mostly works on military subjects, but also some novels. He willingly lent them, never demanding them back; on the other hand, he never returned a book he had borrowed. His chief occupation consisted of pistol shooting. The walls of his room were so riddled with bullet holes they looked like honeycombs. A valuable collection of pistols was the only article of luxury in the poor, mud-walled hut where he lived. The level of skill that he had attained was unbelievable: if he had expressed a wish to shoot a pear off the top of somebody's cap, no one in our regiment would have hesitated to offer his head. Our conversation often touched on duels; Silvio (or so I will call him) never discussed that topic. Asked whether he had ever fought a duel, he answered dryly that he had, but he never went into detail, and it was obvious that he found such questions unpleasant. We supposed that some hapless victim of his terrifying skill lay on his conscience. I must remark that we never dreamed of suspecting anything in him that resembled timidity. There are people whose mere appearance precludes such suspicion. But one unexpected incident caught us all by surprise.

One day about ten of us officers were having dinner at Silvio's house. We drank as usual, that is, a great deal; after dinner we begged the host to hold the bank for us. He remained adamant for a long time, since he almost never played; but at last he sent for the cards, piled fifty or so gold coins on the table, and sat down to deal. We took our places around him, and the game got under way. Silvio had the habit of observing complete silence during a game. He never argued or entered into explanations. If the punter happened to miscalculate, Silvio instantly corrected him, either paying him the difference or writing up the extra amount of his stake. We already knew this and let him play the master as he would; but this time there was an officer with us who had just recently been transferred to our regiment. Playing along with the rest of us, he absentmindedly bent down the corner of a card. Silvio took the chalk and adjusted the stake accordingly, as was his habit. The officer thought that it was Silvio who had made an error, and he started arguing the matter. Silvio continued dealing without a word. The officer finally lost his patience, took the brush, and erased what he thought had been added unnecessarily.[6] Silvio took the chalk and wrote the figure down once more. The officer, incensed by the wine, the game, and the laughter of his comrades, supposed himself terribly insulted; in his rage he picked up a heavy brass candleholder from the table and hurled it at Silvio, who just barely managed to dodge the blow. We all gasped. Silvio stood up, pale with anger, his eyes flashing:

"Sir, be so good as to leave, and thank God this has happened at my own house."

We had no doubt about the consequences and already viewed our new comrade as a dead man. The officer left, saying he was ready to answer for the offense in whatever way the honorable banker deemed fit. The game continued for a few more minutes, but sensing that the host was no longer in the mood for it, we quit one after the other and went home talking about the likelihood that there would soon be a vacancy in the regiment.

The next day, during the riding exercises, we were asking each other whether the poor lieutenant was still alive when he himself appeared among us; we put the same question to him. He answered that so far he had heard nothing from Silvio. This astonished us. We went to Silvio's house and found him in the yard, firing bullet on bullet at an ace glued to the gate. He received us in the usual way, not breathing a word about the previous night's incident. Three days passed, and the lieutenant was still alive. We kept asking with incredulity: was it possible that Silvio would not fight? But Silvio did not. He was satisfied with a casual explanation and made it up with the lieutenant.

It seemed likely at the time that the incident would considerably hurt his reputation among the young officers. A lack of courage is something the young can least forgive; they consider valor the height of human virtue and an excuse for all possible vices. But the matter was gradually forgotten, and Silvio regained his former influence.

I was the only one who could not warm up to him again. Endowed with a romantic imagination by nature, I had been his greatest admirer before the incident, for the life of this man was an enigma, and he himself had struck me as the hero of some mysterious story. He had seemed fond of me; at least I had been the only person in whose company he would refrain from his customary acid vilifications and talk about different subjects with candor and exceptional cordiality. But after that unfortunate evening the thought that his honor had been tarnished, and that the stain had been allowed to remain on it through his own fault, stuck in my mind and prevented me from behaving toward him as before; I felt too embarrassed to look at him. He was too intelligent and too experienced not to notice this and not to guess its cause. It seemed to pain him; at least I noticed on a couple of occasions that he would have liked to explain things to me; but I did not give him an opportunity and he withdrew. From then on, I saw him only in the presence of my comrades, and our former frank conversations came to an end.

Citizens of the capital, with so many different things on their minds, have no conception of certain experiences familiar to residents of villages and small towns, such as waiting for mail delivery days. On Tuesdays and Fridays our regimental headquarters was always full of officers: some expected money, some letters, some newspapers. They usually opened packages on the spot and exchanged news. The office represented a truly lively scene. Silvio used to have his letters addressed to our regiment, and he was usually at the office on delivery days. One day he was handed an envelope, from which he tore the seal with a look of utmost impatience. His eyes sparkled as he read through the letter. The officers, busy with their own letters, noticed nothing.

"Gentlemen," Silvio turned to them, "circumstances demand my immediate departure; I am leaving tonight; I hope you will not refuse to dine with me one last time. I'll expect you too," he continued, addressing me; "be sure to come." With these words he hastily departed; we too, agreeing to gather at Silvio's, each went our separate ways.

I came to Silvio's at the appointed time and found almost the whole regiment there. All his belongings were already packed; nothing remained but the bare bullet-riddled walls. We sat down at the table; the host was in exceptionally good spirits, and his cheerfulness was contagious; corks were popping by the minute, the glasses ceaselessly fizzed and foamed; and we zealously wished our departing host a pleasant journey and all the best. We rose from the table quite late in the evening. As people were sorting out their caps, Silvio said goodbye to all, but he caught hold of my arm and stopped me just as I was about to leave.

"I have to talk to you," he said softly. I stayed.

The guests had all left; we were alone. We sat down facing each other, and lit our pipes in silence. Silvio seemed preoccupied; there was no trace of his feverish gaiety. His grim pallor, his flashing eyes, and the dense smoke issuing from his mouth lent him a truly diabolical appearance. Several minutes went by before he broke the silence.

"We may never meet again," he said to me, "and before we part I would like you to understand me. You may have noticed that I have little regard for other people's opinions, but I am fond of you, and would hate to leave you with a false impression of me."

He paused and started filling his pipe, which had gone out; I gazed at the floor in silence.

"You found it strange," he continued, "that I did not demand satisfaction from that drunken lout R. You will agree that since I had the right to choose weapons, his life was in my hands while mine was hardly in jeopardy. I could claim that my moderation was motivated by generosity, but I don't want to lie to you. If I had been able to punish R. without the slightest risk to my own life, nothing could have persuaded me to let him get away."

I looked at Silvio in amazement. Such a confession confounded me altogether. Silvio went on:

"Exactly so: I have no right to risk my life. Six years ago I received a slap on the face, and my enemy is still alive."

My curiosity was very much aroused.

"Didn't you fight him?" I asked. "Circumstances, I suppose, must have separated you?"

"I did fight him," answered Silvio, "and here is a memento of our duel."

Silvio got up and took out of a cardboard box a red hat with a golden tassel and a galloon (what the French call a *bonnet de police*); he put it on; it had been shot through an inch or so above the forehead.

"You know," continued Silvio, "that I used to serve in the X. Hussar Regiment. You are familiar with my character; I am accustomed to taking the lead; in my youth this was a passion with me. In my day rowdiness was in fashion: I was the foremost troublemaker in the whole army. We flaunted our drunkenness: I outdrank the famous Burtsov, celebrated in Denis Davydov's songs.[7] Duels were fought daily in our regiment: I participated in each and every one, either as second or as principal. My comrades adored me, and the regimental commanding officers, who were frequently replaced, regarded me as a necessary evil.

"I was quietly (or not so quietly) enjoying my fame when a young man from a rich and distinguished family (I don't want to mention his name) joined our regiment. I had never met such a brilliant child of fortune. Picture in your mind youth, intelligence, good looks, the most frenzied vivacity, the most lighthearted courage, an exalted name, and money, more than he could count, in an inexhaustible supply—and then imagine what impression he was bound to make on us. My superior position was shaken. Intrigued by my reputation, he tried to seek my friendship, but I received him coldly; he withdrew without the slightest regret. I grew to hate him. His success in the regiment and in the company of women threw me into utter despair. I began trying to pick a quarrel with him; he responded to my epigrams with epigrams of his own, which always seemed to me more striking and witty than mine, and which were, of course, incomparably more amusing, for he was joking while I seethed. At last, at a ball given by a Polish landowner, where I saw that he was the center of attention of all the ladies and especially of the hostess herself, with whom I was having an affair, I whispered some unsavory insulting remark into his ear. He flared up and slapped me on the face. We each rushed for our swords; the ladies fainted one after the other; we were pulled apart, but we went to fight a duel that same night.

"Dawn was breaking. I stood in the designated place with my three seconds and waited for the arrival of my opponent with indescribable impatience. The sun rose; it was going to be a hot spring day. I saw him at a distance. He was coming on foot, carrying his coat on the tip of his sword, and there was just one second with him. We walked toward them. He approached, holding his cap, which was full of cherries. The seconds measured off twelve paces for us. I was supposed to shoot first, but I was so incensed that I did not trust the steadiness of my hand, and in order to give myself time to cool off, I yielded the first shot to my opponent. He refused. We decided to draw lots, and he—ever favored by fortune—drew the lucky number. He took aim, and his bullet went through my cap. It was my turn. At last his life was in my hands; I eyed him hungrily, trying to detect at least a shade of worry in his expression... He stood there facing my pistol, selecting ripe cherries from his cap and spitting out the stones, which landed near me. His indifference enraged me. What's the use of depriving him of his life, thought I, if he himself doesn't cherish it? A spiteful thought flashed through my mind. I lowered my pistol.

" 'You evidently cannot spare the time to die just now,' I said to him, 'since it is your pleasure to be eating your breakfast; I do not wish to disturb you.'

" 'You're not disturbing me in the least,' he rejoined; 'go ahead and shoot whenever you please. But, of course, it's up to you: you can retain your right to the shot, and I'll be at your service at any time.' I turned to the seconds, announcing that I did not intend to fire my shot just then, and with this the duel stopped.

"I resigned my commission and retired to this village. Since then not one day has gone by without my thinking of revenge. And now my time has come..."

Silvio took from his pocket the letter he had received that morning, and gave it to me to read. Someone (evidently an agent of Silvio's) had written to him from Moscow that a *certain person* was soon to become the lawful wedded husband of a young and beautiful girl.

"You can guess," said Silvio, "who this *certain person* is. I am going to Moscow. We shall see whether he can take death with as much indifference now, just before his wedding, as he did earlier, over a capful of cherries."

With these words Silvio got up, threw his cap on the floor, and started pacing up and down the room, like a tiger in a cage. I listened to him without stirring; strange, contradictory feelings agitated me.

The servant came in to announce that the horses were ready. Silvio grasped my hand firmly; we kissed. He climbed into the cart, which was loaded with two trunks: one holding his pistols, the other one his belongings. We said good-bye once more, and the horses galloped off.[8]

2

Some years went by, and my domestic circumstances forced me to settle in a poor little village in P. District. Busy managing my estate, I could not help secretly sighing for my former noisy and carefree existence. The most difficult task was to get used to spending fall and winter evenings in complete solitude. Until dinner I could fill the time in one way or another, now talking with the village elder, now riding out to supervise work in the fields, now looking at a new building project; but as soon as dusk fell I had no idea what to do with myself. The few books I had found under cupboards or in the storeroom I could soon recite by heart. My housekeeper Kirilovna told me over and over again all the stories she could remember. The songs the peasant women sang made me melancholy. Once or twice I tried an unsweetened home brew, but it gave me a headache, and I must also confess that I was afraid of becoming a *doldrums drunkard*, in other words an *inveterate inebriate* of the kind that is so amply represented in our district.[9] I had no neighbors close by, except for two or three of those *inveterate* ones, whose conversation consisted chiefly of hiccups and moans. Solitude was more bearable.

Four versts from my house there was a prosperous estate belonging to the Countess B., but it was occupied only by the manager. The Countess herself had visited it only once, in the first year of her marriage, but even then she stayed just a month. In the second year of my reclusion, however, a rumor spread that the Countess and her husband were coming to spend the summer on her estate. And indeed they arrived at the beginning of June.

The arrival of a rich neighbor is a historical occasion for people living in the country. The landowners and their domestics speak of nothing else for two months before the event and for three years after. As for me, I must confess that the news about the arrival of my young and beautiful neighbor affected me strongly: I burned with impatience to see her, and on the first Sunday after her arrival, I set out after dinner for the village of R. in order to pay my respects to Their Excellencies as their closest neighbor and most humble servant.

The butler conducted me to the Count's study and went to announce my arrival. The spacious study was furnished with all possible luxury: bookcases with bronze busts on top lined the walls; a broad mirror hung over the marble mantelpiece; the floor was covered with green carpeting and strewn with rugs. Having grown unaccustomed to luxury in my poor corner and not having seen other people's riches for a long time, I now felt timid and awaited the Count with a certain trepidation, as a provincial petitioner awaits the appearance of a Minister. The doors opened, and a handsome man of about thirty-two entered. He approached me in an unpretentious, friendly way; I tried to gather courage and began to introduce myself, but he anticipated me. We sat down. His free and amiable conversation soon dispelled my cloddish shyness; I was beginning to regain my usual composure when suddenly the Countess came in, throwing me into even greater confusion. She was indeed a beauty. The Count introduced me; I wanted to appear free and easy, but the more I tried to assume a casual air the more awkward I felt. In order to give me time to recover myself and get used to my new acquaintances, they began talking between themselves, treating me as an indulgent neighbor with whom you do not have to stand on ceremony. Meanwhile, I started walking up and down the room, looking at books and pictures. I am not a connoisseur of paintings, but one of them attracted my attention. It showed a Swiss landscape. What awoke my interest in it, however, was not the painter's art, but the fact that the picture was pierced by two bullets, one just above the other.

"That's a good shot," I said, turning to the Count.

"Yes," he answered, "a remarkable shot. Are you a good marksman?" he added.

"Not too bad," I answered, pleased that the conversation had at last touched on a subject familiar to me. "I can hit a card without fail from a distance of thirty paces, assuming, of course, that I am using pistols I am accustomed to."

"Is that so?" said the Countess with a look of great interest. "And you, my dear, can you hit a card at thirty paces?"

"We'll try some time," answered the Count. "In my earlier days I was a fair shot, but I haven't had a pistol in my hand for some four years now."

"Oh, if that's the case," I remarked, "then I bet Your Excellency could not hit a card even at twenty paces, because pistol shooting requires daily practice. I know this from experience. In my regiment I was regarded as one of the best marksmen. But once it so happened that I hadn't handled a pistol for a month because mine were being repaired, and what do you think was the result, Your Excellency? The first time I started shooting again I missed a bottle at twenty-five paces four times in a row. There was a captain in our regiment, a great wit and wag, who happened to be there; he says to me: 'I see, brother, you just cannot raise your hand against a bottle.' No, Your Excellency, you must not neglect practicing, otherwise you lose your touch in no time. The best shot I've ever had a chance to meet practiced every day, at least three times before dinner. It was a daily routine with him, just like his glass of vodka."

The Count and Countess were glad that I had begun talking.

"And what were the results?" asked the Count.

"Well, this is what, Your Excellency: he would notice, for instance, that a fly had landed on the wall—are you laughing, Countess? I swear to you, it's true. He would see the fly and call out: 'Kuzka, fetch me a pistol!' Kuzka would bring it to him loaded. He would go bang, and ram the fly into the wall."

"That's astonishing," said the Count. "And what was his name?"

"Silvio, Your Excellency."

"Silvio!" exclaimed the Count, springing to his feet. "You knew Silvio?"

"I did indeed, Your Excellency; we were friends. He was treated in our regiment as a brother officer, but for the last five years or so I have heard nothing about him. Your Excellency, I take it, knew him?"

"I did, all too well. Didn't he tell you—no, I suppose he wouldn't have—but, still, didn't he tell you about a very strange incident?"

"You don't mean the slap on the face, Your Excellency, that he received from some scamp at a ball?"

"Did he ever tell you the name of that scamp?"

"No, Your Excellency, he never did... But oh, Your Excellency," I continued, beginning to guess the truth, "forgive me... I didn't know... Was it you by any chance?"

"Yes, it was," answered the Count, looking acutely distressed, "and the picture with the bullets through it is a memento of our last meeting."

"Please, my dear," said the Countess, "for heaven's sake, do not tell the story: I should be frightened even to listen to it."

"No," rejoined the Count, "I will tell it all: he knows how I insulted his friend; let him learn how Silvio took revenge on me."

The Count pulled up an armchair for me, and I listened with the liveliest curiosity to the following story.

"We were married five years ago. We spent the first month, *the honey-moon*,[10] here, on this estate. I am bound to this house both by memories of the best moments in my life and by one of the most painful recollections.

"One evening my wife and I were out riding together; her horse became restive, which frightened her; she gave me the reins and started to walk back to the house. I rode ahead. In the courtyard I saw a cart, and I was told that there was a man sitting in my study who would not reveal his name but would only say that he had business with me. I came into this room and in the obscure light saw a man covered with dust and unshaven; he stood right there by the mantelpiece. I went up to him, trying to see if I could recognize his features.

" 'Don't you recognize me, Count?' " he said in a trembling voice.

" 'Silvio!' I exclaimed, and I must confess I could feel my hair standing on end.

" 'Exactly,' he continued. 'It's my turn to shoot; I have come to fire my pistol; are you ready?'

"A pistol was sticking out of his side pocket. I measured off twelve paces and took up my position in that corner, asking him to shoot me as soon as possible, before my wife's return. He stalled, asked for a light. Candles were brought in. I locked the doors, gave orders not to admit anybody, and asked Silvio once more to shoot. He drew his pistol and aimed... I counted the seconds... I thought of her... A terrifying minute went by. Silvio lowered his hand.

" 'I regret,' he said, 'that the pistol is not loaded with cherry stones... the bullet is heavy. I keep thinking, though, that this is not a duel but a murder: I am not used to aiming at an unarmed man. Let's start all over again; let's draw lots to decide who should shoot first.'

"My head was swimming... I think I objected... But at last we loaded another pistol, rolled up two pieces of paper; he placed them in the cap that I had once shot through; again I drew the lucky number.

"'Count, you are devilishly lucky,' he said with a leer that I shall never forget.

"I don't know what possessed me and how he managed to talk me into it, but I did fire a shot and hit this picture." The Count pointed with his finger at the perforated picture; his face burned like fire; the Countess was paler than her handkerchief; I could not restrain an exclamation.

"I fired a shot," continued the Count, "and, thank God, I missed; then Silvio (at that moment he was truly terrifying) began taking aim at me. Suddenly the door opens, and Masha runs in and throws herself on my neck with a shriek. Her presence restored to me all my courage.

"'Dear heart,' I said to her, 'can't you see we're just joking? How frightened you look! Go, drink a glass of water and then come back to join us: I'll introduce an old friend and fellow officer to you.'

"Masha still refused to believe me. 'Tell me, is my husband telling the truth?' she asked, turning to the ferocious-looking Silvio. 'Is it true that you're both joking?'

"'He's always joking, Countess,' Silvio answered her. 'He once jokingly slapped me on the face, he jokingly sent his bullet through this cap of mine, and a minute ago his shot jokingly just missed me. Now I feel like cracking a joke...' With these words he made as if to take aim at me—in her presence! Masha threw herself at his feet.

"'Get up, Masha, for shame!' I shouted in rage. 'And you, sir, will you stop taunting a poor woman? Are you going to shoot or not?'

"'I'm not,' answered Silvio. 'I'm perfectly satisfied: I've seen your confusion and fright, and I've made you shoot at me; that is quite enough for me. You will remember me. I leave you to your conscience.'

"He was on the point of leaving, but he stopped in the doorway, looked back at the picture that had my bullet in it, fired at it almost without taking aim, and vanished. My wife lay in a swoon; the servants, not daring to stop Silvio, just stared at him in horror; he walked out to the front steps, called his driver, and rode away before I could recover my senses."

The Count fell silent. This was how I came to know the end of the story whose beginning had at one time made such a deep impression on me. I never was to see its hero again. I have heard said that Silvio commanded a detachment of Hetairists during the uprising led by Alexander Ypsilanti, and that he was killed in the battle near Skuliany.[11]

The Blizzard

> Over hillocks deep in snow
> Speeding horses trample,
> In a clearing off the road
> Winks a lonely temple.
> . . .
>
> All at once a blizzard flings
> Drifts across the way,
> And a wheeling raven's wings
> Rasp above the sleigh.
> Sorrow spell the gusty wails,
> And the hasting horses
> Scan the darkness, manes and tails
> Bristling in their courses...
> ZHUKOVSKII [12]

Toward the end of the year 1811—a memorable time for us—there lived in his own village of Nenaradovo a good man called Gavrila Gavrilovich R. He was renowned throughout the region for his hospitality and cordiality: neighbors came to his house all the time, some to eat and drink well, others to play Boston for five-kopeck stakes with his wife, Praskovia Petrovna, and still others to see the couple's daughter, Maria Gavrilovna, a slender and pale girl of seventeen. She was considered a good match, and quite a few men marked her out either for themselves or for their sons.

Maria Gavrilovna had been brought up on French novels and was consequently in love. The object she had chosen for her affections was a penniless sublieutenant of infantry, who at the time was staying in his village on a furlough. It goes without saying that the young man was aflame with an equal passion, and that the parents of his beloved, as soon as they noticed the young couple's mutual inclinations, forbade their daughter even to think about him. They began receiving him at their home with less kindness than they would have shown a retired assessor.

Our lovers were engaged in correspondence, and they met alone every day either in the pine grove or by the ancient chapel. There they swore eternal love for each other, lamented their fate, and discussed different possible courses of action. As a result of such correspondence and meetings, they arrived (which was quite natural) at the following consideration: if we cannot breathe without each other, yet the will of cruel parents stands in the way of our happiness, should we not disregard that will? It is easy to guess that this felicitous idea occurred to the young man first and was then heartily embraced by Maria Gavrilovna's romantic imagination.

Winter set in and put a stop to the young couple's meetings; their correspondence, on the other hand, grew all the more lively. Vladimir Nikolaevich entreated Maria Gavrilovna in each letter to give herself to him and wed him in secret; they would remain in hiding for a while, then throw themselves at the feet of her parents, who of course would at last be moved by the lovers' heroic constancy and unhappy state, and would inevitably say, "Children! Come to our bosoms!"

Maria Gavrilovna hesitated for a long while; many a plan for elopement was rejected. At last she gave her consent: on an appointed day she was to miss supper and retire to her room on the pretext of a headache. Her maid was in collusion with her; they were both to go into the garden by way of the back porch, find the sleigh waiting for them behind the garden, get in and ride five versts from Nenaradovo to the village of Zhadrino, and once there, go straight to the church, where Vladimir would be expecting them.

The night before the decisive day Maria Gavrilovna could not sleep a wink; she packed, tied up her linen and clothes into bundles, wrote a long letter to a friend—a sentimental young lady—and another one to her parents. She took leave of them in the most touching terms, excused her act by the irresistible force of her passion, and concluded with the assertion that it would be the happiest moment of her life if she were allowed to throw herself at the feet of her dearest parents. Having sealed both letters with a seal from Tula that showed two flaming hearts with an appropriate inscription, she threw herself on her bed just before dawn and dozed off, but terrible dreams kept waking her even then. At first she fancied that just as she was getting into the sleigh to ride to her wedding, her father stopped her, dragged her across the snow with excruciating speed, and threw her into a bottomless pit... She was falling headlong with indescribable palpitations of the heart... Then she saw Vladimir lying in the grass pale and bloodied. Dying, he begged her in a piercing voice to hurry up and marry him... Still other visions, equally hideous and absurd, flitted before her in quick succession. At last she got up, paler than usual and with a genuine headache. Her father and mother noticed her anxious state; their tender solicitude and never-ending questions—"What's the matter with you, Masha?" "Are you ill, Masha?"—lacerated her heart. She tried to reassure them, tried to appear happy, but could not. Evening came. The thought that she was spending her last day in the midst of her family weighed on her heart. She was more dead than alive; in her mind she was saying good-bye to all the people and objects surrounding her. Supper was served; her heart began to beat violently. She declared in a trembling voice that she did not feel like eating supper, and wished her father and mother good night. They kissed her and, as usual, blessed her, which almost made her cry. On reaching her room, she threw herself in an armchair and burst into a flood of tears. Her maid pleaded with her to calm herself and summon up her courage. Everything was ready. In another half hour Masha was to leave forever her parents' home, the tranquil life of a maiden... Outside a blizzard was whirling; the wind howled, the shutters shook and rattled; all of which seemed a threat and a bad omen to her. The house soon grew quiet: everybody was asleep. Masha wrapped herself in a shawl, put on a warm coat, picked up her bandbox, and went out on the back porch. The maid came after her, carrying two bundles. They descended into the garden. The blizzard was not letting up; the wind met Masha head-on as if trying to stop the young malefactress. They could hardly reach the other end of the garden. The sleigh was waiting for them on the road. The horses, frozen through, could not stand still; Vladimir's coachman walked up and down in front of the shafts of the sleigh trying to restrain the restless animals. He helped the young lady and her maid climb in and find room for the two bundles and the box, then he took the reins, and the horses dashed off. But let us entrust the young lady to her lucky stars and to the skill of Tereshka the coachman, while we turn our attention to our young paramour.

Vladimir had been on the road all day. In the morning he went to see the priest at Zhadrino and could just barely prevail on him; then he went in search of potential witnesses among the landowners of the neighborhood. The first one he called on, a forty-year-old retired cavalry officer by the name of Dravin, consented with pleasure. This adventure, he kept saying, reminded him of his earlier days and his pranks in the hussars. He persuaded Vladimir to stay for dinner, assuring him that finding two more witnesses would be no problem at all. Indeed a land surveyor named Schmitt, wearing mustachios and spurs, and the son of the police superintendent, a boy of sixteen who had recently joined the uhlans, appeared on the scene right after dinner. Not only did they accede to Vladimir's request, but they even swore they would sacrifice their lives for him. Vladimir embraced them with fervor and went home to get ready.

It was already quite dark. He sent his reliable Tereshka to Nenaradovo with his troika and with detailed, thorough instructions. For himself he had a small one-horse sleigh harnessed, and set out alone, without a driver, for Zhadrino, where Maria Gavrilovna was due to arrive in another couple of hours. He knew the road well, and it was only a twenty-minute ride.

But no sooner had he left the village behind and entered the fields than the wind rose, and such a blizzard developed that he could not see anything. In one minute the road was covered over; the surrounding landscape disappeared in a thick yellowish mist driven through with white flakes of snow; the sky merged with the earth. Vladimir found himself in the middle of a field, and his attempts to get back on the road were all in vain. The horse trod at random, now clambering up a pile of snow, now tumbling into a ditch; the sleigh kept turning over; all Vladimir could do was to try not to lose the right direction. It seemed to him, however, that more than half an hour had passed, yet he had still not reached the Zhadrino woods. Another ten minutes or so went by, but the woods still did not come within his view. He rode across a field intersected by deep gullies. The blizzard would not let up; the sky would not clear. The horse began to get tired, and Vladimir perspired profusely, even though he kept sinking into the snow up to his waist.

At last Vladimir realized he was going in the wrong direction. He stopped, began to think, to recollect, to consider, and became convinced that he should have turned to the right. He started off to the right. His horse could hardly move. He had already been on the road for over an hour. Zhadrino should not have been very far. Yet though he rode on and on, there was no end to the open country. Snowdrifts and gullies at every step; the sleigh kept turning over; he had to lift it upright every minute. The time was passing; he began to worry in earnest.

At last something dark came into his view on one side. He turned toward it. Coming closer, he could make out a wood. Thank God, he thought, I am close now. He drove along the edge of the wood, hoping presently to meet the familiar road, or else to go around the wood and find Zhadrino right behind it. He soon found the road and advanced into the darkness under the trees bared by winter. Here the wind could not blow quite so fiercely; the road was even; the horse perked up, and Vladimir felt reassured.

He rode on and on, however, yet there was no sign of Zhadrino; nor was there an end to the woods. He realized with horror that he had driven into an unfamiliar forest. Despair took possession of him. He whipped the horse; the poor animal tried to break into a trot but soon gave in to fatigue, and within a quarter of an hour slowed down to a snail's pace despite every effort on the part of the unfortunate Vladimir.

Gradually the trees thinned out, and Vladimir emerged from the forest, but there was still no sign of Zhadrino. It must have been around midnight. Tears gushed from his eyes; he drove forward haphazardly. The weather had by now grown calm, the clouds were breaking up, and a broad, flat field, covered with a white undulating carpet, stretched out before Vladimir. The night was quite clear. A short distance away Vladimir saw a hamlet consisting of four or five houses. He rode up to it. At the first hut he jumped out of the sleigh, ran up to the window, and started knocking. In a few minutes the wooden shutter opened and an old man thrust his gray beard out of the window.

"What d'ya want?"

"Is Zhadrino far from here?"

"If Zhadrino's far?"

"Yes, yes. Is it far?"

"Not that far; it'll be ten versts or thereabouts."

Hearing this answer, Vladimir clutched his head and remained motionless like a man condemned to die.

"And where would you be coming from?" continued the old man.

Vladimir was not in a state to answer questions.

"Listen, old man," he said, "can you procure some horses that will take me to Zhadrino?"

"Horses, here?"

"Could I at least take a guide with me? I will pay him as much as he wants."

"Wait," said the old man, letting the shutter down. "I'll send my son out. He'll show you the way."

Vladimir waited a little, but scarcely a minute had gone by when he started knocking again. The shutter was raised, and the beard came in view.

"What d'ya want?"

"What about your son?"

"He'll be out in a minute. Tying up his shoes. You're frozen, I trow; come inside to warm up."

"No, thank you, just send your son out as soon as possible."

The gate creaked; a lad came out with a cudgel in his hand; he went ahead of Vladimir, either leading him along the road or searching for it where it was covered by snowdrifts.

"What is the time?" Vladimir asked him.

"It'll soon be getting light," answered the young peasant. Vladimir no longer said anything.

The cocks were crowing, and it was already daylight by the time they reached Zhadrino. The church was locked. Vladimir paid his guide and drove to the priest's house. His troika was not in the courtyard. What news awaited him!

But let us return to the good proprietors of Nenaradovo and take a look: what might be happening at their house?

Well, nothing.

The old couple woke up and came down to the living room. Gavrila Gavrilovich wore his nightcap and a flannel jacket, Praskovia Petrovna was in her quilted dressing gown. The samovar was lit, and Gavrila Gavrilovich sent a little handmaid to find out how Maria Gavrilovna felt and whether she had slept well. The little girl came back with the answer that the young mistress had slept badly but was by now feeling better and, so please Your Honor, would soon come down to the living room. Indeed, the door opened, and Maria Gavrilovna came up to her papa and mama in turn to wish them good morning.

"How's your head, Masha?" asked Gavrila Gavrilovich.

"It's better, papa," answered Masha.

"It must have been the fumes from the stove that made you feel poorly last night," said Praskovia Petrovna.

"It may have been," answered Masha.

The day passed without any incident, but during the night Masha fell ill. They went to town for the doctor. He arrived toward evening and found the invalid in a state of delirium. A high fever had developed, and the poor girl hovered on the brink of the grave for two weeks.

Nobody in the household knew about the intended elopement. The letters Masha had written the night before were burned, and her maid, fearing the anger of her masters, did not breathe a word to anybody. The priest, the retired officer, the mustachioed land surveyor, and the juvenile uhlan were all discreet, and for good reason. Tereshka the coachman never used an extra word, even in his cups. Thus the secret was kept by more than half a dozen conspirators. It was only Maria Gavrilovna who revealed her secret in her continual state of delirium. Her words, however, were so incongruous that her mother, who never for a moment left her bedside, could make out only that Masha was fatally in love with Vladimir Nikolaevich, and that her love was probably the cause of her illness. She consulted her husband and some neighbors, and they all came to the unanimous conclusion that this was evidently Masha's destiny, that marriages were made in heaven,[13] that poverty was no shame, that you have to live with the man, not with his money, and so forth. Moral maxims are surprisingly useful on occasions when we can invent little else to justify our actions.

In the meanwhile the young lady began to get better. Vladimir had not been seen at Gavrila Gavrilovich's house for a long time. He was afraid of getting the usual reception. They decided to send for him and notify him of his unexpected luck—their consent to his marriage to Masha. How immensely astonished were the proprietors of Nenaradovo, however, when in answer to their invitation they received a half-insane letter from him! He declared he would never set foot in their house again and asked them to forget the unhappy man for whom death was the only remaining hope. In a few days they learned that he had returned to the army. This was in the year 1812.

For a long time they did not dare give the news to the convalescent Masha. She never mentioned Vladimir. She did faint, a few months later, when she saw his name on a list of those who had distinguished themselves and been severely wounded at Borodino, and it was feared that her fever might return, but, thank God, her fainting had no consequences.

Another grief was visited on her; Gavrila Gavrilovich died, leaving his whole fortune to her as his sole heiress. Her inheritance did not console her; she sincerely shared poor Praskovia Petrovna's grief and vowed never to part with her; together they left Nenaradovo, the scene of so many sad memories, and settled on an estate in N. Guberniia.[14]

Here, too, eligible young men came whirling around the charming rich maiden, but she did not give the slightest encouragement to any of them. Her mother would try on occasion to persuade her to make a choice, but Maria Gavrilovna would only shake her head and grow pensive. By this time Vladimir was not among the living: he had died in Moscow on the eve of its occupation by the French. His memory seemed to be sacred to Masha; at least she faithfully kept everything that could remind her of him—books he had read at one time, his drawings, the music or poetry he had copied out for her. The neighbors, hearing all about it, wondered at her constancy and awaited with curiosity the appearance of the hero who would eventually triumph over the sad fidelity of this virginal Artemisia.[15]

Meanwhile, the war had come to a glorious end. Our regiments were returning from abroad. Crowds rushed out to meet them on the way. The bands were playing songs captured in the war: "Vive Henri Quatre," Tyrolean waltzes, and arias from *Joconde*.[16] Officers who had left for the campaign almost as adolescents were returning as men seasoned in war and decorated with crosses all over their chests. Soldiers chatted gaily, constantly mixing German and French words into their speech. Unforgettable time! A time of glory and ecstasy! How mightily beat the Russian heart at the word Fatherland! How sweet were the tears of reunion! How unanimously did we ally our feeling of national pride with our love for the Emperor! And what a moment it was for him!

The women, Russian women, were inimitable then. Their usual coldness disappeared. Their enthusiasm was truly intoxicating when they met the victors, shouted "hurray!"

And tossed their caps into the air.[17]

Who, among the officers of the time, will deny that he was indebted to Russian womanhood for the best, most precious reward he had ever received?

Maria Gavrilovna and her mother lived through these glorious days in N. Guberniia and did not witness how the two capitals celebrated the return of the troops. But the general enthusiasm was possibly even greater in the provincial towns and villages. Arriving in one of these places was a veritable triumph for an officer; and a lover in a frock coat fared poorly in his vicinity.

We have already mentioned that her coldness notwithstanding, Maria Gavrilovna was surrounded by suitors as before. All had to give up, however, when a wounded hussar colonel called Burmin—with the St. George Cross in his buttonhole and an *interesting pallor* on his face, as young ladies of the time used to say—presented himself at the manor house. He was about twenty-six. He came to spend his furlough on his estate, adjacent to Maria Gavrilovna's village. Maria Gavrilovna bestowed special attention on him. In his presence her mood, usually pensive, grew lively. You could not say she was flirting with him, but a poet observing her demeanor with him would have said:

Se amor non e, che dunque?[18]

Burmin was indeed a very appealing young man. His mind was just the kind women like: it was a mind at once delicate and observant, without the slightest pretensions, and with a penchant for lighthearted banter. His mien with Maria Gavrilovna was simple and free; he followed with his eyes and all his feelings whatever she said or did. He seemed to be of a quiet and modest disposition, but the gossips insisted that in his earlier days he had been a frightful rake, which actually did not lower him in Maria Gavrilovna's opinion because she (like almost all young ladies) readily excused mischiefs that revealed a daring and ardent nature.

But the aspect of the young hussar's behavior that piqued her curiosity and imagination more than anything else (more than his tenderness, his pleasant conversation, his interesting pallor and bandaged arm) was his failure to declare himself. She could not help recognizing that he liked her very much; it was likely that he too, with his intelligence and experience, had noticed the special attention she was giving him: why then had she still not seen him at her feet, why had she still not heard his confession? What held him back? Was it shyness, inseparable from true love, or pride, or the flirtatiousness of a wily skirt chaser? It was a puzzle to her. Having thoroughly considered the matter, she decided that shyness was the sole cause of his silence, and she resolved to encourage him by more attention and—if circumstances so demanded—perhaps even by tenderness. She was setting the stage for the most unexpected denouement and impatiently awaited the moment of romantic explanation. A secret, of whatever kind it might be, is always hard for a female heart to bear. Her maneuvers achieved the desired effect: at least Burmin fell into such reveries and his dark eyes came to rest on Maria Gavrilovna with such ardency that the decisive moment seemed to be near. The neighbors talked about the wedding as a matter already settled, and the good Praskovia Petrovna rejoiced over her daughter's having at last found a worthy suitor.

One day the old lady was sitting in the living room playing solitaire when Burmin came in and immediately asked after Maria Gavrilovna.

"She is in the garden," answered the old lady. "Go and join her; I'll wait for you here."

Burmin went out, and the old lady made the sign of the cross, saying to herself: God willing the matter will be settled today!

Burmin found Maria Gavrilovna by the pond, under a willow tree, with a book in her hands and in a white dress—a veritable heroine out of a novel. After the initial exchange of questions, Maria Gavrilovna deliberately failed to keep up the conversation, thereby heightening the mutual embarrassment from which the only escape was a sudden and decisive declaration. And indeed Burmin, feeling the awkwardness of his situation, announced that he had long been seeking an opportunity to open his heart to her, and requested a moment's attention. Maria Gavrilovna closed her book and cast her eyes down as a sign of consent.

"I love you," said Burmin. "I love you passionately." Maria Gavrilovna blushed and lowered her head even further. "It has been imprudent of me to indulge in the enchanting habit of seeing you and listening to you daily..." Maria Gavrilovna remembered St. Preux's first letter.[19] "It is now too late to struggle against my fate; your memory, your dear incomparable image, will remain both the torment and the joy of my life; but I must still perform my painful duty of revealing a horrible secret to you and placing an insurmountable barrier between us."

"It has always been there," interrupted Maria Gavrilovna intensely; "I could never be your wife..."

"I know," he answered softly, "I know you loved at one time, but death and three years of grieving... Dear, kind Maria Gavrilovna, don't try to deprive me of my last solace, the thought that you would have agreed to make me happy, if... Keep silent, for heaven's sake, keep silent. You are lacerating my heart. Yes, I know, I sense, that you would have been mine, but I am the most unhappy creature... I am married!"

Maria Gavrilovna looked at him in astonishment.

"I am married," continued Burmin. "I have been married for close to four years and I don't know who my wife is, where she is, and whether I am ever to meet her!"

"What are you saying?" exclaimed Maria Gavrilovna. "How strange this is! But continue; I'll tell you afterwards... please continue."

"At the beginning of 1812," related Burmin, "I was hurrying to Vilno, where my regiment was stationed. Late one evening I came to a post station and was about to have fresh horses harnessed when a terrific blizzard blew up; both the stationmaster and the drivers advised me to stay until it passed over. I followed their advice, but an inexplicable restlessness took hold of me; it was almost as if somebody was pressing me forward. Although the blizzard had not abated, I could not wait any longer: I had the horses harnessed again and rode off straight into the storm. The driver took it into his head to go on the ice of a river, which was supposed to shorten our route by three versts. The banks were piled high with snow, and the driver missed the point where one could get back on the road; we ended up in an unfamiliar place. The storm was not letting up; I saw a faint light and ordered the driver to head for it. We entered a village; the light came from the wooden church. The church was open; several sleighs stood behind the fence; people were going up and down the porch.

" 'Here! Here!' shouted several voices. I told the driver to drive up to them.

"'For God's sake, where have you been?' somebody said to me. 'Your bride has fainted, the priest doesn't know what to do; we were just about ready to go back home. Get out quickly.'

"I jumped out of the sleigh without a word and entered the church, which was dimly lit by two or three candles. A girl was sitting on a bench in a dark corner of the church; another one was rubbing her temples.

"'Thank God,' said the second one, 'you have at last arrived. You've nearly killed the young mistress.'

"The old priest came up to me with the question, 'Do you wish me to begin?'

"'Yes, do, Father, by all means do,' I answered absently.

"They lifted up the girl. She seemed quite pretty to me... Inexplicable, unexcusable recklessness... I stood by her before the lectern; the priest was in a hurry; the three men and the maid supported the bride and were busy only with her. We were married.

"'Kiss each other,' we were told.

"My wife turned her pale face toward me. I wanted to kiss her... She shrieked, 'Oh, that's not him! It's not him,' and collapsed unconscious.

"The witnesses fixed their frightened eyes on me. I turned around, left the church without the slightest hindrance, flung myself into the sleigh and yelled out 'Go!'"

"Good heavens!" exclaimed Maria Gavrilovna, "and you don't know what's become of your poor wife?"

"No, I don't," answered Burmin. "I don't know the name of the village where I was married, I don't remember which post station I had been coming from. At the time I attached so little importance to my wicked prank that, since I left the church, I fell asleep and didn't wake up until the morning, when we were already at the third station. The orderly who was with me then died later in the war, and therefore I have no hope of finding her on whom I played such a cruel joke and who is now so cruelly avenged."

"Oh my God, oh my God," said Maria Gavrilovna, seizing his hand, "so it was you? And you don't recognize me?"

Burmin blanched and threw himself at her feet...

The Undertaker

Do we not daily gaze on coffins,
The silver thatch of earth decaying?
DERZHAVIN [20]

The last lot of the undertaker Adrian Prokhorovich's belongings was piled up on the hearse, and the pair of rawboned horses trudged for the fourth time from Basmannaia to Nikitskaia Street, where the undertaker was moving with all his household. Locking his office, he nailed a notice on the gate advising that the house was available for sale or rent, and set out on foot for his new domicile. As he approached the little yellow house that had enthralled his imagination for so long, and that he had at last bought for a considerable sum, the old undertaker noticed with surprise that his heart was not rejoicing. Stepping across the unfamiliar threshold and finding his new home in utter confusion, he sighed for his decrepit little cottage, where everything had been arranged in the strictest order for eighteen years. He started scolding his two daughters and the housemaid for their sluggishness, and set about helping them himself. Order was soon established. The icons were in their case and the crockery in the cupboard; the table, the sofa, and the bed took up the corners assigned to them in the back room; and the kitchen and living room were filled with the master's wares—coffins of all colors and sizes as well as cupboards full of mourning hats and cloaks and torches. Above the gate a sign was suspended showing a chubby Cupid,[21] with a torch held askew in his hand, and the inscription "Plain and Colored Coffins Sold and Upholstered; Available for Rent; Used Ones Repaired." The girls retired to their bedrooms. Adrian made an inspection tour of the house, sat down by the window, and gave orders to light the samovar.

The educated reader knows that both Shakespeare and Walter Scott presented their gravediggers as merry and jocular people, in order to strike our imagination all the more by this contrast.[22] Our respect for truth forbids us to follow the example of these authors; indeed we are obligated to admit that our undertaker's temper fully corresponded to his gloomy profession. Adrian Prokhorov was usually morose and pensive. He broke his silence only in order to rebuke his daughters when he found them idly eyeing the passersby from the window, or in order to demand exorbitant prices for his wares from those who had the misfortune (or sometimes pleasure) of needing them. On this occasion, too, as he sat by the window drinking his seventh cup of tea, he was sunk in sad thoughts. He thought of the pelting rain of the week before, which had caught the funeral procession of a retired brigadier at the city gates. Many cloaks had shrunk, many hats had lost their shape. He foresaw inevitable expenses, for his old stock of funereal apparel was deteriorating into a pitiful condition. He was planning to make up for the loss at the expense of Triukhina, a merchant's old widow, who had been on the brink of the grave for about a year. But she lay dying in Razguliai, and Prokhorov was afraid that her heirs, despite their promise, would not take the trouble to send for him to such a distant place and would make arrangements with an undertaker nearby.

These reflections were suddenly interrupted by three masonic knocks on the door.

"Who's there?" asked the undertaker.

The door opened, and a man instantly recognizable as a German artisan came into the room. He approached the undertaker with a cheerful countenance.

"Forgive me, dear neighbor," he said with the kind of Russian accent that we to this day cannot hear without laughter, "forgive me for disturbing you... I wanted to make your acquaintance as soon as possible. I am a shoemaker, my name is Gottlieb Schulz, and I live across the street, in that little house which is just opposite your windows. I will be celebrating my silver wedding anniversary tomorrow, and would like to ask you and your daughters to come and dine with us just like friends of the family."

The invitation was cordially accepted. The undertaker asked the shoemaker to sit down and have a cup of tea, and thanks to Gottlieb Schulz's convivial nature, they were soon conversing amicably.

"How's Your Honor's business?" asked Adrian.

"Oh, well," answered Schulz, "so-so. I can't complain. Though, of course, my wares are not the same as yours: a man alive can go without shoes, but a dead man can't live without a coffin."

"That's true enough," remarked Adrian. "On the other hand, if the live man cannot afford to buy shoes, he can, forgive my saying so, just as well go barefooted; but a beggar's corpse will take a coffin free of charge."

The conversation continued in this vein for some time longer; at last the shoemaker rose and said good-bye to the undertaker, repeating his invitation.

The next day, at exactly twelve o'clock, the undertaker and his daughters left their newly acquired house, passed through the wicket gate and directed their steps toward the neighbor's. Deviating for the nonce from the manner adopted by today's novelists, I will not describe Adrian Prokhorov's Russian caftan or the European attire of

Akulina and Daria. I do not deem it superfluous, however, to mention that both girls had put on yellow hats and red shoes, which they did only on festive occasions.

The shoemaker's small apartment was full of guests, mostly German artisans with their wives and apprentices. The only Russian official there was a police guard, a Finn called Iurko who, despite his humble title, enjoyed the special favor of the host. He had served in his vocation for some twenty-five years steadfastly and dependably, just like Pogorelskii's mailman.[23] The conflagration of 1812, which destroyed Russia's ancient capital, also annihilated Iurko's sentry box. But as soon as the enemy was chased out,[24] a new box appeared in the place of the old, this one gray with white Doric columns, and Iurko began once more to pace to and fro before it with "poleax in hand, wearing a coarse frieze coat."[25] He was acquainted with most of the Germans living near the Nikitskii Gate; some had even had occasion to be his guests from Sunday night till Monday morning. Adrian immediately made his acquaintance, for Iurko might sooner or later prove to be useful; and when the guests went to the dinner table Adrian and Iurko sat down side by side. Mr. and Mrs. Schulz and their daughter, the seventeen-year-old Lottchen, while dining with their guests, were also busy offering the food and helping the cook serve it. The beer flowed abundantly. Iurko ate for four; Adrian did not lag behind him, though his daughters put on a more modest show; the conversation, conducted in German, was getting noisier by the minute. Presently the host asked for attention and, uncorking a bottle sealed with pitch, uttered in loud Russian, "To the good health of my dear Louisa!"

The sparkling wine, almost like champagne, bubbled over. The host implanted a tender kiss on his forty-year-old helpmate's fresh cheek, and the guests noisily drank the good-natured Louisa's health.

"To the health of my dear guests!" exclaimed the host, opening a second bottle, and the guests expressed their gratitude by draining their glasses once more. One toast followed another: they drank to each guest separately; to Moscow and to a round dozen small towns in Germany; to all guilds in general and to each in particular; to the masters and to the apprentices. Adrian drank diligently and got so merry that he himself proposed a humorous toast. Suddenly one of the guests, a fat baker, raised his glass and cried out:

"To the health of those we work for, *unserer Kundleute!*"

This toast, like all the others, was accepted joyously and unanimously. The guests started bowing one to the other, the tailor to the shoemaker, the shoemaker to the tailor, the baker to both, the whole

company to the baker, and so forth. In the midst of all these salutations Iurko cried out, turning to his neighbor, "And how about you?
Drink, brother, to the health of your corpses."

Everybody laughed, but the undertaker felt offended and frowned.
Nobody noticed this, however; the guests continued to drink, and the
bells were already ringing for vespers when the company rose from
the table.

The guests left late, most of them in a mellow mood. Heeding the
adage, "One good turn deserves another,"[26] the fat baker and a book-
binder, whose face seemed to have been bound in reddish morocco,
led Iurko to his sentry box, supporting him by his arms. The undertaker arrived home drunk and angry.[27]

"What's all this really?" he argued aloud. "In what way is my profession less honorable than others? Or is the undertaker a brother to
the hangman? What are the infidels laughing about? Or is an undertaker a clown in a yuletide show? I was going to invite them to a
housewarming party, spread out a sumptuous feast, but none of that
after this! I will issue an invitation, but it will be to those for whom I
work: the Russian Orthodox dead."

"What is this, master?" said the serving woman who was pulling
the boots off his feet just then. "What nonsense are you saying? Make
the sign of the cross! To invite the dead to a housewarming party!
Holy horrors!"

"God be my witness, I am going to invite them," continued Adrian,
"and invite them for tomorrow. Do me the honor, my benefactors,
come to feast at my house tomorrow evening; I will treat you to all
that God has sent me." With these words the undertaker got into bed
and soon started snoring.

It was still dark outside when Adrian was roused from his sleep.
The merchant's widow Triukhina had died during the night, and her
steward sent a special emissary on horseback to bring Adrian the
news. The undertaker tipped the man ten kopecks for it, then dressed
quickly, took a cab, and drove to Razguliai. Police were already posted
at the dead woman's gate, and merchants were roving about like ra-
vens scenting a corpse. The deceased was laid out on the table; she
was yellow as wax but not yet disfigured by decomposition. Relatives,
neighbors, and domestics crowded around her. All the windows were
open; candles burned; priests were reading prayers. Adrian went up to
Triukhina's nephew, a callow little tradesman in a fashionable coat,
and informed him that the coffin, candles, shroud, and other funereal
accessories would be delivered immediately in perfect order. The heir
thanked him distractedly, saying that he would not wrangle about the

price but would fully rely on the undertaker's conscience. The latter, as was his wont, swore he would not charge a kopeck too much; he exchanged meaningful glances with the steward and went to see to the arrangements. He spent the whole day riding back and forth between Razguliai and the Nikitskii Gate; he settled everything by the evening and, dismissing his cabdriver, returned home on foot. It was a moonlit night. He got as far as the Nikitskii Gate without any incident. Near the Church of the Ascension our acquaintance Iurko challenged him and, recognizing him, wished him good night. It was late. The undertaker was approaching his house when suddenly he fancied he saw somebody go up to his gate, open the wicket, and disappear through it.

"What could this mean?" thought Adrian. "Who else needs my services? Or has a thief crept into my house? Or could it be lovers sneaking in to my silly lasses? Anything can happen."

The undertaker was on the point of calling out to his friend Iurko for help. At that moment, however, somebody else came up to the wicket and was about to enter, but seeing the master of the house running toward him, he stopped and took off his three-cornered hat. His face seemed familiar, but in his hurry Adrian could not examine his features closely.

"You've honored me with your visit," said Adrian out of breath, "so please come in, do me the favor."

"Don't stand on ceremony, my good fellow," answered the other, with a hollow ring to his voice; "just step forward briskly and show the way to your guests."

Adrian had indeed no chance to stand on ceremony. The wicket was open; he went up the steps, the other man right behind him. Adrian fancied that people were walking about his rooms.

"What the devil!" he thought and hurried in... But there his knees almost gave way under him. The room was full of corpses. The moon shining through the windows lit up their yellow and blue faces, gaping mouths, murky half-closed eyes, and protruding noses... To his horror Adrian recognized in them the people who had been buried through his efforts, and in the guest entering with him, the brigadier whose funeral had taken place in the pelting rain. All of them, male and female, surrounded the undertaker with bows and salutations; only one pauper, who had been buried gratis a little while back, stood humbly in the corner, feeling too awkward and ashamed of his rags to come forward. All the others were properly dressed, the lady corpses in caps and ribbons, the gentlemen of rank in uniform, though with their chins unshaven, and the merchants in their holiday caftans.

"As you see, Prokhorov," said the brigadier in the name of the whole honorable company, "we have all risen in response to your invitation; only those stayed at home who are by now really incapacitated, who have entirely gone to pieces or have only their bones left without skin; but even among those there was one who could not restrain himself, so badly did he want to visit with you…"

At this moment a small skeleton pushed his way through the crowd and approached Adrian. His skull smiled affably and threadbare linen hung on him here and there as if on a pole, and the bones of his legs rattled in his jackboots like pestles in mortars.

"You don't recognize me, Prokhorov," said the skeleton. "Can't you remember retired Sergeant of the Guards Petr Petrovich Kurilkin, the one to whom you sold your first coffin in 1799, pretending it was oak though it was pine?"

With these words the corpse sought to enfold Prokhorov in his osseous embrace, but the undertaker gathered all his strength, screamed, and pushed him away. Petr Petrovich lost his balance, fell over, and crumbled. A murmur of indignation rose among the corpses; they all stood up in defense of their fellow corpse's honor and drew near Adrian with abuse and threats, so that their poor host, deafened by their shouts and almost crushed by their throng, lost his presence of mind, collapsed on the bones of the retired sergeant of the guards, and fainted.

The sun had long been shining on the undertaker's bed. At last he opened his eyes and saw before him the serving woman, who was blowing into the samovar to quicken its flame. With horror, he recalled all the events of the preceding night. Blurred images of Triukhina, the brigadier, and Sergeant Kurilkin floated before his mind's eye. He waited in silence for the woman to begin a conversation and tell him how the night's incident had concluded.

"How very long you've slept, dear master Adrian Prokhorovich!" said Aksinia as she gave him his dressing gown. "The tailor from next door has been to see you, and the local guard has dropped in to tell you that today is the district police officer's name-day, but you pleased to sleep so soundly that we didn't want to wake you."

"And has anybody been from the late Triukhina's family?"

"The late Triukhina's? Has she died then?"

"What a silly woman! Didn't you yourself help me yesterday with the arrangements for her funeral?"

"What's this, dear master? Have you lost your mind, or are you still befuddled by yesterday's wine? What funeral was there yesterday? You gorged yourself at the German's all day, came home drunk, tum-bled into bed, and have been sleeping until this very minute, though the bells have already rung for mass."

"Is that so?" said the undertaker, much gladdened.

"Of course it is so," answered the serving woman.

"Well, if it is, then make that tea quickly and call my daughters."

The Stationmaster

Fiscal clerk-of-registration,
Despot of the posting station.
PRINCE VIAZEMSKII [28]

Who has not cursed stationmasters?—who has not quarreled with them frequently? Who has not demanded the fateful book from them in moments of anger, in order to enter in it a useless complaint against their highhandedness, rudeness, and negligence? Who considers them anything but a blemish on the human race, as bad as the chancery clerks of yore or at least as the robbers of the Murom Forest? Let us be fair, however, and try to imagine ourselves in their position: then, perhaps, we shall judge them with more lenience. What is a stationmaster? A veritable martyr of the fourteenth class, whose rank is enough to shield him only from physical abuse, and at times not even from that. (I appeal to my reader's conscience.) What are the duties of this despot, as Prince Viazemskii playfully calls him? Are they not tantamount to penal servitude? Day or night, he does not have a moment's quiet. The traveler takes out on him all the irritation accumulated during a tedious ride. Should the weather be unbearable, the highway abominable, the coachdriver intractable, should the horses refuse to pull fast enough—it is all the stationmaster's fault. Entering the stationmaster's poor abode, the traveler looks on him as an enemy; the host is lucky if he can get rid of his unwanted guest fast, but what if he happens to have no horses available? God! What abuses, what threats shower on his head! He is obliged to run about the village in rain and slush; he will go out on his porch even in a storm or in the frost of the twelfth day of Christmas just to seek a moment's rest from the shouting, pushing, and shoving of exasperated travelers. A general arrives: the trembling stationmaster lets him have the last two teams of horses, including the one that should be reserved for couriers. The general rides off without a word of thanks. Five minutes have scarcely gone by when bells tinkle and a state courier tosses his order for fresh horses on the stationmaster's desk!... Let us try to comprehend all this in full, and our hearts will be filled with sincere compassion instead of resentment. Just a few more words: in the course of twenty years I have traveled Russia in all directions; I know almost all the postal routes; I have been acquainted with several generations of coachdrivers; it is a rare postmaster whose face I do not recognize, and there are few I have not had dealings with. In the not too distant future I hope to publish a curious collection of observations I have made as a traveler; for now I will only say that postmasters as a group are usually presented to the public in an unfair light. These maligned public servants are usually peaceable people, obliging by nature, inclined to be sociable, modest in their expectations of honors, and not too greedy for money. From their conversations (which traveling gentlemen are wrong to ignore) one can derive a great deal that is interesting and instructive. For my part, I must confess that I would rather talk with them than with some official of the sixth class traveling on government business.

It will not be difficult to guess that I have some friends among the honorable estate of stationmasters. The memory of one of them is indeed precious to me. Circumstances drew us together at one time, and it is he of whom I now intend to talk to my amiable readers.

In 1816, in the month of May, I happened to be traveling through N. Guberniia, along a route that has since been abandoned. Of low rank at the time, I traveled by post, hiring two horses at each stage.[29] As a result, stationmasters treated me with little ceremony, and I often had to take by force what I thought should have been given me by right. Being young and hotheaded, I felt indignant over the baseness and pusillanimity of the stationmaster who gave away to some high-ranking nobleman the team of horses that had been prepared for me. It also took me a long time to get used to being passed over by a snobbish flunkey at the table of a governor. Nowadays both the one and the other seem to me to be in the order of things. Indeed what would become of us if the rule convenient to all, "Let rank yield to rank," were to be replaced by some other, such as "Let mind yield to mind"? What arguments would arise? And whom would the butler serve first? But let me return to my story.

It was a hot day. When we were still three versts away from the station of P. it started sprinkling, and in a minute a shower drenched me to the skin. On my arrival at the station, my first concern was to change into dry clothes as soon as possible, and the second, to ask for some tea.

"Hey, Dunia!" called out the stationmaster. "Light the samovar and go get some cream." As these words were pronounced, a little girl aged about fourteen appeared from behind the partition and ran out on the porch. I was struck by her beauty.

"Is that your daughter?" I asked the stationmaster.

"Aye, truly she is," answered he, with an air of satisfaction and pride, "and what a sensible, clever girl, just like her late mother."

He started copying out my order for fresh horses, and I passed the time by looking at the pictures that adorned his humble but neat dwelling. They illustrated the parable of the Prodigal Son. In the first one, a venerable old man, in nightcap and dressing gown, was bidding farewell to a restless youth who was hastily accepting his blessing and a bag of money. The second one depicted the young man's lewd behavior in vivid colors: he was seated at a table, surrounded by false friends and shameless women. Farther on, the ruined youth, in rags and with a three-cornered hat on his head, was tending swine and sharing their meal;[30] deep sorrow and repentance were reflected in his features. The last picture showed his return to his father: the warm-hearted old man, in the same nightcap and dressing gown, was running forward to meet him; the Prodigal Son was on his knees; in the background the cook was killing the fatted calf, and the elder brother was asking the servants about the cause of all the rejoicing.[31] Under each picture I read appropriate verses in German. All this has remained in my memory to this day, together with the pots of balsam, the motley curtain of the bed, and other surrounding objects. I can still see the master of the house himself as if he were right before me: a man about fifty years of age, still fresh and agile, in a long green coat with three medals on faded ribbons.

I had scarcely had time to pay my driver for the last stage when Dunia was already returning with the samovar. The little coquette only had to take a second glance at me to realize what an impression she had made on me; she cast down her big blue eyes; but as I started up a conversation with her she answered without the slightest bashfulness, like a young woman who has seen the world. I offered a glass of rum punch to her father and a cup of tea to her, and the three of us conversed as if we had long been acquainted.

The horses had been ready for quite some time but I did not feel like parting with the stationmaster and his daughter. At last I said good-bye to them; the father wished me a pleasant journey, and the daughter came to see me to the cart. On the porch I stopped and asked her to let me kiss her; she consented... I have accumulated many recollections of kisses

> Since I took up the occupation,[32]

but none has made such a lasting and delightful impression on me as the one I received from Dunia.[33]

Some years went by, and circumstances brought me once more to the same places, along the same route. I remembered the old station-master's daughter, and the thought of seeing her again gave me joy. I told myself that the old stationmaster might well have been replaced, and that Dunia was likely to have married. It even occurred to me that one or the other might have died, and I approached the station with rueful premonitions.

The horses stopped by the small building of the station. As I entered the room, I immediately recognized the pictures illustrating the parable of the Prodigal Son; the table and the bed stood in their former places; but there were no longer any flowers on the windowsills, and everything around betrayed dilapidation and neglect. The stationmaster himself slept under a fur coat; my arrival woke him; he got up... It was indeed Samson Vyrin, but how he had aged![34] While he set about entering my order for horses, I looked at his gray hair, the deep furrows lining his face, which had not been shaven for a long time, his hunched back, and I could hardly believe that three or four years could have changed a stalwart fellow into such a feeble old man.

"Do you recognize me?" I asked him. "You and I are old acquaintances."

"That may well be," he answered sullenly; "this is a busy highway; many travelers come and go."

"How's your Dunia?" I pursued the conversation. The old man frowned.

"God knows," he answered.

"So she's married, is she?" I asked.

The old man pretended not to have heard my question and continued muttering details of my travel document. I refrained from further questions and had the kettle put on for tea. Burning with curiosity, I hoped that some rum punch might loosen my old acquaintance's tongue.

I was right; the old man did not refuse the glass I offered him. The rum noticeably dissipated his gloom. Over the second glass he became talkative: he either remembered me or pretended to, and I heard from him the following story, which captured my imagination and deeply moved me at the time.

"So you knew my Dunia?" he began. "Aye, verily, who didn't know her? Oh, Dunia, Dunia! What a fine lass she was! No matter who'd pass through here, in the old days, they'd all praise her; no one ever said a word against her. The ladies would give her presents, now a kerchief, now a pair of earrings. Gentlemen passing through would deliberately stay on, as if to dine or sup, but really only to look at her a little longer. It often happened that a gentleman, however angry he was, would calm down in her presence and talk to me kindly. Faith, sir, couriers, government emissaries, would converse with her for as long as half an hour at a time. The whole household rested on her: be it cleaning or cooking, she'd see to it all. And I, confound me for a fool, just doted on her, just did not know how to treasure her enough; who'd dare say I didn't love my Dunia, didn't cherish my child? Who had a good life if she didn't? But no, you cannot drive off evil by curses: you cannot escape your fate."

He began telling me about his grief in detail. Three years before, one winter evening when the stationmaster was lining his new register with a ruler and Dunia was sewing a dress behind the partition, a troika drove up, and a traveler, wearing a Circassian hat and military coat, and wrapped in a scarf, came into the room demanding horses. All the horses were out. Hearing this news, the traveler was about to raise both his voice and his whip, but Dunia, who was used to such scenes, ran out from behind the partition and sweetly asked the man if he would like to have something to eat. Dunia's appearance produced its usual effect. The traveler's anger dissipated; he agreed to wait for horses and ordered supper. When he had taken off his wet shaggy hat, unwound his scarf, and thrown off his coat, he turned out to be a slim young hussar with a little black mustache. He made himself at home at the stationmaster's, and was soon merrily conversing with him and his daughter. Supper was served. In the meanwhile some horses arrived, and the stationmaster gave orders to harness them to the traveler's carriage immediately, without even feeding them; but when he returned to the house he found the young man lying on the bench almost unconscious; he was feeling sick, he had a headache, he could not travel on... What could you do? The stationmaster yielded his own bed to him, and it was resolved that if he did not get any better by the morning, they would send to the town of S. for the doctor.

The hussar felt even worse the next day. His orderly rode to town to fetch the doctor. Dunia wrapped a handkerchief soaked in vinegar around the hussar's head and sat by his bed with her sewing. In the stationmaster's presence, the patient groaned and could hardly utter a word; but he drank two cups of coffee nonetheless and, groaning, ordered himself dinner. Dunia did not leave his bedside. He kept asking for something to drink, and Dunia brought him a jug of lemonade prepared by her own hand. The sick man took little sips, and every time he returned the jug to Dunia, he squeezed her hand with his enfeebled fingers in token of gratitude. The physician arrived by dinner time. He felt the patient's pulse and spoke with him in German; in Russian he declared that all the sick man needed was rest, and he would be well enough to continue his journey in a couple of days. The hussar handed him twenty-five rubles in payment for his visit and invited him to stay for dinner; the physician accepted; both ate with excellent appetite, drank a bottle of wine, and parted highly satisfied with each other.

Another day passed, and the hussar recovered entirely. He was extremely cheerful; joked incessantly, now with Dunia, now with her father; whistled little tunes; talked with the travelers; entered their orders in the postal register; and made himself so agreeable to the warmhearted stationmaster that on the third day he was sorry to part with his amicable lodger. It was a Sunday: Dunia was preparing to go to mass. The hussar's carriage drove up. He took leave of the stationmaster, generously rewarding him for his bed and board; he said goodbye to Dunia, too, and offered to take her as far as the church, which was on the edge of the village. Dunia stood perplexed.

"What are you afraid of?" said her father. "His Honor's not a wolf; he won't eat you: go ahead, ride with him as far as the church."

Dunia got into the carriage next to the hussar, the orderly jumped up next to the driver, the driver whistled, and the horses started off at a gallop.

Later the poor stationmaster could not understand how he could have permitted Dunia to go off with the hussar; what had blinded him? what had deprived him of reason? Half an hour had scarcely passed when his heart began to ache and ache, and anxiety overwhelmed him to such a degree that he could no longer resist setting out for the church himself. He could see as he approached the church that the congregation was already dispersing, but Dunia was neither in the churchyard nor on the porch. He hurried into the church: the priest was leaving the altar, the sexton extinguishing the candles, and two old women still praying in a corner; but Dunia was not there. Her poor father could hardly bring himself to ask the sexton if she had been to mass. She had not, the sexton replied. The stationmaster went home more dead than alive. The only hope he had left was that Dunia, with a young girl's capricious impulse, might have decided to ride as far as the next station, where her godmother lived. He waited in a state of harrowing agitation for the return of the team of horses that had driven her off. But the driver did not come back for a long time. At last toward evening he arrived, alone and drunk, with the appalling news:

"Dunia went on with the hussar past the next station."

The old man could not bear his misfortune: right there and then, he took to the same bed in which the young deceiver had lain the night before. Turning all the circumstances over in his mind, he could now guess that the hussar had only feigned illness. The poor old man developed a high fever; he was taken to S. and temporarily replaced by another person at the station. The same physician who had been to see the hussar was treating him. He assured the stationmaster that the young man had been perfectly healthy, and that he, the doctor, had guessed his evil intentions even then but had kept his silence, fearing the young man's whip. Whether the German spoke the truth or just wished to boast of his foresight, what he said certainly did not console the poor patient. The latter, having scarcely recovered from his illness, asked the district postmaster in S. for a two-month leave of absence, and without saying a word to anyone about his intentions, set out on foot to find his daughter. He knew from the travel document that Captain Minskii had been traveling from Smolensk to Petersburg. The driver who had driven them said that Dunia had wept during the whole journey, though it did seem that she was going of her own free will.

"Perchance," the stationmaster said to himself, "I shall bring my lost sheep home."

He arrived in Petersburg with this in mind, put up in the barracks of the Izmailovskii Regiment, at the lodging of a retired noncommissioned officer who was a former comrade, and began his search. He soon found out that Captain Minskii was in Petersburg and lived at the Hotel Demuth. The stationmaster decided to call on him.

He presented himself at the captain's anteroom early one morning and asked the orderly to announce to His Honor that an old soldier begged to see him. The orderly, who was cleaning a boot on a last, declared that his master was asleep, and that he never received anybody before eleven o'clock. The stationmaster went away and came back at the appointed time. Minskii himself came out to him in his dressing gown and red skullcap.

"What can I do for you, brother?" he asked.

The old man's heart seethed with emotion, tears welled up in his eyes, and he could only utter in a trembling voice, "Your Honor!... Do me the Christian favor!..."

Minskii took a quick glance at him, flushed, seized him by the hand, led him to his study, and locked the door.

"Your Honor," continued the old man, "what is done cannot be undone;[35] but at least give me back my poor Dunia. You have had your fun with her; do not ruin her needlessly."

"What can't be cured must be endured,"[36] said the young man in extreme embarrassment. "I stand guilty before you and I ask for your pardon, but don't think I could abandon Dunia: she will be happy, I give my word of honor. What would you want her for? She loves me; she has grown away from her former station in life. Neither you nor she could ever forget what has happened."

Then, thrusting something into the cuff of the stationmaster's sleeve, he opened the door, and the old man found himself on the street again, though he could not remember how he had got there.

He stood motionless for a long time; at last he took notice of a roll of some kind of paper in the cuff of his sleeve; he pulled it out, and unrolling it, discovered several crumpled five- and ten-ruble notes. Tears welled up in his eyes once more, tears of indignation. He pressed the notes into a lump, threw them on the ground, trampled on them with his heel, and walked away... Having gone a few steps, however, he stopped, thought for a while... returned... but by then the banknotes were gone. A well-dressed young man ran up to a cab as soon as he noticed the stationmaster returning, got in quickly, and shouted: "Go!" The stationmaster did not chase after him.[37] He decided to return home to his station, but before doing so, he wished to see his poor Dunia just once more. To this end, he returned to Minskii after a couple of days, but the orderly told him sternly that his master was not receiving anybody, gave him a push with his chest to get him out of the anteroom, and slammed the door in his face. The stationmaster stood there for a while, but finally went away.

In the evening of that same day, having attended service at the Church of All the Afflicted,[38] he walked along Liteinaia Street. Suddenly a garish droshky dashed by him, and he recognized Minskii seated in it. It stopped before the entrance of a three-story building, and the hussar ran up the steps. A felicitous thought flashed through the stationmaster's mind. He walked back, and when he came alongside the driver, he said:

"Whose horse is this, my good man? Isn't it Minskii's?"

"Just so," answered the driver, "and what do you want?"

"Here's what: your master gave me a note to take to his Dunia, but I went and forgot where this Dunia lives."

"She lives right here, on the second floor. But you're tardy with your note, brother: he himself is up there now."

"No matter," rejoined the stationmaster, with an inexpressible leap of the heart. "Thanks for telling me, but I'll do my job anyway." With these words he went up the stairs.

The door was locked; he rang, and a few seconds of painful anticipation followed. The clanking of a key could be heard, and the door opened.

"Does Avdotia Samsonovna live here?" he asked.

"Yes, she does," answered the young maidservant. "What do you want with her?" The stationmaster went through to the hall without answering. "You can't, you mustn't!" shouted the maid after him. "Avdotia Samsonovna has visitors."

But the stationmaster pressed forward, paying no attention. The first two rooms were dark, but there was a light in the third one. He walked up to the open door and stopped. In the room, which was elegantly furnished, he saw Minskii seated, deep in thought. Dunia, dressed in all the finery of the latest fashion, sat on the arm of his easy chair like a lady rider on an English saddle. She was looking at Minskii with tenderness, winding his dark locks around her fingers, which glittered with rings. Poor stationmaster! Never had his daughter appeared so beautiful to him; he could not help admiring her.

"Who is there?" she asked without raising her head. He remained silent. Receiving no answer, Dunia raised her head... and fell to the carpet with a shriek. Minskii, alarmed, rushed to lift her up, but when he caught sight of the old stationmaster standing in the doorway, he left Dunia and came up to him, trembling with rage.

"What do you want?" he hissed at him, clenching his teeth. "Why do you steal after me like a brigand? Do you intend to cut my throat? Get out of here!"—and with his strong hand he grabbed the old man by the collar and flung him out on the staircase.

The old man returned to his lodgings. His friend advised him to file a complaint, but the stationmaster, after considering the matter, gave it up as a lost cause and decided to retreat. In another two days he left Petersburg for his post station, and took up his duties once more.

"It's almost three years now," he concluded, "that I've been living without Dunia, having no news of her whatsoever. Whether she is alive or dead, God only knows. Anything can happen. She is not the first, nor will she be the last, to be seduced by some rake passing through, to be kept for a while and then discarded. There are many of them in Petersburg, of these foolish young ones: today attired in satin and velvet, but tomorrow, verily I say, sweeping the streets with the riffraff of the alehouse. Sometimes, when you think that Dunia may be perishing right there with them, you cannot help sinning in your heart and wishing her in the grave..."

Such was the story of my friend, the old stationmaster—a story often interrupted by tears, which he wiped away with the skirt of his coat in a graphic gesture, like the zealous Terentich in Dmitriev's beautiful ballad.[39] These tears were partly induced by the five glasses of rum punch that he had swilled down while he told his story; but for all that they deeply moved my heart. After I parted with him, I could not forget the old stationmaster, nor could I stop thinking about poor Dunia for a long time...

Just recently, passing through the small town of R., I remembered my old friend; I was told, however, that the station he had ruled over had been abolished. To my question, "Is the old stationmaster still alive?" nobody could give a satisfactory answer. I decided to visit the place I had known so long, hired private horses, and set out for the village of P.

This took place in the fall. Grayish clouds covered the sky; a cold wind blew from the reaped fields, stripping the roadside trees of their red and yellow leaves. I arrived in the village at sundown and stopped before the building of the former station. A fat woman came out on the porch (where poor Dunia had at one time kissed me) and explained in response to my questions that the old stationmaster had died about a year before, that a brewer had settled in his house, and that she was the brewer's wife. I began to regret the useless journey and the seven rubles I had spent in vain.

"What did he die of?" I asked the brewer's wife.

"A glass or two too many, Your Honor," answered she.

"And where is he buried?"

"Yonder past the village, next to his late wife."

"Could somebody lead me to his grave?"

"That'd be easy enough. Hey, Vanka! Leave that cat alone and take the gentleman to the graveyard, show him where the stationmaster's buried."

At these words a red-haired, one-eyed little boy in tatters ran up and led me straight to the edge of the village.

"Did you know the late stationmaster?" I asked him on the way.

"Aye, sir, I did. He taught me how to whittle flutes, he did. Sometimes (Lord bless him in his grave!) he'd be coming from the pothouse and we'd be after him, 'Grandpa, grandpa, give us nuts!' and he'd just scatter nuts among us. He used to always play with us."

"And do any of the travelers mention him?"

"There's few travelers nowadays; the assessor'll turn up sometimes, but his mind is nowise on the dead. There was a lady, though, traveled through these parts in the summer: she did ask after the old stationmaster and went a-visiting his grave."

"What sort of a lady?" I asked with curiosity.

"A wonderful lady," replied the urchin; "she was traveling in a coach-and-six with three little masters, a nurse, and a black pug; when they told her the old stationmaster'd died, she started weeping and said to the children, 'You behave yourselves while I go to the graveyard.' I offered to take her, I did, but the lady said, 'I know the way myself.' And she gave me a silver five-kopeck piece—such a nice lady!"

We arrived at the graveyard, a bare place, exposed to the winds, strewn with wooden crosses, without a single sapling to shade it. I had never seen such a mournful cemetery.

"Here's the old stationmaster's grave," said the boy to me, jumping on a mound of sand with a black cross bearing a brass icon.

"And the lady came here, did she?" I asked.

"Aye, she did," replied Vanka; "I watched her from afar. She threw herself on the grave and lay there for a long time. Then the lady came back to the village, sent for the priest, gave him some money, and went on her way, and to me she gave a silver five-kopeck piece—a wonderful lady!"

I too gave five kopecks to the urchin, and no longer regretted either the journey or the seven rubles spent on it.[40]

The Squire's Daughter

Fair art thou, Dushenka, in any garb.
BOGDANOVICH [41]

In one of our remote *guberniias* there was an estate owned by Ivan Petrovich Berestov. In his youth he had served in the Guards; he retired at the beginning of 1797,[42] settled in his village; and from then on never stirred abroad. He married a noblewoman of humble means, but she died in childbirth at a time when he was out on a hunt. He soon found consolation in various undertakings around the estate. He built a house, which he himself had designed, founded a textile mill, trebled his income, and began to consider himself the cleverest man in the neighborhood—an opinion that was not refuted by his neighbors, who came for frequent visits with their families and hunting dogs. On weekdays he went about in a short velveteen jacket, and on holidays put on a coat made of a cloth of domestic manufacture; he kept the record of his expenses himself and read nothing except for the *Senate Register*. He was generally liked, though considered a little haughty. The only person who could not get on with him was his closest neighbor, Grigorii Ivanovich Muromskii. This latter was a true Russian nobleman. Having squandered the larger part of his fortune in Moscow and lost his wife just then, he came to live in his last remaining village, where he continued to indulge in follies, only this time of a different nature. He laid out an English garden, spending on it almost all of his remaining revenue. His grooms were dressed like English jockeys. His daughter had an English *madam*[43] for a governess. He tilled his land according to the English method,

> But Russian grain won't grow after a foreign fashion,[44]

and even though Grigorii Ivanovich curtailed his expenses considerably, his revenues refused to increase. He managed to get into new debts even in the country. Despite all this, however, he enjoyed the reputation of a man not altogether stupid because he was the first landowner in the *guberniia* to think of taking out a mortgage on his estate from the State Board of Trustees—an operation that seemed extremely complex and daring at that time.[45] Among those people who disapproved of him, Berestov was the most vociferous. A hatred for innovations was one of the distinguishing traits of his character. He could not speak of his neighbor's Anglomania with equanimity, and found occasion to criticize him at every step. If Berestov was showing a guest around his estate, for instance, and the guest praised his managerial skills, his response, pronounced with a cunning smile, would be:

"Yes, sir! We don't do business like our neighbor Grigorii Ivanovich. We are too stodgy to go to ruin according to the English method. It's enough for us to be well-fed in the Russian way."

Thanks to the neighbors' zeal, such witticisms, with supplements and exemplifications, always reached the ears of Grigorii Ivanovich. The Anglophile bore the criticism about as patiently as our journalists do. He raged and called his vilifier a boor and a country bumpkin.

Such were the relations of the two landowners when Berestov's son came home to stay with him. He had been educated at the University of N.[46] and intended to enter the military service, but his father would not consent to it. Of entering the civil service, the young man considered himself absolutely incapable. Neither of them would yield, and so young Aleksei came home to live as a country gentleman for the time being, though he did grow a mustache just in case.[47]

Aleksei was truly a splendid young fellow. It would indeed have been a great pity if no military uniform were ever to hug his slim waist, and if, instead of parading on horseback, he were to spend his youth hunched over papers in a chancery. Seeing how he would always ride first during a hunt, with no concern for where he was going, the neighbors said in unison that he would never make a department head worth his salt. The young ladies eyed him; there were even some who could not take their eyes off of him; but Aleksei paid little attention to them. They attributed his coldness to a romantic attachment. Indeed the following address, copied from a letter he had mailed, was circulating among the neighbors: "To Akulina Petrovna Kurochkina, Moscow, straight across from the St. Aleksei Monastery, care of the brazier Savelev, and I humbly beg you to forward this letter to A.N.R."[48]

Those of my readers who have not lived in the country cannot imagine how charming those provincial misses are. Brought up in fresh air, in the shade of the apple trees in their orchards, they acquire all their knowledge of the world and life from books.[49] Solitude, freedom, and reading early develop in them feelings and passions that are unknown to our scatterbrained debutantes.[50] For the provincial miss the jingling of a coach bell is an adventure; she considers a trip to the nearest town a milestone in history; and the visit of a guest leaves behind a lingering, sometimes ever-lasting memory. Of course, anybody is free to laugh at some of their oddities, but the jeers of a superficial observer cannot efface their essential virtues, the chief one of which is a "distinctiveness of character, originality (*individualité*)"— a quality considered by Jean-Paul a prerequisite of human greatness.[51] I will allow that women receive a better education in the capitals, but the habits of social intercourse soon flatten out their character and make their minds just as uniform as their headdresses. I am not trying to judge anybody, less even to censure, but still, as an ancient commentator says, *nota nostra manet*.[52]

It is easy to imagine what impression Aleksei made among our young ladies. He was the first ever to appear in their company morose and disillusioned, the first ever to speak to them about a loss of zest for life and about his youth wasting away; moreover, he wore a black ring engraved with a death's head. All this was extremely new in that *guberniia*. The young ladies were raving about him.

But the person whose imagination was most exercised by him was the daughter of our Anglophile, Liza (or Betsy, as Grigorii Ivanovich usually called her). Since her father and his did not visit each other, she had not had a chance to meet him, while all her young neighbors could speak of nothing but him. She was seventeen years old. Dark eyes animated her dusky, very attractive face. She was her father's only child and therefore a spoiled one. Her playfulness and perpetual pranks delighted her father but drove to distraction her governess, a prim and proper forty-year-old maiden lady called Miss Jackson, who powdered her face, penciled her eyebrows, read through *Pamela* twice a year,[53] received two thousand rubles for it, and was dying of boredom in *this barbarous Russia.*

Liza had a maid called Nastia; she was a little older but just as giddy as her young mistress. Liza loved her very much, let her in on all her secrets, and planned her pranks with her aid; in other words, Nastia was a personage of considerably greater importance in the village of Priluchino than the confidante in a French tragedy.

"Please let me go visiting today," said Nastia one time, as she was dressing her young mistress.

"You may go if you want to: but where?"

"To Tugilovo, to the Berestovs'. It's their cook's wife's name-day, and she came over yesterday to invite us to dinner."

"So that's how it is," said Liza. "The masters have quarreled, but the servants treat each other to dinners."

"It's not our business what the masters do," rejoined Nastia. "And besides, I'm yours, not your papa's. You haven't yet quarreled with the young Berestov, have you? Let the old ones have their scuffles if that's what makes them happy."

"Do try to meet with Aleksei Berestov, Nastia, and tell me all about what he looks like and what kind of a person he is."

Nastia promised to do so, and Liza impatiently waited for her return all day. Nastia came back in the evening.

"Well, Lizaveta Grigorevna," she said coming into the room, "I've seen the young Berestov. Indeed I had my fill of seeing him: we spent the whole day together."

"How come? Tell me, tell me all as it happened."

"Just as you please, miss. We set out, that is, Anisia Egorovna, Nenila, Dunka, and I..."

"All right, I know. And what happened then?"

"Please, miss, I'll tell everything as it happened. So we arrived just before dinner. The room was full of people. There were some from Kolbino, some from Zakharevo, the steward's wife was there with her daughter, there were people from Khlupino..."

"Yes, yes. And Berestov?"

"Wait a minute, miss. So we sat down to table, the bailiff's wife in the place of honor and I next to her... Her daughters turned up their noses but I didn't care a rap..."

"Oh, Nastia, you're so boring with your interminable details!"

"And how impatient are you! Well, so we got up from the table... we had sat there a good three hours, you know, and the dinner was splendid; we had blue-and-red marbled blancmange for dessert... So we got up from the table and went out in the garden to play tag, and it was there that the young master came to join us."

"And what's he like? Is it true he's handsome?"

"Amazingly handsome, a real dazzler. Slim, tall, with rosy cheeks..."

"Really? And I thought he had a pale face. In any case, what did he seem like? Melancholy, pensive?"

"What? I've never seen such a rambunctious one in my life. He took it into his head to play tag with us."

"To play tag with you! Impossible!"

"I swear it's possible! And do you know what other trick he was up to? He'd catch you and start kissing you!"

"Nastia, you're telling fibs."

"I'm not telling fibs, say what you like. I could barely get away from him. All day he fooled around with us."

"Then why do they say he's in love and won't look at anybody?"

"I don't know about that, miss, but I do know he looked at me, too much even; and at Tania, the steward's daughter, too, and at Pasha from Kolbino. To tell the truth he didn't spurn any one, such a rascal!"

"How astonishing! And what are the servants saying about him?"

"He's a wonderful master, they say; such a good-natured and cheerful one. There's only one trouble: he's too fond of chasing the girls. But I'd say that's no great crime: he'll settle down once he's finished sowing his wild oats."

"How I'd love to meet him!" said Liza with a sigh.

"What's so difficult about that? Tugilovo is not far from us, only three versts: go on a walk that way or ride out on horseback; you will probably meet him. He takes his gun and goes out hunting every day, early in the morning."

"No, that's no good. He may think I am chasing after him. Besides, our fathers are on bad terms, so I can't just go and make his acquaintance... You know what, Nastia? I will dress up as a peasant girl!"

"Yes, do, miss: put on a coarse shirt and a *sarafan*, and go boldly to Tugilovo; I'll vouch Berestov will not let you go by unnoticed."

"And I can speak the way the local folks do, too. Ah, Nastia, my dear Nastia! What a wonderful idea!" And Liza went to bed determined to carry out her playful plan without fail.

The next morning she set about putting her scheme into practice. She sent to the market for some coarse linen, blue nankeen, and brass buttons, cut out a shirt and a *sarafan* with Nastia's help, and put all the maids in the house to work, and by evening the sewing was all done. As she tried on her new costume in front of the mirror, she had to confess to herself that she had never before seemed quite so sweet. She rehearsed her role: curtsied deeply while walking, let her head rock from side to side like the head of a porcelain cat, spoke in a peasant dialect, and covered her mouth with her sleeve when she laughed, all of which earned Nastia's full approval. There was only one difficulty: she tried to cross the yard barefooted, but the lawn felt prickly to her tender feet, not to mention the sand and pebbles, which seemed intolerable. Nastia, however, helped her out of this difficulty, too: she measured Liza's foot, ran to the meadow to find Trofim the shepherd, and ordered from him a pair of bast slippers of the right size. The next morning Liza was up at the crack of dawn. The whole house was asleep. Nastia waited for the shepherd by the gate. The horn sounded, and the village herd filed by the manor house. Passing by Nastia, Trofim handed her a pair of small motley bast slippers and received a fifty-kopeck piece as a reward. Liza quietly dressed up as a peasant girl, whispered instructions to Nastia concerning Miss Jackson, stepped out on the back porch, and ran through the vegetable garden into the field.

The dawn was radiant in the east, and the golden ranks of clouds seemed to be awaiting the sun like courtiers their sovereign; the clear sky, the morning freshness, the dew, the light breeze, and the singing of the birds filled Liza's heart with childlike joy; afraid of meeting somebody she knew, she seemed not to walk, but to fly. As she approached a grove that stood on the boundary of her father's property, she slackened her pace. This was where she was supposed to wait for Aleksei. Her heart beat fast, she did not know why; the fear that accompanies our youthful pranks is also their greatest charm. Liza entered the darkness of the grove. She was greeted by the deep rolling rumble of the wind among the trees. Her high good humor became subdued. She sank more and more into a pleasant reverie. She thought about—but can one determine with precision what is on the mind of a seventeen-year-old miss when she is by herself in a grove before six o'clock on a spring morning? And so she was walking, deep in thought, along the road under the canopy of tall trees overhanging from either side, when suddenly a sleek pointer barked at her. Frightened, Liza cried out. At the same moment a voice called:

"*Tout beau, Sbogar, ici...*"[54] and a young sportsman appeared from behind the shrubbery. "Don't be scared, sweetheart," he said to Liza; "my dog doesn't bite."

Liza had already recovered from her fright, and immediately took advantage of the situation.

"But I am frightened, Your Honor," she said, pretending to be half-frightened, half-bashful. "Look how mean she is, leaping at me again."

Aleksei (whom the reader has already recognized) was meanwhile taking full measure of the young peasant girl.

"I'll accompany you if you're afraid," he said to her. "Will you allow me to walk by your side?"

"There's nobody will hinder you," answered Liza. "Each goes where he likes; the road belongs to everybody."

"Where are you from?"

"From Priluchino; I'm the blacksmith Vasilii's daughter; I'm going to pick mushrooms." She was carrying a basket on a rope. "And you, Your Honor? From Tugilovo, I trow."

"Exactly," answered Aleksei. "I am the young squire's valet."

Aleksei wanted to appear on an equal footing with her. But Liza glanced at him and burst into laughter.

"That's a lie if I ever heard one," she said, "but you can't fool me. I can see you're the squire himself."

"What makes you think so?"

"Well, everything."

"But what exactly?"

"Nay, how could I not tell the master from the servant? You're got up differently, you don't talk like folks do, you call your dog different like."

Aleksei felt drawn to Liza more and more by the minute. Accustomed to standing on no ceremony with pretty lasses, he wanted to put his arm around her waist, but Liza jumped away from him and instantly assumed such a stern and cold expression that Aleksei, though he was amused by it, refrained from further advances.

"If you wish us to remain friends," she said gravely, "be good enough not to forget yourself."

"Who taught you such prudence?" asked Aleksei, amid peals of laughter. "Was it Nastenka, my acquaintance, the maid of your young mistress? So this is the way enlightenment spreads!"

Liza felt she had risked stepping out of her role, and she checked herself immediately.

"Lack-a-day, and who do you think I am?" she said. "Do you think I've never been to the manor house? Faith, sir: I've heard and seen plenty. But," she added, "if I keep a-prattling with you, I'll never pick any mushrooms. Go your own way, Your Honor, and I'll go mine. God bless you..."

Liza wanted to leave him, but Aleksei held her back by the hand.

"What is your name, precious heart?"

"Akulina," replied Liza, trying to extricate her fingers from Aleksei's grasp. "Let me go, Your Honor, it's time I went home even."

"Well, my friend Akulina, I will make sure to visit your dad, the blacksmith Vasilii."

"What are you saying?" Liza returned with alarm. "In the name of Christ, don't you come. If they hear at home as how I idly prated with a gentleman, all alone with him in the woods, I'll get into deep trouble; my father, the blacksmith Vasilii, will thrash me to death."

"But I must see you again without fail."

"There'll be occasions when I come here to pick mushrooms again."

"When will that be exactly?"

"Tomorrow, perhaps."

"Sweet Akulina, I'd kiss you all over but I daren't. So you say tomorrow, at the same time?"

"Yes, yes."

"You will not deceive me?"

"I won't."

"Swear to it."

"Cross my heart I'll come."

The young couple parted ways. Liza came out of the wood, scampered across the field, crept into the garden, and dashed headlong to the outbuilding where Nastia was waiting for her. There she changed, giving offhanded answers to her impatient confidante's questions, and soon made her appearance in the living room. The table was laid, the breakfast ready, and Miss Jackson, who had already powdered her face and laced herself into the shape of a liqueur glass, was cutting bread into tiny thin slices. Her father praised Liza for her early morning walk.

"There is nothing healthier," he said, "than getting up at daybreak."

He cited several examples of human longevity that he had read about in English journals, and remarked that all centenarians abstained from vodka and rose at dawn come winter or summer. Liza did not listen to him. She turned over in her mind all the details of her early morning encounter, all the words that had passed between Akulina and the young hunter, and she began to feel a twinge of conscience. In vain did she repeat to herself that their conversation had not transgressed the limits of propriety, and her prank could not have any serious consequences: the voice of her conscience was louder than that of her reason. The promise she had made about the following day worried her most of all, and she almost decided not to keep her solemn vow. But Aleksei, having waited for her in vain, might come to the village to look for the blacksmith Vasilii's daughter—the real Akulina, who was a fat wench with a pockmarked face—and might in that way uncover her irresponsible prank. This thought terrified Liza, and she decided to make her way to the grove next morning, once more in the disguise of Akulina.

As for Aleksei, he was enchanted; he thought about his new acquaintance all day, and the image of the dark-complexioned beauty haunted him even in his dreams at night. The first blush of dawn had hardly spread across the horizon when he was already dressed. Not giving himself enough time even to load his gun, he went out into the fields with his faithful Sbogar and rushed to the place where they had agreed to meet. About half an hour passed in unbearable suspense, but at last he caught a glimpse of a blue *sarafan* through the shrubs and ran to meet his sweet Akulina. She smiled on seeing him in raptures of gratitude, but Aleksei instantly detected traces of dejection and worry on her face. He wanted to know the reason. Liza confessed that she thought she had taken an irresponsible step, that she was regretting it, that just this once she had come, not wanting to break her promise, but this meeting would have to be the last one. She asked him to discontinue their acquaintance, which could lead to nothing good. All this, of course, was pronounced in a peasant dialect, but Aleksei was struck all the more by such ideas and sentiments, so unusual for a simple girl. He employed all his eloquence in an attempt to sway Akulina from her resolution; he assured her of the innocence of his desires, promised never to give her cause for regret and to obey her in everything, and entreated her not to deprive him of his only joy: of meeting her possibly every day or at least twice a week. He spoke the language of genuine passion and at that moment was truly in love. Liza listened to him in silence.

"Give me your word," she said at last, "that you will never look for me in the village or ask questions about me. Give me your word that you will never seek meetings with me apart from those that I myself assign." Aleksei was about to swear and cross his heart, but Liza stopped him with a smile. "I don't need a vow," she said; "your promise alone will be enough."

After this they had a friendly conversation, strolling about the woods, until Liza said, "It's time to go." They parted, and Aleksei, left by himself, pondered how a simple village girl had managed to acquire such unmistakable power over him in the course of two meetings. These relations with Akulina had the charm of novelty for him, and though the rules the unusual peasant girl had prescribed were onerous to him, it never entered his mind that he might not keep his word. The fact is that Aleksei, despite his ominous ring, his secret correspondence, and his somber disenchantment, was a good-natured and full-blooded young fellow with a pure heart, capable of enjoying innocent pleasures.

Were I to follow my own inclinations, I would describe in full detail the meetings of the two young people, their growing fondness of, and trust in, each other, their occupations, and their conversations, but I am aware that the majority of my readers would not share my enjoyment of such details.[55] Such details must seem cloying to people in general, and I will therefore leave them out, saying simply that before two months had elapsed Aleksei was head over heels in love, and Liza was no less involved, though less vocal, than he. They both enjoyed the present and gave little thought to the future.

The thought of an indissoluble bond passed through the mind of each quite frequently, but neither said anything on the subject. There were good reasons for this: Aleksei, however strongly he might have been attached to his sweet Akulina, could nevertheless not forget the distance separating him from a poor peasant girl; and Liza, knowing what deep hatred their fathers harbored against each other, did not dare hope for their reconciliation. Moreover, her vanity was secretly tempted by the dim romantic hope that the landlord of Tugilovo might in the end throw himself at the feet of the Priluchino blacksmith's daughter. Suddenly, an important event occurred that threatened to change their relationship.

One clear cold morning (one of the many our Russian autumn can boast of) Ivan Petrovich Berestov went out on a pleasure ride, taking with him, just in case, three pairs of greyhounds, a groom, and some footboys with clappers. At the same time Grigorii Ivanovich Muromskii, tempted by the good weather, gave orders to have his dock-tailed filly saddled and set out at a gallop around his Anglicized domains. As he approached the wood he noticed his neighbor proudly sitting on his horse in a Circassian coat, lined with fox fur, and waiting for a hare, which the boys were chasing out of a thicket with shouts and claps. If Grigorii Ivanovich had foreseen such a meeting, he would of course have turned aside, but he came across Berestov entirely unexpectedly, suddenly finding himself no farther than a pistol shot away from him. There was no way to escape a meeting. Muromskii, as a civilized European, rode up to his adversary and greeted him courteously. Berestov returned the greeting with as much enthusiasm as a chained bear bows to the *ladies and gentlemen* under orders from its trainer. Just at that moment the hare darted out of the wood and ran across the field. Berestov and the groom yelled out with all their might, let the dogs loose, and galloped after them at full speed. Muromskii's horse, which had never participated in a chase, bolted with fright. Her owner, who had proclaimed himself an excellent rider, gave her free rein and was secretly glad of the opportunity to rid himself of a disagreeable companion. But the horse, reaching the edge of a ravine that she had not noticed earlier, suddenly flung herself around, throwing Muromskii off. Having fallen rather hard on the frozen ground, he lay cursing his dock-tailed filly, which, as if coming to her senses, stopped in her tracks as soon as she felt herself free of a rider. Ivan Petrovich rode up to him, asking if he had hurt himself. Meanwhile, the groom brought the culprit around, holding her by the bridle. He helped Muromskii climb into the saddle, and Berestov invited him to his house. Muromskii felt that he was obligated and could not refuse, and so Berestov returned home in full glory, bringing back not only the hare he had caught, but also his adversary, wounded and almost a prisoner of war.

The two neighbors, eating lunch together, got into quite a friendly conversation. Muromskii, confessing that his fall made him incapable of returning home on horseback, asked Berestov to lend him a carriage. Berestov saw him off all the way to the porch, and Muromskii left only after he had extracted a promise from his neighbor that he (together with Aleksei Ivanovich) would come to Priluchino the very next day to dine together as old friends. Thus it appeared that an ancient and deeply rooted enmity was about to end, thanks to the skittishness of a dock-tailed filly.

Liza ran outside to meet Grigorii Ivanovich.

"What does all this mean, papa?" she asked in astonishment. "Why are you limping? Where is your horse? Whose carriage is this?"

"You will never guess, *my dear*,"[56] answered Grigorii Ivanovich, and told her everything that had happened.

Liza could hardly believe her ears. Her father, giving her no time to recover herself, declared that both Berestovs were coming to dinner the next day.

"What are you saying?" she exclaimed, blanching. "The Berestovs, both father and son! For dinner tomorrow! No, papa; say what you please, I will not show myself for anything!"

"What? Have you lost your mind?" rejoined her father. "Since when have you become so shy? Or are you bound by a hereditary feud like a romantic heroine? We've had enough of that; don't be silly."

"No, papa, nothing in the world, not all the treasures of the world, can persuade me to show myself before the Berestovs."

Grigorii Ivanovich shrugged his shoulders and did not argue with her any further, knowing that one could gain nothing by contradicting her. He retired to take a rest after his memorable ride.

Lizaveta Grigorevna went to her room and summoned Nastia. The two of them spent a long time discussing the impending visit. What would Aleksei think if in the well-bred young lady he recognized his Akulina? What opinion would he form of her conduct and principles, of her prudence? On the other hand, Liza very much wanted to see just what effect such an unexpected meeting would have on him... Suddenly an idea occurred to her. She immediately communicated it to Nastia; they both rejoiced over it as a godsend, and resolved to put it into practice without fail.

The next morning Grigorii Ivanovich asked his daughter over breakfast if she was still planning to hide from the Berestovs.

"Papa," answered Liza, "I will receive them if that is your wish, but only under one condition: in whatever shape I appear before them or whatever I do, you must not scold me, or give any sign of astonishment or displeasure."

"Yet another prank," said Grigorii Ivanovich, laughing. "Well, all right, all right, I consent: do as you like, my black-eyed prankster." With these words he kissed her on the forehead, and Liza ran off to get ready.

At nearly two o'clock a carriage of domestic manufacture drawn by six horses rolled into the courtyard and rounded the dense green circle of the lawn. Berestov the elder came up the steps aided by two liveried lackeys of Muromskii's. Berestov the younger, who had ridden after his father on horseback, entered the dining room with him. The table was already laid. Muromskii received his neighbors with the greatest possible kindness. He suggested they make a tour of the garden and the menagerie before dinner, and led them along the carefully raked and sanded paths. The elder Berestov inwardly disapproved of so much time and effort being wasted on such useless trifles, but he kept quiet out of politeness. His son could share neither the thrifty landowner's disapproval nor the vainglorious Anglophile's enthusiasm: he was impatiently waiting for the appearance of his host's daughter, about whom he had heard a great deal. Although his heart, as we know, was already engaged, a beautiful young woman could always make a claim on his imagination.

At last the three of them returned to the living room and sat down. While the two old men recalled earlier times and told anecdotes of their days in the service, Aleksei pondered what role he should assume in the presence of Liza. He decided that cold inattention would be most appropriate, whatever the circumstances, and he prepared himself accordingly. When the door opened he turned his head in that direction with such indifference, with such arrogant lack of concern, that it would have sent a shudder through even the most indurate coquette's heart. Unfortunately, the person who entered was not Liza, but the old Miss Jackson, powdered and laced, curtsying slightly, with her eyes cast down; and thus Aleksei's splendid stratagem had been employed in vain. He had hardly had time to collect himself when the door opened once more, this time admitting Liza herself. Everybody rose; the father was about to introduce the guests to his daughter, but he stopped and, checking himself, bit his lip... Liza, his dark-complexioned Liza, was covered with white powder up to her ears, and her eyebrows were painted even worse than those of Miss Jackson; she had on a wig whose artificial locks, much lighter than her own hair, were swept up like those of Louis XIV's peruke; her sleeves *à l'imbécile* stuck out as far as Madame de Pompadour's hooped skirt;[57] her waist was laced into the shape of the letter X; and all the diamonds of her late mother that had not yet been carried off to the pawnshop sparkled· on her fingers, around her neck, and in her ears. Aleksei could not recognize his Akulina in this ridiculous and glittering young lady. His father bent down to kiss her hand, and he followed his example grudgingly; when he touched her white little fingers, it seemed to him that they were trembling. He did find occasion, however, to notice her small foot, clad in the most coquettish shoe imaginable, which she had deliberately stuck out. This feature reconciled him somewhat to the rest of her attire. As for the powder and paint, it must be admitted that in the simplicity of his heart he neither noticed them at first glance nor suspected their presence later. Grigorii Ivanovich remembered his promise and tried not to show any sign of surprise, but his daughter's trick seemed so funny to him that he could hardly control himself. By contrast, the prim and proper Englishwoman was in no mood for laughter. She could guess that the paint and powder had been stolen from her chest of drawers, and a crimson hue of annoyance shone through the artificial whiteness of her face. She looked daggers at the young prankster, who, deferring any and all explanations till another time, pretended to notice nothing.

They sat down to table. Aleksei continued to play the role of a distracted man, sunk in his thoughts. Liza put on airs, speaking in a singsong through her teeth, and that only in French. Her father kept staring at her, not fathoming her purpose but finding it all very amusing. The Englishwoman was in a rage and remained silent. Ivan Petrovich alone felt perfectly at home: he ate for two, drank his fair share, laughed over his own jokes, and chatted and chortled more and more jovially by the minute.

At last they got up from the table; the guests went home; and Grigorii Ivanovich was free to laugh and ask questions.

"What gave you the idea of playing this trick on them?" he asked Liza. "And you know what? Face powder suits you; I am no judge of the secrets of ladies' toilette, but if I were you I would powder my face regularly; not too much, of course, but I would do it lightly."

Liza was thrilled with the success of her scheme. She embraced her father, promised to think about his advice, and dashed off to pacify the incensed Miss Jackson, who could hardly be persuaded to open her door to her and listen to her excuses. She had felt so embarrassed to show her dusky face to these strangers, Liza was saying; she had not dared to ask... she had been sure that dear, kind Miss Jackson would forgive her... and so on and so forth. Miss Jackson, concluding that ridiculing her had not been Liza's intention, calmed down, kissed Liza, and gave her as a token of reconciliation a jar of English ceruse, which Liza accepted with expressions of sincere gratitude.

The reader will easily guess that the next morning Liza did not delay coming to the grove where they usually met.

"Your Honor went to our masters' last night, didn't you?" she asked Aleksei immediately. "How did you like our young mistress?"

Aleksei answered that he had hardly taken notice of her.

"That's a pity," rejoined Liza.

"And why is it a pity?" asked Aleksei.

"Because I wanted to ask you, is it true, what they say?..."

"What do they say?"

"Is it true, as they say, that I'm like the young missus?"

"What nonsense! Compared to you she is a freak."

"Oh, Your Honor, you mustn't speak like that: our mistress has such delicate white skin and she's such a lady of fashion! How can I be compared with her?"

Aleksei swore to her that she was prettier than all the fair-complexioned young ladies in creation, and, in order to reassure her completely, began painting her mistress in such funny colors that Liza laughed with all her heart.

"All the same," she said with a sigh, "though the young missus may be funny, I'm an illiterate fool compared with her."

"Oh!" said Aleksei, "is that any cause for grief? If you want me to, I can teach you how to read and write in next to no time."

"Maybe you're right," said Liza. "Maybe we should really try."

"As you please, sweetheart; shall we begin at once?"

They sat down. Aleksei took a pencil and notebook from his pocket, and Akulina learned the alphabet amazingly fast. Aleksei marveled at her quick mind. The next morning she wanted to try her hand at writing as well; at first the pencil would not obey her fingers, but in a matter of a few minutes she could already draw her letters quite tolerably.

"What a miracle!" Aleksei was saying. "This is going faster than it could under the Lancasterian system."[58]

And indeed at the third lesson Akulina was already reading "Natalia the Boyar's Daughter" syllable for syllable,[59] interrupting her reading by remarks that truly astonished Aleksei, and scribbling aphorisms from the same story on a sheet of paper.

Another week went by, and a correspondence got under way between the two young people. A post office was established in the hollow of an old oak. Nastia performed the duties of the surreptitious mailman. Aleksei brought here his letters written in a bold hand, and found the plain blue sheets that carried the scribble-scrabble of his beloved. Akulina was evidently getting used to more refined language, and her mind was perceptibly developing, becoming cultivated.

Meanwhile Ivan Petrovich Berestov's recent acquaintance with Grigorii Ivanovich Muromskii became more and more firmly grounded and, thanks to certain considerations, soon turned into friendship. Muromskii often contemplated the circumstance that after Ivan Petrovich's death his whole fortune would pass on to Aleksei Ivanovich, making the young man one of the richest landowners of the province, in which case there would be no reason why he should not marry Liza. On his part the elder Berestov, though he recognized a certain extravagance in his neighbor (what he called his neighbor's English folly), could not deny that he had many excellent qualities. Grigorii Ivanovich was, for example, exceptionally resourceful; he was closely related to Count Pronskii, a distinguished and powerful man who could prove to be very useful to Aleksei; and finally (so argued Ivan Petrovich) Muromskii would probably be pleased with such an advantageous match for his daughter. The two elderly gentlemen kept turning the matter over in their heads until at last they exchanged views on it, embraced, agreed to take whatever steps were necessary, and set about accomplishing the task. Muromskii faced the difficulty of persuading his Betsy to become better acquainted with Aleksei, whom she had not seen since the memorable dinner party. They did not seem to like each other very much: at least Aleksei never returned to Priluchino, and Liza retired to her room every time Ivan Petrovich honored them with a visit. But, thought Grigorii Ivanovich, if Aleksei started coming over every day, Liza would be bound to fall in love with him. That was in the nature of things: time is the best match-maker.

Ivan Petrovich worried less about the success or failure of his scheme. The same evening he had made his agreement with Murom-skii he summoned his son to his study, lit his pipe, paused for a moment, and said, "What's happened to you, Alesha, that you no longer talk about military service? Doesn't the hussar uniform tempt you any more?"

"No, father," answered Aleksei respectfully. "I can see you don't want me to join the hussars, and it's my duty to obey you."

"Very good," answered Ivan Petrovich. "I see you're an obedient son; that's a comfort to me; I don't want to force you into anything either. I will not compel you... for the time being... to enter the civil service; instead, I intend to get you a wife."

"Who would that be, father?" asked the astonished Aleksei.

"Lizaveta Grigorevna Muromskaia," answered Ivan Petrovich; "you couldn't find a better bride, could you now?"

"Father, I haven't thought of marrying yet."

"You haven't, but I have, and I've thought it over thoroughly, too."

"That's all very well, but I don't like Liza Muromskaia in the least."

"You'll grow to like her later. Love comes with time."

"I don't think that I can make her happy."

"Her happiness is not your headache. So this is how you respect your father's wishes? Very well!"

"You may say what you please, I do not want to get married, and I will not get married."

"You will marry or I shall curse you and, God be my witness, I shall sell and squander the family property and not leave you a penny. I'll give you three days to think the matter over; until then I want you to keep out of my sight."

Aleksei knew that once his father took an idea into his head, you could not—to use Taras Skotinin's expression—poke it out of there with a nail;[60] but Aleksei took after his father, and it was just as difficult to sway him. He retired to his room and started thinking about the limits of paternal power, Lizaveta Grigorevna, his father's solemn promise to make him a beggar, and finally Akulina. For the first time he could see clearly that he was passionately in love with her. The romantic idea of marrying a peasant girl and supporting himself by work crossed his mind, and the more he thought about such a decisive step the more reasonable it seemed to him. Their meetings in the grove had been suspended for some time because of the rainy weather. He wrote a letter to Akulina in a clear hand but a frantic style, telling her about the disaster that was threatening them and directly asking for her hand. He immediately mailed the letter, that is, put it in the hollow of the tree, and went to bed entirely satisfied with himself.

Early next morning Aleksei, firm in his resolve, went to see Muromskii in order to explain matters frankly. He hoped to awaken his generosity and win him over.

"Is Grigorii Ivanovich at home?" he asked, as he stopped his horse by the front steps of the Priluchino mansion.

"No, he is not," answered the footman. "Grigorii Ivanovich pleased to ride out early."

"How annoying!" thought Aleksei, and turned to the footman once more. "Is at least Lizaveta Grigorevna at home?"

"She is, Your Honor."

Aleksei jumped off his horse, handed the reins to the footman, and went into the house unannounced.

"All will be settled," he thought, directing his steps toward the living room, "I will explain matters to Lizaveta herself."

He entered... and stopped dumbfounded! Liza... or no: Akulina, his sweet, dark-complexioned Akulina, not in a *sarafan* but in a white morning frock, sat by the window reading his letter; she was so engrossed in it that she had not even heard him enter. Aleksei could not hold back a joyous shout. Liza started, raised her head, cried out, and wanted to run away. He rushed to hold her back.

"Akulina! Akulina!"

Liza tried to tear herself away from him...

"Mais laissez-moi donc, monsieur; mais êtes-vous fou?"⁶¹ she repeated, turning away from him.

"Akulina! My dearest Akulina!" he kept exclaiming, kissing her hands.

Miss Jackson, who was a witness to this scene, did not know what to think. At this moment the door opened and in came Grigorii Ivanovich.

"Oho!" said he. "I see you've already settled matters between yourselves."

My readers will no doubt excuse me from the unnecessary chore of relating the denouement.

A History of the Village of Goriukhino
(1830)[1]

If God sends me readers they may wish to learn how I came to write
this *History of the Village of Goriukhino*. For this purpose I must recount some preliminary details.

I was born of honest and noble parents in the village of Goriukhino
on April 1, 1801, and received my elementary education from our sexton. It is to this estimable man that I owe both my love of reading and
the general interest in literary pursuits that I later developed. Although my progress was slow, it was not without promise, for by the
age of ten I had already acquired almost all the knowledge that I was
going to retain, to this day, in memory—a memory that was weak by
constitution, and that my parents did not allow me to overburden
with knowledge in view of my equally weak physical health.

The calling of a man of letters has always seemed most enviable to
me. My parents, honorable but simple people raised in the old way,
never read anything, and the only books in the whole house were a
primer they had bought for me, some calendars, and the *Latest Handbook of Composition*. Reading the latter was my favorite pursuit for a
long time. I knew it by heart, yet I could find new, previously unnoticed beauties in it every day. Its author, Kurganov, seemed to me
one of the greatest men on earth, second only to General Plemianni-
kov, under whom my father had at one time served as an adjutant. I
asked everybody for information about him, but nobody could satisfy
my curiosity, nobody knew him personally, and nobody told me anything about him except that he had authored the *Latest Handbook of
Composition*, which I already knew very well.[2] A mist of obscurity
surrounded him as if he were an ancient demiurge; at times I even
doubted his very existence. His name seemed to me to have been invented, and the legend about him appeared to be a mere myth, awaiting the investigations of a new Niebuhr.[3] But since he ceaselessly
haunted my imagination, I tried to attach some image to his myste-

rious personality, and finally decided that he must have looked like the assessor of the district court, Koriuchkin—a small old man with a red nose and flashing eyes.

I was taken to Moscow and enrolled in Karl Ivanovich Meyer's boarding school in 1812, but ended up spending no more than three months there because we were dismissed when the enemy approached.[4] I returned to the country. After the armies of a dozen nations had been expelled, there was talk of taking me back to Moscow to see if Karl Ivanovich had by some chance re-established himself on the ashes of his former school, or, in case he had not, to enroll me in a different institution; but I persuaded my dear mother to let me stay in the country, because my state of health did not allow me to get up at seven in the morning, the usual time of rising in boarding schools. Thus I reached my sixteenth birthday without advancing beyond an elementary education and spending my time playing tag ball with playmates from the village—the only science in which I had acquired ample knowledge during my sojourn at the boarding school.

At that age I enrolled as a cadet in the X. Infantry Regiment, in which I remained until last year, 18—. Serving in that regiment left few pleasurable impressions on my memory other than my promotion to the rank of officer and a win of 245 rubles at cards just at a time when I had a mere ruble-sixty left in my pocket. The death of my dear parents forced me to retire and settle on my ancestral estate.

That period of my life is so significant to me that I intend to enter into some detail about it, asking in advance for my gentle reader's indulgence in case he should think I am abusing his patient attention.

It was an overcast autumnal day. Having come to the station at which I had to turn off the main highway for Goriukhino, I hired private horses and set out along a country lane. Although I am generally of a calm disposition, this time I was seized by such an uncontrollable desire to see again the places where I had spent my best years that I kept urging my driver forward, now promising him a tip, now threatening to beat him. Since it was more expedient for me to poke him in the back than to pull out and untie my purse, I must confess I hit him on some three occasions, which I had never done before, since for some reason I had always had a soft spot for the estate of coach drivers. The man drove his team forth, yet to me it seemed that despite his goading the horses and waving the whip at them, he was actually reining them in—as coachdrivers were wont to do. At last I caught sight of the Goriukhino wood, and in another ten minutes we drove into the courtyard of the manor house. My heart pounded; I looked around with indescribable emotion. I had not seen Goriukhino for eight years. The little birches that had been planted along the fence when I was still living there had grown into tall trees with branches spread wide. The yard, which used to be ornamented with three neat flower beds, a broad sanded path running among them, had by now turned into an unmowed pasture, on which a dun-brown cow was grazing.[5] My carriage stopped by the front porch. My servant tried to open the door, but it was boarded up, even though the shutters were open and the house seemed to be inhabited. A woman came out of the servants' quarters and asked me whom I wanted to see. On learning that her master had arrived, she ran back into the servants' quarters, and soon I was surrounded by domestics. Seeing all these faces—some familiar, some new to me—and exchanging friendly kisses with them all touched me to the core of my heart. My former playmates were now grown muzhiks, and the little girls who used to sit around on the floor waiting to be sent on errands were now married women. The men wept. To the women I would say without ceremony, "How you've aged," to which they would reply with emotion, "And how you've lost your looks, Your Honor." They led me around to the back porch, where my old nurse met me—much enduring Odysseus—with cries and sobs. They ran to light the stove in the bathhouse. The cook, who had grown a beard in his idleness,[6] offered to prepare my dinner, or supper to be exact, since it was already getting dark. Soon the living apartments, in which my nurse had been staying with my late mother's maidservants, were cleaned up; I found myself in my humble ancestral abode and went to sleep in the same room in which I had been born twenty-three years before.

Some three weeks passed in toil and trouble: I had to fuss with assessors, marshals of the nobility, and all manner of provincial civil servants. At last I received my inheritance and was installed as proprietor of my ancestral estate; I felt reassured, but the boredom of inactivity soon began to torment me. At that time I was not yet acquainted with my good-hearted and honorable neighbor N.[7] Managing an estate was an occupation entirely alien to me. The conversation of my nurse, whom I had promoted to housekeeper and estate manager, consisted, in total, of fifteen domestic anecdotes, which held great interest for me but were told by her always in exactly the same manner, so much so that she soon became in my eyes just like the *Latest Handbook of Composition*, in which I knew what line I would find on which page. As for the actual time-honored *Handbook*, I found it in the store room, among other rubbish, in a pitiful condition. I brought it out into the daylight and set to reading it; but Kurganov had lost his previous charm for me; I read through it once more and never opened it again.

In this extremity the question occurred to me whether I myself should try to write something. My gentle reader already knows that I had been educated on a shoestring budget and subsequently had no opportunity to acquire by myself what had been omitted, for until age sixteen I had played around with the village boys and afterwards marched from one province to another, moving from lodging to lodging, spending my time with Jews and sutlers, playing on dilapidated billiard tables, and trudging in the mud.

Moreover, being an author seemed so very difficult to me, so unattainable for us amateurs, that at first the mere thought of taking up pen frightened me. Could I dare hope ever to join the ranks of writers, when even my fervent wish to meet with just one of them had never been fulfilled? But this reminds me of an incident, which I intend to relate as proof of my ever-burning passion for our native literature.

In 1820, when I was still a cadet, official duty took me to Petersburg. I stayed for a week, and despite the fact that I did not know a single soul there, I had an exceedingly good time, for I stole off to the theater, to the fourth-tier gallery, every day. I learned the names of all the actors and fell passionately in love with Y., who one Sunday played with great art the role of Amalia in the drama *Misanthropy and Repentance*.[8] In the morning, as I returned from General Headquarters, I usually went to a low-ceilinged confectionary shop and read the literary magazines over a cup of hot chocolate. On one occasion I was sitting engrossed in a critical review in *The Steadfast* when someone in a pea-colored coat came up to my table and gently pulled the *Hamburg Gazette* from under my journal.[9] I was so preoccupied that I did not even raise my eyes. The stranger ordered a beefsteak and sat down in front of me. I continued reading, paying no attention to him. Meanwhile he finished his lunch, angrily scolded the boy for poor service, drank half a bottle of wine, and left. Two young people were also having lunch there.

"Do you know who that was?" one of them said to the other. "It was B., the author."[10]

"Author!" I cried out involuntarily; leaving my journal half-read and my cup half-drained, I dashed to pay my check and, not waiting for the change, ran out on the street. I looked in all directions, spotted the pea-colored coat at a distance, and hurried after it, almost running, along Nevskii Avenue. But I had only taken a few steps when I suddenly felt somebody stopping me: turning around, I found myself face to face with an officer of the Guards, who pointed out to me that instead of pushing him off the sidewalk, I should have halted and stood to attention. After this reprimand I grew more cautious; to my misfortune, I met more officers and had to halt every moment, while the author went forward, leaving me farther and farther behind. My soldier's uniform had never been so burdensome to me, and the epaulets of an officer had never seemed more enviable. We were already at Anichkin Bridge when I caught up with the pea-colored coat at last.

"Allow me to ask," I said saluting, "whether you are Mr. B., whose excellent articles I have had the pleasure of reading in the *Votary of Enlightenment*?"[11]

"Umph—no, sir," he answered. "I am not an author but a solicitor. I do, however, know the author Z.; I met him at the Politseiskii Bridge just fifteen minutes ago."

Thus my zeal for Russian literature had cost me thirty kopecks of forfeited change, a reprimand by a superior, almost an arrest—and all of it in vain.

Against my better judgment, the bold idea of becoming a writer kept recurring to me. At last, no longer able to resist my natural inclination, I sewed sheets of paper together into a thick notebook with the firm resolve to fill it with anything whatever. All the genres of poetry (for I had not yet contemplated humble prose) were analyzed and evaluated by me, and I resolutely settled on an epic poem, its subject to be drawn from our national history. It did not take a long time to search for a hero. I chose Riurik[12]—and set to work.

In versification I had acquired some facility while copying the notebooks that had been passed around among us officers, such as "The Dangerous Neighbor," "A Critique on the Moscow Boulevard," "A Critique on the Presnia Ponds," and the like.[13] In spite of this, my poem progressed slowly, and I abandoned it on the third verse. I concluded that the epic was not my genre, and commenced the tragedy of Riurik. The tragedy did not work out. I tried to turn it into a ballad, but that did not seem to suit my talent either. At last inspiration came to me: I began, and successfully completed, an inscription for the portrait of Riurik.

Even though my inscription was not altogether unworthy of note, especially as the first work of a young versifier, I nevertheless felt that I had not been born a poet, and contented myself with this first effort. But through these creative experiments I grew so attached to literary work that I could no longer part with the notebook and the inkwell. I

wanted to descend to prose. At first, not wishing to engage in preliminary study, plot structure, the linking of component parts, and the
like, I proposed to write down separate thoughts, with no connection
or order, just as they presented themselves to me. Unfortunately, no
thoughts came to my head, and all I could devise in two full days was
the following dictum:

> He who does not obey the dictates of reason
> and is accustomed to following the induce-
> ments of passion will often err and subject
> himself to later repentance.

The thought was, of course, correct, but not quite new. Leaving
aside thoughts, I began writing tales, but because of my lack of experience I did not know how to string fictitious events together, and
therefore chose some remarkable anecdotes I had heard in the past
from various people. I tried to embellish the truth by lively narration
and sometimes even by the flowering of my own imagination. Composing these tales, I gradually formed my style, until I had learned to
express myself correctly, pleasantly, and fluently. My stock was soon
exhausted, however, and once more I began to seek a subject for my
pen.

The idea of relinquishing trivial and dubious anecdotes in favor of
relating true and great events had long been stirring my imagination.
To be the judge, observer, and prophet of centuries and peoples seemed
to me the highest achievement attainable to a writer. But given my
pitiable education, what kind of history could I write that would not
already have been surpassed by learned and conscientious men of science? Which branch of history had not already been explored by
them? Suppose I were to start writing a universal history; but does
not the immortal work of the Abbé Millot already exist? [14] Suppose I
turned to the history of my own fatherland; but what could I add
to Tatishchev, Boltin, and Golikov? [15] And was it for me to delve
into chronicles, trying to divine the arcane meaning of an ancient
tongue, when I was not even able to master the Old Slavic numerals? I
thought of a history of a lesser scope, such as that of the capital of our
guberniia; but how many unsurmountable obstacles would I meet
even in that undertaking! A trip to the city, visits to the governor and
to the archbishop, applying for admission to the archives and to the
repositories of monasteries, etc. A history of our county seat would
have been more manageable for me, but it could have had no interest
either for the philosopher or for the pragmatist; nor could it have

provided food for eloquence: Y. was not chartered as a town until 17—, and the only significant event recorded in its annals was a terrible conflagration that destroyed its marketplace and courthouse ten years ago.

An unexpected occurrence settled the issue for me. A serving woman, as she was hanging up linen in the attic, found an old basket full of wood shavings, trash, and books. Everybody in the house knew about my fondness for reading. Just as I sat chewing my pen over my notebook, attempting to compose a sermon to my villagers, my housekeeper triumphantly dragged the basket into my room and shouted with joy: "Books! books!" "Books!" I repeated in raptures and threw myself on the basket. Indeed I beheld a whole heap of books in green and blue paper covers. It was a collection of old calendars. This latter discovery cooled my enthusiasm somewhat, but I was still pleased with the unexpected find, since these were after all books of sorts. The washerwoman was generously rewarded for her zeal with a silver half-ruble piece. Once left alone, I set to examining my calendars, and soon my interest was greatly aroused. They comprised an unbroken chain of years from 1744 to 1799, that is, a total of fifty-five. The sheets of blue paper—the kind usually bound into calendars—were all covered with writing in an old-fashioned hand. Glancing at these lines, I discovered with astonishment that they contained not only observations about the weather and financial accounts, but also brief items of historical information about the village of Goriukhino. I set to deciphering these precious notations without delay and soon ascertained that they represented a full history of my ancestral estate for almost a whole century, given in the strictest chronological order. In addition, they contained an inexhaustible store of economical, statistical, meteorological, and other scholarly observations. From that time on, I devoted myself exclusively to the study of these notations, for I detected the possibility of extracting from them a well-proportioned, interesting, and instructive narrative. Having sufficiently acquainted myself with these precious memorabilia, I set about searching for new sources for this history of the village of Goriukhino. And soon the abundance of such materials astounded me. Having devoted a full six months to a preliminary study, at last I set to work on my long-desired opus and with God's help completed it on this third day of November, 1827.

And now, having finished my difficult task, I shall put my pen down and—like a certain historian similar to me whose name I forget[16]—sadly proceed to my garden in order to contemplate what I have accomplished. To me, too, it seems that having written the *His-*

tory of Goriukhino I am no longer necessary to the world, my duty has been done, and it is time for me to betake myself to my final rest!

Herewith I attach a list of the sources I have used in compiling the *History of Goriukhino*:

1. A collection of old calendars, in fifty-four issues. The first twenty issues bear writing in an old-fashioned hand, with Old Church Slavic abbreviations.[17] This chronicle was composed by my great-grandfather Andrei Stepanovich Belkin. It is distinguished by its clarity and laconic style. For example:

> May 4. Snow. Trishka thrashed for rudeness.
> 6. The dun cow has died. Senka thrashed for drunkenness.
> 8. Clear skies.
> 9. Rain and snow. Trishka thrashed on account of the weather.[18]
> 11. Clear skies. Fresh snow on the ground. Killed three rabbits.

And some more in this vein, with no reflection on the events... The remaining thirty-five issues, bearing different kinds of handwriting, mostly the so-called tradesman's script with or without Old Church Slavic abbreviations,[19] tend to be wordy, disconnected, and full of misspellings. A woman's hand is noticeable here and there. With this group belong notes written by my grandfather, Ivan Andreevich Belkin, and by my grandmother, that is, his wife, Evpraksia Alekseevna, as well as by the steward Garbovitskii.

2. A chronicle written by the Goriukhino sexton. I unearthed this fascinating manuscript at the house of my priest, who is married to the chronicler's daughter. Its first pages had been torn out and used by the priest's children for so-called kites. One of these kites fell down in the middle of my yard. I picked it up and was about to return it to the children when I noticed that it had been written all over. I could see from the first lines that the kite had been made of a chronicle; fortunately, I was able to save the remainder. This chronicle, which I subsequently obtained for a quarter-measure of oats, is distinguished by its profundity of thought and extraordinary magniloquence.

3. Oral traditions. I did not scorn any kind of information. But I am especially indebted to Agrafena Trifonova, mother of the elder Avdei, who was rumored to have been the mistress of the steward Garbovitskii at one time.

4. Census registers (and accounting and housekeeping books), with notes by former village elders on the mores and living conditions of the peasants.

The country that is named Goriukhino after its capital occupies more than two hundred and forty *desiatinas* on the terrestrial globe.[20] The number of male serfs living in it reaches sixty-three.[21] To the north it borders on the territory of the villages of Deriukhovo and Perkukhovo, whose inhabitants are poor, thin, and small of stature, and whose proud owners are devoted to the martial exercise of rabbit hunting.[22] On the south side, the Sivka River separates it from the lands of the Karachevo freeholders—restless neighbors who are famous for the savage cruelty of their ways. On the western side, it is embraced by the flourishing fields of Zakharino, which prosper under the rule of wise and enlightened landowners. On the east, it adjoins a wild uninhabited region, an impassable swamp, where only cranberries grow and frogs monotonously croak, and where, according to superstitious tradition, a certain demon is supposed to dwell.

N.B. This swamp is in fact called Demon's Swamp. They say that a half-witted girl used to tend a herd of swine not far from this forlorn region. She became pregnant and could give no satisfactory explanation for this occurrence. By popular belief, the demon of the swamp was to blame; but this tale is not worthy of the attention of a historian, and after Niebuhr it would be inexcusable to give it any credit.

From ancient times Goriukhino has been renowned for the fecundity of its land and for its healthful climate. Rye, oats, barley, and buckwheat grow on its fertile fields. A birch wood and a fir forest supply its inhabitants with timber and firewood for the construction and heating of their dwellings. There is no shortage of nuts, cranberries, cowberries, and bilberries. Mushrooms grow in unusual quantities; broiled with sour cream they make a tasty, albeit unhealthy, dish. The pond is full of carp, and the Sivka River teams with pike and burbot.

The male inhabitants of Goriukhino are mostly of medium height, strongly built and virile, with gray eyes and either blond or red hair. The distinguishing features of the women are somewhat turned-up noses, prominent cheekbones, and corpulence. *N.B.* The expression strapping wench often occurs in the village elder's notes to the census registers.[23] The men are well-behaved, industrious (especially in their own fields), brave, and combative: many of them will set on a bear singlehanded and many are famous throughout the district as fist-fighters. They are, by and large, all inclined to the sensual delights of drunkenness. The women, in addition to their household duties, take a share in most of the men's work; they do not lag behind the men in courage; you will rarely find one afraid of the village elder. Nicknamed battle-axes (a combination of the words battle and ax),[24] they constitute a mighty civil guard that untiringly watches over the courtyard of the manor. The battle-axes' chief duty is to beat an iron plate with a stone as often as possible, in order to ward off evil-doing. They are as chaste as they are beautiful; they have a stern and expressive response to the advances of the daring.

The inhabitants of Goriukhino have since ancient times carried on an abundant trade in phloem fiber, baskets, and bast shoes. This is facilitated by the Sivka River, which they cross in boats in the spring, like the ancient Scandinavians, and ford in other seasons of the year, with their trousers rolled up to their knees.

The Goriukhino language has definitely branched out of common Slavic, but is as far from it as Russian. It abounds in abbreviations and ellipses; some letters have been either entirely eliminated from it or replaced by others. A Great Russian can, however, easily understand a Goriukhinian, and vice versa.

The men used to marry twenty-year-old women at age fourteen.[25] The wives beat their husbands for four or five years, after which it was the husbands who beat the wives; thus each sex had its period of domination, and a certain balance was achieved.

Funeral rites took place in the following fashion. The deceased was carried off to the cemetery on the very day of his death so that he would not unnecessarily occupy space in the cottage. For this reason it has happened that the deceased would sneeze or yawn, to his relatives' indescribable joy, just as he was being carried in his coffin past the edge of the village. Wives would bemoan the death of their husbands by wailing and chanting: "My precious brave one, why didst thou leave me? To whom hast thou forsaken me? How shall I mourn thee?" After the mourners returned from the cemetery, a funeral feast would begin, and the dead man's relatives and friends would be drunk for two or three days, or even for a whole week, depending on their zeal and on how much they cherished the dead man's memory. These ancient rites have been preserved to this day.

The Goriukhinian men's attire consisted of a shirt worn over the trousers, a distinctive feature that revealed their Slavic origin. In the winter they wore sheepskin coats, but more for adornment than out of real need, since they would fling the coat over one shoulder only and would throw it off altogether for the slightest job that required physical exertion.

The sciences, arts, and poetry have from ancient times found themselves in quite a flourishing state in Goriukhino. In addition to the priest and church readers, it has always counted some literate people among its population. The chronicles mention a certain village notary called Terentii, who lived around 1767 and could write not only with his right hand but also with his left. This unusual person acquired fame in the district by fashioning letters of all kinds, petitions, homemade passports, and the like. Having more than once suffered for his art, for his readiness to oblige, and for his participation in various remarkable incidents, he died in ripe old age, just when he was learning to write with his right foot in consideration of the fact that the writing produced by both of his hands had become too well known. He plays, as the reader will see below, an important part in the history of Goriukhino.

Music has always been a favorite art among the educated in Goriukhino: even today the balalaika and the bagpipe resound, delighting sensitive hearts, throughout the village, especially in the ancient public building adorned with a fir tree and with the image of a double-headed eagle.[26]

At one time poetry, too, flourished in ancient Goriukhino. The poems of Arkhip the Bald have been preserved in the memory of posterity to this day.

In tenderness of feeling they do not yield to the Eclogues of the well-known Virgil; in beauty of imagery they are far superior to the idylls of Mr. Sumarokov.[27] And though they fall behind the latest productions of our muses in stylistic affectation, they equal them in inventiveness and wit.

Let us quote the following satirical poem as an example:

> Anton, village elder,
> To the manor goes,
> And a bunch of tallies
> To the master shows.
> Master takes a look at them,
> Can't make head or tail of them.
> Anton doesn't mind,
> Steals the gentry blind,
> Squanders all the manor grows,
> Buys his woman fancy clothes.

Having thus acquainted my reader with the ethnographical and statistical state of affairs in Goriukhino and with the mores and customs of its inhabitants, I will now begin the narrative proper.

FABULOUS TIMES

The Village Elder Trifon

The form of government in Goriukhino has changed several times. It has in turns been under the rule of elders chosen by the village commune, under that of stewards appointed by the landowner, and finally under the immediate power of the landowners themselves. The advantages and disadvantages of these different forms of government will be expatiated on in the course of our narrative.

The founding of Goriukhino and its original settlement are shrouded in a mist of uncertainty. Legends from the dim past claim that at one time Goriukhino was a large prosperous village, that all its inhabitants were wealthy, and that the quitrent was collected once a year and sent off to some unknown person in a few carts. At that time everything was bought cheaply and sold at high prices. Stewards did not exist, the elders did not mistreat anybody, the inhabitants worked little yet lived in clover, and even shepherds wore boots while tending their herds. We must not be deluded by this enchanting picture. The idea of a golden age is inherent in the tradition of every people, which proves nothing except that people are never satisfied with the present, and since their experience gives them little hope for the future, they adorn the irrevocable past with all the flowers of their imagination. What can be ascertained is as follows.

The village of Goriukhino has belonged to the illustrious family of Belkin since ancient times. But my ancestors, possessing many other estates, did not pay attention to this remote land. Goriukhino was lightly taxed, and governed by elders elected by the people at meetings called village assemblies.

With the passage of time, however, the Belkins' ancestral possessions became fragmented and fell into decline. The impoverished grandsons of a rich grandfather were unable to give up their habits of luxury, and they demanded the former full income from an estate that had shrunk to one-tenth of its original size. Threatening commands followed one after the other. The elder read them to the assembly; the aldermen waxed eloquent, and the commune grew agitated; yet the landlords, instead of a double amount of quitrent, received only sly excuses and humble complaints written on wax-spattered paper and sealed with a half-kopeck piece.

A dark cloud hung over Goriukhino, but nobody gave it a thought. In the last year of the reign of Trifon—the last elder elected by the people—on the very day of the village's patron saint, when the whole populace either noisily crowded around the recreational building (called pothouse in the vernacular) or roamed the streets arm in arm loudly singing the songs of Arkhip the Bald, a wicker-covered carriage, drawn by a pair of nags just barely alive, drove into the village; a Jew in tatters sat on the box; a head in a visored cap appeared from inside and looked at the festive crowd with, it seemed, some interest. The citizens met the carriage with laughter and rude jokes. (*N.B.* The imbeciles teased the Jewish driver by rolling up the hems of their garments into tubes and exclaiming gleefully, "Yid, Yid, eat a pig's ear!" —from *The Chronicle of the Goriukhino Sexton.*) But how great was their surprise when the carriage stopped in the middle of the village, and the newcomer, jumping out, demanded in a stentorian voice to see the elder Trifon! That dignitary was at the time in the recreational building, whence two aldermen escorted him out respectfully, supporting him by the arm. The stranger looked at him menacingly, handed him a letter, and commanded him to read it without delay. The Goriukhino elders had the habit of never reading anything themselves. Indeed the elder was illiterate. They sent for the notary Avdei. He was discovered not too far away, asleep under a fence in a side street, and was brought into the stranger's presence. But on his arrival, he thought—either from sudden fright or from a woeful presentiment—that the characters in the letter, though clearly traced, were somehow blurred, and was unable to decipher them. With horrendous curses the stranger sent both the elder Trifon and the notary Avdei off to sleep, postponed the reading of the letter till the next day, and went to the estate office, where the Jew carried his small suitcase after him.

The Goriukhinians watched these unusual proceedings in silent wonderment, but soon the carriage, the Jew, and the stranger were all forgotten. The day ended with much noise and merriment, and Goriukhino fell asleep not suspecting what was awaiting it.

When the sun rose, the inhabitants were awakened by a knock on their windows and a summons to a village assembly. The citizens came one after the other to the courtyard of the estate office, which served as a communal meeting place.[28] Their eyes were bleary and red, their cheeks puffy; yawning and scratching themselves, they looked at the man in the visored cap and worn blue caftan who stood on the porch of the estate office with an air of importance, and tried to recall if they had seen his features before. The elder Trifon and the notary Avdei stood by him with their hats off, and with a look of servility and deep sorrow.

"Is everybody here?" asked the stranger.

"Everybody here?" repeated the elder.

"We are," answered the citizens.

Then the elder announced that a letter had been received from the landlord, and he ordered the notary to read it aloud to the commune. Avdei stepped forward and read in a thunderous voice what follows below. (*N.B.* "I copied this document of ill omen at the house of the elder Trifon where it was being kept in the icon-case together with other memorabilia of his reign over Goriukhino"—from *The Chronicle of the Goriukhino Sexton*. I myself have been unable to unearth the original of this curious letter.)

Trifon Ivanov,

The bearer of this letter, my representative P., is being sent to my ancestral estate, the village of Goriukhino, in order to take over its management. Immediately after his arrival all the peasants are to be called together and their master's will is to be announced to them, namely: that they, the peasants, are to obey the commands of my representative P. like my very own. And they are to carry out unquestioningly everything he demands, or else he is to treat them with all necessary severity. I have been forced to take this step by their unconscionable disobedience and by your, Trifon Ivanov's, knavish connivance with them.

Signed NN

After the reading of this, P., spreading his legs like the letter X and placing his arms akimbo to form the letter ф, uttered the following brief but expressive speech:

"Look you here: don't try any of your smart tricks on me; I know you're a spoiled lot, but I'll beat the nonsense out of your heads I dare say faster than last night's drunkenness."

There was no drunkenness left in a single head. As if thunderstruck, the Goriukhinians hung their heads low and dispersed in horror.

The Rule of the Steward P.

P. took up the reins of government and set about putting into practice his political theory—a theory that deserves special analysis.

Its chief foundation was the following axiom: the richer the peasant, the more recalcitrant, and, conversely, the poorer the humbler.

Consequently, P. encouraged humility in the community as the cardinal peasant virtue. He demanded an inventory of the peasant households and divided them into the rich and the poor. 1. Arrears of rent from the village were apportioned among the rich peasants and exacted from them with utmost severity. 2. Paupers and idlers were immediately put behind plows, and if according to his reckoning their work did not prove satisfactory, he hired them out as farmhands to other peasants, for which the latter paid him voluntary tribute. Those given over into bondage had every right to ransom themselves by paying twice the amount of their annual rent in addition to their arrears. All communal obligations fell on the shoulders of the rich peasants. The recruitment of soldiers was a veritable triumph for the greedy steward, for all the well-to-do peasants, one after the other, bought themselves off, until at the last the choice fell on some rascal or poor devil.* The meetings of the village assembly were abolished. The steward collected the quitrent little by little, all the year around. In addition, he introduced supplemental collections. The peasants, it seems, were not paying all that much more than they had before, but they could never earn or save sufficient money. Within three years Goriukhino was completely impoverished.

The village lost its liveliness, the marketplace grew deserted, the songs of Arkhip the Bald could no longer be heard. The lads and lasses went a-begging. Half of the peasants worked on the landlord's fields, the other half served as farmhands; and the day of the village's patron saint became, as the chronicler says, not a day of joy and jubilation, but an anniversary of sorrow and a commemoration of mournful events.[29]

* "The accursed steward put Anton Timofeev in fetters until old Timofei ransomed his son for 100 rubles; then the steward clapped Petrushka Eremeev in irons until he was bought off by his father for 68 rubles; next the accursed one wanted to shackle Lekha Tarasov, but the latter ran away into the forests, which distressed the steward so utterly that he ranted and raved; the person who was finally taken to the city and inducted into the army was Vanka the drunkard."—From a complaint lodged by the Goriukhino peasants.

Roslavlev
(1831)[1]

As I was reading *Roslavlev*[2] I realized with astonishment that its plot is based on a real-life incident all too well known to me. At one time I was a close friend of the unfortunate woman whom Mr. Zagoskin has made the heroine of his novel. He has drawn anew the attention of the public to a forgotten event, reawakening feelings of indignation that time had lulled, and disturbing the tranquility of a grave. I will undertake to defend her shade, and trust that the reader, bearing in mind the sincerity of my motives, will excuse the feebleness of my pen. I shall be compelled to speak quite a lot about myself, because my poor friend's fate was closely linked with mine for a prolonged period.

I was brought out in the winter season of 1811. I shall not go into the details of my first impressions. It is easy to imagine the feelings of a girl of sixteen who has just exchanged her schoolroom and teachers for an uninterrupted series of balls. Not yet a thinking person, I threw myself into the whirl of gaiety with all the liveliness of my years... This was a pity, because those times were worth observing.

Among the debutantes who were brought out with me that season, Princess N. was particularly notable. (Since Mr. Zagoskin gave her the name Polina, I will call her the same.) She and I soon became friends as a result of the following circumstances.

My brother, a fine fellow of twenty-two at the time, belonged to the order of coxcombs; he was listed as an employee at the Ministry of Foreign Affairs but lived in Moscow, dancing and sowing his wild oats. He fell in love with Polina, and asked me to effect a closer friendship between her family and ours. My brother was the idol of our whole family, and he could make me do whatever he liked.

Having formed closer ties to Polina as a favor to my brother, I soon grew genuinely attached to her. There was much in her that seemed strange, but even more that was appealing. I was not yet able to understand her, but I already loved her. Unconsciously, I began to look at the world with her eyes and her thoughts.

Polina's father was a man who had rendered the state considerable service—in other words, he rode around in a tandem and was decorated with a key and a star[3]—though actually he was a frivolous and simple-minded fellow. Her mother, by contrast, was a sensible woman, distinguished by dignity and good judgment.

Polina was present at all the social functions; she was surrounded by admirers; everybody paid court to her. But she was bored, and boredom lent her an air of haughtiness and coldness. This suited extremely well her Grecian profile and dark eyebrows. I felt triumphant whenever my satirical observations brought a smile to those regular features frozen by boredom.

Polina read exceptionally large numbers of books, without at all discriminating. She kept the key to her father's library, which consisted of works by eighteenth-century authors. She was well-versed in French literature from Montesquieu to the novels of Crébillon.[4] She knew Rousseau by heart.[5] The library contained no Russian books, except the works of Sumarokov, which Polina never opened.[6] She told me she could hardly make out the Russian script; she evidently never read anything in Russian, not even the doggerel presented to her by Moscow versifiers.

Here I will allow myself a brief digression. It has been, by God's mercy, some thirty years since they started scolding us poor Russian women for not reading in Russian and allegedly not being able to express ourselves in our native tongue. (*N.B.*: It is unjust on the part of the author of *Iurii Miloslavskii* to repeat these banal accusations.[7] We have all read his novel, and if I am not mistaken, he is indebted to one of us for its French translation.[8]) The truth is that we would be glad to read in Russian, but our literature, as far as I know, goes back only as far as Lomonosov and has until now been extremely limited in scope.[9] It has, of course, presented us with some excellent poets, but you cannot expect all readers to have an exclusive taste for poetry. In prose, all we have is Karamzin's *History*.[10] It is true that the last two or three years have seen the appearance of the first two or three Russian novels;[11] but look at France, England, and Germany, where one remarkable book comes out after the other. We do not even see translations; and if we do, well, say what you like, I still prefer the originals. Our journals are of interest only to our men of letters. We are forced to derive everything—both information and concepts—from foreign books, and therefore we also think in a foreign language (those of us, that is, who do think and keep up with the ideas of humankind). Our

best-known literati have admitted this much to me. Our writers' perpetual lamentations about our negligence of Russian books are like
the complaints of the Russian tradeswomen who resent that we buy
our hats at Sichler's instead of being content with the creations of the
milliners of Kostroma.[12] But let us return to our subject.

Recollections of society life, even of a historical epoch, are usually
vague and insignificant. But the arrival of one lady visitor in Moscow
did leave a deep impression on my mind. This visitor was Madame de
Staël.[13] She arrived in the summer, when the majority of Moscow's
inhabitants had already left for the country. Yet a great bustle of Russian hospitality arose; people went all out to entertain the famous foreigner. It goes without saying that there were dinner parties in her
honor. Ladies and gentlemen gathered to gape at her, but most went
away dissatisfied with her. All they saw in her was a fat woman of
fifty, whose dress was inappropriate for her years. Her manners did
not please; people found her speeches too long and her sleeves too
short. Polina's father, who had met Madame de Staël in Paris, gave a
dinner for her, convoking all our Moscow wits. It was at this dinner
party that I met the author of *Corinne*. She sat in the place of honor,
resting her elbows on the table, furling and unfurling a piece of paper
between her lovely fingers. She seemed to be in low spirits; made several attempts at conversation, but could not warm to her theme. Our
wits ate and drank their measure, appearing more satisfied with the
Prince's fish soup than with Madame de Staël's conversation. The
ladies looked all starched. Convinced of the insignificance of their
thoughts and overawed by the presence of a European celebrity, the
guests in general spoke very little. Polina was on tenterhooks all
through the dinner. The attention of the guests was divided between
the sturgeon and Madame de Staël. All the while they were waiting
for her to toss out a *bon mot*; at last a double entendre, and rather a
daring one at that, escaped her lips. Everyone snatched it up, bursting out in laughter; a general murmur of amazement went round the
table; the Prince was beside himself with rapture. I glanced at Polina.
Her face was aflame, and tears appeared in her eyes. The guests rose
from the table entirely reconciled to Madame de Staël: she had made
a pun that they could carry all over town at a gallop.

"What's the matter with you, *ma chère*?" I asked Polina. "Could
that joke, admittedly a rather bold one, have embarrassed you to such
a degree?"

"Oh, my dear," answered Polina, "I am in despair! How insignificant our high society must have seemed to this unusual woman! She
is used to being surrounded by people who understand her, on whom

a brilliant remark, a powerful sentiment, an inspired word, are never lost; she is used to fascinating conversations in the most highly cultured circles. But here—my God! Not one thought, not one memorable word in the course of three hours! Dull faces, dull pomposity, and nothing else! How bored she was! How weary she seemed! She realized what they needed, what these apes of civilization were capable of understanding, and she tossed them a pun. How they threw themselves on it! I burned with shame and was ready to burst into tears... But let her," continued Polina heatedly, "let her go away thinking of our aristocratic rabble what it deserves. At least she has seen our good-natured simple people and understands them. You heard what she said to that insufferable old buffoon who, trying to play up to a foreigner, started cracking jokes at the expense of Russian beards: 'People who were able to defend their beards a hundred years ago, will be able to defend their heads today.'[14] How charming she is! How I love her! How I hate her persecutor!"[15]

I was not the only one to notice Polina's embarrassment. Another pair of penetrating eyes rested on her at that same moment: the dark eyes of Madame de Staël. I do not know what she thought was the matter, but after dinner she came over to my friend and engaged her in a long conversation. A few days later she sent her the following note:

> Ma chère enfant, je suis toute malade. Il serait bien aimable à vous de venir me ranimer. Tâchez de l'obtenir de m-me votre mère et veuillez lui présenter les respects de votre amie
>
> *de S.*[16]

This note has survived in my safekeeping. Despite all my curiosity, Polina never told me what further contact she had with Madame de Staël; but she certainly adored this distinguished woman, who was as kindhearted as she was gifted.

How people love to slander! Just recently, I recounted all this at a highly respectable social gathering.

"It is quite possible," I was told, "that Madame de Staël was nothing but a spy for Napoleon, and Princess N. was supplying her with information she needed."

"For pity's sake," said I. "Madame de Staël, who had been hunted by Napoleon for ten years; the kind, noble Madame de Staël who had barely managed to escape under the Russian Emperor's protection; Madame de Staël the friend of Chateaubriand and Byron; would Madame de Staël become Napoleon's spy?"

"Quite, quite possible," rejoined the sharp-nosed Countess B. "Napoleon was such a devil, and Madame de Staël such a cunning creature."

At the time Madame de Staël visited Moscow everybody was talking about the impending war and, as far as I remember, talking rather lightheartedly. Aping French manners of the time of Louis XV was in fashion. Love of one's fatherland seemed like pedantry. The savants of the day glorified Napoleon with fanatical obsequiousness and jested over our defeats. Unfortunately, those who championed the fatherland were somewhat simple-minded; they were ridiculed rather amusingly, and had no influence. Their patriotism was limited to violent denunciations of the use of French in society, to a condemnation of foreign loanwords, to fearful sallies against the Kuznetskii Bridge,[17] and the like. Young people spoke about everything Russian either with contempt or with indifference, and jokingly predicted that Russia would become another Confederation of the Rhine.[18] In other words, society was rather repugnant.

Suddenly we were staggered by the news of the invasion, and the Emperor's appeal. Moscow was shaken up. Count Rastopchin's folksy posters appeared;[19] fury gripped the masses. The high-society jesters grew humble; the ladies were frightened. The detractors of the French language and Kuznetskii Bridge were decisively taking the upper hand, and the drawing rooms became filled with patriots: some poured French tobacco out of their snuffboxes and started sniffing a Russian brand; others burned at least ten French brochures; still others renounced Château Lafite and took to drinking sour kvass. All swore to abstain from the French language; all started shouting about Pozharskii and Minin and advocating a people's war,[20] while at the same time getting ready to leave for their estates in the Saratov Guberniia.

Polina could not hide her contempt any more than she had been able to hide her indignation before. Such an expeditious change of tune and such cowardice made her lose patience. She deliberately spoke French on the boulevards and by the Presnia Ponds;[21] and over the dinner table, in the presence of servants, she deliberately disputed vainglorious patriotic claims, deliberately spoke of the large number of Napoleon's troops and of his military genius. Those present blanched, fearing a denunciation, and hastened to censure her for her devotion to the enemy of the fatherland. Polina smiled with contempt. "May God grant," she would say, "that all Russians should love their fatherland as I do." She astonished me. I had always known her to be modest and quiet, and could not understand what made her so audacious.

"For goodness' sake," I said to her once, "why on earth should you meddle in matters that don't concern us? Let men fight and shout about politics; women don't go to war and have nothing to do with Bonaparte."

Her eyes flashed. "Shame on you," she said. "Don't women have native lands according to you? Don't they have fathers, brothers, and husbands? Is Russian blood alien to us? Or do you suppose we were born only to be whirled around in Scottish square dances and to sit at home embroidering little dogs on canvas? No, I know how much influence a woman can have on public opinion, or at least, if you please, on the heart of one man. I do not accept the humble position to which they try to relegate us. Consider Madame de Staël: Napoleon fought against her as he would fight an enemy force. And my uncle has the face to laugh at her when she is frightened of the approach of the French army! 'Be reassured, Madame: Napoleon is fighting against Russia, not against you...' Yes, indeed! If uncle fell into the hands of the French, they would let him walk about the Palais Royal, but if they caught Madame de Staël, she would die in a state prison. And how about Charlotte de Corday? And our Mayoress Marfa? And Princess Dashkova?[22] In just what way am I inferior to them? Surely not in daring of spirit and resoluteness!"

I listened to Polina in amazement. I had never suspected so much ardor and so much ambition in her. But alas! Where did the extraordinary qualities of her soul and the masculine loftiness of her mind lead her? My favorite writer was correct to say: "Il n'est de bonheur que dans les voies communes."*

The arrival of the Emperor increased the general agitation. At last patriotic fervor took possession of the best society, too. Drawing rooms turned into chambers of debate.[23] Everywhere there was talk about patriotic contributions to the war effort. Young Count Mamonov's immortal speech, pledging the whole of his fortune, was being recited.[24] Some mammas remarked afterwards that the Count was no longer such an enviably eligible young man, but we all idolized him. Polina raved about him.

"What are you pledging?" she once asked my brother.

"I have not yet come into possession of my estate," answered my rakish brother. "All I have is a debt of thirty thousand rubles; I will offer it as a sacrifice on the altar of the fatherland."

---

*These appear to be the words of Chateaubriand.—The Publisher. [The footnote is Pushkin's. The quote is from the very end of Chateaubriand's *René* (1802). The exact words, however, are "Il n'y a de bonheur que dans les voies communes" ("Happiness can only be found along the trodden path")—Trans.]

Polina lost her temper. "To some people," she said, "honor and fatherland are mere trifles. While their brothers are dying on the battlefields, they play the fool in drawing rooms. I wonder if any woman would sink so low as to allow such a buffoon to pretend to be in love with her."

My brother colored. "You expect too much, Princess," he rejoined. "You demand that everyone see a Madame de Staël in you and declaim to you tirades from *Corinne.* You should realize that a man, just because he jokes with a woman, may not be inclined to jest when it comes to his fatherland or its enemies."

With these words he turned away. I thought they had quarreled forever, but I was wrong: my brother's insolence appealed to Polina. His noble outburst of indignation made her forgive him for his clumsy joke; and when she heard a week later that he had joined Mamonov's regiment, she herself asked me to bring about a reconciliation between them. My brother was in raptures. He asked for her hand immediately. She gave her consent, but postponed the wedding until after the war. The next day my brother set off for his regiment.

Napoleon was marching on Moscow; our troops were retreating; the city grew alarmed. Its citizens fled one after another. The Prince and Princess persuaded my mother to accompany them to their estate in X. Guberniia.

We arrived at Y., an enormous agricultural town twenty versts from the capital of the *guberniia*. We had lots of neighbors all around, mostly recent arrivals from Moscow. There were daily social gatherings: our life in the provincial town resembled city life. Letters from the front came almost every day; old ladies searched for a place called *bivouac* on the map and were angry when they could not find it. Polina devoted herself exclusively to politics, reading nothing but newspapers and Rastopchin's posters, and not opening one single book. Surrounded by people whose understanding was limited, and perpetually hearing preposterous conclusions and unfounded reports, she fell into a deep depression; a weariness took possession of her spirit. She despaired of the deliverance of her fatherland; it seemed to her that Russia was fast approaching final collapse; every report received deepened her despondence; and Count Rastopchin's police bulletins drove her out of her mind. Their jocular tone struck her as the height of indecency, and the measures he took, as intolerable barbarity. She could not comprehend the idea underlying that historic epoch, so great in its horror—the idea whose bold execution was to save Russia and liberate Europe.[25] She spent hours on end with her elbow on the map of Russia, counting versts and tracing the rapid movements of troops. Strange notions would sometimes enter her mind. Once she informed me of her intention to abscond from town, present herself in the midst of the French army, find a means to get close to Napoleon, and kill him with her own hands. It was not difficult to convince her of the madness of such an undertaking. But the thought of Charlotte de Corday haunted her mind for a long time.

Her father, as you already know, was a rather frivolous man, whose only concern in the country was to come as close to a Moscow way of life as possible. He gave dinners, set up a *théâtre de société* that staged representations of French *proverbes*, and employed every other means to vary our entertainments. Some captive officers arrived in town. The Prince, glad to see new faces, persuaded the governor to quarter them in his house.

There were four of these prisoners of war—three of them rather insignificant people, fanatic champions of Napoleon and insufferable braggarts, who had, it must be admitted, paid for their boastfulness by honorable wounds. The fourth one was an exceptional, remarkable man.

He was twenty-six years old at the time. He came from a good family. He had a pleasant face and excellent manners. We singled him out at once. He received our kindness with dignified modesty. He spoke little, but his remarks were always sound. He found favor with Polina as the first person able to give her clear explanations of military maneuvers and troop movements. He set her mind at ease, assuring her that the retreat of the Russian army was not a senseless flight, and that it worried the French as much as it embittered the Russians.

"And what about you?" Polina asked him. "Aren't you confident of your Emperor's invincibility?"

Sénicour (I will call him by the name given by Mr. Zagoskin)[26] thought for a while, then answered that in his situation it would be awkward for him to be frank. Polina persisted in demanding an answer. Sénicour eventually divulged his opinion that the French army's thrust into the heart of Russia could prove to be a dangerous move, and that the campaign of 1812 appeared to be over, though it had not produced any decisive results.

"Over?" retorted Polina. "Over, when Napoleon is still advancing and we are still retreating?"

"All the worse for us," answered Sénicour, and changed the subject.

Polina, who was tired of both the fearful predictions and the stupid braggadocio of our neighbors, avidly listened to these conclusions, based on knowledge and objectivity. From my brother I received letters that one could not make head or tail of. They were filled with jokes—some clever, others flat—with questions about Polina, with banal protestations of love, and the like. Reading them, Polina grew irritated, and shrugged her shoulders.

"You must admit," she said, "your Aleksei is the most trivial man. Even under the present circumstances, from the very fields of battle, he manages to write letters totally lacking in meaning. What sort of conversation will he have for me in the course of quiet family life?"

She was mistaken. My brother's letters were trivial, not because he himself was empty-headed, but because of a prejudice that, by the way, is most offensive to us: he supposed it incumbent on him, when addressing women, to adapt his language to their feeble understanding, and imagined that serious matters did not concern us. Such an opinion would be boorish anywhere in the world; in our country it is also stupid. There is no doubt that in Russia the women are better educated, read more, and think more than the men, who are preoccupied with heaven knows what.

News of the Battle of Borodino arrived. Everybody talked about it; everybody had his own most reliable information and his own list of the dead and wounded. My brother was not writing. We were extremely worried. At last one of those newsmongers arrived to inform us that he had been taken prisoner; to Polina, however, he whispered the news of his death.[27] Polina was deeply distressed. She was not in love with my brother and had often been annoyed with him, but at that moment she saw him as a martyr and a hero, and wept over him, hiding her grief from me. I caught her with tears in her eyes several times. This did not surprise me, since I knew how keenly she felt the plight of our suffering land. I did not suspect this additional cause of her grief.

One morning I was walking in the garden; Sénicour accompanied me, and we talked about Polina. I noticed how deeply he appreciated her unusual qualities, and what a strong impression her beauty had made on him. I hinted jokingly that his situation was most romantic. Captured by the enemy, the wounded knight falls in love with the castle's noble proprietress, touches her heart, and eventually wins her hand.

"No," said Sénicour, "the Princess sees in me an enemy of Russia, and will never consent to leaving her fatherland."

At that moment Polina appeared at the end of the avenue, and we went to meet her. She approached us with hasty steps. I was struck by her paleness.

"Moscow has been taken," she said to me without acknowledging Sénicour's bow. My heart sank, and tears started streaming from my eyes. Sénicour kept silent, casting his eyes down.

"The noble, enlightened French,"[28] she continued in a voice trembling with indignation, "have celebrated their triumph in a befitting manner. They have set Moscow on fire. Moscow has been burning the last two days."

"What are you saying?" cried Sénicour. "That is impossible."

"Wait until night," she answered dryly, "and you may be able to see the glow."

"My God! He is done for," said Sénicour. "How can you fail to see that the burning of Moscow means the destruction of the whole French army, that Napoleon will have nothing to hold on to, nothing to sustain his troops with, and will be compelled to retreat as fast as he can across a ravaged wasteland with a disorganized and disaffected army under the threat of approaching winter? How could you believe that the French would have dug their own grave? No, no, it was the Russians; the Russians set Moscow on fire! What horrifying, barbarous prodigality! Now it's all decided: your country is out of danger. But what will become of us, what will happen to our Emperor?"

He left us. Polina and I could not recover our senses.

"Could he," she said, "could Sénicour be right? Could the burning of Moscow be the work of our own hands? If that is so... Oh, then I can feel proud to be a Russian woman! The whole world will marvel at such tremendous sacrifice! Now even our ruin cannot daunt me, since our honor has been saved: never again will Europe dare fight against a people who hack their own hands off and set their own capital on fire."

Her eyes flashed and her voice had a metallic ring to it. I embraced her; we blended our tears of noble exaltation and fervent prayers for the fatherland.

"You don't know," said Polina with an inspired look on her face, "but your brother... he is happy, he is not a prisoner of war. Be glad: he has died for the deliverance of Russia."

I cried out and fell into her arms unconscious...

Dubrovskii
(1832–33)[1]

Volume One

I

A few years back, there lived on one of his feudal estates a Russian landowner of the old type, Kirila Petrovich Troekurov. Owing to his wealth, distinguished birth, and connections, he carried great weight in the *guberniias* where his estates lay. His neighbors were ready to cater to his slightest whim; civil officials of those *guberniias* trembled at the mere mention of his name; he himself accepted all gestures of servility as his due. His house was always full of guests, willing to provide diversion for their lordly host's idle days and participating in his noisy, sometimes even riotous, amusements. No one dared to refuse an invitation from him or to not pay his respects at the manor house in Pokrovskoe on certain days. In his domestic circle Kirila Petrovich displayed all the vices of an uncultivated man. Spoiled by his surroundings, he was accustomed to give free rein to every impulse of his ardent nature and to every caprice of his rather limited mind. Despite his exceptionally strong constitution, he suffered from the effects of gluttony once or twice a week, and was drunk every evening. In one wing of his house, there lived sixteen chambermaids, engaged in handicrafts appropriate to their sex.[2] The windows in that wing were protected by wooden bars, and the doors padlocked, with the keys in Kirila Petrovich's safekeeping. The young recluses came down into the garden at appointed hours to walk under the eyes of two old women. Every so often Kirila Petrovich married some of them off and new ones took their places. He was severe and arbitrary with his peasants and house serfs; yet they were devoted to him: they were proud of their master's wealth and reputation, and in their turn took many a liberty with their neighbors, trusting in their master's powerful protection.[3]

Troekurov usually spent his time riding about his extensive estates, feasting at length, and playing pranks, newly invented by the day, whose victims as a rule were new acquaintances, though even old friends were not always spared—with the one exception of Andrei Gavrilovich Dubrovskii. The latter, a retired lieutenant of the Guards, was Troekurov's nearest neighbor, and the owner of seventy serfs. Troekurov, haughty in his relations with people of the highest rank, treated Dubrovskii with respect despite the latter's humble circumstances. They had at one time been together in the service, and Troekurov knew from experience how impetuous and determined his friend was. They had been separated by circumstances for a long time.[4] Dubrovskii, with his property in disarray, had been forced to retire from the service and settle in his last remaining village. Having heard of this, Kirila Petrovich offered him his good offices, but Dubrovskii, though expressing his gratitude, preferred to remain poor and independent. A few years later Troekurov, retiring with the rank of General of the Army, came to live on his estate; they met again and were delighted with each other. From that time on they became daily companions; and Kirila Petrovich, who had never in his life condescended to visit anyone else, frequently called at his old friend's cottage unannounced. Of the same age, born of the same social class, and educated the same way, they were to some extent similar in character and disposition. In certain respects, even fate had treated them similarly: both had married for love and soon lost their wives; and each was left with a child. Dubrovskii's son was being educated in St. Petersburg, while Kirila Petrovich's daughter was growing up under her father's eyes. Kirila Petrovich often said to Dubrovskii, "Listen, brother Andrei Gavrilovich: if your Volodka grows into a sensible lad, I'll let him marry Masha; never mind if he's poor as a churchmouse."[5]

Andrei Gavrilovich usually shook his head and answered, "No, Kirila Petrovich: my Volodka is no match for your Maria Kirilovna. A poor nobleman like him should marry a poor noblewoman and be the head of his household, rather than become the steward of a spoiled female."

Everybody envied the accord reigning between the haughty Troekurov and his poor neighbor, and everybody marveled at the latter's boldness when he unceremoniously announced his opinions at Kirila Petrovich's table, not caring whether they contradicted those of his host. Some attempted to imitate him, stepping over the boundaries of required subservience, but Kirila Petrovich put them in such fear that they lost forever the desire for any such attempts; and thus Dubrovskii alone remained outside the general law. An unexpected occurrence unsettled and changed all this.

One time, early in the fall, Kirila Petrovich was preparing to ride out for a hunt. On the eve of the occasion the kennelmen and grooms were given orders to be ready by five o'clock in the morning. A tent and a field kitchen were sent ahead to the place where Kirila Petrovich intended to dine. The host and his guests came out to the kennels, where over five hundred harriers and borzois lived in comfort and contentment, lauding Kirila Petrovich's generosity in their canine tongue. The kennels included a hospital for dogs, supervised by the chief of the veterinary staff, Timoshka, and a maternity ward, where noble bitches whelped and suckled their puppies. Kirila Petrovich was proud of this fine establishment and never omitted an opportunity to show it off to his guests, each of whom had already inspected it at least twenty times. He walked about the kennels, surrounded by his guests and escorted by Timoshka and the chief kennelmen; he stopped in front of some of the doghouses, now inquiring after the condition of the sick, now handing out reprimands, more or less strict and just, now calling to him some dogs by name and fondly talking to them. The guests considered it their duty to be enthusiastic about Kirila Petrovich's kennels. Dubrovskii alone kept silent, frowning. He was a passionate hunter; and since his circumstances allowed him to keep only two harriers and one pack of borzois, he could not help feeling a certain envy at the sight of this magnificent establishment.

"Why are you frowning, brother?" Kirila Petrovich asked him. "Don't you like my kennels?"

"I do indeed," he answered morosely. "Your kennels are marvelous; I doubt whether your servants live as well as your dogs."

One of the kennelmen felt insulted.

"Thanks to God and our master," he said, "we have no complaints; but if the truth be told, there's many a gentleman who'd be better off if he exchanged his homestead for any one of these doghouses. He'd be both fed better and kept warmer."

Kirila Petrovich burst into loud laughter at his serf's insolent remark, and his guests followed suit, even though they felt that the hounds keeper's joke might well have applied to them. Dubrovskii blanched and did not say a word. At this moment some newborn pups were brought to Kirila Petrovich in a basket, and he turned his attention to them, choosing two to keep and ordering the rest to be drowned. In the meantime Andrei Gavrilovich disappeared, unnoticed by anyone.

On returning with his guests from the kennels, Kirila Petrovich sat down to supper, and only then, not seeing Dubrovskii, did he realize that his friend was missing. The servants reported that Andrei Gavrilovich had gone home. Troekurov gave orders to go after him immediately and bring him back without fail. Never had he ridden out on a hunt without Dubrovskii, who was an experienced and acute judge of canine virtues and an unerring arbiter of all manner of huntsmen's disputes. The servant sent after him came back while the company was still at table, and reported to his master that Andrei Gavrilovich, defying orders, had refused to return. Kirila Petrovich, flushed with liquor as usual, grew angry and sent the same servant off for a second time to tell Andrei Gavrilovich that if the latter did not come at once to spend the night at Pokrovskoe, he would break off all relations with him forever. The servant galloped off once more, while Kirila Petrovich rose from the table, dismissed his guests, and went to bed.

The next morning his first question was whether Andrei Gavrilovich was there. Instead of an answer, they handed him a letter folded into a triangle; he ordered his scribe to read it, and heard the following:

Most gracious sir,

I do not intend to come to Pokrovskoe until you send me your kennelman Paramoshka with an admission of his guilt; and it will be my pleasure to punish him or spare him; and I do not intend to tolerate jests from your serfs, nor will I tolerate them from you, for I am not a buffoon but a nobleman of ancient lineage. I remain your humble servant.

Andrei Dubrovskii

By today's code of etiquette this letter would be considered extremely boorish; what angered Kirila Petrovich, however, was not its strange style and composition, but simply its substance.

"What's this?" thundered Troekurov, jumping out of bed on his bare feet. "That I should send him my men with an admission of guilt, and that it should be his pleasure to punish them or spare them! What the devil's got into him? Who does he think he's locking horns with? I'll show him... I'll make him cry himself blind; I'll teach him what it's like to affront Troekurov!"

Kirila Petrovich got dressed and rode out in his usual splendor, but the hunt did not turn out well. They saw only one hare the whole day, and let even that one escape. The dinner under the tent in a field was unsuccessful, or at least it was not to the taste of Kirila Petrovich, who beat up his cook, tongue-lashed his guests, and on his way home deliberately rode over Dubrovskii's fields with his whole cavalcade.

Several days passed, but the hostility between the two neighbors did not abate. Andrei Gavrilovich continued to stay away from Pokrovskoe; and Kirila Petrovich, bored without him, poured out his annoyance in the most insulting expressions, which thanks to the diligence of the local gentry, reached Dubrovskii's ears with amendments and supplements. Any hope that might have still remained for a reconciliation was extinguished by a new incident.

One day Dubrovskii was driving about his small estate. Approaching a copse of birches, he heard the sound of an ax and, a minute later, the crash of a falling tree. He rushed into the copse and came upon some peasants from Pokrovskoe, who were calmly stealing his timber. Seeing him, they tried to run away, but he and his coachman caught two of them and brought them back to his house in bonds. Three enemy horses were also among the spoils of the victor. Dubrovskii was exceedingly angry: never before had Troekurov's men, brigands as everyone knew, dared to play their pranks within the boundaries of his property, since they were aware of his friendly relations with their master. Dubrovskii realized that they were now taking advantage of the breach of friendship that had recently occurred, and he decided, against all military conventions, to teach his prisoners of war a lesson with the same switches that they themselves had cut in his copse, and to set the horses to work, adding them to his own livestock.

A report about this incident reached Kirila Petrovich that same day. He flew into a rage, and in the first moment of anger wanted to gather all his men and fall upon Kistenevka (as his neighbor's village was called), raze it to the ground, and besiege the landlord in his manor house. Such exploits were not unusual with him. But his thoughts were soon drawn in a different direction.

Pacing up and down the hall with heavy steps, he accidentally glanced through the window and caught sight of a troika stopped by the gate. A small man in a leather cap and a frieze coat climbed out of the wagon and went to see the steward in a wing of the house: Troekurov recognized the assessor Shabashkin and sent for him. In another minute Shabashkin stood before Kirila Petrovich, scraping and bowing and reverently awaiting his orders.

"Hullo, my man, what's-your-name," said Troekurov. "What brought you to us?"

"I was driving to town, Your Excellency," answered Shabashkin, "and dropped by Ivan Demianov's to see if Your Excellency had any instructions for me."

"You came just at the right time, what's-your-name; I need you. Have a glass of vodka and listen to me."

The assessor was pleasantly surprised by such a warm welcome. He refused the vodka and listened to Kirila Petrovich with all his attention.

"I have a neighbor," said Kirila Petrovich. "He's a boor of a smallholder. I want to take away his estate. What do you think?"

"Well, Your Excellency, if there are some documents, or..."

"Nonsense, brother; what documents do you want? What are court orders for? The crux of the matter is precisely to take away his estate without any rights. Wait a minute, though. That estate used to belong to us at one time; it was bought from somebody called Spitsyn and then sold to Dubrovskii's father. Couldn't we make a case out of that?"

"It'd be difficult, Your Excellency: that sale was probably effected in a legal manner."

"Think about it, brother; search around a little."

"If, for instance, Your Excellency could somehow obtain from your neighbor the record or deed that entitles him to his estate, then, of course..."

"I understand, but the trouble is that all his documents were burned in a fire."

"What, Your Excellency, were his documents burned? You couldn't wish for anything better! In that case you may proceed according to the law, and you will without any doubt find complete satisfaction."

"Do you think so? Well, take good care of the matter. I rely on your zeal, and you can rest assured of my gratitude."

Shabashkin bowed almost to the floor and left. That same day he busied himself with the concocted case, and thanks to his dexterity, in exactly two weeks Dubrovskii received from town an order to present at once an appropriate clarification with regard to his possession of the village of Kistenevka.

Astonished by the unexpected request, Andrei Gavrilovich wrote a rather rude reply the same day, declaring that the village of Kistenevka had come into his possession after his father's death, that he held it by right of inheritance, that Troekurov had nothing to do with it, and that any other party's claims to his property amounted to chicanery and fraud.

This letter made a highly agreeable impression on the assessor Shabashkin. He could see, first, that Dubrovskii had little comprehension of legal matters, and, second, that it would not be difficult to get such a hot-tempered and incautious man into a very disadvantageous situation. Andrei Gavrilovich, when he had considered the assessor's request with a cool head, did see the need to reply in greater detail and did write quite a businesslike communication, but subsequently even this turned out to be insufficient.

The business dragged on. Convinced of the rightness of his case, Andrei Gavrilovich paid little further attention to it. He had neither the desire nor the means to throw money about, and although he had always been the first to crack jokes about the venality of the tribe of scriveners, it never occurred to him that he might become a victim of chicanery. Troekurov, on his part, cared just as little about winning the case he had initiated. It was Shabashkin who kept busy on his behalf, acting in his name, intimidating and bribing judges, and interpreting every possible edict every which way.

In any case, on February 9, 18.., Dubrovskii received through the town police a summons to appear before the N. district judge to hear his ruling with regard to the estate contested between him (Lieutenant Dubrovskii) and General of the Army Troekurov, and to sign it, indicating either his concurrence or his exception. Dubrovskii left for town that same day; on the road he was overtaken by Troekurov. They glanced at each other haughtily, and Dubrovskii noticed a malicious smile on his adversary's face.

2

On his arrival in town Andrei Gavrilovich stopped at the house of a merchant he knew and spent the night there, and the next morning he presented himself at the district courthouse. No one paid any attention to him. Right after him Kirila Petrovich arrived. The clerks rose and stuck their pens behind their ears. The panel of judges welcomed Troekurov with abject subservience, pulling up an armchair for him in consideration of his rank, years, and portliness; he sat down close to the door, which was left open. Andrei Gavrilovich stood, leaning against the wall. Profound silence ensued, and the secretary began to read the court's ruling in a ringing voice. We will cite that ruling in full, assuming that it will be gratifying to every reader to be apprised of one of the means whereby we in Holy Russia can lose property to which we have an indisputable right:

On the 27th day of October in the year 18.., the N. District Court examined the case of the adverse possession by Lieutenant of the Guards Andrei Dubrovskii, son of Gavrila Dubrovskii, of an estate belonging to General of the Army Kirila Troekurov, son of Petr Troekurov, which comprises the village of Kistenevka situated in P. Guberniia, with X number of serfs of the male sex and Y *desiatinas* of land, including meadows and appurtenances.[6] From which case it is evident that: on the 19th day of June in the past year of 18.., said General of the Army Troekurov instituted at this Court a possessory action setting forth that on the 14th day of August, 17.., his father, Collegiate Assessor and Cavalier Petr Troekurov, son of Efim Troekurov, deceased, who was at that time serving as provincial secretary in the chancery of the governor-general of S., purchased by an act of sale from the clerk Fadei Spitsyn, son of Egor Spitsyn, of the nobility, an estate, comprising, in said village of Kistenevka of R. region (which village, according to census No. X, was called Kistenevo Settlements), a total of Y number of male serfs registered in census No. 4, with all the peasants' chattels, with a farmstead, with arable and nonarable land, woods, meadows, fishing rights in the Kistenevka River, with all appurtenances attached to the estate, and with a wooden manor house—in other words everything without exclusion that Fadei Spitsyn had inherited from his father, Sergeant Egor Spitsyn, son of Terentii Spitsyn, of the nobility, and which he held in his possession, excluding not one of his serfs nor any measure of land—for a price of 2,500 rubles, for which a deed of sale was validated the same day at N. courthouse, and after which, on the 26th day of the same month of August, Troekurov's father was duly placed in possession of said estate by the N. District Court, and a livery of seizin was executed. And at last on the 6th day of September in the year 17.., his father by God's will deceased, while he, said Plaintiff, General of the Army Troekurov, from the year 17.., almost from infancy, had been in military service, mostly participating in campaigns abroad, for which reason he received no intelligence either of his father's death or about the estate left after him. Having now finally retired from the service and returned to his father's estates, comprising a total of 3,000 serfs in different villages situate in R. and S. districts of N. and P. *guberniias*, he finds that one of said estates with the above-mentioned number of serfs according to census No. X (of whom, according to the current census, Y number belong to this one estate) is being held, together with its land and all appurtenances, without any legal proof of possession by the aforementioned Lieutenant of the Guards Andrei Dubrovskii; for which reason he, Troekurov, attaching to his petition the original deed of sale given to his father by the vendor Spitsyn, petitions that the aforementioned estate be removed from Dubrovskii's wrongful possession and placed, according to its proper pertinence, at his, Troekurov's, disposal in full. As for Dubrovskii's wrongfully entering upon said estate, from which he has enjoyed revenues, petitioner prays the Court that, the appropriate interrogatories having been processed, lawful damages be assessed against Dubrovskii, wherewith restitution to Troekurov be effected.

The investigations conducted by N. District Court with regard to the above cause of action have revealed that: aforementioned current possessor of the disputed estate, Lieutenant of the Guards Dubrovskii, has deposed before the assessor in charge of affairs of the nobility that the estate currently in his possession, comprising said village of Kistenevka, with X number of serfs, land, and appurtenances, had been conveyed to him as inheritance after the death of his father, Second Lieutenant of the artillery Gavrila Dubrovskii, son of Evgraf Dubrovskii; that his father had acquired it through purchase from said plaintiff's father, Troekurov, who had earlier been a provincial secretary and later a collegiate assessor; and that said purchase had been effected through the services of Titular Councillor Grigorii Sobolev, son of Vasilii Sobolev, to whom plaintiff's father had given power of attorney on 30 August 17.., notarized at the N. District Court, according to which a deed of sale was to be issued to his, Dubrovskii's, father, because in said power of attorney it is stated that he, Troekurov's father, had sold to Dubrovskii's father the whole estate, comprising X number of serfs and land, bought earlier from the chancery clerk Spitsyn; and that Troekurov's father had received in full from Dubrovskii's father and had not returned the 3,200 rubles that were due to him according to the sales agreement; and that he wished the aforementioned agent, Sobolev, to convey to Dubrovskii's father the title to the property. Moreover, according to the same power of attorney, Dubrovskii's father, by virtue of having paid the whole sum, was to take possession of the estate bought by him and was to be in charge of it as its full owner even before the transference to him of said title, and neither the vendor Troekurov nor anyone else was henceforth to interfere with it. But when exactly and at which court of law the aforesaid deed of sale was issued by the agent Sobolev to his father, this he, Andrei Dubrovskii, did not know, because at that time he was a small child, and because after his father's death he could not find the title; for which reason he supposes that it might have burned along with other documents and property in a fire that occurred in their house in the year 17.., about which the inhabitants of said village also knew. As for the Dubrovskiis' undisputed possession of said estate from the day of its sale by Troekurov or from the day of the issuance of a power of attorney to Sobolev—that is, from the

year 17.. till the death of his father in 17.. and thereafter—he calls
to witness inhabitants of the neighborhood, who, fifty-two in number, have testified under oath that indeed, as far as they could remember, the said noblemen Dubrovskii came into possession of
the aforementioned disputed estate without any dispute about seventy years ago, but that they could not tell by exactly what deed or
title. As for the aforementioned previous vendee of said estate, former Provincial Secretary Petr Troekurov, they could not remember
whether he had owned it. The house of the noblemen Dubrovskii
did burn down about thirty years ago in a fire that had started in the
village at night; and the witnesses confirmed the assumption that
the estate sued for could produce revenue, counting from that time
on, of no less than 2,000 rubles a year.

In response, on 3 January of the current year General of the Army
Kirila Troekurov, son of Petr Troekurov, filed at this Court the
pleading that although aforementioned Lieutenant of the Guards
Andrei Dubrovskii had, in the course of the investigation of the
present action, adduced as evidence the power of attorney given by
his, plaintiff's, father to Titular Councillor Sobolev for effecting
the purchase of said estate, he had not, by this document, shown
clear proof—as required by Chapter 19 of the General Regulations
and by the edict of 19 November 1752—either of the actual deed of
sale or of its execution at any time. Therefore this power of attorney
today, after the death of its issuer, his father, is, according to the
decree of the Nth day of May, 1818, completely null and void.
Moreover: it has been decreed that properties sued for shall be restored to their proprietors—those with deeds under titles, according to the titles, and those without deeds, according to the results of
an investigation.

For said estate, which had belonged to his father, he, Troekurov,
has already shown the deed of sale as proof, and therefore it should,
on the basis of aforementioned laws, be recovered from said Dubrovskii's wrongful possession and restored to him by right of inheritance. And since said landowners, having in their possession,
without color of title, an estate that did not belong to them, have
also wrongfully enjoyed revenues from it to which they have not
been entitled, it should be established according to the law to what
sum said revenues amount, and damages should be assessed against
the landowner Dubrovskii, wherewith restitution to him, Troekurov, be effected.

Having investigated said cause of action and having cited plaintiff's and defendant's averments as well as the relevant statutes of law, the N. District Court *orders, adjudges, and decrees* that:

It is evident from said action that with regard to the aforementioned estate sued for, which is currently in the possession of Lieutenant of the Guards Andrei Dubrovskii, son of Gavrila Dubrovskii, and which comprises the village of Kistenevka with X number of male serfs according to the latest census, and with land and appurtenances, General of the Army Kirila Troekurov, son of Petr Troekurov, has shown a valid deed of sale, proving that said estate was conveyed in the year 17.. to his late father, provincial secretary and subsequently collegiate assessor, from chancery clerk Fadei Spitsyn, of noble birth; and that, furthermore, said vendee of the estate, Troekurov, was, as can be seen from a notation entered on the deed of sale, placed in possession of said estate by the N. District Court the same year, with a livery of seizin executed. Lieutenant of the Guards Andrei Dubrovskii, on the other hand, has adduced as evidence a power of attorney given by said vendee Troekurov, deceased, to Titular Councillor Sobolev, authorizing him to issue a deed of sale to his, Dubrovskii's, father, but it is forbidden by edict No. X not only to confirm proprietorship of immovable property, but even to permit temporary possession thereof on the basis of such transactions; moreover, the death of its issuer has rendered said power of attorney completely null and void. Furthermore Dubrovskii has failed, from the commencement of the present action in 18.. to date, to present clear evidence about when and where a deed of sale for said disputed estate, in accordance with the power of attorney, was actually issued. Therefore this Court orders, adjudges, and decrees: that said estate, with X number of serfs, land, and appurtenances, in whatever condition it may now be, shall be confirmed, on the basis of the deed of sale presented by him, as the property of General of the Army Troekurov; that Lieutenant of the Guards Dubrovskii shall be removed from the management of said estate; and that P. local court shall be instructed duly to place Mr. Troekurov, by virtue of his having inherited the estate, in possession thereof, and to execute a livery of seizin. General of the Army Troekurov has furthermore sued for damages from Lieutenant of the Guards Dubrovskii for having enjoyed revenues from his inherited estate, wrongfully in the possession of Dubrovskii; but since said estate, according to the testimony of inhabitants of long standing, has been in the undisputed possession of the noblemen Dubrovskii for several years; since the evidence as presented does not show that Mr. Troekurov had before now sued Dubrovskii in any way for his wrongful possession of said estate; and since it has been decreed that

if anyone should sow a crop in a track of land or enclose a farm-stead that does not belong to him, and an action be brought, with pretension to direct damages, against him for his wrongfully having taken possession, then the party adjudged right shall have that land with the crop sown in it, and the enclosure, and other improvements;

therefore General of the Army Troekurov shall be denied the damages for which he has sued Lieutenant of the Guards Dubrovskii in view of the circumstances that the estate belonging to him is being restored to his possession without any diminution. At the time said estate is being taken into possession, no part thereof may be found missing; if, on the other hand, General of the Army Troekurov should have clear and legitimate cause for claims in that regard, he shall have the right to sue separately at the appropriate court. This decision is to be communicated in advance both to plaintiff and to defendant in a legal manner, and with opportunity for appeal; said plaintiff and defendant shall furthermore be summoned through the police to this Court in order to hear the decision and sign it, respectively indicating either their concurrence or their exception.

The aforegoing decision has been signed by all members of this Court.

The secretary grew silent; the assessor rose and turned to Troekurov with a low bow, offering him the document to sign. Troekurov, triumphant, took the pen from him and signed the Court's "decision," indicating his complete concurrence.

It was Dubrovskii's turn. The secretary brought the document to him. But Dubrovskii remained motionless, with his head lowered.

The secretary repeated to him his invitation to sign, indicating either his full and complete concurrence or his explicit exception in case he should feel with a clear conscience, against the court's expectations, that his case was just, and should wish to file an appeal at the appropriate court within the legally allotted time. Dubrovskii remained silent... Then suddenly he raised his head with eyes flashing, stomped his foot, shoved the secretary aside with such force that the man fell to the ground, and seizing an inkpot, hurled it at the assessor.[7] Everyone was terrified.

"What! To defile the church of God! Away with you, band of flunkies!" Then he turned to Kirila Petrovich and continued: "What infamy, Your Excellency: the kennelmen are bringing dogs into God's church! Dogs are running all over the church. Just wait, I'll teach you..."

The guards, who had run in on hearing the noise, were just barely able to overpower him. They led him out and put him in his sleigh. Troekurov came out after him, accompanied by the whole court. Dubrovskii's sudden fit of insanity made a powerful impression on him and poisoned his triumph.

The judges, who had been hoping for an expression of his gratitude, were not favored with as much as one word of appreciation. He left for Pokrovskoe the same day. Dubrovskii, meanwhile, was lying in bed: the district doctor, who was fortunately not a complete ignoramus, had successfully let his blood and applied leeches and Spanish flies to him. By the evening the patient's condition improved, and he regained consciousness. The next day he was driven back to Kistenevka —hardly his own property any more.

3

Some time passed, but poor Dubrovskii's state of health was still bad. Although no more fits of madness recurred, he was visibly losing his strength. He began to forget his earlier occupations, rarely left his room, and fell into reverie for days at a time. The good-hearted old woman Egorovna, who had at one time looked after his son, now became his nurse too. She took care of him as if he were a child: reminded him of mealtimes and bedtime, fed him, and put him to bed. Andrei Gavrilovich obeyed her quietly, and had no contact with anyone except her. Since he was in no shape to take care of his affairs or manage his estate, Egorovna thought it necessary to write about it all to the young Dubrovskii, who was in St. Petersburg at the time, serving in one of the regiments of the Foot Guards. Tearing a page out of a housekeeping book, she dictated a letter to the cook Khariton, who was the only literate person in Kistenevka, and sent it off to town the same day for mailing.

It is time, however, to acquaint the reader with the actual hero of our narrative.

Vladimir Dubrovskii had been educated at a military academy, and after graduation appointed an officer in the Guards. His father spared nothing to support him in proper style, and the young man received more from home than he had a right to expect. Prodigal and ambitious, he indulged himself in extravagant habits, played at cards, got into debt, and gave no thought to the future, anticipating that sooner or later he would find a rich bride—the usual dream of poor youths.

One evening, as several officers sat in his apartment, sprawled on sofas and smoking his amber pipes, his valet Grisha handed him a letter, whose address and seal immediately struck the young man. He broke the seal hurriedly and read the following:

> Our gracious master, Vladimir Andreevich,
>
>   I, your old nurse, have decided to inform you of your dear father's state of health. He is very poorly, sometimes he drivels, and sits all day like an idiot child—but life and death are in the hands of the Lord. Come home to us, my dearest, we'll even send horses for you to Pesochnoe. They say the local court is going to put us under the mastership of Kirila Petrovich Troekurov, because, they say, we are his, but we have always been yours, and I have never even heard such a thing since the day I was born. Living in Petersburg, you could report it to the Tsar our father, and he would not let us be wronged. I remain your faithful slave and nurse,
>
> Orina Egorovna Buzyreva
>
>   I send my motherly blessing to Grisha; is he serving you well? Here, it has been two weeks already as the rains would not stop, and the shepherd Rodia died close upon St. Mikola's Day.

Vladimir Dubrovskii read these rather incoherent lines several times with extreme agitation. He had lost his mother in infancy and, scarcely knowing his father, had been sent to Petersburg in his eighth year. Nevertheless he had a romantic attachment to him, and he loved family life all the more for having never enjoyed its quiet pleasures.

The thought of losing his father lacerated his heart, and the state of the poor sick man, which he could picture to himself from his nurse's letter, appalled him. He imagined his father, foresaken in a remote village, under the care of a foolish old woman and his other domestics, threatened by some calamity and languishing without succor in the midst of both physical and mental torments. Vladimir reproached himself for his criminal neglect. He had not heard from his father for a long time, yet he had not thought of inquiring after him, supposing him to be either traveling about or engrossed in the care of his estate.

He decided to go and see him, and even to retire in case his father's condition should require his presence. His friends noticed his agitation and departed. Left by himself, Vladimir wrote an application for leave of absence, lit his pipe, and sank into deep thought.

He handed in his application that same evening, and in another three days was already on the highway.

He was approaching the station at which he had to turn off the highway toward Kistenevka. His heart was full of sad forebodings: he feared his father might be dead by the time he reached home; and he imagined the dreary life awaiting him in the country—backwoods, loneliness, poverty, and troubles over business, about which he did not know the first thing. When he arrived at the station, he went to ask the stationmaster if there were private horses available for hire. The stationmaster, learning his destination, told him that a team of horses sent from Kistenevka had been waiting for him for more than three days. Soon the old coachman Anton, who used to take Vladimir around the stables and look after his pony, presented himself to him. Tears welled up in Anton's eyes on seeing him; he bowed to the ground and reported that his old master was still alive. He hurried off to harness the horses. Vladimir Andreevich refused the breakfast offered him and hastened to depart. Anton drove him along the country lanes, and conversation began between them.

"Please tell me, Anton, what's this business between my father and Troekurov?"

"Heaven only knows, young master Vladimir Andreevich... The master, they say, fell foul of Kirila Petrovich, who then took him to court, as if he weren't his own judge anyway! It's not for us serfs to remark on what our masters wish to do, but, by God, your dear father shouldn't have set himself against Kirila Petrovich; whether the pitcher strikes the stone or the stone the pitcher, it's bad for the pitcher."[8]

"So evidently this Kirila Petrovich does just what he likes in these parts?"

"Aye, so he does, young master: he snaps his fingers at the assessor, and the police superintendent is his errand boy. As for the gentlefolks hereabout, they gather at his house to pay their respect: verily I say, he that hath a full purse never wanted a friend."[9]

"Is it true that he's taking away our property?"

"Even so, young master, that's what we hear tell. Just the other day the sacristan from Pokrovskoe said at a christening held at our elder's house: 'The good times are over: you'll see what it's like when Kirila Petrovich takes you in hand.' Mikita the blacksmith answered him. 'Enough of that, Savelich,' he says, 'don't sadden the godfather, don't upset the guests. Kirila Petrovich is one master, Andrei Gavrilovich another; and we're all in the hands of God and the Tsar.' But people will talk."[10]

"You don't wish, then, to pass into Troekurov's possession?"

"To pass into Kirila Petrovich's possession! The Lord save and preserve us from that! His own people have a rough enough deal at times: if he gets his hand on strangers, he'll not only skin them, but tear their very flesh off. Nay, God grant a long life to Andrei Gavrilovich, and if it's His will to gather him to his fathers, then we wish for no other master but you, our provider. Don't abandon us, and we'll stand up for you." With these words, Anton brandished his whip and shook the reins; the horses broke into a brisk trot.

Touched by the old coachman's loyalty, Dubrovskii fell silent and once more gave himself up to reflections. More than an hour passed. Suddenly Grisha awakened him with the exclamation, "Here's Pokrovskoe!"

Dubrovskii raised his head. They were riding along the shore of a wide lake, drained by a stream that flowed meandering among hills at a distance; on one of these hills there arose, above the dense great foliage of a grove, the green roof and belvedere of an enormous stone house; on another one, there stood a five-domed church and an ancient bell tower; and all around were scattered peasant cottages with their vegetable gardens and wells. Dubrovskii recognized all these landmarks: he recalled that on that hill he used to play with the little Masha Troekurova, two years his junior, who was already then promising to grow into a beauty. He wanted to ask Anton about her, but a sense of reserve held him back.

As he drew closer to the manor house, he saw a white dress flitting among the trees of the park. At this moment Anton lashed at the horses and, obeying a vanity common to both country coachmen and city drivers, dashed across the bridge, past the village. Leaving the village behind, they climbed a slope. Vladimir soon caught sight of a birch wood and, in a clearing to its left, a little gray house with a red roof. His heart pounded: he saw before him Kistenevka and his father's humble house.

In ten minutes he drove into the courtyard. He looked about him with indescribable emotion: he had not seen his home for twelve years. The little birches that had only just been planted along the fence when he was still living there had grown into tall trees with branches spread wide. The yard, which used to be ornamented with three neat flower beds, a well-swept broad path running among them, had by now turned into an unmowed pasture, on which a hobbled horse was grazing. The dogs began to bark but, recognizing Anton, grew quiet, wagging their shaggy tails. The domestics all poured out of the servants' quarters and surrounded their young master with loud manifestations of joy. He was barely able to push his way through their eager crowd in order to ascend the dilapidated porch; in the anteroom Egorovna met him, embracing her former charge with sobs.[11]

"How are you, nurse? It's so good to see you," he kept repeating while pressing the good old woman to his heart. "But what about father? Where is he? How is he?"

At this moment a tall old man, pale and thin, wearing a dressing gown and a nightcap, entered the room, though hardly able to drag his feet one after the other.

"Hullo, Volodka!" he said in a weak voice, and Vladimir warmly embraced his father. The joy of seeing his son was too much of a shock for the sick man: he grew faint, his legs gave way under him, and he would have collapsed had his son not caught him up.

"Why did you get out of bed?" Egorovna said to him. "He can't stand on his legs, yet he's itching to go where other people go."

The old man was carried off to his bedroom. He tried to talk to his son, but his thoughts became confused and his words were incoherent. He fell silent and soon dozed off. Vladimir was dismayed by his condition. He installed himself in his father's bedroom and asked to be left alone with him. The domestics obeyed and now turned to Grisha, whom they carried off to the servants' quarters, giving him a hearty welcome, feasting him in a rustic manner, and exhausting him with questions and greetings.

4

On the table once laden with victuals
now stands a coffin.[12]

A few days after his arrival, the young Dubrovskii wanted to turn to business matters, but his father was in no state to provide the necessary explanations, nor did he have an attorney. Going over his father's papers, Vladimir found only the assessor's first letter and a draft of Andrei Gavrilovich's answer, from which he could not derive a clear idea of the lawsuit. He decided to await further developments, placing his hopes in the rightness of his family's cause.

In the meantime, Andrei Gavrilovich's condition worsened by the hour. Vladimir saw that his end was not far off, and he never left the side of the old man, now fallen into a state of complete infancy.

Meanwhile, the deadline for an appeal lapsed, with none filed. Kistenevka now belonged to Troekurov. Shabashkin came to him with bows and congratulations; and to ask when it would suit His Excellency to be placed in possession of his newly acquired estate, and whether he would wish to participate in the transaction in person or would prefer to give power of attorney to someone else. Kirila Petrovich felt embarrassed. He was not avaricious by nature: his desire for vengeance had carried him too far, and now he had pangs of conscience. He knew about the condition of his adversary—the old comrade of his youth—and his victory brought no joy to his heart. He glanced at Shabashkin menacingly, searching for some reason to heap curses on him, but finding no sufficient pretext, angrily said: "Go away, I'm not in the mood for you."

Seeing that he was indeed not in a good mood, Shabashkin bowed and hastily withdrew. Left by himself, Kirila Petrovich started pacing up and down, whistling "May thou, thunder of victory, rumble,"[13] which, with him, was always a sign of extraordinary agitation.

At last he gave orders to have the racing droshky harnessed, dressed warmly (it was already the end of September), and rode out, driving himself.

He soon beheld Andrei Gavrilovich's little house, and contradictory feelings filled his heart. Satisfied vengeance and a love of power had smothered his more noble sentiments up to a point, but at long last these latter triumphed. He resolved to make it up with his old neighbor, erasing all traces of the quarrel and returning his property to him. His feelings alleviated by this commendable decision, he approached his neighbor's house at a trot and drove straight into the courtyard.

At this time the sick man was seated by his bedroom window. He recognized Kirila Petrovich, and his face assumed an expression of terrible confusion: a purple flush suffused his usually pale cheeks, his eyes flashed, and he uttered some incomprehensible sounds. His son, seated in the same room over some ledgers, raised his head and was struck by the old man's condition. The patient pointed at the courtyard with a look of horror and anger. He hastily gathered the skirts of his dressing gown, preparing to get up from his armchair; he rose... and suddenly collapsed. His son rushed to him. The old man had lost consciousness and was not breathing; he had suffered a stroke.

"Quick, quick, send to the city for the doctor!" Vladimir cried.

"Kirila Petrovich is asking for you," said a servant, entering.

Vladimir threw a terrifying glance at him.

"Tell Kirila Petrovich to clear out of here before I have him thrown out... Off you go!"

The servant gladly rushed from the room to fulfill his master's command. Egorovna clasped her hands.

"Young master," she said in a squeaky voice, "you're bringing ruin on your head! Kirila Petrovich will swallow us all up!"

"Be quiet, nurse," said Vladimir angrily. "Send Anton to the city for the doctor at once."

Egorovna left.

There was nobody in the entrance hall: all the servants had gathered in the courtyard to look at Kirila Petrovich. Egorovna, going out on the porch, heard the servant deliver his young master's reply to the visitor. The latter heard him out, seated in his droshky. His face turned darker than night, then a contemptuous smile came over it; he glanced at the servants menacingly and slowly drove past the house. He also glanced at the window where Andrei Gavrilovich had been seated but could no longer be seen. The nurse stood on the porch, forgetting her master's order. The servants started a noisy discussion of what had happened. Suddenly Vladimir appeared among his servants and abruptly declared, "There's no need for a doctor; father has died."

There was general confusion. The servants rushed into their old master's room. He lay in the armchair where Vladimir had placed him; his right arm dangled over the floor and his head hung over his chest; there was not the least sign of life left in his body, still warm but already disfigured by death. Egorovna burst into sobs, and the servants crowded around the corpse left to their care; they washed it, dressed it in a uniform made back in 1797; and laid it out on the same table at which they had served their master for so many years.

5

The funeral was held three days later. The poor old man's body lay on the table wrapped in a shroud and surrounded by candles. The dining room was full of servants. They were getting ready for the funeral procession. Vladimir and three servants lifted the coffin. The priest went first, accompanied by the sexton, singing dirges. The master of Kistenevka passed over the threshold of his house for the last time. They carried the coffin through the woods to where the church stood. It was a clear, cold day. The autumn leaves were falling from the trees.

Past the wood, the Kistenevka village church and the cemetery, shaded by old lime trees, came into view. The body of Vladimir's mother lay there, and next to her tomb a new grave had been dug the day before.

The church was full of Kistenevka peasants who had come to pay their last respects to their master. The young Dubrovskii stood in the chancel; he neither wept nor prayed, but his face looked frightening. The somber service came to an end. Vladimir went up first to take leave of the corpse; all the servants followed after him. The lid was brought in, and the coffin nailed shut. The village women wailed loudly, and the men once in a while wiped away their tears with their fists. Vladimir and the same three servants, accompanied by the whole village, carried the coffin to the cemetery. The coffin was lowered into the grave; each person present threw a handful of soil on it; they filled the pit, bowed down, and dispersed. Vladimir left hastily, before anybody else, and disappeared into the Kistenevka wood.

Egorovna, in the name of the young master, invited the priest and all the clergy to a funeral dinner, at the same time informing them that he himself would not be present. Father Anton, his wife Fedotovna, and the sexton walked back to the house, talking with Egorovna about the virtues of the departed and discussing what was likely to happen to his heir. The whole neighborhood already knew about Troekurov's visit and the reception he got, and every local know-it-all was predicting that the incident would have grave consequences.

"What is to be, will be," said the priest's wife. "It would be a pity, though, if Vladimir Andreevich weren't to be our landlord. Such a fine fellow, I declare!"

"Who else could be our landlord, if not he?" interrupted Egorovna. "It's no use Kirila Petrovich getting all worked up. He's not dealing with a child: my precious one can stand up for himself, and, God helping, his protectors won't turn their backs upon him neither. He's uncommon high and mighty, ain't he, Kirila Petrovich! But I'll be sworn he stuck his tail between his legs when my Grishka yelled at him: 'Out with you, old dog! Out of this yard!' "

"Mercy on us, Egorovna," said the sexton, "it's a wonder Grigorii's tongue didn't refuse to obey him. For my part I'd sooner affront the bishop than look askance at Kirila Petrovich.[14] You only have to catch sight of him, and you're already cringing with fear and trembling; before you know it, your back is bending on its own hook."

"Vanity of vanities," said the priest.[15] "One day the burial service will be read over Kirila Petrovich, just as it was over Andrei Gavrilovich this morning; only perhaps the funeral will be more sumptuous and more people will be invited, but isn't it all the same to God?"

"Aye, truly, Father, we too wanted to invite the whole neighborhood, but Vladimir Andreevich refused to. I'll be sworn we have plenty to do the honors with, but what can you say if he doesn't want to? Even if there's no other people, though, I'll have a nice spread at least for you, dear guests."

This cordial invitation and the hope of laying their fingers on some delectable pies helped quicken the steps of the conversing party; they soon arrived at the house, where the table was already laid and the vodka served.

In the meanwhile Vladimir, trying to muffle the voice of sorrow in his heart by physical exertion and tiredness, had gotten himself deep into the thickets. He walked at random, off the beaten path, brushing against branches and getting scratched, while his feet kept sinking into bogs, to none of which did he pay any attention. At length he came on a little hollow, surrounded by woods on all sides, and a brook that meandered silently under the trees, half-stripped of their leaves by the autumn. He stopped and sat down on the cold turf. His mind was full of thoughts, one gloomier than the other. He keenly felt his loneliness. Storm clouds seemed to be gathering over his future. The feud with Troekurov foretokened new misfortunes. His modest property might pass into another's hands, in which case poverty awaited him. For a long time he sat motionless in the same place, watching the brook's quiet flow as it carried away some withered leaves—a faithful, all too familiar likeness of life. At last he noticed it was getting dark: he rose and set out to find the way home, but it took him a great deal of straggling about unfamiliar woods before he stumbled on the path that led straight to the gates of his house.

It so happened that the priest and his retinue were just then coming up the path. The idea that this was a bad omen crossed Vladimir's mind. He could not help turning aside and hiding behind a tree. Not noticing him, they talked excitedly among themselves as they passed by.

"Depart from evil, and do good,"[16] the priest was saying to his wife. "There's no reason for us to tarry here. Whatever transpires is not our business."

His wife said something in answer, which Vladimir could not make out.

As he approached his house he saw a great many people: peasants and servants were crowding in the courtyard. Loud voices and much noise could be heard even at a distance. Two carriages stood by the barn. On the porch several strangers in uniform seemed to be discussing something.

"What does all this mean?" he crossly asked Anton, who was running to meet him. "Who are these people and what do they want?"

"Alas the day, young master Vladimir Andreevich," answered the old man, catching his breath. "The court's come. They're giving us over to Troekurov, taking us away from Your Honor!"

Vladimir hung his head; the servants crowded around their unfortunate master.

"Father and benefactor," they cried, kissing his hands, "we don't want no master but you; just give us the word and we'll take care of the court. We'd sooner die than betray you."

Vladimir looked at them with strange feelings stirring in his soul. "Just stand quietly," he told them. "I'll talk the matter over with the officials."

"Do, young master, do talk it over," they shouted to him from the crowd. "Awaken their conscience, the damned rascals!"

Vladimir went up to the officials. Shabashkin, his cap on his head, stood with his arms akimbo and haughtily looked about him. The police superintendent, a tall, corpulent man of about fifty with a red face and mustachios, cleared his throat as he saw Dubrovskii approach, and called out in a hoarse voice:

"And so I repeat what I've already told you: by the decision of the district court, from now on you belong to Kirila Petrovich Troekurov, whose person is represented here by Mr. Shabashkin. Obey all his commands; and you, women, love him and respect him, for he's got a great fondness for you."

The superintendent burst into laughter over his witty joke; Shabashkin and the other officials followed his example. Vladimir seethed with indignation.

"Allow me to ask," he addressed the merry superintendent with pretended calmness, "what all this means."

"What all this means," answered the resourceful official, "is that we have come to place Kirila Petrovich Troekurov in possession of this estate, and to request *all other parties* to clear out of here while the going is good."

"It seems to me, though, that you might have turned to me before my peasants, and announced to a landowner that he has been deprived of his possessions."

"And who might you be?" asked Shabashkin with an insolent look. "The former landowner, Andrei Dubrovskii, son of Gavrila Dubrovskii, has passed away by the will of God, and as for you, we neither know you nor desire to."

"Vladimir Andreevich is our young master," said a voice from the crowd.

"Who was it dared open his mouth over there?" asked the superintendent menacingly. "What master? What Vladimir Andreevich? Your master is Kirila Petrovich Troekurov, d'ye hear, you blockheads?"

"Not likely," said the same voice.

"But this is a riot!" shouted the superintendent. "Hey, elder, come here!"

The village elder stepped forward.

"Find the man at once who dared talk back to me. I'll teach him!"

The elder turned to the crowd, asking who had spoken, but everyone kept quiet. Soon, however, a murmur began to rise from the back of the crowd, and in one minute it had grown into a horrendous uproar. The superintendent lowered his voice and tried to calm the crowd down.

"What are we looking at him for?" shouted the servants. "Throw him out, fellows!"

The whole crowd lurched forward. Shabashkin and the others lost no time in dashing into the anteroom and locking the door behind them. "Tie them up, fellows," shouted the voice previously heard, and the crowd began to press on the house.

"Stop!" yelled Dubrovskii. "Idiots! What are you up to? You'll ruin yourselves, and me too. Go back to your cottages and leave me in peace. Don't be afraid: the Sovereign has a kind heart; I will appeal to him. He will not let us be harmed. We're all his children. But how can he protect you if you're rioting and housebreaking?"

The young Dubrovskii's speech, his ringing voice and majestic air, produced the desired effect. The people calmed down and dispersed; the courtyard became empty. The officials sat in the anteroom. At last Shabashkin cautiously unlocked the door, came out on the porch, and, bowing and scraping, thanked Dubrovskii profusely for his kind intervention. Vladimir listened with contempt and made no answer.

"We have decided," continued the assessor, "to spend the night here if you'll allow us: it's already dark, and your peasants might fall upon us on the highway. Do us a great favor: give orders to spread at least some hay on the drawing-room floor for us to sleep on; as soon as the day breaks, we'll be on our way."

"Do what you like," answered Dubrovskii dryly. "I'm no longer master here." With these words he retired to his father's room and locked the door behind him.

6

"All is finished, then," said Vladimir to himself. "This morning I still had a roof over my head and a piece of bread; tomorrow I shall have to leave the house where I was born and my father died—and leave it to the man who caused his death and made me a pauper." He fixed his eyes on his mother's portrait. The painter had depicted her with her elbow resting on a balustrade, in a white morning dress, and with a scarlet rose in her hair. "This portrait, too, will fall into the hands of my family's foe," he thought further. "It will be tossed into a storeroom among broken chairs, or else will be hung in the entrance hall, to be ridiculed and commented on by his kennelmen. In her bedroom, where father died, his steward will take up residence, or his harem will be installed. No, and a thousand times no! He shall not have the woeful house from which he is evicting me." Vladimir clenched his teeth: terrible thoughts came to his mind. He could hear the voices of the officials: they were behaving like masters of the house, demanding now this, now that, and unpleasantly distracting his mind from his melancholy reflections. At last all grew quiet.

Vladimir unlocked the chests and cabinets, and began to sort out his late father's papers. They consisted mostly of accounts and business correspondence. Vladimir tore them up without reading them. Among them, however, he found a package with the inscription "Letters from my wife." His feelings deeply stirred, Vladimir set to reading these: they were written during the Turkish campaign and addressed from Kistenevka to the army.[17] She described to her husband her lonely life and domestic occupations, gently lamenting their separation and urging him to come home, into the arms of a loving wife. In one letter she voiced her anxiety over little Vladimir's health; in another, expressed her joy over early signs of his abilities, predicting a bright and happy future for him. Vladimir read on and on, letting his memory plunge into a world of family happiness and oblivious to everything else; he did not notice how time passed. The grandfather clock struck eleven. Vladimir put the letters in his pocket, took the candle, and left the study. The officials were sleeping on the floor in the drawing room. Their empty glasses stood on the table, and the whole room smelled strongly of rum. Walking past them with disgust, Vladimir went out into the entrance hall. The outside door was locked. Not finding the key, he returned to the drawing room: it lay on the table. He opened the door and stumbled on a man crouching in the corner; an ax glinted in his hand. Turning the candle toward him, Vladimir recognized Arkhip the blacksmith.

"What are you doing here?" he asked.

"Oh, it's you, Vladimir Andreevich," whispered Arkhip. "Thank gracious goodness heavens! It's a good thing you came with a candle!"

Vladimir looked at him in astonishment.

"Why are you hiding here?" he asked.

"I wanted... I came to... to see if they're all inside," answered Arkhip in a low, faltering voice.

"And why are you carrying an ax?"

"An ax? Why, these days a body can't stir abroad without one. These officials, you see, are into such mischief—a man can never tell..."

"You must be drunk. Put away that ax and go sleep it off."

"Me drunk? Vladimir Andreevich, young master, God is my witness I haven't had one drop in my mouth. Nay, how could one think of liquor when the officials want to lay their hands on us; have you ever seen such infamy, chasing our masters off their property?... Snoring in there, aren't they, the damned rascals: I'd put them all away at once, and none would be the wiser."

Dubrovskii frowned.

"Listen, Arkhip," he said after a short pause, "you're barking up the wrong tree. It's not the officials' fault. Light a lantern and follow me."

Arkhip took the candle from his master's hand, found a lantern behind the stove, and lit it; both quietly descended the steps and proceeded down the courtyard. A guard began to beat an iron plate, and the dogs started barking.

"Who is on watch?" asked Dubrovskii.

"It's us, young master," answered a thin voice, "Vasilisa and Lukeria."

"Go home," he said; "we don't need you."

"That'll do," added Arkhip.

"Thank you, kind sir," replied the women and went home immediately.

Dubrovskii proceeded farther. Two men approached him and called to him. He recognized the voices of Anton and Grisha.

"Why aren't you sleeping?" he asked them.

"How could we sleep?" answered Anton. "What we've lived to see... Who would have thought?"

"Quietly," said Dubrovskii. "Where is Egorovna?"

"She's at the manor house, in her little corner," replied Grisha.

"Go and bring her here, and get all our people out of the house, leaving not a soul in it except the officials. And you, Anton, get a cart ready."

Grisha left and soon reappeared with his mother. The old woman had not undressed for the night; except for the officials, nobody in the house had closed an eye.

"Is everybody here?" asked Dubrovskii. "Is there no one left in the house?"

"No one except the officials," answered Grisha.

"Bring some hay or straw," said Dubrovskii.

The servants ran to the stables and returned with their arms full of hay.

"Pile it under the porch. That's right. And now, fellows, give me a light!"

Arkhip opened the lantern, and Dubrovskii lit a splinter. "Wait a minute," he said to Arkhip; "I think in my hurry I locked the door of the entrance hall: go and unlock it quickly."

Arkhip ran up to the entrance hall and found the door unlocked. He locked it with the key, murmuring under his breath, "Unlock it! Not likely!" And he returned to Dubrovskii.

Dubrovskii put the splinter to the hay, which flared up; the flames soared high, illuminating the whole courtyard.

"Mercy on us," cried Egorovna in a plaintive voice. "Vladimir Andreevich, what are you doing?"

"Be quiet," said Dubrovskii. "Farewell, my good people: I'm going where God will guide me. Be happy with your new master."

"Father and provider," answered the servants, "we'd sooner die than leave you: we're coming with you."

The cart drew up; Dubrovskii climbed into it with Grisha, and to the others assigned the Kistenevka wood as a meeting place. Anton lashed the horses, and they left the courtyard.

A wind blew up. In one minute the flames engulfed the whole house. Red smoke rose writhing over the roof. The window panes cracked and shattered; flaming beams were falling; and plaintive cries and howls could be heard:

"Help, we're burning, help!"

"Not likely," said Arkhip, eyeing the fire with a malicious smile.

"Arkhipushka," called out Egorovna, "save them, the damned rascals; God will reward you."

"Not likely," answered the blacksmith.

At this moment the officials appeared in the windows, trying to break the double frames. But the roof caved in with a crash just then, and the howls died away.

Soon all the servants poured out into the courtyard. The women, crying, rushed to save their pitiable belongings, while little boys and girls jumped up and down, enjoying the fire. The sparks flew in a blazing blizzard, and the cottages caught fire.

"All set, now," said Arkhip. "It's burning nicely, ain't it? A fine sight from Pokrovskoe, I'll vow."

At this moment, however, something new attracted his attention: a cat was running about on the roof of the blazing barn, not knowing where to jump; flames surrounded it on all sides. The poor animal was calling for help with pitiful meows. Some little boys rolled with laughter, watching her despair.

"You devils, what are you laughing at?" said the blacksmith angrily. "Don't you fear the Lord: God's creature's a-perishing, and you're glad, you blockheads."

With these words he placed a ladder against the burning roof and climbed up to rescue the cat. The animal understood his intention and clutched his sleeve with a look of eager gratitude. The blacksmith, half-burned, climbed down with his catch.

"Fare you well, good people," he said to the bewildered servants. "There's nothing else for me to do here. Live happily and remember me kindly."

The blacksmith left; the fire raged for some time longer. At last it abated; only heaps of embers glowed flameless but bright in the dark of the night, with Kistenevka's burnt-out inhabitants wandering around them.

7

News of the fire spread throughout the neighborhood the next day. Everybody talked about it, offering different guesses and suppositions. Some claimed that Dubrovskii's servants, having got drunk at the funeral feast, had set the house on fire through carelessness; others blamed the officials, who must have had a drop too much as they took possession of the house; still others maintained that Dubrovskii, too, had perished in the flames, together with the officials and all the servants. There were some, however, who guessed the truth, asserting that Dubrovskii himself, driven by spite and despair, was the instigator of the awful calamity. Troekurov came the very next day to the site of the conflagration and conducted an investigation. It was established that the police superintendent and the assessor, scribe, and clerk of the district court, as well as Vladimir Dubrovskii, the nurse Egorovna, the house serf Grigorii, the coachman Anton, and the blacksmith Arkhip were all missing. Further the servants testified that the officials had burned at the time the roof caved in; and their charred bones were indeed found in the ashes. The serving women Vasilisa and Lukeria also declared that they had seen Dubrovskii and the blacksmith Arkhip just a few minutes before the fire started. The latter, according to the general testimony, was alive and had been the chief, if not the only, instigator of the fire. But strong suspicion fell on Dubrovskii too. Kirila Petrovich sent the governor a detailed account of the incident, and new legal proceedings started.

Soon other reports aroused curiosity and gave rise to gossip. Robbers cropped up in the N. District, spreading terror throughout the environs. The measures the authorities took against them proved ineffective. Robberies, each more spectacular than the last, followed in succession. There was no safety either along the highways or in the villages. Carts filled with robbers crisscrossed the whole *guberniia* in broad daylight, waylaying travelers and the mail, coming into villages, pillaging landowners' houses and consigning them to flames. The band's chief gained a reputation for intelligence, daring, and a certain magnanimity. Wondrous tales circulated about him; the name of Dubrovskii was on everybody's lips, all being convinced that it was he and no other who commanded the daring brigands. One circumstance that amazed everybody was that Troekurov's estates were spared: the robbers did not plunder one single barn or waylay one single cart that belonged to him. With his usual arrogance, Troekurov ascribed this exceptional treatment to the fear he inspired throughout the *guberniia*, and also to the exceptionally good police force that he had organized in his villages. At first the neighbors chuckled among themselves over Troekurov's loftiness and daily expected the uninvited guests to arrive in Pokrovskoe, where there was plenty to plunder, but at last they had to come around to his interpretation of the matter and admit that even robbers, inexplicably, showed him respect. Troekurov was triumphant, and every time he heard about a new robbery by Dubrovskii he showered witticisms on the heads of the governor, the police superintendents, and the platoon commanders from whom Dubrovskii invariably got away unharmed.

In the meanwhile October 1, which was celebrated in Troekurov's village as the patron saint's day, arrived. But before we embark on a description of this celebration or relate the ensuing events, we must acquaint the reader with certain personages who are either new to him or have been mentioned only passingly at the beginning of our narrative.

8

In all likelihood the reader has already guessed that Kirila Petrovich's daughter, about whom we have so far said only a few words, is the heroine of our tale. At the time we are describing she was seventeen years old, in the full bloom of her beauty. Her father loved her to distraction but treated her with his usual capriciousness, now trying to cater to all her wishes, now frightening her with his stern, sometimes even cruel, ways. Although sure of her affections, he could never gain her confidence. She developed the habit of concealing her feelings and thoughts from him, because she could never be sure how he would receive them. Growing up in solitude, she had no girl friends. The neighbors' wives and daughters rarely came to Kirila Petrovich's house, because his usual conversation and amusements called more for male company than for the presence of ladies. Seldom did our young beauty appear among guests feasting with Kirila Petrovich. The huge library, consisting mostly of French authors of the eighteenth century, was placed at her disposal. Her father, who never read anything except *The Complete Art of Cookery*, could not guide her in her choice of books, and Masha, having sampled works of all kinds, naturally gave her preference to novels. It was with their aid that she completed her education, begun at one time under the guidance of Mlle. Mimi, whom Kirila Petrovich completely trusted and favored, and whom he was obliged in the end to transfer surreptitiously to another of his estates, since the consequences of his friendship had become all too apparent. Mademoiselle Mimi left behind a rather pleasant memory. She was a good-hearted girl who never abused the influence she obviously had over Kirila Petrovich, in which respect she greatly differed from his other mistresses, who had replaced each other in quick succession. It seemed that Kirila Petrovich himself loved her more than the others, for a black-eyed naughty little boy of nine, whose face bore the traces of Mademoiselle Mimi's southern features, was being brought up in the house as his son, even though a great many other barefooted little children, all the spit and image of Kirila Petrovich, were running about under his windows, regarded as house serfs. Kirila Petrovich had a French tutor sent down from Moscow for his little

Sasha; and this tutor arrived in Pokrovskoe just at the time of the events we are describing.

Kirila Petrovich was favorably impressed with the tutor's pleasant appearance and simple conduct. The Frenchman presented him his credentials and a letter from a relative of the Troekurovs at whose house he had served as a tutor for four years. Kirila Petrovich looked at all this carefully, and was dissatisfied only with the Frenchman's youth: not because he thought this enviable shortcoming indicated that the young man would lack the patience and experience so very necessary in a tutor's unfortunate profession, but because he had his own doubts in this connection, which he decided to voice at once. To this end, he sent for Masha. (Since he himself did not speak French, she served as an interpreter for him.)

"Come here, Masha: tell this *monsieur* that, all right, I'll take him on, but only under the condition that he doesn't start running after my girls, or else I'll teach him, the son of a bitch... Translate this for him, Masha."

Masha blushed and, turning to the tutor, said to him in French that her father counted on his modest and proper behavior.

The Frenchman bowed and answered that he hoped he would deserve respect, even if he did not win favor.

Masha translated his answer word for word.

"Very well, very well," said Kirila Petrovich. "He needn't bother about either favor or respect. His business is to look after Sasha, and teach him grammar and geography. Translate this for him."

Maria Kirilovna softened her father's rude expressions in her translation, and Kirila Petrovich let his tutor proceed to the wing of the house where a room had been assigned to him.

Masha paid no attention to the young Frenchman: brought up with aristocratic prejudices, she regarded a tutor as a kind of servant or artisan, who were not men in her eyes. She noticed neither the impression she made on Monsieur Desforges, nor his embarrassment, nor his trembling, nor his changed voice. During the days following his arrival she met him quite frequently, but did not bestow any greater attention on him. As a result of an unexpected incident, however, she formed an entirely new idea of him.

Several bear cubs were usually being raised at Kirila Petrovich's house, serving as one of the chief sources of amusement for the master of Pokrovskoe. When still little, they were brought into the living room daily, where Kirila Petrovich played with them for hours at a time, setting them at cats and puppies. When they grew up, they were put on a chain, awaiting the real baitings they were destined for. From time to time they were led out in front of the windows of the manor house, where an empty wine barrel studded with nails was rolled out toward them: the bear would sniff at the barrel, then gently touch it, which would hurt its paw; angered, it would push the barrel with greater force, and the pain would become greater. It would get into a blind rage and keep throwing itself on the barrel with growls until at last they separated the poor beast from the target of its futile frenzy. At other times a pair of bears would be harnessed to a cart, and some guests, put in the cart against their will, would be driven off heaven knows where. But the joke Kirila Petrovich considered best was the following.

They would lock a hungry bear in an empty room, tying it with a rope to a ring screwed into the wall. The rope would be long enough to reach to any point in the room except the opposite corner, which would be the only place safe from the ferocious beast's attack. They would lead some novice up to the door of this room, suddenly push him in, and lock the door behind him, leaving the hapless victim alone with the shaggy hermit. The poor guest, with the skirt of his coat torn and he himself bleeding from scratches, would soon find the safe corner, but would be compelled, sometimes for as long as three hours, to stand there, two steps from the bear, flattening himself against the wall, and from this position to watch the frenzied beast growl, leap, and rear up, tearing at its rope and straining to reach him. Such were the noble pastimes of a Russian gentleman! Some days after the tutor's arrival it occurred to Troekurov to entertain him, too, with a visit to the bear's room. With this purpose in mind, he summoned the Frenchman one morning, and led him along some dark corridors; suddenly a side door opened, two servants pushed the Frenchman in, and locked the door after him. Recovering his senses, the tutor caught sight of the tied-up bear, which began to snort and sniff at its visitor from a distance, then suddenly reared up and advanced on him. The Frenchman, unruffled, did not flee, but awaited the attack. When the bear came close, he pulled a small pistol from his pocket, held it to the hungry beast's ear, and fired. The bear rolled over. People came running to open the door; Kirila Petrovich appeared, astonished by the outcome of his joke. He demanded a full explanation of the whole business, wanting to know if someone had alerted Desforges to the practical joke set up for him, and if not, why he was carrying a loaded pistol in his pocket. Masha was sent for. She came running, and translated her father's questions to the Frenchman.

"I had not heard of the bear," answered Desforges, "but I always carry a pistol on me because I do not intend to tolerate offenses for which, in view of my position, I cannot demand satisfaction."

Masha looked at him in amazement and translated his words for Kirila Petrovich. The latter made no answer. He gave orders to have the bear removed and skinned, and then, turning to his men, said, "Quite a character, isn't he! He didn't funk, did he, I'll be sworn."

From that time on he took a liking to Desforges and never thought of testing him again.

The incident made an even deeper impression on Maria Kirilovna. It stirred her imagination: she kept seeing in her mind's eye the dead bear, and Desforges, as he calmly stood over it and calmly conversed with her. She came to realize that courage and proud self-respect were not the exclusive attributes of one social class; and from that time on she began to show the young tutor her esteem, which was fast turning into favor. A certain relationship was established between them. Masha had a beautiful voice and great musical talent; Desforges offered to give her lessons. The reader will easily guess that after this Masha fell in love with the Frenchman, though for the time being she did not confess it even to herself.

Volume Two

9

The guests began to arrive the day before the holiday. Some stayed at the manor house or in one of its wings; others were put up at the steward's, or at the priest's, or at the houses of well-to-do peasants. The stables were full of horses, the yards and barns crowded with carriages of different shapes and sizes. At nine o'clock in the morning the bells rang for mass: everyone streamed toward the new stone church, built by Kirila Petrovich and annually improved by his new gifts. It was filled with such a large crowd of the honorable faithful that the simple peasants could not get in and had to stand either on the porch or in the churchyard. The mass had still not begun: they were waiting for Kirila Petrovich. At length he arrived in a coach-and-six and solemnly took his place, accompanied by Maria Kirilovna. The eyes of both men and women turned on her, the former marveling at her beauty, the latter carefully examining her dress. The mass commenced; the landlord's private singers sang in the choir, reinforced by his own voice now and then. Kirila Petrovich prayed, looking neither to the right nor to the left, and bowing to the ground with proud humility when the deacon referred, in a thunderous voice, to *the founder of this house of God.*

The mass was over. Kirila Petrovich went up to kiss the crucifix first. Everyone lined up after him; then all the neighbors filed by him to pay their respects. The ladies surrounded Masha. On leaving the church, Kirila Petrovich invited everybody to dine at his house, got into his carriage, and drove home. The whole crowd followed him. The rooms were soon filled with guests. New people arrived every minute and could hardly push their way through to the master of the house. The ladies, dressed according to yesterday's fashion, in expensive but worn garments, and bedecked with pearls and diamonds, sat decorously in a semicircle, while the men crowded around the caviar and the vodka, talking in loud, discordant tones. In the hall the table was laid for eighty. The servants were busily rushing about, arranging bottles and decanters and smoothing out tablecloths. At last the butler announced, "Dinner is served," and Kirila Petrovich went to take his place at the table first. The ladies followed after him, the matrons solemnly taking their places according to a system of seniority, while the unmarried girls huddled together like a flock of timid kids, and chose places next to one another. The men seated themselves on the opposite side. The tutor sat at the end of the table, next to little Sasha.

The waiters began to serve the dishes according to rank, resorting, in case of doubt, to guesses based on Lavater's system, and almost always hitting the mark.[18] The clinking of plates and spoons mingled with the guests' loud conversation. Kirila Petrovich looked merrily round the table, fully enjoying his happy role as a generous host. At this time a coach-and-six drove into the courtyard.

"Who is that?" asked the host.

"It's Anton Pafnutich," answered several voices.

The door opened and Anton Pafnutich Spitsyn, a fat man of fifty with a round, pockmarked face adorned with a triple chin, burst into the room, bowing and smiling, and ready to offer his apologies.

"Set a place right here," cried Kirila Petrovich. "Welcome, Anton Pafnutich; sit down and tell us what the meaning of all this is: you didn't come to my mass and are late for dinner. This is most unlike you, for you're both pious and fond of your stomach."

"Forgive me, please," answered Anton Pafnutich, tucking his napkin into a buttonhole of his pea-colored coat. "Excuse me, dear sir Kirila Petrovich: I did set out early for the journey, but I'd scarcely traveled ten versts when the rim on one of my front wheels broke into two: what was there to do? Fortunately, we weren't too far from a village, but even so, by the time we dragged the carriage there, sought out the blacksmith, and made repairs as best we could, full three hours had passed, there was no helping it. Not daring to drive straight across Kistenevka wood, I made a detour..."

"Aha!" interrupted Kirila Petrovich, "I see you're not a valiant knight. What are you afraid of?"

"What indeed, dear sir Kirila Petrovich! Dubrovskii, that's what! You can never tell when you might fall into his clutches. He's nobody's fool: he doesn't let people off lightly; and especially me, heaven help me, he would skin twice."

"Why, brother, such a distinction?"

"Why indeed, dear sir Kirila Petrovich! For the lawsuit, of course, against the late Andrei Gavrilovich. Wasn't I the one who, in order to please you, that is, according to my conscience and the truth, testified that the Dubrovskiis held possession of Kistenevka without any rights, thanks merely to your generosity? Already the late Andrei Gavrilovich (may he rest in peace) promised to have a word with me in his own fashion; do you think his son won't keep his father's promise? By God's grace I've been spared until now. So far they've plundered only one of my granaries, but you can never tell when they might find their way to the manor house."

"And when they do, they'll have a merry time," remarked Kirila Petrovich. "The little red coffer, methinks, is full to the brim."

"How could it be, my dear sir Kirila Petrovich? It used to be full, but by now it's entirely empty."

"Enough of fibbing, Anton Pafnutich. We know you all too well: what would you be spending money on? You live at home like a pig in a sty, never inviting anybody and fleecing your peasants; you do nothing but scrape and save, I'll vow."

"Surely, most worthy sir Kirila Petrovich, you are but jesting," muttered Anton Pafnutich with a smile. "God is my witness, I've been ruined."

Anton Pafnutich proceeded to swallow down his host's high-handed joke with a greasy mouthful of fishpie. Kirila Petrovich let him be, and turned to the new police superintendent, a guest at his house for the first time, and seated at the far end of the table, next to the tutor.

"Well, Mr. Superintendent, will you at last catch Dubrovskii?"

The superintendent winced, bowed, smiled, and said at length in a faltering voice, "We will do our best, Your Excellency."

"Hm, do your best. All of you have been doing your best for a long time, yet we've seen no results. And why should you wish to catch him, come to think of it? His robberies are sheer blessings for police superintendents: journeys, investigations, expeditions, all of it bringing grist to the mill. Why snuff out such a benefactor? Isn't that true, Mr. Superintendent?"

"That is the plain truth, Your Excellency," answered the superintendent, totally confused.

The guests burst into laughter.

"I like the lad for his sincerity," said Kirila Petrovich. "It's a pity they burned our late superintendent, Taras Alekseevich: the neighborhood would be more peaceful with him around. By the way, what do you hear about Dubrovskii? Where was he seen last?"

"At my house, Kirila Petrovich," resounded a lady's booming voice. "He dined at my house last Tuesday."

All eyes turned toward Anna Savishna Globova, a simplehearted widow whom everybody loved for her kind and cheerful disposition. Everyone waited for her story with interest.

"I should mention that three months ago I sent my steward to the post office to forward some money to my Vaniusha. I don't indulge my son, and wouldn't have the means for it even if I wanted to; but as you all know, an officer of the Guards must live decently, and so I try to share with my Vaniusha what little income I have. This time I sent him two thousand rubles. Dubrovskii did cross my mind more than once, but I say to myself: the town's close by, a mere seven versts; the money'll get through with God's help. But, come evening, I see my steward returning pale, all tattered, and on foot. 'Souse!' I cry. 'What's the matter? What's happened to you?' 'Dear ma'am Anna Savishna,' says he, 'the bandits robbed me; they all but killed me; Dubrovskii himself was there; he wanted to hang me, but took pity on me and let me go, but not before robbing me clean, and taking away even the horse and the cart.' My heart stood still: gracious goodness heavens, what'll my Vaniusha do? But there was no helping it: I wrote my son a letter, telling him all about it and sending him my blessing without as much as half a kopeck.

"A week went by, then another—suddenly a carriage drives into my yard. Some general's asking if he could see me: welcome, show him in. A man enters, aged about thirty-five, swarthy, with black hair, mustachios, and beard, just like a portrait of Kulnev;[19] introduces himself as a friend and former comrade of my late husband Ivan Andreevich. He was riding by, says he, and couldn't miss visiting his friend's widow, knowing that I live here. I treated him to whatever was in the house, and we talked about this and that, mentioning at last Dubrovskii, too. I told him about my misfortune. My general frowned. 'That's strange,' says he. 'What I've heard is that Dubrovskii attacks, not just anybody, but only men known for their riches; and even with them he divides the spoils, not robbing them clean; and as for murder, he's never been accused of that. Isn't there some mischief in this? Pray send for your steward.' We sent for the steward; he appeared; seeing the general he just stood rooted to the ground. 'Would you mind telling me, brother, just how it was Dubrovskii robbed you and wanted to hang you?' My steward went all a-tremble and threw himself at the general's feet. 'Gracious sir, I am guilty: it was the devil's work—I lied.' 'If that's so,' replied the general, 'then please be good enough to tell your lady how the whole thing happened, while I listen.' The steward could not recover his senses. 'Well,' continued the general, 'do tell us: where was it you met Dubrovskii?' 'At the two pines, my gracious sir, at the two pines.' 'And what did he say to you?' 'He asked me, whose man are you, where are you going, and what for?' 'Very well, and then?' 'And then he demanded the letter and the money.' 'Well?' 'I gave him the letter and the money.' 'And he? Well, and what did he do?' 'Gracious sir, I am guilty.' 'But what did he do?' 'He returned the money and letter to me, saying, move on, and God be with you; take them to the post office.' 'And what did you do?' 'Gracious sir, I am guilty.' 'I'll settle with you, friend,' said the general menacingly. 'And you, madam, be so good as to give orders to have this rascal's trunk searched; as for him, give him to me, I'll teach him a lesson. I want you to know that Dubrovskii used to be an officer of the Guards himself, and he would do no wrong to a former comrade.' I guessed who His Excellency was, but I wasn't going to enter into a discussion on that score. His coachmen tied the steward to his carriage box. The money was found; the general stayed to dine with me, and left right after dinner, taking the steward with him. They found the steward the next day in the woods, tied to an oak and stripped like a lime sapling."

Everybody, especially the young ladies, listened to Anna Savishna's story with bated breath. Many of them wished Dubrovskii well, seeing a romantic hero in him; this was especially true of Maria Kirilovna, an ardent dreamer, brought up on Radcliffe's mysterious horrors.[20]

"And you suppose, Anna Savishna, that it was Dubrovskii himself who visited you?" asked Kirila Petrovich. "You couldn't be further from the truth. I don't know who visited you, but it certainly wasn't Dubrovskii."

"How now, my dear sir? Who else if not Dubrovskii would take to the highways, stopping and searching travelers?"

"I don't know, but surely not Dubrovskii. I remember him as a child: he may have become dark haired since, though at that time he was a little boy with curly blond hair. But this I do know, that he was five years older than my Masha: consequently, he's not thirty-five, but about twenty-three."

"Exactly so, Your Excellency," declared the superintendent of police. "I have in my pocket Vladimir Dubrovskii's description, and it says precisely that he's in his twenty-third year."

"Ah!" said Kirila Petrovich. "Would you read that description while we listen: it wouldn't be amiss to know his distinctive marks, in case we run into him; we wouldn't want to let him slip away, would we?"

The superintendent drew from his pocket a rather soiled sheet of paper, solemnly unfolded it, and read in a singsong voice:

"Vladimir Dubrovskii's distinctive marks, taken down from the words of his former house serfs: He is in his twenty-third year of life, of medium *height*, with a clear *complexion*; he shaves his *beard*, his *eyes* are brown, his *hair* dark blond, and his *nose* straight. *Special distinctive marks*: said to have none."

"And that's all," said Kirila Petrovich.

"That is all," replied the superintendent, folding up the paper.

"Congratulations, Mr. Superintendent. What a splendid document! It'll indeed be a simple matter to find Dubrovskii by these distinctive marks. Who else, after all, is of medium height, with dark blond hair, straight nose, and brown eyes! I'll bet you could talk with Dubrovskii himself for three full hours, and not guess with whom fate has thrown you together. Verily I say, these officials are cunning fellows."

The superintendent meekly put the document in his pocket and silently turned to his goose with cabbage. The servants, in the meanwhile, had gone around the table several times, filling up glasses. Several bottles of Caucasian and Tsimlianskoe wines had been popped open and graciously accepted under the name of champagne;[21] the faces began to glow, and the conversation grew more and more noisy, disconnected, and merry.

"Nay," continued Kirila Petrovich, "we'll never see another superintendent like the late Taras Alekseevich! He was nobody's fool, nor an idiot. It's a pity they burned the lad: he wouldn't let a single one get away from the whole band. He would catch them to a man; even Dubrovskii himself couldn't slip away from him, or bribe his way out. Taras Alekseevich would take the money from him all right, but still wouldn't let him go: such was the character of the deceased. There's no other way, it seems: I'll have to take the matter into my own hands and go after the robbers with my servants. I'll dispatch twenty men to begin with; [22] they'll clean up the robbers' woods, for they're not what you might call timid fellows: each will take on a bear single-handed, so they're not likely to turn tail on some robbers."

"How is your bear, dear sir Kirila Petrovich?" asked Anton Pafnutich, reminded of a shaggy acquaintance and a certain practical joke of which he had once been the victim.

"Misha has succumbed," replied Kirila Petrovich. "He died an honorable death, at the hands of an adversary. And there sits his vanquisher." Kirila Petrovich pointed at Desforges. "You should buy a holy picture of the Frenchman's saint, for he's avenged your... craving your pardon... Do you remember?"

"How could I not remember?" said Anton Pafnutich, scratching himself. "I do, only too well. So Misha's dead. I'm sorry for him, upon my word I am. What a jester he was! and what a clever fellow! You'll never find another bear like him. And why did the *monsieur* kill him?"

Kirila Petrovich launched with great pleasure into the story of his Frenchman's exploit, for he had the happy faculty of priding himself on everything that surrounded him. The guests listened attentively to the tale of Misha's demise, and looked with surprise at Desforges, who, not suspecting that the subject of the conversation was his courage, calmly sat in his place, handing out admonitions to his restive charge.

The dinner, which had lasted about three hours, came to an end; the host put his napkin on the table; everyone rose and repaired to the drawing room, where coffee and cards were waiting for them, and where the drinking, so gloriously begun in the dining hall, continued.

10

About seven o'clock in the evening some of the guests wanted to leave, but the host, merry with drink, gave orders to lock the gates, letting nobody leave the house till morning. Soon, thunderous notes of music were heard; the doors were opened into the hall, and the dancing commenced. The host and his intimate circle sat in a corner, drinking glass after glass and watching with delight the gaiety of the young. The old ladies played cards. As usual, except where a brigade of uhlans is quartered, there were fewer cavaliers than ladies, and therefore every man at all fit to dance was recruited. The tutor distinguished himself above everybody, dancing more than anybody else;

the young ladies kept choosing him, and found him an adroit waltzing partner. He whirled around with Maria Kirilovna several times, so much so that the other young ladies began to make derisive comments about them. At length, about midnight, the tired host stopped the dancing, giving orders to serve supper, while he himself retired to bed.

Kirila Petrovich's absence lent a freer and livelier spirit to the company. The cavaliers took the liberty of sitting next to their ladies; the girls laughed and whispered comments to their neighbors; and the married women loudly conversed across the table. The men drank, argued, and roared with laughter—in other words, the supper turned out to be exceedingly joyous, leaving behind many pleasant memories.

There was only one person who did not take part in the general merriment: this was Anton Pafnutich, sitting in his place, gloomy and silent, eating absently and looking extremely worried. All that talk about robbers had stirred up his imagination. As we shall soon see, he had plenty of reason to fear them.

He had not sworn falsely in invoking God as his witness that his little red coffer was empty: it indeed was empty, because the money he used to keep in it had been transferred to a leather pouch, which he was wearing under his shirt around his neck. Only by this precaution was he able to still his suspicions and constant fear. Compelled to spend the night in a strange house, he was afraid that he might be assigned a bed somewhere in a remote room, easily accessible to thieves. He looked around for a roommate to protect him, and his choice fell on Desforges. The Frenchman's appearance, exuding strength, and, even more, the courage he had displayed in his encounter with the bear—a creature that Anton Pafnutich could not recall without trembling—were the decisive factors in his choice. When everybody rose from the table, Anton Pafnutich started circling around the young Frenchman, coughing and clearing his throat, until at last he turned to him with his request:

"Hm, hm, couldn't I, *monsieur*, spend the night in your little room, because, you see..."

"Que désire monsieur?" asked Desforges with a polite bow.

"Alack, it's a pity you haven't learned Russian yet, brother monsieur. Je veux, mois, chez vous coucher,[23] do you understand?"

"Monsieur, tres volontiers," replied Desforges. "Veuillez donner des ordres en conséquence."[24]

Anton Pafnutich, highly satisfied with his ability to communicate in French, immediately went off to make the necessary arrangements.

The guests wished one another good night, each going to the room assigned to him. Anton Pafnutich proceeded with the tutor to his wing. It was a dark night. Desforges lit the way with a lantern, and Anton Pafnutich followed behind him quite cheerfully, occasionally pressing the secret sum against his chest in order to be sure that the money was still there.

Arriving at the room, the tutor lit a candle, and both started undressing. In the meantime, Anton Pafnutich walked about the room to check on the door locks and the windows, and shaking his head at the disheartening results of his inspection. The only lock on the door was a latch, and the windows had not yet been fitted with double frames. He tried to complain about it to Desforges, but his knowledge of French was insufficient to convey such a complex matter; since the Frenchman did not understand him, he was compelled to stop complaining. Their beds stood opposite each other; both men lay down; and the tutor blew out the candle.

"Pourquoi vous touchez, pourquoi vous touchez," cried Anton Pafnutich, trying somehow to conjugate the Russian verb *tushu* in a French manner.[25] "I can't *dormir* in the dark."

But Desforges did not understand his exclamations and wished him good night.

"The damned infidel," grumbled Spitsyn, wrapping himself in his blanket. "Why did he have to blow out that candle? So much the worse for him. I can't sleep without a light. Monsieur, monsieur," he went on, "je veux avec vous parler."[26]

But the Frenchman did not answer and soon started snoring.

"Snoring, isn't he, the French beast," said Anton Pafnutich to himself. "And I can't even think of sleep. Thieves might come in through the unlocked door or climb through the window, and this beast couldn't be waked with a cannon."

"*Monsieur! Monsieur!* The deuce take you!"

At last Anton Pafnutich fell silent: fatigue and the effects of alcohol gradually overcame his fear; he dozed off and soon fell into a deep slumber.

A strange awakening came upon him. He felt, still in sleep, that someone was gently pulling at the collar of his shirt. Opening his eyes, he saw Desforges before him in the pale light of the autumn dawn: the Frenchman was holding a pocket pistol in one hand and unfastening the cherished treasure with the other. Anton Pafnutich's heart stood still.

"Qu'est-ce que c'est, monsieur, qu'est-ce que c'est?" he uttered in a trembling voice.[27]

"Hush, be quiet," answered the tutor in pure Russian. "Be quiet, or you're done for. I am Dubrovskii."

11

We shall now ask the reader for permission to explain the last events of our tale by certain previous occurrences that we have not yet had occasion to relate.

One day at the P. station, inside the house of the stationmaster whom we have mentioned earlier, there sat in a corner a traveler with a meek and patient air, which betrayed either a member of the third estate or a foreigner—in any case a person unable to assert his rights on the mail route. His carriage stood in the yard, waiting to be greased. A small suitcase—a meager token of less-than-comfortable circumstances—reposed in the carriage. The traveler did not ask for either tea or coffee; he just looked through the window and whistled—an action that greatly annoyed the stationmaster's wife, who was sitting behind the partition.

"The Lord blessed us with a whistler," she muttered. "Ugh, he does whistle, may he be struck dumb, the damned infidel."

"Surely, now" said the stationmaster, "it's no great matter: let him whistle."

"No great matter?" rejoined his wife crossly. "And don't you know what they say?"

"What do they say? That whistling drives money away? Nay, Pakhomovna, where there's no money, there's nobody'll drive it away. Where there isn't, there isn't."

"But let him go anyway, Sidorych. What makes you keep him here? Give him some horses and let him go to the devil!"

"He can wait, Pakhomovna: I've only three teams of horses in the stables, the fourth is resting. You can never tell, some better sort of traveler may turn up: I don't want to stick my neck out for a Frenchman. Ha! Just as I said! Here they come galloping. And how fast, too! As I live, it's a general!"

A carriage stopped by the porch. A footman jumped off the box and opened the door: soon a young man in a military coat and white cap came in to see the stationmaster; the footman brought in a traveling box after him and put it on the windowsill.

"Horses!" said the officer in an imperious voice.

"In just one moment," answered the stationmaster. "May I have your order?"

"I don't carry an order. I'm going to take a byroad. Don't you recognize me?"

The stationmaster began to bustle about and ran to hurry the coachmen. The young man paced up and down the room, then went behind the partition and softly asked the stationmaster's wife who the other traveler was.

"Heaven knows," she answered. "Some sort of Frenchman. He's been waiting for horses these five hours, whistling. I'm sick to death of the damned fool."

The young man addressed the traveler in French.

"May I ask where you are going?" he inquired.

"To the town nearby," replied the Frenchman, "and from there to a landowner who's hired me unseen as a tutor. I thought I'd reach my destination today, but evidently *monsieur* the stationmaster has decided otherwise. It's hard to find horses in this country, officer."

"And who among the local landowners has hired you?" asked the officer.

"Mr. Troekurov," replied the Frenchman.

"Mr. Troekurov? What sort of man is this Troekurov?"

"*Ma foi, mon officier...* I've heard little good about him. They say he's a proud and willful gentleman, cruel in his treatment of those in his service; apparently no one can get along with him; everyone trembles at the very sound of his name; and he's reported not to stand on ceremony with his tutors (*avec les outchitels*),[28] having already flogged two of them to death."

"Heaven help me! And you've decided to accept a position at the house of such a monster?"

"What else can I do, officer? He's offering me a good salary: three thousand rubles a year, plus room and board. Perhaps I'll be luckier than the others. I have an aged mother, for whose keep I shall be sending off half of my salary; from the rest I can accumulate in five years sufficient capital to secure my independence; and then, *bonsoir*, I'm going to Paris and set up in business."

"Does anybody know you at Troekurov's house?" asked the officer.

"Nobody," the tutor answered. "He had me sent down from Moscow through the good offices of an acquaintance, whose cook, a compatriot of mine, recommended me. I should mention that I had intended to become a confectioner, not a tutor, but I was told that in your country the calling of tutor is far more lucrative..."

The officer was lost in deep thought.

"Listen," he interrupted the Frenchman, "what would you say if instead of this prospective position someone offered you ten thousand rubles ready cash on condition that you immediately return to Paris?"

The Frenchman looked at the officer in astonishment, broke into a smile, and shook his head.

"The horses are ready," said the stationmaster, entering. The footman came in to confirm the same.

"Presently," said the officer. "Leave the room for a minute." The stationmaster and the footman both left. "I'm not joking," he continued in French. "I can pay you ten thousand rubles; all I ask in exchange are your absence and your papers." With these words he opened the traveling box and drew out several bundles of bank notes.

The Frenchman's eyes bulged. He did not know what to think.

"My absence and my papers..." he repeated in amazement. "Here are my papers... But you must be joking. What would you want my papers for?"

"That is my own business. I ask you: do you agree, or don't you?"

The Frenchman, still not believing his ears, handed his papers to the young officer, who examined them quickly.

"Your passport... That's good. A letter of recommendation. Let's see. Birth certificate: that's splendid. Well, here's your money; return home. Good-bye."

The Frenchman stood as if rooted to the ground.

The officer returned.

"I almost forgot the most important thing. Give me your word of honor that all this will remain between us. Your word of honor."

"I give you my word of honor," replied the Frenchman, "but what about my papers? How do I get by without them?"

"Report in the first town you come to that you were robbed by Dubrovskii. They will believe you and give you the necessary attestation. Farewell; may God grant you a safe and speedy journey to Paris, and may you find your mother in good health."

Dubrovskii left the room, got into his carriage, and galloped away.

The stationmaster looked out of the window, and when the carriage drove away, he turned to his wife with the exclamation, "What do you know, Pakhomovna! That was Dubrovskii!"

The postmistress dashed to the window, but it was already too late: Dubrovskii was far away. She started scolding her husband. "Don't you fear the Lord, Sidorych? Why didn't you tell me before, so I could've taken a good look at Dubrovskii? Now you can wait until kingdom come, he'll never drop in again. You have no conscience, have you?"

The Frenchman still stood as if rooted to the ground. The agreement with the officer, the money, and all the rest still seemed like a dream to him. But the bundles of bank notes were there, in his pocket, eloquently confirming that the amazing incident was real.

He decided to hire horses to the nearest town. The coachman drove him at a snail's pace, and it was night by the time they got there.

Before reaching the town gate, at which a broken sentry box stood instead of a guard, the Frenchman ordered the driver to stop, got out of the carriage, and set out to go the rest of the way on foot, explaining to the coachman by hand signs that he was giving him both the carriage and the suitcase as a tip. The driver was as much astounded by the Frenchman's generosity as the Frenchman had been by Dubrovskii's offer. He came to the conclusion, however, that the *German* had gone out of his mind; he thanked him with a profound bow and, not thinking it wise to ride into town, proceeded to a house of entertainment he knew, whose landlord was an intimate friend of his. There he spent the night; the next morning he went on his way with his team of horses, without the carriage or the suitcase, but with swollen cheeks and red eyes.

Dubrovskii, having obtained the Frenchman's papers, boldly presented himself, as we have seen, at Troekurov's house and settled there. Whatever his secret intentions might have been (we shall learn them later), his conduct was blameless. It is true that he did not pay much attention to little Sasha's education, giving free rein to the boy's pranks and leniently listening to recitations of lessons that had been assigned only for appearances' sake, but he followed with particular attention his female pupil's progress in music, sitting with her by the piano for hours at a time. Everyone liked the young tutor: Kirila Petrovich for his daring agility in hunting; Maria Kirilovna for his boundless zeal and timid attentiveness; Sasha for his lenience toward his pranks; and the servants for his good nature and a generosity that seemed incompatible with his station. He himself appeared to have grown attached to the whole family and regarded himself as one of its members.

About a month had passed between the time he had taken up the calling of tutor and the memorable holiday feast; yet no one suspected that the modest young Frenchman was in fact the dreaded robber whose name alone was enough to strike terror in the hearts of all the landowners of the neighborhood. All through that month Dubrovskii had not left Pokrovskoe, yet rumors about his robberies did not stop circulating, thanks perhaps to the inventive imagination of local people, or perhaps because his band continued its exploits even in the absence of its chief.

When, however, he found himself spending the night in the same room with a man whom he had every reason to regard as a personal enemy and one of the chief architects of his misfortune, Dubrovskii could not resist the temptation: he knew about the existence of the pouch and resolved to lay his hands on it. We have seen how he astounded poor Anton Pafnutich by his unexpected metamorphosis from tutor into robber.

At nine o'clock in the morning the guests who had spent the night at Pokrovskoe began to gather in the drawing room, where a samovar was already boiling; seated before it were Maria Kirilovna, in her morning dress, and Kirila Petrovich, in a flannel jacket and slippers, drinking his tea from a cup as wide as a slopbasin. The last to appear was Anton Pafnutich; he looked so pale and seemed so downcast that everybody was struck by his appearance, and Kirila Petrovich even inquired after his health. Spitsyn gave an incoherent answer and kept glancing with horror at the tutor, who sat there as if nothing had happened. In a few minutes a servant came in to announce that Spitsyn's carriage was ready; Anton Pafnutich hastened to make his farewell bows and, despite his host's protestations, hurried from the room in order to drive off immediately. Nobody could understand what had happened to him; Kirila Petrovich eventually decided that he must have overeaten. After tea and a farewell breakfast, the other guests began to take their leave, and Pokrovskoe became deserted, everything returning to normal.

12

Nothing remarkable happened for several days. Life at Pokrovskoe had its routine. Kirila Petrovich rode out to hunt every day; and Maria Kirilovna was occupied with reading, walks, and above all, music lessons. She was beginning to understand her own heart, confessing to herself with involuntary vexation that she was by no means indifferent to the young Frenchman's good qualities. On his part he never allowed himself to step beyond the limits of respect and strict propriety, which both flattered her pride and reassured her, beset as she was with alarming doubts. She gave herself over to her days' absorbing routine with more and more confidence. She felt listless when Desforges was not there; and in his presence gave him her full attention, wishing to know his opinion about everything, and always agreeing with him. Maybe she was not yet in love, but her passion was ready to flare up at the first sign of an accidental obstacle or an unexpected twist of fate.

One day, as she entered the room where the tutor waited for her, she was surprised to see signs of confusion on his pale face. She lifted the lid of the piano and sang a few notes, but Dubrovskii, excusing himself with a headache, interrupted the lesson; and as he folded over the sheet of music he surreptitiously slipped a letter into her hand. Maria Kirilovna, given no time to refuse it, took the letter; she immediately regretted it, but by that time Dubrovskii had left the room. She went to her room, opened the letter, and read the following: "Come to the arbor by the brook at seven o'clock this evening. I must speak to you."

Her curiosity was strongly piqued. She had long expected a confession, both wishing for it and fearing it. She would have enjoyed hearing a confirmation of what she had suspected, but she was conscious that it would be improper for her to listen to such a declaration on the part of a man who, due to his station, could never hope to gain her hand. She resolved to go to the rendezvous, but was not sure how to receive the tutor's confession: whether to respond with aristocratic indignation, friendly remonstrances, light banter, or silent sympathy. In the meanwhile she kept looking at the clock every minute. It grew dark; the candles were lit; Kirila Petrovich sat down to play Boston with some neighbors who had driven over. The clock on the table struck a quarter to seven. Maria Kirilovna inconspicuously stepped out on the porch, looked around her in all directions, and ran into the garden.

The night was dark, the sky covered with clouds, and one could not see two steps ahead, but Maria Kirilovna could make her way along familiar paths even in the dark. It took her only a minute to reach the arbor. Here she stopped to catch her breath so as to be able to meet Desforges with an indifferent and unhurried air. But Desforges was already standing before her.

"I am grateful to you," he said in a low and sad tone, "for not refusing my request. I would have fallen into despair if you had decided not to come."

Maria Kirilovna answered with the ready phrase, "I hope you will not make me regret my compliance."

He stood in silence, as if to gather his thoughts.

"Circumstances demand... I must leave you," he said at last. "Soon, you will probably learn the reason yourself... But before we part I owe you an explanation."

Maria Kirilovna made no answer. She took these words as an introduction to the confession she had expected.

"I am not who you think I am," he confessed, lowering his head. "I am not the Frenchman Desforges: I am Dubrovskii."

She let out a shriek.

"Don't be afraid, for heaven's sake: you need not fear my name. Yes, I am the unfortunate person whom your father has deprived of his last piece of bread, driven from his parental home, and sent on the highways to rob. But you need not fear me, either for yourself or for him. The matter is closed. I have forgiven him, and mark you, it was you who saved him. My first bloody act ought to have been directed against him. I prowled around his house, determining where the fire should start, which way to get into his bedroom, and how to cut off all his routes of escape, but at that moment you passed by me like a heavenly vision, and forgiveness filled my heart. I understood that the house where you lived was sacred, and that no being related to you by the bond of blood could be subject to my curse. I renounced vengeance as madness. For days I roamed near the Pokrovskoe gardens in the hope of catching sight of your white dress at a distance. I followed you on your incautious walks, stealing from bush to bush and feeling elated at the thought that I was guarding you, that there could be no danger for you where I was secretly present. At last an opportunity presented itself. I came to live in your house. These three weeks have been a period of happiness for me. Recalling them will always be a consolation amid my sad days... News that I have received today makes it impossible for me to stay here any longer. I take leave of you today... at this very moment... But first I had to reveal my thoughts to you, so that you might not curse or despise me. Think of Dubrovskii sometimes; be assured that he was born for a different destiny, that his soul was capable of loving you, that he would never..."

Just then a low whistle was heard, and Dubrovskii fell silent. He seized her hand and pressed it to his burning lips. The whistle was repeated.

"Farewell," said Dubrovskii; "they're calling me, and a minute's delay may bring my downfall."

He walked away, while Maria Kirilovna stood motionless. Then he came back and took her hand again.

"If any time in the future," he said to her in a gentle, touching voice, "if at any time misfortune befalls you and you cannot expect help or protection from anyone, will you promise me that in such a case you will turn to me and demand all that I am capable of, in order to rescue you? Will you promise not to scorn my devotion?"

Maria Kirilovna wept in silence. The whistle was heard a third time.

"You're bringing my downfall on me!" cried Dubrovskii. "I will not leave you until you give me an answer. Will you, or will you not, promise?"

"I promise," whispered the poor beauty.

Maria Kirilovna, agitated by her meeting with Dubrovskii, walked back toward the house. She realized that the servants were all running about; the whole house was in a commotion; there were a lot of people in the courtyard; and a carriage stood by the porch. She could hear Kirila Petrovich's voice at a distance, and she hurried inside, fearing that her absence might be noticed. She was met by Kirila Petrovich in the hall. His guests stood around the superintendent of police—our acquaintance—and showered him with questions. The superintendent, dressed for the road and armed to the teeth, gave his answers with a mysterious and preoccupied air.

"Where've you been, Masha?" asked Kirila Petrovich. "Did you happen to see Monsieur Desforges?"

Masha could just barely utter a negative reply.

"Just imagine," continued Kirila Petrovich, "the superintendent's come to capture him, and he's trying to convince me that the man is Dubrovskii himself."

"He fits the description exactly, Your Excellency," said the superintendent respectfully.

"Pooh, friend!" interrupted Kirila Petrovich. "I'll tell you where to go with your descriptions! I'm not going to hand my Frenchman over to you until I've sorted this matter out myself. You can't take on trust what Anton Pafnutich says, for he's a coward and a liar: he must have just dreamed that the tutor wanted to rob him. Why didn't he say a single word about it to me that morning?"

"The Frenchman scared the life out of him, Your Excellency," answered the superintendent, "and made him swear to keep mum..."

"A pack of lies," declared Kirila Petrovich. "I'll clear up the matter this minute. Where's that tutor?" he said, turning to a servant who was just entering.

"He can't be found anywhere, sir," answered the servant.

"Then go and search for him," shouted Troekurov, beginning to entertain some doubts. "Show me your touted description," he said to the superintendent, who immediately produced the paper. "Hm, hm. Twenty-three years... Well, that's correct, but it doesn't prove anything by itself. Well, where is that tutor?"

"They can't find him," was the answer once more.

Kirila Petrovich began to grow anxious. Maria Kirilovna looked more dead than alive.

"You're pale, Masha," remarked her father. "You've been frightened."

"No, papa," replied Masha, "I just have a headache."

"Go to your room, Masha, and don't be alarmed."

Masha kissed his hand and retired to her room, where she threw herself on the bed and burst into hysterical sobs. The maidservants came running; they undressed her, and with difficulty managed to calm her by means of cold water and all kinds of spirits. They put her to bed, and she finally settled into sleep.

The Frenchman had still not been found during all this time. Kirila Petrovich paced up and down the hall, dourly whistling "May thou, thunder of victory, rumble." The guests whispered among themselves; the superintendent looked foolish; and the Frenchman was still not to be found. Evidently he had managed to escape, having been warned. But by whom and how—that remained a mystery.

The clock struck eleven, but nobody even thought of going to bed. At length Kirila Petrovich angrily said to the superintendent, "Surely now, you can't stay here till morning. My house is not a tavern. It'd take a smarter man than you, lad, to catch Dubrovskii, if he is indeed Dubrovskii. Off with you now, and be a little quicker in the future. And it's time for you, too, to go home," he continued, turning to his guests. "Give orders to have your horses hitched up: I want to go to bed."

It was in this ungracious manner that Troekurov parted with his guests.

13

Some time went by without anything remarkable happening. At the beginning of the following summer, however, some great changes occurred in Kirila Petrovich's family life.

At a distance of thirty versts from Pokrovskoe there was a prosperous estate owned by Prince Vereiskii. The Prince had spent a long time abroad, leaving the management of his estate to a retired major, and thus there had been no commerce between Pokrovskoe and Arbatovo. At the end of May, however, the Prince returned from abroad and came to live on his estate, which he had never seen before. Used to a life full of distractions, he could not bear solitude, and on the third day after his arrival he came over to dine with Troekurov, whom he used to know at one time.

The Prince was about fifty but looked much older. Excesses of all kinds had undermined his health and left on him their indelible

mark. His outward appearance was nevertheless pleasant, even remarkable; and having spent his whole life in society, he had acquired
a certain charm, especially in his dealings with women. He had a constant need for distractions and was constantly bored. Kirila Petrovich
was highly gratified by his visit, taking it as a mark of respect from a
man who mingled in high society; and he treated him, as was his
habit, to a tour of his various establishments, including his dog kennels. But the Prince almost suffocated in the canine atmosphere and
hastened to quit it, holding a scented handkerchief to his nose. The
old-fashioned garden with its pruned lime trees, square-shaped pond,
and symmetrical paths did not please him, since he was fond of English gardens and so-called nature; but he nonetheless handed out
compliments and showed enthusiasm. A servant came to announce
that the meal was served. They went to dine. Exhausted by his walk,
the Prince limped along, already regretting his visit.

In the dining hall, however, Maria Kirilovna met them, and the old
skirt chaser was struck by her beauty. Troekurov seated his guest next
to her. Her presence revived the Prince: he was cheerful company and
managed to capture her attention several times with interesting anecdotes. After dinner Kirila Petrovich suggested a ride on horseback, but
the Prince excused himself, pointing at his velvet boots and half-
jokingly complaining of gout; in fact he preferred a pleasure ride in a
carriage, which would not separate him from his charming neighbor.
The horses were hitched to the carriage. The two old men and the
young beauty got in and rode off. The conversation never flagged. Maria Kirilovna was listening with pleasure to the flattering and humorous compliments this man of the world was offering her, when suddenly Vereiskii turned to Kirila Petrovich and asked him what that
burned-down building was and to whom it belonged. Kirila Petrovich
frowned: the recollections evoked by the burned-down homestead
were unpleasant to him. He answered that the land was now his, but
earlier it used to belong to Dubrovskii.

"To Dubrovskii?" repeated Vereiskii. "To the famous robber?"

"To the robber's father," answered Troekurov, "who was pretty
much of a robber himself."

"Incidentally, what's become of our Rinaldo?[29] Is he alive? Has he
been captured?"

"Both alive and at large; and won't be caught either, whilst we have
police superintendents who are in collusion with brigands. By the
way, Prince, Dubrovskii has paid a visit to your Arbatovo, hasn't he?"

"Yes, last year, if I'm not mistaken, he burned down something or

plundered something. Wouldn't it be interesting, though, Maria Kirilovna, to make the acquaintance of this romantic hero?"

"Wouldn't it, indeed!" said Troekurov. "She is acquainted with
him: he gave her music lessons for three weeks, without, thanks to
God, taking any wages."

Kirila Petrovich launched into his story about the French tutor. Maria Kirilovna sat on pins and needles. Vereiskii listened to it all with
great interest, found it all very strange, and changed the topic. On
their return to the house, he gave orders to have his carriage made
ready and, despite Kirila Petrovich's earnest entreaties to stay the
night, left right after tea. Before he did so, however, he had asked
Kirila Petrovich to pay him a visit with Maria Kirilovna; and the
haughty Troekurov had accepted the invitation because, considering
the Prince's title, two stars, and ancestral estate with 3,000 serfs, he
regarded him to some degree as his equal.

Two days after this occasion Kirila Petrovich set out with his
daughter to repay the visit. Approaching Arbatovo, he could not help
admiring the peasants' clean and cheerful cottages and the landlord's
stone house, built in the style of an English castle. Before the house
there stretched a rich green meadow, on which Swiss cows grazed,
tinkling their bells. An extensive park surrounded his house on all
sides. The host came out on the porch to greet his guests, and shook
hands with the beautiful young girl. They entered the magnificent
dining hall, where the table was set for three. The host led his guests
up to a window, from which they beheld a charming view. The Volga
flowed below; heavily loaded barges under full sail floated on it; and
here and there small fishing vessels, aptly called smack boats,[30] could
be glimpsed fleetingly. Hills and fields stretched beyond the river,
with some villages enlivening the landscape. Then the host and his
guests went to look at the gallery of paintings the Prince had bought
abroad. The Prince explained to Maria Kirilovna what the different
pictures signified; told her the life stories of the painters; and pointed
out the merits and shortcomings of their canvases. He spoke about
the paintings, not in the pedant's abstract language, but with feeling
and imagination. Maria Kirilovna listened to him with pleasure. They
went in to dine. Troekurov fully appreciated both the wines of this
Amphitryon and the artistry of his cook;[31] and Maria Kirilovna did
not feel the slightest embarrassment or constraint in conversing with
a man whom she had seen only once before. After dinner the host proposed that they repair to the garden. They drank coffee in an arbor on
the shore of a wide lake, which was strewn with islands. Suddenly the

sound of a wind ensemble could be heard, and a six-oared boat drew up to moor right by the arbor. They went boating on the lake, passing by some islands and landing on others. On one they found a marble statue, on another a secluded cave, and on a third a monument with a mysterious inscription that piqued Maria Kirilovna's curiosity, but she was left to wonder by the Prince's polite half-explanations. Time passed imperceptibly; it began to grow dark. The Prince, under the pretext of chill and damp air, urged them to return home, where the samovar was waiting for them. He asked Maria Kirilovna to assume the role of hostess in the house of an old bachelor. She poured the tea, listening to the amiable chatterer's endless stories; suddenly a shot was heard and a rocket illuminated the sky. The Prince handed Maria Kirilovna her shawl, inviting her and her father to come out on the balcony. In the dark, in front of the house, fireworks of different colors flared up, began to spin, rose upward in the shape of ears of grain, palm trees, fountains, then scattered like drops of rain or falling stars, now extinguished, now flaring up anew. Maria Kirilovna enjoyed herself like a child. Prince Vereiskii was pleased with her delight; and Troekurov felt no less satisfied, for he took *tous les frais*[32] of the Prince as gestures of respect and homage paid to him.

The quality of the supper was in no way inferior to that of the dinner. The guests retired to the rooms assigned to them, and in the morning took leave of their amiable host amidst mutual promises to meet again.

14

Maria Kirilovna was sitting over her embroidery by the open window of her room. Unlike Konrad's mistress, who in her amorous distraction embroidered a rose in green,[33] Maria did not get her silk mixed up. Under her needle, the canvas unerringly reproduced the features of the original, even though her thoughts were far away.

Suddenly a hand was thrust through the window, quietly depositing a letter on her embroidery frame and disappearing again, before Maria Kirilovna realized what was happening. At the same moment a servant entered to call her to Kirila Petrovich. She hid the letter under her kerchief with a trembling hand and hurried to her father's study.

Kirila Petrovich was not by himself. Prince Vereiskii sat with him. When Maria Kirilovna appeared, the Prince stood up and silently bowed to her with an air of embarrassment that was unusual for him.

"Come here, Masha," said Kirila Petrovich. "I have some news, which, I hope, will gladden you. Here is a suitor for you; the Prince is asking for your hand."

Masha stood rooted to the ground; a deathly pallor spread over her face. She kept her silence. The Prince went up to her, took her hand, and asked in a touched tone whether she would consent to make him happy. Masha kept her silence.

"Consent? Of course, she'll consent," said Kirila Petrovich. "But you know, Prince, how difficult it is for a girl to pronounce that word. Well, children, kiss each other and be happy."

Masha stood motionless; the old Prince kissed her hand; then suddenly tears coursed down her pale cheeks. The Prince frowned slightly.

"Go to your room, go to your room," said Kirila Petrovich; "wipe your tears and join us again all happy. They all cry when they get engaged," he continued, turning to Vereiskii. "This is a custom with them. And now, Prince, let's talk business, that is, let's discuss the dowry."

Maria Kirilovna eagerly availed herself of the opportunity to retire. She ran to her room, locked herself in, and let her tears flow freely as she imagined herself in the position of the old Prince's wife: he had suddenly become repugnant and hateful to her, and the thought of marrying him was as terrifying as the executioner's block or the grave...

"No, and a thousand times no," she repeated to herself in despair. "I'd sooner die, I'd sooner retire to a convent, I'd sooner marry Dubrovskii."

This reminded her of the letter, and she eagerly started reading it, sensing that it must be from him. It was indeed written by him and consisted only of the following words:

"Ten o'clock this evening at the same place."

15

The moon was shining. It was a still July night. The wind rose now and then, and a light rustle ran over the entire garden.

Like a light shadow, the young beauty drew near the appointed meeting place. Nobody was yet in sight. Suddenly Dubrovskii, coming out from behind the arbor, appeared in front of her.

"I know all about it," he said to her in a soft, sad voice. "Do remember your promise."

"You are offering me your protection," answered Masha. "Don't feel offended, but that frightens me. In what way can you help me?"

"I could rid you of the hateful man."

"For heaven's sake, don't touch him, don't dare touch him if you love me. I don't want to be the cause of some horrible deed..."

"I will not touch him: your wish is sacred to me. He owes his life to you. No evil deed will ever be committed in your name. You must remain blameless, whatever my crimes are. But how can I save you from a cruel father?"

"There is still some hope. Perhaps I can touch him with my tears and despair. He is obstinate, but he loves me so much."

"Do not hope in vain: in your tears he will see only the usual timidity and revulsion common to young girls when they marry not from love but from careful calculation. What if he takes it into his head to make you happy despite yourself? What if they lead you to the altar by force, putting your life forever into the hands of an old husband?"

"Then... then there is nothing else we can do: come for me, and I will be your wife."

Dubrovskii trembled. A crimson flush spread across his pale face, which, in the next moment, became even paler than before. He remained silent for a long time, with his head bent.

"Summon up all your spiritual strength, beseech your father, throw yourself at his feet, depict for him the full horror of the future, your youth fading by the side of a decrepit and corrupt old man; bring yourself even to a cruel explanation: tell him that if he remains unbending, then... then you will find a terrible deliverance; tell him that riches will not bring you one moment of happiness; that luxury gladdens only the poor, and even them for only a short time while they are still not used to it; don't stop pestering him, don't be afraid of his anger or threats while there is still a faint glimmer of hope, for heaven's sake, don't stop pestering him. But if there is really no other way..."

Here Dubrovskii covered his face with his hands and seemed to be gasping for air. Masha wept...

"My unhappy, unhappy destiny," he said with a bitter sigh. "I would give my life for you; just to see you from a distance, to touch your hand used to be ecstasy for me. And now, when there might be an opportunity for me to clasp you to my agitated heart and say, 'Angel! Let us die together!'—now I have to beware of happiness, have to avoid it, unlucky creature that I am, by every means possible. I dare not throw myself at your feet and thank heaven for an inexplicable, undeserved reward. Oh, how I ought to hate the man who... but I feel that at this moment there can be no room for hatred in my heart."

He gently put his arm around her slender waist and gently drew her to his heart. She leaned her head trustingly on the young robber's shoulder. Both were silent.

Time flew.

"I must go," said Masha at last.

Dubrovskii seemed to be waking from a trance. He took her hand and slipped a ring on her finger.

"If you decide to resort to my help," he said, "bring this ring here and drop it into the hollow of this oak. Then I shall know what to do."

Dubrovskii kissed her hand and disappeared among the trees.

16

Prince Vereiskii's marriage proposal was no longer a secret in the neighborhood. Kirila Petrovich received congratulations, and preparations for the wedding were going forward. Day after day Masha postponed making a decisive declaration. In the meanwhile her manner with her old suitor was cold and strained. The Prince did not seem to mind. He made no effort to inspire love: all he wished for was her tacit consent.

But time was passing. At length Masha decided to act, and wrote a letter to Prince Vereiskii: she tried to awaken magnanimity in his heart, openly confessing that she had not the least inclination toward him, and beseeching him to give her up himself and thereby protect her from the tyranny of her father. She surreptitiously handed the letter to Prince Vereiskii. He read it in private and was not in the least touched by his fiancée's frankness. On the contrary, he realized that it was necessary to hold the wedding earlier, and for that reason thought it advisable to show the letter to his future father-in-law.

Kirila Petrovich flew into a rage; the Prince had great difficulty persuading him not to let on to Masha that he had been informed of the letter. Eventually Kirila Petrovich agreed not to speak about it to her, but he resolved not to waste time and fixed the wedding for the next day. The Prince found the idea well-advised. He came to see his fiancée and told her that her letter had greatly saddened him, but that he was hoping to win her affections with time; that the thought of losing her would be too much for him to bear; and that he simply did not have the strength to sign his own death warrant. After this he respectfully kissed her hand and left for home, not saying a word to her about her father's decision.

He was scarcely past the gate, however, when her father entered her room and commanded her without further ado to be ready for the next day. Maria Kirilovna, already agitated by Prince Vereiskii's explanation, burst into tears and threw herself at her father's feet.

"Papa," she cried in a plaintive voice, "papa, don't ruin me; I don't love the Prince and don't want to be his wife."

"What is the meaning of this?" said Kirila Petrovich sternly. "Until now you've kept silent and been in agreement, but now, when everything is decided, you take it into your head to behave capriciously and start refusing him. Don't play the fool: it'll get you nowhere with me."

"Don't ruin me," repeated poor Masha. "Why are you driving me from you, handing me over to a man I don't love? Have you grown so tired of me? I want to remain with you as before. Papa, it'll be sad for you without me, and sadder still when you remember that I'm unhappy, papa; don't force me, I don't want to get married..."

Kirila Petrovich was touched, but concealed his feelings and pushed her away, saying severely, "All this is nonsense, do you hear? I know better than you what you need for happiness. Your tears won't help: your wedding will be the day after tomorrow."

"The day after tomorrow!" exclaimed Masha. "My dear God! No, no, that's impossible, it cannot be. Papa, listen to me, if you are resolved to ruin me, I will find a protector, one you can't even think of, and you will see, you will be horrified to see, what you have driven me to."

"What? What is this?" said Troekurov. "Threats? Are you threatening me, insolent wench? Well, let me tell you, I'm going to do something with you that you haven't even dreamed of. You dare try to scare me with a protector? We will see who this protector will be."

"Vladimir Dubrovskii," replied Masha in her despair.

Kirila Petrovich thought she must have lost her mind and stared at her in astonishment.

"Very well," he said to her after a pause. "Wait for whoever you think will deliver you; but in the meanwhile sit in this room, which you're not going to leave until the very moment of your wedding."

With these words Kirila Petrovich left and locked the door behind him.

The poor girl wept for a long time, imagining the fate awaiting her. The tempestuous exchange with her father had, however, lightened her heart; she could now view her situation more calmly and consider what she needed to do. The main thing was to escape the odious wedding: the life of a robber's wife seemed like paradise to her in comparison with the fate they were preparing for her. She glanced at the ring

Dubrovskii had left with her. She fervently wished to see him alone and consult with him once more before the decisive moment. A presentiment told her that she could find him in the garden near the arbor that evening, and she resolved to wait for him there as soon as it became dark. It grew dark. Masha got ready to go, but her door was locked. The chambermaid answered from behind it that Kirila Petrovich had given orders not to let her out. She was under arrest. Deeply insulted, she sat down by her window and stayed there late into the night without undressing, with her eyes fixed on the dark sky. At dawn she dozed off, but her light sleep was troubled by melancholy visions, and the rays of the rising sun soon awakened her.

17

Her first waking thought brought back to mind the full horror of her situation. She rang for her maid, who came in and told her in response to her questions that last night Kirila Petrovich had driven over to Arbatovo and returned late; that he had given strict instructions not to let her out of her room and not to let her speak with anyone; and that, incidentally, no particular preparations for the wedding were evident except for an order given to the priest not to leave the village under any circumstances. After communicating these pieces of information the maid left Maria Kirilovna, once more locking the door on her.

The maid's words embittered the young prisoner. Her brain seething and her blood boiling, she resolved to let Dubrovskii know about everything, and began to look for some means of conveying the ring into the secret hollow of the oak. At that moment a pebble hit her window, clinking against the pane. Looking out into the yard, Maria Kirilovna saw little Sasha making furtive signs at her. Sure of his attachment to her, she was glad to see him and opened the window.

"Hello, Sasha," she said. "Why are you calling me?"

"I came to find out, sister, if you need anything. Papa is cross and forbade the whole household to take orders from you, but you just tell me what you want, and I'll do anything."

"Thank you, my dear Sashenka. Listen: do you know the old hollow oak close to the arbor?"

"Yes, sister, I do."

"Well, then, if you love me, run down there and put this ring in the hollow. Take care, though, not to let anybody see you."

With these words she threw the ring to him and closed the window.

The boy picked up the ring, dashed off with all his might, and in three minutes reached the secret tree. Once there, he stopped, caught his breath, looked around on every side, and placed the ring in the hollow. Having safely accomplished his task, he was about to report back to Maria Kirilovna, but suddenly a little red-haired, cross-eyed boy, in tattered clothes, darted out from behind the arbor, dashed to the oak, and thrust his hand into the hollow. Sasha, faster than a squirrel, pounced on him and dug his nails into him.

"What are you doing here?" he asked menacingly.

"None of your business," answered the boy, trying to get away from him.

"Leave that ring alone, ginger-head," shouted Sasha, "or else I'll show you who you've picked a fight with."

Instead of answering him, the boy struck him in the face, but Sasha did not let go and started yelling with all his might, "Help, thief! Help, thief!"

The boy struggled to free himself. He was, apparently, a couple of years older and much stronger than Sasha, but Sasha was more agile. They fought for several minutes, until at last the red-haired boy gained the upper hand. He threw Sasha on the ground and seized him by the throat.

At this moment, however, a strong hand grabbed the boy by his frizzy red hair, and the gardener Stepan lifted him off the ground by half an *arshin*.[34]

"You red-haired devil," said the gardener. "How dare you beat the young master?"

By this time, Sasha had jumped to his feet and recovered himself.

"You got me under my arms," he said; "otherwise you'd never have thrown me down. Give me the ring at once and get out of here."

"Not likely," answered the redhead and, suddenly twisting himself around, he freed his frizzy locks from Stepan's hand. He tried to run away, but Sasha caught up with him and pushed him in the back so that the boy fell flat on his face. The gardener seized him once more and tied him up with his belt.

"Give me the ring!" shouted Sasha.

"Wait, young master," said Stepan. "Let's take him to the steward for him to sort this matter out."

The gardener led the prisoner into the courtyard, accompanied by Sasha, who kept anxiously looking at his trousers, torn and stained by grass. Suddenly all three found themselves face to face with Kirila Petrovich, who was on his way to inspect the stables.

"What's going on?" he asked Stepan.

Stepan described the incident in a few words. Kirila Petrovich listened attentively.

"You scapegrace," he turned to Sasha. "Why did you get into a fight with him?"

"He stole the ring from the hollow of the tree, papa; tell him to give it back to me."

"What ring, from what hollow?"

"Well, the one Maria Kirilovna... the ring that..."

Sasha became confused, and stammered. Kirila Petrovich frowned and said, shaking his head, "So Maria Kirilovna is mixed up in this. Confess everything, or else I'll give you such a thrashing that your own mother won't recognize you."

"I swear by God, papa, I, papa... Maria Kirilovna didn't send me on any errands, papa."

"Stepan, go and cut me some good fresh birch switches."

"Wait, papa, I'll tell you everything. As I was running about the yard today, Sis Maria Kirilovna opened her window, and I ran under it, and she accidentally dropped a ring, and I hid it in the hollow of the tree, and... and... this redhead wanted to steal it..."

"She dropped it accidentally, did she? And you wanted to hide it? Stepan, go and get those switches."

"Wait, papa, I'll tell you everything. Sis Maria Kirilovna told me to run down to the oak and put the ring in the hollow, and I ran and put it in, but this horrid boy..."

Kirila Petrovich turned to the horrid boy and asked menacingly, "Whose are you?"

"I am a house serf of the masters Dubrovskii," answered the red-haired boy.

A cloud came over Kirila Petrovich's face.

"So you don't acknowledge me as your master. Very well. And what were you doing in my garden?"

"I was stealing raspberries," answered the boy with perfect equanimity.

"Aha, like master, like servant; like priest, like people. And do you find raspberries growing on oak trees in my garden?"

The boy made no reply.

"Papa, tell him to give me the ring," said Sasha.

"Be quiet, Aleksandr," answered Kirila Petrovich, "and don't forget I'm still planning to settle accounts with you. Go to your room. And you, squint-eyes, it seems to me you're nobody's fool. Give me the ring and go home."

The boy opened his fist to show that there was nothing in his hand.

"If you confess everything to me, I will not thrash you; I shall even give you a five-kopeck piece to buy some nuts with. But if you don't, I'll do something to you that you've never even imagined. Well?"

The boy made no reply; just stood with his head inclined and with the air of a perfect simpleton.

"Very well," said Kirila Petrovich, "lock him up somewhere, but watch out, don't let him run away, or else I'll skin every one of you."[35]

Stepan led the boy off to the dovecote, locked him up there, and posted the old poultrywoman Agafia to watch over him.

"And now we must send to town for the superintendent," said Kirila Petrovich as he followed the boy with his eyes, "and do it as fast as possible."

"There can be no doubt. She has kept in touch with that damned Dubrovskii. But was she really trying to call for his help?" mused Kirila Petrovich, pacing up and down his room and angrily whistling "May thou, thunder of victory..." "But perhaps I am at last hot on his track, and from us he won't slip away. We'll seize the opportunity. Ha! A bell! Thank God, this must be the superintendent.—Hey, bring that captured boy in here!"

In the meanwhile a cart had driven into the courtyard, and our acquaintance the superintendent, all covered with dust, came into the room.

"Wonderful news," said Kirila Petrovich to him. "I've caught Dubrovskii."

"Praises be to God, Your Excellency," said the superintendent, overjoyed. "Where is he?"

"Well, not exactly Dubrovskii, but one of his band. They'll bring him in presently. He'll help me catch the robber chief himself. Here he is."

The superintendent, who had expected a ferocious brigand, was astonished to see a thirteen-year-old boy of rather puny appearance. He turned to Kirila Petrovich in bewilderment, waiting for an explanation. Kirila Petrovich related what had happened in the morning, without any mention, however, of Maria Kirilovna.

The superintendent listened to him attentively, casting frequent glances at the little miscreant, who, pretending to be a simpleton, seemed to be paying no attention to what was going on around him.

"Allow me, Your Excellency, to speak with you in private," said the superintendent at last.

Kirila Petrovich led him into an adjacent room and locked the door.

Half an hour later they came back to the hall, where the captive was waiting for his fate to be decided.

"The master wanted you to be put in the city jail, lashed with the whip, and then deported," said the superintendent, "but I've interceded on your behalf and persuaded him to pardon you.—You can untie him."

They untied the boy.

"Well, thank your master, won't you?" asked the superintendent.

The boy went up to Kirila Petrovich and kissed his hand.

"Very well, go home," said Kirila Petrovich to him, "and in the future don't steal raspberries from hollow trees."

The boy went outside, joyfully jumped off the porch, and without looking back, set out at a gallop across the field toward Kistenevka. When he reached it, he stopped by a little tumbledown hut at the edge of the village and knocked at the window. The window was raised, and an old woman appeared in it.

"Granny, some bread," said the boy. "I haven't eaten since the morning; I'm starving."

"Oh, it's you, Mitia. Where did you vanish to, you little devil?"

"I'll tell you later, granny, but give me some bread for God's sake."

"Well, come inside, won't you?"

"I haven't got time, granny; I must still run to another place. Bread, for Christ's sake, bread!"

"Always itching to go," grumbled the old woman. "Here, take this hunk," and she handed him a piece of black bread through the window.

The boy eagerly bit into it and, chewing, immediately set out on his further errand.

It was beginning to grow dark. Mitia made his way to the Kistenevka wood, stealing past barns and vegetable gardens. Reaching two pine trees that stood at the edge of the wood like sentries at an outpost, he stopped, looked about him on every side, let out a brief, shrill whistle, and started to listen. A long, soft whistle answered him; someone came out of the wood and approached him.

18

Kirila Petrovich paced up and down the hall, whistling his march more loudly than usual; the whole house was in commotion, the servants dashing to and fro, the maids bustling about, the coachmen getting the carriage ready in the shed. A crowd gathered in the courtyard. In the young mistress's boudoir, a lady surrounded by maids stood before the mirror, and dressed the pale, motionless Maria Kirilovna. Masha's head bent languidly under the weight of diamonds; she started slightly each time a careless hand pricked her, but otherwise silently and absently stared at herself in the mirror.

"How much longer?" sounded Kirila Petrovich's voice from behind the door.

"Just one minute," answered the lady. "Maria Kirilovna, stand up and take a look: is everything right?"

Maria Kirilovna rose and made no answer. The door opened.

"The bride is ready," said the lady to Kirila Petrovich. "Please order the carriage."

"With God's grace," answered Kirila Petrovich, and took an icon from the table. "Come here, Masha," he said to her with emotion, "and receive my blessing."

The poor girl collapsed at his feet and burst into sobs.

"Papa... papa," she repeated in tears, and her voice died away. Kirila Petrovich hastened to bless her; she was lifted up and almost borne to the carriage. Her mother by proxy and a maid sat with her. They drove to the church. The bridegroom was already waiting there. He came out to greet his bride and was struck by her paleness and strange look. They entered the cold empty church together, and the doors were locked behind them. The priest emerged from the sanctuary and began the ceremony without delay. Maria Kirilovna neither saw nor heard anything. Her mind was fixed on one idea: she had been waiting for Dubrovskii every since the morning, not giving up hope for one minute. When the priest turned to her with the customary questions, she shuddered and froze with fear, but she still hesitated, still did not give up hope. However, the priest, not waiting for her reply, pronounced the irrevocable words.

The ceremony was over. She felt her unloved husband's cold kiss and heard those present joyfully congratulating her, but she still could not believe that her life was fettered forever, and that Dubrovskii had not come flying to deliver her. The Prince turned to her with tender words, which she did not comprehend. They came out on the porch, where the peasants of Pokrovskoe were crowding. Her glance quickly ran over them, then she resumed her air of indifference. The newlyweds got into the carriage together and drove off to Arbatovo; Kirila Petrovich had set out ahead of them in order to greet the young couple there. Left alone with his young wife, the Prince did not in the least feel discomfited by her cold look. He did not importune her with unctuous explanations or ludicrous raptures: his words were simple and required no reply. They covered about ten versts this way; the horses ran fast over the bumps of the country lanes, but the carriage hardly rocked on its English springs. Suddenly the shouts of a pursuing party could be heard; the carriage stopped; a band of armed men surrounded it; and a man in a half-mask, opening the door on the young Princess' side, said to her, "You are free: alight."

"What does this mean?" shouted the Prince. "Who the devil are you?"

"It is Dubrovskii," said the Princess.

The Prince did not lose his presence of mind, but drew from his side pocket a traveling pistol and shot at the masked bandit. The Princess screamed and, horror-stricken, covered her face with both hands. Dubrovskii was wounded in the shoulder,[36] and the blood was beginning to show through. The Prince, losing no time, drew another pistol, but he was given no opportunity to fire it: the door on his side opened and several strong hands pulled him out of the carriage and took the pistol from him. Knives flashed above him.

"Don't touch him!" shouted Dubrovskii, and his fearsome companions drew back.

"You are free," resumed Dubrovskii, turning to the pale Princess.

"No," she answered. "It's too late. I am already married. I am the wife of Prince Vereiskii."

"What are you saying?" cried Dubrovskii in despair. "No, you are not his wife, you were coerced, you could never give your consent..."

"I did consent. I made my vow," she rejoined resolutely. "The Prince is my husband; please give orders to let him go, and leave me with him. I did not deceive you. I waited for you till the last moment... But now, I am telling you, it's too late. Let us go free."

Dubrovskii could no longer hear her: the pain of his wound and the violent agitation of his soul had taken away his strength. He collapsed by the wheel; his bandits gathered around him. He had managed to say a few words to them, and they put him on his horse, two of them supporting him, while a third led the animal by the bridle. They all rode off across the fields, leaving the carriage in the middle of the road, with the men tied up and the horses unharnessed, but without plundering anything or shedding one drop of blood in revenge for the blood of their chief.

19

In a narrow clearing in the middle of a dense forest there was a small earthwork, consisting of a rampart and a trench, behind which a few huts and dugouts could be seen.

In the enclosure a large number of people, readily identifiable by their varied dress and uniform weaponry as bandits, were eating their dinner, with their heads bare, seated around a shared cauldron. On the rampart a sentry sat cross-legged at a small cannon. He was sewing a patch on his garment, plying his needle with the skill of an experienced tailor; at the same time he kept glancing around on every side.

Although a dipper had gone around from hand to hand several times, a strange silence reigned over the crowd; the bandits finished their dinner, rose to their feet, and said their prayers one after the other; some dispersed among the huts, while others straggled into the woods or lay down for a nap according to the Russian custom.

The sentry finished his work and shook his tattered garment, admiring the patch on it; then stuck his needle into his sleeve, sat astride the cannon, and burst into a sad old song at the top of his voice:

> Do not rustle your leaves, dear oak tree, green mother,
> Do not disturb me, brave young lad, in thinking my thoughts.[37]

On the instance the door of one of the huts opened, and an old woman in a white cap, dressed neatly and properly, appeared on the threshold.

"Enough of that, Stepka," she said angrily. "The master's asleep, but you must bawl: have you no conscience or pity?"

"I beg pardon, Egorovna," answered Stepka. "I won't any more. Let the young master sleep and get better."

The old woman withdrew, and Stepka started pacing to and fro on the rampart.

In the hut from which the old woman had emerged, on a camp bed behind a partition, lay the wounded Dubrovskii. His pistols sat on a small table next to him and his saber hung on the wall at the head of the bed. The mud hut was covered and hung all over with luxurious carpets; and in the corner there was a woman's silver wash basin with a cheval glass. Dubrovskii held an open book in his hands, but his eyes were closed. The old woman, who kept peeping at him from behind the partition, could not be sure whether he was asleep or just lost in thought.

Suddenly Dubrovskii started: an alarm was sounded in the fortification, and Stepka poked his head through the window.

"Vladimir Andreevich, young master," he shouted, "our men have given the signal: a search party is coming."

Dubrovskii jumped off his bed, seized his weapons, and stepped outside the hut. The bandits were noisily gathering in the enclosure; but as soon as he appeared among them deep silence set in.

"Is everyone here?" asked Dubrovskii.

"Everyone except the sentries," was the answer.

"Take up your positions!" shouted Dubrovskii.

Each bandit took up his assigned position. At this moment the three sentries came running to the gates. Dubrovskii went forward to meet them.

"What is it?" he asked them.

"There are soldiers in the woods," they replied. "They're encircling us."

Dubrovskii gave orders to lock the gates and went to check the small cannon. Several voices could be heard in the woods; they came closer; the bandits waited silently. Suddenly three or four soldiers emerged from the woods, but they immediately withdrew, signaling to their comrades by shots.

"Prepare for combat!" said Dubrovskii, and a murmur passed through the bandits' ranks, after which all grew quiet again.

Then the noise of an approaching detachment could be heard; weapons flashed among the trees; some one hundred and fifty soldiers poured out of the woods and dashed for the rampart with shouts. Dubrovskii held the fuse to the cannon, and fired successfully: one soldier's head was torn off, and two others were wounded. The soldiers were thrown into confusion, but when their officer dashed forward, they followed, and jumped into the trench. The bandits shot at them with rifles and pistols, and were ready with axes in hand to defend the rampart, which the frenzied soldiers stormed, leaving behind some twenty comrades in the trench, wounded. A hand-to-hand battle ensued. The soldiers were already on the rampart, forcing the bandits to retreat, but Dubrovskii went right up to their officer and shot him point-blank in the chest. The officer fell over backward. Some soldiers picked him up in their arms, hastening to carry him off into the woods, while the others, deprived of their commander, stopped. The emboldened bandits took advantage of this moment of confusion and crushed the soldiers' ranks, forcing them back into the trench. The besiegers took flight, and the bandits pursued them with shouts. The battle was won. Trusting that the enemy had been thrown into complete disorder, Dubrovskii stopped his men and withdrew behind the locked gates of the fort, giving orders to gather up the wounded, to double the guard, and not to leave the fort.

These last developments drew the government's serious attention to Dubrovskii's bold robberies. Intelligence was gathered concerning his whereabouts. A company of soldiers was dispatched to capture him dead or alive. It was learned, however, from some of his followers who had been caught, that he was no longer with the band. And indeed, a few days after the last battle, he had gathered all his followers, declaring to them that he would leave them for good, and advising them that they, too, should change their way of life.

"You've grown rich under my command and each of you has a false passport with which you can make your way to some remote *guberniia* and live for the rest of your life in honest work and prosperity. But you are all ruffians and will probably not want to give up your trade."

After this speech he left them, taking with him only R. Nobody knew where he had disappeared to. The authorities at first doubted the truth of these depositions, for the bandits' attachment to their chief was well known. It was supposed that they were only trying to save him. But subsequent events proved the depositions right. The awesome raids, burnings, and plunders ceased. The highways became safe again. From other reports it was learned that Dubrovskii had escaped abroad.[38]

The Queen of Spades

(1833)[1]

The queen of spades signifies
secret ill-will.

FROM A RECENT
FORTUNE-TELLING BOOK

I

And in rainy weather,
They gathered together
And squandered,
God pardon their sin,
From fifty a win
To a hundred;
Won many a pot
And tallied the lot
On a board.
Thus in rainy weather
Many workdays together
They scored.[2]

There was a card party at the house of Narumov, an officer of the Horse Guards. The long winter night passed imperceptibly; it was close to five in the morning when the company sat down to supper. Those who had won were eating with good appetite; the others sat lost in thought before their empty plates. But champagne was brought in, and the conversation grew lively, with everyone joining in.

"How did you do, Surin?" asked the host.

"Lost, as usual. You must admit I have no luck: I play a *mirandole* game,[3] always keep cool, never let anything confuse me, and yet I lose all the time!"

"Have you never been tempted? Have you never risked *routé*?[4] Your firmness amazes me."

"And what about Hermann?" said one of the guests, pointing at a young engineer. "He's never in his life had a card in his hand, never bent down a *paroli*,[5] yet he will sit with us until five in the morning watching our game!"

"The game interests me very much," said Hermann, "but I am not in a position to sacrifice the necessary in the hope of gaining the superfluous."

"Hermann is a German: he's thrifty, that's all," remarked Tomskii.

"If there's anybody I don't understand, it's my grandmother, Countess Anna Fedotovna."

"Why? How is that?" cried the guests.

"I cannot fathom," continued Tomskii, "why my grandmother never punts."

"Well, what's so surprising about it," said Narumov, "that an old lady of eighty doesn't punt?"

"So you don't know anything about her?"

"No, not a thing."

"Well, in that case, listen. I should mention, to begin with, that about sixty years ago my grandmother went to Paris, where she created quite a sensation. People ran after her, just to catch a glimpse of *la Vénus moscovite*; Richelieu paid court to her,[6] and grandmother asserts that he almost shot himself because of her cruelty.

"Ladies used to play *pharaon* in those days.[7] On one occasion at the Court my grandmother lost a very large sum, on word of honor, to the Duke of Orleans.[8] After she arrived home, as she was peeling off her beauty spots and untying her hooped petticoat, she informed my grandfather of her loss and ordered him to pay.

"My late grandfather, as far as I remember, played the part of a butler to my grandmother. He feared her like fire; but when he heard about such a terrible loss, he flew into a rage, brought in the ledgers, demonstrated to her that in half a year they had spent half a million, pointed out that around Paris they did not possess the kind of estates they had around Moscow and Saratov, and absolutely refused to pay. Grandmother slapped him on the face and went to bed by herself as an indication of her displeasure.

"The next day she sent for her husband, hoping that the domestic punishment had had its effect on him, but she found him unshaken. For the first time in her life she went as far as to argue with him and offer him explanations; she thought she could awaken his conscience if she condescended to demonstrate to him that not all debts were alike, and that there was a difference between a duke and a cartwright. But all in vain! Grandfather had risen in rebellion. No, and no! Grandmother did not know what to do.

"She was on friendly terms with a very remarkable man. You have heard of Count Saint-Germain, the hero of so many miraculous tales.[9] You know he pretended to be the Wandering Jew, the inventor of the elixir of life and of the philosopher's stone, et cetera. He was ridiculed as a charlatan, and Casanova called him a spy in his *Memoirs*;[10] be that as it may, despite his mysteriousness Saint-Germain was a man of highly respectable appearance and had excellent manners. To this day grandmother loves him with a passion and gets cross if she hears disrespectful talk about him. She knew that Saint-Germain had a large fortune at his disposal. She decided to turn to him for help and sent him a note asking him to call on her without delay.

"The old eccentric came at once and found her terribly upset. Depicting her husband's barbarity in the darkest colors to him, she concluded that she was placing all her hope in his friendship and kindness.

"Saint-Germain became thoughtful.

" 'I could accommodate you with the required sum,' he said, 'but I know you would not rest until you repaid me, and I wouldn't want to inflict new worries upon you. There is another way out: you can win the money back.'

" 'But my dear Count,' answered grandmother, I'm telling you we've run out of money altogether.'

" 'It requires no money,' rejoined Saint-Germain. 'Pray, hear me out.' And he revealed to her a secret for which any of us would be willing to pay a high price..."

The young gamblers listened with doubled attention. Tomskii lit his pipe, took a puff, and continued.

"That same evening grandmother presented herself at Versailles, *au jeu de la Reine.*[11] The Duke of Orleans was holding the bank; grandmother casually excused herself, spinning some little yarn, for not bringing what she owed, and set down to punt against the Duke. She chose three cards and bet on them in sequence: all three won *sonica,*[12] and grandmother regained everything she had lost."

"Mere chance!" said one of the guests.

"A fairy tale!" remarked Hermann.

"Perhaps they were powdered cards,"[13] joined in a third.

"I don't think so," Tomskii replied in a serious tone.

"How now!" said Narumov. "You have a grandmother who can predict three winning cards in a row, and you have still not tried to snatch her cabalistic power from her?"

"The devil I haven't!" answered Tomskii. "She has four sons, including my father: all four are desperate gamblers, but she has not revealed her secret to any one of them, even though it would be handy for each—or for me, for that matter. But I'll tell you what my uncle, Count Ivan Ilich, has told me, and what he swears on his honor is true. The late Chaplitskii—the one who died in poverty, having squandered millions—once in his youth lost 300,000 to Zorich if I am not mistaken.[14] He was in despair. Grandmother, though she usually viewed young people's pranks with severity, somehow took pity on Chaplitskii. She named him three cards with the instruction to play them one after the other, and she made him give his word of honor that he would never again play afterwards. Chaplitskii went back to his vanquisher; they sat down to play. Chaplitskii staked 30,000 on the first card and won *sonica*; he bent down a *paroli*, then a *paroli-paix*;[15] he won back what he had lost, and even went away a winner...

"But it's time to go to bed: it is already quarter of six."

Indeed it was already getting light: the young men emptied their glasses and left.

2

"Il paraît que monsieur est
décidément pour les suivantes."
"Que voulez-vouz, madame? Elles
sont plus fraîches."
CONVERSATION AT
A SOCIAL GATHERING[16]

The old Countess N. sat in front of the mirror in her boudoir. Three chambermaids surrounded her. One was holding a jar of rouge, the second one a box of pins, and the third one a tall bonnet with flame-colored ribbons. The Countess did not have the slightest pretensions to beauty, which had long since faded from her face, but she adhered to all the habits of her youth, strictly following the fashions of the 1770's, spending just as much time on, and paying just as much attention to, her toilette as she had sixty years before. A young lady, her ward, was seated over an embroidery frame by the window.

"Good morning, *grand'maman*," said a young officer, entering. "*Bonjour, mademoiselle* Lise. *Grand'maman*, I have a favor to ask of you."

"What is it, Paul?"

"Let me introduce one of my friends to you and bring him to your ball on Friday."

"Bring him directly to the ball, and introduce him right there and then. Were you at X.'s last night?"

"How could I have missed it! We had a very jolly time: danced until five o'clock in the morning. Wasn't Eletskaia fabulous!"

"La, my dear! What do you see in her? She couldn't hold a candle to her grandmother, Princess Daria Petrovna... By the way, methinks she must be getting on, Princess Daria Petrovna?"

"What do you mean getting on?" Tomskii answered absentmindedly. "She's been dead these seven years."

The young lady raised her head and signaled to him. He remembered that the old Countess was never informed of the death of any of her contemporaries, and he bit his lip. But the Countess took the tidings, new to her, with perfect equanimity.

"Dead!" she said. "And I didn't even know! We were appointed maids of honor together, and as we were being presented, the Empress..."

For the hundredth time, the Countess related the anecdote to her grandson.

"And now, Paul," she said afterwards, "help me get up. Lizanka, where is my snuffbox?"

She proceeded behind the screen with her chambermaids in order to complete her toilette. Tomskii remained alone with the young lady.

"Who is it you want to introduce?" asked Lizaveta Ivanovna softly.

"Narumov. Do you know him?"

"No, I don't. Is he an officer or a civilian?"

"An officer."

"An engineer?"

"No, a cavalryman. What made you think he was an engineer?"

The young lady laughed and did not answer a word.

"Paul!" called the Countess from behind the screen. "Send me a new novel, will you, but please not the kind they write nowadays."

"What do you mean, *grand'maman*?"

"I mean a novel in which the hero does not strangle either his mother or his father, and which describes no drowned bodies. I am terribly scared of drowned bodies."

"There are no such novels these days. Would you perhaps like some Russian ones?"

"You don't mean to say there are Russian novels?... Send some to me, my dear, send some by all means!"

"I'm sorry, I must go now, *grand'maman*: I'm in a hurry... Goodbye, Lizaveta Ivanovna! I still want to know why you thought Narumov was an engineer."

And Tomskii left the boudoir.

Lizaveta Ivanovna remained by herself; she laid aside her work and looked out of the window. Soon a young officer appeared from behind a corner on the other side of the street. A blush spread over her cheeks; she took up her work again and bent her head right over the canvas. At that moment the Countess entered, fully dressed.

"Lizanka," she said, "would you give orders to have the horses harnessed; we'll go out for a ride."

Lizanka rose from behind the embroidery frame and began putting her work away.

"What's the matter with you, child? Are you deaf?" the Countess shouted. "Tell them to harness the horses at once."

"Yes, ma'am," the young lady answered softly and ran into the anteroom.

A servant came in and handed the Countess some books from Prince Pavel Aleksandrovich.

"Very well. Give him my thanks," said the Countess. "Lizanka! Lizanka! Where are you running now?"

"To get dressed."

"You'll have plenty of time for that. Sit down here. Open the first volume and read to me..."

The young lady took the book and read a few lines.

"Louder!" said the Countess. "What's with you, child? Have you lost your voice or something?... Wait a minute: pull up that footstool for me, closer... Well now!"

Lizaveta Ivanovna read two pages. The Countess yawned.

"Put that book down," she said. "What nonsense! Send it back to Prince Pavel with my thanks... But what's happened to the carriage?"

"The carriage is ready," said Lizaveta Ivanovna, looking out on the street.

"And why aren't you dressed?" said the Countess. "One always has to wait for you! This, my dear, is unbearable."

Liza ran to her room. Two minutes had not gone by when the Countess started ringing with all her might. Three maids ran in through one door, and a footman through the other.

"It's totally impossible to get anyone's attention around here," the Countess said to them. "Go and tell Lizaveta Ivanovna that I am waiting for her."

Lizaveta Ivanovna came in, wearing a cape and a bonnet.

"At long last, child!" said the Countess. "But what finery! What's all this for? Whose head do you want to turn?... And what's the weather like?—There is a wind, it seems to me."

"No, there isn't, so please your ladyship. It's entirely calm," said the footman.

"You always say what comes into your head first! Open the transom window. Just as I thought: there is a wind! Chilling to the bones! Have the horses unharnessed! Lizanka, we're not going; you needn't have decked yourself out so."

"This is my life," thought Lizaveta Ivanovna.

In truth, Lizaveta Ivanovna was the unluckiest of creatures. "How the bread of others savors of salt," says Dante, "and how hard is the descending and the mounting of another's stairs."[17] Who indeed would be more familiar with the bitter taste of dependence than the poor ward of an aristocratic old lady? The Countess N was, of course, not an evil soul, but as the spoiled pet of society, she was capricious; she had grown mean and sunk into a cold egoism, like all old people whose fondest memories lay in the past and to whom the present was alien. She participated in all the trivial events of high society life, dragging herself to balls, where she would sit in a corner, all painted up and dressed according to an ancient fashion, like a misshapen but obligatory ornament of the ballroom; the guests, as they arrived, would go up to her bowing low, as if performing an established rite, but afterwards would pay no attention to her. She was scrupulous in receiving the whole city as etiquette decreed, but hardly recognized any of her guests. Her numerous domestics, grown fat and gray in her entrance hall and maids' quarters, did what they pleased, robbing the moribund old woman left, right, and center. Lizaveta Ivanovna was the martyr of the household. She poured the tea and was scolded for using too much sugar; read novels aloud and was blamed for all the faults of the authors; accompanied the Countess on her rides and was held responsible for both the weather and the condition of the pavement. She had a fixed salary, but it was never paid in full; at the same time she was expected to be dressed like everyone else, that is, like the very few. In society she played the most pitiable role. Everybody knew her, but nobody took any notice of her; at the balls she danced only when an extra partner was needed for a *vis-à-vis;* and ladies took her by the arm every time they needed to go to the dressing room in order to adjust something in their costume. She was proud; she felt her position keenly, and looked around impatiently waiting for a deliverer; but the young men, calculating in their whimsical vanity, did not honor Lizaveta Ivanovna with their attention, though she was a hundred times more appealing than the brazen and coldhearted debutantes on whom they danced attendance. How many times did she steal out of the tedious though sumptuous salon in order to weep in her own poor room, furnished with a paper screen, a chest of drawers, a small mirror, a painted bedstead, and a tallow candle faintly burning in its brass holder!

One time—this happened two days after the party described at the beginning of our story and a week before the scene that we have just detailed—one time Lizaveta Ivanovna, sitting over her embroidery frame by the window, happened to glance at the street and caught sight of a young engineering officer who was standing there motionless with his eyes fixed on her window. She lowered her head and resumed her work; five minutes later she looked again; the young officer was standing in the same place. Since it had never been her way to flirt with unknown officers, she stopped looking at the street and embroidered for about two hours without raising her head. Dinner was announced. She stood up, started putting away her embroidery frame, and inadvertently glancing at the street, caught sight of the officer once more. This seemed rather strange to her. After dinner she went to the window with a certain feeling of apprehension, but the officer was no longer there, and she soon forgot about him...

About two days later, as she and the Countess came out of the house to get into their carriage, she saw him again. He was standing right by the entrance, his face hidden in his beaver collar, his dark eyes sparkling from under his cap. Lizaveta Ivanovna was frightened, though she did not know why, and got into the carriage, shaking inexplicably.

After she returned home she ran up to the window: the officer was standing in his former place, gazing at her; she turned away, tormented by curiosity and agitated by a feeling that was entirely new to her.

From that time on, not one day passed without the young man arriving, at a certain hour, under the windows of the house. An undefined relationship was established between him and her. Sitting in her place over her work, she could sense his approach; she raised her head and looked at him longer with each day. The young man seemed to be grateful for it: she could see with her keen young eyes that a sudden blush spread over his pale cheeks each time their glances met. By the end of the week she gave him a smile...

When Tomskii asked for the Countess's permission to introduce a friend, the poor girl's heart gave a thump. Having learned, however, that Narumov was not an engineer, but a cavalryman, she regretted the indiscreet question that had betrayed her secret to the flighty Tomskii.

Hermann was the son of a Russified German, who had left him a little capital. Firmly resolved to ensure his independence, Hermann did not touch even the interest earned by these funds; he lived on his salary alone, denying himself even the slightest extravagance. Since he was also reserved and proud, his comrades rarely had occasion to laugh at his excessive thriftiness. He had strong passions and a fiery imagination, but his resoluteness saved him from the usual lapses of youth. He was, for example, a gambler at heart but never touched a card, reckoning that his circumstances did not allow him (as he was fond of saying) *to sacrifice the necessary in the hope of gaining the superfluous.* Yet at the same time he would sit by the card table whole nights and follow with feverish trembling the different turns of the game.

The anecdote about the three cards fired his imagination; he could not get it out of his head all night. "What if," he thought as he wandered about Petersburg the following evening, "what if the old Countess revealed her secret to me? If she named the three reliable cards for me? Why not try my luck?... I could be introduced to her, get into her good graces, become her lover if need be; but all this requires time, and she is eighty-seven: she may die in a week—in a couple of days!... And what about the anecdote itself? Can one put any faith in it? No! Calculation, moderation, and industry; these are my three reliable cards. They will treble my capital, increase it sevenfold, and bring me ease and independence!"

Lost thus in thought, he found himself on one of the main streets of Petersburg, in front of an old-style house. The street was crowded with carriages; one equipage after another rolled up to the lighted entrance. Now a young beauty's shapely leg, now a clinking riding boot, now a striped stocking and a diplomat's shoe emerged from the carriages. Fur coats and cloaks flitted by the stately doorman. Hermann stopped.

"Whose house is this?" he asked the sentry on the street.

"The Countess N.'s," answered the sentry.

A shiver ran down Hermann's spine. The marvelous anecdote arose in his imagination once more. He began to pace up and down by the house, thinking about its owner and her miraculous talent. It was late when he returned to his humble lodging; he could not go to sleep for a long time, and when he finally dropped off, he dreamed of cards, a green table, heaps of bank notes, and piles of gold coins. He played one card after another, bent the corners resolutely, and kept winning, raking in the gold and stuffing the bank notes in his pockets. Waking up late, he sighed over the loss of his illusory riches; once more he went wandering about the city and once more found himself in front of Countess N.'s house. A mysterious force, it seemed, had drawn him there. He stopped and started looking at the windows. Behind one of them he noticed a dark-haired young head, bent, evidently, over a book or some work. The head was raised. Hermann beheld a fresh young face and dark eyes. That moment sealed his fate.

3

Vous m'écrivez, mon ange, des lettres de
quatres pages plus vite que je ne puis les lire.
FROM A CORRESPONDENCE [18]

No sooner had Lizaveta Ivanovna taken off her cape and bonnet than the Countess sent for her and once more ordered the carriage. They went downstairs to get in. Two servants had just lifted up the old lady and pushed her through the door of the carriage, when Lizaveta Ivanovna beheld her engineer right by the wheel; he seized her hand; before she had time to recover from her fright, the young man had put a letter in her palm and was gone. She slipped it inside her glove, and was unable to hear or see anything during the whole ride. The Countess had a habit of constantly asking questions as she rode along: "Who was it we just passed?" "What's the name of this bridge?" "What's written on that sign?" This time Lizaveta Ivanovna answered at random and wide of the mark, making the Countess angry.

"What's the matter with you, child? Are you in a trance or something? Don't you hear me or understand what I'm saying?... Thank God, I don't slur my words and I'm not yet a dotard!"

Lizaveta Ivanovna paid no attention to her. As soon as they returned home she ran to her room and drew the letter out of her glove: it was not sealed. She read it. It contained a confession of love; it was tender, respectful, and translated word for word from a German novel. But Lizaveta Ivanovna did not know German and found it very satisfactory.

For all that, her acceptance of the letter worried her in the extreme. For the first time in her life she was entering into a secret, close relationship with a young man. His boldness terrified her. She reproached herself for her imprudent conduct and did not know what to do: should she leave off sitting by the window and try, by her lack of attention, to discourage the young officer from further advances? Should she return his letter to him? Or should she answer him, coldly and resolutely? She had no one to turn to for advice; she had neither a friend nor a counselor. In the end she decided to reply.

She sat down at her small desk, took out pen and paper—and fell to thinking. She began her letter several times but each time tore it up: her phrases seemed to her either too encouraging or too forbidding. At last she succeeded in writing a few lines that left her satisfied. "I am convinced," said the letter, "that you have honorable intentions and did not wish to offend me with a thoughtless act; but this is not the way to begin an acquaintance. I return your letter and hope to have no cause in the future to complain of an unwarranted disrespect."

The next day, as soon as she saw Hermann walking below, she rose from her embroidery frame, went out to the reception hall, opened the transom, and threw her letter into the street, trusting in the young officer's agility. Hermann dashed for it, picked it up, and went to a confectionary shop. Tearing off the seal, he found his own letter as well as Lizaveta Ivanovna's answer. That was just what he had expected, and he returned home very much absorbed in his intrigue.

Three days later, a pert young *mam'selle* from a ladies' dress shop brought a note to Lizaveta Ivanovna. She opened it with anxiety, anticipating a demand for payment, but suddenly recognized Hermann's hand.

"You've made a mistake, precious," she said, "this note is not for me."

"Yes, it really is," answered the bold little girl, not concealing a sly smile. "Please read it!"

Lizaveta Ivanovna read through the note quickly. Hermann was demanding a rendezvous.

"Impossible!" said Lizaveta Ivanovna, frightened by both the rashness of Hermann's demand and the means he had chosen to convey it. "This is surely not written to me!" And she tore the letter into small pieces.

"If the letter was not for you, why did you tear it up?" said the little *mam'selle*. "I could've returned it to the sender."

"Please, precious," said Lizaveta Ivanovna to the girl, whose remark made her blush, "in the future do not bring notes to me. And tell him who sent you that he should be ashamed of himself..."

But there was no stopping Hermann. Lizaveta Ivanovna received letters from him every day, sent now in this way, now in that. They were no longer translations from German. Inspired by passion, Hermann wrote them in a style that was characteristic of him, expressing both the uncompromising nature of his desires and the confusion of his unbridled imagination. It no longer occurred to Lizaveta Ivanovna to send them back: she reveled in them and began to answer them, her notes growing longer and tenderer by the day. In the end she threw the following letter to him from the window:

Tonight the Ambassador of Y. is giving a ball. The Countess is planning to attend. We shall stay there until about two in the morning. Here is an opportunity for you to see me alone. As soon as the Countess leaves, her servants will probably scatter in all directions; the doorman will remain by the entrance, but even he is likely to retreat, as is his habit, into his cubicle. Come at half past eleven.

Walk straight up the staircase. If you find anybody in the anteroom, inquire whether the Countess is at home. You will be told she is not—and that will be the end of that. You will have to turn back. But it is likely that you will meet no one. The maids sit in their room, all of them together. From the anteroom turn left and walk straight through, all the way to the Countess's bedroom. In her bedroom, behind a screen, you will see two small doors: the one on the right leads to a study, which the Countess never enters; the one on the left opens into a corridor, where you will find a narrow winding staircase: this leads to my room.

Hermann waited for the appointed time, trembling like a tiger. At ten o'clock in the evening he was already in front of the Countess's house. The weather was terrible: the wind howled, wet snow fell in large flakes; the lights shone dimly; the streets were deserted. Only occasionally did a cabdriver shamble by with his scrawny nag, on the lookout for a late passenger. Hermann stood wearing only a jacket, yet feeling neither wind nor snow. At last the Countess's carriage drew up. Hermann watched as the servants, grasping her by the arms, carried out the hunched-up old lady, wrapped in a sable coat. Right behind her, her ward flitted by, dressed in a light cloak, her head adorned with fresh flowers. The doors of the carriage were slammed to. The carriage rolled off heavily in the soft snow. The doorman shut the front door. The lights in the windows went out. Hermann started pacing up and down before the lifeless house. He went up to a streetlamp and looked at his watch: it was twenty past eleven. He stayed under the lamp with his eyes fixed on the hands of his watch, waiting for the remaining minutes to pass. At exactly half past eleven he stepped on the porch and went up to the brightly lit entrance hall. The doorman was not there. Hermann ran up the stairs, opened the door of the anteroom, and saw a servant asleep in an ancient soiled armchair under a lamp. Hermann walked past him with a light but firm step. The reception hall and the drawing room were dark, with only a feeble light falling on them from the lamp in the anteroom. Hermann entered the bedroom. A gold sanctuary lamp burned in front of an icon-case filled with ancient icons. Armchairs with faded damask upholstery and down-cushioned sofas, their gilt coating worn, stood in melancholy symmetry along the walls, which were covered with Chinese silk. Two portraits, painted in Paris by Mme. Lebrun,[19] hung on the wall. One of them showed a man about forty years old, red-faced and portly, wearing a light green coat with a star; the other a beautiful young woman with an aquiline nose, with her hair combed back over her temples, and with a rose in her powdered locks. Every nook and corner was crowded with china shepherdesses, table clocks made by the famous Leroy,[20] little boxes, bandalores, fans, and diverse other ladies' toys invented at the end of the last century, along with Montgolfier's balloon and Mesmer's magnetism.[21] Hermann went behind the screen. A small iron bedstead stood behind it; on the right there was the door leading to the study; on the left, another one leading to the corridor. Hermann opened the latter and saw the narrow winding staircase that led to the poor ward's room... But he drew back and went into the dark study.

Time went slowly. Everything was quiet. A clock struck twelve in the drawing room, and following it, all the clocks in all the rooms announced the hour; then everything grew quiet again. Hermann stood leaning against the cold stove. He was calm: his heart beat evenly, like that of a man embarked on a dangerous but unavoidable mission. The clocks struck one, then two in the morning; at last he heard the distant rumble of a carriage. An involuntary agitation seized him. The carriage drove up to the house and stopped. He heard the thump of the carriage's steps being lowered. The house began stirring. Servants were running, voices resounded, and lights came on. Three old chambermaids ran into the bedroom, and the Countess, barely alive, came in and sank into a Voltairean armchair. Hermann watched through a crack in the door: Lizaveta Ivanovna passed by him. He could hear her hasty steps up her staircase. Something akin to a pang of conscience stirred in his heart, but was soon stilled. He stood petrified.

The Countess began to undress in front of the mirror. The maids unpinned her bonnet bedecked with roses and removed the powdered wig from her closely cropped gray head. Pins came showering off her. Her yellow dress, embroidered with silver, fell to her swollen feet; Hermann became privy to the loathsome mysteries of her dress. At last she put on her bed jacket and nightcap: in these clothes, more appropriate for her age, she seemed to be less frightening and hideous.

Like most old people, the Countess suffered from insomnia. Having undressed, she sat in the Voltairean armchair by the window and dismissed her chambermaids. The candles were taken away and once more the room was lit only by the sanctuary lamp. The Countess sat, all yellow, mumbling with her flabby lips and swaying right and left. Her dim eyes were completely empty of thought; looking at her, one might assume that the swaying of this horrifying old woman was caused, not by her own will, but by the action of a hidden galvanism.[22]

Suddenly an inexpressible change came over her lifeless face. Her lips stopped mumbling, and her eyes lit up: a strange man stood before her.

"Don't be frightened, for heaven's sake, don't!" he said in a clear but low voice. "I have no intention of harming you: I've come to beg a favor of you."

The old lady looked at him in silence and did not seem to hear him. Hermann assumed she was deaf and repeated his phrases, bending down toward her ear. The old lady kept silent as before.

"It is in your power to make my life happy," continued Hermann, "and it will cost you nothing: I know you are able to predict three winning cards in a row..."

Hermann stopped. The Countess seemed to have understood what was demanded of her; she seemed to be searching for words to reply.

"That was a joke," she said at last. "I swear to you it was only a joke!"

"It is no joking matter," rejoined Hermann angrily. "Remember Chaplitskii, whom you helped to win back his loss."

The Countess grew visibly confused. Her features betrayed a profound stirring of her heart, but she soon relapsed into her former numbness.

"Can you," continued Hermann, "can you name those three reliable cards for me?"

The Countess kept silent; Hermann went on:

"For whom are you saving your secret? For your grandsons? They are rich as it is, and they don't even know the value of money. A spendthrift will not benefit by your three cards. He who cannot guard his patrimony will die in poverty, whatever demonic machinations he may resort to. I am not a spendthrift; I know the value of money. Your three cards will not be wasted on me. Well, then..."

He stopped, trembling in anticipation of her answer. The Countess was silent; Hermann knelt down before her.

"If your heart ever knew the feeling of love," he said, "if you remember its ecstasies, if you once in your life smiled hearing the cry of a newborn son, if anything human has ever pulsated within your bosom, then I beseech you, appealing to the feelings of a wife, mistress, mother—to everything that is sacred in life—do not refuse my request! Reveal your secret to me! Of what use is it to you?... Maybe it is linked with a terrible sin, a forfeiture of eternal bliss, a covenant with the devil... Consider: you are old, you will not live long—I am willing to take your sin on my soul. Only reveal your secret to me.

Consider that the happiness of a man is in your hands; not only I, but my children, grandchildren, and great-grandchildren will bless your memory and hold it sacred..."

The old woman did not answer a word.

Hermann stood up.

"You old witch!" he said, clenching his teeth. "Then I will make you answer."

With these words he drew a pistol from his pocket.

At the sight of the pistol the Countess once more betrayed strong emotion. She jerked back her head and raised her hand as if to shield herself from the shot... Then she rolled over backwards... and remained motionless.

"Stop this childish game," said Hermann, grasping her hand. "I am asking you for the last time: will you or will you not name your three cards for me? Yes or no?"

The Countess did not answer. Hermann realized that she was dead.

4

7 mai 18—
Homme sans moeurs et sans religion!
FROM A CORRESPONDENCE[23]

Lizaveta Ivanovna sat in her room deep in thought, still wearing her evening gown. On her arrival home she had hastened to dismiss the sleepy maid who begrudgingly offered her services; she said she would undress by herself and went to her room trembling, both hoping to find Hermann there and wishing not to. One glance was enough to convince her of his absence, and she thanked her fate for the obstacle that had prevented their meeting. She sat down without undressing and began to recollect all the circumstances that had led her so far in such a short time. Less than three weeks had passed since she had first caught sight of the young man through the window, and she was already corresponding with him, he had already made her consent to a nocturnal assignation! She knew his name only because some of his letters were signed; she had never spoken with him, never heard his voice, nor heard anything about him... until that evening. A strange thing! That very evening, at the ball, Tomskii was in a huff with the young Princess Polina, who had for the first time flirted with someone other than he; and wishing to take revenge on her by a show of indifference, he kept Lizaveta Ivanovna engaged in an endless mazurka. All through it he joked about her partiality for engineering officers, trying to convince her that he knew much more than she might suppose. Some of his jeers were so well aimed that several times Lizaveta Ivanovna thought her secret was known to him.

"Who told you all this?" she asked, laughing.

"A friend of a person you know," answered Tomskii, "a very remarkable man."

"And who is this remarkable man?"

"His name is Hermann."

Lizaveta Ivanovna did not say anything, but her hands and feet felt like ice...

"This Hermann," continued Tomskii, "is a truly romantic character: he has the profile of Napoleon and the soul of Mephistopheles. I think he has at least three crimes on his conscience. But how pale you've turned!..."

"I have a headache... What did this Hermann, or whatever his name is, tell you?..."

"Hermann is very dissatisfied with his friend: he says that in his friend's place he would have acted entirely differently... I even suspect that Hermann himself has an eye on you: at least he cannot remain calm listening to his friend's amorous exclamations."

"But where has he seen me?"

"At church, maybe, or when you went on a ride... Heaven only knows! Perhaps in your room while you were asleep: I wouldn't put it past him..."

The conversation, which was becoming painfully fascinating to Lizaveta Ivanovna, was interrupted by three ladies who approached to ask, "oubli ou regret?"[24]

The lady Tomskii chose turned out to be Princess Polina. She gave herself an opportunity to explain things to Tomskii by running an extra circle and spinning in front of her chair longer than usual. By the time Tomskii returned to his seat he had neither Hermann nor Lizaveta Ivanovna on his mind. The latter was determined to resume the interrupted conversation, but the mazurka came to an end, and soon afterwards the old Countess was ready to leave.

Tomskii's words had been no more than a mazurka partner's chitchat, but they sank deep into the young dreamer's soul. The portrait Tomskii sketched in was rather like the image she herself had formed, and thanks to the latest novels, her imagination was both daunted and enchanted by this type—actually quite hackneyed by now. She sat with her bare arms crossed and her head, still adorned with flowers, bent over the deep decolletage of her dress... Suddenly the door opened and Hermann came in. She shuddered...

"Where have you been?" she asked in an alarmed whisper.

"In the old Countess's bedroom," answered Hermann. "I have just left her. She is dead."

"My God!... What are you saying?..."

"And it seems to me," Hermann continued, "that I caused her death."

Lizaveta Ivanovna looked at him, and Tomskii's words echoed in her mind: *This man has at least three crimes on his conscience!* Hermann sat down on the windowsill by her and told her the full story.

Lizaveta Ivanovna listened to him in horror. And so, those passionate letters, those ardent demands, that bold and dogged pursuit—all that was not love! Money was what his soul was craving! It was not in her power to quench his passion and make him happy. The poor ward had turned out to be no more than the blind accomplice of a burglar, of the murderer of her aged benefactress!... She shed bitter tears of agonizing, belated remorse. Hermann regarded her in silence: his heart was also crushed, but neither the poor girl's tears nor the wondrous charm of her sorrow could move his icy soul. He felt no pang of conscience over the old woman's death. The one thought appalling him was the irretrievable loss of the secret that he had expected to make him rich.

"You are a monster!" said Lizaveta Ivanovna at last.

"I did not wish her death," Hermann answered. "My pistol is not loaded."

They both grew silent.

It was getting toward morning. Lizaveta Ivanovna extinguished the burned-down candles; a pale light spread across her room. She wiped her eyes, red from crying, and fixed them on Hermann: he was sitting on the windowsill with arms folded and brows fiercely knitted. In this pose he bore an amazing resemblance to Napoleon's portrait. Even Lizaveta Ivanovna was struck by the likeness.

"How are you going to get out of the house?" she broke the silence.

"I thought of leading you out by a secret staircase, but we would have to go past the bedroom, which scares me."

"Just tell me how to find this secret staircase, and I'll go out by myself."

Lizaveta Ivanovna got up, took a key from her chest of drawers, handed it to Hermann, and gave him detailed instructions. Hermann pressed her cold, unresponsive hand, kissed her bowed head, and went out.

He descended the winding staircase and once more entered the Countess's bedroom. The dead old woman sat petrified; profound tranquility was reflected in her face. Hermann stopped before her, looked at her for a long time as if wishing to ascertain the terrible truth; at last he stepped into the study, felt for the door behind the wall hanging, and began to descend the dark staircase, his mind agitated by strange feelings. "Perhaps," he thought, "up this very staircase, about sixty years ago, into this same bedroom, at this same hour, dressed in an embroidered coat, with his hair combed *à l'oiseau royal,* pressing his three-cornered hat to his heart, there stole a lucky young man, now long since turned to dust in his grave; and the heart of his aged mistress has stopped beating today..."

At the bottom of the stairs Hermann opened another door with the same key, and found himself in a passageway leading to the street.

5

> That night the late Baroness von W. appeared
> to me. She was dressed all in white, and
> said, "How do you do, Mr. Councillor?"
>   SWEDENBORG[25]

Three days after the fatal night, at nine o'clock in the morning, Hermann set out for the Z. Monastery, where the funeral service for the deceased Countess was to be performed. Although he did not feel repentant, he could not completely silence the voice of his conscience, which kept telling him, "You are the old lady's murderer!" Deficient in true faith, he was nevertheless subject to many superstitions. He believed that the dead Countess could exercise an evil influence on his life, and he decided to go to her funeral in order to ask her pardon.

The church was full. Hermann had difficulty pushing his way through the crowd. The coffin lay on a sumptuous catafalque under a velvet canopy. The deceased lay in her coffin with her arms folded over her chest, in a lace cap and white atlas dress. She was surrounded by her domestics and relations: her servants dressed in black caftans with the family's coat of arms on the shoulders and holding candles in their hands, and her family—children, grandchildren, great-grandchildren—dressed in deep mourning. Nobody wept: tears would have been *une affectation.* The Countess was so very old that her death could not have come as a surprise to anyone; her relatives had considered her on the edge of the grave for quite some time. A young bishop gave the funeral sermon. He depicted in simple, moving words the peaceful ascent into heaven of the righteous, whose long years had been a serene, inspiring preparation for a Christian end. "The angel of death found her," said the orator, "waiting for the midnight bridegroom, vigilant in godly meditation."[26] The service was concluded in an atmosphere of somber propriety. The relatives went first to pay their last respects to the deceased. Then came the numerous guests, filing by in order to take their last bow before her who had so long participated in their frivolous amusements. Then all the domestics followed. Finally came the old housekeeper, a contemporary of the deceased. Two young girls led her by the arms. She was too weak to bow all the way to the ground; she alone shed a few tears as she kissed her mistress's cold hand. After her Hermann, too, decided to go up to the coffin. He bowed to the ground and lay for several minutes on the cold floor strewn with fir branches. At last he rose to his feet, pale as the deceased herself, mounted the steps of the catafalque, and bent over... At that moment it seemed to him that the deceased cast a mocking glance at him, screwing up one of her eyes. He moved back hastily, missed his step, and crashed to the ground flat on his back. As he was lifted to his feet, Lizaveta Ivanovna had to be carried out on the porch, unconscious. This incident disturbed for a few minutes the solemnity of the somber rite. A muffled murmur arose among those in attendance, and a gaunt chamberlain—a close relative of the deceased— whispered into the ear of an Englishman standing by him that the young officer was the dead woman's illegitimate son, to which the Englishman responded with a cold "Oh?"

Hermann was extremely distressed that whole day. Dining at a secluded tavern, he drank too much, which was not his wont, in the hope of calming his inner agitation. But the wine only further inflamed his imagination. Returning home, he threw himself on his bed fully clothed, and fell into a deep sleep.

It was night when he woke up; the moon was shining into his room. He glanced at his watch: it was a quarter to three. Not feeling sleepy any more, he sat on his bed and thought about the old Countess's funeral.

Just then somebody looked in from the street through the window, and immediately went away. Hermann paid no attention. A minute later he could hear the door of the anteroom open. His orderly, thought Hermann, was returning from a nocturnal outing, drunk as usual. But he heard unfamiliar steps: somebody was softly shuffling along in slippers. The door opened, and a woman in a white dress came in. Hermann took her for his old nurse and wondered what could have brought her here at this time of night. But the woman in white glided across the room and suddenly appeared right before him: Hermann recognized the Countess in her!

"I have come to you against my will," she said to him in a firm voice. "I have been ordered to grant your request. The trey, the seven, and the ace will win for you in succession, but only under the condition that you play no more than one card within one day, and that afterwards you never play again for the rest of your life. I will forgive you my death under the condition that you marry my ward, Lizaveta Ivanovna..."

After these words she quietly turned around, went to the door, and left, shuffling her slippers. Hermann heard the front door slam and once more saw someone looking in through his window.

Hermann was unable to regain his senses for a long time. He went into the other room. His orderly was asleep on the floor; Hermann had great difficulty waking him up. The orderly was drunk as usual: it was impossible to get any sense out of him. The front door was locked. Hermann returned to his own room, lit a candle, and jotted down his vision.

6

> "*Attendez!*"
> "How dare you say *attendez* to me?"
> "Your Excellency, I said *attendez, sir!*"[27]

Two fixed ideas can no more coexist in the moral sphere than can two bodies occupy the same space in the physical world. The trey, the seven, and the ace soon overshadowed the image of the dead old woman in Hermann's mind. Trey, seven, ace—the threesome haunted him and was perpetually on his lips. Seeing a young girl, he would say, "How shapely! Just like a trey of hearts." If anybody asked him what time it was, he would answer, "Five to the seven." Every portly man reminded him of an ace. The trey, the seven, and the ace hounded him even in his dreams, taking on every imaginable form: the trey blossomed before him like a great luxuriant flower; the seven appeared as a Gothic gate; and the ace assumed the shape of an enormous spider. All his thoughts converged on the one idea of using the secret for which he had paid so dearly. He began to consider retirement and travel. It was his intention to wrest a fortune from the hands of an enchanted Fate in the public gambling casinos of Paris. But chance saved him from any such effort.

Wealthy gamblers formed a group in Moscow under the deanship of the famous Chekalinskii, who had spent all his life over the card table and had at one time made millions, even though he had been winning promissory notes while losing ready cash. His many years of experience had earned him the trust of his fellow gamblers; his open door, excellent cook, cordiality, and cheerfulness had won him universal admiration. He came to St. Petersburg. Young men thronged to his house, forgetting the balls for the sake of cards and preferring the seductions of faro to the enticements of gallantry. Narumov brought Hermann to him.

The two young men passed through a series of magnificently furnished rooms, well attended by polite waiters. Some generals and privy councillors were playing whist; there were young people eating ice cream or smoking their pipes, sprawled on damask-upholstered sofas. In the drawing room twenty or so players crowded around a long table, behind which sat the host, holding the bank. He was about sixty, of a highly respectable appearance. Silver hair covered his head; his fresh-complexioned round face reflected good nature; his eyes sparkled, animated by a continual smile. Narumov introduced Hermann. Chekalinskii cordially shook the young man's hand, asked him not to stand on ceremony, and continued dealing.

The deal lasted a long time. There were more than thirty cards on the table. Chekalinskii stopped after each turn to give the players time to make their wishes known; he jotted down losses, courteously listened to requests, and even more courteously straightened out the odd corner that had been bent down incorrectly by a roaming hand. At last the deal was completed. Chekalinskii shuffled the deck and was about to begin a new deal.

"Allow me to place a bet," said Hermann, reaching over from behind a corpulent gentleman who was punting at the table. Chekalinskii gave a smile and a silent bow in token of his humble compliance. Narumov laughingly congratulated Hermann on breaking his long-sustained fast and wished him beginner's luck.

"Ready," said Hermann, writing the amount above his card in chalk.[28]

"How much is that, sir?" the banker asked, screwing his eyes. "Forgive me, I cannot make it out."

"Forty-seven thousand," said Hermann.

At these words all heads turned, and all eyes fastened on Hermann. "He has lost his mind," thought Narumov.

"Allow me to remark," said Chekalinskii, with his immutable smile, "that your game is bold. So far no one here has placed more than two hundred and seventy-five on a *simple.*"[29]

"What of it?" rejoined Hermann. "Will you make the play or not?"

Chekalinskii bowed with the same air of humble compliance. "All I wished to bring to your attention was," he said, "that, deemed worthy of my friends' confidence as I am, I can hold the bank only against ready cash. I am of course personally convinced that your word suffices, but for the sake of order in the game and the accounts, I ask you to place the money on the card."

Hermann took a bank note out of his pocket and gave it to Chekalinskii, who after a quick glance at it placed it on Hermann's card.

Chekalinskii proceeded to deal. A nine fell to his right, and a trey to his left.

"It's a winner," said Hermann, showing his card.

A murmur arose among the players. Chekalinskii frowned for a moment, but the usual smile soon returned to his face.

"Do you wish to receive your winnings now?" he asked Hermann.

"If you please."

Chekalinskii took several bank notes out of his pocket and immediately settled his account. Hermann took the money and left the table. Narumov could hardly recover his senses. Hermann drank a glass of lemonade and went home.

The next evening he was at Chekalinskii's again. The host was dealing. The punters made room for Hermann as soon as he approached the table. Chekalinskii bowed to him affably.

Hermann waited until a new deal began; then he led a card, placing both his original forty-seven thousand and his win of the previous night on it.

Chekalinskii began dealing. A jack fell to his right and a seven to his left.

Hermann turned his seven face up.

Everybody gasped. Chekalinskii was visibly flustered. He counted out ninety-four thousand and handed it over to Hermann. The latter took it with equanimity and left at once.

The following evening Hermann once more presented himself at the table. Everybody had been expecting him. The generals and privy councillors abandoned their whist in order to watch such an extraordinary game. The young officers jumped up from their sofas, and all the waiters gathered in the drawing room. Everyone crowded around Hermann. The other players made no wagers, impatiently waiting to see the outcome of his play. Hermann stood by the table, ready to punt against the pale, though still smiling, Chekalinskii. Each unsealed a new pack of cards. Chekalinskii shuffled. Hermann picked a card and placed it on the table, covering it with a stack of bank notes. It was like a duel. A profound silence reigned over the gathering.

Chekalinskii started dealing with trembling hands. On his right showed a queen, on his left an ace.

"The ace has won!" said Hermann and turned his card face up.

"Your lady has been murdered," said Chekalinskii affably.[30]

Hermann shuddered: indeed, instead of an ace, the queen of spades lay before him. He could not believe his eyes; he could not fathom how he could possibly have pulled the wrong card.[31]

Suddenly, it seemed to him that the queen of spades had screwed up her eyes and grinned. An extraordinary likeness struck him...

"The old woman!" he cried out in terror.

Chekalinskii gathered in the bank notes lost by Hermann. The young man stood by the table, motionless. When at last he left the table, the whole room burst into loud talk. "Splendid punting!" the players kept saying. Chekalinskii shuffled the cards anew: the game resumed its usual course.

Conclusion

Hermann has lost his mind. He is at the Obukhov Hospital, ward number 17; he doesn't answer questions, just keeps muttering with uncommon rapidity, "Trey, seven, ace! Trey, seven, queen!"

Lizaveta Ivanovna has married a very pleasant young man; he holds a position somewhere in the civil service and has a handsome fortune of his own: he is the son of the old Countess's former steward. Lizaveta Ivanovna is bringing up the daughter of a poor relation.

Tomskii has been promoted to captain and is engaged to marry Princess Polina.

Kirdzhali
(1834)[1]

Kirdzhali was a Bulgarian by birth. The word *kirdzhali* in Turkish means warrior, daredevil.[2] Kirdzhali terrorized the whole of Moldavia with his robberies. Let me recount one of his exploits, just to give an idea of them. One night he and the Albanian Mihajllaki between the two of them attacked a Bulgarian village. They set it on fire from either end, and went from hut to hut. Kirdzhali murdered while Mihajllaki carried the loot. They both shouted, "Kirdzhali! Kirdzhali!" The villagers scattered in all directions.

When Alexander Ypsilanti proclaimed his uprising and began to recruit troops, Kirdzhali joined up with several of his old comrades. They had no clear notion of what the Hetairia was actually striving for, but they could plainly see that the war presented an opportunity to get rich at the expense of the Turks, and possibly of the Moldavians.

Alexander Ypsilanti was a courageous individual, but he did not possess the qualities required for the role he had so fervently and rashly undertaken. He could not cope with the men he was supposed to lead. They neither respected nor trusted him. After the unfortunate battle in which the flower of Greek youth perished, Yorghakis Olympios advised him to step down and took his place.[3] Ypsilanti rode off to the borders of Austria and sent back a curse on his men, calling them insubordinate cowards and scoundrels. Most of these cowards and scoundrels had perished either within the walls of the Seku Monastery or on the banks of the Prut, desperately trying to fight off an enemy that outnumbered them ten to one.[4]

Kirdzhali served in the detachment of Georgii Kantakuzen,[5] about whom one could repeat what has already been said of Ypsilanti. On the eve of the battle near Skuliany, Kantakuzen asked the Russian authorities for permission to enter our compound. The detachment remained without a commander, but Kirdzhali, Saphianos, Kantagoni, and their comrades did not see any need for a commander.

No one, it seems, has described the battle near Skuliany in its full pathetic reality. Imagine seven hundred men—Arnauts, Albanians, Greeks, Bulgarians, and every other kind of rabble[6]—who had no concept of military art and were retreating in the face of a Turkish cavalry of fifteen thousand. This detachment drew back to the bank of the Prut and set up two tiny cannon, brought along from the hospodar's courtyard at Jassy, where they had been used for firing salvos during dinner parties on the hospodar's saint's day.[7] The Turks would have no doubt liked to fire grapeshot, but did not dare to without permission from the Russian authorities, for some would have inevitably hit our side of the river. The commander of the compound (deceased by now), who had served in the military for forty years but had never heard a bullet whistle, at last had a God-given opportunity to hear some.[8] Several whizzed by his ears. The old man lost his temper and gave the major of the Okhotsk Infantry Regiment, guarding the compound, a thorough dressing-down. The major, not knowing what to do, ran down to the river, on the other side of which the Turkish cavalrymen were wheeling their horses, and shook his finger at them. Seeing his gesture, the Turkish cavalry turned around and galloped off, followed by the whole detachment. The major who shook his finger at them was called Khorchevskii. I do not know what became of him later.

Nevertheless, the next day the Turks attacked the Hetairists. Afraid to use either grapeshot or ball, as they normally would, they decided to use cold steel. The battle was ruthless. Both sides fought chiefly with yataghans. On the Turkish side, however, some spears could be seen as well, though the Turks had not been known to use that weapon. They turned out to be Russian spears: Nekrasa's descendants were fighting in the Turks' ranks.[9] The Hetairists had our Emperor's permission to cross the Prut and seek asylum in our compound. They began to move across. Kantagoni and Saphianos were the last ones to stay on the Turkish side. Kirdzhali, who had been wounded the evening before, was already abed in the compound station. Saphianos was killed. Kantagoni, a very fat man, was stabbed in the stomach by a spear. He raised his saber with one hand, and he grasped his enemy's spear and thrust it deeper into himself; in this way he was able to reach his murderer with his saber, and the two of them fell together.

It was all over. The Turks were the victors. Moldavia was cleared of the Hetairists. About six hundred Albanians were scattered throughout Bessarabia; although they had no livelihood, they were nevertheless grateful to Russia for her protection. They led an idle but by no means reprobate existence. One could always see them in the coffeehouses of semi-Turkish Bessarabia, with their long-stemmed pipes in their mouths, sipping thick coffee from tiny cups. Their embroidered jackets and red pointed slippers were beginning to look worn, but their tufted calots still sat on their heads aslant, and their yataghans and pistols still protruded from their wide belts. Nobody had any complaints against them. It was impossible even to think that these poor, peaceful people had been the most notorious brigands of Moldavia, comrades of the ferocious Kirdzhali, and that he himself was among them.

The pasha serving as governor of Jassy learned of this fact and, citing the provisions of the peace treaty, demanded the extradition of the brigand.

The police began an investigation. They learned that Kirdzhali was indeed in Kishinev, and captured him at the house of a runaway monk one evening when he was eating his supper, sitting in the dark with seven comrades.

He was put under arrest. Without the slightest attempt to conceal the truth, he admitted he was Kirdzhali.

"But," he added, "since the time I crossed the Prut I have not touched a grain of anyone else's property, have not harmed the lowliest Gypsy. To the Turks, the Moldavians, and the Wallachians I am, of course, a brigand, but among the Russians I am a guest. When Saphianos, having used up all his grapeshot, came into the compound to take the buttons, nails, chains, and yataghan handles from the wounded to be used for the last shots, I gave him twenty *beşliks* and was left without any money.[10] God is my witness that I, Kirdzhali, have been living on alms! Why, then, are the Russians handing me over to my enemies?"

From then on Kirdzhali kept silent and calmly awaited the resolution of his fate.

He did not have to wait long. The authorities, not obliged to regard brigands in their romantic aspect and convinced that the demand for extradition was just, gave orders to transport Kirdzhali to Jassy.

A man of intelligence and sensitivity—at that time an unknown young civil servant, today an important official—has described to me in vivid colors Kirdzhali's departure.[11]

A mail *căruță* stood by the prison gate... (Perhaps you do not know what a *căruță* is. It is a low wicker-covered cart, to which even recently six or eight jades were usually harnessed. A mustachioed Moldavian, wearing a sheepskin hat, would sit astride one of them, constantly shouting and cracking his whip, and the little jades would run at quite a lively trot. If one of them began to lag behind, he would unharness it with horrible oaths and abandon it on the road, not caring what became of it. On his way back he would be sure to find it calmly grazing in a green pasture near the same place. It happened quite frequently that a traveler who had left one post station with eight horses would arrive at another with only a pair. Nowadays, in Russified Bessarabia, Russian harness and Russian carts have taken over.)

Such a *căruță* stood by the prison gate one day toward the end of September 1821.[12] Jewesses, nonchalantly flopping their slippers, Albanians in their tattered colorful costumes, and shapely Moldavian women with black-eyed babies in their arms surrounded the *căruță*. The men were silent, the women eagerly waited for something to happen.

The gate opened, and several police officers came into the street; two soldiers followed them, bringing out Kirdzhali in fetters.

He seemed to be about thirty years old. The features of his swarthy face were regular and stern. He was tall and broad-shouldered, and in general appeared to possess uncommon physical strength. A colorful turban sat obliquely on his head; a wide belt hugged his narrow waist; a dolman of thick blue cloth, a shirt with ample folds that hung almost to his knees, and handsome slippers made up the rest of his costume. The expression on his face was dignified and calm.

One of the officials, a red-faced little old man in a faded uniform with only three buttons dangling on it, pinched with his nickel-framed glasses the purple lump that passed as his nose, unfolded a document, and began reading it in Moldavian with a nasal twang. From time to time he cast a haughty glance at the fettered Kirdzhali, to whom the document evidently referred. Kirdzhali listened attentively. The official finished his reading, folded the document, bellowed menacingly at the crowd, commanding it to make way, and ordered the *căruță* to be brought up. At this time Kirdzhali turned to him and said a few words in Moldavian; his voice trembled and the expression on his face changed; he burst into tears and, clanking his chains, threw himself at the police official's feet. The official, frightened, jumped back; the soldiers were about to lift Kirdzhali up, but he rose to his feet himself, gathered up his shackles, stepped into the *căruță*, and cried out, "Go!" A gendarme got in next to him, the Moldavian cracked his whip, and the *căruță* rolled off.

"What was it Kirdzhali said to you?" the young civil servant asked the police official.

"He asked me, my dear sir," replied the official laughing, "if I would protect his wife and child, who live not far from Kilia in a Bulgarian settlement: he is afraid that they will suffer *because of him*. Stupid people, my dear sir."

The scene the young civil servant had related profoundly moved me. I felt sorry for poor Kirdzhali. For some time I knew nothing about his subsequent fate. It was several years later that I met the young civil servant again. We started talking about the past.

"And what about your friend Kirdzhali?" I asked. "Do you know what has become of him?"

"I do indeed," he answered, and told me the following.

Brought to Jassy, Kirdzhali was delivered over to the pasha, who sentenced him to be impaled. The execution was postponed until some holiday. For the time being he was locked up in a prison.

The captive was guarded by seven Turks (simple people, and brigands at heart, just like Kirdzhali); they respected him and listened to his marvelous stories with the characteristic eagerness of people of the East.

A close friendship developed between the guards and the captive. One day Kirdzhali said to them, "Brothers! My hour is drawing close. No one can escape his fate. I shall soon part with you. I would like to leave something to you to remember me by."

The Turks pricked up their ears.

"Brothers," continued Kirdzhali, "three years ago, when I was marauding with the late Mihajllaki, we buried in the steppe, not far from Jassy, a pot full of *galbens*.[13] It is evident that neither of us is destined to make use of that pot. Since that can't be helped, you take it for yourselves and divide it with brotherly love."

The Turks practically went out of their minds. There began a discussion of how they could find the hidden place. They considered, and considered, and resolved that Kirdzhali himself should lead them there.

Night fell. The Turks took the fetters off the captive's feet, tied his hands with a rope, and decamped with him, heading for the steppe.

Kirdzhali led them, keeping to the same direction, from one burial mound to the next.[14] They walked for a long time. At last Kirdzhali stopped by a wide rock, measured off twenty paces to the south, stamped his foot, and said, "Here."

The Turks set about the task. Four of them drew out their yataghans and began digging. Three of them kept guard. Kirdzhali sat on the rock and watched their work.

"Well, and how much longer?" he kept asking. "Haven't you reached it yet?"

"Not yet," answered the Turks, and labored so hard that sweat came pouring off them.

Kirdzhali began to show impatience.

"What dumb people," he said. "They don't even know how to dig properly. I would have finished the whole business in two minutes. Look here, lads! Untie my hands and give me a yataghan!"

The Turks pondered and debated the matter.

"Why not?" they decided. "Let us untie his hands and give him a yataghan. What harm could there be? He is just one man, and there are seven of us." And they untied his hands and gave him a yataghan.

Kirdzhali was at last free and armed. What a feeling it must have been! He began to dig briskly, with the guards helping... Suddenly he stuck his yataghan into one of them, left the blade in his chest, and grabbed the two pistols from the man's belt.

The other six, seeing Kirdzhali armed with two pistols, ran away.

Nowadays Kirdzhali preys upon the environs of Jassy. Not long ago he wrote to the hospodar, demanding five thousand lei and threatening, in case the payment should not be forthcoming, to burn Jassy and lay his hands on the hospodar himself. The five thousand lei were delivered to him.

Isn't Kirdzhali something?

A Tale of Roman Life
(1833, 1835)[1]

Caesar was traveling; a number of us, with Titus Petronius, were following him at a distance.[2] When the sun set, the slaves erected the tent and arranged the couches; we lay down to feast and engaged in cheerful conversation. At dawn we resumed our journey and, fatigued by the heat and the night's amusements, pleasantly dozed off, each on his litter.

We reached Cumae and were about to proceed farther when a messenger from Nero arrived. He brought Petronius an order from Caesar to return to Rome and there to await word about his fate—the consequence of an invidious denunciation.

We were horror-stricken. Petronius alone listened to the verdict with equanimity; he dismissed the courier with a gift and announced to us that he intended to remain in Cumae. He sent off his favorite slave to choose and rent a house for him, while he waited in a cypress grove consecrated to the Eumenides.[3]

We gathered around him anxiously. Flavius Aurelius asked him how long he intended to stay in Cumae and whether he was not afraid of rousing Nero's ire by his disobedience.

"Not only do I not intend to disobey him," answered Petronius with a smile, "but I propose to anticipate his wishes. As for you, my friends, I advise you to return. On a clear day a traveler will rest in the shade of an oak, but in a storm he will be wise to move away from it for fear of thunderbolts."

We all declared our wish to remain with him, and he thanked us warmly. The servant returned and led us to the house he had chosen. It was on the outskirts of the city. An old freedman was looking after it in the absence of its owner, who had left Italy a long time ago. A few slaves, under his supervision, kept the rooms and the gardens tidy. On the wide portico we found images of the Nine Muses, and two centaurs stood at the entrance.

Petronius stopped at the marble threshold and read the greeting carved on it: "Welcome!" A sad smile came over his face. The old custodian led him to the bibliotheca, where we inspected some scrolls; then we proceeded to the master bedroom. It was appointed simply, with only two statues, both of the family. One represented a matron seated in an armchair, the other a little girl playing with a ball. A small lamp stood on the bedside table. Petronius stayed here for a rest, dismissing us and inviting us to gather in his room toward evening.

My heart was so full of sorrow that I could not go to sleep. I regarded Petronius not only as a generous patron, but also as a friend, genuinely attached to me. I respected his capacious mind and loved his exquisite soul. My conversations with him gave me a knowledge of the world and people—subjects I otherwise knew more from the teachings of the divine Plato than from my own experience. His judgment was usually quick and sure. His indifference to everything saved him from bias, and his forthright attitude toward himself made him perspicacious. Life could no longer present anything new to him; he had experienced all its pleasures; his feelings were dormant, dulled by habit, but his mind had preserved an astonishing freshness. He loved the free play of ideas as much as the euphony of words. An avid listener to philosophical discussions, he himself composed poems no worse than those of Catullus.

I went out into the garden and spent a long time walking along the paths, which meandered under old trees. I sat down on a bench, in the shade of a tall poplar, next to the statue of a young satyr carving a reed pipe. Wishing somehow to dispel my sad thoughts, I took out my writing tablet and translated one of Anacreon's odes. Here is my translation, preserved in memory of that sad day:[4]

> Ever rarer, ever paler
> Grow the locks that grace my skull,
> In my jaws the teeth are frailer,
> In my eyes the spark grows dull.
> A few days are left me merely
> Till sweet life is due to fade,
> Atropos keeps count severely,
> Tatarus awaits my shade.—
> Dread the nether vault and chilly,
> Whither all the entrance find,
> None the exit; willy-nilly
> All descend—and pass from mind.

The sun was declining toward the west; I went to Petronius. I found him in the library. He was pacing up and down: his personal physician, Septimius, was with him. Seeing me, Petronius stopped and jokingly recited the following lines:[5]

> Any highly mettled steed
> By the branded haunch is known.
> And the boastful Parthian's breed
> By the hood which forms a cone.
> For a happy pair you need
> Look into their eyes alone.

"You have guessed correctly," I answered him, handing him my tablet. He read my verses. A cloud of pensiveness passed over his features but immediately dispersed.

"When I read poems like these," he said, "I am always curious to know about the fate of those who had been so struck by the thought of death: how did they actually die? Anacreon insists that the Tatar frightened him, but I don't believe him any more than I believe in Horace's faintheartedness. Do you know this ode of his?[6]

> Which god has brought you back again,
> The one with whom I shared the random
> Affright of arms, my first campaign,
> When desperate Brutus chased the phantom
> Of liberty for us in vain?
> You, in whose tent I sat, in lively
> Carousal drowning war's alarm,
> And ringlets garlanded with ivy
> Anointed with the Syrian balm?
> Recall the battle to perdition,
> When shamefully I dropped my shield,
> All vows and prayers, and quit the field,
> A pusillanimous patrician!
> Oh, how I trembled, how I fled!
> But Hermes, sudden vapors shaping,
> Enwrapped me and to safety sped
> From death which seemed beyond escaping...

"The shrewd versifier wanted to make Augustus and Maecenas laugh at his faintheartedness only because he did not want to remind them that he had been a comrade-in-arms of Cassius and Brutus. I don't know how you feel, but I find more sincerity in his exclamation: 'A sweet and seemly thing is death for country.' "[7]

We Were Spending the Evening
at Princess D.'s Dacha
(1835?)[1]

We were spending the evening at Princess D.'s dacha.

The name of Madame de Staël happened to come up in the conversation. Baron Dahlberg very badly, in broken French, recited the well-known anecdote of how she asked Bonaparte whom he considered the most outstanding woman in the world, and his amusing answer, "The one who has borne the most children" ("Celle qui a fait le plus d'enfants").

"What a splendid epigram!" remarked one of the guests.

"And she deserves it, too!" said one of the ladies. "How could she fish for compliments so clumsily?"

"To me it seems," said Sorokhtin, who had been taking a nap in an armchair from Hambs',[2] "to me it seems that neither was Madame de Staël asking for a madrigal, nor did Napoleon have an epigram in mind. She asked her question out of simple curiosity, which was perfectly understandable, and Napoleon expressed literally what he thought. But you don't trust the simplemindedness of geniuses."

The guests began to argue, and Sorokhtin dozed off again.

"But really," said the hostess, "whom do you consider the most outstanding woman in the world?"

"Watch it: you're fishing for compliments, too..."

"No, seriously..."

A discussion ensued: some named Madame de Staël, others the Maid of Orleans, still others Queen Elizabeth, Madame de Maintenon, Madame Roland, and so forth.[3]

A young man standing by the open fireplace (for a fireplace is never superfluous in Petersburg) decided to join the conversation for the first time.

"To my mind," he said, "the most outstanding woman ever was Cleopatra."

"Cleopatra?" responded the guests. "Well, of course... but why in particular?"

"There is one episode in her biography that has so gripped my imagination I can hardly look at a woman without thinking of Cleopatra."

"What episode is that?" asked the hostess. "Tell us."

"I can't: it's a queer story to tell."

"In what sense? Is it improper?"

"Yes, like almost everything that vividly depicts the terrifying mores of antiquity."

"Oh! Tell us, please tell us!"

"Oh no, don't tell us," interrupted Volskaia, a widow by divorce, primly casting down her fiery eyes.

"Come, come!" cried the hostess with impatience. "Qui est-ce donc que l'on trompe ici?[4] It was only yesterday that we watched *Antony*, and a copy of *Le Physiologie du mariage* is lying right here on the mantelpiece.[5] Improper! Whom are you trying to frighten? Stop playing tricks on us, Aleksei Ivanych! You're not a journalist. Tell us simply what you know about Cleopatra; be proper, though, if possible..."

Everyone laughed.

"God be my witness," said the young man, "I quail: I've become as bashful as the censorship. But if you wish... I must mention that among the Latin historians there is a certain Aurelius Victor, of whom you have probably never heard."

"Aurelius Victor?" interrupted Vershnev, who had at one time studied under the Jesuits. "Aurelius Victor was a writer of the fourth century. His works have been ascribed to Cornelius Nepos and even to Suetonius; he wrote the book *De Viris Illustribus*—about the noteworthy men of the city of Rome—I'm familiar with it."[6]

"Exactly so," continued Aleksei Ivanovich. "His little book is rather insignificant, but it contains the legend about Cleopatra that has so captured my imagination. And what is most remarkable, in this particular passage the dry and boring Aurelius Victor equals Tacitus in force of expression: 'Haec tantae libidinis fuit ut saepe prostiterit; tantae pulchritudinis ut multi noctem illius morte emerint.'"[7]

"Splendid!" cried Vershnev. "It reminds me of Sallustius—do you recall? 'Tantae...'"

"What is this, gentlemen?" asked the hostess. "Now you think fit to converse in Latin! How very amusing for the rest of us! Tell us, what does your Latin phrase mean?"

"The crux of the matter is that Cleopatra offered her beauty for sale, and many bought her nights at the price of their lives."

"How horrible!" said the ladies. "But what did you find so marvelous about it?"

"So marvelous? It seems to me that Cleopatra was not a trivial flirt, and that the price she attached to herself was not low. I suggested to N. that he write a narrative poem about it; he did start one, but gave it up."

"Very wisely so."

"What did he think he could get out of this subject? What was his main idea, do you remember?"

"He begins with a description of a feast in the Egyptian Queen's garden:

Dark, sultry night has invested the African sky; Alexandria has fallen asleep; its squares and streets have become quiet, and its houses have faded into shadows. Only the faraway light of Pharos burns in solitude amidst the city's spacious harbor, like a lamp at a sleeping beauty's bedside.

Bright and noisy are the halls of Ptolemy: Cleopatra is spreading a feast before her friends; the table is set with ivory spoons; three hundred youths are waiting on the guests; three hundred maidens are bearing amphorae full of Greek nectar around the table, under the silent, watchful gaze of three hundred eunuchs.

The colonnade of porphyry, exposed to the south and to the north, awaits the breath of Eurus; but the air is still, the lanterns' flame-tongues are burning still; the smoke from the incense-burners is borne aloft in a straight, still column; the sea, like a mirror, lies still by the steps of the rose-colored semicircular portico. In it the gilded claws and granite tails of guardian sphinxes find themselves reflected. Only the strains of the cithara and the lute ruffle the flames, the air, and the sea.

Suddenly the Queen became pensive and hung her exquisite head low; her sadness cast a gloom over the bright feast, as a cloud casts gloom over the sun.

What makes her sad?

> Why is a melancholy racking
> Her soul? Whatever could be lacking

The heir to Egypt's wealth of ages?
Securely walled by guards and pages,
Her Highness holds by languid reins
The jewel of the coastal plains.
The deities of earth attend her,
Her palaces abound in splendor.
Let blaze with heat the Nubian day,
Let cool nocturnal breezes play,
What art with luxury dispenses
Combines to court her dreamy senses,
All lands, the swells of every sea,
Bear her their toll of finery,
An endless choice of rich attire;
Now she will gleam with ruby fire,
Now robed and cloaked in purple shades
Aglow with dyes of Tyrian maids;
Then she may board her golden bark
And in the sail's translucent dark
Hoar Nilus' silver waters roam,
Like Aphrodite born of foam.[8]
Her days are gorged with sights and sounds
By feast on feast in ceaseless rounds,
Her nights—no fancy yields the keys
To all their sultry mysteries...

But all in vain! Her heart is wrenched
By nameless thirsting, never quenched;
Her oversated senses sicken,
With barrenness of feeling stricken...

Cleopatra awakens from her pensiveness.

Bedazed, the guests fall silent now;
But once again she lifts her brow,
And searing fire is in her gaze
As with a haughty smile she says:
"Do I not haunt your dreams like Venus?
Mark what I choose to tell you, then.
I may forget the gulf between us
And make you happiest of men.
Here is my challenge—who will meet it?
For sale I offer peerless nights.

Who will step forward—I repeat it—
And pay with life for his delights?"

"This subject should be brought to the attention of Marquise George Sand, who is as shameless as your Cleopatra. She would adapt your Egyptian anecdote to contemporary mores."

"That would be impossible. It would completely lack verisimilitude. This is an anecdote exclusively of the ancient world; a bargain of this kind would be as impractical today as the erection of pyramids."

"Why impractical? Couldn't you find one among today's women who would want to test in deed the truth of what men repeat to her every minute—that her love is dearer to them than their lives?"

"That would be interesting to find out, I suppose. But how could you carry out your scientific experiment? Cleopatra had at her disposal all the necessary means to make her debtors pay. But do we? After all, you cannot draw up such agreements on legal paper and have them notarized in civil court."

"In that case it would be possible to rely on the man's *word of honor*."

"How would that be?"

"A woman could accept a man's word of honor that he would shoot himself the following day."

"And the following day he could leave for foreign lands, making a fool of his lady."

"Yes, if he was willing to remain forever dishonest in the eyes of the woman he loves. When you consider, is the condition itself so hard to accept? Is life such a treasure that one would begrudge sacrificing it for happiness? Just think of it: the first scamp happening by, whom I despise, says something about me that cannot hurt me in any way, yet I expose my forehead to his bullet. I have no right to deny this satisfaction to the first bully coming my way who takes it into his head to test my sangfroid. And yet you think I would act like a coward when my bliss is at stake? What is life worth if it is poisoned by dejection and unfulfilled desires? What remains in it if all its delights have been sapped?"

"Would you really be capable of entering into such a contract?"

At this moment Volskaia, who had been sitting silently with her eyes cast down, quickly glanced at Aleksei Ivanovich.

"I am not speaking about myself. But a man truly in love would not hesitate for a moment."

"Is that so? Even for a woman who didn't love you? (If she agreed to such a proposal she would certainly not be in love with you.) The very thought of such bestial cruelty would be enough to destroy the most reckless passion."

"No: in her agreement I would see only an ardency of imagination. As for requited love... that I do not demand: why should it be anyone's business if I am in love?"

"Oh, stop it—heaven knows what you're saying. So that's the anecdote you didn't want to tell us."

The young Countess K., a homely, plump little woman, tried to lend an air of importance to her nose, which looked like an onion stuck into a turnip, and said, "There are women even today who value themselves highly."

Her husband, a Polish Count who had married her out of (they say mistaken) calculation, cast his eyes down and drank up his tea.

"What do you mean by that, Countess?" asked the young man, hardly able to restrain a smile.

"What I mean is," answered the Countess K., "that a woman who respects herself, who respects..." But she became entangled in her thought. Vershnev came to her rescue.

"You think that a woman who respects herself will not wish death on the sinner, right?"

The conversation changed course.

Aleksei Ivanych sat down next to Volskaia and, leaning over as if examining her needlework, said in a whisper, "What do you think of Cleopatra's contract?"

Volskaia remained silent. Aleksei Ivanych repeated his question.

"What shall I say? Today, too, some women value themselves highly. But the men of the nineteenth century are too cold-blooded and sober-minded to enter into such contracts."

"You think," said Aleksei Ivanych in a voice that had suddenly changed, "you really think that in our time, in Petersburg, one can find a woman who has enough pride and spiritual strength to demand Cleopatra's condition of her lover?"

"I think so; I am even convinced."

"You're not deceiving me? Just consider: that would be too cruel, more cruel even than the condition itself."

Volskaia looked at him with her fiery, penetrating eyes and pronounced in a firm voice, "No, I am not."

Aleksei Ivanych rose and disappeared on the instant.

Egyptian Nights
(1835?)[1]

I

"Quel est cet homme?"
"Ha, c'est un bien grand
talent, il fait de sa voix tout
ce qu'il veut."
"Il devrait bien, madame,
s'en faire une culotte."[2]

Charskii was a kind of person indigenous to St. Petersburg. He was
not quite thirty; not married; and held a position in the civil service
that placed no great burden on him. His late uncle, who had been a
vice-governor at a prosperous time, had left him a handsome estate.[3]
He was in a position to lead a very pleasant life; but he had the unfortunate habit of writing and publishing poetry. In the journals they
called him a poet, in the servants' quarters, a scribbler.

Despite all the great advantages enjoyed by versifiers (it must be admitted that apart from the privileges of using the accusative instead of
the genitive case and one or two other acts of so-called poetic license,
we do not know of any particular advantages Russian versifiers could
be said to enjoy)—however that may be, despite all their advantages
these people are subject to a great deal of trouble and unpleasantness.
The most bitter and intolerable bane of the poet is his title, his sobriquet, with which he is branded and of which he can never rid himself.
The reading public look on him as though he were their property: in
their opinion, he was born for their *benefit and pleasure.*[4] If he has
just returned from the country, the first person he runs into will ask
him, "Have you brought with you a new little something for us?" If he
is sunk in thought about his tangled finances or about the illness of
someone close to his heart, this will immediately provoke the inane
exclamation, accompanied by an inane smile, "No doubt you are
composing something!" And should he fall in love, the lady of his
heart will promptly buy an album at the English store and be ready to
receive an elegy. If he goes to see a man whom he hardly knows, about

an important business matter, the man will inevitably call in his young son, ordering him to recite some poetry; and the lad will treat the poet to the latter's own verses, with distortions. And these are only the laurels of his profession! What must its pains be like? The salutations, inquiries, albums, and little boys irritated him so much, Charskii confessed, that he constantly had to be on his guard lest he make some rude response.[5]

Charskii did everything in his power to rid himself of the insufferable sobriquet. He avoided the company of his fellow men of letters, preferring to them people of high society, even the shallowest. His conversation was of the most commonplace character, and he never touched on questions of literature. In his dress he always followed the latest fashion with great diffidence and veneration, as if he were a young Muscovite visiting Petersburg for the first time in his life. In his study, furnished like a lady's bedroom, nothing betrayed the habits of a writer: there were no books scattered about, on or under the tables; the sofa was not stained with ink; there was no sign of the sort of disorder that reveals the presence of the muse and the absence of broom and brush. He was thrown into despair if any of his society friends caught him with pen in hand. It was hard to believe to what pettiness he could stoop, even though, as a matter of fact, he was a gifted man, endowed with ready wit and feeling. He always pretended to be something else: now a passionate lover of horses, now a desperate gambler, now the most discriminating gastronome, though he could in no way tell a mountain pony from an Arabian steed, could never remember the trump cards, and secretly preferred baked potatoes to all the inventions of French cuisine. He led the most distracted existence: he hung about all the balls, overindulged himself at all the diplomatic dinners, and was just as unavoidable at every reception as Rezanov's ice cream.[6]

He was a poet nevertheless, and his passion for poetry was indomitable: when he felt this *nonsense* approach (that was what he called inspiration), he locked himself in his study and wrote from morning till late night. He confessed to his genuine friends that he knew true happiness only at such times. The rest of the time he led his dissipated life, put on airs, dissembled, and perpetually heard the famous question, "Have you written a new little something?"

One morning Charskii felt he was in that exuberant state of mind when fantasies arise before you in clear outline, when you find vivid, unexpected words in which to incarnate your visions, when verses readily flow from your pen, and when resonant rhymes run up to meet well-ordered thoughts. His spirit was immersed in sweet oblivion... Society, the opinions of society, and his own conceits were all banished from his mind. He was writing a poem.

Suddenly the door of his study creaked and an unfamiliar face appeared in it. Charskii started and frowned.

"Who is it?" he asked with irritation, mentally cursing his servants who never stayed put in his anteroom.

The stranger entered.

He was tall and thin, and looked about thirty. The features of his swarthy face were distinctive: his pale high forehead, framed in black locks, his sparkling black eyes, his aquiline nose, and his thick beard, which encircled his sunken, tawny cheeks, all revealed the foreigner in him. He wore a black frock coat, already graying along the seams, and a pair of summer trousers (though the season was well into the autumn); a fake diamond glittered on the yellowing shirtfront under his worn black tie; his fraying hat appeared to have seen both rain and sunshine in its day. If you had met this man in the woods, you would have taken him for a robber; in society, for a political conspirator; and in an anteroom, for a charlatan peddling elixirs and arsenic.

"What do you want?" Charskii asked him in French.

"Signor," answered the foreigner with low bows, "lei voglia perdonarmi se..."[7]

Charskii did not offer him a chair but stood up himself; the exchange continued in Italian.

"I am a Neapolitan artist," said the stranger. "Circumstances forced me to leave my country. I have come to Russia hoping to make use of my talent here."

Charskii thought that the Neapolitan intended to give some cello concerts and was selling tickets door to door. He was about to hand the man his twenty-five rubles, hoping to get rid of him fast, but the stranger added:

"I hope, *signor*, that you will do a brotherly favor for a fellow artist and will introduce me to the houses to which you yourself have access."

It would have been impossible to deliver a sharper blow to Charskii's vanity. He cast a haughty glance at the man who called himself his fellow artist.

"Allow me to ask who you are and what you take me for," he said, making a great effort to keep his indignation under control.

The Neapolitan noticed his irritation.

"Signor," he answered faltering, "ho creduto... ho sentito... la Vostra Eccelenza mi perdonera..."[8]

"What do you want?" Charskii repeated dryly.

"I have heard a great deal about your marvelous talent, and I am convinced that men of quality in this country consider it an honor to offer their patronage in every way to such an excellent poet," answered the Italian, "and therefore I have taken the liberty of presenting myself to you..."

"You are mistaken, *signor*," Charskii interrupted him. "The calling of poet does not exist in our country. Our poets do not receive the patronage of men of quality: our poets are men of quality themselves, and if any Maecenas here (devil take them all!) should fail to realize this, so much the worse for him. With us there are no tattered abbés whom a composer might pick up on a street corner to write a libretto. With us, poets do not walk door to door soliciting donations. As for my being a great poet, somebody must have been pulling your leg. It is true that I wrote a few bad epigrams at one time, but, thank heavens, I have nothing to do, nor wish to have anything to do, with *Messieurs les poètes*."

The poor Italian became confused. He gazed around him. The pictures, marble statuettes, bronze busts, and expensive gewgaws, arranged inside a Gothic display cabinet, amazed him. He understood that the arrogant dandy who stood before him wearing a tufted brocade skullcap and a gold-embroidered Chinese dressing gown, girded by a Turkish sash, could have nothing in common with him, a poor itinerant artist, in a frayed cravat and worn frock coat. He uttered some incoherent apologies, bowed, and made as if to leave. His pathetic figure moved Charskii who, despite the petty vanities of his character, had a warm and noble heart. He felt ashamed of his irritable sense of self-pride.

"Where are you going?" he said to the Italian. "Wait a minute... I had to decline the title undeservedly conferred on me and had to declare to you that I was no poet. But let us now speak about your affairs. I am willing to be at your service in whatever way I can. Are you a musician?"

"No, Eccelenza!" answered the Italian. "I am a penniless improvisatore."

"Improvisatore?" exclaimed Charskii, fully realizing the cruelty of his conduct. "Why didn't you tell me sooner that you were an improvisatore?" And Charskii pressed his hand with a feeling of sincere regret.

His friendly air reassured the Italian. He launched trustingly into details of what he contemplated doing. His outward appearance was not misleading: he did need money, and he was hoping in some way to improve his affairs in Russia. Charskii listened to him attentively.

"I hope," he said to the poor artist, "that you will have success: our society here has never heard an improvisatore. People's curiosity will be aroused; it is true that Italian is not in use among us, and therefore you will not be understood, but that doesn't matter: the main thing is that you should be in vogue."

"But if nobody among you understands Italian," said the improvisatore, pondering the matter, "who will come to listen to me?"

"They will come, don't worry: some out of curiosity, others just to kill the evening somehow, still others in order to show that they understand Italian; the only important thing, I repeat, is that you should be in vogue, and you will be, I give you my word."

Charskii parted with the improvisatore amiably, taking down his address, and he set about making arrangements for him that same evening.

2

> "I'm king and slave, I'm worm and god."
> DERZHAVIN[9]

The next day Charskii sought out room No. 35 along the dark and dirty corridor of a tavern. He stopped at the door and knocked. The Italian opened it.

"Victory!" said Charskii to him. "It's all arranged. The Princess N. will let you have her reception room; I already had occasion at last night's reception to recruit half of Petersburg; you must have your tickets and announcements printed. I can guarantee you, if not triumph, at least some profit..."

"And that is the main thing!" cried the Italian, demonstrating his joy by lively gestures, characteristic of his southern race. "I knew you would help me. *Corpo di Bacco!* You are a poet, just as I am; and say what you like, poets are splendid fellows! How can I express my gratitude? Wait a second... Would you like to hear an improvisation?"

"An improvisation?... Surely, you can't do without an audience, music, and the thunder of applause, can you?"

"All that's nonsense. Where could I find a better audience? You are a poet, you will understand me better than any of them, and your quiet encouragement will be dearer to me than a whole storm of applause... Sit down somewhere and give me a theme."

Charskii sat down on a trunk. (Of the two chairs in the cramped cubicle one was broken, the other one laden with a heap of papers and linen.) The improvisatore picked up a guitar from the table and stationed himself before Charskii, strumming on the strings with his bony fingers and waiting for his request.

"Here is a theme for you," said Charskii: *"a poet chooses the subjects of his songs himself: the crowd has no right to command his
inspiration."*

The Italian's eyes flashed; he played a few chords, proudly raised his
head, and impassioned stanzas, the expression of his momentary feeling, rose from his lips harmoniously... Here they follow—a free tran-
scription by a friend of what Charskii could recall: [10]

> The poet walks: his lids are open,
> But to all men his eyes are blind;
> Then by a ruffle of his robing
> Someone detains him from behind...
> "Why do you roam so void of purpose?
> Your eye no sooner scales a height
> Than you recall it to the surface
> And netherward direct your sight.
> Your view of the fair world is blurred.
> You are consumed by idle flames;
> Each minute you are lured and stirred
> By petty subjects' fancied claims.
> A genius soars above the earthy,
> The genuine poet ought to deem
> Of his exalted anthems worthy
> None but an elevated theme."
>
> "Why does the wind revolve inanely
> In hollows, raining leaves and dust,
> While vessels in the doldrums vainly
> Await its animating gust?
> Why, spurning mountain crag and tower,
> Does the great eagle's fearsome power
> Light on a withered stump? Ask him!
> Ask Desdemona why her whim
> Did on her dusky moor alight,
> As Luna fell in love with night?
> Like wind and erne, it is because
> A maiden's heart obeys no laws.
> Such is the poet: like the North,
> Whate'er he lists he carries forth,
> Wherever, eagle-like, he flies,
> Acknowledging no rule or owner,
> He finds a god, like Desdemona,
> For wayward heart to idolize."

The Italian grew silent... Charskii sat without a word, astonished and moved.

"Well?" asked the improvisatore.

Charskii grasped his hand and pressed it firmly.

"Well?" asked the improvisatore. "How was it?"

"Astonishing," answered the poet. "How can it be that someone else's idea, which had only just reached your ear, immediately became your own property, as if you had carried, fostered, and nurtured it for a long time? Does this mean that you never encounter either difficulty, or a dampening of spirit, or the restlessness that precedes inspiration?... Astonishing, astonishing!..."

The improvisatore's reply was:

"Every talent is inexplicable. How can a sculptor see a Jupiter hidden in a slab of Carrara marble and bring it to light, chipping off its shell with chisel and hammer? Why is it that a thought emerging from a poet's head is already equipped with four rhymes and measured in concordant, uniform feet? Similarly, no one except the improvisatore himself can comprehend this alacrity of impressions, this close tie between one's own inspiration and another's external will:[11] it would be in vain even if I tried to explain it to you. However... it's time to think about my first evening. What do you think? What should be the price of a ticket that would neither burden the public too much nor leave me out of pocket? *La signora* Catalani, they say, charged twenty-five rubles.[12] That's not a bad price..."

It was unpleasant for Charskii to fall so suddenly from the height of poetry into the bookkeeper's office, but he understood the demands of everyday life very well, and plunged into mercantile calculations with the Italian. The occasion revealed so much unbridled greed in the Italian, such simplehearted love of profit, that Charskii became disgusted with him and hastened to leave him, in order not to lose altogether the feeling of elation that the brilliant improvisation had aroused in him. The preoccupied Italian did not notice this change, and accompanied his guest along the corridor and down the staircase with deep bows and assurances of his everlasting gratitude.

3

The tickets are 10 rubles
each; the performance begins at 7 P.M.
FROM A POSTER

Princess N.'s reception room had been put at the improvisatore's disposal. A platform had been erected, and the chairs had been arranged in twelve rows. On the appointed day, at seven in the evening, the room was illuminated, and an old lady with a long nose, wearing a gray hat with drooping feathers and a ring on every finger, sat by the door behind a little table, charged with the sale and collection of tickets. Gendarmes stood by the main entrance. The audience was beginning to gather. Charskii was one of the first to arrive. Very much concerned with the success of the performance, he wanted to see the improvisatore in order to find out if he was satisfied with everything. He found the Italian in a little side room, impatiently glancing at his watch. He was dressed in a theatrical fashion: he wore black from head to foot; the collar of his shirt was thrown open; the unusual whiteness of his neck contrasted sharply with his thick black beard; and loosely hanging locks framed his forehead and brows. Charskii found it very disagreeable to see a poet dressed as an itinerant mountebank. After a brief exchange of words, he returned to the reception room, which was filling up with more and more people.

Soon all the rows of armchairs were occupied by brilliant ladies; the men, as though forming a tight frame around them, stood by the platform, along the walls, and behind the last row of chairs. The musicians with their stands took up the space on either side of the platform. A porcelain vase stood on a table in the center of the room. The audience was sizable. Everybody waited impatiently for the beginning of the performance; at last the musicians began to stir at half past seven, getting their bows ready, and then started playing the overture to *Tancredi*.[13] Everybody settled down and grew quiet; the overture's last thunderous notes resounded... And then the improvisatore, greeted with deafening applause on all sides, advanced to the very edge of the platform with deep bows.

Charskii had anxiously waited to see what impression the first minute would create, but he noticed that the costume, which had appeared so inappropriate to him, was not having the same effect on the audience. He himself found nothing ludicrous in the man when he saw him on the platform, his pale face brightly illuminated by a multitude of lamps and candles. The applause died away; all conversation ceased... The Italian, speaking in broken French, asked the ladies and gentlemen present to set a few themes for him, writing them down on pieces of paper. At this unexpected invitation, the guests all looked at one another in silence, not one person making any response. The Italian, after waiting a little, repeated his request in a timid and humble voice. Charskii stood right below the platform; he grew anxious; he could see that the affair could not be carried through without him, and that he would be compelled to write down a theme. Indeed several ladies turned their heads toward him and began calling out to him, at first in a low tone, then more and more loudly. Hearing Charskii's name, the improvisatore looked for him and, seeing him at his feet, gave him a pencil and a piece of paper with a friendly smile. Charskii found it very unpleasant to have to play a role in this comedy, but there was no getting around it: he took the pencil and paper from the Italian's hand and wrote a few words on it; the Italian picked up the vase from the table, came down from the platform, and held the vase out to Charskii, who dropped his theme into it. His example had its effect: two journalists, in their capacity as men of letters, felt duty-bound to write a theme; the secretary of the Neapolitan Embassy and a young man who had just returned from a journey and was still raving about Florence both placed their rolled-up slips of paper in the urn.[14] Finally, at her mother's insistence, a plain-looking girl with tears in her eyes wrote a few lines in Italian and, blushing to her ears, handed them to the improvisatore, while other ladies watched her in silence, with a barely perceptible smile of contempt. Returning to his platform, the Italian placed the urn on the table and started drawing the pieces of paper out, one after the other, reading each aloud:

The Cenci family (La famiglia dei Cenci)
L'ultimo giorno di Pompeïa
Cleopatra e i suoi amanti
La primavera veduta da una prigione
Il trionfo di Tasso [15]

"What is the pleasure of the honorable company?" asked the humble Italian. "Do you wish to select one of the suggested themes, or let the matter be decided by lot?"

"By lot!" said a voice from the crowd.

"By lot, by lot!" was repeated throughout the audience.

The improvisatore came down from the platform once more, holding the urn in his hands, and asked, "Who will be so good as to draw a theme?"

He searched the front rows with an imploring glance. Not one of the brilliant ladies seated there would move a finger. The improvisatore, unaccustomed to northern reserve, seemed distressed... but suddenly he noticed that on one side of the room a small hand in a tight-fitting white glove was raised: he swiftly turned and walked up to a majestic young beauty seated at the end of the second row. She rose without the slightest embarrassment, put her small aristocratic hand into the urn with the most natural gesture, and drew out a rolled-up piece of paper.

"Would you be kind enough to unroll it and read it?" the improvisatore asked her.

The beautiful girl unrolled the paper and read the words out: "Cleopatra e i suoi amanti."

She read these words in a soft tone, but the silence reigning over the room was so complete that everybody could hear her. The improvisatore bowed deeply, with a look of profound gratitude, to the beautiful lady, and returned to his platform.

"Ladies and gentlemen," he said turning to the audience, "the lot bids me to improvise on the theme of Cleopatra and her lovers. I humbly ask the person who suggested this theme to elucidate the idea: which of her lovers are in question, *perché la grande regina n'aveva molto!*..."[16]

Several men burst into loud laughter at these words. The improvisatore appeared somewhat confused.

"I would like to know," he continued, "what historical episode the person suggesting the theme was alluding to... I should be most grateful if that person would kindly explain."

Nobody hastened to answer. Some ladies directed their glance toward the plain girl who had written down a theme at her mother's command. The poor girl noticed this malevolent attention and became so embarrassed that tears welled up in her eyes...

Charskii could not bear this any longer. Turning to the improvisatore, he said in Italian: "I was the one who suggested the theme. I had in mind the testimony of Victor Aurelius, who claims that Cleopatra named death as the price of her love, and that some admirers were found to whom such a condition was neither frightening nor repellent...[17] But maybe the subject is somewhat embarrassing... Would you rather choose another one?"

But the improvisatore already sensed the divine presence... He signaled to the musicians to play... His face grew alarmingly pale; he trembled as if in fever; his eyes sparkled with wondrous fire; he smoothed his black hair back with his hand, wiped the beads of sweat off his high forehead with a handkerchief... and suddenly stepped forward, folding his arms across his chest... The music stopped... The improvisation began:[18]

> The palace gleamed. From jubilant choirs
> Of bards re-echoed hymns of praise;
> The joyous strains of lutes and lyres
> The Queen enhanced by voice and gaze.
> All hearts in transports thronged to seek her,

When of a sudden she stopped short
And mused above the golden beaker,
Her wondrous forehead dropped in thought.

The festive turmoil ceases shifting,
The choir stands mute as in a daze;
At last the Queen pronounces, lifting
Her brow again, with cloudless gaze:
"Is not my love your dreamed-of treasure?
Well—you may buy such bliss divine.
Hear me! This night it is my pleasure
To grant you equal rank to mine.
Behold the marketplace of passion!
For sale is now my love divine;
Who dares to barter in this fashion
His life against one night of mine?"

Thus she. All hearts are set aflutter
By passion blent with dreadful qualm.
To their abashed and doubtful mutter
She listens with a brazen calm.
Her scornful glances sweep the verges
Of her admirers' silent throng...
There—of a sudden one emerges,
Two others follow soon along.
Their step is bold, their eyes unclouded;
The Queen arises to their stride;
Three nights are bought: the couch is shrouded
For deadly raptures at her side.

"Thee, Holy Goddess of the Senses,
I vow to serve like none before,
A venal passion's recompenses
To gather like a common whore.
Oh hearken Thou, Our Cyprian Lady's
High Grace, and hear, in realms forlorn,
Ye dreaded deities of Hades,
My oath: unto the morning's dawn
My sovereign rulers' burning wishes
With rich fulfillment I will quench,
Slake them with ecstasies delicious,
With magical caresses drench.
But mark! as soon as to Aurora's

Renascent blush this night shall fade,
The happy heads of my adorers
Shall leap beneath the deadly blade."

By holy augurs blessed and chosen,
There issue from the fateful urn,
While the assembled guests stand frozen,
The lots assigned to each in turn.
First, Flavius, grayed amidst the laurels
And scars of Rome's historic quarrels;
His pride resolved to bear no more
A female's challenge to his mettle,
He bridled, as in days of war
He used to rise to calls of battle.
Crito was next, young sage who, raised
In shady groves Epicurean,
Had chosen Love his god and praised
The Graces and the Cytherean.
Appealing both to eye and heart,
The last to have his doom awarded,
Like vernal petals shy to part,
Has never had his name recorded
By scribes. His tender cheek a start
Of downy beard but faintly bordered...
Untasted passion flared and tested
His heart with unaccustomed blaze...
And softly touched, the Queen's eyes rested
Upon him with a gentler gaze.

Already daylight, swift to fade,
To Luna's golden horn surrenders,
And Alexandria's high splendors
Lie sunken in a balmy shade.
The lights are glowing, fountains playing,
Sweet incense wafting from a hearth,
A breeze, voluptuous cool conveying,
Is promised to the gods of earth.
And in that velvet dusk, all heady
With lures of luxury untold,
The gleaming ottoman of gold,
In purple canopied, stands ready.

Maria Schoning

(1834 or 1835?)[1]

Anna Harlin to Maria Schoning; W., April 25

My dear Maria,

What has happened to you? For more than four months I have not
received a single line from you. Are you in good health? If I had not
been so busy all the time, I would have come to visit you, but as you
know, twelve miles is not a joke. Without me the household would
come to a dead stop: Fritz is no good at it; he is just like a child. Have
you perhaps married? No, I am sure you would have thought of me
and not neglected to delight your friend with the news of your happiness. In your last letter you wrote that your poor father was still sickly;
I hope the spring has helped him, and he is better now. About myself I
can say that, thanks to God, I am well and happy. My work brings in
little; but I am still incapable of bargaining or charging too much. It
might be just as well to learn how to. Fritz is also quite well, though
lately his wooden leg has been causing him trouble. He gets about
very little, and in bad weather wheezes and groans. Otherwise he is
just as cheerful as before, still likes his glass of wine, and has still not
finished telling me the story of his campaigns. The children are growing and getting more and more beautiful. Frank is turning out a clever
little fellow. Just imagine, dear Maria, he is already running after girls,
though he is not yet three. What do you think of that? And what a
mischief-maker he is! Fritz can't rejoice in him enough and spoils
him terribly: instead of checking the child, he goads him on and delights in his every prank. Mina is much calmer; but then of course she
is a year older. I have begun teaching her to read. She is very sharp-
witted and, it seems, will be pretty. But what is the good of being
pretty? If she will just grow into a good and sensible girl, she will no
doubt be happy.

P.S. I am sending you a scarf as a little present: wear it for the first
time next Sunday, when you go to church. It was a present to me from
Fritz, but red goes better with your black tresses than with my blonde

hair. Men do not understand such things. Blue and red are all the same to them. Farewell, my dear Maria; I have chattered long enough. Do write as soon as you can. Give my sincere regards to your dear father. Let me know how he is doing. I shall never forget the three years spent under his roof, during which he treated me, a poor orphan, not as a hired servant but as a daughter. The mother of our pastor advises him to drink red chamomile instead of tea: it is a very common herb—I have even found out its Latin name—any apothecary can point it out to you.

Maria Schoning to Anna Harlin; April 28

I received your letter last Friday but have not read it until today. My poor father died just that day, at six o'clock in the morning, and yesterday was his funeral.

I never thought his death was so imminent. Lately he had been doing much better, so much so that Herr Költz had hopes for his complete recovery. On Monday he even took a walk in our little garden and got as far as the well without running out of breath. When he returned to his room, however, he felt slightly shivery; I put him into bed and ran off for Herr Költz. He was not at home. When I returned to my father I found him asleep. Sleep, I thought, might relax him and make him feel entirely better. Herr Költz called on us in the evening. He examined the patient and was unhappy with his condition. He prescribed a new medicine for him. Father awoke in the middle of the night and asked for something to eat; I gave him some soup; he swallowed one spoonful, but did not feel like any more. He dozed off again. The next day he had spasms. Herr Költz did not leave his bedside. Toward evening his pain abated, but he was seized by such restlessness that he could not lie in the same position for more than five minutes at a time. I had to keep turning him from one side to the other... Toward morning he grew calm and slept for a couple of hours. Herr Költz left his room, promising to return in about two hours. Suddenly father sat up and called for me. I came and asked what he wanted. He said, "Maria, how come it is so very dark? Open the shutters."

I answered in alarm, "Dear father, can't you see? The shutters are open."

He started searching about him, grasped my hand, and said, "Maria, Maria, I feel very bad—I am dying... Let me give you my blessing while I can."

I threw myself on my knees and placed his hand on my head. He said, "Oh Lord, reward her; oh Lord, I put her in your hands."

He grew quiet; then suddenly his hand felt heavy. Thinking he had fallen asleep again, I did not dare stir for several minutes. Presently Herr Költz entered, took my father's hand off my head, and said, "Leave him alone now, go to your room."

I glanced at father: he lay there pale and motionless. It was all over.

The good-hearted Herr Költz did not leave our house for two full days, and made all the necessary arrangements, for I was not in a state to do so. Lately I have been looking after the patient by myself, since there was no one to relieve me. I often thought of you and bitterly regretted that you were not with us...

Yesterday I got up and was preparing to follow the coffin, but all of a sudden felt bad. I went down on my knees in order to take leave of my father at least from a distance. Frau Rotberch remarked, "What a comedienne!" These words, just imagine, my dear Anna, returned my strength to me. I followed the coffin with surprisingly little difficulty. In the church, it seemed to me, everything was exceedingly bright, and everything around me was reeling. I did not weep. I felt suffocated and wanted to burst out laughing all the time. They bore him to the cemetery behind St. Jacob's Church and lowered him into the grave under my eyes. Suddenly I felt like digging it up again, for I had not quite taken my leave of him. But there were still many people walking about the cemetery, and I was afraid Frau Rotberch might remark again, "What a comedienne!"

How cruel it is not to let a daughter say good-bye to her dead father the way she wants to...

Returning home, I found several strangers, who told me it was necessary to seal all my father's property and papers. They let me stay in my little room, but they carried everything out of it except for the bed and a chair. Tomorrow is Sunday. I shall not be able to wear the scarf you gave me, but I want to thank you for it very much. Give my regards to your husband and kiss Frank and Mina for me. Farewell.

I am writing standing by the windowsill; I have borrowed an inkpot from the neighbors.

Maria Schoning to Anna Harlin

My dear Anna,

An official came to me yesterday and declared that all of my late father's property must be sold at auction to the benefit of the city treasury, because he had not been taxed according to his financial status: the inventory showed that he had been much wealthier than they had thought. I cannot understand any of this. Lately we had spent a great deal on medicine. All the ready cash I had left was twenty-three thalers; I showed it to the officials, but they said I could keep it, since the law did not require me to surrender it.

Our house will be auctioned off next week, after which I have no idea where I shall go. I have been to see Herr Bürgermeister. He received me kindly but declared that there was nothing he could do to help me. I do not know where I could take service. Write to me if you need a maidservant: as you know, I can help you around the house and with needlework; moreover, I can look after the children and Fritz in case he should fall ill. I have learned how to look after the sick. Please let me know whether you need me. And do not feel embarrassed about it. I feel sure that it will not change our relationship in the least: in my eyes you will always remain the same good and kind friend.

The old Schoning's house was full of people. They crowded around the table over which the auctioneer presided. He shouted:

"A flannel camisole with brass buttons: X thalers. One—two: anybody with a higher offer? A flannel camisole: X thalers—three."

The camisole passed into the hands of its new owner.

The buyers examined the exhibited items with curiosity and abusive comments. Frau Rotberch scrutinized the dirty linen left unwashed after Schoning's death; she pulled at it and shook it open, repeating, "What trash, what rubbish, what old rags," at the same time raising her bid by one more penny. The innkeeper Hürtz bought two silver spoons, half a dozen napkins, and two china cups. The bed in which Schoning had died was bought by Karoline Schmidt, a girl heavily made up but otherwise of a modest and humble appearance.

Maria, pale as a shadow, stood there silently watching the pillage of her poor belongings. She held X thalers in her hand, ready to buy something from the spoils, but she did not have the courage to outbid the other buyers. People were leaving, carrying their purchases. Two portraits, in frames that had once been gilt-edged but were now flyspecked, were still unsold. One showed Schoning as a young man, in a red coat; the other, his wife Christiana with a lapdog in her arms. Both portraits were painted in sharp, bright outlines. Hürtz wanted to buy these, too, in order to hang them in the corner room of his inn, whose walls were too bare. The portraits were valued at X thalers. Hürtz drew out his purse; but this time Maria overcame her timidity and raised the bid in a trembling voice. Hürtz threw a contemptuous glance at her and began to haggle. Little by little the price reached Y thalers. Maria at last bid Z. Hürtz gave up, and the portraits remained in her possession. She handed over the price, put the remainder of her money in her pocket, picked up the two portraits, and left the house, not waiting for the end of the auction.

Having walked out on the street with a portrait under each arm, she stopped in bewilderment: where was she to go?

A young man with gold-framed glasses came up to her and very politely offered to carry the portraits for her wherever she wished to take them...

"I am much obliged to you... but I truly don't know."

She kept wondering where to take the portraits for the time being, until she found a position.

The young man waited a few moments, then went on his way. Maria decided to take the portraits to Költz, the physician.[2]

The Captain's Daughter
(1836)[1]

Cherish your honor from a tender age.

A PROVERB

I. The Sergeant of the Guards

"In no time he'll be a captain in the Guards."
"No need for that; I had the ranks in mind."
"Handsomely said: they'll put him through the grind.
. . .
"And who's his father?"

KNIAZHNIN[2]

My father, Andrei Petrovich Grinev, served under Count Münnich in his youth.[3] He returned with the rank of major in 17—.[4] From then on, he lived on his estate in Simbirsk Province, where he married the maiden Avdotia Vasilevna Iu., daughter of an impecunious local squire. They had nine children, but all my brothers and sisters died in infancy.

I was still in my dear mother's womb when they registered me as a sergeant in the Semenovskii Regiment, thanks to the good offices of Major of the Guards Prince B., a close relative of ours.[5] If against all expectations my mother had delivered a baby girl, my father would have simply informed the appropriate authorities that the sergeant could not report for duty because he had died, and that would have been the end of that. I was considered to be on leave until the completion of my studies. But in those days schooling was not what it is today. At the age of five I was entrusted to the care of the groom Savelich, appointed to be my personal attendant in recognition of his sober conduct. Under his supervision I had learned to read and write Russian by the age of twelve, and acquired a sound judgment of the qualities of chase hounds. Then my dear father hired a Frenchman for me, Monsieur Beaupré, who had been ordered by mail from Moscow along with our annual supply of wine and cooking oil. This man's arrival greatly displeased Savelich.

"Heaven be thanked," he muttered under his breath, "the child's kept clean, well-combed, and fed. What need is there to throw away money hiring this *mounseer*,[6] as if there weren't enough of our own folk?"

In his homeland Beaupré had been a barber; then he did some soldiering in Prussia; and finally he came to Russia *pour être outchitel,*[7] though he did not quite understand the meaning of that title. He was a good-natured fellow, but irresponsible and dissolute in the extreme. His main weakness was a passion for the fair sex; his amorous advances frequently earned him raps and knocks that would make him groan for days. Moreover, he was (as he himself put it) "no enemy of the bottle," that is (in plain Russian), he loved to take a drop too much. In our house, however, wine was served only with dinner, a glass at a time, and they usually forgot to offer even that to the tutor. For this reason he soon grew accustomed to homemade Russian vodka, eventually even preferring it to the wines of his homeland as a drink incomparably better for the stomach. He and I hit it off immediately. Although by his contract he was supposed to teach me "French, German, and all the sciences,"[8] in practice he chose to learn Russian from me, soon acquiring enough to prattle after a fashion; and from then on we each went about our own business. We lived in perfect harmony. I could not have wished for a better mentor. Fate, however, soon separated us, due to the following incident.

The washerwoman Palashka, a fat and pockmarked wench, and the one-eyed dairymaid Akulka somehow decided to throw themselves at my mother's feet at the same time, confessing to a reprehensible weakness and complaining in tears against the *mounseer,* who had seduced their innocence. My mother did not treat such things lightly, and complained to my father. He brought the matter to a fast conclusion. He immediately sent for that rascal of a Frenchman, and when he was told that *monsieur* was giving me a lesson, he came to my room. Beaupré at this time was sleeping the sleep of the innocent on my bed. I was engrossed in work. It must be mentioned that a map had been obtained for me from Moscow and had been hanging on the wall of my room without being of the slightest use to anyone; it had been tempting me with the width and quality of its paper for a long time. I decided to make it into a kite and, taking advantage of Beaupré's sleep, had set about the task. At the time my father entered the room I was just fixing a bast tail to the Cape of Good Hope. Seeing me thus engaged in the study of geography, my father pulled my ear, then stepped up to Beaupré, woke him none too gently, and showered reproaches on him. Beaupré, all confused, tried to get up but could not: the hapless Frenchman was dead drunk. As well be hanged for a sheep as for a lamb:[9] my father lifted him off the bed by the collar, shoved him through the door, and that very day banished him from the house, to Savelich's indescribable joy. Thus ended my education.

I lived the life of a young oaf, chasing pigeons and playing leapfrog with the serving boys. Meanwhile I had turned sixteen. Then the course of my life changed.

One autumn day my mother was making preserves with honey in the parlor, while I, licking my chops, was watching the boiling froth. My father was seated by the window, reading the *Court Calendar*, which he received each year. This book always had a strong effect on him; he could never leaf through it without getting involved, and reading it never failed to rouse his spleen. My mother, who knew all his habits inside out, always tried to tuck away the unfortunate book in some hidden corner, and therefore the *Court Calendar* sometimes did not catch his eye for whole months. But if he did chance to come across it, he did not let it out of his hands for hours on end. This time, too, he kept reading it, occasionally shrugging his shoulders and muttering:

"Lieutenant general! He used to be a sergeant in my platoon! Decorated with both Russian crosses![10] It was only the other day that he and I..."

At length father tossed the *Calendar* on the sofa, and sank into a reverie that augured little good.

Suddenly he turned to mother. "Avdotia Vasilevna, how old is Petrusha?"

"He's going on seventeen," answered mother. "Petrusha was born the same year that Auntie Nastasia Gerasimovna lost an eye and when..."

"Very well," interrupted father, "it's time for him to enter the service. He's had quite enough of hanging around the maidservants' quarters and climbing up to the pigeon lofts."

The idea of soon having to part with me upset my mother so much that she dropped the spoon into the saucepan, and tears started streaming from her eyes. By contrast, my rapture would be hard to describe. The thought of entering the service was connected in my mind with notions of freedom and the pleasures of Petersburg life. I imagined myself an officer of the Guards—a status that in my opinion was the ultimate in the wellbeing of men.

Father did not like either to change his mind or to postpone carrying out his decisions. The day for my departure was fixed. The evening before I was to leave, father declared his intention to furnish me with a letter to my future commanding officer, and he asked for pen and paper.

"Don't forget to give my regards to Prince B.," said mother. "Tell him I hope he'll take Petrusha under his protection."

"What nonsense is this?" father answered, frowning. "Why should I be writing to Prince B.?"

"Why, you did say it was your pleasure to write to Petrusha's commander."

"That's right. And what then?"

"Well, isn't Prince B. his commander? He is, after all, registered with the Semenovskii Regiment."

"Registered! What business of mine is it that he's registered? Petrusha is not going to Petersburg. What would he learn if he served there? To squander and to sow wild oats? No, let him serve in the army, let him learn to sweat and get used to the smell of gunpowder, let him become a soldier, not an idler. Registered with the Guards! Where is his passport? Give it here."

Mother searched out my passport, which she kept in a box together with my baptismal shirt, and gave it to father with a trembling hand. He read it carefully, put it on the table in front of him, and began his letter.

Curiosity was tormenting me; where was I being sent if not to Petersburg? I could not take my eyes off father's pen, which was moving rather slowly. At last he finished and sealed the letter in an envelope along with my passport. He took his glasses off, called me over to him, and said, "Here's a letter to Andrei Karlovich R., my old comrade and friend. You're going to Orenburg to serve under his command."

All my brilliant hopes were dashed to the ground! Instead of a merry life in St. Petersburg, boredom awaited me in some remote, godforsaken region. The service, which I had contemplated with such enthusiasm even a minute before, now seemed like a burdensome chore. But there was no arguing with my father. The next morning a covered wagon was brought up to the front porch, and the servants piled into it my trunk, a hamper with a tea service, and bundles with rolls and pies—the last tokens of a pampered domestic life. My parents blessed me. Father said, "Good-bye, Petr. Serve faithfully the Sovereign to whom you swear allegiance; obey your superiors; don't curry favor with them; don't volunteer for duty, but don't shirk it either;[11] and remember the proverb, 'Take care of your clothes while they're still new; cherish your honor from a tender age.' "

My dear mother admonished me in tears to take care of my health and exhorted Savelich to look after her child. They helped me into a hareskin coat and a fox overcoat. I got into the wagon with Savelich and set out on my journey, shedding floods of tears.

That night I arrived in Simbirsk, where I was supposed to stay for a day while various necessary items were procured—that task having been entrusted to Savelich. We put up at an inn. Savelich left for his shopping expedition in the morning. Bored with looking at the muddy side street from my window, I went wandering about the rooms of the inn. Reaching the billiard room, I spied a tall gentleman, about thirty-five years old, with long black mustachios, wearing a dressing gown and holding a cue in his hand and a pipe between his teeth. He was playing against the marker, who received a glass of vodka each time he won and had to crawl under the table on all fours every time he lost. I stopped to watch their game. The longer it lasted the more frequently the marker went crawling, until at last he remained under the table. The gentleman uttered a few pithy phrases over him by way of a funeral oration, and asked me if I would like to have a game. I refused since I did not know how to play. This evidently struck him as rather strange. He cast a pitying look at me; but we nevertheless got into a conversation. He told me that his name was Ivan Ivanovich Zurin, and that he was a captain in the X. Hussar Regiment, had come to Simbirsk to receive new recruits,[12] and was staying at the inn. He invited me to take potluck with him as a fellow soldier. I agreed with pleasure. We sat down to the meal. Zurin drank a great deal and treated me generously too, saying that I had to get used to the service. He told me anecdotes of army life that made me roll with laughter; by the time we got up from the table we were bosom friends. He offered to teach me how to play billiards.

"It's essential for the likes of us in the service," he said. "Suppose you're on the march, you come to a small village: what's there to do? You can't be beating up the Yids all the time. Willynilly you end up at an inn playing billiards: but for that you must know how to play!"

I was entirely won over, and embarked on the course of instruction with great diligence. Zurin encouraged me vociferously, marveled at the fast progress I was making, and after a few lessons suggested that we play for money, just for half a kopeck at a time, not with gain in mind, but simply to avoid playing for nothing—which, in his words, was the nastiest of habits. I agreed to this proposition, too. Zurin ordered some rum punch and persuaded me to give it a try, saying once more that I had to get used to the service: what sort of service would it be without punch! I obeyed him. In the meantime we continued our game. Every sip from my glass made me bolder. I sent the balls flying over the edge every minute; all excited, I cursed the marker who was keeping the score in heaven knows what outlandish fashion; and I kept increasing the stake: in other words, I behaved like a young whelp who had broken loose for the first time. The hours passed imperceptibly. Zurin looked at his watch, put down his cue, and declared that I had lost a hundred rubles. This embarrassed me a little because my money was in Savelich's hands. I started apologizing, but Zurin interrupted me:

"For pity's sake! Don't give it a thought. I can wait. And now let's go to Arinushka's."

What can I say? I concluded the day just as dissolutely as I had begun it. We ate supper at Arinushka's. Zurin kept filling my glass, repeating that I had to get used to the service. I could hardly stand on my feet when we got up from the table; it was midnight when Zurin drove me back to the inn.

Savelich was waiting for us on the porch. He groaned on seeing the unmistakable signs of my zeal for the service.

"What's happened to you, my dear sir?" he said in a pathetic tone. "Where did you get fuddled like that? My goodness gracious! I've never seen such infamy in my whole life."

"Shut up, old sot!" I replied, stammering. "You must be drunk, go to bed... put me to bed."

The next morning I woke with a headache and could only dimly recall what had happened the day before. My reflections were interrupted by Savelich, who came in with a cup of tea.

"You're beginning early, Petr Andreich," he said, shaking his head. "You're beginning to play your pranks early. Who are you taking after? Neither your father nor your grandfather was a drunkard, I daresay; not to mention your dear mother, who's never touched anything but kvass since the day she was born. And who's to blame for it all? That damned *mounseer*, that's who. How many's the times, I remember, as he'd run to Antipevna: 'Madame, je vous prie vottka!' Well, here's the result of *je vous prie*! He set you a good example, didn't he, the son of a bitch! Did they really need to hire an infidel to look after the child, as if the master didn't have enough of his own folk!"

Ashamed of myself, I turned away from him and said, "Go away, Savelich: I don't want any tea."

But it was not easy to silence Savelich once he had started on a sermon.

"Now you can see, Petr Andreich, what it's like when you go on a spree. An aching head and no appetite. A drinking man's no good for nothing... Drink a glass of pickle juice with honey, or better yet, take a hair of the dog that bit you: have half a glass of vodka. What do you say?"

At this moment a boy came in with a note from I. I. Zurin. I opened it and read the following lines:

My dear Petr Andreevich,

Be so good as to send me by my serving boy the hundred rubles I won from you yesterday. I am in extremely straitened circumstances.

Ever at your service,
Ivan Zurin

There was no way out of it. Assuming an air of equanimity, I turned to Savelich—that "zealous guardian of all my cash and linen, indeed of all my business"[13]—and ordered him to hand the boy a hundred rubles.

"Why? What for?" asked the astonished Savelich.

"I owe it to the gentleman," I countered with utmost coolness.

"Owe it to him?" asked Savelich, more and more amazed by the minute. "And when was it, sir, you found the time to get into this debt? Something's got to be fishy about this business. Say what you will, sir, I'm not paying a kopeck."

I thought that if at this decisive moment I did not gain the upper hand over the obstinate old man, it would be difficult to free myself from his tutelage later on, and therefore I said, casting a haughty glance at him, "I am your master, you are my servant. The money is mine. I lost it at billiards because that was my pleasure. As for you, I advise you not to try to be clever, but to do what you're told to."

Savelich was so struck by my words that he just threw up his hands and stood rooted to the ground.

"What are you waiting for?" I bawled at him angrily.

He burst into tears. "Petr Andreich, young master," he uttered in a trembling voice, "don't break my heart. Light of my life, listen to me, an old man: write to this brigand that you were only joking, and we just don't have that kind of money. A hundred rubles! Gracious Lord! Tell him that your parents strictly forbade you to play for anything but nuts..."

"Enough of this nonsense," I interrupted sternly. "Bring the money here, or else I'll throw you out by the scruff of your neck."

Savelich looked at me in deep sorrow and went to fetch my debt. I felt sorry for the poor old man, but I wanted to shake myself loose and prove that I was no longer a child. The money was delivered to Zurin. Savelich hurried to get me out of the accursed inn. He came to report that the horses were ready. I left Simbirsk with a troubled conscience and silent remorse, without saying good-bye to my mentor, nor imagining that I would ever see him again.

II. The Guide

Land, dear land,
Strange land,
I did not come here of my own will;
It was not my brave horse that
    brought me here:
What brought me here, brave young
    lad,
Was reckless folly, dauntless
    bravery,
And drunken revelry.

AN OLD SONG[14]

My reflections, as we rode along, were not very pleasant. I had lost, according to the value of money at that time, a considerable sum. Deep down I could not help recognizing that my behavior at the Simbirsk inn had been foolish, and I also felt guilty about Savelich. All this was tormenting me. The old man sat on the box by the driver in a state of gloom, with his back to me, and kept silent except for clearing his throat occasionally. I was determined to make up with him, but did not know how to begin. At last I said:

"Listen, Savelich, that's enough. Let's make up. I'm sorry: I admit I was at fault. I misbehaved yesterday and unjustly offended you; I promise I'll be more sensible from now on and will listen to you. Don't be angry any more; let's make up."

"Oh, young master Petr Andreich," he answered, heaving a deep sigh, "it's with myself I'm angry; I'm to blame for everything. How could I leave you all by yourself at the inn! What can I say! It was the devil's work: he put the thought in my head to drop in on the sexton's wife, mother of my godchild. Talk much and err much, just as they say.[15] Devil's own luck! How can I ever face the master and mistress? What'll they say when they hear that their child drinks and gambles?"

In order to reassure poor old Savelich, I gave him my word that from then on I would not dispose of one kopeck without his consent. He gradually calmed down, though he still muttered from time to time, shaking his head: "A hundred rubles! No trifle, is it!"

I was approaching my destination. A dreary wilderness, crosscut with ridges and ravines, extended all around me. It was all covered with snow. The sun was setting. Our wagon traveled along a narrow road or, to be exact, along tracks left by peasants' sleighs. Suddenly the driver began casting frequent glances over to the side, until at last he turned to me, taking his hat off, and said, "Please, master, wouldn't it be better to turn back?"

"What for?"

"The weather's fickle: the wind's freshening up—see how it's blowing the snow."

"What does that matter?"

"But can't you see what's over there?" He pointed to the east with his whip.

"I don't see anything except the white steppe and the clear sky."

"But over there, there: that little cloud."

I did indeed see on the horizon a small white cloud, which I had at first mistaken for a distant hill. The driver explained that a small cloud like that betokened a blizzard.

I had heard of snowstorms in that region and knew that they could bury whole wagon trains. Savelich, in agreement with the driver, advised me to turn back. But the wind did not seem to me very strong; I hoped we could reach the next station in good time, and therefore I gave orders to press forward as fast as possible.

The driver made the horses go at a gallop, but kept looking to the east. The animals moved along rapidly. The wind, however, was becoming stronger by the minute. The little cloud turned into a white cumulus, billowing upward, growing, and gradually covering the whole sky. Snow began to fall, at first lightly, then suddenly in large flakes. The wind howled: we were in the middle of a snowstorm. In one minute the dark sky merged with the sea of snow. You couldn't see a thing.

"Well, master," shouted the driver, "we're in trouble: it's a blizzard."

I looked out of the wagon: all I could see was darkness and whirling snow. The wind howled with such ferocity that it seemed alive; both Savelich and I were covered with snow; the horses could move only at a walk; they soon came to a standstill.

"Why aren't you going on?" I asked the driver impatiently.

"What's the good of going?" he answered, climbing off the box. "There's no telling as where we've got to, even now: there's no road, just darkness all around."

I started berating him, but Savelich took his part.

"Why didn't you listen to him?" he said crossly. "We could've returned to the wayside inn, filled up with tea, and slept till the morning; the blizzard would've calmed down, and we could've gone on. Why the great haste? It'd be something else if you were hurrying to your wedding!"

Savelich was right. There was nothing we could do. The snow was falling thick and fast. It was piling up alongside the wagon. The horses stood with their heads down and shuddered from time to time.

The driver walked about, adjusting the harnesses for lack of anything better to do. Savelich grumbled; I looked in all directions, hoping to see some sign of human habitation or a roadway, but could not discern anything except the turbid whirl of the snowstorm... Suddenly I caught sight of something dark.

"Hey, driver," I called out, "what's that dark shape over there?"

The driver strained his eyes. "Heaven only knows, my lord," he said, climbing back in his seat; "perhaps a cart, perhaps a tree; but it moves, I fancy: it must be either wolf or man."

I ordered him to drive toward the undiscernible object, which in its turn started moving toward us. In two minutes we met up with a man.

"Hullo, my good man," the driver called to him; "can you tell us where the road is?"

"The road's here all right: I'm standing on a firm strip of ground," the traveler answered, "but what's the use?"

"Listen, muzhik," I said to him, "do you know this land? Will you guide me to a shelter for the night?"

"As for knowing this land," the traveler answered, "by the mercy of God I've traveled the length and breadth of it, on horseback and on foot, but you see what the weather's like: it doesn't take much to lose your way. It'll be best to stay here and wait; perhaps the blizzard will calm down, the sky will clear, and then we'll find the way by the stars."

His equanimity reassured me. I was already prepared, resigning myself to God's will, to spend the night in the middle of the steppe when suddenly the traveler climbed nimbly on the box and said to the driver, "Thank God, we're not far from habitation: turn to the right and go."

"Why should I turn to the right?" asked the driver with annoyance. "Where do you see the road? It's easy to whip another man's horses."[16]

It seemed to me the driver was right.

"Why indeed do you think that there is habitation not far off?" I asked the traveler.

"Because there was a gust of wind from over there," he answered, "and I smell smoke, and so, there's a village nearby."

His cleverness and his keen sense of smell amazed me. I told the driver to go forward. It was hard for the horses to trudge through the deep snow. The wagon moved slowly, now gliding over a snowdrift, now falling into a gully and keeling over on this or that side. It was like the tossing of a ship on a stormy sea. Savelich groaned, constantly knocking into my side. I lowered the blind, wrapped myself in my fur coat, and dozed off, lulled by the singing of the storm and the rocking of the slow-moving wagon.

I had a dream that I was never to forget, and that I still see as prophetic when I relate it to the events of my life. I hope the reader will forgive me, for he probably knows from experience how easy it is for people to fall into superstition, however great their contempt for unfounded beliefs may be.

I was in that state of mind and feeling in which reality yields to reveries and merges with them in the nebulous vision of approaching sleep. The blizzard, I fancied, was still raging, and we were still floundering in the snow-covered wilderness, but I suddenly beheld a gate and was driven into the courtyard of our manor house. My first thought was an apprehension that my father might be angry with me for this unintentional reentrance under the paternal roof, construing it as deliberate disobedience. I jumped out of the wagon with anxiety and saw my mother coming off the porch to meet me with an air of deep sorrow.

"Quiet," she says to me, "your father is on his deathbed and wants to bid farewell to you."

Struck by fear, I follow her into the bedroom. I see a dimly lit chamber and people standing around the bed with a sad expression on their faces. I tiptoe up to the bed; mother raises the bedcurtain and says, "Andrei Petrovich, Petrusha has arrived: he's heard of your illness and come back home; give him your blessing."

I go down on my knees and raise my eyes to the invalid. But what do I see? Instead of my father I behold a muzhik with a black beard, looking at me gaily. I turn to mother in bewilderment, saying, "What's the meaning of this? This is not father. And why should I ask a muzhik for his blessing?"

"It's all the same, Petrusha," answers mother; "this is your father by proxy: kiss his dear hand and let him bless you."

I could not agree to that. The muzhik jumps off the bed, draws an ax from behind his back, and starts flourishing it in all directions. I want to run, but I can't; the room is filling with dead bodies; I stumble over the corpses and slip in the pools of blood. The terrifying muzhik calls out to me kindly, "Don't be afraid, come to receive my blessing."

Horror and bewilderment overwhelm me...[17] At this moment I woke up: the horses had stopped, and Savelich was nudging my arm, saying, "Get out, sir, we've arrived."

"Arrived where?" I asked, rubbing my eyes.

"At the wayside inn. God saved us, we drove right into the fence. Quick, Your Honor, get out and warm yourself."

I stepped out of the wagon. The blizzard was still blowing, though with lesser force by now. It was pitch-dark: you couldn't see your hand before your face. The innkeeper came out to meet us at the gate, holding a lantern under the skirt of his coat. He led me into the front room, small but quite clean and lit by a torch. A rifle and a tall Cossack hat hung on the wall.

The innkeeper, a Iaik Cossack by origin,[18] seemed to be about sixty years old, still hale and hearty. Savelich brought in the hamper with my tea service and asked that a fire be made for tea, for which I thirsted more than I had ever done before. The innkeeper went to attend to the matter.

"And where is our guide?" I asked Savelich.

"Right here, Your Honor," answered a voice from above. Looking up at the bunk, I saw a black beard and two shining eyes.

"How are you doing, my good fellow? Are you all frozen?"

"I should think I am, in nothing but a thin jerkin. I had a sheepskin jacket, but, why deny it, I pawned it at a tavern last night: the frost didn't seem that fierce then."

At this moment the innkeeper brought in the boiling samovar, and I offered our guide a cup of tea; he climbed down from the bunk. His appearance struck me as rather remarkable: he was about forty, of medium height, lean and broad-shouldered. Some gray streaks were showing in his black beard, and his large lively eyes were wide awake. His face bore a rather pleasant though roguish expression. His hair was cropped close around the crown, after the Cossack fashion; he wore a ragged jerkin and Tatar trousers. When I handed him a cup of tea, he took a sip and made a wry face.

"Your Honor, be so kind, let them give me a glass of vodka: we Cossacks don't drink tea."

I readily fulfilled his wish. The innkeeper took a bottle and a glass from the cupboard, and went up to him, looking in his face.

"Ah," he said, "so you're in these parts again, are you? Where have you sprung from?"

My guide winked at the innkeeper suggestively and answered with the proverb, "'I flew about the garden, pecking at the hemp; grandmother saw me, threw a stone at me, but missed.' And how are your fellows doing around here?"

"Our fellows!" the innkeeper answered, also in an allegorical manner. "They were about to ring the bell for evening service, but the priest's wife wouldn't let them: the priest's away visiting, the devil's in the churchyard."

"Hold your tongue, uncle," retorted my vagabond. "When the rain falls, there'll be mushrooms; when the mushrooms grow, there'll be a basket. But now," he winked once more, "hide the ax behind your back: the ranger's making his rounds. Your Honor, here's to your good health!" With these words he took the glass, crossed himself, and drank the vodka down in one gulp. Then he bowed to me and returned to his bunk.

I could not understand any of this thieves' cant at the time but later gathered that they had been alluding to the affairs of the Iaik Host, which had only just been pacified after the revolt of 1772.[19] Savelich listened with an air of great disapproval. He kept glancing suspiciously now at the innkeeper, now at our guide. This wayside inn, or *umet* as they call them in that region, was in a remote place, in the middle of the steppe, far from any habitation, and seemed very like a robbers' den. But there was nothing we could do. It was unthinkable to continue the journey. Savelich's anxiety amused me a great deal. In the meantime, I prepared for the night and lay down on a bench. Savelich decided to climb up on the stove; the innkeeper stretched out on the floor. Soon the whole houseful of us were snoring; I slept like a log.

Waking rather late the next morning, I saw that the storm had passed. The sun was shining. The snow covered the boundless steppe like a dazzling blanket. The horses were harnessed. I settled accounts with the innkeeper, who charged such a modest sum that Savelich did not even argue or start his usual haggling with him, and quite forgot his suspicions of the night before. I called for our guide, thanked him for his help, and told Savelich to give him half a ruble for vodka. Savelich knitted his brows.

"Half a ruble for vodka!" he exclaimed. "And why? Because you kindly drove him to the inn? Craving your pardon, sir, we don't have any half-ruble pieces to spare. If you tip every man you meet, you'll soon go hungry yourself."

I could not argue with Savelich. I had promised that he would have full control of my money. It vexed me, however, that I was unable to reward the man who had saved me, if not from disaster, at least from a very unpleasant situation.

"All right," I said with full composure, "if you don't want to give him half a ruble, pull something out from among my clothes. He is dressed too lightly. Give him my hareskin coat."

"Have mercy on me, young master Petr Andreich!" said Savelich.

"What does he need your hareskin coat for? He'll sell it for drink, the dog, at the first tavern."

"It's not your headache, graybeard," my vagabond said, "whether I sell it for drink or not. His Honor's giving me a coat off his own shoulders: that's his pleasure as master. You keep your peace and obey: that's your duty as servant."

"Don't you fear the Lord, you brigand?" responded Savelich, raising his voice. "You can see the child's not yet sensible enough, so you're glad to rob him, making the most of his innocence. What do you want the young master's little coat for? You can't even stretch it across your damned hulking shoulders."

"Don't try to be clever," I said to my attendant. "Bring the coat here right now."

"God Almighty!" groaned Savelich. "A hareskin coat, as good as new! And to whom? Not to anyone deserving, but to a threadbare drunkard!"

He did, however, produce the hareskin coat. The muzhik proceeded to try it on right then and there. Sure enough the coat, which even I had outgrown, was on the tight side for him. But by hook or crook he managed to put it on, ripping it at the seams. Savelich almost burst out sobbing when he heard the stitches tearing. The vagabond was exceedingly happy with my present. He saw me to the wagon and said with a low bow, "Thank you, Your Honor! May the Lord reward you for your charity! I'll never forget your kindness."

He went on his own way, and I continued my journey, ignoring Savelich's vexation and soon forgetting all about yesterday's blizzard, my guide, and the hareskin coat.

As soon as I arrived in Orenburg I presented myself to the general. The man I found myself facing was of great stature but already bent with old age. His long hair was entirely white. His old faded uniform reminded one of a warrior of the times of Anna Ivanovna,[20] and he had a heavy German accent. I handed him my father's letter. As soon as he saw the name he cast a quick glance at me.

"Gottness gracious," he said. "It vass only ze ozer day Andrei Petrovich vass your age, and now hass he such a big lad! Ach, time flies!" He broke the seal and started reading the letter under his breath, making comments as he read on. " 'My Gracious Sir, Andrei Karlovich, I trust that Your Excellency...' Stands he on tseremonies! Hass he no conscience? Discipline, of course, commes first, but is zis any vay to write to an old kamerad? 'Your Excellency has not forgotten...' Hmm, hmm... 'and when... the late Fieldmarshal Mün... during his campaign... and we also with Karolinka...' Acha, bruder! Doess he still remember our old pranks! 'And now, turning to business... my rascal to your care'... hmm... 'hold him in a mailed fist.'[21] Vot's a mailed fist? It musst be Russisch saying. Vot does it mean hold him in a mailed fist?'"

"It means," I answered with as innocent an air as I could put on, "to treat kindly, not too severely, to allow as much freedom as possible, in other words, to hold in a mailed fist."

"Hmm, I understand... 'and not to allow him much freedom...' No, mailed fist musst mean somesing else... 'enclose his passport'... Where is it? Oh, here... 'to notify Semenovskii...' Very goot, very goot, efrysing will be done. 'You will allow me to put rank aside and embrace you as a comrade and friend'... At last hass he the sense... And so on, and so forth... Well, young friend," he said to me, having finished the letter and put the passport aside, "everything will be done: you will be transferred to X. Regiment as an officer, and in order not to waste time, you will set out tomorrow for Fort Belogorsk, where you will serve under the command of Captain Mironov, a good, honest man. There you will experience real service and learn discipline. In Orenburg there is nothing for you to do: dissipation is not good for a young man. As for today, you're cordially invited to dine with me."

"From bad to worse," thought I. "What use is it to me that I was a sergeant of the Guards already in my mother's womb? Where did it take me? To the X. Regiment and to a godforsaken fort on the edge of the Kirgiz-Kaisak steppes!"[22] I had dinner at Andrei Karlovich's house, in company with his old adjutant. Strict German economy reigned over his table, and I suspect that his fear of occasionally having to share his bachelor repast with an extra guest was one of the reasons why he dispatched me to the garrison with so much haste. The next morning I said good-bye to the general and set out for the fort to which I had been assigned.

III. The Fort

In the fort we make our quarter,
Eating bread and drinking water,
And if foemen, cruel ones,
Come to call and share our buns,
We will make their welcome hot:
Powder, canister, and shot.

A SOLDIER SONG [23]

Old-fashioned people, my dear sir.

The Young Hopeful [24]

Fort Belogorsk was situated at a distance of forty versts from Orenburg.[25] The highway led along the steep bank of the Iaik. The river was not yet frozen over, and the leaden waters formed a sad, dark contrast to its unvaried banks, covered with white snow. On the other side stretched the Kirgiz steppes. I sank into reflections, mostly melancholy. Life in a garrison held little attraction for me. I tried to picture to myself Captain Mironov, my future commanding officer, and the image that came to mind was that of a stern, short-tempered old man, ignorant of everything except the service, and ready to put me under arrest on bread and water for the merest trifle. In the meantime it was beginning to get dark. We were riding along quite fast.

"Is it far to the fort?" I asked my driver.

"It isn't," he answered; "you can already see it yonder."

I looked in every direction, expecting to see fearsome bastions, towers, and a rampart, but I could not see anything except a small village bounded by a palisade. On one side of it there were three or four haystacks, half-buried in snow, on the other a sagging windmill with idly drooping bast sails.

"Where *is* the fort?" I asked in amazement.

"Right here," answered the driver, pointing at the little village, and as he spoke we had already driven in.

By the gate I saw an old cast-iron cannon; the streets were narrow and winding, the cottages low and mostly with thatched roofs. I gave orders to drive to the commandant's, and in a minute the wagon stopped in front of a small frame house, built on a hill near a wooden church.

Nobody came out to meet me. I went up to the porch and opened the door leading into the anteroom. A veteran of advanced years sat on a table, sewing a blue patch on the elbow of a green uniform coat. I told him to announce me.

"Just go in, Your Honor," replied the veteran; "the family's at home."

I entered a small room, very clean and furnished in the old style. In the corner there stood a cupboard with crockery; on the wall hung an officer's diploma, framed and glazed; next to it the place of pride was occupied by popular prints, some depicting the taking of Küstrin and Ochakov, others showing the selection of a bride and the burial of a cat.[26] An old lady in a padded jacket and with a scarf over her head was seated by the window. She was winding a hank of yarn, which a one-eyed old man, wearing an officer's uniform, held stretched out on his hands.

"What can we do for you, young man?" she asked without interrupting her work.

I answered that I had arrived to serve in the fort and had come to report for duty to my captain; and with these words I was about to turn to the one-eyed little old man, taking him for the commandant, but the lady of the house interrupted my prepared speech.

"Ivan Kuzmich isn't at home," she said. "He's visiting with Father Gerasim, but it's all the same, young man, I'm his wife. You're very welcome: make yourself at home. Do sit down."

She called her maid and told her to fetch the Cossack sergeant. The little old man looked me up and down inquisitively with his one eye.

"May I be so bold as to ask," he said, "in which regiment you've served?"

I satisfied his curiosity.

"May I also inquire," he continued, "why it was your pleasure to transfer from the Guards to a garrison?"

I answered that that was the wish of my superiors.

"For conduct unbecoming an officer of the Guards, I suppose," continued my untiring interrogator.

"That's enough of your nonsense," the captain's wife said to him. "You can see the young man's tired after his journey: he's in no mood to prattle with you... Hold your hands straight... As for you, my dear young man," she turned to me, "don't be disheartened that they've shipped you off to us, behind the beyond: you aren't the first, nor will be the last. You'll like it when you get used to it. It's been near five years since Shvabrin, Aleksei Ivanych, was transferred to us for manslaughter by murder. Heaven knows what got into him—it must've been the devil's work—but he went, you see, outside the city with a certain lieutenant, and they took their swords with them, and what do you know, they started jabbing at each other until Aleksei Ivanych cut down the lieutenant, and in front of two witnesses to boot! What can you say? The wiles of the devil are many."

At this moment the sergeant, a well-built young Cossack, came into the room.

"Maksimych," said the captain's wife to him, "assign this officer to a lodging, but mind you, a clean one."

"Yes, madam, Vasilisa Egorovna," replied the sergeant. "Should we perhaps billet His Honor at Ivan Polezhaev's?"

"Nonsense, Maksimych," said the captain's wife. "Polezhaev's house is crowded as it is; besides, I'm the godmother of his child, and he's never forgotten that we're his betters. Take the officer... What's your name and patronymic, dear? Petr Andreich? Take Petr Andreich to Semen Kuzov's. The scoundrel has let his horse into my vegetable garden. How are things otherwise, Maksimych? Everything all right?"

"Everything's been peaceful, thank God," said the Cossack, "except that in the bathhouse Corporal Prokhorov got into a scuffle with Ustinia Negulina over a tubful of hot water."[27]

"Ivan Ignatich," the captain's wife turned to the one-eyed little old man, "please sort out the matter between Prokhorov and Ustinia: who's right, who's to blame. Then punish them both. Well, Maksimych, you may go now, God be with you. Petr Andreich, Maksimych will take you to your lodging."

I bowed and took my leave. The sergeant led me to a cottage on the high riverbank, at the very edge of the fort. One half of the cottage was occupied by Semen Kuzov's family; the other half was given to me. It consisted of the cottage's one front room, tolerably neat, divided into two by a partition. Savelich started unpacking, and I looked out of the narrow window. A melancholy steppe stretched out before me. On one side I could see a few huts; some chickens were roaming about the street. An old woman was standing on her porch with a trough in her hands calling her pigs, which responded with friendly grunts. This was the place where I was condemned to spend my youth! I was overcome by dejection; I left the window and went to bed without supper, despite the exhortations of Savelich, who kept saying in deep distress, "God Almighty! Won't eat anything! What'll the mistress say if the child fall sick?"

The next morning I had only just begun to dress when the door opened and a young officer, not very tall, with a swarthy face that was strikingly unattractive but exceptionally lively, came into the room.

"Please forgive me," he said in French, "for coming to introduce myself without ceremony. I heard of your arrival yesterday: the urge to see a human face at last so overwhelmed me that I couldn't restrain myself. You'll understand what I mean when you've been here for some time."

I could guess that this was the officer discharged from the Guards for a duel. We proceeded to introduce ourselves. Shvabrin was by no means a stupid man. His conversation was witty and entertaining. He described to me with great mirth the commandant's family and social circle, and the region where fate had brought me. I was roaring with laughter when the same veteran who had been mending his uniform in the commander's anteroom the day before came in to convey Vasilisa Egorovna's invitation to dinner. Shvabrin volunteered to come with me.

As we approached the commandant's house, we saw in a small square some twenty doddering veterans wearing three-cornered hats over their long hair. They were lined up, standing at attention. Facing them stood the commandant, a tall, well-preserved old man, wearing a nightcap and a cotton dressing gown. He came up to us as soon as he saw us, said a few kind words to me, then went back to drilling his men. We stopped to watch the drill, but he told us to go on in to Vasilisa Egorovna, and promised to come soon after us.

"There's not much for you to see here," he added.

Vasilisa Egorovna received us informally and cordially, treating me like an old friend of the family. The veteran and Palashka were laying the table.

"What's the matter with my Ivan Kuzmich today, that he can't stop that drilling?" said the captain's wife. "Palashka, go call the master to dinner. And where's Masha?"

At that moment a girl of about eighteen, with round rosy cheeks and light brown hair combed smoothly behind her blushing ears, came into the room. At first glance she did not make a great impression on me. I looked at her with prejudice because Shvabrin had described Masha, the captain's daughter, as a perfect ninny. She sat down in the corner and started sewing. In the meanwhile the cabbage soup had been put on the table. Vasilisa Egorovna, still not seeing her husband, sent Palashka for him a second time.

"Tell the master that the guests are waiting, the cabbage soup's getting cold: with God's help there'll be plenty more occasion for him to do his drilling; there'll be plenty more chance to yell himself hoarse."

The captain soon arrived, accompanied by the one-eyed little old man.

"What's this, my dear?" the captain's wife said to him. "The food's been served for ages, but there's no way to get you in here."

"Aye, you know, Vasilisa Egorovna," answered Ivan Kuzmich, "duty kept me: I was drilling my old soldiers."

"Don't tell me that," she retorted. "Great glory, drilling your soldiers, indeed; they aren't able to learn the routines, and you don't know the first thing about them, either. It'd be far better if you sat at home and prayed to God. Dear guests, please come and be seated."

We sat down to dinner. Vasilisa Egorovna did not keep quiet for a moment, showering me with her questions: who were my parents, were they still alive, where did they live, and what were their circumstances? Informed of my father's three hundred serfs, she said: [28]

"Fancy that! There are some rich people in this world, aren't there? All we have, my dear, is the one Palashka, but thank God we manage to make ends meet. There's just one problem: Masha. She's of marriageable age, but what does she have for a dowry? A fine-tooth comb, a besom, and a three-kopeck piece (God forgive me) to go to the bathhouse with. All will be fine if a good man turns up; otherwise she'll remain a marriageable maiden for the rest of her life."

I glanced at Maria Ivanovna: her face was aflame, and tears were even dropping on her plate. I felt sorry for her and quickly changed the subject.

"I've heard," I said apropos of nothing, "that some Bashkirs are planning to attack your fort."

"Who told you that, my dear fellow?" asked Ivan Kuzmich.

"I heard it in Orenburg," I replied.

"Nonsense!" said the commandant. "We haven't heard of any such thing for a long time. The Bashkirs are a frightened lot. Don't worry; they won't poke their noses in here, and if they do, I'll give them a rap that'll keep them quiet for ten years."

"Is it not frightening to you," I continued, turning to the captain's wife, "to stay in the fort when it is exposed to such dangers?"

"It's a matter of getting used to it, my dear young man," answered she. "Twenty years ago, when we were transferred here from the regiment, these unbaptised dogs scared me out of my wits. I'd only have to see their lynx-fur hats and hear their war cries, and my heart'd stop beating, can you believe it? But by now I've got so used to them that I don't stir an inch when it's reported that the scoundrels are roving around the fort."

"Vasilisa Egorovna is a stouthearted lady," remarked Shvabrin, with an important air. "Ivan Kuzmich is a witness to that."

"You'd better believe it," said Ivan Kuzmich. "The woman's no sissy."

"And how about Maria Ivanovna?" I asked. "Is she just as brave as you?"

"Masha brave?" responded her mother. "No, she's a coward. To this day she can't hear a gunshot without palpitations. And a couple of years ago, when Ivan Kuzmich took it into his head to fire our cannon on my saint's day, Masha, my poor darling, almost quit this world with fright. We've stopped firing the accursed cannon since then."

We rose from the table. The captain and his wife retired to lie down. I went to Shvabrin's and spent the whole evening with him.

IV. The Duel

> If you will, get in position for my trigger.
> You will observe me puncturing your figure.
>
> KNIAZHNIN [29]

A few weeks went by, and my life in Fort Belogorsk became not only tolerable, but even pleasant. At the commandant's I was treated like a member of the family. The master of the house and his wife were highly respectable people. Ivan Kuzmich, a private's son who had risen from the ranks, was a simple, uneducated, but honest and kind-hearted man. He was under his wife's thumb, which suited his easy-going disposition. Vasilisa Egorovna regarded matters connected with the service just as if they were affairs of her household. It did not take long for Maria Ivanovna to overcome her shyness with me. We got to know each other. I found her to be a sensible and sensitive young woman. I myself hardly noticed how attached I was growing to the good-hearted family, even to Ivan Ignatich, the one-eyed garrison lieutenant, about whom Shvabrin invented the tale that he had an illicit liaison with Vasilisa Egorovna. There was not a shade of truth in this fabrication, but that did not worry Shvabrin.

I was commissioned as an officer. My duties were no great burden. In our fort, entrusted to God's mercy, there were neither reviews, nor training, nor patrols. The commandant did drill his soldiers from time to time for his own amusement, but he had not yet succeeded in teaching all of them which was the right-hand side and which the left, even though, in order to avoid mistakes, they usually crossed themselves before about-faces.[30] Shvabrin had a few books in French. I began reading, and developed a taste for literary pursuits. In the morning I usually read, polished my style through translations, and sometimes even wrote verses. For dinner I almost always went to the commandant's house and stayed on, as a rule, for the rest of the day; some evenings Father Gerasim would also drop in with his wife Akulina Pamfilovna—the foremost bearer of tidings in the whole district. I did, of course, see A. I. Shvabrin every day, too, but his conversation was becoming less and less agreeable to me. His perpetual jokes about the commandant's family did not appeal to me, and I particularly disliked his caustic remarks at the expense of Maria Ivanovna. There was no other society in the fort, and I wished for no other.

Despite the predictions, the Bashkirs were not stirring. Tranquility reigned around our fort. But the peace was disturbed by unexpected internal strife.

As I have mentioned, I developed an interest in literary pursuits. My efforts, judging by the standards of the time, were tolerable: Aleksandr Petrovich Sumarokov was some years later to accord much praise to them.[31] One day I succeeded in writing a little song that I thought was satisfactory. As is well known, authors will sometimes, pretending to be asking for advice, seek a well-disposed listener. I too, having made a clean copy of my song, took it to Shvabrin, the only person in the fort who could appreciate the efforts of a poet. After a brief introduction I drew my notebook out of my pocket and read the following verses aloud:[32]

> Oh, the thought of Masha banning,
> How I struggle to forget;
> And, the lovely maiden shunning,
> Free again my thoughts to set!

> But the wondrous eyes that drew me
> Ever stay before me yet,
> Haunt my peace and still pursue me,
> Never letting me forget.

> Thou, perceiving this my anguish,
> Pity, Masha, take on me,
> Seeing how I vainly languish
> In my sad captivity.

"What do you think of it?" I asked, expecting the praise that I thought was unquestionably due to me. But to my great disappointment Shvabrin, who had generally been indulgent, this time unhesitatingly declared that my song was no good.

"And why?" I asked, concealing my annoyance.

"Because," he replied, "such verses are worthy of my former teacher, Vasilii Kirilych Trediakovskii, and strongly remind me of his amatory couplets."[33]

He took my notebook and began mercilessly picking apart every line and every word, making fun of me in the most sarcastic manner. I could bear it no longer: I tore my notebook out of his hands and declared that I would never again show him my literary works. Shvabrin laughed at this threat.

"We'll see," he said, "whether you'll keep your word. A poet needs a listener as much as Ivan Kuzmich needs his glass of vodka before dinner. And who is that Masha to whom you confess your tender passion and amorous woes? Could it be Maria Ivanovna by any chance?"

"None of your business," I answered, frowning, "whoever that Masha may be. I don't need either your opinion or your guesses."

"Oho! A vain poet and a discreet lover!" continued Shvabrin, irritating me more and more. "But take some friendly advice from me: if you want to succeed, don't limit your maneuvers to mere songs."

"Just what do you mean, sir? Please be so kind as to explain yourself."

"With pleasure. What I mean is that if you want Masha Mironova to come visiting you at dusk, give her a pair of earrings instead of tender verses."

My blood began to boil.

"And why are you of such an opinion about her?" I asked, suppressing my indignation with difficulty.

"Because," he answered with an infernal grin, "I know her ways and habits from experience."

"You're lying, scoundrel!" I exclaimed in a rage. "You're lying in the most shameless manner."

Shvabrin changed color.

"You are not going to get away with that," he said, seizing my arm. "You'll give me satisfaction."

"Just as you wish, any time," I answered with joy. At that moment I could have torn him to pieces.

I immediately went to Ivan Ignatich, whom I found with a needle in hand: he had been entrusted by the captain's wife with stringing some mushrooms to be dried for the winter.

"Ah, Petr Andreich," said he, as he saw me, "come right in. What good fortune brings you here? What's on your mind, if I may ask?"

I explained to him in a few terse words that I had quarreled with Aleksei Ivanych, and that I would like to ask him, Ivan Ignatich, to be my second. He listened to me attentively, with his one eye wide open.

"It is your pleasure to be saying," he responded, "that you want to slay Aleksei Ivanych and you wish me to be present as a witness? Is that it, if I may ask?"

"Exactly so."

"Have mercy on us, Petr Andreich! What an idea! You've quarreled with Aleksei Ivanych? Not the end of the world. A quarrel isn't cast in stone.[34] If he swore at you, you curse him back; if he hit you in the mug, you bash him on the ear; and once more, and again; and then go your separate ways; we'll see to it that you make up. But slaying your neighbor—is that a decent thing to do, if I may ask? That's supposing that you slay him; so much the worse for him—I'm not so fond of Aleksei Ivanych myself. But what if he punctures your hide? How'll that feel? Who'll look a fool then, if I may ask?"

The arguments of the prudent lieutenant had no effect on me: I remained firm in my resolve.

"Just as you wish," said Ivan Ignatich. "Do what you think is best. But why should I be a witness to it? What business is it of mine? Two people get into a scuffle: is that something to gape at, if I may ask? By God's will I fought against the Swedes and the Turks; I've seen enough."

I tried to explain the role of a second to him as best I could, but Ivan Ignatich was incapable of comprehending it.

"Say what you will," he declared, "if I'm to get mixed up in this business at all, it will be to go and report to Ivan Kuzmich, as my duty requires, that an evil scheme, injurious to the interests of the state, is being hatched in the fort: would the commandant deem it advisable to take the necessary measures?"

I was alarmed, and besought Ivan Ignatich not to say anything to the commandant. I could just barely dissuade him from doing so, but at last he gave me his word, whereupon I beat a quick retreat.

As usual, I spent the evening at the commandant's house. I tried to appear cheerful and nonchalant so as not to arouse any suspicions and not to invite importune questions, but I must admit I did not possess the kind of composure that people in such a position almost always boast of. I was easily moved and inclined to tenderness that evening. I found Maria Ivanovna even more appealing than usual. The thought that this might be the last time I would ever see her lent a touching aspect to her presence. Shvabrin also came by. I took him aside and told him about my conversation with Ivan Ignatich.

"What do we need seconds for?" he asked dryly. "We'll do without them."

We agreed to fight behind the haystacks outside the fort toward seven o'clock the next morning. To all appearances we were chatting so amiably that Ivan Ignatich, delighted, let the cat out of the bag.

"This is how it should have been all along," he said with a look of satisfaction. "Better a lean peace than a fat victory; better a tarnished honor than a bruised skin."[35]

"What was that you said, Ivan Ignatich?" asked the captain's wife, who was telling fortunes by cards in the corner. "I didn't quite catch it."

Ivan Ignatich, noticing displeasure on my face and remembering his promise, grew confused and did not know what to answer. Shvabrin was quick enough to come to his aid.

"Ivan Ignatich approves of our reconciliation," he said.

"And who was it, dear, you quarreled with?"

"Petr Andreich and I had a rather nasty argument."

"What about?"

"A mere trifle, a song, Vasilisa Egorovna."

"Could you find nothing else to quarrel about? A song! And how did it happen?"

"This is how: Petr Andreich started singing in my presence a song he had recently composed, while I struck up my own favorite one:

> Captain's daughter, from home
> At the midnight don't roam.[36]

A disagreement arose between us. Petr Andreich was angry at first, but later came to the conclusion that everybody is free to sing what he wants to. With that the whole thing was over."

I almost exploded with rage over Shvabrin's shameless indelicacy, but no one except me understood his rude allusion: at least no one seemed to pay any attention to it. From songs the conversation turned to poets, with the commandant remarking that they were all inveterate drunkards and debauchers. He advised me as a friend to leave versifying well alone as a pursuit incompatible with the service and one that had never led anyone to any good.

Shvabrin's presence was unbearable to me. I soon took my leave of the commandant and his family. When I got home, I inspected my sword, tested its point, and went to bed, ordering Savelich to wake me after six.

Next morning at the appointed time I was behind the haystacks waiting for my adversary. He, too, appeared soon.

"They might catch us at it," he said; "we must hurry."

We took off our uniform coats and, wearing our vests only, drew our swords. At this moment Ivan Ignatich and five or so veterans appeared from behind the haystack. He summoned us to the commandant. We obeyed grudgingly. Surrounded by the soldiers, we marched behind Ivan Ignatich, who led the way to the fort in triumph, striding along with an air of remarkable self-importance.

We arrived at the commandant's house. Ivan Ignatich opened the door and announced triumphantly, "The prisoners!"

We were met by Vasilisa Egorovna.

"How now, my good sirs! What's this I hear? Plotting manslaughter in our fort? Ivan Kuzmich, lock them up at once! Petr Andreich, Aleksei Ivanych, hand over your swords, hand them over this instant! Palashka, take these swords to the storeroom. Petr Andreich, I didn't expect this of you! Aren't you ashamed of yourself? Aleksei Ivanych is of another sort: it was bloody murder he was discharged from the Guards for, and he doesn't fear the Lord God; but you should have known better! Are you going to follow in his footsteps?"

Ivan Kuzmich, in complete agreement with his spouse, kept repeating: "Yes, d'ye hear, Vasilisa Egorovna's right. Military regulations explicitly prohibit duels."

In the meanwhile Palashka had taken our swords and carried them off to the storeroom. I could not help bursting into laughter. Shvabrin maintained a solemn air.

"With all due respect to you, madam," he said to the captain's wife coolly, "I cannot refrain from remarking that you put yourself in unnecessary trouble setting yourself up as a judge over us. I suggest that you leave the matter to Ivan Kuzmich, within whose authority it lies."

"Ah, my dear sir!" retorted the captain's wife. "Are not husband and wife one flesh and one soul? Ivan Kuzmich! Why d'ye stand there gaping? Coop 'em up, each in a different corner, and keep 'em on bread and water until they're cured of this folly. And let Father Gerasim impose a penance on them, so they'll pray to God for forgiveness and show themselves repentant before men."

Ivan Kuzmich did not know what to do. Maria Ivanovna was extremely pale. By and by the storm blew over: the captain's wife calmed down and made us kiss each other. Palashka brought our swords back. We left the commandant's house to all appearances perfectly reconciled. Ivan Ignatich accompanied us.

"Didn't you feel any shame in denouncing us to the commandant," I asked him angrily, "when you'd given your word that you wouldn't?"

"God is my witness, I said nothing to Ivan Kuzmich," he replied. "Vasilisa Egorovna wormed the secret out of me. It was she who saw to it all without the commandant's knowledge. But it's all over now: thank God it's ended as it has." With these words he turned off toward his house, leaving Shvabrin and me by ourselves.

"We can't just leave it at that," I said to him.

"Of course not," replied Shvabrin; "you shall answer with your blood for your impertinence. But they're likely to keep an eye on us: for a few days we'd better put on a show. Good-bye!" And we parted as if nothing was the matter.

Returning to the commandant's house, I sat down next to Maria Ivanovna as usual. Ivan Kuzmich was out, and Vasilisa Egorovna was busy with her chores. Maria and I talked in a low tone. She tenderly reproached me for the anxiety I had caused them all by my quarrel with Shvabrin.

"I almost fainted," she said, "when I was told that the two of you were going to fight with swords. How strange men are! For one word, which they would probably have forgotten in another week, they're ready to shed blood and to sacrifice not only their lives, but also their clear conscience and the happiness of those who... But I'm convinced it wasn't you who started the quarrel. Aleksei Ivanovich was probably to blame."

"Why do you think so, Maria Ivanovna?"

"I just do... He always sneers at everything. I don't like Aleksei Ivanych. I find him offensive; yet, strangely, I'd be really upset if I thought he disliked me as much as I dislike him. Such a thought would worry me dreadfully."

"And what do you think, Maria Ivanovna? Does he like you or not?"

Maria Ivanovna was taken aback; she blushed.

"It seems to me..." she said, "indeed I do think he likes me."

"Why do you think so?"

"Because he once asked for my hand."

"Asked for your hand? He asked for your hand? When?"

"Last year. About two months before your arrival."

"And you refused?"

"As you can see. Aleksei Ivanych is, of course, an intelligent man, of good family and comfortable circumstances, but the mere thought of having to kiss him publicly before the altar... No, not for anything! Not for all the riches in the world!"

Maria Ivanovna's words opened my eyes and shed light on a great many things. Now I could understand Shvabrin's relentless campaign of vilification. He had no doubt noticed our mutual attraction and tried to set us against each other. The words that had led to my quarrel with him appeared to me even more despicable now, when I saw them as a deliberate slander rather than just a coarse and indecent joke. My desire to punish the insolent slanderer grew even stronger, and I waited for an opportunity with impatience.

I did not have to wait long. The next day, as I sat composing an elegy and biting my pen in the hope that a rhyme would come my way, Shvabrin knocked at my window. I put down my pen, picked up my sword, and went out to him.

"Why delay the matter?" said Shvabrin. "They're not watching us. Let's go down to the river. No one will disturb us there."

We set out in silence. Having descended by a steep path, we stopped at the very edge of the river and drew our swords. Shvabrin was more skilled, but I was stronger and bolder; and I could also make good use of the few fencing lessons Monsieur Beaupré, a former soldier, had given me. Shvabrin had not expected to encounter such a dangerous adversary in me. For a long time we were unable to inflict any harm on each other. At length, noticing that Shvabrin was beginning to get tired, I advanced on him vigorously and drove him into the very river. Suddenly I heard someone shout my name. I glanced back and saw Savelich running down the steep path toward me. At that moment I felt a sharp stab in my chest just under the right shoulder; I fell down and lost consciousness.

V. Love

> Oh, you maiden, pretty maiden,
> Do not get married, maiden:
> Ask for your father's and mother's
>   advice,
> Your father's and mother's and all
>   your kinfolk's;
> Store up, maiden, some wisdom,
> Some wisdom and a dowry.
>
> A FOLK SONG

> If you find one better than me,
>   you will forget me;
> If you find one worse than me,
>   you will remember me.
>
> ANOTHER FOLK SONG [37]

When I came around, for a while I could not remember where I was and what had happened to me. I was lying in bed in an unfamiliar room, feeling very weak. Savelich stood before me with a candle in his hand. Someone was gently unwinding the bandages that had been tightly wrapped around my chest and shoulder. Gradually I regained full consciousness. Remembering my duel, I guessed I must have been wounded. At that moment the door creaked.

"Well, how is he?" whispered a voice that sent a thrill through my frame.

"Still the same," Savelich answered with a sigh. "Still unconscious, and it's already the fifth day."

I wanted to turn on my side but could not.

"Where am I? Who's here?" I said with an effort. Maria Ivanovna came up to my bed and bent over me.

"Well, how do you feel?" she asked.

"Heaven be praised!" I replied in a weak voice. "Is that you, Maria Ivanovna? Tell me..." Not strong enough to continue, I fell silent.

Savelich cried out. His face beamed with joy.

"He's come around! He's come around!" he kept repeating. "Thanks to Thee, O Lord! Well, young master Petr Andreich, I vow you've scared me. No trifle, is it: the fifth day already!"

Maria Ivanovna interrupted him. "Don't speak too much to him, Savelich," she said; "he's still weak."

She went out and gently closed the door behind her.

My thoughts were in turmoil. Evidently I was at the commandant's house; Maria Ivanovna had just been in to see me. I wanted to put some questions to Savelich, but the old man shook his head and covered his ears with his hands. I closed my eyes with annoyance and soon fell into a deep sleep.

Waking, I called Savelich, but instead of him I saw Maria Ivanovna before me; her angelic voice greeted me. I cannot express the joyous feeling that overwhelmed me at that moment. I seized her hand and pressed my face against it, bathing it in tears of emotion. Masha did not take it away... Suddenly her lips touched my cheek, and I felt a fresh, burning kiss. Fire shot through my veins.

"Dear, kind Maria Ivanovna," I said to her, "be my wife, consent to make me happy."

She recovered herself.

"For heaven's sake, calm yourself," she said, withdrawing her hand. "You're still not out of danger: your wound may reopen. Take care of yourself, if only for my sake."

With these words she went out, leaving me in raptures. Happiness was reviving me. She would be mine! She loved me! The thought filled my whole being.

From that time on, I got better by the hour. There being no other medical men in the fort, the regimental barber attended to my wound, and fortunately he did not try to be too clever. Youth and nature speeded my recovery. The commandant's whole family was nursing me. Maria Ivanovna hardly ever left my bedside. It goes without saying that as soon as another opportunity presented itself I resumed my interrupted declaration of love; this time Maria Ivanovna heard me out with more patience. She acknowledged her heartfelt attachment to me without any affectation and said that her parents would certainly be glad of her happiness.

"But consider carefully," she added; "won't your family raise any objections?"

I pondered. I had no doubt about my mother's loving considerateness, but familiar with my father's nature and way of thinking, I suspected that my love would not move him much, and that he would view it as a young man's folly. I frankly admitted as much to Maria Ivanovna, and resolved to write to my dear father as eloquently as I possibly could, asking for his paternal blessing. I showed the letter to Maria Ivanovna, who found it so convincing and touching that she did not have the slightest doubt about its effect, and she abandoned herself to the feelings of her tender heart with all the trustfulness of youth and love.

With Shvabrin I made matters up during the first days of my convalescence. Ivan Kuzmich, scolding me for the duel, had said, "Aye, Petr Andreich, I should really throw you in prison, but you've already been punished as it is. As for Aleksei Ivanych, he's been shut in the granary under guard, and Vasilisa Egorovna's locked his sword away. Let 'im reflect and repent at his leisure."

I was too happy to harbor resentment in my heart. I pleaded for Shvabrin, and the good-hearted commandant, with his wife's consent, set him free. Shvabrin came to see me: he expressed deep regret over what had happened between us; he admitted it had been his fault entirely, and begged me to forget all about it. Not being rancorous by nature, I sincerely forgave him, both for our quarrel and for the wound he had inflicted on me. Ascribing his slander to the chagrin of wounded pride and scorned love, I generously excused my luckless rival.

I soon recovered fully and was able to move back to my lodging. I waited impatiently for an answer to my letter, not daring to hope but trying to suppress dark forebodings. I had not yet spoken with Vasilisa Egorovna and her husband, but I knew it would not come as a surprise to them. Certain of their consent before we ever asked for it, Maria Ivanovna and I did not try to conceal our feelings from them.

At last one evening Savelich came into my room holding a letter in his hand. I seized it with trembling fingers. The address was written in my father's hand. This indicated something important, since it was usually my mother who wrote to me, with my father adding only a few lines at the end. I could not bring myself to open the envelope for a long time: I just kept reading and rereading the formal superscription: "To my son Petr Andreevich Grinev, Fort Belogorsk, Orenburg Guberniia." I tried to divine by the handwriting in what spirit the letter had been written. When I did break the seal at last, I could see at first glance that the devil had confounded the whole matter. The contents of the letter were as follows:

My son Petr,

Your letter in which you ask for our parental blessing and consent to your marriage to Mironov's daughter Maria Ivanovna arrived on the 15th of this month, and not only do I not intend to give you my blessing or consent, but I have a mind to get hold of you and teach you a lesson in a way befitting a whelp, despite your rank as an officer: for you have proven that you are as yet unworthy to carry a sword, which was presented to you for the defense of the fatherland and not for duels with other scamps like yourself. I will immediately write to Andrei Karlovich asking him to transfer you as far away from Fort Belogorsk as possible, where you will be cured of this folly. Your dear mother, on hearing of your duel and wound, was taken ill with grief and is still in bed. What will become of you? I pray to God that you shall reform, although I hardly dare trust in such divine mercy.

Your father, A. G.

Reading this letter evoked several feelings in me. The harsh expressions that my father had so unsparingly indulged in offended me deeply. The disdain with which he had referred to Maria Ivanovna seemed to me both improper and unjust. The thought of being transferred from Fort Belogorsk terrified me. What distressed me most, however, was the news of my mother's illness. I was indignant with Savelich, for I did not doubt that my parents had learned of my duel through him. After pacing up and down my narrow room for some time, I stopped before him and said with a menacing air:

"It clearly hasn't been enough for you that I was wounded because of you and teetered on the brink of the grave for a whole month: you also wish to destroy my mother."

Savelich was thunderstruck.

"Have mercy on me, sir," he said, almost sobbing. "What is this you're saying? That you were wounded because of me? God be my witness, I was a-running to throw my own breast between you and Aleksei Ivanych's sword! It's just that my accursed old legs couldn't carry me fast enough. And what did I do to your dear mother?"

"What did you do?" said I. "Who told you to write and inform on me? Or were you assigned to spy on me?"

"Me write and inform on you?" Savelich replied in tears. "God Almighty! Just read, if you please, what the master writes to me: you'll see if I've been informing on you."

He took a letter from his pocket and gave me the following to read:

You ought to be ashamed of yourself, old cur, that despite my strict orders you failed to report on my son Petr Andreevich, and that strangers have had to inform me of his pranks. Is this how you carry out your duty and the will of your master? I will send you, old cur, into the fields to herd swine for concealing the truth and pandering to youth. Immediately upon receipt of this letter I order you to give me an account of his health, which I am told has improved, and of where exactly he has been wounded and whether he has received proper treatment.

It was obvious that Savelich had a clear conscience and I had unjustly offended him with my reproaches and suspicions. I apologized to him, but the old man remained inconsolable.

"I never thought I'd live to see this," he repeated. "This is the reward I get from my masters. I'm an old cur and a swineherd, am I? And the cause of your wound? Nay, young master Petr Andreich! Not me, it's that accursed *mounseer* who's to blame: 'twas him taught you how to poke others with iron skewers and stamp your foot, as if poking 'n' stamping could drive an evil man away! Much need there was to throw away money, hiring that *mounseer*!"

But who then took it on himself to inform my father of my conduct? The general? He did not seem to pay much attention to me; and in any case Ivan Kuzmich had not thought it necessary to report my duel to him. I was at a loss. Finally my suspicions fastened on Shvabrin. He alone could have profited by the denunciation, which could have led to my removal from the fort and my separation from the commandant's family. I went to report all this to Maria Ivanovna. She met me on the porch.

"What's happened to you?" she asked as soon as she saw me. "How pale you are!"

"It's all over!" I answered, handing her my father's letter. It was her turn to blanch. Having read the letter, she returned it to me with a trembling hand and said in a faltering voice:

"Evidently, fate has ordained otherwise... Your parents do not wish to receive me into their family. The Lord's will be done! God knows better than we do what is good for us. There's nothing to be done, Petr Andreich: I hope you at least will find happiness..."

"This is not to be!" I exclaimed, seizing her hand. "You love me: I am ready for anything. Let's go and throw ourselves at my parents' feet: they're simple people, not coldhearted snobs. They will give us their blessing, we'll get married, and with time, I'm sure, we'll soften my father's heart. My mother will be on our side, and he'll forgive me."

"No, Petr Andreich," Masha replied. "I will not marry you without your parents' blessing. Without their blessing you'll never find happiness. Let us acquiesce in the Lord's will. If you find the one destined

for you, if you give your heart to another: God be with you, Petr Andreich, I will pray for you both..."

She burst into tears and left me. I had an impulse to follow her into
the house, but realizing that I would not be able to control myself, I
went back to my lodging.

I was sitting deep in thought; suddenly Savelich interrupted my
reflections.

"Here, sir," he said, handing me a piece of paper covered with writing, "see if I'm an informer against my master and if I try to set father
and son against each other."

I took the paper from his hand: it was his answer to the letter he
had received. Here it is, word for word:

Andrei Petrovich, Sir, Our Gracious Master,

I am in receipt of your gracious letter in which it pleases you to be
angry with me, your serf, and in which you say that I ought to be
ashamed of myself for not carrying out my master's orders; but I,
not an old cur but your faithful servant, do obey my master's orders,
and my hair has turned gray in your zealous service. About Petr Andreevich's wound I did not write to you in order not to affright you
unnecessarily; they say that the mistress, Avdotia Vasilevna, pro-
tectress of us all, has taken to bed with grief as it is, and I will pray
to God to restore her to health. And Petr Andreich was wounded
under the right shoulder, in the chest just under the bone, the cut
being a *vershok* and a half deep,[38] and he lay in bed at the commandant's house, where we had brought him from the riverbank, and he
was treated by the local barber Stepan Paramonov; and by now Petr
Andreich, heaven be thanked, has entirely recovered, and one can
write nothing but good about him. The commandant, I hear, is satisfied with him, and Vasilisa Egorovna treats him as if he were her
own son. And if a little incident befell him: youth will have its
fling; the horse has four legs, and yet he stumbles. And if it please
you, as you wrote, to send me into the fields to herd swine, it is
within your lordly power. Herewith I humbly bow down before you,
                                    Your faithful servant,
                                    Arkhip Savelev

I could not help smiling several times as I read the good-hearted old
man's epistle. I was not in a condition to reply to my father; as for
reassuring my mother, it seemed to me that Savelich's letter was
sufficient.

From that time my situation changed. Maria Ivanovna hardly ever spoke to me and made every effort to avoid my company. The commandant's house became a disagreeable place for me. Gradually I got used to sitting at home by myself. Vasilisa Egorovna reproached me for it at first, but, seeing my stubbornness, left me in peace. I saw Ivan Kuzmich only when duty required it. With Shvabrin I seldom came into contact, and then only reluctantly, all the more so since I noticed in him a veiled hostility toward me, which confirmed my suspicions. My life became unbearable. I fell into a despondent brooding, made worse by solitude and idleness. In my isolation, my love for Maria blazed out of control and became more and more of a torment. I lost the taste for reading and literary pursuits. I became dejected. I was afraid I would either lose my mind or throw myself into dissipation. But some unexpected developments, which were to have a profound effect on the whole of my life, suddenly gave my soul a powerful and salutary shock.

VI. The Pugachev Rebellion

You, young lads, listen to the tales
That we, old men, will be telling you.
A SONG [39]

Before I relate the strange events that I was to witness, I must say a few words about the conditions prevailing in Orenburg Guberniia at the end of 1773.

This extensive and rich *guberniia* was inhabited by a number of semi-barbarian peoples who had only recently accepted the Russian Emperors' suzerainty. Because of their frequent revolts, their ways unaccustomed to law and civilized life, and their instability and cruelty, the government could keep them under control only by maintaining constant surveillance over them. Forts were built in convenient locations and settled mostly by Cossacks, who had for a long time held possession of the banks of the Iaik. But these Iaik Cossacks, whose duty it was to guard the peace and safety of the region, had themselves for some time been restless subjects, posing a threat to the government. In 1772 a revolt broke out in their main town. Its cause lay in the strict measures taken by Major General Traubenberg to bring the Host to a proper state of obedience. As a result, Traubenberg was brutally murdered; the Cossacks took full control of their own governance again; and finally their revolt was crushed by grapeshot and ruthless punishments.

All this had happened a short time before my arrival at Fort Belogorsk. By now everything was quiet or at least seemed so; the authorities, however, had too easily given credence to the wily rebels, who feigned repentance but who in fact harbored a secret resentment and were waiting for a suitable opportunity to renew their disturbances.

I return to my narrative.

One evening (this was at the beginning of October 1773) I was sitting at home by myself, listening to the howl of the autumn wind and gazing through my window at the clouds speeding past the moon, when a messenger came to call me to the commandant. I set out at once. Shvabrin, Ivan Ignatich, and the Cossack sergeant were with him. Neither Vasilisa Egorovna nor Maria Ivanovna was in the room. The commandant greeted me with an anxious look. He locked the door, seated everyone except the sergeant, who remained standing by the door, and taking a sheet of paper from his pocket, said to us, "Gentlemen, fellow officers, I have received important news. Listen to what the general writes."

He put on his glasses and read the following:

To Captain Mironov, Commandant of Fort Belogorsk—
Confidential:

Herewith I wish to inform you that the fugitive Don Cossack Emelian Pugachev, a schismatic, has with unpardonable insolence assumed the name of the late Emperor Peter III, has gathered a villainous horde and incited riots in settlements along the Iaik, and has already occupied and destroyed several forts, looting and murdering everywhere. For this reason you are commanded, Captain, to take immediately on receipt of this letter all necessary measures to repulse, and if possible entirely destroy, the above-mentioned villain and impostor in case he should march on the fort entrusted to your care.

"To take all necessary measures indeed!" said the commandant, removing his glasses and folding the letter. "Easier said than done. The villain is evidently strong, and we have only a hundred and thirty men, not counting the Cossacks, who cannot be relied on, if you'll excuse my saying so, Maksimych." The sergeant grinned. "But we have no other choice, gentlemen: be meticulous in carrying out your duties, send out patrols and post guards at night; and in case of an attack lock the gates and assemble the men. You, Maksimych, keep a sharp eye on your Cossacks. The cannon must be inspected and thoroughly cleaned. And first and foremost, keep all this a secret, so that nobody in the fort learns of it sooner than necessary."

Having given these orders, Ivan Kuzmich dismissed us. I went out with Shvabrin, turning over in my mind what I had just heard.

"What do you think?" I asked him. "How's this going to end?" "God only knows," he replied. "We'll see. For the time being I see nothing that should give us concern. And in case..." On that word he fell to thinking and started distractedly whistling an aria from a French opera.

Despite all our precautions, the news of Pugachev's appearance on the scene spread through the fort. Although Ivan Kuzmich had great respect for his wife, he would not for anything have revealed to her an official secret entrusted to him. Having received the general's letter, he rather craftily got her out of the house by telling her that Father Gerasim had received some exciting news from Orenburg, which he was keeping in great secret. Vasilisa Egorovna immediately felt like visiting the priest's wife, and, on Ivan Kuzmich's advice, took Masha along, lest she should be bored left alone at home.

Having taken sole possession of the house, Ivan Kuzmich immediately sent for us and in the meanwhile locked Palashka in the storeroom to prevent her from eavesdropping on us.

Vasilisa Egorovna had no success trying to pry the secret out of the priest's wife, and when she returned home, she learned that Ivan Kuzmich had called a meeting and locked Palashka up in her absence. She guessed that she had been duped by her husband, and she besieged him with questions. But Ivan Kuzmich was prepared for the assault. He betrayed no confusion and briskly answered his inquisitive helpmate, "You know, mother dear, the women in the fort have taken up the habit of burning straw in the stoves, which might cause some accidents, and so I gave strict orders that in the future they should burn not straw, but twigs and fallen branches."

"But why did you have to lock up Palashka?" asked the captain's wife. "Why did the poor wench have to sit in the storeroom until we came home?"

For this question Ivan Kuzmich was not prepared: he became confused and muttered something incomprehensible. Vasilisa Egorovna could see through her husband's perfidy, but knowing well that she could not get anything out of him, she cut the interrogation short and switched to the topic of pickled cucumbers, for which Akulina Pamfilovna had a most unusual recipe. Vasilisa Egorovna could not sleep all night for trying to guess what could be on her husband's mind that she was not allowed to know.

The next day, as she was returning from mass, she saw Ivan Ignatich plucking out of the cannon rags, pebbles, bits of wood and bone, and other rubbish that the children had thrown in there.

"What could these military preparations mean?" pondered the captain's wife. "Could it be that a Kirgiz raid is expected? But would Ivan Kuzmich conceal such trifles from me?" She called out to Ivan Ignatich, firmly resolved to worm out of him the secret that tormented her feminine curiosity.

At first she made some observations concerning household matters, like a magistrate who begins an interrogation with irrelevant questions in order to put the defendant off his guard. Then, after a pause, she heaved a deep sigh and said, shaking her head, "Oh, Lord God! What news! What'll come of all this?"

"Never fear, good madam," answered Ivan Ignatich. "The Lord is merciful: we have enough soldiers and plenty of powder, and I've cleaned out the cannon. With a little luck we'll drive back Pugachev. God tempers the wind to the shorn lamb." [40]

"And what sort of a man is this Pugachev?" asked the captain's wife.

Ivan Ignatich now realized that he had let the cat out of the bag, and he bit his tongue. But it was too late. Vasilisa Egorovna, giving her word not to pass the secret to anyone, made him reveal the whole thing.

She kept her promise, not breathing a word to anyone except the priest's wife, and to her only because her cow was still grazing on the steppe and might be captured by the villains.

Soon the whole fort was buzzing with talk about Pugachev. There were several rumors. The commandant dispatched the sergeant to find out what he could from neighboring settlements and forts. The sergeant came back two days later, reporting that about sixty versts from the fort he had seen a large number of campfires, and that according to the Bashkirs an army of unprecedented proportions was approaching. But he could not say anything more positive, because he had not dared venture farther afield.

Unusual agitation could be observed among the Cossacks of the fort: they gathered in groups in every street and talked in a low tone, but dispersed as soon as they saw a dragoon or a garrison soldier. Spies were sent to mingle with them. The baptised Kalmyk Iulai brought important intelligence to the commandant. The sergeant's report, according to Iulai, was false: on his return, the shifty Cossack had told his comrades that he had in fact been to the rebels' camp and presented himself to their leader, who let him kiss his hand and had a long talk with him. The commandant immediately took the sergeant into custody and appointed Iulai in his place. The Cossacks took this new development with manifest displeasure. They grumbled loudly, so much so that Ivan Ignatich, who executed the commandant's order, heard with his own ears, "You'll live to regret that, garrison rat!" The commandant was planning to interrogate his prisoner the same day, but he escaped, no doubt with the aid of accomplices.

Another development increased the commandant's anxiety. A Bashkir carrying copies of a seditious manifesto was captured. In view of this, the commandant wanted to convene his officers again and to get Vasilisa Egorovna out of the house again under some plausible pretext. But since he was a simplehearted and straightforward man, he could think of no ruse except the one he had already employed.

"Listen, Vasilisa Egorovna," he said clearing his throat, "Father Gerasim, I hear, has received from the city..."

"That's enough of your lies, Ivan Kuzmich," his wife interrupted him; "I can see you want to call a meeting and to talk about Emelian Pugachev without me, but this time you're not going to trick me."

Ivan Kuzmich opened his eyes wide. "Well, mother dear," he said, "stay if you already know all about it: we can just as well talk in your presence."

"That's more like it, there's a good man," she answered. "Cunning doesn't befit you. Just send for those officers."

We assembled once more. Ivan Kuzmich, in the presence of his wife, read aloud Pugachev's manifesto, written by some semiliterate Cossack. The impostor declared his intention to march on our fort immediately; he invited the Cossacks and soldiers to join his band and admonished the commanders not to offer any resistance on pain of death. The manifesto was written in a crude but forceful language that was bound to make a dangerous impression on the minds of simple people.

"What a scoundrel!" exclaimed the captain's wife. "How does he dare propose such things to us! To meet him outside the fort and lay our flags at his feet! Oh, the son of a bitch! Doesn't he realize that we've been in the service for forty years and have, by the mercy of God, seen a thing or two? Can there be commanders who've obeyed the impostor?"

"There shouldn't be, certainly," Ivan Kuzmich answered. "But I hear that the villain has already taken many forts."

"He does seem to be really strong," remarked Shvabrin.

"We will learn about his actual strength right now," said the commandant. "Vasilisa Egorovna, give me the key to the barn. Ivan Ignatich, bring the Bashkir here and tell Iulai to fetch a whip."

"Wait a minute, Ivan Kuzmich," said the commander's wife, getting up. "Let me take Masha somewhere out of the house: I don't want her to be terrified by the screams. And to tell you the truth, I haven't much of a taste for torture either. I wish you the best."

Torture was so deeply ingrained in judicial procedure in the old days that the noble decree by which it was eventually abolished remained without effect for a long time.[41] It was thought that the offender's own confession was indispensable if his guilt was to be fully established—an idea that not only lacks foundation, but is diametrically opposed to sound legal thinking; for if a denial by the accused is not accepted as proof of his innocence, then an admission by him should be even less of a proof of his guilt. Even today I sometimes hear old judges express regret over the abolition of this barbaric practice. In the days of my youth no one—neither the judges nor the accused—doubted that torture was necessary. Therefore the commandant's order neither surprised nor troubled any of us. Ivan Ignatich went to fetch the Bashkir, who was locked in Vasilisa Egorovna's barn, and in a few minutes the captive was led into the anteroom. The commandant ordered him to be brought before him.

The Bashkir stepped across the threshold with difficulty (he was in irons) and, taking off his tall hat, remained standing by the door. I glanced at him and shuddered. I shall never forget this man. He appeared to be over seventy. His nose and ears were missing. His head was shaved; in place of a beard he had a few gray hairs sticking out; he was small, thin, and bent; but fire still sparkled in his narrow slit eyes.

"Aha!" said the commander, recognizing by the terrible marks one of the rebels punished in 1741. "So you're an old wolf who's been caught in our traps before. I can tell by your well-shorn nob, it's not the first time you've rioted. Come a little closer and tell me who sent you."

The old Bashkir remained silent and stared at the commandant with an air of total incomprehension.

"Why are you silent?" continued Ivan Kuzmich. "Or don't you understand Russian? Iulai, ask him in your tongue who's sent him into our fort?"

Iulai repeated Ivan Kuzmich's question in Tatar. But the Bashkir gazed back at him with the same expression and did not answer a word.

"*Iakshi,*"[42] said the commandant. "I'll make you speak up if that's what you want. Fellows, take this clownish striped gown off him and hemstitch his back. But mind, Iulai, don't spare him!"

Two veterans started undressing the Bashkir. He kept glancing about him like a little wild animal caught by children. But when one of the veterans grabbed the Bashkir's arms and, twining them around his own neck, lifted the old man on his shoulders, while Iulai picked up the whip and flourished it, the Bashkir gave out a moan in a weak, imploring voice and, shaking his head, opened his mouth, in which there was a truncated stump instead of a tongue.

When I reflect that this happened in my own lifetime, and that since then I have lived to see Emperor Alexander's mild reign, I cannot help marveling at the rapid progress of enlightenment and the spread of humane principles. Young man! If my memoirs fall into your hands, remember that the best and most enduring changes are those arising from a betterment of mores without violent shocks.

We were all horror-stricken.

"Well," said the commander, "we'll obviously not get any sense out of him. Iulai, take the Bashkir back to the barn. With you, gentlemen, I have a few more things to talk over."

We were just beginning to discuss our situation when Vasilisa Egorovna burst into the room, breathless and beside herself with alarm.

"What's happened to you!" asked the commandant in astonishment.

"My dear sirs, calamity's upon us!" Vasilisa Egorovna answered. "Fort Nizhne-Ozernaia was taken this morning. Father Gerasim's hired man has just returned from there. He saw them take it. The commandant and all the officers have been hanged. All the soldiers have been taken prisoner. It won't be long before the villains are here."

This unexpected news was a great shock to me. I knew the commandant of Fort Nizhne-Ozernaia, a quiet and modest young man: only two months before he and his young wife had passed through our fort on their way from Orenburg and spent the night at Ivan Kuzmich's house.[43] Nizhne-Ozernaia was about twenty-five versts from our fort. We could expect Pugachev's attack at any moment. I vividly imagined the fate awaiting Maria Ivanovna, and my heart sank.

"Listen, Ivan Kuzmich," I said to the commandant, "it is our duty to defend the fort to our last breath;[44] that goes without saying. But we must think of the safety of the women. Please send them off to Orenburg, if the road is still open, or to a more secure fort somewhere far away, out of the brigand's reach."

Ivan Kuzmich turned to his wife and said, "Indeed, mother dear, wouldn't it be better to send you to some place farther off while we take care of these rebels?"

"Nonsense!" replied the commander's wife. "Where's a fort that bullets can't reach? What's wrong with the safety of Belogorsk? Thank God, we've lived in it for close to twenty-two years. We've seen the Kirgiz and the Bashkir: we'll sit out Pugachev's siege too."

"Well, mother dear," rejoined Ivan Kuzmich, "stay, if you trust our fort; but what are we going to do with Masha? All well and good, if we sit out the siege or relief comes in time; but what if the villains take the fort?"

"Well, then..." Vasilisa Egorovna stopped short, falling silent with an extremely anxious look.

"No, Vasilisa Egorovna," continued the commandant, noticing that his words had made an impression, perhaps for the first time in his life, "it won't do to let Masha stay here. Let's send her to Orenburg, to her godmother: there they have enough troops and cannon, and the walls are of stone. And I'd advise you to go there too: old woman or not, just look at what might happen to you if they storm the fort."

"All right," she said, "let it be so: we'll send Masha off. As for me, don't even try asking me; I won't go. There's no earthly reason why I should part with you in my old age and seek a lonely grave in a strange place. Together we have lived, together we will die."

"You may be right about that," said the commandant. "But we've no time to lose: go and get Masha ready for the journey. We'll send her off at daybreak tomorrow, and we'll provide her with a convoy, as well, though we hardly have men to spare. But where is she?"

"She's at Akulina Pamfilovna's," the commandant's wife replied. "She felt faint on hearing about the fall of Nizhne-Ozernaia: I hope she won't fall sick. God Almighty, what times we've lived to see!"

Vasilisa Egorovna left to see to her daughter's departure. The discussions with the commandant were still going on, but I no longer participated in them or listened to what was being said. Maria Ivanovna came to supper, her face pale and her eyes red with weeping. We ate in silence and rose from the table earlier than usual. Wishing the whole family good night, all of us left. I had deliberately left my sword behind, however, and went back for it: I had a premonition that I would find Masha alone. Indeed she met me at the door and handed me my sword.

"Good-bye, Petr Andreich!" she said in tears. "They're sending me to Orenburg. Take care of yourself and be happy: perhaps the Lord will so ordain that we'll meet again; if not..." She burst into sobs. I embraced her.

"Farewell, my angel," I said, "farewell, my darling, my beloved one!

Whatever happens to me, you can be sure that my last thought and last prayer shall be for you!"

Masha sobbed, resting her head on my breast. I kissed her fervently and hurried out of the room.

VII. The Assault

> My head, my dear head,
> My head, grown gray in service!
> You have served, my head,
> Thirty-three years, no more, no less.
> Oh, you have not earned by your service
> Either fortune or joy,
> Or a kind word,
> Or any high rank;
> All you have earned, my head,
> Are two tall posts,
> A transom of maple
> And a noose of silk.
>
> A FOLK SONG [45]

That night I did not sleep, nor did I undress. At daybreak I intended to go to the gate of the fort through which Maria Ivanovna would be leaving, and say farewell to her for the last time. I felt a great change in myself: my agitated state of mind was much less onerous than the dejection that had overwhelmed me of late. Vague but alluring dreams mingled in my thoughts with the sadness of separation; and I awaited danger impatiently, with a feeling of noble ambition. The night passed imperceptibly. I was just about to leave the house when my door opened and a corporal came in to report that our Cossacks had left the fort during the night, forcibly taking Iulai with them, and that strange men were reconnoitering the area around the fort. The thought that Maria Ivanovna would not be able to get away terrified me; I hastily gave some instructions to the corporal and rushed to the commandant's.

It was already getting light. As I sped along the street I heard someone call me. I stopped. "Where are you running?" asked Ivan Ignatich, catching up with me. "Ivan Kuzmich is on the rampart and has sent me to fetch you. Pugach has arrived." [46]

"Has Maria Ivanovna got away?" I asked with a fluttering heart.

"She couldn't," replied Ivan Ignatich. "The road to Orenburg is cut off, and the fort is surrounded. Things are looking bad, Petr Andreich!"

We went to the rampart, which was a natural elevation reinforced by a palisade. All of the inhabitants of the fort were already crowding there. The garrison stood under arms. The cannon had been hauled here the night before. The commandant paced up and down before his little troop. The approach of danger inspired the old warrior with unusual vigor. Some twenty people were riding about on the steppe, not far from the fort. They appeared to be Cossacks, but there were also some Bashkirs among them, easily distinguishable by their lynx hats and quivers. The commandant inspected his troop, saying to the soldiers, "Well, my lads, we'll stand up today for our Mother the Empress and show the world we're courageous people, true to our oath."

The soldiers loudly voiced their zeal. Shvabrin stood next to me, with his gaze fixed on the enemy. The people riding about on the steppe noticed some movement in the fort; they gathered in a group and began talking among themselves. The commandant ordered Ivan Ignatich to aim the cannon at the group, and he himself applied the fuse. The ball whizzed over their heads, causing no harm to anyone. The horsemen scattered and instantly galloped out of sight: the steppe became empty.

At this moment Vasilisa Egorovna appeared on the rampart, accompanied by Masha, who did not want to be left alone.

"Well," asked the commandant's wife, "how's the battle going? And where's the enemy?"

"The enemy isn't far off," Ivan Kuzmich replied. "With God's help we'll be all right. Well, Masha, are you frightened?"

"No, papa," answered Masha, "it's more frightening to be left alone at home."

She looked at me and made an effort to smile. I involuntarily grasped the hilt of my sword, remembering that I had received it from her hands the evening before, as if for the defense of my beloved. My heart glowed. I imagined myself her knight-protector. I longed to prove that I was worthy of her trust, and waited impatiently for the decisive moment.

At this point new mounted hordes appeared from behind a ridge half a verst from the fort, and soon the whole steppe was covered with multitudes, armed with lances and bows and arrows. Among them, on a white horse, rode a man in a red caftan, with his saber drawn: this was Pugachev himself. He stopped; his men gathered around him; and evidently by his command, four of them peeled off from the group and galloped right up to the fort at full speed. We recognized them as defectors from our own fort. One of them brought a sheet of paper under his hat; another held, stuck on the point of his lance, the head of Iulai, which he swung in a broad arc and hurled to us over the palisade. The poor Kalmyk's head fell at the commandant's feet. The traitors were shouting, "Don't shoot: come out of the fort to greet the Sovereign. The Sovereign is here!"

"I'll teach you who's here!" cried Ivan Kuzmich. "Ready, lads, fire!"

Our soldiers fired a volley. The Cossack holding the letter swayed in his saddle and fell off his horse; the others galloped back. I looked at Maria Ivanovna. Terror-stricken by the sight of Iulai's bloody head and deafened by the volley, she seemed bedazed. The commandant summoned the corporal and ordered him to take the sheet of paper from the dead Cossack's hand. The corporal went out into the field and came back leading the dead man's horse by the bridle. He handed the letter to the commandant. Ivan Kuzmich read it to himself and tore it to pieces. In the meantime the rebels were plainly preparing for action. Soon bullets came whizzing by our ears, and several arrows fell close to us, sticking in the ground or in the palisade.

"Vasilisa Egorovna," said the commandant, "this is no place for women. Take Masha away: as you can see, the poor girl's more dead than alive."

Vasilisa Egorovna, tamed by the bullets, glanced at the steppe, which was all astir, and turned to her husband, saying, "Ivan Kuzmich, life and death are in God's hands: give your blessing to Masha. Masha, go to your father."

Masha, pale and trembling, went up to Ivan Kuzmich, dropped to her knees, and bowed to the ground before him. The old commandant made the sign of the cross over her three times, then raised her up and kissed her, saying in a voice of deep emotion:

"Well, Masha, be happy. Pray to God: he will not forsake you. If a good man should come along, God grant you peace and happiness. Live with him as I have lived with Vasilisa Egorovna. And now, farewell, Masha. Vasilisa Egorovna, do take her away, won't you?"

Masha threw her arms around his neck and burst into sobs.

"Let me kiss you, too," said the commandant's wife, weeping. "Farewell, my dear Ivan Kuzmich! Forgive me if I've ever vexed you in any way!"

"Farewell, farewell, mother dear," said Ivan Kuzmich, embracing his old woman. "But that's enough, now. Go home, please do; and if there's time, dress Masha in a *sarafan*."[47]

The commandant's wife and daughter walked away. I followed Maria Ivanovna with my eyes; she glanced back and nodded to me. Then Ivan Kuzmich turned toward us and directed all his attention to the enemy. The rebels gathered around their leader and suddenly began dismounting.

"Steady now," said the commandant, "the assault is coming."

At that moment the rebels burst into terrifying shrieks and screams and rushed toward the fort. Our cannon was loaded with grapeshot.

The commandant let the rebels come up close and suddenly fired again. The shot tore into the middle of the crowd. The rebels scattered right and left, and fell back. Their leader alone remained at the front... He brandished his saber and appeared to be fervently exhorting the others... The shrieks and the screams, which had died down for a moment, instantly revived.

"Now, lads," said the commandant, "open the gate and beat the drum! Forward, lads! Charge! Follow me!"

The commandant, Ivan Ignatich, and I were outside the rampart in no time, but the intimidated garrison did not budge. "What's the matter, lads, why are you standing?" shouted Ivan Kuzmich. "We can die but once: it's a soldier's duty."

At that moment the rebels charged and burst into the fort. The drum fell silent; the garrison threw down their weapons; I was hurled to the ground, but I got up and entered the fort with the rebels. The commandant, wounded in the head, stood in the midst of a group of villains, who were demanding the keys from him. I was on the point of rushing to his aid, but some hefty Cossacks seized me and bound me with their belts, repeating, "You'll get your deserts for disobeying His Majesty!" They dragged us through the streets; the inhabitants of the fort came out of their houses offering bread and salt. The church bells rang. Suddenly a shout came from the throng that the Sovereign was in the square awaiting the prisoners and receiving oaths of allegiance. The crowd surged toward the square; we were hustled there too.

Pugachev sat in an armchair on the porch of the commandant's house. He was wearing a red Cossack caftan edged with galloons. His tall sable hat with golden tassels was pulled right down to his flashing eyes. His face seemed familiar to me. He was surrounded by Cossack leaders. Father Gerasim, pale and trembling, stood by the porch with a cross in his hands and appeared to be silently imploring him to spare the lives of the victims who were to be brought before him. Gallows were being hastily erected in the square. The Bashkirs drove the crowd back as we approached, and we were brought before Pugachev. The bells stopped ringing; deep silence enveloped the scene.

"Which one is the commandant?" the pretender asked.

Our sergeant stepped forward and pointed at Ivan Kuzmich. Pugachev looked at the old man menacingly and asked him, "How did you dare oppose me, your Sovereign?"

The commandant, languishing from his wound, gathered his last strength and replied in a firm voice, "You're no sovereign to me, you're a pretender and an impostor, d'ye hear?"

Pugachev sullenly knitted his brows and waved a white handkerchief. Several Cossacks grabbed the old captain and dragged him to the gallows. We saw the mutilated Bashkir we had interrogated the day before astride the transom. He held a rope in his hand, and in another minute I saw poor Ivan Kuzmich hoisted into the air. Then Ivan Ignatich was led before Pugachev, who said to him, "Swear your allegiance to your Sovereign, Petr Feodorovich!"

"You're not our sovereign," replied Ivan Ignatich, repeating his captain's words. "You, fellow, are an impostor and a pretender!"

Pugachev waved his handkerchief once more, and the good lieutenant was soon hanging by his old commander.

It was my turn. I was looking at Pugachev boldly, ready to repeat the answer my noble comrades had given him. At that moment, to my indescribable astonishment, I beheld among the rebel leaders Shvabrin, his hair cropped close around the crown after the Cossack fashion, and wearing a Cossack caftan. He approached Pugachev and whispered a few words in his ear.

"Hang him!" said Pugachev, not even looking at me. They threw the noose around my neck. I prayed silently, offering God sincere repentance for all my sins and imploring Him to save all those dear to my heart. I was dragged under the gallows.

"Don't be scared, don't be scared!" repeated my executioners, wishing, in all truth perhaps, to give me courage.

Suddenly I heard a shout:

"Stop, damn you! Hold it!"

The hangman stopped. I glanced around: Savelich was prostrate at Pugachev's feet.

"Father to us all!" my poor old attendant was saying. "What good'll the death of the noble child do to you? Let 'im go; they'll pay you a ransom for 'im, they will; and for fear and example have me, an old man, hanged."

Pugachev gave a signal; they immediately untied me and set me free.

"The Tsar Our Father has pardoned you," they told me.

I cannot say at that moment I was pleased to be spared; but neither can I say that I regretted it. My feelings were too confused. I was brought to the pretender once more and made to kneel before him. Pugachev held out his sinewy hand to me.

"Kiss his hand! Kiss his hand!" they were saying around me.

But I would have preferred the cruelest death to such a foul humiliation.

"Petr Andreich, young master!" whispered Savelich, standing behind me and nudging me. "Don't be obstinate! What does it matter to you? Don't give a damn, just kiss the scound... Whew! Kiss his dear hand."

I did not stir. Pugachev let his hand fall and said mockingly, "His Honor, I see, is dazed with joy. Raise him up!"

They lifted me up and released me. I watched the rest of the horrifying comedy.

The inhabitants of the fort came up to take the oath. One by one they approached, kissed the crucifix, and then bowed to the pretender. The garrison soldiers also stood there. The tailor of the platoon, armed with his blunt scissors, was snipping off their locks. They shook their clipped hair off and went up to kiss the hand of Pugachev, who pronounced them pardoned and accepted them into his band. All this lasted for about three hours. At last Pugachev rose from the armchair and came down from the porch, accompanied by his chiefs. His white horse with its richly ornamented harness was brought to him. Two Cossacks grasped him by the elbows and lifted him into the saddle. He announced to Father Gerasim that he would dine at his house. At this moment a woman's scream was heard. Several brigands had just dragged Vasilisa Egorovna, disheveled and stripped naked, out on the porch. One of them had already decked himself out in her padded jacket. Others were lugging featherbeds, chests, a tea service, linen, and all manner of other spoils.

"Please, my dear fellows," shouted the poor old woman, "let me be. Dear sirs, take me to Ivan Kuzmich." Suddenly she glanced at the gallows and recognized her husband. "Blackguards!" she screamed in a frenzy. "What have you done to him? Ivan Kuzmich, light of my life, brave soldier heart! You escaped both the Prussians' bayonets and the Turks' bullets unscathed; it was not your lot to lay down your life in honest battle; you had to perish at the hands of an escaped convict!"

"Make the old witch shut up!" said Pugachev.

A young Cossack struck her on the head with his saber, and she fell dead on the steps of the porch. Pugachev rode away; the crowd surged after him.

VIII. An Uninvited Guest

An uninvited guest is worse than a Tatar.
A POPULAR SAYING

The square was deserted. I remained standing in the same place and could not gather my thoughts, thrown into disarray by all these horrifying experiences.

Uncertainty about the fate of Maria Ivanovna troubled me most. Where was she? What had happened to her? Had she managed to hide? Was her hiding place safe? My head full of alarming thoughts, I went into the commandant's house. It had been completely laid waste: the chairs, tables, and chests were broken; the crockery smashed; everything ransacked. I ran up the narrow staircase leading to the bedchambers, and for the first time ever entered Maria Ivanovna's room. Her bed had been turned upside down; her wardrobe was broken and plundered; a sanctuary lamp was still burning in front of the empty icon-holder. A mirror on the wall between the windows had also escaped destruction. Where was the inhabitant of this humble virginal cell? A terrible thought passed through my mind: I imagined her in the hands of the marauders. My heart sank. I burst into bitter, bitter tears and loudly called out the name of my beloved. At that moment I heard a slight noise: Palashka, pale and trembling, came out from behind the wardrobe.

"Oh, Petr Andreich!" she said, clasping her hands. "What a day! What horrors!"

"And Maria Ivanovna?" I asked impatiently. "What's happened to Maria Ivanovna?"

"The young mistress is alive," replied Palashka. "She's hiding at Akulina Pamfilovna's."

"With the priest's wife?" I exclaimed in horror. "My God! But Pugachev is there!"

I rushed out of the room, was on the street in a flash, and ran headlong to the priest's house, oblivious to everything around. From inside the house shouts, laughter, and songs could be heard: Pugachev was feasting with his comrades. Palashka ran up behind me. I sent her in to call Akulina Pamfilovna out without attracting attention. In a minute the priest's wife came out to the anteroom with an empty decanter in her hand.

"For heaven's sake, where is Maria Ivanovna?" I asked her with inexpressible agitation.

"She's lying on the bed, my little lamb, right there behind the partition," answered the priest's wife. "We almost had a mishap, Petr Andreich, but thank God it's turned out all right. The villain had just sat down to dinner when my poor darling came to, and gave out a groan! My heart stood still: he heard it!

"'And who's groaning back there, goodwife?'

"I doubled over before the impostor: 'That's my niece, Your Majesty; she's very poorly; she's been lying in bed these two weeks.'

"'And is your niece young?'

" 'She is, Your Majesty.'

" 'Let me see her, goodwife, this niece of yours.'

"My heart leapt into my throat, but there was nothing I could do.

" 'Just as you wish, Your Majesty: only the poor girl can't get up and come to Your Highness.'

" 'That's all right, goodwife, I'll go and take a look at her myself.'

"And that's just what he did, damnation on him: he went behind the partition and, just imagine, pulling the curtain aside, laid his hawk-eyes on her! But the Lord saved us; nothing happened. My goodman and I, can you believe it, were already preparing for martyrdom, but fortunately Masha, my little lamb, didn't recognize him. God Almighty, what days we've lived to see! I'll never! Poor Ivan Kuzmich! Who would have thought? And Vasilisa Egorovna! And Ivan Ignatich! Why him, too? But how come they spared you? And what do you think of Shvabrin, Aleksei Ivanych? Do you know he's had his hair cut like a Cossack and is sitting right in there with them, feasting? Nimble, ain't he? And when I said that about my sick niece, he looked at me, can you imagine, as if piercing me through with a knife, but he didn't give us away, for which, at least, we should be grateful to him."

At this time we heard the guests' drunken shouts and Father Gerasim's voice. The guests were demanding more wine, and the host was calling his spouse. She fell into a flutter.

"Go home now, Petr Andreich," she said; "I've no time for you: the brigands are on a binge. If you don't watch it, you'll fall into some drunkards' hands. Good-bye, Petr Andreich! What's to be, will be: we're all in God's hands."

The priest's wife left me. Somewhat reassured, I went back to my lodging. As I passed by the square I saw a number of Bashkirs crowding around the gallows and pulling the boots off the hanged men's feet: I could hardly restrain my indignation, but I knew it would be useless to try to interfere. Plunderers were roaming the fort, robbing the houses of the officers. The place resounded with shouts of drunken rebels. I reached home. Savelich met me on the threshold.

"Thank God!" he exclaimed when he saw me. "I was afeared the brigands have laid hands on you agin. Well, young master Petr Andreich! Can you believe it? They've robbed us clean, the scoundrels: clothes, linen, crockery, everything—they've left nothing. But never mind! Thank God they've let you off in one piece. By the way, sir, you recognized the ataman, didn't you?"

"No, I didn't. Who is he?"

"You didn't, young master? Have you forgotten the drunkard who swindled you out of your jacket at the wayside inn? That little hareskin jacket was still quite new, but the bastard ripped it apart, struggling into it."

I was astounded. Indeed, the similarity between Pugachev and my guide was striking. I came to realize that the two were one and the same person, which explained why I had been spared. I could not help marveling at such a strange coincidence: my childhood jacket, given as a present to a vagabond, saved me from the noose, and the drunkard who had been loafing around wayside inns was now setting siege to forts and shaking an empire to its foundations!

"Would you like to have something to eat?" asked Savelich, unswerving in his habits. "There's nothing at home, but I can hunt up something and cook it for you."

Left alone, I sank into reflections. What was I to do? Both remaining in a fort occupied by the brigand and following after his band were unbecoming to an officer. My duty demanded that I present myself where my service could still be useful to the fatherland under the given critical circumstances... But love eloquently counseled me to stay close to Maria Ivanovna, to be her defender and protector. Although I anticipated that the course of affairs could not fail to change soon, I could still not help trembling when I thought of the dangers of her present situation.

My reflections were interrupted by the arrival of one of the fort's Cossacks with the announcement that "His Imperial Highness demands your presence."

"Where is he?" I asked, getting ready to obey the command.

"At the commandant's house," answered the Cossack. "After dinner the Tsar Our Father went to the bathhouse, and now he's resting. Well, Your Honor, everything shows that he's a person of distinction: at dinner he was pleased to eat two roast suckling-pigs, and he had his steambath so hot that even Taras Kurochkin couldn't bear it: he had to hand the besom to Fomka Bikbaev and could just barely revive himself with cold water. All his ways are dignified, there's no denying... In the bathhouse, they say, he was showing his royal marks on his chest: a two-headed eagle the size of a five-kopeck piece on one side, and his own image on the other."

I did not think it necessary to dispute the Cossack's opinions, and proceeded with him to the commandant's house, trying to anticipate what my meeting with Pugachev would be like and to guess how it would end. As the reader can imagine, I was not altogether composed.

It was beginning to get dark when I arrived at the commandant's house. The gallows with its victims loomed dark and terrifying. The body of the commandant's poor wife still lay by the porch, which was guarded by two Cossack sentries. The Cossack who accompanied me went to announce me and, returning immediately, led me into the room where I had taken such tender farewell of Maria Ivanovna the evening before.

An extraordinary picture greeted my eyes: at the table, covered with a cloth and laden with bottles and glasses, sat Pugachev and about ten Cossack chiefs, with their hats on, in colorful shirts, their cheeks flushed with wine and their eyes sparkling. Neither Shvabrin nor our sergeant—newfangled traitors—was there among them.

"Ah, Your Honor!" said Pugachev on seeing me. "Welcome. Please be seated."

His companions moved over to make room for me. I sat down silently at the end of the table. My immediate neighbor, a well-built, handsome young Cossack, poured a glass of ordinary vodka for me, which I did not touch. I surveyed the gathering with curiosity. Pugachev sat in the place of honor, with his elbow on the table, resting his black beard on his broad fist. His features, regular and rather pleasant, had nothing ferocious about them. He often turned to a man of about fifty, calling him Count or Timofeich, and sometimes honoring him with the title of uncle.[48] All present treated one another as comrades, showing no particular deference to their leader. They talked about that morning's assault, the success of the uprising, and their future operations. Each swaggered, offered his opinions, and freely disputed those of Pugachev. It was at this strange military council that they decided to march on Orenburg—a bold decision, but one that was almost to be crowned with calamitous success! It was declared that the campaign would begin the next morning.

"Well, brothers," said Pugachev, "let's sing my favorite song before we break up for the night. Chumakov, you start!"

My neighbor struck up a doleful barge hauler's song in a high-pitched voice, and the others joined him in chorus:[49]

> Do not rustle your leaves, dear oak tree, green mother,
> Do not disturb me, brave young lad, in thinking my thoughts.
> In the morning I, brave young lad, must go to be questioned,
> Before a stern judge, the Tsar himself.
> And the Sovereign Tsar will question me:
> You tell me, tell me, lad, peasant's son,
> With whom you went robbing and plundering,
> Did you have many other fellows with you?
> I will tell you, Our Hope, Orthodox Tsar,
> I will tell you the full truth, and nothing but the truth,
> That it was four fellows that I had with me:

My first fellow was the dark night,
My second fellow was a damask steel knife.
My third fellow was my brave horse,
My fourth fellow was a taut bow,
And my errand boys were red-hot arrows.
And the Tsar, Our Hope, will speak:
Well done, young lad, peasant's son,
You knew how to rob and how to answer me,
For which I will reward you, young lad,
With a tall dwelling in the middle of a field,
That will have two posts and a transom.

I cannot describe what effect this folk song about the gallows, sung by people destined for the gallows, had on me. Their stern faces, their harmonious voices, and the doleful intonation they gave to the song's already expressive words—all this inspired me with poetic awe.

The guests drank one more glass, rose from the table, and wished Pugachev good night. I wanted to leave with them, but Pugachev said to me, "Don't go: I want to have a talk with you."

We remained face to face.

For some minutes both of us sat silent. Pugachev fixed his gaze on me, occasionally screwing up his left eye with a wonderfully roguish and mocking expression. At last he burst into laughter with such unaffected merriment that looking at him I started laughing myself, not knowing why.

"Well, Your Honor?" he said to me. "You got scared, didn't you, when my lads threw the rope around your neck? Frightened out of your wits, weren't you?[50] And I vow you would've dangled from the transom if it hadn't been for your servant. I recognized the old devil immediately. Well, Your Honor, did you think that the man who guided you to the wayside inn was your Sovereign Master?" He assumed a solemn and mysterious air. "You'd committed a serious offense against me," he continued, "but I pardoned you for your charity, for doing me a favor at a time when I was forced to hide from my enemies. But that is just the beginning. You'll see how I reward you when I regain my empire! Do you promise to serve me with zeal?"

The rogue's question and boldness seemed so amusing to me that I couldn't restrain a smile.

"What are you smiling at?" he asked, frowning. "Or don't you believe that I am your Sovereign Majesty? Give me a straight answer."

I was perplexed. I could not acknowledge a vagabond as my Sovereign—that would have seemed inexcusable cowardice to me—but to call him an impostor to his face was to invite my own ruin. It seemed to me that to make the gesture now that I had been ready to make under the gallows, in front of the whole crowd, in the first heat of indignation, would be useless braggadocio. I wavered. Pugachev was sullenly waiting for my reply. At length (and to this day I remember the moment with pride) my sense of duty triumphed over my human frailty. I replied to Pugachev:

"Listen, let me tell you the honest truth. Think of it yourself, can I acknowledge you as my sovereign? You're a sharp-witted person: you'd be the first to realize that I was faking."

"And who am I then, in your opinion?"

"God only knows; but whoever you may be, you're playing a dangerous game."

Pugachev cast a quick glance at me.

"So you don't believe," he said, "that I am your Sovereign Petr Fedorovich? All right. But isn't it true that fortune favors the bold?[51] Didn't Grishka Otrepev reign in days of old?[52] Take me for what you wish, but don't desert me. Why should you worry whether I'm this person or that? Whoever's the priest, he's called father. Serve me with faith and truth, and I'll make you a field marshal and a Prince. What do you say?"

"No," I replied firmly. "I was born a nobleman; I swore allegiance to Her Majesty the Empress; I cannot serve you. If you really wish me well, let me go to Orenburg."

Pugachev thought for a while.

"But if I let you go," he asked, "will you promise at least not to fight against me?"

"How could I promise such a thing?" I answered. "You know yourself it doesn't depend on my own wishes: if I'm commanded to go against you, I'll go, there's nothing else I can do. You're a leader now; you demand obedience from your men. Indeed what would it look like if I refused to serve when my services were needed? My life is in your hands: if you let me go, I'll be grateful; if you execute me, God shall be your judge; in any case, I've told you the truth."

My sincerity impressed Pugachev.

"Be it so," he said, slapping me on the shoulder. "Hang him or spare him: don't do things by halves.[53] Go wherever you want, and do what you like. Come and say good-bye tomorrow; and now go to bed: I'm beginning to feel sleepy myself."

I left Pugachev and went out on the street. The night was still and frosty. The moon and the stars shone brightly, illuminating the square and the gallows. In the fort everything was quiet and dark. Only in the tavern was there still a light; shouts of dallying drunkards could be heard from time to time. I looked at the priest's house. The shutters and the gate were closed. Everything seemed to be quiet inside.

Arriving at my lodging, I found Savelich worrying over my absence. He was overjoyed when he heard I was allowed to go free. "Thank gracious heavens!" he said, crossing himself. "We'll leave the fort at the crack of dawn tomorrow and go where our feet'll carry us. I've prepared a little something for you: eat, young master, and sleep the sleep of the just till morning."

Following his advice, I ate my supper with good appetite and, worn out in both body and mind, fell asleep on the bare floor.

IX. Separation

Sweet it was to be united
With you then, my lovely heart;
Bitter now to be divided,
As for flesh and soul to part.
KHERASKOV [54]

Early next morning I was awakened by the beating of drums. I went to the place of assembly. Pugachev's hordes were already lined up next to the gallows, where the victims of the previous day were still hanging.[55] The Cossacks sat on horseback, the soldiers stood under arms. Banners were flying. Several cannon, among which I recognized ours, were placed on gun carriages. All the inhabitants of the fort were here, too, waiting for the pretender. In front of the porch of the commandant's house a Cossack was holding a beautiful white Kirgiz horse by the bridle. I looked about for the corpse of the commandant's wife. It had been pushed somewhat to the side and covered with a piece of matting. At last Pugachev appeared in the doorway. All the people bared their heads. Pugachev stopped on the porch and exchanged greetings with everyone. One of his chiefs gave him a bag filled with copper coins, which he proceeded to scatter about by the handful. People threw themselves on the coins with shouts: the transaction did not pass without some bodily injury. Pugachev was surrounded by his chief followers, including Shvabrin. Our eyes met: the contempt he could read in mine made him turn away with an expression of genuine spite and affected scorn. Seeing me in the crowd, Pugachev nodded to me and called me to him.

"Listen," he said to me, "set out for Orenburg at once, and tell the governor and all the generals to expect me in a week. Counsel them to meet me with filial love and submission: otherwise they won't escape merciless execution. Have a pleasant journey, Your Honor!" Then he turned to the people and said, pointing to Shvabrin, "Here, my children, is your new commander: follow his orders in everything; he's answerable to me for you and the fort."

I heard these words with horror: Shvabrin was to be commander of the fort, and Maria Ivanovna to remain under his power! Lord, what was to become of her! Pugachev came down from the porch. His horse was brought to him. He deftly leapt into the saddle, not waiting for his Cossacks to help him.

At this moment I saw Savelich step out of the crowd, go up to Pugachev, and hand him a sheet of paper. I could not imagine what would come of this.

"What is this?" asked Pugachev gravely.

"Read, if you please, and you will see," answered Savelich.

Pugachev took the paper and scrutinized it for a long time with an air of importance.

"What strange handwriting," he said at last. "Our regal eyes cannot make out any of it. Where's my chief scribe?"

A young fellow in a corporal's uniform swiftly ran up to Pugachev.

"Read it aloud," said the pretender, handing him the paper.

I was extremely curious to learn what my attendant could possibly have written to Pugachev. The chief scribe began to read the following in a thunderous voice, drawing out each word syllable by syllable:

"Two dressing gowns, one of calico and one of striped silk, worth six rubles."

"What does this mean?" asked Pugachev, frowning.

"Just tell 'im to read further," Savelich calmly replied.

The chief scribe continued:

A uniform coat made of fine green cloth, seven rubles.
A pair of white broadcloth pantaloons, five rubles.
Twelve Dutch linen shirts with ruffles, ten rubles.
A hamper with a tea service, two and a half rubles.

"What nonsense is all this?" interrupted Pugachev. "What business of mine are hampers and pantaloons with ruffles?"

Savelich cleared his throat and began to explain.

"This, so please Your Honor, is an inventory of my master's goods that the brigands made off with."

"What brigands?" Pugachev asked menacingly.

"I crave pardon: my tongue slipped," Savelich answered. "Brigands or no brigands, but it was your lads as went ransacking and plundering. Don't be angry with 'em: the horse has four legs and yet he stumbles. But tell 'im to finish the list."

"Read on," said Pugachev.

The scribe continued:

A chintz coverlet, and another one, of taffeta quilted with cotton wool, four rubles.

A fox fur coat, lined with woolen cloth, forty rubles.

And finally a hareskin coat, given to Your Grace at the wayside inn, fifteen rubles.[56]

"And what else!" exclaimed Pugachev, his eyes flashing.

I must confess I felt extremely alarmed for my poor attendant. He was about to launch into further explanations, but Pugachev cut him short.

"How dare you pester me with such trifles?" he cried, tearing the paper from the scribe's hand and flinging it in Savelich's face. "Stupid old idiot! They've been robbed: so what? You should pray for me and my men for the rest of your life, old sod: you and your dear master could both be hanging here among the others who've disobeyed me... Hareskin coat! I'll give you a hareskin coat! Before you know it, I'll have you flayed alive and a coat made of your skin!"

"Do as you please," replied Savelich, "but I'm a man in bondage, responsible for my master's chattels."

Pugachev was apparently in a fit of generosity.

He turned away and rode off without saying another word. Shvabrin and the chiefs followed him. The band marched out of the fort in orderly fashion. The crowd went to see Pugachev off. I remained alone with Savelich in the square. My attendant held the inventory in his hands, reading it over and over with a look of deep regret.

Seeing my good relations with Pugachev he had hit on the idea of putting this to good use, but his artful stratagem had not worked. I thought of scolding him for his inappropriate zeal, but I could not refrain from laughing.

"Aye, you can laugh, sir," he responded, "you can laugh, but when it comes to having to buy all of 'em things anew, you won't find it funny."

I hurried to the priest's house to see Maria Ivanovna. The priest's wife met me with sad news: during the night Maria Ivanovna had developed a high fever. She was lying unconscious, in a delirium. The priest's wife led me into the girl's room. I tiptoed up to her bed. I was struck by the change in her face. She did not recognize me. Gloomy thoughts troubled my mind. The plight of the poor defenseless orphan, left amongst the vicious rebels, and my own inability to help her filled me with horror. Shvabrin, it was above all Shvabrin who preyed on my thoughts. Invested with authority by the pretender, put in charge of the fort where the unfortunate girl—an innocent target of his hatred—was remaining, he might resolve to do anything. But what could I do? How could I help her? How could I free her from the villain's hands? There was only one means left to me: I decided to set out for Orenburg immediately in order to hasten the deliverance of Belogorsk and if possible to assist in it. I said farewell to the priest and Akulina Pamfilovna, fervently entreating the good woman to take care of her whom I already regarded as my wife. I took the poor girl's hand and kissed it, bathing it in tears.

"Farewell," said the priest's wife as she saw me off, "farewell, Petr Andreich. Perhaps with God's help we'll meet in better times. Don't forget us and write to us as often as you can. Poor Maria Ivanovna has no one now but you to comfort and protect her."

When I reached the square, I stopped for a moment, looked at the gallows, and bowed down before it.[57] Then I left the fort, setting out along the Orenburg highway, accompanied by Savelich, who never lagged far behind.

I was walking on, immersed in my thoughts, when I suddenly heard the clatter of horses' hooves behind me. As I looked around I saw a Cossack galloping from the fort, pulling along a Bashkir horse by the reins and making signs to me from afar. I stopped and soon recognized our sergeant. When he reached us, he got off his horse and said, handing me the reins of the other one, "Your Honor, the Tsar Our Father is sending you as a present this horse and a fur coat off his own back." (There was a sheepskin coat tied to the saddle.) "And," the sergeant added with a stammer, "he's also made a present of half a ruble to you... but I seem to have lost it along the way: please generously forgive me."

Savelich eyed him askance and growled, "Lost it along the way indeed! And what's jingling under your shirt? Don't you have no shame?"

"Jingling under my shirt?" rejoined the sergeant without the slightest embarrassment. "What are you talking about, graybeard? The bridle was jingling, not any coins."

"All right," I said, putting an end to the dispute. "Please give my thanks to him who sent you; as for the half-ruble you've lost, try to find it on your way back and keep it for your services."

"Most grateful to Your Honor," he replied, turning his horse around. "I will forever be praying for you."

With these words he galloped off, holding his shirt against his chest with one hand. In a minute he disappeared from our sight.

I put the fur coat on and got on the horse, seating Savelich behind me.

"D'ye see now, sir," said the old man, "I didn't petition the rascal for nothing: the impostor felt ashamed of himself, though I will say that a lanky Bashkir jade and a sheepskin coat ain't worth half what the rascals stole from us and what you yourself gave 'im. But they'll do, I s'pose: we mustn't look a gift horse in the mouth." [58]

X. The Siege of a City

> Fields and hills in hand,
> On high with eagle eyes the city's site he scanned.
> Beyond the camp he had a cloud of thunder wrought
> And, charged with bolts, at night against the bastion
> brought.
>
> KHERASKOV [59]

As we approached Orenburg we saw a group of convicts, their heads shaved and their faces disfigured by the executioner's tongs. They were working around the fortifications under the supervision of veterans from the garrison. Some were carting away the trash that had accumulated in the trench; others were digging with spades; on the ramparts masons were carrying bricks and repairing the city walls. At the gate the sentries stopped us and demanded our passports. As soon as the sergeant heard that I was coming from Belogorsk, he took me straight to the general's house.

I found him in his garden. He was inspecting some apple trees, already bared by the breath of autumn, and with the aid of an old gardener, was carefully wrapping them in warm straw. His face wore an expression of calm, good health, and benevolence. He was glad to see me and questioned me about the horrible events I had witnessed. I told him about everything. He listened to me attentively, though he continued to cut back dead branches all the while.

"Poor Mironov!" he said when I had finished my sad story. "I am sorry about him: he was a good officer. And Madame Mironova was a good-hearted lady, and what an expert at pickling mushrooms! But what happened to Masha, the captain's daughter?"

I replied that she had remained at the fort, in the care of the priest's wife.

"Oh, that's bad," remarked the general, "that's very bad. You cannot count on any discipline among the brigands. What'll become of the poor girl?"

I answered that Fort Belogorsk was not far off, and that His Excellency would presumably not wait long before dispatching troops to liberate its poor inhabitants. The general shook his head doubtfully. "We'll see, we'll see," he said. "We'll have a chance to talk more about that. Come over for a cup of tea: a council of war is to be held at my house today. You can give us reliable information about this rascal Pugachev and his army. In the meanwhile go and take a rest."

I retired to the lodging assigned to me, where Savelich had already set up house. I waited impatiently for the appointed time. As the reader can imagine, I did not fail to appear at the council that was to have such great influence on my fate. I was at the general's before the appointed hour.

I found one of the city officials with him—the director of the customhouse if I rightly remember—a rotund, high-colored little old man wearing a brocade caftan. He asked me many questions about the fate of Ivan Kuzmich, who, he said, had been the godfather of one of his children. He often interrupted me with additional questions and moral observations, which revealed him as a man, if not well versed in the military arts, at least endowed with shrewdness and native wit. Meanwhile the other people who had been invited to the council arrived. Except for the general himself, there was not one military man among the members of the council.[60] When everybody was seated and tea had been served, the general gave a very clear and detailed account of the situation.

"And now, gentlemen," he continued, "we must decide in what way to operate against the rebels: *offensively* or *defensively*? Each of the two methods has its advantages and disadvantages. Offensive action offers more hope for a speedy annihilation of the enemy, whereas defensive action is safer and more reliable. Well, let us put the question to the vote according to the established rules of order, that is, beginning with those holding the lowest ranks. Ensign," he continued, turning to me, "be so good as to give us your opinion."

Rising, I first described Pugachev and his band in a few words, then resolutely declared that the pretender could in no way stand up to a regular army.

The officials listened to my opinion with obvious disapproval. They regarded it as evidence of a young man's impetuosity and daring. There arose a murmur, and I could distinctly hear somebody pronouncing under his breath the word "greenhorn." The general turned to me and said with a smile:

"Ensign, at councils of war the first votes are usually cast in favor of offensive operations: this is in the order of things. Let us now continue with the polling of opinions. Mr. Collegiate Councillor, would you tell us what you think?"

The little old man in the brocade caftan quickly downed his third cup of tea, much diluted with rum, and gave the general the following answer:

"I think, Your Excellency, that our action should be neither offensive nor defensive."

"How now, Mr. Collegiate Councillor," rejoined the surprised general, "the science of tactics knows no other way: you take either offensive or defensive measures."

"Your Excellency, take bribing measures."

"Oho-ho! Your idea is quite sensible. Bribing is allowed in tactics, and we will take your advice. We can offer an award of, say, seventy, or perhaps even a hundred, rubles for the rascal's head, from the secret funds."

"For that award," interrupted the director of the customhouse, "the brigands will surrender their ataman, his hands and feet clapped in iron, or I'll be a Kirgiz ram, not a collegiate councillor."

"We will think about this and discuss it some more," answered the general. "But to be on the safe side, we must also take military measures. Gentlemen, cast your votes according to the rules of order."

All opinions turned out to be contrary to mine. All the officials spoke about the unreliability of our troops, the uncertainty of success, the need for caution, and the like. All thought it more prudent to stay under the protection of the cannon, behind sturdy stone walls, than to test our luck at arms in the open field. At last the general, having listened to all the opinions, shook the ashes out of his pipe and made the following speech:

"My dear sirs, I must declare on my part that I am in full agreement with the ensign, for his opinion is based on the rules of sound tactics, which almost always prescribe offensive rather than defensive action."

He stopped to fill his pipe. My vanity received a boost. I cast a proud glance at the officials, who were whispering among themselves with a look of disappointment and alarm.

"But, my dear sirs," he continued, emitting a thick puff of tobacco smoke as well as a deep sigh, "I cannot take such a great responsibility on myself when the stake is the safety of the provinces entrusted to me by Our Most Gracious Sovereign, Her Imperial Majesty. Therefore I cast my vote with the majority, which has resolved that it is most prudent and least dangerous to await the siege inside the city, and to repulse the attack of the enemy by the force of artillery and, if possible, by sorties."

It was the officials' turn to look at me derisively. The council dispersed. I could not help deploring the weakness of the venerable warrior, who was, against his own conviction, following the advice of untrained and inexperienced people.

A few days after this memorable meeting of the council, we learned that Pugachev was approaching Orenburg just as he had promised. I could see the rebel army from the top of the city walls. It seemed to me that it had increased tenfold since the time of the assault I had witnessed. The rebels also had artillery, taken from the small forts they had conquered. Remembering the council's decision, I could foresee a long confinement within the walls of Orenburg, and almost wept with resentment.

I will not describe the siege of Orenburg, which belongs to history rather than to a family chronicle.[61] I will only say briefly that this siege, due to the carelessness of the local authorities, was calamitous for the citizens, who suffered from hunger and all kinds of other deprivations. It should be easy to imagine that life in Orenburg was wellnigh intolerable. All were waiting for their destiny in a state of despondency; all bemoaned the high prices, which were terrible indeed. The citizens grew accustomed to the cannonballs that landed in their yards; even Pugachev's attacks did not arouse interest any more. I was dying of ennui. Time wore on. No letters came from Belogorsk. All the roads were cut off. Separation from Maria Ivanovna was becoming unbearable to me. I was tormented by uncertainty about her fate. Sorties were my only diversion. By the kindness of Pugachev, I had a good horse, with which I shared my meager rations and on which I rode out daily to exchange shots with Pugachev's flying squadrons. In these skirmishes the advantage was usually on the side of the villains, who sat well-fed and drunk on their excellent horses. The garrison's emaciated cavalry could not cope with them. At times our starving infantry also sallied out into the field, but the deep snow prevented it from operating successfully against the flying squadrons, which were scattered far and wide. The artillery thundered in vain from the high walls, and if taken into the field, the guns sank into the snow and could not be moved by the exhausted horses. Such was the nature of our military operations! This was what the officials of Orenburg called caution and prudence!

One day, when we had somehow succeeded in scattering and putting to flight quite a dense throng, I rode up against a Cossack who had fallen behind his comrades; I was about to strike him with my Turkish saber when he took his hat off and cried, "Good day to you, Petr Andreich! How do you do?"

Looking at him, I recognized our sergeant. I was overjoyed to see him.

"Good day to you, Maksimych," I said to him. "How long ago did you leave Belogorsk?"

"Not long, Your Honor, Petr Andreich; I came back only yesterday. I've brought along a little letter for you."

"Where is it?" I cried, suddenly all flushed.

"It's right here on me," replied Maksimych, thrusting his hand under his shirt. "I promised Palashka I'd get it to you somehow."

With these words he handed me a folded piece of paper and galloped off immediately. I unfolded it and, trembling, read the following lines:

It was God's will that I should be deprived of both my father and mother at once; I have not one relation or protector in the whole world. I am turning to you, knowing that you have always wished me well, and that you are ever ready to help others. I pray to God that this letter may somehow reach you! Maksimych has promised to deliver it to you. Palashka has heard from him that he often sees you from a distance in sallies, and that you do not take the least care of yourself, forgetting those who pray to God with tears in their eyes for you. I was ill for a long time, and when I recovered, Aleksei Ivanovich, who is the fort's commandant in place of my dear late father, forced Father Gerasim, threatening him with Pugachev, to hand me over to him. I live in our house under guard. Aleksei Ivanovich is trying to compel me to marry him. He says he saved my life by not exposing Akulina Pamfilovna's hoax, when she told the villains that I was her niece. But I would sooner die than marry a man like Aleksei Ivanovich. He treats me very cruelly and threatens that if I don't change my mind and consent to his proposal, he will bring me to the villain's camp, and there "you'll meet the fate of Lizaveta Kharlova."[62] I have asked Aleksei Ivanovich to let me think it over. He has agreed to wait another three days; but if I am still not willing to marry him then, there will be no mercy. Petr Andreich, dear friend, you are my only protector: please help a poor girl! Please implore the general and all the commanders to send a liberating force to us as soon as possible, and come yourself if you can. I remain your poor humble orphan,

Maria Mironova

I almost went out of my mind when I read this letter. I galloped toward the city, unmercifully spurring my poor horse. On the way I turned over in my mind several schemes for rescuing the poor girl, but could not think of anything practicable. Reaching the city, I went straight to the general's and burst into his room.

He was pacing up and down his room, smoking his meerschaum pipe. On seeing me, he stopped. He must have been struck by the expression on my face, for he anxiously inquired after the reason for my precipitate visit.

"Your Excellency," I said to him, "I am turning to you as I would to my own father; for the love of God, please do not refuse my request: the happiness of my whole life is at stake."

"What's the matter, my dear fellow?" asked the old man, astonished. "What can I do for you? Speak your mind."

"Your Excellency, would you give me permission to take a platoon of garrison soldiers and about fifty Cossacks to liberate Fort Belogorsk?"

The general stared at me, obviously assuming that I had lost my mind (in which he was not far wrong).

"How now? To liberate Fort Belogorsk?" he asked at last.

"I'll vouch for our success," I answered fervently. "Just let me go, please!"

"No, young man," he said, shaking his head. "Over such a long distance the enemy could easily cut you off from communication with your headquarters and achieve a decisive victory over you. When communication is interdicted..."

I was alarmed to see him getting involved in tactical considerations, and I hastened to interrupt him.

"Captain Mironov's daughter," I told him, "has sent me a letter asking for help: Shvabrin is trying to force her to marry him."

"Is he indeed? Oh, that Shvabrin is a great *Schelm*,[63] and if he ever falls into my hands, I'll have him tried within twenty-four hours, and we'll shoot him on the parapet of the fortress! But for the time being we must be patient..."

"Be patient!" I cried, completely beside myself. "And in the meanwhile let him marry Maria Ivanovna!"

"Oh, that's no great tragedy," retorted the general. "It's better for her to be Shvabrin's wife for the time being, since he can protect her under the present circumstances; and after we've shot him, God will provide other suitors for her. Sweet little widows don't remain maidens for long; or what do I mean? A young widow finds herself a husband sooner than a maiden does."

"I'd sooner die," I cried in a fury, "than yield her to Shvabrin!"

"Oho-ho!" said the old man. "Now I understand: evidently you're in love with Maria Ivanovna. Oh, that's a different matter. My poor lad![64] But even so I cannot give you a platoon of soldiers and fifty Cossacks. Such an expedition would not be prudent, and I cannot take the responsibility for it."

I lowered my head; despair overcame me. Suddenly an idea flashed through my mind. What it entailed, the reader will see in the next chapter—as old-fashioned novelists used to say.

XI. The Rebel Village

> The lion, though by nature fierce, was sated then.
> "What prompted your resolve to seek me in my den?"
> he mildly asked.
>   A. SUMAROKOV [65]

I left the general and hurried back to my lodging. Savelich met me with his usual remonstrances.

"Law, dear sir, what is it makes you jostle with drunken brigands? Is that worthy of a gentleman? You'll be done for, before you know it, without no use. It'd be something else if you were marching against 'em Turks or Swedes, but one's ashamed even to say who you're tussling with."

I interrupted his discourse with a question: how much money did I have, all told?

"There'll be enough," he answered with a look of satisfaction. "Much as the rascals rummaged, I managed to hide some."

With these words he drew from his pocket a long knitted purse full of silver.

"Well, Savelich," I said to him, "give me half now and keep the other half for yourself. I am going to Fort Belogorsk."

"Petr Andreich, young master!" said my good-natured attendant in a trembling voice. "Don't tempt the Lord! How could you set out now, when all the roads are cut off by the brigands? Pity at least your parents, if you don't pity yourself. Where would you go? What for? Wait a spell: troops'll be coming a-catching the rascals, and then you can go where your feet'll carry you."

But I was firm in my resolve.

"It's too late to discuss it," I said to the old man. "I must go: I simply cannot do otherwise. Don't be upset, Savelich: God is merciful, perhaps we'll meet again. But listen, don't have scruples now, don't be sparing. Buy yourself what you need, even if the price is three times what it should be. I'm giving you the money. In case I don't return in three days..."

"What's that you're saying, sir?" Savelich interrupted me. "That I should let you go by yourself? Don't even dream of it! If you're so set on going, I'll follow after you on foot if need be, but I won't desert you.

That I should sit here, behind 'em stone walls without you! I haven't yet gone off my head, have I? Say what you will, sir, I'm not budging from your side."

Knowing well that I could not outargue Savelich, I let him get ready for the journey. In half an hour I mounted my good horse, while Savelich got on an emaciated, lame jade, which a citizen had given him free, having nothing to feed it with. We rode to the city gates; the sentries let us through; we left Orenburg behind.

It was beginning to get dark. We had to pass by the village of Berda, Pugachev's den. The road there was buried under snow, but one could see tracks made by horses, renewed daily, all over the steppe. I rode at a full trot. Savelich could just barely follow me at a distance, and kept shouting after me every minute, "Easy, sir, for God's sake, easy! My damned nag can't keep up with your long-legged devil. Where you hurrying to? It'd be something else if we were rushing to a feast, but hark my word, we're going to put our heads in a noose... Petr Andreich! Young master, Petr Andreich! Don't ruin us!... God Almighty, the noble child's going to perish!"

We could soon see the lights of Berda twinkle. We approached the ravines—natural lines of defense for the village. Savelich would not be left behind and did not cease his plaintive entreaties. I had hoped to skirt the village unnoticed, but suddenly I beheld, right in front of me in the dusk, five or so peasants armed with cudgels: these were sentries at the outer edge of Pugachev's camp. They challenged us. Not knowing the password, I wanted to ride by them in silence, but they immediately surrounded me, and one of them caught my horse by the bridle. I drew my saber and struck the peasant on the head: his hat saved his life, but he staggered and let go of the bridle. The others fell back in confusion: I took advantage of this moment and galloped off spurring my horse.[66]

The darkness of the descending night might have saved me from any further danger, but looking back I suddenly noticed that Savelich was not following me. On his lame horse the poor old man had not been able to get away from the brigands. What was I to do? Having waited a few minutes and ascertained that he had been held up, I turned my horse around and went to try to rescue him.

As I approached the ravine, I could hear in the distance some noise, shouts, and the voice of my Savelich. I rode on faster and soon found myself in the midst of the peasant sentries who had stopped me a few minutes before. They had Savelich with them. They had dragged the old man off his jade and were getting ready to tie him up. My arrival greatly pleased them. They threw themselves on me with shouts and pulled me off my horse in no time. One of them, evidently their leader, declared that he would take us directly to the Sovereign.

"It's up to Our Father the Tsar," he added, "whether he'll order you to be hanged now or upon the morn."

I did not resist; Savelich followed my example; and the sentries led us away in triumph.

We crossed the ravine and entered the village. There were lights in every cottage. Noise and shouts could be heard everywhere. We came across many people on the streets, but in the dark nobody paid any attention to us, and nobody realized I was an officer from Orenburg. We were led straight to a cottage situated at the crossroads. There were several barrels of liquor and two cannon by the gate.

"Here's the palace," said one of the peasants. "We'll announce you at once."

He went inside. I glanced at Savelich: the old man was crossing himself and muttering a prayer. We waited for a long time; at last the peasant returned and said to me, "Follow me: Our Father has said to let the officer in."

I entered the cottage—or palace, as the peasants called it. It was lit by two tallow candles, and its walls were hung with golden paper; otherwise, the benches, the table, the washbasin hanging on a rope, the towel on a nail, the oven-fork in the corner, and the board hearth covered with pots—everything was just as it would be in an ordinary cottage. Pugachev, dressed in a red caftan and a tall hat, sat under the icons, with his arms akimbo in a self-important manner. Some of his chief associates stood by him with a feigned look of servility. It was evident that the news of the arrival of an officer from Orenburg had aroused great curiosity in the rebels, and they had prepared to receive me with pomp. Pugachev recognized me at first glance. His assumed self-importance disappeared immediately.

"Ah, Your Honor," he said to me gaily, "how do you do? What brought you to these parts?"

I replied that I had been traveling on my own business but his men had stopped me.

"And what business is that?" he asked me.

I did not know what to reply. Assuming that I did not want to enter into explanations before witnesses, Pugachev turned to his comrades, telling them to leave. All of them obeyed except for two, who did not stir from their places.

"You can safely talk in their presence," Pugachev told me; "I hide nothing from them."

I threw a sidelong glance at the pretender's confidants. One of them, a frail, hunched-over little old man with a meager gray beard, had nothing noteworthy about him except for a blue ribbon draped across his shoulder, over his gray tunic. But I shall never forget his companion. He was tall, burly, and broad-shouldered, and appeared to be about forty-five years of age. His thick red beard, his gleaming gray eyes, his nose with the nostrils slit, and the red marks on his forehead and cheeks lent an indescribable expression to his broad pockmarked face. He wore a red shirt, a Kirgiz robe, and Cossack trousers. The former (as I was to learn) was the runaway corporal Beloborodov, and the latter Afanasii Sokolov (nicknamed Khlopusha), a criminal sentenced to penal servitude who had escaped from Siberian mines three times.

Despite the worries that had an almost exclusive claim on my attention, the company in which I unexpectedly found myself profoundly stirred my imagination. But Pugachev soon roused me with a question: "Tell us then: what business brought you out of Orenburg?"

A strange thought entered my mind: it seemed to me that providence, bringing me face to face with Pugachev for the second time, was presenting me with an opportunity to execute my plans. I resolved to take advantage of it, and, with no time to reflect on what I was getting into, replied to Pugachev, "I was going to Fort Belogorsk to rescue a mistreated orphan."

Pugachev's eyes flashed.

"Who among my men dares mistreat an orphan?" he cried. "Be he as shrewd as a fox, he won't escape my judgment![67] Speak: who's the culprit?"

"Shvabrin is the culprit," was my answer. "He's keeping as his prisoner the maiden you saw lying ill at the priest's house. He wants to force her to marry him."

"I'll teach Shvabrin a lesson or two," Pugachev said menacingly. "He'll learn what rewards arbitrary mistreatment of the people earns under my rule. I'm going to hang him."

"Allow me to put in a word," Khlopusha said in a hoarse voice. "You were in a hurry to appoint Shvabrin commander of a fort; now you're in a hurry to hang him. You already offended the Cossacks when you put a nobleman over them; now you want to frighten the nobles by executing them at the first accusation."

"No need either to pity or to favor them!" said the little old man with the blue ribbon. "There'll be no harm in hanging Shvabrin; and it wouldn't be amiss, either, to question this here officer thoroughly: why he's honored us with his visit. If he doesn't recognize you as his sovereign, why's he seeking justice from you, and if he does recognize you, what's he been doing sitting in Orenburg with your foes till the present day? Wouldn't you like to have him taken down to the chancery and get a good fire going in the furnace? His Grace, I suspect, has been sent by the commanders of Orenburg to spy on us."

The old villain's logic seemed quite convincing to me. A shiver ran down my spine when I reflected in whose hands I was. Pugachev noticed my confusion.

"How about that, Your Honor?" he asked, winking at me. "My field marshal, it seems to me, is talking sense. What do you think?"

Pugachev's taunting manner restored my courage. I answered calmly that I was in his power and he was free to deal with me in whatever way he thought fit.

"All right," said Pugachev. "Now tell us, in what condition is your city?"

"Thank God," I answered, "all is well."

"All is well!" repeated Pugachev. "And what about the people dying of hunger?"

The pretender spoke the truth, but I felt duty-bound to assert that all that was just empty rumor, and that in fact there was enough of all kinds of supplies in Orenburg.

"You can see," the little old man chimed in, "that he's lying right to your face. All the fugitives have consistently reported that there is famine and death in Orenburg, that they're feeding on carrion, thinking themselves lucky for it, yet His Grace asserts that there's enough of everything. If you want to hang Shvabrin, hang this pretty young man, too, on the same gallows, so that neither of them could feel envious of the other."

The words of the accursed old man seemed to be swaying Pugachev. Fortunately, Khlopusha contradicted his companion.

"That's enough, Naumych," he said. "All you ever want is to strangle and slaughter. A great hero, aren't you? Look at you, your body and soul are scarcely held together. One foot's already in the grave, but you still cut other people's throats. Haven't you already got enough blood on your conscience?"

"And since when have you become a saint?" retorted Beloborodov. "Whence this sudden compassion?"

"Of course," answered Khlopusha, "I'm also a sinner. This hand," here he clenched his bony fist and, rolling up his sleeve, bared his hairy arm, "this hand, too, is guilty of shedding Christian blood. But I've slain foes, not guests; at the crossroads and in the dark forest, not at home while sitting by the stove; with bludgeon and ax, not with slander like an old woman."

The old man turned away and muttered the words, "slit nostrils!"

"What are you whispering there, old devil?" yelled Khlopusha. "I'll give you slit nostrils; just wait, your time's coming too: God willing, you will yet feel the kiss of the executioner's tongs... And in the meanwhile take care lest I pluck your scraggly beard!"

"Generals!" exclaimed Pugachev solemnly. "That's enough of your quarrels. There'd be no harm in it if all the Orenburg dogs dangled from the same transom, but we'll come to a bad end if our own hounds start snapping and snarling at one another. Please make up."

Khlopusha and Beloborodov did not say a word, just glared at each other sullenly. I felt the necessity of changing the topic of the conversation, which could have ended in a way very unfavorable to me, and I turned to Pugachev, saying with a cheerful expression, "Oh, I almost forgot to thank you for the horse and the coat. Without your help I would've never reached the city and would've frozen on the highway."

My ruse worked. Pugachev cheered up.

"One good turn deserves another," he said with a wink and a twinkle in his eyes. "Tell me now, why are you so concerned about the girl Shvabrin is mistreating? Has she kindled a flame in your young heart? Has she?"

"She's my fiancée," I answered Pugachev, seeing a favorable change in the weather and having no reason to conceal the truth.

"Your fiancée!" cried Pugachev. "Why didn't you tell me before? We'll have you married and feast at your wedding!" Then he turned to Beloborodov: "Listen, field marshal, His Honor and I are old friends: let's sit down to supper and then sleep on the matter. We'll see in the morning what we should do with him."

I would have been glad to decline the honor, but there was no way to get out of it. Two young Cossack girls, daughters of the owner of the cottage, laid the table with a white cloth, bringing in some bread and fish soup and several bottles of vodka and beer: once more I found myself sharing a table with Pugachev and his terrifying comrades.

The orgy to which I became an involuntary witness lasted well into the night. At length befuddlement began to get the better of the members of the party. Pugachev fell asleep in his chair; his comrades rose and signaled to me to leave him. I went out with them. By Khlopusha's order the sentry led me to the cottage of the chancery, where I found Savelich and where they locked us in. My attendant was so confounded by all that had happened that he did not even ask me any questions. He lay down in the dark, sighing and moaning for a long time; at last he started snoring, while I gave myself over to musings, which did not allow me a wink of sleep all night.

The next morning Pugachev sent for me. As I approached his quarters, I saw at the gate a covered wagon, with a troika of Tatar horses harnessed to it. There was a crowd in the street. I met Pugachev at the entrance: he was dressed for the road, in a fur coat and a Kirgiz hat. His companions of the night before surrounded him, assuming an air of submission that was in sharp contrast with all I had witnessed the previous evening. Pugachev greeted me merrily and ordered me to get into the wagon with him.

We took our seats.

"To Fort Belogorsk!" said Pugachev to the broad-shouldered Tatar driver standing at the front of the wagon. My heart pounded. The horses hurtled forward, the bells jingled, the wagon dashed forth...

"Stop! Stop!" I heard an all-too-familiar voice, and I caught sight of Savelich running toward us in the street. Pugachev gave orders to stop.

"Petr Andreich, young master!" cried my attendant. "Don't forget me in my old age among these scoundr..."

"Oh, the old devil!" said Pugachev. "Fate's brought us together again. All right, sit on the box."

"Thank you, My Sovereign, thank you, Father," said Savelich taking his seat. "May the Lord keep you in good health for a hundred years for taking pity on an old man and comforting him. I'll pray for you all my life, and I'll never even mention the hareskin coat again."

That hareskin coat might have at last made Pugachev angry in earnest. But happily he either did not hear the unfortunate allusion or chose to ignore it. The horses set off at a gallop; the people in the street stopped and bowed from the waist. Pugachev nodded to them right and left. In another minute we left the village behind and went whizzing over the smooth surface of the highway.

The reader can easily imagine what I felt at that moment. In a few hours I was to see her whom I had already considered lost to me forever. I imagined the moment of our reunion... I also thought about the man in whose hands my fate rested and with whom, by a series of strange coincidences, I was mysteriously linked. I remembered the wanton cruelty and bloodthirsty ways of this same man—who was now volunteering to deliver my beloved one! Pugachev did not know that she was the daughter of Captain Mironov; an exasperated Shvabrin could reveal it all to him; or he might find out the truth in some other way... What would then become of Maria Ivanovna? A shiver ran down my spine, and my hair stood on end at the very thought...

Suddenly Pugachev interrupted my thoughts, turning to me to ask, "What is Your Honor brooding over?"

"How could I not be brooding?" I answered. "I am an officer and a nobleman; only yesterday I was fighting against you; yet today I'm riding in the same wagon with you, and the happiness of my whole life depends on you."

"And what about it?" asked Pugachev. "Are you scared?"

I answered that having already been spared by him once, I was hoping not only for his mercy but even for his help.

"And you're right, by God, you're right!" said the pretender. "You saw how my fellows scowled at you; even this morning the old man insisted that you were a spy and should be tortured and hanged; but I wouldn't consent," he added, lowering his voice so that Savelich and the Tatar would not be able to hear, "because I remembered your glass of vodka and hareskin coat. You can see I'm not as bloodthirsty as your people claim."

I remembered the taking of Fort Belogorsk, but I did not think it necessary to contradict him, and made no answer.

"What do they say about me in Orenburg?" asked Pugachev, after a pause.

"Well, they say that coping with you is no easy matter; you've certainly made your mark."

The pretender's face showed that his vanity was gratified.

"Yes!" he said with a cheerful expression. "I fight with skill, don't I? Have your people in Orenburg heard about the battle at Iuzeeva?[68] Forty generals killed, four armies taken captive. What do you think: could the Prussian King stand up to me?"

The impostor's bragging amused me.

"What do you think yourself?" I said. "Could you get the better of Frederick?"[69]

"Of Fedor Fedorovich? And why not? After all, I'm getting the better of your generals, and they've beaten him more than once. Fortune has favored my arms so far; but it's been nothing yet: just wait and see how I'll march on Moscow."

"So you're proposing to march on Moscow?"

The pretender pondered a little and said in an undertone, "Heaven only knows. My path is narrow:[70] I've little freedom. My fellows are always trying to be clever. They're crooks. I've got to keep my ears pricked: at the first sign of failure they'll try to save their necks in exchange for my head."

"Exactly so!" I told him. "Wouldn't it be better if you yourself left them before it was too late, and threw yourself on the Empress's mercy?"

Pugachev's face broke into a bitter smile.

"No," he answered. "It's too late for me to repent. There'll be no mercy for me. I'm going to continue as I began. You can never be sure: perhaps I'll succeed! After all, Grishka Otrepev reigned over Moscow, didn't he?"

"And do you know how he ended up? He was thrown out of a window, slaughtered, and burned, and his ashes were fired from a cannon!"

"Listen," said Pugachev with frenzied inspiration. "I'll tell you a tale that I heard from an old Kalmyk woman when I was a child. Once the eagle asked the raven, 'Tell me, raven-bird, why is it that you live three hundred years in this bright world, and I am allotted only three and thirty?' 'It's for this reason, my friend,' answered the raven, 'that you drink live blood while I feed on carrion.' Thought the eagle, 'Let me try to feed on the same.' Very well. Off flew the eagle and the raven. Suddenly they saw a fallen horse; they descended and alighted on it. The raven started tearing at it, praising it. The eagle pecked at it once, pecked at it twice, then flapped its wings and said to the raven, 'No, friend raven: rather than live on carrion for three hundred years, I'll choose one good drink of blood, and then what'll come will come.' How do you like this Kalmyk tale?"[71]

"Clever," I replied. "But in my opinion, to live by murder and plunder is the same as pecking carrion."

Pugachev looked at me with surprise and did not answer. We both fell silent, each engrossed in his thoughts. The Tatar struck up a melancholy tune; Savelich swayed from side to side on the box, asleep. The wagon dashed along the smooth, snow-covered highway... Then I caught sight of a little village on the steep bank of the Iaik, with its palisade and bell tower—and in another quarter of an hour we rode into Fort Belogorsk.

XII. The Orphan

> Even as our apple tree
> Has neither leafy top nor spreading branches,
> So has our little princess
> Neither father nor mother.
> There is no one to dress her.
> There is no one to bless her.
> A WEDDING SONG[72]

The wagon drew up to the porch of the commandant's house. The people recognized Pugachev's bell and ran crowding after us. Shvabrin met the pretender on the porch. He was dressed like a Cossack and had grown a beard. The traitor helped Pugachev out of the wagon, voicing his joy and zeal in obsequious terms. When he saw me he became confused, but he soon recovered himself and offered his hand, saying, "So you, too, are on our side? High time!"

I turned away and did not answer anything.

My heart ached when we entered the long-familiar room, where the late commandant's commission still hung on the wall as a melancholy epitaph upon the past. Pugachev sat down on the same sofa on which Ivan Kuzmich used to be lulled to sleep by the grumbling of his spouse. Shvabrin himself brought in some vodka to offer to the pretender. Pugachev emptied his glass and said to him, pointing at me, "Offer some to His Honor, too."

Shvabrin came up to me with his tray, but I turned away from him once more. He seemed to be extremely ill at ease. With his usual perceptiveness he could, of course, guess that Pugachev was dissatisfied with him. He was cringing with fear before the pretender and kept glancing at me with suspicion. Pugachev asked him how things were at the fort, what he had heard about enemy troops, and so forth, and then suddenly turned on him with a question:

"Tell me, brother, what girl is this you're keeping here locked up? Show her to me."

Shvabrin turned pale as a corpse.

"Your Majesty," he said in a trembling voice, "Your Majesty, she's not locked up... She's sick... She's in bed in her room."

"Lead me to her, then," said the pretender, rising from his seat.

There was no way to refuse him. Shvabrin went forward to lead Pugachev to Maria Ivanovna's room. I followed behind.

Shvabrin stopped on the stairs.

"Your Majesty," he said, "you're free to demand of me whatever you wish, but do not order me to let a stranger into my wife's bedroom."

I shuddered.

"So you're married!" I said to him, ready to tear him into pieces.

"Quiet!" Pugachev interrupted me. "This is my business. And you," he continued, turning to Shvabrin, "stop making excuses and raising difficulties: whether she's your wife or not, I will bring in whoever I please. Follow me, Your Honor."

Shvabrin stopped once more at the door of the bedroom and said in a faltering voice, "Your Majesty, I must warn you that she's in a delirium and has been raving incessantly for the last three days."

"Open the door!" said Pugachev.

Shvabrin searched his pockets and declared that he had not brought the key with him. Pugachev kicked the door; the lock flew off, the door flung open, and we entered.

I took one look and froze with fright. Maria Ivanovna, in a tattered peasant dress, pale and thin, with her hair disheveled, sat on the floor. A jug of water covered with a chunk of bread stood before her. Seeing me, she shuddered and cried out. What I felt at that moment I cannot describe.

Pugachev looked at Shvabrin and said with a sarcastic smile, "Nice sick ward you have!" Then, approaching Maria Ivanovna: "Tell me, dear heart, what's your husband punishing you for? What have you done to offend him so?"

"My husband!" she repeated. "He's not my husband. I'll never be his wife! I've resolved I'd sooner die, and will die if I'm not set free."

Pugachev looked at Shvabrin menacingly.

"How dare you deceive me?" he asked him. "Do you know, rascal, what you deserve for this?"

Shvabrin fell on his knees... At that moment my contempt of him muffled all the hatred and anger I bore him. I was disgusted to see a nobleman groveling at the feet of a fugitive Cossack. Pugachev relented.

"I'll pardon you this time," he said to Shvabrin, "but bear in mind that one more offense, and this one will also be remembered." Then he turned to Maria Ivanovna, saying to her kindly, "Go free, pretty maiden: I grant you freedom. I am your Sovereign."

Maria Ivanovna cast a quick glance at him and guessed that the murderer of her parents was standing before her. She covered her face with both hands and fainted away. I rushed to her side; but at this moment my old acquaintance Palashka pushed her way into the room boldly and took over the care of her young mistress. Pugachev left the bedroom, and the three of us went to the parlor.

"Well, Your Honor," said Pugachev, laughing, "we've delivered the pretty maiden! What do you think, should we send for the priest and make him marry his niece to you? I'll be father by proxy, if you like, and Shvabrin can be your best man: we'll feast and drink and banish sorrow!"

What I had been afraid of, now happened. Hearing Pugachev's suggestion, Shvabrin flew into a passion.

"Your Majesty!" he shouted, beside himself. "I'm guilty, I lied to you, but Grinev is also deceiving you. This girl is not the niece of the Belogorsk priest: she's the daughter of Ivan Mironov, who was executed when the fort was taken."

Pugachev fixed his fiery eyes on me.

"What's this now?" he asked me, bewildered.

"Shvabrin is telling the truth," I answered firmly.

"You didn't mention this to me," Pugachev remarked, and a cloud came over his features.

"Just consider," I replied, "could I have declared in front of your men that Mironov's daughter was alive? They would've torn her to pieces. Nothing could've saved her!"

"That's true enough," laughed Pugachev. "My drunkards wouldn't have spared the poor girl. That old dear, the priest's wife, did right to deceive them."

"Listen," I continued, seeing his favorable mood, "I don't know what to call you, and I don't wish to know... But God is my witness, I'd be glad to repay you with my life for what you've done for me. Only don't demand of me anything that is against my honor and Christian conscience. You are my benefactor. Please conclude the matter as you began it: let me and the poor orphan go free, wherever God will guide us. And wherever you may be, whatever may happen to you, we will pray to God every day to save your sinful soul..."

Pugachev's hardened soul, it seemed, was touched.

"Oh, well, let it be as you say," he said. "Hang him or spare him: don't do things by halves. That is my principle. Take your beautiful one, go with her where you want, and may God grant you peace and happiness!"

Then he turned to Shvabrin and ordered him to issue me a pass for all the outposts and forts he had occupied. Shvabrin, entirely crushed, stood rooted to the ground. Pugachev went to inspect the fort. Shvabrin followed him, while I stayed under the pretext of making preparations for our departure.

I ran to the bedroom. The door was locked. I knocked.

"Who's there?" asked Palashka.

I called out my name. Maria Ivanovna's sweet voice answered from behind the door. "Wait a moment, Petr Andreich. I'm changing. Go to Akulina Pamfilovna's: I'll be there in a minute."

I obeyed and went to Father Gerasim's house. Both he and his wife ran out to greet me. Savelich had already informed them of what had happened.

"Welcome, Petr Andreich," said the priest's wife. "It was God's will that we should meet again. How are you? We've been talking about you every day. And Maria Ivanovna, my little lamb, what has she gone through without you! But tell me, dear, how come you get on so well with Pugachev? How is it that he didn't dispatch you to kingdom come? For that at least we should be grateful to the villain."

"That'll do, old woman," Father Gerasim interrupted her. "There's no need to gabble about everything that comes into your head. Do not speak in vain as the heathens do.[73] Petr Andreich, sir! Welcome, step right in. It's been a long, long time since we saw you last."

The priest's wife invited me to partake in whatever food there was in the house, and talked incessantly. She told me how Shvabrin had forced them to surrender Maria Ivanovna to him; how Maria Ivanovna had wept, unwilling to part with them; how she had managed to keep in touch with them through Palashka (a sprightly wench, who made even the sergeant dance to her tune); how she had advised Maria Ivanovna to write a letter to me, and so forth. I told her my own story briefly. The priest and his wife both crossed themselves when they heard that Pugachev had found out about their deception.

"May the Lord God protect us!" said Akulina Pamfilovna. "May the storm pass over! Oh, but that Aleksei Ivanych: a nasty bit of work, I'll vow!"

At that moment the door opened, and Maria Ivanovna came in with a smile on her pale face. She had shed her peasant costume and was dressed as always before, simply and tastefully.

I seized her hand and for a long time could not utter a single word. We both kept silent from a fullness of heart. Our host and hostess, feeling their presence superfluous, both left the room. We remained all alone. The whole world was forgotten. We talked and talked, and could not talk enough. Maria Ivanovna related to me everything that had happened to her since the taking of the fort; she described the full horror of her situation and all the torments she had experienced at the hands of the detestable Shvabrin. We recalled the earlier happy days too... We both wept... At length I started outlining my plans to her. She could certainly not stay in the fort, under Pugachev's authority and Shvabrin's command. It would also have been senseless to go to Orenburg, subjected as it was to all the vicissitudes of a siege. She had not one relation in the whole wide world. I suggested to her that she go and stay with my parents in their village. At first she hesitated: she was afraid of my father since she knew about his unkindly feelings toward her. I reassured her. I knew that my father would consider it a blessing and an obligation to shelter the daughter of an honored warrior who had given his life for the fatherland.

"My dear Maria Ivanovna!" I said at last. "I regard you as my wife. Our strange circumstances have united us inseparably: nothing in the world can make us part."

She listened to me simply, without affected bashfulness or coy reluctance. She felt that her fate was linked with mine. But she repeated that she would be my wife only if my parents gave their consent. I did not contradict her. We kissed fervently, with all our heart—and thus everything was settled between us.

After an hour the sergeant brought along my pass, with the pretender's signature scrawled on it, and told me that Pugachev wished to see me. I found him ready to leave. I cannot describe what I felt as I said farewell to this terrifying man, a monster and a blackguard to everyone except me. Why not confess the truth? At that moment I was drawn to him by a strong sense of sympathy. I ardently wished to extricate him from the company of the villains whose leader he was, and to save his head before it was too late. Shvabrin and the people crowding around us prevented me from expressing to him all the feelings that filled my heart.

We parted as friends. Seeing Akulina Pamfilovna in the crowd, Pugachev shook his finger at her and winked at her significantly; then he climbed into his wagon, giving orders to drive to Berda, and as the horses started off, he leaned out once more, shouting to me, "Farewell, Your Honor! Perhaps we'll see each other again!"

I was indeed to see him again, but under what circumstances!

Pugachev was gone. For a long time I gazed at the white steppe as his troika rapidly crossed it. The people dispersed. Shvabrin disappeared. I returned to the priest's house. Everything was ready for our departure, and I did not want to delay it any longer. Our belongings were all placed in the commandant's old carriage. The drivers harnessed the horses in no time. Maria Ivanovna went to pay a farewell visit to her parents' grave in the churchyard. I wanted to accompany her, but she asked me to let her go by herself. She returned in a few minutes, shedding silent tears. The carriage drew up. Father Gerasim and his wife came out on the porch. Three of us—Maria Ivanovna, Palashka, and I—took our seats inside the carriage, while Savelich climbed up on the box.

"Farewell, Maria Ivanovna, my little lamb! Farewell, Petr Andreich, my brave falcon!" said the good-hearted Akulina Pamfilovna. "Have a safe journey, and may God grant happiness to you both!"

We set off. I caught sight of Shvabrin standing at the window in the commandant's house. His face wore a surly expression of spite. I did not wish to appear to be triumphing over an annihilated enemy and turned my eyes the other way. At last we passed through the gate and left Fort Belogorsk behind forever.

XIII. The Arrest

"Pray, be not angry, sirrah: but my duty calls
On me to send you straight behind the dungeon walls."
"You may, and I stand ready; but before you do,
Let me by your kind leave explain the case to you."

KNIAZHNIN [74]

I could hardly believe my good fortune at being so unexpectedly reunited with the dear girl whose fate had so terribly worried me even that morning: it seemed as though it had all been just an empty dream. Maria Ivanovna gazed pensively now at me, now at the highway; she had evidently not had enough time to come to her senses and recover her old self. Drained of emotions, we were both silent. In a couple of hours, which had gone by almost unnoticed, we were at the next fort, also under Pugachev's rule. Here we changed horses. The speed with which they were harnessed and the eagerness with which the bearded Cossack, appointed commandant by Pugachev, tried to oblige us seemed to indicate that, thanks to the loquacity of our driver, I was being taken for a courtier of the pretender.

We continued our journey. It was beginning to get dark. We approached a small town, which the bearded commandant had reported to be occupied by a strong detachment on its way to join forces with the pretender. We were stopped by the sentries. To the challenge, "Who goes there?" our driver replied in a thunderous voice, "The Sovereign's trusty friend with his bride." Suddenly a throng of hussars surrounded us, swearing frightfully.

"Get out of there, devil's trusty friend!" the sergeant said to me. "A nice hot bath is waiting for you, and for your bride."

I got out of the carriage and demanded to be taken to their commander. Seeing an officer, the soldiers stopped swearing. The sergeant proceeded to conduct me to the major. Savelich followed right behind me, muttering to himself, "So much for the Sovereign's trusty friend! Out of the frying pan into the fire! God Almighty! How's all this going to end?" The carriage followed us at a walking pace.

In five minutes we reached a brightly lit little house. The sergeant left me guarded by the sentries and went in to announce me. He returned immediately, declaring that His Honor had no time to receive me, and had ordered him to take me off to prison and to bring my bride to him.

"What does this mean?" I shouted in a rage. "Has he lost his mind?"

"That I daren't judge, Your Honor," answered the sergeant, "but His Honor's given orders that Your Honor should be taken off to prison and Her Honor should be brought before His Honor, Your Honor."

I sprang onto the porch. The sentries did not attempt to stop me, and I dashed straight into the room where the hussar officers, some six of them, were playing cards. The major was dealing. How great was my surprise when at the first glance I recognized Ivan Ivanovich Zurin, who had at one time fleeced me in the Simbirsk tavern!

"Is it possible?" I cried. "Ivan Ivanych! Is it you?"

"Gads so! Petr Andreich! What brings you here? Where've you come from? Welcome, brother. Would you like a card?"

"Thank you kindly. I'd rather you'd assign me to a lodging."

"What lodging? Stay with me."

"I can't: I'm not by myself."

"Well, bring your comrade, too."

"I'm not with a comrade. I'm... with a lady."

"With a lady? Where did you get your hands on her? Oho, brother!" Here Zurin whistled so expressively that everybody burst into laughter, and I was thoroughly embarrassed.

"Well," continued Zurin, "be it as you wish. You'll have lodgings. It's a pity, though... We could've had a good time, as of old... But say, boy, why aren't they bringing in Pugachev's little lady friend? Or is she balking? Tell 'er not to be afraid: the gentleman is handsome and will do no harm to her; and give 'er a good hearty slap."

"What do you mean?" I said to Zurin. "What little lady friend of Pugachev's? It's the daughter of the late Captain Mironov. I rescued her from captivity, and I'm now taking her to my father's village, where I intend to leave her."

"How? Is it you then whose arrival they just announced? For pity's sake, what does all this mean?"

"I'll tell you about it later. But now, for heaven's sake, reassure the poor girl, whom your hussars have frightened so."

Zurin immediately proceeded to make the necessary arrangements. He himself came out in the street to apologize to Maria Ivanovna for the accidental misunderstanding and ordered the sergeant to assign to her the best apartment in town. I myself stayed to spend the night with him.

We had supper, and when we were left alone, I related my adventures to him. He listened to me attentively. When I finished, he shook his head, saying:

"All this is fine, brother, except for one thing: what the devil do you want to get married for? Honest officer that I am, I don't want to deceive you: you must believe me that marriage is folly. Why would you want to trifle with a wife and waste your time looking after babies? A plague on them! Take my advice: shake off this captain's daughter.

I've cleared the highway to Simbirsk: it's safe now. Send her off to your parents by herself tomorrow, and stay with my detachment. There's no point in trying to return to Orenburg. If you fall into the rebels' hands again, you'll hardly be able to extricate yourself yet another time. That way this amorous folly will pass of itself, and all will be fine."

Although I did not quite agree with him, I nevertheless recognized that duty and honor demanded my presence in the Empress's army. I decided to follow Zurin's advice and send Maria Ivanovna to my parents' village while I stayed with his detachment.

Savelich came in to help me undress: I told him to be ready to set out for the journey with Maria Ivanovna the next morning. At first he balked at the idea.

"What d'ye mean, sir? That I should forsake you? Who'd be looking after you? What 'ud your parents say?"

Knowing my attendant's stubborn nature, I resolved to get around him by soft words and candor.

"Arkhip Savelich, my friend," I said to him, "don't refuse me your favor, be my benefactor: I don't need any servants here, and I'd be worried if Maria Ivanovna were to set out on the road without you. Serving her, you'll be serving me, for I've firmly resolved to marry her as soon as circumstances permit."

Savelich clasped his hands with a look of indescribable astonishment.

"To marry!" he repeated. "The child wants to marry! And what'll your dear father say? And your dear mother, what'll she think?"

"They'll consent," answered I; "they'll be sure to consent when they get to know Maria Ivanovna. I'm placing my hopes in you, too. Father and mother trust you: you'll plead for us, won't you?"

The old man was touched.

"Oh, dear master, Petr Andreich," he replied, "early though you've taken it into your head to marry, it's true that Maria Ivanovna is such a good-hearted young lady that it'd be a crime to miss the opportunity. Egad, be it as you wish! I'll accompany her, God's little angel, and will humbly tell your parents that such a bride doesn't even need a dowry."

I thanked Savelich and went to bed, sharing Zurin's room. All wrought up and excited, I chattered away. At first Zurin conversed with me willingly, but gradually his answers grew less and less frequent and coherent, until at last he answered one of my questions with a snore and a whistle. I stopped talking and soon followed his example.

I went to see Maria Ivanovna the next morning. I told her about my intentions. She acknowledged them to be prudent and immediately consented. Zurin's detachment was to leave the town that same day. There was no reason to delay matters. I parted with Maria Ivanovna right then and there, entrusting her to Savelich's care and furnishing her with a letter to my parents. She burst into tears.

"Farewell, Petr Andreich," she said in a soft voice. "God only knows if we'll see each other again, but I will never forget you: till my dying day you alone shall live in my heart."

I was unable to reply. There were people around us, and in their presence I did not wish to give full rein to the emotions stirring within me. At last she left. I returned to Zurin sad and silent. He wanted to cheer me up, and I myself was seeking distraction: we spent the day wildly and noisily. In the evening we set out on our march.

This was at the end of February. Winter, which had hindered military operations, was drawing to its close, and our generals were preparing for joint action. Pugachev was still encamped below Orenburg. In the meantime the various government troops scattered about him were joining forces and converging on the robbers' den. The rebel villages submitted to legal authority at the first sight of our troops; the bands of brigands were fleeing from us everywhere; and all signs pointed to an early and happy conclusion of the affair.

Prince Golitsyn soon beat Pugachev at Fort Tatischev, scattering his hordes and lifting the siege of Orenburg.[75] The rebellion, it appeared, had been dealt the last, decisive blow. At this time Zurin's detachment was ordered out against a band of Bashkirs, who scattered before we could set eyes on them. Spring caught us in a Tatar hamlet. The rivers overflowed, and the roads became impassable. Our only comfort in our idleness was the thought that this tedious and petty war against brigands and savages would soon be over.

But Pugachev had not been captured. He reemerged in the area around the Siberian metalworks, gathered new bands there, and recommenced his villainous acts. Reports about his success were making the rounds again. We learned that he had destroyed several Siberian forts. Soon after, rumors of the taking of Kazan and of the pretender's intention to march on Moscow awakened the commanders of the various troops, who had been carelessly slumbering, trusting in the despised rebel's incompetence. Zurin received orders to cross the Volga.[76]

I will not go into the details of our campaign and of the end of the war. I will only say that the disaster reached extreme proportions. We passed through villages ravaged by the rebels and, despite our best intentions, took away from the poor villagers whatever they had managed to salvage.[77] Law and order were suspended everywhere; landowners were hiding in the forests. Bands of brigands dealt destruction everywhere; the commanding officers of various government troops arbitrarily meted out punishment or mercy; conditions were terrible in the whole vast region engulfed in the conflagration... May the Lord save us from another such senseless and ruthless Russian rebellion!

Pugachev fled, pursued by Ivan Ivanovich Mikhelson.[78] Soon afterwards we heard about his complete defeat. Finally Zurin received news of the pretender's capture, and orders not to proceed any farther. The war was over. I could at last return to my parents! I went into raptures at the thought of embracing them and seeing Maria Ivanovna, of whom I had not had any news. I leapt with joy like a child. Zurin laughed and said, shrugging his shoulders, "Mark my word, you'll come to a bad end! You'll marry—and perish for no good reason!"

At the same time, however, a strange emotion poisoned my joy: I could not help feeling disturbed whenever I thought of the villain, bespattered by the blood of so many innocent victims and awaiting execution. "Emelia, Emelia," I said to myself with vexation, "why couldn't you fall on a bayonet or cross the path of a grapeshot! That would have been the best solution." How could I feel otherwise? His image was joined in my mind with a recollection of the mercy he had shown me at one of the most terrible moments of my life and with the memory of my fiancée's deliverance from the hands of the detestable Shvabrin.

Zurin granted me a furlough. In a few days I was to be in the bosom of my family and to see my Maria Ivanovna again... But suddenly an unexpected storm burst on me.

On the appointed day of my departure, at the very moment I was about to leave, Zurin came into my cottage holding a piece of paper in his hand and wearing an extremely serious look. A pang shot through my heart. I felt alarmed, though I did not know why. He sent my orderly out and declared that he had to talk to me about an official matter.

"What is it?" I asked anxiously.

"A slight unpleasantness," he answered, handing me the piece of paper. "Read what I've just received."

I began to read it: it was a secret order to the commanders of all army units to arrest me wherever I might be caught and to convey me immediately under guard to Kazan, to appear before the Secret Commission established to investigate Pugachev's case.

The paper almost fell out of my hands.

"There's nothing I can do," said Zurin. "It's my duty to obey the order. Evidently, rumors about your friendly travels with Pugachev have somehow reached the government. I hope the matter will have no serious consequences and you will be able to justify yourself before the Commission. Don't feel dejected, but rather set out at once."

My conscience was clear, and I did not fear the trial, but the thought that my cherished reunion with my beloved one would have to be postponed by possibly several months appalled me. The wagon was ready. Zurin bade me a friendly farewell. I took my seat in the wagon. Two hussars with their swords drawn sat beside me, and we set out along the main highway.

XIV. The Trial

Speech on earth—
Ocean surf.
A PROVERB [79]

I was sure that the cause of the whole affair was my unauthorized departure from Orenburg. I could easily justify myself, for not only had sorties never been forbidden, they had been fully encouraged. I could be accused of unwise impetuosity but not of disobedience. On the other hand, my friendly relations with Pugachev might have been reported by a number of witnesses and might have seemed, to say the least, highly suspicious. All during the journey I thought about the investigation awaiting me, turned over in my mind the answers I would give, and resolved to tell the plain truth before the tribunal, feeling certain that this was the simplest and at the same time the most reliable way to justify myself.

I arrived in Kazan, laid waste and ravaged by fire. Heaps of charcoal lined the streets instead of houses; blackened walls stuck out here and there, without roofs or windows. Such were the traces Pugachev had left behind! I was brought to the fortress, which had remained intact in the midst of the burned-down city. The hussars delivered me over to the officer of the guard. He sent for a blacksmith. Fetters were put around my ankles and hammered tight. Then I was taken to the prison and left alone in a narrow, dark, kennel-like cell, with bare walls and a tiny window crisscrossed by iron bars.

Such a beginning was not a good omen. But I did not lose either courage or hope. I resorted to the consolation of all those in distress, experiencing for the first time the comfort derived from prayer that pours forth from a pure but lacerated heart. I went to sleep calmly, not worrying about what the future would bring.

The next morning the prison guard woke me with a summons from the Commission. Two soldiers conducted me across the yard to the commandant's house; they stayed in the entrance hall and let me proceed into the inner rooms by myself.

I entered a good-sized chamber. Two men were seated behind a table covered with papers: a general of advanced years, who looked stern and cold, and a young captain of the Guards, aged about twenty-eight, who had a pleasant appearance and smooth, easy manners. Behind a separate desk by the window sat the secretary, with a quill stuck behind his ear, bending over his paper, ready to take down my deposition. The interrogation began. I was asked my name and title. The general inquired if I was the son of Andrei Petrovich Grinev, and when he heard my answer, he sternly rejoined, "A great pity that such an honorable man should have such an unworthy son!"

I calmly replied that whatever the accusations leveled against me were, I hoped to refute them by a sincere recounting of the truth. He did not like my assurance.

"You're a sharp fellow," he said, frowning, "but we've dealt with sharper ones before now."

Then the young man asked me when and under what circumstances I had entered Pugachev's service, and what commissions I had carried out for him.

I answered with indignation that as an officer and a nobleman I could not have entered Pugachev's service and could not have accepted any commissions from him.

"How did it happen, then," rejoined my interrogator, "that this nobleman and officer was spared by the pretender while all his fellow officers were bestially murdered? How did it happen that this same officer and nobleman feasted with the rebels as their friend and accepted presents, such as a fur coat, a horse, and half a ruble, from the chief villain? What gave rise to this strange friendship, and what were its foundations if not treason or at least despicable and inexcusable cowardice?"

I was deeply offended by the words of the officer of the Guards and fervently began my justification. I related how my acquaintance with Pugachev had begun on the steppe during a blizzard, and how he had recognized and spared me after the taking of Fort Belogorsk. I said that I had indeed not scrupled to accept the sheepskin coat and horse from the pretender, but I had defended Fort Belogorsk against him to the last extremity. Finally I made reference to my general, who could testify to my zeal during the calamitous Orenburg siege.

The stern old man picked up an opened letter from the table and read aloud the following:

In answer to Your Excellency's letter of inquiry with regard to Ensign Grinev, according to which he had involved himself in the recent uprising and had entered into such dealings with the villain as constitute a breach of duty and a breaking of his oath of allegiance, I have the honor to report that the above-named Ensign Grinev served in Orenburg from the beginning of October 1773 till February 24 of the current year, on which date he departed from the city, never again reporting for duty under my command. Further, it has been reported by fugitives that he visited Pugachev in the village and rode together with him to Fort Belogorsk, where he had earlier been stationed; as for his conduct, I can...

Here the old man interrupted his reading and said to me grimly, "What can you say in your defense now?"

I was going to continue as I had begun, explaining my relations to Maria Ivanovna just as frankly as I had explained everything else, but suddenly I was overcome by an uncontrollable feeling of disgust. It occurred to me that if I named her, the Commission would summon her to testify: the thought of getting her name entangled with the vile denunciations of scoundrels, and of bringing her here for a confrontation with them, struck me as so horrible that I started to stammer in confusion.

My judges, who it seemed to me had begun listening to my answers with a little more benevolence, grew prejudiced against me once more as they saw my confusion. The officer of the Guards requested that I be confronted with the principal witness who had denounced me. The general ordered "yesterday's scoundrel" brought in. I turned toward the door with great interest, awaiting the appearance of my accuser. In a few minutes there was a clanking of chains, the door opened, and—Shvabrin entered. I was astonished to see how much he had changed. He was terribly thin and pale. His hair, jet-black only a short while before, had turned entirely gray, and his long beard was disheveled. He repeated his accusations in a weak but defiant voice. According to his testimony, I had been sent to Orenburg by Pugachev as a spy; had sallied out daily in order to pass written reports to the rebels about conditions in the city; and in the end had openly gone over to the pretender's side, traveling with him from fort to fort and doing everything in my power to cause harm to my fellow traitors so as to occupy their places and gain more favors from the pretender. I listened to him silently and was satisfied on one score: the vile scoundrel had not pronounced the name of Maria Ivanovna. I do not know whether his vanity forbade any thought of her who had rejected him with contempt or whether he harbored in his heart a spark of the same feeling that made me silent—in any case, the name of the Belogorsk commandant's daughter was not mentioned before the Commission. I grew even more firm in my resolve, and when the judges asked me what I had to say in refutation of Shvabrin's testimony, I replied that I wished to stand by my previous statement and had nothing else to add in self-justification. The general ordered us to be conducted from the room. We went out together. I looked at Shvabrin calmly and did not say a single word to him. He broke into a spiteful grin, lifted his shackles, and hurried past me. I was led back to prison and was not summoned for further interrogation.

I was not a witness to everything that I still have to relate to the reader, but I have heard it told so many times that even the minutest details have been engraved on my memory, as if I myself had been invisibly present at the events.

My parents received Maria Ivanovna with the sincere cordiality characteristic of people in the olden times. They regarded the opportunity to shelter and comfort the poor orphan as God's blessing. They soon grew genuinely fond of her, for it was impossible not to love her once you came to know her. My father no longer regarded my love as mere folly, and my mother could not wait to see her Petrushka married to the captain's charming daughter.

The whole family was thunderstruck by the news of my arrest. Maria Ivanovna had related my strange acquaintance with Pugachev so innocently that it not only did not worry my parents, but even made them laugh heartily. My father was loath to think that I could possibly have been involved in a vile rebellion aimed at overthrowing the monarchy and exterminating the nobility. He closely interrogated Savelich. My attendant did not conceal that his master had visited with Pugachev, and that the villain had indeed shown him favor, but he swore that there had never been even a suspicion of treason. My old ones felt reassured and waited impatiently for more favorable tidings. Maria Ivanovna was extremely worried, but being endowed with modesty and caution to the highest degree, she kept silent.

A few weeks passed... Then, unexpectedly, my father received a letter from Petersburg, from our relation Prince B. The Prince was writing about me. After the usual introductory remarks, he informed my father that the suspicions concerning my participation in the rebels' evil designs had unfortunately proved to be all too well founded, and that I ought to have been subject to exemplary execution; but the Empress, in consideration of the father's services and advanced years, had pardoned the guilty son, exempting him from shameful execution but ordering him exiled to a distant part of Siberia for permanent settlement.

This unexpected blow almost killed my father. He lost his usual firmness of character, and his sorrow (which he would normally have borne in silence) poured forth in bitter lamentations.

"What!" he would repeat, working himself into a rage. "My son was a party to Pugachev's evil designs! Merciful God, what have I lived to see! The Empress is exempting him from execution! Will that make me feel any easier? It's not the execution that's horrible: one of my forefathers lost his head on the block defending his sacred convictions; and my father suffered along with Volynskii and Khrushchev.[80] But that a nobleman should break his oath and ally himself with brigands, murderers, and runaway serfs!... It's a shame and disgrace to our family!"

Alarmed by his despair, my dear mother did not dare weep in his presence and tried to console him by talking about the unreliability of rumors and the fickleness of the world's opinions. But my father was inconsolable.

The person who suffered most, however, was Maria Ivanovna. Convinced that I could have vindicated myself if I had wanted to, she guessed the truth and blamed herself for my misfortune. She concealed her tears and torments from everybody, but incessantly brooded over what means she could employ to rescue me.

One evening my father sat on the sofa leafing through the pages of the *Court Calendar*. His thoughts, however, were far away, and the reading did not produce the usual effect on him. From time to time he would whistle an old military march. My mother was knitting a woolen jersey in silence, occasionally dropping a tear on her work. Suddenly Maria Ivanovna, who was also sitting over her work, declared that her affairs required her to travel to Petersburg, and asked if they could provide her with the means to undertake the journey. It saddened my mother very much.

"Why do you need to go to Petersburg?" she asked. "Do you too want to forsake us?"

Maria Ivanovna answered that her whole future depended on this trip, and that she was going to seek protection and help from the powers that be, as the daughter of a man who had suffered for his faithful service.

My father lowered his head: every word that reminded him of his son's presumed crime pained him and sounded like a bitter reproach to him.

"Go, my dear, go," he said with a sigh. "We wouldn't want to stand in the way of your happiness. God grant you a good man, not a publicly dishonored traitor, for a husband."

He rose and went out of the room.

Left alone with my mother, Maria Ivanovna explained something of her plans to her. Mother embraced her with tears in her eyes and prayed to God for the success of her undertaking. They equipped Maria Ivanovna for the journey, and in a few days she set out, accompanied by her faithful Palashka and by the equally faithful Savelich, who, separated from me by force, was comforted by the thought that he was at least serving my betrothed.

Maria Ivanovna arrived safely in Sofia,[81] and hearing at the post station that the Court currently resided at Tsarskoe Selo, she stopped there. They let her have a corner of a room behind a partition. The stationmaster's wife immediately entered into a conversation with her, informing her that she was a niece of the Court stoker, and initiating her into all the mysteries of Court life. She told her what time the Empress usually woke up, drank her coffee, and went out walking; which dignitaries were currently surrounding her; what she had graciously said over the table the day before; and whom she had received in the evening—to put it briefly, Anna Vlasevna's conversation was worth several pages of historical memoirs and, if preserved, would have been a precious gift to posterity. Maria Ivanovna listened to her attentively. They walked out into the park. Anna Vlasevna related the history of every avenue and every little bridge. Having walked to their hearts' content, they returned to the post station highly satisfied with each other.

The next morning Maria Ivanovna woke early, got dressed, and stole out into the park. It was a beautiful morning; the rays of the sun fell on the tops of the lime trees, whose leaves had already turned yellow under autumn's fresh breath. The wide pond glittered motionless. The swans, just awakened, majestically swam out from behind the bushes that overhung the banks. Maria Ivanovna walked by the lovely field where a monument commemorating Count Petr Aleksandrovich Rumiantsev's recent victories had just been erected.[82] Suddenly a little white dog of English breed ran barking toward her.

Frightened, Maria Ivanovna stopped. At the same moment she heard a pleasant feminine voice say, "Don't be afraid; she won't bite you."

Maria Ivanovna caught sight of a lady seated on a bench opposite the monument. She sat down on the other end of the bench. The lady looked at her intently, and on her part Maria Ivanovna, casting a few oblique glances at her, also managed to size up the lady from head to foot. She wore a white morning dress, a nightcap, and a padded sleeveless jacket. She seemed to be about forty. Her round, rosy cheeks expressed dignity and calm; and her blue eyes, together with the shadow of a smile playing on her lips, were inexpressibly charming. The lady was the first to break the silence.

"You do not live around here, I take it," she said.

"No, ma'am: I arrived from the country only yesterday."

"Did you come with your parents?"

"No, ma'am, I came by myself."

"By yourself! But you're so young!"

"I have neither father nor mother."

"You must have come on some business, of course?"

"Yes, ma'am. I have come to present a petition to the Empress."

"As an orphan, you're probably complaining against injustice and maltreatment?"

"No, ma'am. I have come to ask for mercy, not for justice."

"Allow me to ask, who are you?"

"I am the daughter of Captain Mironov."

"Captain Mironov! The same who was commandant of one of the forts in the Orenburg region?"

"Yes, ma'am."

The lady appeared to be moved.

"Forgive me," she said in an even kinder voice, "if I'm meddling in your affairs, but I'm frequently at Court: do tell me what it is you're petitioning for, and perhaps I'll be able to help."

Maria Ivanovna rose to her feet and thanked her respectfully. She was instinctively drawn to this unknown lady, whose every gesture inspired confidence. Maria Ivanovna drew from her pocket a folded piece of paper and handed it to her unknown benefactress, who proceeded to read it to herself.

As she started reading, she had an attentive and benevolent air, but suddenly her countenance changed, and Maria Ivanovna, who had been following all her movements with her eyes, was alarmed to see a stern expression come over her features, which had been so pleasant and serene only a moment before.

"So you're asking mercy for Grinev?" she asked coldly. "The Empress cannot pardon him. He went over to the pretender, not out of ignorance or gullibility, but as an immoral and ill-meaning scoundrel."

"Oh, that's not true!" cried Maria Ivanovna.

"What do you mean not true?" rejoined the lady, coloring.

"It isn't true, God is my witness, it isn't! I know all about it, I'll relate it all to you. Only for my sake did he expose himself to the misfortunes that befell him. And if he didn't vindicate himself before the court, it was only because he didn't want to involve me."

She then ardently related everything that is already known to the reader.

The lady listened to her with attention. Then she asked, "Where are you staying?" When she heard that Maria had put up at Anna Vlasevna's, she added with a smile, "Oh, yes, I know her. Good-bye, and don't tell anyone about our meeting. I hope you won't have to wait long before you receive an answer to your letter."

With these words, she rose and proceeded on through an arbor, while Maria Ivanovna, filled with joyous hope, returned to Anna Vlasevna's.

Her hostess scolded her for taking an early morning walk in this fall season, claiming that it was bad for a young girl's health. She brought in the samovar and was about to embark, over a cup of tea, on her interminable stories about the Court when a carriage from the palace drove up to the porch, and the Empress's chamberlain came in to announce that Her Majesty graciously summoned to her presence the maiden Mironova.

Anna Vlasevna was astonished and fell into a flutter.

"Bless me!" she cried. "Her Majesty is summoning you to Court! How did she learn about you? And how can you, my dear child, present yourself before her? I'll warrant you don't even know how to carry yourself at Court... Hadn't I better accompany you? I could at least give you a few hints. And how can you go in your traveling robe? Hadn't we better send to the midwife for her yellow dress that's got a hoop skirt?"

The chamberlain declared that it was the Empress's wish that Maria Ivanovna come by herself and in whatever she happened to be wearing. There was no helping it: Maria Ivanovna got into the carriage and set out for the palace, accompanied by Anna Vlasevna's advice and blessings.

Maria Ivanovna had a presentiment that our fate was about to be decided: her heart throbbed violently and irregularly. In a few minutes the carriage stopped in front of the palace. Maria Ivanovna mounted the stairs with trepidation. The doors opened wide before her. She passed through a long row of magnificent rooms with no one present; the chamberlain showed her the way. At length, when they came to a closed door, he said he would announce her and left her alone.

The thought of finding herself face to face with the Empress frightened her so much that she could hardly stand on her feet. After a moment the door opened, and she was admitted into the Empress's boudoir.

The Empress was busy with her toilette. She was surrounded by several courtiers, who respectfully made way for Maria Ivanovna. The Empress turned toward her kindly, and Maria Ivanovna recognized the lady to whom she had so candidly told her story only a little while before. The Empress bade her come closer and said with a smile:

"I am glad I have been able to keep my word and grant your request. The matter has been seen to. I have become convinced of the innocence of your fiancé. Here is a letter; I would be grateful if you would personally deliver it to your future father-in-law."

Maria Ivanovna took the letter with a trembling hand, burst into tears, and fell at the Empress's feet. The latter lifted her up and kissed her. She entered into a conversation with her.

"I know you are not rich," she said, "but you should not worry about the future, for I feel indebted to the daughter of Captain Mironov. I will undertake to see to your welfare."

Having showered her affections on the poor orphan, the Empress let her go. Maria Ivanovna left in the same palace carriage she came in. Anna Vlasevna, who had been waiting for her return with impatience, smothered her with questions but received only halfhearted answers. She was dissatisfied with the young woman's inability to recollect details, but she attributed it to her provincial shyness and generously forgave her. Maria Ivanovna set out to return to the country the same day, without as much as taking one curious look at Petersburg...

With this the memoirs of Petr Andreevich Grinev come to an end. Family tradition has it that he was released from confinement at the end of 1774 by highest order; and that he was present at the execution of Pugachev, who recognized him in the crowd and acknowledged him with a nod of his head, which in another minute was displayed to the people lifeless and bloodied. Soon afterwards Petr Andreevich married Maria Ivanovna. Their progeny thrives to this day in Simbirsk Guberniia. Thirty versts from X. there is a village that now belongs to ten proprietors.[83] In one wing of the mansion a letter from Catherine II, written in her own hand, is displayed, framed and glazed.

Addressed to Petr Andreevich's father, it vindicates his son and praises the heart and mind of Captain Mironov's daughter. Petr Andreevich Grinev's manuscript was given to me by one of his grandsons, who had heard that I was engaged in a historical study of the times described by his grandfather. I have decided, with the permission of his descendants, to issue Grinev's manuscript as a separate publication, choosing an appropriate epigraph for each chapter and taking the liberty of changing some of the proper names.[84]

October 19, 1836   The Publisher

PART TWO

A History of Pugachev

A History of Pugachev
(1833–34)[1]

Preface

This incomplete piece of historical research was to form part of a larger project, which I have since abandoned.[2] Here I have brought together everything about Pugachev that the government has made public and everything that I have found trustworthy in the foreign authors treating him.[3] I have also had an opportunity to make use of some manuscripts, oral traditions, and accounts of eyewitnesses still alive.[4]

The legal case against Pugachev, still sealed as of this writing, used to be kept at the State Archives in St. Petersburg, among other important documents that were at one time secret government papers but have subsequently become source materials for the historian. On ascending the throne, His Imperial Majesty issued a decree to have these documents put in order. Out came all these treasures from the cellars, where they had been inundated several times and nearly destroyed.

The future historian who has permission to unseal Pugachev's case will easily be able to correct and augment my work—which is of necessity imperfect but at least conscientious.[5] A page of history on which the names of Catherine, Rumiantsev, two Panins, Suvorov, Bibikov, Mikhelson, Voltaire, and Derzhavin occur must not be lost for posterity.[6]

November 2, 1833
The Village of Boldino

A. Pushkin

To render a proper account of all the designs and adventures of this impostor would, it seems, be almost impossible not only for a historian of average abilities but even for the most excellent one, because all of this impostor's undertakings depended, not on rational considerations or military precepts, but on daring, happenstance, and luck. For this reason (I think) Pugachev himself not only would be unable to recount all the details of these undertakings, but would not even be aware of a considerable portion of them, since they were initiated, not just by him directly, but by many of his unbridled daredevil accomplices in several locations at once.

ARCHIMANDRITE PLATON LIUBARSKII[7]

Chapter One

The origin of the Iaik Cossacks.—A poetic legend.—The Tsar's charter.—Piracy on the Caspian Sea.—Stenka Razin.—Nechai and Shamai.—Peter the Great's intentions.—Internal disturbances.—The flight of a nomadic people.—The Iaik Cossacks' riot.—Their suppression.

The Iaik River, renamed Ural by Catherine II's decree, issues from the mountains that have given it its present name. It flows southward along the mountain range to the point where Orenburg was at one time to be founded and where Fort Orsk is now located. Here it turns to the west, dissecting the rocky mountain ridge, and follows a course of more than 2,500 versts to the Caspian Sea. It irrigates part of Bashkiriia; it serves as the southeastern boundary of almost all of Orenburg Guberniia; the trans-Volga steppes stretch up to its right bank; and from the left bank extends the gloomy wilderness where the primitive tribes known to us as the Kirgiz Kaisaks lead their nomadic existence.[8] Its current is swift; its murky waters abound in fish of all kinds; its banks are mostly clayey or sandy and treeless, in places expanding into water meadows suitable for cattle-raising. Near its delta it is overgrown with tall reeds—a hiding place for boars and tigers.

The Don Cossacks, who had been crossing the Khvalinsk [Caspian] Sea, appeared on the banks of this river in the fifteenth century. They spent the winters on its banks, at that time still wooded and safe due to the river's remoteness. They set sail for the sea in the spring, plundered until late fall, and returned to the Iaik with the onset of winter. Moving farther and farther upstream from one place to the next, they at last chose for permanent settlement Kolovratnoe Point, sixty versts from today's Uralsk.

Some Tatar families, split off from the nomad camps of the Golden Horde and seeking free pastures on the banks of the same Iaik, roamed the new settlers' neighborhood. At first the two tribes were at enmity, but with the passage of time they entered into friendly dealings: the Cossacks began to take wives from the Tatar camps. According to a poetic legend, the Cossacks, passionately attached to their unmarried life, resolved among themselves that each time they embarked on a new campaign they would kill all the newborn infants and abandon their wives. One of their atamans, by the name of Gugnia, was the first to take pity on his young wife and break this cruel resolution; the rest of the Cossacks, following his example, submitted to the yoke of family life. To this day the people living on the banks of the Ural, by now civilized and hospitable, drink to the health of Grandmother Gugnikha at their feasts.

Living by plunder and surrounded by hostile tribes, the Cossacks felt the need for a powerful protector, and during the reign of Mikhail Fedorovich they sent an envoy to Moscow with the request that the Sovereign take them under his mighty patronage.[9] Settling the Cossacks on the unclaimed lands along the Iaik was probably regarded as a gain of obvious significance. The Tsar received his new subjects kindly and presented them with a charter for the Iaik River, granting it to them from its upper reaches to its delta, and permitting them to *bring any free people there for settlement.*

Their number grew rapidly. They continued crossing the Caspian Sea, joining up with the Don Cossacks to raid Persian merchant ships and plunder seaside settlements. The Shah complained to the Tsar. Admonitions were sent from Moscow to both the Don and the Iaik.

The Cossacks sailed up the Volga to Nizhnii Novgorod in boats still loaded with loot; whence they proceeded to Moscow and presented themselves at Court, pleading guilty and each carrying an ax with an executioner's block. They were sent to Poland and to Riga in order to earn pardon for their misdeeds. Some Streltsy, who were later to merge into one tribe with the Cossacks, were dispatched to the Iaik region.[10]

Stenka Razin visited the settlements along the Iaik. According to the testimony of chronicles, the Cossacks received him as an enemy.[11] Their town was taken by this daring mutineer, and the Streltsy stationed there were either slain or drowned.

According to tradition, confirmed by a Tatar chronicler, the campaigns of two Iaik atamans, Nechai and Shamai, took place in this same period. The first, having collected a band of volunteers, went to Khiva in the hope of rich loot. Luck was on his side. After a difficult passage, the Cossacks reached Khiva. The Khan with his army was away at war just then. Nechai occupied the city, meeting no resistance; but he gave himself over to the good life and set out for the return march too late. Loaded down with loot, the Cossacks were overtaken by the Khan who had come home; they were defeated and annihilated on the bank of the Syr Daria. No more than three returned to the Iaik with the news that the brave Nechai had perished. A few years later another ataman, named Shamai, set out in the tracks of the first. But he was taken captive by the K⁻ᵐyks of the steppe. Meanwhile, his Cossacks proceeded farther, lost their way, and never reached Khiva, arriving instead at the Aral Sea, on whose shore they were forced to spend the winter. Hunger overtook them. The luckless adventurers killed and ate one another. The majority perished. The survivors at last sent a message to the Khan of Khiva, asking him to receive them and save them from starvation. The Khiva Tatars came out for them, captured them all, and took them back to their city as slaves. There they all vanished. As for Shamai, the Kalmyks brought him back to the Iaik Host a few years later, evidently to be ransomed. After this, the Cossacks lost their taste for far-flung campaigns. They gradually grew accustomed to civilized family life.

The Iaik Cossacks obediently bore offices according to the hierarchy of ranks issued by Moscow, but at home they preserved their original mode of government. A perfect equality of rights; atamans and elders, elected by the community as temporary executors of communal resolutions; circles, or meetings, at which each Cossack had a free voice and where all public issues were decided by majority vote; no written resolutions; *into a sack and into the water* for treason, cowardice, murder, and theft—these were the main features of their polity. To the simple, crude laws brought along from the Don the Iaik Cossacks added others of local importance, relating to fishing, which was the main source of their revenue, and to the right of hiring the necessary number of Cossacks for service—extremely complex laws, defined with the greatest attention to detail.

Peter the Great introduced the first measures aimed at incorporating the Iaik Cossacks into the general system of state government. In 1720 the Iaik Host was put under the authority of the War College. The Cossacks rioted and burned their town with the intention of fleeing into the Kirgiz steppes, but were cruelly brought to heel by Colonel Zakharov. A census was taken, services were defined, and wages were set. The Sovereign appointed the ataman of the Host himself.

Under the reigns of Anna Ivanovna and Elisaveta Petrovna, the government intended to complete the actions initiated by Peter. This was facilitated by the discord that had arisen between the Host's ataman Merkurev and its elder Loginov, dividing the Cossacks into two factions: the ataman's on the one hand and Loginov's, or the people's, on the other. In 1740 it was decided that the Iaik Cossacks' polity should be reorganized, and Nepliuev, the governor of Orenburg at the time, submitted a project for new laws to the War College. For the most part, however, the plans and directives were not carried out until the accession to the throne of the Empress Catherine II.

As early as 1762 the Iaik Cossacks of the Loginov faction began complaining about the oppressive measures taken by the chancery officials whom the government had imposed on the Host: they complained about the withholding of allotted wages, about arbitrary taxes, and about infringements of ancient fishing rights and customs. The civil servants sent to investigate their complaints were either unable or unwilling to placate them. The Cossacks rioted several times, so much so that Major Generals Potapov and Cherepov (the first in 1766, the second in 1767) were obliged to resort to the force of arms and to the horror of executions. An investigating commission was set up in the Cossacks' town, Iaitskii Gorodok. Among its members were Major Generals Potapov, Cherepov, Brümfeld, and Davydov, and Captain of the Guards Chebyshev. The Host's ataman, Andrei Borodin, was dismissed; Petr Tambovtsev was elected in his place; and the chancery officials were enjoined to pay, over and above the sums withheld, a considerable fine to the Host. The officials, however, managed to evade obeying this injunction. The Cossacks did not lose heart: they attempted to bring their legitimate complaints to the attention of the Empress herself. But the men they sent on this secret mission were arrested in Petersburg on the orders of Count Chernyshev, president of the War College; they were put in fetters and punished as mutineers. In the meanwhile an order was issued to detail several hundred Cossacks for service in Kizliar. The local authorities used this opportunity to take new oppressive measures against the people in revenge for its resistance. It became known that the government intended to press the Cossacks into cavalry squadrons, and that orders had already been given to have their beards shaved. The sending of Major General Traubenberg to Iaitskii Gorodok for this purpose aroused general indignation. The Cossacks were in a state of turmoil. At last, in 1771, mutiny burst out with full force.

What had set it off was another event of equal importance. Peaceful Kalmyks, who had come from the borders of China at the beginning of the eighteenth century to live under the white Tsar's suzerainty, were roaming about in the immense steppes of Astrakhan and Saratov, in the region between the Volga and the Iaik. Ever since their arrival they had served Russia faithfully, guarding her southern borders. Russian police officials, taking advantage of their simplicity and remoteness from the central institutions of government, began to oppress them. The complaints of these peaceable and well-meaning people did not reach the higher administration. At last, having lost their patience, they decided to leave Russia and to enter into secret negotiations with the Chinese government. It was easy for them to move right up to the bank of the Iaik without arousing suspicions. Then, suddenly, all 30,000 of them forded the river and set out across the Kirgiz steppes toward the boundaries of their former homeland. The government took hasty measures to stop the unexpected flight. The Iaik Host was ordered to pursue the fugitives, but the Cossacks (with very few exceptions) failed to obey, and openly refused to perform any service.

The local authorities resorted to the strictest measures in an attempt to end the mutiny, but by now no punishment could subdue the embittered Cossacks. On January 13, 1771, they gathered in the town square, took the icons from the church, and went, under the leadership of the Cossack Kirpichnikov, to the house of Captain of the Guards Durnovo, who was in Iaitskii Gorodok at the time, involved in the business of the investigating commission. They demanded the dismissal of the chancery officials and the payment of withheld wages. Major General Traubenberg confronted them with troops and cannon, and ordered them to disperse, but neither his commands nor the admonitions of the ataman had any effect. Traubenberg gave orders to open fire; the Cossacks rushed the cannon. A battle ensued; the mutineers gained the upper hand. Traubenberg tried to flee but was killed at the gate of his house; Durnovo was covered with wounds, Tambovtsev hanged, the chancery officials put under arrest, and new officials appointed in their place.

The mutineers triumphed. They sent elected representatives to Petersburg, delegated to explain and justify the bloody incident. In the meanwhile Major General Freymann had been dispatched from Moscow with a company of grenadiers and artillery to subdue them. Freymann arrived in Orenburg in the spring, waited there until the rivers subsided, and then, taking two light field detachments and a few Cossacks with him, went on to Iaitskii Gorodok.[12] The mutineers, numbering 3,000, came out to face him: the two sides met at a point 70 versts from the town. Hot battles took place on June 3 and June 4. Freymann cleared his path with grapeshot. The mutineers galloped home to gather up their wives and children, and they started crossing the Chagan River with the intention of escaping to the Caspian Sea. Freymann, who entered the town right on their heels, managed to hold the populace back by threats and remonstrances. Those who had already left were pursued and captured almost to a man. An investigating commission was set up in Orenburg under the chairmanship of Colonel Neronov. A good many of the mutineers were brought there. Since the prisons were overflowing, some were kept in stalls at the market hall and barter court. The earlier Cossack polity was liquidated. Leadership was put in the hands of the commandant of Iaitsk, Lieutenant Colonel Simonov. The Host elder Martemian Borodin and the other (civil) elder, Mostovshchikov, were commanded to assist at his chancery. The ringleaders of the riot were whipped; about 140 people were exiled to Siberia; others were conscripted (*N.B.* all of them deserted); the rest were pardoned and administered a second oath of allegiance. Outwardly, these strict and necessary measures restored order, but the peace was uncertain. "Just watch out," the pardoned mutineers kept saying, "we shall yet lay our hands on Moscow." The Cossacks were still divided into two factions: the acquiescent and the dissident (or, as the War College aptly translated these terms, the obedient and the disobedient). Secret conferences took place at taverns and remote hamlets across the steppe. Everything portended a new mutiny. Only a leader was missing. A leader was soon found.

Chapter Two

Pugachev's arrival on the scene.—His escape from Kazan.—Kozhevnikov's testimony.—The Pretender's first successful steps.—The Ilek Cossacks' treason.—The taking of Fort Rassypnaia.—Nurali-Khan.—Measures taken by Reinsdorp.—The taking of Nizhne-Ozernaia.—The taking of Fort Tatishchev.—The council in Orenburg.—The taking of Chernorechenskaia.—Pugachev in Sakmara.

In this time of trouble an unknown vagrant drifted about among the Cossack homesteads, taking jobs now with this, now with that master, and dabbling in all manner of handicrafts. Having witnessed the suppression of the mutiny and the chastisement of its ringleaders, he went to a schismatic community on the Irgiz for a while. This community sent him at the end of 1772 to buy a supply of fish in Iaitskii Gorodok, where he stayed at the house of the Cossack Denis Pianov. He was noted for the boldness of his statements—for heaping abuse on the authorities and inciting the Cossacks to flee to the lands of the Turkish Sultan. He claimed that the Don Cossacks would not take long in following them, that at the border he had 20,000 rubles in cash and 70,000 rubles' worth of goods waiting for him, and that some pasha or other was to supply the Cossacks with 5,000,000 after their arrival, until which time he had promised to pay each of them a monthly wage of 12 rubles. Further, the vagrant claimed that two regiments had set out from Moscow against the Iaik Cossacks, and that a riot around Christmas or Epiphany was inevitable. Some of the "obedient" Cossacks wanted to take him prisoner and hand him over as a

Map 1. Area of the first two phases of the Pugachev Rebellion

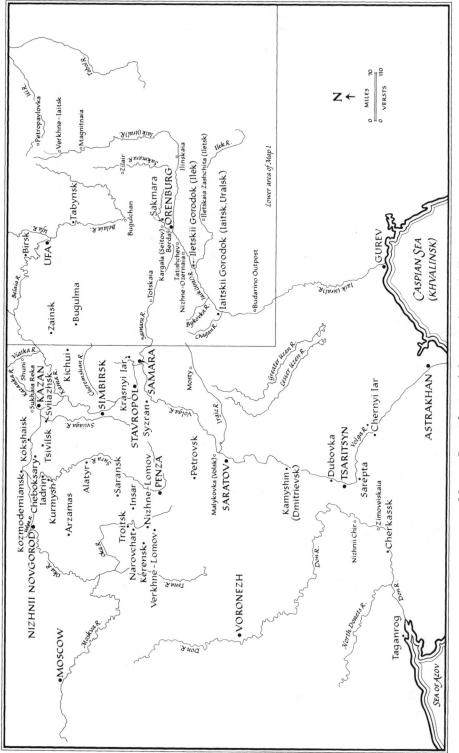

Map 2. General area of the Pugachev Rebellion

rabble-rouser to the commandant's chancery, but he vanished, along with Denis Pianov, and was caught only later in the village of Malykovka (today's Volsk), where a peasant, with whom he had traveled the same road, pointed him out. This vagrant was Emelian Pugachev, a Don Cossack and schismatic who had come from Poland with false documents intending to settle among the schismatics living on the Irgiz River.[13] Taken into custody, he was conveyed first to Simbirsk and then to Kazan; and since everything concerning the affairs of the Iaik Host could be important under those circumstances, the governor of Orenburg deemed it necessary to send a report about his arrest, dated January 18, 1773, to the State War College.

Mutineers from the Iaik region were no rarity in those days, and therefore the Kazan authorities paid no particular attention to the offender sent to them. Pugachev was not confined with any greater strictness than the other prisoners. In the meanwhile his followers were not asleep. One day, escorted by two soldiers of the garrison, he walked about town collecting alms. At the corner of Zamochnaia Reshetka (as one of the main streets of Kazan was called) stood a troika, ready to take off. Pugachev stepped up to it and, suddenly pushing one of his escorts aside, got into the wagon aided by the other, who went galloping out of town with him. This happened on June 19, 1773. Petersburg's sanction of Pugachev's sentence—flogging and exile to Pelym for penal servitude—was received in Kazan three days later.

Pugachev turned up on the farmlands of a retired Cossack, Danila Sheludiakov, for whom he had previously worked as a farmhand. On these farms the conspirators gathered to confer.

At first the possibility of fleeing to Turkey—an idea long entertained by all discontented Cossacks—was discussed. Under the reign of Anna Ivanovna, as is well known, Ignatii Nekrasov [Nekrasa] put that idea into practice, carrying off a large number of Don Cossacks. Their descendants are still living in territories under Turkish rule, preserving in an alien country the faith, language, and customs of their former homeland. In the last Turkish war they fought against us desperately. Some of them came to the Emperor Nicholas after he had crossed the Danube in a Zaporozhe boat: like the remaining members of the Sech, they pleaded guilty in the name of their fathers and returned under the sovereignty of their legitimate monarch.[14]

But the Iaik conspirators were too strongly attached to their bountiful native riverbanks. Instead of fleeing, they decided to riot again. Imposture, they thought, would be a reliable motive force. All it required was a bold and resolute vagabond not yet known to the people. Their choice fell on Pugachev. It did not take long to persuade him. They immediately started recruiting followers.

The War College circulated information about the escape of the Cossack convict in all the locations where it was thought he might be hiding. Lieutenant Colonel Simonov soon learned that the fugitive had been seen on farms around Iaitskii Gorodok. Detachments were sent to capture Pugachev, but they had no success. Pugachev and his chief associates eluded their pursuers by moving from one place to another, all the while augmenting their band. In the meantime strange rumors were spreading... Many Cossacks were put under arrest. Mikhailo Kozhevnikov was captured and brought to the commandant's chancery, where the following important testimony was extracted from him by torture:

At the beginning of September he was on his farm when Ivan Zarubin came to him and told him confidentially that a highborn person was staying in their region. He asked Kozhevnikov to shelter this person on his farm. Kozhevnikov agreed. Zarubin left and returned that night just before dawn with Timofei Miasnikov and a stranger, all three on horseback. The stranger was of medium height, broad-shouldered, and lean. He had a black beard just beginning to turn gray. He wore a camel's hair coat and a blue Kalmyk hat, and was armed with a rifle. Zarubin and Miasnikov left for the town in order *to notify the people,* while the stranger, remaining at Kozhevnikov's, informed him that he was the Emperor Peter III, that the rumors about his death had been false, and that in fact, with the help of the officer guarding him, he had escaped to Kiev, where he hid for about a year. Then, he continued, he spent some time in Tsaregrad [Constantinople] and served in the Russian army, under an assumed identity, during the last Turkish war; from there he went to the Don region, and was later captured in Tsaritsyn, but his faithful Cossacks soon liberated him. He had spent the last year on the Irgiz and in Iaitskii Gorodok, where he was arrested and subsequently taken to Kazan; once again, he was set free by his guard, bribed with 700 rubles by an unknown merchant. After his escape, he headed for Iaitskii Gorodok, but, having heard from a woman that passports were being very strictly demanded and scrutinized, he turned back and took the highway toward Syzran. He drifted about on this highway until at last Zarubin and Miasnikov met up with him at the Talovin tavern and brought him to Kozhevnikov. Having told his absurd story, the pretender began laying out his plans. In order to circumvent the garrison's resistance and to avoid *unnecessary bloodshed,* he would not reveal his identity until after the Cossack Host had left for *the trip* (the fall fishing expedition). He would appear among the Cossacks during the expedition, have the ataman tied up, head straight for Iaitskii Gorodok, occupy it, and post guards on each highway, so that the news about him would not spread prematurely. Failing to accomplish this, he intended *to fall on Russia,* win over to his side all her inhabitants, appoint new judges everywhere (for, as he said, he had observed much injustice perpetrated by those presently in office), and place the Grand Duke on the throne.[15] "*As for myself,*" he said, "*I no longer wish to reign."* Pugachev spent three days at Kozhevnikov's farm, after which Zarubin and Miasnikov came to take him to Usikhina Rossash, where he was planning to hide until the time of the expedition. Kozhevnikov, Konovalov, and Kochurov accompanied him.

The arrest of Kozhevnikov and of the Cossacks who were implicated by his testimony hastened the unfolding of events. On September 18 Pugachev made his way from the Budarino outpost to the vicinity of Iaitskii Gorodok with a mob numbering 300; he stopped at a distance of three versts from the town, beyond the Chagan River.

The town was thrown into confusion. Inhabitants, only recently pacified, began crossing over to the side of the new rebels. Simonov sent a force of 500 Cossacks, reinforced by infantry and two pieces of artillery and under the command of Major Naumov, to confront Pugachev. Two hundred of the Cossacks, with Captain Krylov in charge, were sent forward as a vanguard. They were met by a Cossack holding a seditious manifesto from the pretender above his head. Krylov's Cossacks demanded that the manifesto be read aloud to them. Krylov refused. A mutiny followed, with half of the detachment deserting to the pretender's side and dragging along 50 loyal Cossacks by the bridles of their horses. Seeing this treason among his troops, Naumov returned to the town. The Cossacks spirited away by force were led before Pugachev, who ordered 11 of them hanged. These first victims of Pugachev's were Lieutenants Vitoshnov, Chertorogov, Rainev, and Konovalov, Sublieutenants Ruzhenikov, Tolstov, Podiachev, and Kolpakov, and Privates Sidorovkin, Larzianev, and Chukalin.

The next day Pugachev approached the town, but when he saw troops coming out to meet him, he began retreating, scattering his band across the steppe. Simonov did not pursue him because he did not want to detach any Cossacks, fearing their betrayal, and he did not dare move the infantry to any distance from the town, whose inhabitants were on the verge of revolt. He sent a report about all of this to the governor of Orenburg, Lieutenant General Reinsdorp, asking him for a troop of light cavalry that could pursue Pugachev. But direct communication to Orenburg was already severed, and Simonov's report did not reach the governor for a whole week.

With his band multiplied by new rebels, Pugachev headed straight for Iletskii Gorodok, sending its commandant, Ataman Portnov, an order to meet him outside the fort and join him. He promised the Cossacks to vouchsafe the cross and the beard (all the Ilek Cossacks, like their Iaik brethren, were Old Believers),[16] and to grant them their rivers, meadows, wages and provisions, lead and gunpowder, and freedom in perpetuity. In case of disobedience he threatened revenge. Faithful to his duty, the ataman tried to resist, but the Cossacks tied him up and received Pugachev with ringing bells and bread and salt. Pugachev hanged the ataman, celebrated his victory for three days, and then, taking all the Ilek Cossacks and the garrison cannon with him, he marched toward Fort Rassypnaia.

The forts erected in that region were no more than villages enclosed by wattle or wooden fences. The handful of aging soldiers and local Cossacks stationed in these forts under the protection of two or three cannon were safe enough from the arrows and lances of the nomadic tribes that roamed the steppes of Orenburg Guberniia and its environs. On September 24 Pugachev besieged Rassypnaia. The Cossacks deserted here, too. The fort was taken. The commandant, Major Velovskii, a few officers, and a priest were hanged; and the garrison platoon and 150 or so Cossacks were enlisted into the insurgents' ranks.

The rumor about the pretender spread quickly. While still at the Budarino outpost, Pugachev had written to the Kirgiz Kaisak Khan, signing himself Emperor Peter III and demanding the Khan's son as a hostage along with an auxiliary corps of 100 men. Nurali Khan went to Iaitskii Gorodok under the pretext of negotiations with the authorities, offering them his services. They thanked him and answered that they hoped they could cope with the rebels without his help. The Khan sent the governor of Orenburg a copy of the pretender's manifesto in Mongolian, containing the first announcement of his arrival in the region. "We people who live on the steppes," Nurali wrote to the governor, "do not know who this person is, riding about the riverbanks: is he an impostor or the real Sovereign? The scout we had sent out came back declaring he had learned nothing except that the man had a light brown beard." Using this opportunity, the Khan demanded that the governor return the hostages he was holding, the cattle that had been driven off the Kirgiz lands, and the slaves who had run away from the Horde. Reinsdorp hastened to reply that the death of the Emperor Peter III was common knowledge throughout the world, that he, Reinsdorp, had himself seen the Sovereign in his coffin and kissed his dead hand. He admonished the Khan to hand the pretender over to the government if he should happen to flee to the Kirgiz steppes; the Empress would not forget such a service, Reinsdorp asserted. The Khan's requests were complied with. In the meanwhile Nurali entered into friendly negotiations with the pretender, though he ceaselessly assured Reinsdorp of his loyalty to the Empress; and the Kirgiz were getting ready to attack.

Right after the communication from the Khan reached Orenburg, the report from the commandant of Iaitsk, sent via Samara, was received. Soon Velovskii's report about the taking of Iletskii Gorodok arrived, too. Reinsdorp hastened to take measures aimed at eradicating the rising evil. He directed Brigadier Baron von Bülow to set out from Orenburg with 400 troops, both infantry and cavalry, and six fieldpieces, and to head for Iaitskii Gorodok, gathering into his troops more people from outposts and forts on the way. The commander of the Verkhne-Ozernaia district, Brigadier Baron Korf, was ordered to come to Orenburg as fast as possible, and Lieutenant Colonel Simonov was to send Major Naumov with a field detachment and Cossacks to join Bülow. The chancery at Stavropol was instructed to supply Simonov with 500 armed Kalmyks.[17] The Bashkirs and Tatars living in the vicinity were to assemble a corps of 1,000 men with the greatest possible speed and to link up with Naumov. Not one of these orders was carried out. Bülow took charge of Fort Tatishchev and was about to move on to Nizhne-Ozernaia, but on hearing some cannonade at night while he was still 15 versts away from his destination, he became frightened and retreated. Reinsdorp ordered him a second time to hasten to defeat the rebels, but Bülow paid no attention and stayed on at Tatishchev. Korf tried to evade action under various pretexts. Instead of 500, fewer than 300 armed Kalmyks were assembled, and even those ran off along the way.The Bashkirs and Tatars paid no heed to the instructions. Major Naumov and the Host elder, Borodin, left Iaitskii Gorodok and trailed Pugachev at a distance; they arrived in Orenburg from the steppe side on October 3, bringing tidings of nothing but the pretender's triumphs.

From Rassypnaia Pugachev proceeded to Nizhne-Ozernaia. On the way there, he crossed paths with Captain Surin, who had been sent to Velovskii's aid by the commander of Nizhne-Ozernaia, Major Kharlov. Pugachev hanged him, and his platoon joined the rebels. Having learned of Pugachev's approach, Kharlov sent his young wife, the daughter of Elagin, commander of Tatishchev, to her father, while he himself made preparations for the defense of his fort. His Cossacks deserted to Pugachev's side. Kharlov was left with a handful of soldiers of advanced age. On the eve of September 26 he hit on the idea of raising his soldiers' morale by firing his two cannon—occasioning the cannonade that scared Bülow and made him retreat. By the morning Pugachev had arrived at the fort. He rode at the head of his troops.

"Take care, Your Majesty," an old Cossack said to him, "lest they kill you with a cannon shot."

376 A HISTORY OF PUGACHEV

"Old age must have gone to your head," answered the pretender; "cannon are not forged to kill Tsars."

Kharlov ran from one soldier to another, commanding them to fire. Nobody obeyed. He grabbed the fuse, fired one cannon, and dashed to the other one. At that moment the rebels occupied the fort, threw themselves on its single defender, and covered him with wounds. Half dead, he thought of ransoming himself, and led his attackers to his cottage, where his possessions were hidden. In the meanwhile the gallows were already being put up outside the fort; Pugachev sat in front of them, receiving oaths of allegiance from the fort's inhabitants and garrison. Kharlov, bedazed by his wounds and bleeding profusely, was led before him. One of his eyes, poked out by a lance, dangled over his cheek. Pugachev ordered him executed, along with Ensigns Figner and Kabalerov, a scribe, and the Tatar Bikbai. The garrison troops started pleading for the life of their good-hearted commander, but the Iaik Cossacks leading the rebellion were implacable. Not one of the victims betrayed a faint heart. Bikbai, a Muhammadan, crossed himself as he mounted the scaffold, and put his neck in the noose himself. The next day Pugachev set out for Tatishchev.

This fort was under the command of Colonel Elagin. The garrison was augmented by Bülow's detachment, since he had sought refuge there. On the morning of September 27 Pugachev's troops appeared on the hills around the fort. All the inhabitants could see him placing his cannon there and aiming them at the fort with his own hands. The rebels rode up to the walls of the fort, trying to persuade the garrison *not to obey the boyars* and to surrender voluntarily. They received fire in response. They retreated. Shooting with no effect continued from noon till evening, when some haystacks close to the fort were set on fire by the besiegers. The flames soon reached the wooden breastwork. The soldiers rushed to put the fire out. Pugachev, taking advantage of the confusion, attacked from the other side. The Cossacks stationed in the fort defected to his side. The wounded Elagin and even Bülow put up a desperate fight. At last the rebels charged into the fort's smoking ruins. The commanders were captured. Bülow was beheaded. Elagin, a corpulent man, was skinned; the scoundrels cut his fat out and rubbed it on their wounds. His wife was hacked to pieces. Their daughter, Kharlov's wife, widowed the day before, was led before the victor who had presided over the execution of her parents. Pugachev was struck by her beauty and decided to make the poor woman his concubine, sparing her seven-year-old brother for her sake. Major Velovskii's widow, who had escaped from Rassypnaia, was also there: they strangled her. All the officers were hanged. A number of regulars and Bashkirs were marshaled into a field and killed by grapeshot. The rest of the soldiers were shorn after the Cossack fashion and signed into the rebel forces. Thirteen cannon came into the victor's possession.

Reports of Pugachev's successes were reaching Orenburg one after the other. No sooner had Velovskii reported the taking of Iletskii Gorodok than Kharlov was reporting the fall of Rassypnaia; right afterwards Bülow reported from Tatishchev that Nizhne-Ozernaia had been taken, and Major Kruse from Chernorechenskaia, that shooting had been heard at Tatishchev. Finally (on September 28) a troop of 300 Tatars, assembled with great difficulty and dispatched to Tatishchev, came back with the news of Elagin's and Bülow's fate. Reinsdorp, alarmed by the speed with which the conflagration was spreading, convened a council consisting of the leading officials of Orenburg, and the following measures were decided on:

1. All the bridges over the Sakmara to be dismantled and sent floating downstream.

2. The Polish Confederates stationed in Orenburg to be disarmed and conveyed to Fort Troitsk under the strictest supervision.[18]

3. People of the third estate who had arms to be assigned places in the defense of the city under the supervision of the commander-in-chief, Major General Wallenstern; the others, to prepare to fight fires under the command of the director of the customhouse, Obukhov.

4. The Seitov Tatars to be brought into the city and placed under the command of Collegiate Councillor Timashev.

5. The artillery to be commanded by Actual State Councillor Starov-Miliukov, who had at one time served as an artilleryman.

In addition Reinsdorp, concerned about the safety of Orenburg itself, ordered the commander-in-chief to repair the fortifications, making them ready for the city's defense. The garrisons of smaller forts not yet taken by Pugachev were ordered to come to Orenburg, either burying or throwing into the rivers whatever heavy equipment and gunpowder they had.

On September 29 Pugachev left Tatishchev and marched on Chernorechenskaia. In that fort there remained a few veterans under the command of Captain Nechaev, replacing the commandant, Major Kruse, who had stolen away to Orenburg. They surrendered without resistance. Pugachev hanged the captain because one of his serfs, a young woman, complained against him.

Pugachev, bypassing Orenburg on the right, proceeded to Sakmara, whose inhabitants were awaiting him impatiently.[19] He went there on October 1 from the Tatar village Kargala, in the company of a few Cossacks. An eyewitness describes his arrival in the following words:

In the fort, before the Cossack command post, carpets were spread out and a table laid with bread and salt. The priest was waiting for Pugachev with cross and holy icons. When he entered, the fort bells were rung and people bared their heads, and when he climbed off his horse, two of his Cossacks supporting him by the arms, all prostrated themselves. He kissed both the cross and the bread and salt, and seating himself in the chair provided for him, said, "Rise, my children." Then they all came to kiss his hand. He inquired about the Cossacks of the town. He was told that some were away in state service; others had been ordered to Orenburg with their ataman, Danilo Donskoi; only 20 men had been left behind for stagecoach duty, but even they had vanished. He turned to the priest and sternly commanded him to find the men, adding, "You are their priest, be their ataman, too. You and all who live here will answer for them with your heads." Then he went to the house of the ataman's father, where dinner had been prepared for him. "If your son were here," he said to the old man, "this dinner would be worthy and honorable, but as it is, your bread and salt are tainted. What kind of an ataman is he, if he has deserted his post?" After dinner, drunk, he was about to have the old man executed, but the Cossacks accompanying him dissuaded him; in the end the old man was just put in fetters and locked up at the Cossack command post for one night. The next day the Cossacks who had been tracked down were brought before Pugachev. He treated them kindly and took them with him. They asked him, "What provisions should we bring with us?"

"Just a hunk of bread," he answered; "you will accompany me only as far as Orenburg."

In the meanwhile the Bashkirs sent by the governor of Orenburg had surrounded the town. Pugachev rode out to meet them and without a gunshot attached them all to his own troops. On the bank of the Sakmara he had six people hanged.[20]

Thirty versts away from Sakmara there was a fort called Prechisten-skaia. The major part of its garrison had been taken by Bülow on his march to Tatishchev. Pugachev with one of his detachments occupied it without a fight. The officers and the garrison came out to meet the victors. The pretender, as usual, attached the soldiers to his own troops and, for the first time, disgraced the officers by sparing them.

Pugachev gathered strength: it had only been two weeks since he had arrived below Iaitskii Gorodok with a handful of rebels, yet he now had as many as 3,000 men, both infantry and cavalry, with more than 20 cannon. Seven forts had been either taken by him or surrendered to him. His army grew by the hour at an incredible pace. He decided to take advantage of his good luck, and during the night of October 3, crossing the river below Sakmara by a bridge that had been left standing despite Reinsdorp's orders, he marched on Orenburg.

Chapter Three

Measures taken by the government.—The state of Orenburg.—Reinsdorp's manifesto about Pugachev.—The bandit Khlopusha.—Pugachev below Orenburg.—The village of Berda.—Pugachev's companions.—Major General Kar.—His lack of success.—The demise of Colonel Chernyshev.—Kar leaves the army.—Bibikov.

The affairs of Orenburg Guberniia took a bad turn. A general mutiny of the Iaik Host was expected at any moment; the Bashkirs, stirred up by their elders (whom Pugachev had already managed to endow richly with camels and goods wrested from Bukhara merchants), began to raid Russian villages and to join up, in large numbers, with the rebel forces. Kalmyks on military duty at the outposts were running off. The Mordvin, the Chuvash, and the Cheremis no longer obeyed Russian authorities. Seignorial serfs openly showed their allegiance to the pretender, and soon not only Orenburg Guberniia, but other, adjacent *guberniias* were showing an alarming instability.

Various governors—von Brandt of Kazan, Chicherin of Siberia, and Krechetnikov of Astrakhan in addition to Reinsdorp—were sending reports to the State War College about the events in the Iaik region. The Empress anxiously turned her attention to the emerging calamity. The conditions that prevailed at the time favored disorders. Troops had been drawn away from every region to Turkey and to a seething Poland. Because of the strict measures taken all over Russia in an attempt to curb the plague that had only recently raged, there was widespread discontent among the rabble. Recruiting levies added to the problems. Several platoons and squadrons from Moscow, Petersburg, Novgorod and Bakhmut were ordered to hasten to Kazan. They were put under the command of Major General Kar, who had distinguished himself in Poland by an unwavering execution of the strict measures that his superiors had prescribed. He was in St. Petersburg at the time, enlisting new recruits. He was ordered to hand his brigade over to Major General Nashchokin and to hurry to the endangered regions. Major General Freymann, who had already pacified the Iaik Host once and was familiar with the theater of the new disturbances, was to be attached to his staff. The military commanders of neighboring *guberniias* were also ordered to take appropriate measures. On October 15 the government issued a proclamation announcing the appearance of a pretender and admonishing those deceived by him to renounce their criminal error before it was too late.

Let us return to Orenburg.

There were up to 3,000 troops and 70 cannon in the city. Such resources not only made it possible to liquidate the rebels, but put the
commanders under an obligation to do so. Unfortunately, however,
not one among the military commanders knew his business. Frightened from the beginning, they gave Pugachev time to gather momen-
tum and deprived themselves of the opportunity for offensive action.
Orenburg suffered through a calamitous siege, of which Reinsdorp
himself has left a curious record.

For some days, Pugachev's appearance as a pretender remained a secret to the citizens of Orenburg, but rumors about the taking of forts
soon spread, and Bülow's hasty departure confirmed them. There was
unrest in Orenburg itself: the Cossacks grumbled menacingly, and the
terrified citizens talked of surrender. The instigator of the disturbances, a retired sergeant sent by Pugachev, was caught. He confessed
during the interrogations that he had intended to assassinate the governor. Agitators began operating in villages around Orenburg. Reinsdorp published a manifesto about Pugachev, revealing the pretender's
true identity and earlier crimes. This manifesto, however, was written in a tangled, obscure style. It stated that *"the man engaged in villainous acts in the Iaik region is rumored to be of an estate different
from the one to which he truly belongs,"* and that in fact he was a Don
Cossack, Emelian Pugachev, who had been flogged and had his face
branded for previous crimes. This allegation was incorrect. Reinsdorp
had given credit to a false rumor, thereby enabling the rebels triumphantly to accuse him of slander.

It seemed that every measure Reinsdorp had taken was working
against him. In the Orenburg prison there was at this time a villain
kept in irons who was known by the name of Khlopusha. He had been
committing robberies in those parts for 20 years, had been banished to
Siberia three times, and had found a way to escape three times. Reinsdorp took it into his head to use this sharp-witted convict to transmit
some admonitory leaflets to Pugachev's band. Khlopusha swore he
would fulfill his mission faithfully. Set free, he went directly to Pugachev and handed all the governor's leaflets to him.[21]

"I know what's written on them, brother," said the illiterate Pugachev, presenting Khlopusha with half a ruble and the clothes of a recently hanged Kirgiz. Since Khlopusha was thoroughly familiar with
the region, which he had so long terrorized with his robberies, he became indispensable to Pugachev. He was appointed to the rank of
colonel and entrusted with pillaging and stirring up factories. He
lived up to Pugachev's expectations. He proceeded along the Sakmara

River, inciting rebellion in the villages of the area. He descended on the landings at Bugulchan and Sterlitamak,[22] and on factories in the Urals, whence he sent Pugachev cannon, ball, and powder. His band grew, swelled with serfs assigned to factory work and with Bashkirs— his accomplices in brigandage.

On October 5 Pugachev and his forces pitched camp on a Cossack pasture five versts from Orenburg. They immediately moved on the city, setting up, under gunfire, one battery on the portico of a church in a suburb and another at the governor's suburban house. The heavy cannonade, however, drove them back. That same day the suburb was burned down at the governor's orders. The only two buildings left standing were a cottage and Saint Georgii's Church. The inhabitants, who had been moved to the city, were promised full compensation for their losses. The moat ringing the city was cleaned out and chevaux-de-frise were set up around the ramparts.

During the night stacks of hay, stored for the winter outside the city, flared up all around. The governor had not had time to have them transferred within the city walls. The next morning Major Naumov (who had only just arrived from Iaitskii Gorodok) led an offensive against the incendiaries. He had 1,500 troops with him, both cavalry and infantry. Encountering artillery, they stopped, exchanged fire with the rebels for a while, and eventually withdrew without any success. His regular soldiers were fearful, and he did not trust his Cossacks.

Once more Reinsdorp convened his council, now consisting of both military and civil officials, and asked them to submit written opinions on whether to attempt another offensive against the villain or to await the arrival of new troops under the protection of the city's fortifications. At this council meeting Actual State Councillor Starov-Miliukov was the only one to voice an opinion worthy of a military man, namely, *"To march against the rebels."* All the others, fearing that a new failure might throw the citizens into utter despondency, thought only of defense. Reinsdorp agreed with them.

On October 8 the rebels raided the barter court, three versts outside the city.[23] A detachment sent out against them routed them, killing 200 people on the spot and taking 116 prisoners. Reinsdorp, wishing to take advantage of an event that had raised the morale of his troops a little, wanted to take the field against Pugachev the next day, but his senior officers unanimously reported that the troops were entirely un-reliable: the soldiers, disheartened and confused, fought unwillingly; and the Cossacks might cross over to the rebel side on the very field of battle, which could lead to the fall of Orenburg. Poor Reinsdorp was at a loss. Eventually he managed to awaken his subordinates' conscience, and on October 12 Naumov made another sally out of the city with his unreliable troops.

A battle ensued. Pugachev's artillery pieces outnumbered those brought out of the city. The Orenburg Cossacks, intimidated by the unfamiliar cannon fire, stayed close to the city, under the protection of the cannon ranged on the ramparts. Naumov's detachment was surrounded by multitudes on all sides. He drew up his troops in square formation and began retreating while maintaining fire. The engagement lasted four hours. Counting those who had deserted as well as the dead and the wounded, he lost a total of 117 men.

Not one day passed without an exchange of fire. Mobs of rebels rode around the city ramparts attacking foraging detachments. Pugachev went right up to Orenburg with all his forces several times, but he had no intention of storming it.

"I will not waste men," he said to some Cossacks from Sakmara. "I'll wipe the city out by famine."

He found many an opportunity to get his inflammatory leaflets into the hands of Orenburg citizens. Several rascals sent by the pretender and equipped with explosives and fuses were caught in the city.

Orenburg was soon gripped by a shortage of fodder. Since all military and civilian horses were emaciated and incapacitated, it was decided to round them up and send them off, some to Iletskaia Zashchita, others to Verkhne-Iaitsk, still others to the Ufa area. But rebel peasants and Tatars captured the horses a few versts from the city and brought their Cossack drivers before Pugachev.

Cold weather set in earlier than usual that fall. The first frost came on October 14, and on the 16th it snowed. On the 18th Pugachev, having burned his camp, left the Iaik with his full train and headed for the Sakmara. He camped outside the village of Berda, close to the summer road along the Sakmara, seven versts from Orenburg. His flying squadrons, based here, relentlessly harassed the city, attacking foraging detachments and posing a constant threat to the garrison.

On November 2 Pugachev moved up to Orenburg with all his forces once more, and having positioned batteries all around the city, began a fearful bombardment. He was answered in kind from the city walls. In the meanwhile 1,000 men from Pugachev's infantry crept into the burned-down suburb from the side of the river, up almost to the rampart and the chevaux-de-frise and, hiding in cellars, pelted the city with bullets and arrows. Pugachev himself led them. The jaegers of the field command drove them out of the suburb. Pugachev was almost taken prisoner. The firing ceased in the evening, but all through the night the rebels answered the chiming of the cathedral clock, marking each hour with a burst of gunfire.

The next day the firing resumed despite the cold and a blizzard. The rebels took turns warming themselves by a campfire lit in the church and by the stove of the one cottage that had been left standing in the burned-down suburb. Pugachev had one cannon placed on the portico of the church and another hoisted up to the bell tower. The rebels' main battery was positioned on top of a tall target that had been set up at a verst from the city for artillery practice. Both sides continued firing all day. At nightfall Pugachev drew back, having suffered some insignificant losses and having caused virtually no harm to the city's defenders. In the morning a group of convicts, guarded by Cossacks, was sent out of the city to raze the target and other barricades, and to demolish the cottage. In the chancel of the church, where the rebels had been bringing their wounded, there were puddles of blood. The frames of icons had been ripped off, and the altar cloth had been torn to pieces. The church had also been desecrated by horse dung and human excrement.

The frosts were intensifying. On November 6 Pugachev and his Iaik Cossacks moved from their new camp into the village of Berda proper. The Bashkirs, Kalmyks, and factory peasants stayed at the camp, in covered wagons and dugouts. The movement of flying squadrons, the raids, and the skirmishes went on relentlessly. Pugachev's forces grew by the day. His army numbered 25,000 at this point. The Iaik Cossacks and the regular soldiers commandeered from forts formed its nucleus, but an unbelievable multitude of Tatars, Bashkirs, Kalmyks, rioting peasants, escaped convicts, and vagabonds of all kinds gathered around the main body. All this rabble was armed in a makeshift fashion: some with spears, pistols, or swords taken from officers, others with bayonets stuck into long staffs, still others with clubs. But a good many had no weapon at all. The army was divided into regiments of 500 each. Only the Iaik Cossacks received regular pay; the rest had to content themselves with plunder. Vodka was purchased *from the state*. Horses and fodder were obtained from the Bashkirs. Desertion, it was announced, would be punished by death. Each corporal answered for his men with his own head. Frequent patrolling and the posting of guards were instituted. Pugachev strictly supervised the guards, riding around to check them himself, sometimes even at night. Drills (especially in the artillery units) were held almost every day. There was a daily church service. During *ektenia* prayers were offered for Emperor Petr Fedorovich and his wife, Empress Ekaterina Alekseevna.[24] Pugachev, a schismatic, never went to church. Riding around the market or the streets of Berda, he always scattered copper coins among the populace. He held court and pronounced judgment seated in an armchair in front of his cottage. On either side of him there sat a Cossack, one with a mace, the other with a silver ax in hand. Those approaching him had to bow to the ground, make the sign of the cross, and kiss his hand. Berda was a veritable den of vice and murder. The camp was full of officers' wives and daughters, given over to the bandits to violate at will. There were executions every day. The ravines outside Berda were filled with the corpses of victims shot to death, strangled, or quartered. Bands of marauders swarmed in all directions, carousing in the villages, and robbing public coffers and the possessions of the nobility, but never touching the property of peasants. Some daredevils would ride right up to the chevaux-de-frise by the Orenburg walls; others would shout, waving their hats stuck on the tip of their spears, "Cossack sirs! It is time to come to your senses and serve your Emperor Petr Fedorovich!" Still others clamored for the extradition of Martiushka Borodin (the Host elder who had come from Iaitskii Gorodok to Orenburg with Naumov's detachment) or issued invitations to the Cossacks, saying, "Our Father doesn't spare his wine!"[25] Sorties were made against them from the city, resulting in skirmishes, at times quite hot ones. Pugachev himself was frequently there to show how plucky he was. Once he arrived drunk, hatless and swaying in his saddle; but for some Cossacks who dragged his horse away by the bridle, he would have fallen into the garrison's hands.

Pugachev was not despotic. The Iaik Cossacks who had instigated the revolt controlled the actions of the vagabond, whose only merits were a degree of military know-how and exceptional daring. He never undertook anything without their consent, whereas they frequently acted without his knowledge and sometimes even against his wishes. Outwardly, they showed him respect, baring their heads in his presence and bowing down before him in public, but in private they treated him as a comrade, getting drunk with him, sitting in their shirt-sleeves and with their hats on in his company, and singing barge haulers' songs. Pugachev chafed at their guardianship. "My path is narrow," he once said to Denis Pianov, as they were feasting at the wedding of Pianov's younger son. Distrustful of outside influences on the tsar they had created, they did not allow him to have other favorites or confidants. At the beginning of the revolt Pugachev had made Sergeant Karmitskii his scribe, having pardoned him under the very gallows. Karmitskii had soon become his favorite. The Iaik Cossacks strangled the man during the taking of Tatishchev and threw him into the river with a rock tied to his neck. Pugachev inquired after him. "He left," they answered him "to visit his mother down the Iaik." Pugachev let the matter go without a word. The young Kharlova had the misfortune of winning the pretender's affections. He kept her at his camp below Orenburg. She was the only person allowed to enter his covered wagon at any time; and at her request he gave orders to bury the bodies of all those who had been hanged at Ozernaia at the time the fort was taken. She became suspect in the eyes of the jealous villains and Pugachev, yielding to their demand, gave his concubine up to them. Kharlova and her seven-year-old brother were shot. Wounded, they crawled up to each other and embraced. Their bodies, thrown into the bushes, remained there in each other's arms for a long time.

Most prominent among the chief rebels was Zarubin (nicknamed Chika), Pugachev's mentor and close associate from the very beginning of the revolt. He had the title of field marshal and held the highest office next to the pretender. Ovchinnikov, Shigaev, Lysov, and Chumakov commanded the army. They were all nicknamed after grandees surrounding Catherine's throne at the time: Chika was called Count Chernyshev, Shigaev Count Vorontsov, Ovchinnikov Count Panin, and Chumakov Count Orlov. The pretender had full confidence in the retired artillery corporal Beloborodov, who, together with Padurov, looked after all paperwork for the illiterate Pugachev and introduced strict order and discipline into the rioters' bands. Perfilev, sent to Petersburg on behalf of the Iaik Host at the beginning of the uprising, had promised the government to bring the Cossacks under control and to hand Pugachev over to the legal authorities, but after he arrived in Berda he proved to be one of the most desperate rebels, linking his fate with that of the pretender. The robber Khlopusha, just recently flogged and branded by the executioner's hand, with nostrils slit to the very cartilage, was one of Pugachev's favorites. Ashamed of his mutilated features, he either wore a loosely woven cloth over his face or held his sleeve over it as if protecting it from the frost. These were the people who rocked the state to its foundations!

In the meanwhile Kar arrived at the boundary of Orenburg Guberniia. Before Kar's arrival the governor of Kazan had managed to assemble a few hundred soldiers, some retired, some brought in from garrisons and military settlements, and had deployed some of them near the Kichui entrenchment, and some along the Cheremshan River, halfway between Kichui and Stavropol. On the Volga there were about 30 regulars, commanded by one officer, whose task was to catch plunderers and to keep an eye on the rebels' movements. Von

Brandt had written to the commanding general of Moscow, Prince Volkonskii, to ask for troops, but the whole of Moscow garrison was away on a recruiting mission, and the Tomsk Regiment, which had been brought to Moscow, was manning the sentry posts around the city that had been instituted during the raging plague of 1771. Prince Volkonskii was able to release only 300 regulars and one fieldpiece, but he sent these off in a wagon train to Kazan without delay.

Kar instructed the commandant of Simbirsk, Colonel P. M. Chernyshev, who was proceeding up the Samara Line toward Orenburg, to take Tatishchev as soon as possible.[26] Kar's intention was to reinforce Chernyshev's troops with those of Major General Freymann as soon as the latter returned from Kaluga, where he had gone to receive new recruits. Kar had full confidence in victory. "The only thing I am afraid of," he wrote to Count Z. G. Chernyshev, "is that as soon as these bandits get wind of the troops' approach they will flee to the places where they came from, not giving the troops an opportunity to get close to them." He foresaw difficulties in pursuing Pugachev only because of the winter and a shortage of horses.

Kar began pressing forward at the beginning of November, without waiting for the artillery, for the 170 grenadiers sent off from Simbirsk, or for the armed Bashkirs and Meshcheriaks dispatched from Ufa to join him. On his way, at about 100 versts from Orenburg, he learned that the convicted robber Khlopusha, having cast some cannon at the Avziano-Petrovsk ironworks, and having rallied the factory peasants as well as the Bashkirs of the vicinity—all at Pugachev's behest—was returning to Orenburg. Anxious to cut Khlopusha off, on November 7 Kar sent Second Major Shishkin with 400 regulars and two fieldpieces to the village of Iuzeeva, while he himself, accompanied by General Freymann and First Major F. Warnstedt who had just come from Kaluga, set out from Sarmanaeva. Shishkin ran into 600 rebels right outside of Iuzeeva. The Tatars and armed peasants who were with him defected immediately, yet Shishkin managed to disperse the whole mob by a few shots. He occupied the village, where Kar and Freymann also arrived toward four in the morning. The troops were so exhausted that it was impossible even to detail mounted patrols. The generals decided to wait till daylight to make their assault on the rebels. When dawn broke, they saw before them the same mob that had been dispersed the day before. An admonitory manifesto was delivered to the rebels; they took it, but rode off swearing and saying that their own manifestos were more trustworthy; they started firing from a cannon. They were dispersed once more... At this point Kar heard four distant bursts of cannon fire in the rear of his position. He grew alarmed and beat a hasty retreat, supposing himself cut off from Kazan. Suddenly over 2,000 rebels galloped up from all sides and opened fire from nine fieldpieces. Pugachev himself was leading them. He and Khlopusha had managed to join forces. Scattered about the fields just within cannon range, they were perfectly safe. Kar's cavalry was exhausted and small in number. The rebels, who had good horses, fell back from the infantry charges, deftly hauling their fieldpieces down one hill and up another. They accompanied the retreating Kar in this manner for 70 versts. He tried to return the fire from his five fieldpieces for a full eight hours while retreating. He abandoned his supply train; and up to 120 of his men (if one can believe his own report) were either killed or wounded or had deserted. There was no sign of the Bashkirs expected from Ufa; and those under Prince Urakov's command, who were by now not far away, took to their heels as soon as they heard the gunfire. Kar's soldiers, the majority of whom were either advanced in years or just recently conscripted, grumbled loudly and were ready to surrender; their young officers, who had never been under fire, did not know how to raise their morale. The grenadiers who had been dispatched from Simbirsk under Lieutenant Kartashov's command were traveling in so lax a manner that they did not even have their guns loaded and they all slept in their sleighs. They surrendered after the rebels' first four cannon shots—the same shots that Kar heard from Iuzeeva.

Kar suddenly lost his self-assurance. Reporting his losses, he declared to the War College that in order to defeat Pugachev they needed, not small detachments, but whole regiments, with reliable cavalry and strong artillery. He also hastily dispatched an order to Colonel Chernyshev not to leave Perevolotskaia but to try to fortify it while awaiting further instructions. The emissary carrying this order was, however, too late to catch up with Chernyshev.

Chernyshev left Perevolotskaia on November 11 and arrived at Chernorechenskaia on the night of the 13th. Here two Ilek Cossacks, brought to him by the ataman of Sakmara, informed him of Kar's defeat and of the capture of the 170 grenadiers. Chernyshev could not doubt the truth of this last report, since he himself had sent the grenadiers off from Simbirsk, where they had been on a recruiting assignment. He did not know what to do: whether to draw back to Perevolotskaia or to hurry on to Orenburg, to which he had sent notification of his approach just the night before. At this moment five Cossacks and one regular soldier presented themselves to him, claiming to have defected from Pugachev's camp. One of these people was a Cossack centurion, and another was Padurov, a former delegate to the Legislative Commission.[27] He assured Chernyshev of his loyalty, displaying his commission badge as proof, and advised the colonel to go to Orenburg immediately, along a safe route that he, Padurov, would show him. Chernyshev believed him and left Chernorechenskaia immediately, without beat of drum. Padurov led him across the hills, assuring him that Pugachev's advance patrols were far away, and that even if the patrols should catch sight of them at daybreak, by then they would be out of danger and would be able to get into Orenburg without hindrance. Chernyshev arrived at the Sakmara River by the morning and started crossing it on the ice at Maiak Point, five versts from Orenburg. He had 1,500 regulars and Cossacks, 500 Kalmyks, and 12 fieldpieces with him. Captain Rzhevskii crossed the river first with the artillery train and a light field detachment; reaching the other side, he immediately galloped into Orenburg in the company of just three Cossacks, and presented himself to the governor with the news of Chernyshev's arrival. At that same moment cannon fire could be heard in Orenburg; it continued for a quarter of an hour, then ceased... A little later Reinsdorp received the intelligence that Chernyshev's entire battalion had been captured and was being taken to Pugachev's camp.

Chernyshev had been deceived by Padurov, who in fact led him straight to Pugachev. The rebels suddenly charged at his troops and seized his artillery. The Cossacks and Kalmyks defected. The infantry, exhausted from the cold, hunger, and the night's march, was unable to put up any resistance. All were captured. Pugachev hanged Chernyshev, together with 36 officers, an ensign's wife, and a Kalmyk colonel who had stayed loyal to his unfortunate commander.

Brigadier Korf was approaching Orenburg at the same time with 2,400 troops and 20 fieldpieces. Pugachev attacked him too, but was repulsed by garrison Cossacks.

The Orenburg authorities, it seemed, were panic-stricken. On November 14 Reinsdorp, who only the day before had made no attempt to help the battalion of the unfortunate Chernyshev, took it into his head to make a strong sally. All the troops within the walls of the city (even those who had just arrived) were ordered to take the field under the leadership of the commander-in-chief. The rebels, true to their usual tactics, fought from a distance and from all directions, incessantly firing from their numerous fieldpieces. The garrison's emaciated cavalry could not even hope for success. Wallenstern, who had lost 32 men, was eventually forced to draw his troops into square formation and retreat. That same day Major Warnstedt, dispatched by Kar along the New Moscow Road, ran into a strong rebel force and, after losing some 200 men, hastily retreated.

When Kar learned how Chernyshev's battalion had been captured, he lost heart altogether, and from then on he was concerned, not with defeating the despicable rebel, but only with his own safety. He reported all that had transpired to the War College, voluntarily resigned from the commandership under the pretext of illness, offered a few clever pieces of advice about how to operate against Pugachev, and leaving his army under Freymann's care, left for Moscow, where his arrival raised a general hue and cry. The Empress issued strict orders to discharge him from the service. He spent the rest of his life in his village, where he died at the beginning of Alexander's reign.

The Empress saw that strong measures were called for against the growing evil. She looked for a reliable commander to succeed the pusillanimous Kar, and settled on General of the Army Bibikov. Alexander Ilich Bibikov was one of the most illustrious personalities of Catherine's time, which abounded in remarkable people. While still in his youth he had distinguished himself both on the battlefield and in civic affairs. He served with honor in the Seven Years' War, attracting the attention of Frederick the Great. Important tasks were assigned to him. In 1763 he was sent to Kazan to pacify the rioting factory peasants. By firmness and prudent moderation he soon managed to restore order. In 1766, when the Legislative Commission was initiated, he oversaw the election of delegates in Kostroma. He himself was elected, and later appointed marshal of the commission. In 1771 he replaced Lieutenant General Weimarn as commander-in-chief in Poland, where he not only quickly introduced order into a disorganized state of affairs, but also won the love and trust of the vanquished.

During the period under discussion he was in St. Petersburg. Having recently yielded his commandership of Poland to Lieutenant General Romanius, he was preparing to leave for Turkey, to serve under Count Rumiantsev. The Empress had been cool in her reception of him on this occasion, though heretofore she had always shown kindness toward him. It is possible that she was displeased with some indelicate expressions he had let fly in a moment of irritation; for Bibikov, though diligent in his assignments and sincerely devoted to the Empress, tended to be querulous, and bold in voicing his opinions. But Catherine was able to overcome personal grudges. At a Court ball she approached him with her former affectionate smile and, while graciously conversing with him, gave him his new assignment. Bibikov answered that he had dedicated himself to the service of the fatherland, and cited the words of a folksong that applied to his own situation:

> My *sarafan*, dear *sarafan*,
> You are useful everywhere,
> And if not needed, *sarafan*,
> You just lie under the bench.

He accepted the complex, difficult assignment without any conditions, and on December 9 left Petersburg.

Arriving in Moscow, Bibikov found the ancient capital apprehensive and dejected. Its citizens, who had only recently witnessed riot and plague, trembled at the thought of a new calamity. Many noblemen whose homes had been ravaged by Pugachev or were threatened by the upheaval had fled to Moscow. The serfs they had brought with them filled the streets with rumors about the emancipation of peasants and the extermination of landlords. Moscow's multitudinous rabble, getting drunk and staggering about the streets, awaited Pugachev with obvious impatience. The citizens greeted Bibikov with an enthusiasm that revealed how greatly endangered and threatened they felt. He soon left Moscow, hastening to justify the trust the inhabitants had placed in him.

Chapter Four

The rebels' movements.—Major Zaev.—The taking of Fort Ilinskaia.—The death of Kameshkov and Voronov.—The state of Orenburg.—The siege of Iaitskii Gorodok.—The battle at Berda.—Bibikov in Kazan.—Catherine II as a Kazan landowner.—The opinion of Europe.—Voltaire.—The decree about Pugachev's house and family.

The defeat of Kar and Freymann, the annihilation of Chernyshev, and the unsuccessful sallies of Wallenstern and Korf increased the rebels' boldness and self-assurance. As their ranks surged every which way, ravaging villages and towns and inciting people to rebellion, they met no resistance. Tornov revolted at the head of 600 men and ransacked the whole district of Nagaibak. In the meanwhile Chika marched on Ufa with a 10,000-strong division and invested it by the end of November. The city lacked the kind of fortifications Orenburg had, but its commandant, Miasoedov, together with the noblemen who had sought refuge there, resolved to defend themselves. Chika, not daring to mount a strong offensive, set himself up in the village of

Chesnokovka, 10 versts away from Ufa, rousing the neighboring villages—inhabited mostly by Bashkirs—and cutting the city off from all communication. Ulianov, Davydov, and Beloborodov were operating between Ufa and Kazan. At the same time Pugachev sent Khlopusha with 500 troops and six fieldpieces to take the forts of Ilinskaia and Verkhne-Ozernaia, situated to the east of Orenburg. The governor of Siberia, Chicherin, had detailed Lieutenant General Dekalong and Major General Stanislavskii to defend their region. The former guarded the borders of Siberia; the latter stayed in Fort Orsk, operating timidly, losing heart at the approach of the slightest danger and refusing to carry out his duty under various pretexts. Khlopusha took Ilinskaia, slaying its commandant, Lieutenant Lopatin, in the assault, but sparing its other officers and leaving the fort itself standing. He marched on Verkhne-Ozernaia. The commandant of that fort, Lieutenant Colonel Demarin, repulsed the attack. On learning this, Pugachev himself hurried to Khlopusha's assistance and, joining forces with him on the morning of November 26, laid siege to the fort. The bombardment lasted all day. The rebels made several attempts to storm the fort with spears, but were repulsed each time. In the evening Pugachev drew back to a Bashkir village 12 versts from Verkhne-Ozernaia. Here he learned that Major General Stanislavskii had dispatched three platoons from the Siberian Line to Ilinskaia. He set out to intercept these troops.

The commander of this detachment, Major Zaev, managed, however, to get to Ilinskaia and to occupy it (on November 27). Khlopusha had not burned the fort on vacating it. Its inhabitants had not been forced out. There were a few captive Confederates among them. Some of the walls and a few of the cottages had been damaged. All the garrison had been removed, except for one sergeant and a wounded officer. The storehouse had been left open: some quarter-measures of flour and pieces of rusk were lying about the yard. A cannon was abandoned by the gate. Quickly taking what measures he could, Zaev set up the three cannon he had brought with him on three of the bastions (the fourth was left without one), posted guards and sent out patrols, and awaited the arrival of the enemy.

It was already getting dark when Pugachev appeared at the fort the next day. His men came right up to the fort and, riding around it, shouted to the guards, "Don't shoot; come out: the Emperor is here." A cannon was fired at them. The ball killed a horse. The rebels withdrew, but reappeared from behind a hill an hour later, spread out across the field, and galloped toward the fort under Pugachev's leadership. They were driven off by cannon fire. The soldiers and the captive

Poles (especially the latter) fervently implored Zaev to let them make a sally, but he refused, fearing their betrayal. "Stay here and defend the fort," he said to them. "The general did not commission me to make sallies."

Pugachev approached once more on the 29th, moving up two field-pieces on sleds, behind several wagons of hay. He rushed the bastion that had no cannon. Zaev made a hasty attempt to set up two cannon there, but before the transfer could be accomplished, Pugachev's balls pierced the bastion's wooden facing; the rebels stormed it, tearing down the remaining planks, and rushed into the fort with their usual battle cry. The soldiers, their ranks now broken, began to flee. Zaev, almost all his officers, and 200 of the rank and file were killed. The remaining soldiers were herded to a nearby Tatar village and lined up facing a loaded cannon. Pugachev, accompanied by Khlopusha, rode up dressed in red Cossack attire. As soon as he appeared, the soldiers were ordered to kneel. He said to them, "The Lord God and I, your Emperor Peter III, grant you pardon. Arise." Then he gave orders to turn the cannon around and fire it into the steppe. Captain Kameshkov and Ensign Voronov were brought before him. These modest names must be recorded in history.

"Why did you fight against me, your Sovereign?" asked the victor.

"You're no sovereign to us," answered the captives; "we Russians have our Sovereigns, the Empress Ekaterina Alekseevna and Grand Duke Pavel Petrovich. You are a bandit and an impostor."

They were hanged on the spot. Then Captain Basharin was led forth. Pugachev was about to have him hanged without addressing a word to him, but the captive soldiers began pleading with him for their captain's life. "If he's been good to you," said the pretender, "I'll grant him pardon." He ordered the captain, like his soldiers, to be shorn Cossack-fashion, and he had the wounded carried to the fort. The Cossacks of the detachment were greeted by the rebels as their comrades. When asked why they had not joined the besiegers sooner, they said they had been afraid of the regular soldiers.

From Ilinskaia Pugachev turned toward Verkhne-Ozernaia once more. He wanted to take it at any price, all the more so since Brigadier Korf's wife was there. He threatened to hang her in revenge for her husband's scheme of entrapping him through false negotiations.[28]

On November 30 Pugachev invested the fort again, bombarding it by cannon all day and making attempts to storm it now from this, now from that side. Demarin, in order to keep up his garrison's spirit, stood on the rampart throughout the day, loading the cannon with his own hands. In the end Pugachev withdrew; he was going to march against Stanislavskii, but having intercepted the Orenburg mail, he changed his mind and returned to Berda.

Reinsdorp wanted to make a sally during Pugachev's absence, and a detachment did indeed leave the city on the night of the 30th, but the emaciated horses collapsed and died in the effort to pull the artillery, and some Cossacks defected. Wallenstern was forced to withdraw behind the city walls.

The shortage in provisions was beginning to be felt in Orenburg. Reinsdorp requested some from Dekalong and Stanislavskii. Both found excuses for refusing him. He expected reinforcements to arrive momentarily, but since he was cut off from communication on all sides except Siberia and the Kirgiz Kaisak steppes, he could receive no information about them. In order to take a prisoner who might reveal some news, he had to send out as many as 1,000 men, and at times even such a great effort brought no results. On Timashev's advice he even resorted to setting up traps outside the ramparts in an attempt to catch night-roaming rebels like wolves. The city's defenders themselves laughed at this military ploy, though in general they were not much disposed to laughter; as for the rebels, Padurov in one of his letters sarcastically rebuked the governor for his unsuccessful stratagem, at the same time predicting his ruin and scornfully advising him to capitulate to the pretender.

Iaitskii Gorodok, this first hotbed of rebellion, remained loyal for a long time due to the intimidating presence of Simonov's troops. But Pugachev's followers in the town were emboldened by frequent communication with the rebels and a false rumor about the fall of Orenburg. Cossacks whom Simonov regularly sent out to patrol the environs and catch agitators from Berda began to disobey orders quite openly, letting the captured rebels go, tying up elders loyal to the government, and paying visits to the pretender's camp. A rumor spread about a rebel force approaching. On the night of December 29 the elder Mostovshchikov set out with a detachment to counter it. Scarcely had a few hours passed when three of the Cossacks who had gone with him came back to the fort at a gallop, reporting that Mostovshchikov and his men had been surrounded at a place seven versts from town and had all been taken prisoners by a huge band of rebels. There was great confusion in the town. Simonov lost courage, but fortunately there was a captain in the fort named Krylov, a resolute and level-headed man. From the first moment of the upheaval, he took over command of the garrison and saw to the necessary measures. On December 31 a rebel detachment led by Tolkachev entered the town. The citizens received him with enthusiasm and immediately joined his forces, arming themselves as best they could. They besieged the fort from all the side streets, took up positions in tall houses, and began shooting from windows. A witness says the hail of bullets that hit the fort sounded like the beating of 10 drums. People—not only if they were caught in the open but even if they happened to raise their heads momentarily from behind barriers—fell in large numbers. The rebels were safe at a distance of only 10 *sazhens* from the fort,[29] and since they were mostly hunters, they could hit even the openings through which the defenders were shooting. Simonov and Krylov tried to set the adjacent houses on fire, but either the bombs fell in the snow and fizzled out or else the attackers managed to pour water on them. Not one of the houses started burning. At last three regulars volunteered to set fire to the closest building, and they succeeded. The flames spread quickly. The rebels came out; the cannon from the fort fired at them; they withdrew carrying their dead and wounded. Toward evening the garrison, its spirit buoyed, sallied out and succeeded in setting several other houses on fire.

There were about 1,000 garrison soldiers and obedient Cossacks within the walls of the fort; they had plenty of ammunition but not enough food. The rebels invested the fort; erected log barricades on the burned-out square and across the streets and alleys leading to it; set up 16 batteries behind the barricades; built a second wall in front of the houses exposed to fire, filling the gaps between the walls with dirt; and began digging underground tunnels. The defenders, confining their efforts to keeping the enemy at a distance, periodically cleared the square and stormed the fortified houses. These dangerous sorties took place daily, sometimes even twice daily, and were always crowned with success: the regular soldiers were frenzied, and the obedient Cossacks could hope for no mercy from the rebels.

The situation in Orenburg was becoming terrible. Flour and groats were confiscated from the citizens, and a daily ration was introduced. The horses had been fed with brushwood for some time. Most of them died and were eaten. Hunger was intensifying. A sack of flour sold (on the most secret black market) for 25 rubles. On the advice of Rychkov (an academician living in Orenburg at the time), the citizens started frying bull and horse hides, chopping them into small pieces, and mixing them in dough. People fell ill. The grumbling grew louder. It was feared that a mutiny might break out.

In this extreme situation Reinsdorp decided to try his luck at arms once more, and on January 13 all the troops stationed in Orenburg sallied out in three columns under the command, respectively, of Wallenstern, Korf, and Naumov. But the darkness of the winter dawn, the depth of the snow, and the exhaustion of the horses hindered the coordination of the troops. Naumov arrived at the designated place first. The rebels caught sight of him, which gave them time to take countermeasures. They prevented Wallenstern from occupying, as the plan called for, the hills near the Berda–Kargala road. Korf encountered heavy artillery fire; and bands of rebels were beginning to encircle the columns. The Cossacks, left in reserve, fled from the rebels to Wallenstern's column, causing general confusion. Wallenstern found himself under fire from three directions, and since his soldiers were beginning to flee, he beat a retreat; Korf followed suit; and Naumov, who had been operating quite successfully at first, flung after them, afraid of being cut off. The whole corps ran back to Orenburg in disorder, with the loss of some 400 men killed or wounded, and left 15 fieldpieces in the bandits' hands. After this fiasco Reinsdorp did not dare mount another offensive; he simply waited for liberation under the protection of the city walls and cannon.

Bibikov arrived in Kazan on December 25. He found neither the governor nor the other leading officials in the city. The majority of the noblemen and merchants had fled to *guberniias* not yet threatened. Von Brandt was in Kozmodemiansk. Bibikov's arrival revived the despondent city; citizens who had left were beginning to return. On January 1, 1774, after a mass and a sermon by Archbishop Veniamin of Kazan, Bibikov summoned the nobility to his house and made a clever and effective speech. After describing the widespread calamity and the government's efforts to eliminate it, he addressed his appeal to the class that was as much doomed by the rebellion as the government, requesting its cooperation out of patriotism and loyalty to the crown. His speech made a deep impression. Those gathered pledged to assemble and arm at their own expense a corps of cavalry, furnishing one recruit for each 200 serfs. Major General Larionov, a relative of Bibikov's, was elected commander of the legion. The nobility of Simbirsk, Sviiazhsk, and Penza followed this example, assembling two more cavalry corps, one under the command of Majors Gladkov and Chemesov, the other under that of Captain Matiunin. The Kazan council also outfitted a squadron of hussars at its own expense.

The Empress conveyed to the Kazan nobility her imperial favor, goodwill, and patronage; and in a separate letter to Bibikov, which she signed as a Kazan landowner, offered to add her share to the common effort. Makarov, the marshal of the nobility, answered the Empress with an oration composed by Second Lieutenant of the Guards Derzhavin, who was serving on the staff of the commander-in-chief at the time.[30]

Bibikov, in an attempt to raise the morale of the citizens and his subordinates, put on a show of equanimity and good cheer, but in fact worry, irritation, and impatience were gnawing at him. The difficulty of his position is vividly described in his letters to Count Chernyshev, Fonvizin, and his family. On December 30 he wrote to his wife:

Now that I have become acquainted with all the circumstances here, I find the situation so appalling that I could not find the language to express it even if I were to try: my position is much worse and more vexing than it was on my arrival in Poland. I do everything in my power, writing day and night, never letting the pen out of my hand; and I pray to the Lord for His help. He alone can set matters right with His grace. There's no denying, we wake up a little too late. My troops began arriving yesterday: a battalion of grenadiers, and the two squadrons of hussars I had transported by stage-coach, are come. But they will not suffice for stamping out the pestilence. The evil afflicting us is like the Petersburg fire (you remember), which burned in so many places at once that it was well-nigh impossible to keep pace with it. Despite all, I will do whatever is in my power, and place my hope in the Lord. Poor old Governor von Brandt is so worn out that he can hardly drag himself about. He who confounded the affairs of this region in short order and left his army in the lurch will have to answer before God for innocent blood and the demise of many. My health, incidentally, is fair, only I desire no food or drink, and sugary victuals offend my taste. The evil is great and frightening. I beg my sire, whom I know to be the kindest of fathers, to offer his paternal prayers for me. Pray remember me to the holy Mother Evpraksiia.[31] Oh! I do feel bad!

The situation was indeed terrible. A general uprising by Bashkirs, Kalmyks, and other peoples scattered about the region interdicted communication on all sides. The army was small and unreliable. Commanding officers deserted their posts, fleeing at the sight of a Bashkir with bow and arrows or a factory serf with a club. Winter exacerbated the difficulties. The steppes were blanketed with deep snow. It was impossible to move forward unless one had a good supply of firewood as well as of food. The villages were deserted; the major cities either besieged or occupied by bands of rebels; the factories plundered and burned. The mobs rioted and wrought havoc everywhere. The troops dispatched from different regions of the country were slow in their approach. The evil, unimpeded, spread far and wide with great speed. The Iaik Cossacks were rioting from Iletsk to Gurev. The *guberniias* of Kazan, Nizhnii Novgorod, and Astrakhan were brimming over with bands of brigands; the conflagration threatened to spread into Siberia itself; upheavals were commencing in Perm; Ekaterinburg was in danger. The Kirgiz Kaisaks, taking advantage of the absence of troops, began crossing over the unguarded border, pillaging hamlets, driving off cattle, and taking captives. The trans-Kuban peoples were stirring, incited by Turkey, and even some European powers considered taking advantage of the difficult situation in which Russia had found herself.

The instigator of all this terrible upheaval attracted general attention. In Europe he was considered an instrument of Turkish politics. Voltaire, a typical representative of the public opinion of the time, wrote to Catherine: "C'est apparemment le chevalier de Tott qui a fait jouer cette farce; mais nous ne sommes plus au temps de Demetrius, et telle pièce de théâtre qui reussissait il y a deux cents ans est sifflée aujourd'hui."[32] The Empress, irritated by European gossip, answered with a degree of impatience: "Monsieur, les gazettes seules font beaucoup de bruit du brigand Pougatschef lequel n'est en relation directe, ni indirecte avec m-r de Tott. Je fais autant de cas des canons fondus par l'un que des entreprises de l'autre. M-r de Pougatshcef et m-r de Tott ont cependant cela de commun, que le premier file tous les jours sa corde de chanvre et que le second s'expose à chaque instant au cordon de soie."[33]

Although the Empress despised the chief bandit himself, she seized every opportunity to bring the misguided mob to reason. Admonitory manifestos were widely distributed, and a reward of 10,000 rubles was offered for the capture of the pretender. Intercourse between the Iaik and Don Cossacks was especially feared. Ataman Efremov was dismissed, and Semen Sulin was chosen to replace him. Instructions were sent to Cherkassk to burn Pugachev's house and belongings, and to convey his family, *without insult or injury*, to Kazan, where they could reveal his true identity if he was caught. The local authorities carried out Her Majesty's command to the letter: since Pugachev's house in Zimoveiskaia had been sold by his impoverished wife, and, dismantled, had been transported to another homestead, they had it hauled back to its previous location and burned in the presence of the clergy and the whole village. The executioners scattered the ashes to the winds, dug a trench, and erected a fence around the yard, forever to be left desolate as an accursed place. The officials asked for permission in the name of all the Zimoveiskaia Cossacks to resettle in some other place, *even if it was less well-situated*. The Empress did not permit the villagers to prove their zeal in such a wasteful fashion; she simply renamed their village after Potemkin, erasing the gloomy remembrance of the rebel by the glory of a new name that was already becoming dear to her and to the fatherland. Pugachev's wife and his son and two daughters (all three still minors) were sent to Kazan, together with his brother, who had served as a Cossack in the Second Army. At the same time testimony revealed the following detailed information about the villain who had shaken the foundation of the state.

Emelian Pugachev of the village of Zimoveiskaia, a Cossack formerly in state service, was the son of Ivan Mikhailov, long deceased. He was forty years old, and of medium height, had a dark complexion, and was lean; he had brown hair and wore a small black goatee. He had lost one of his upper front teeth in his adolescence, in a fistfight. He had a white blemish on his left temple and on his chest traces of the so-called Black Death. He was illiterate and crossed himself according to the schismatic practice. Ten years previously he had married the Cossack maiden Sofia Nediuzhina, who subsequently bore him five children. He joined the Second Army in 1770; participated in the taking of Bender; and after a year was furloughed to the Don for reasons of ill health. He took a trip to Cherkassk, seeking a cure. When he returned to his native village, the ataman of Zimoveiskaia asked him at a communal meeting where he had obtained the chestnut horse he had ridden home. Pugachev replied that he had bought it in Taganrog; but the Cossacks, familiar with his dissolute ways, did not believe him, and sent him back to obtain written proof. Pugachev left. While he was away, it became known that he had been inciting the Cossacks who lived near Taganrog to flee beyond the Kuban. It was resolved that Pugachev should be handed over to government authorities. When he returned home in December of that year he tried to hide on his farm but was caught; he did manage to run away, however; he gadded about no one knew where for three months, until at last, during Lent, he came back to his house one evening and rapped on the window. His wife let him in and informed the other Cossacks of his arrival. Pugachev was taken into custody again and was conveyed under guard first to the police investigator, the elder of Nizhnii Chir, Makarov, and then on to Cherkassk. On the way there he managed to escape once more, and after that he never again appeared in the Don region. It was already known from Pugachev's own testimony, which he had given before the Court Chancery at the end of 1772, that after his escape he had gone into hiding beyond the Polish border, in the schismatic settlement of Vetka; then obtained a passport, pretending to be an emigrant from Poland, at the Dobriansk frontier post; and finally journeyed to the Iaik region, begging for food along the way. All this information was made public, but at the same time the government forbade all talk about Pugachev because his name stirred up the rabble. This temporary police measure remained in force until the late Emperor's accession to the throne,[34] at which time permission was granted to write about Pugachev and publish

materials relating to him. Even today, the aged witnesses of that upheaval who are still alive are reluctant to answer questions about it.

Chapter Five

*Measures taken by Bibikov.—The first success.—The taking of Samara and
Zainsk.—Derzhavin.—Mikhelson.—The fortress of Iaitskii Gorodok under
continued siege.—Pugachev's marriage.—The destruction of Iletskaia Zashchita.—Lysov's death.—The battle at Tatishchev.—Pugachev's flight.—
The execution of Khlopusha.—The lifting of the siege of Orenburg.—Pugachev's second defeat.—The battle at Chesnokovka.—The liberation of Ufa
and Iaitskii Gorodok.—The death of Bibikov.*

At last the various forces dispatched against Pugachev from different directions were approaching their destination. Bibikov directed
them toward Orenburg. Major General Prince Golitsyn's assignment
was to secure the Moscow Road from Kazan to Orenburg. Major General Mansurov was entrusted with the right flank, providing coverage
for the Samara Line, where Major Muffel and Lieutenant Colonel
Grinev had been sent with their detachments. Major General Larionov
was dispatched to Ufa and Ekaterinburg. Dekalong shielded Siberia
and was ordered to send Major Gagrin with a field detachment to defend Kungur. Lieutenant of the Guards Derzhavin was transferred to
Malykovka to protect the Volga on the side of Penza and Saratov. Success proved that these were the correct measures. At first Bibikov had
misgivings about the morals of his army. In one corps (the Vladimir
Regiment) there was indeed some indication of the presence of Pugachev's followers. But the commandants of the towns through which
the regiment passed were instructed to send officials disguised as
peasants around the taverns, and with their help the agitators were
discovered and apprehended. Thereafter Bibikov was satisfied with
his regiments. "My affairs, thanks to God, are fast improving," he
wrote in February. "The troops are approaching the robber's den. I can
see from all the letters I receive that they are satisfied with me in Petersburg; I only wish someone had asked the goose, as it toddled on
the ice, whether its feet were not feeling frozen."

On December 29 Major Muffel and his field detachment advanced
on Samara, which had been occupied by a band of rebels the day before. The rebels came out to counter him in the open field; he crushed
them and chased them all the way back to the city. Once inside, they
thought they could hold out under the protection of the city's cannon,
but Muffel's dragoons cut their way into the city with their sabers,
hacking at the fleeing rebels and trampling them underfoot. At this

same moment some Stavropol Kalmyks, coming in to reinforce the rebels, appeared two versts outside Samara; they fled, however, as soon as they saw the cavalry detachment sent against them. The city was cleared of rebels. The victors took six cannon and 200 prisoners. Lieutenant Colonel Grinev and Major General Mansurov arrived in Samara right after Muffel. Mansurov detached a troop to subdue the Kalmyks at Stavropol, but the Kalmyks scattered in all directions, and the detachment had to return to Samara without as much as setting eyes on them.

Colonel Bibikov was detached from Kazan with four platoons of grenadiers and a squadron of hussars to reinforce the troops of Major General Freymann, who had been staying in Bugulma without any action.[35] Bibikov proceeded to march on Zainsk, whose seventy-year-old commandant, Captain Mertvetsov, had received a band of brigands with reverence and put them in full control of the town. The rebels had erected whatever fortifications they could; Bibikov was still five versts from the town when he heard their cannon fire. But their chevaux-de-frise were smashed, their batteries wrested from them, and the outskirts of the town occupied: they all took to their heels. Twenty-five rebel villages were pacified in the area. Up to 4,000 repentant peasants came to Bibikov each day; they were issued documents and allowed to go home.

Derzhavin, who commanded three platoons of musketeers, brought under control the schismatic settlements on the Irgiz and the hordes of nomads that roamed the region between the Iaik and the Volga. Having heard on one occasion that a multitude of common people had gathered in a village with the intention of joining Pugachev's forces, he rode with two Cossacks directly to the meeting place and demanded an explanation from the crowd. Two ringleaders stepped forward, declared their intentions, and started toward Derzhavin leveling accusations and threats. The whole crowd was ready to run riot. But Derzhavin, speaking in a tone of authority, ordered his Cossacks to hang both ringleaders. His order was carried out immediately, and the mob scattered.

Major General Larionov, the commander of the legion sponsored by the nobility, who had been sent to liberate Ufa, did not justify the general trust placed in him. "As a punishment for my sins," wrote General Bibikov, "this cousin of mine A. L. has been foisted on me. He volunteered to command the special detachment himself, but now he won't budge." Larionov stayed in Bakaly, taking no action. His inability to perform his duty forced the commander-in-chief to replace him with an officer who had at one time been wounded under Bibikov's eyes and had distinguished himself in the war against the Confederates—Lieutenant Colonel Mikhelson.

Prince Golitsyn assumed command of Freymann's troops. On January 22 he crossed the Kama. On February 6 Colonel Bibikov joined him, and on the 10th Mansurov. The army was advancing on Orenburg.

Pugachev was aware of its approach, but paid little attention. He trusted that the regulars would defect and the commanding officers would make blunders. "They'll fall into our hands of themselves," he kept telling his associates when they repeatedly advised him to meet the approaching troops midway. In case of a defeat he intended to flee, leaving his horde at the mercy of fate. For this purpose he kept 30 choice fast horses on the best fodder. The Bashkirs suspected what was on his mind, and grumbled. "You roused us up," they said, "but now you want to leave us, letting them hang us as they hanged our fathers." (The executions of 1740 were still fresh in their memory.) The Iaik Cossacks, on the other hand, contemplated handing Pugachev over to the government, thus winning pardon for themselves. They guarded him as if he were a hostage. As the following remarkable lines written to Fonvizin show, Bibikov read both their minds and Pugachev's: "Pugachev is no more than a plaything in the hands of these scoundrels, the Iaik Cossacks: he is not important; what matters is the general discontent."

Pugachev left his camp near Orenburg for Iaitskii Gorodok. His arrival put new life into the rebels' actions. On January 20 he himself led a memorable assault on the fortress. In the night part of the wall was blown off under the battery facing the Staritsa (the Iaik's former riverbed). The rebels, in full battle cry, rushed at the fortress through the smoke and dust, occupied the moat, and tried to scale the wall with ladders, but were toppled and driven back. All the townspeople, including women and children, tried to bolster the assault. Pugachev stood in the moat with spear in hand, first trying to fan the attackers' ardor with blandishments, later stabbing at those who tried to flee. The assault lasted nine hours without interruption, accompanied by the incessant firing of cannon and musketry. At last Second Lieutenant Tolstovalov made a sortie with 50 volunteers, cleared the moat, and drove off the rebels, killing some 400 at the price of no more than 15 of his own men. Pugachev gnashed his teeth. He swore to hang not only Simonov and Krylov themselves, but also Krylov's family, which was in Orenburg at the time. Thus a death sentence was pronounced on a four-year-old boy, who was later to become the famous Krylov.[36]

While in Iaitskii Gorodok, Pugachev saw a young Cossack girl,

Ustinia Kuznetsova, and fell in love with her. He went to ask for her hand. Her amazed mother and father replied, "Have mercy on us, Sovereign! Our daughter is neither princess nor duchess: how could she be your wife? And in any case, how could you marry while the Empress, mother to us all, is still alive?" Nevertheless, Pugachev married Ustinia at the beginning of February, naming her Empress and appointing Cossack women in Iaitsk as her ladies-in-waiting and maids of honor. He expressed his wish that, during *ektenia*, prayers be offered for both the Emperor and Petr Fedorovich and his wife, the Empress Ustinia Petrovna, but his priests refused, saying they had not received permission from the Holy Synod. This upset Pugachev, but he did not persist in his request. His wife remained in Iaitskii Gorodok, where he came to visit her every week. Each time he arrived there was a new attempt on the fortress. But the besieged did not lose heart. Their cannon never grew silent, and their sorties never ceased.

On the night of February 19 a little boy came into the fortress from the town and reported that a tunnel leading to the foundation of the bell tower had been completed the day before, and that 20 *pood* of gunpowder had been placed in it.[37] Pugachev, he said, had chosen the next day for storming the fortress. The report did not seem creditable. Simonov supposed that the urchin had been deliberately sent in order to cause groundless panic. The defenders, though they had engaged in countermining operations, had not heard any sound of excavations; and 20 *pood* of powder would have scarcely sufficed to blow up the tall, six-tiered structure. On the other hand, the fortress's whole powder supply was kept in the cellar under the tower (which the rebels could well have known). The defenders decided to bring the powder out at once; they also tore up the brick floor of the cellar and began countermining. The garrison was all prepared for an explosion and an assault. Two hours had scarcely passed when the mine exploded, causing the bell tower to sway gently. Its lower chamber collapsed and the six upper tiers settled on it, crushing some people who had been standing close by. The stones of the structure, not scattered by the detonation, collapsed into one pile. The six sentries posted at a cannon on the top tier dropped down alive; one of them, asleep at the time, not only did not suffer any harm, but did not even wake up as he fell.

Even as the tower was still in the process of collapsing, the fortress's cannon were already being fired; the garrison troops, who had been standing under arms, immediately occupied the ruins of the tower and set up a battery amid the rubble. The rebels, who had not expected to be met quite this way, stopped in bewilderment; a few minutes later they issued their usual cry, but none went forward. In vain did the leaders shout, "Charge, brave atamans, charge!" No assault transpired. The war cries continued until dawn, when the rebels dispersed, grumbling against Pugachev, who had assured them that when the bell tower blew up, it would shower stones on the fortress and crush the whole garrison.

The next day Pugachev received news from his camp of Prince Golitsyn's approach. He hurriedly left for Berda, taking 500 cavalrymen and a supply train of some 1,500 wagons with him. The news reached the defenders of the fortress too. They rejoiced, calculating that a relief force would reach them in a couple of weeks. But in fact the moment of their liberation was still far off.

During Pugachev's frequent travels, Shigaev, Padurov, and Khlopusha directed the siege of Orenburg. Taking advantage of the leader's absence, Khlopusha concocted a plan for overrunning Iletskaia Zashchita (where rock salt is mined), and at the end of February, he stormed the outpost with 400 men. He was able to occupy it with the help of convicts working there—his own family among them. All government property was plundered; all the officers, except for one saved at the convicts' request, were slaughtered; and the convicts were signed into the rebels' band. When Pugachev returned to Berda, he was piqued at the bold convict's wantonness and reproved him for destroying Zashchita, causing damage to state property. He took the field against Prince Golitsyn with 10,000 selected troops, leaving Shigaev below Orenburg with 2,000 men. On the eve of his departure he gave orders to strangle one of his faithful followers, Dmitrii Lysov. A few days earlier he and Lysov, both drunk, had quarreled on the way from Kargala to Berda. Lysov charged at Pugachev from behind and struck him with his spear. Pugachev fell off his horse, but the coat of mail he always wore under his clothes saved his life. Subsequently their comrades reconciled them, and Pugachev even sat drinking with Lysov a few hours before the latter's death.

Pugachev took forts Totskaia and Sorochinsk, and with his usual boldness, attacked Golitsyn's vanguard at night, in a heavy snowstorm. He was repulsed, however, by Majors Pushkin and Elagin. The courageous Elagin was killed in this battle. Just at this time Mansurov joined forces with Prince Golitsyn. Pugachev retreated to Novosergievskaia, with no time to burn the forts he was vacating. Golitsyn, leaving his supplies at Sorochinsk under the protection of 400 men and eight cannon, marched forward after two days. Pugachev at first moved toward Iletskii Gorodok, but then suddenly turned in the direction of Tatishchev; he took up position there and started improving its defenses. Golitsyn had earlier detached Lieutenant Colonel Bedriaga, with three squadrons of cavalry supported by infantry and artillery, to Iletskii Gorodok, while he himself advanced along a straight route to Perevolotskaia; Bedriaga subsequently rejoined him there. Leaving their supply train under the protection of a battalion commanded by Lieutenant Colonel Grinev, they advanced on Tatishchev on March 22.

Pugachev had taken and burned that fort the year before, but by now it had been restored. The burned-down wooden palisades had been replaced by walls of snow. His preparations astonished Prince Golitsyn, who had not expected him to be so well versed in warcraft. Golitsyn at first detached 300 men to reconnoiter the enemy. The rebels hid, allowing the reconnoiterers to come right up to the fort, and then suddenly made a sally. Their thrust was checked, however, by two squadrons that had been sent forward to reinforce the reconnoiterers. Colonel Bibikov also threw into action his jaegers, who, skiing fast on top of the deep snow, occupied all vantage points. Golitsyn arranged his troops in two columns, advanced on the fort, and opened fire, to which the fort responded in kind. The shooting continued for three hours. Seeing that his cannon alone could not overpower the enemy, Golitsyn threw Freymann with the left column into attack. Pugachev brought seven fieldpieces outside to counter him, but Freymann's forces overran these and stormed the frozen walls. The rebels put up a desperate defense but had to yield to the superiority of a properly trained army; they soon fled in all directions. The cavalry, which until then had been kept in reserve, pursued them along all the roads. The bloodshed was horrendous. Some 1,300 rebels were slaughtered within a radius of 20 versts. Golitsyn lost about 400 men killed or wounded, among them over 20 officers. It was a decisive victory. The victor took 36 cannon and over 3,000 prisoners. Pugachev broke through the enemy lines with 60 Cossacks and arrived in Berda, bringing the news of his defeat, with a total of four companions. The rebels began to flee from the village, some on horseback, some in sleds. They piled their wagons high with their plunder. The women and children went on foot. Afraid of drunkenness and mutiny, Pugachev gave orders to smash the barrels of spirits standing near his house. The spirits poured out on the street. In the meanwhile Shigaev, seeing that all was lost, schemed to earn himself a pardon: he detained Pugachev and Khlopusha, and sent an emissary to the governor of Orenburg offering to hand over the pretender and asking the governor to signal his agreement with two shots from a cannon. The centurion Loginov, who had fled with Pugachev earlier, brought the offer to Reinsdorp. The poor governor could not believe his luck, and for two full hours could not make up his mind whether to give the required signal! In the meanwhile some convicts still in Berda released Pugachev and Khlopusha. Pugachev fled with ten fieldpieces, with his booty, and with the remainder of his mob, numbering 2,000. Khlopusha galloped to Kargala hoping to save his wife and son. The Tatars tied him up and sent word to the governor. The famous convict was brought to Orenburg, where they finally beheaded him in June 1774.

The citizens of Orenburg, learning of their liberation, dashed out of the city in large crowds, close on the heels of the 600 infantry soldiers Reinsdorp dispatched to the abandoned village of Berda, and helped themselves to provisions. Eighteen cannon, 17 barrelfuls of copper coins, and a large quantity of grain were found in the village. The people of Orenburg hastened to offer thanks to God for their unexpected liberation. They exalted Golitsyn. Reinsdorp wrote to him to congratulate him on his victory, calling him the liberator of Orenburg. Supplies began arriving in the city from all directions. Abundance had returned, and the harrowing siege of six months was forgotten in one joyous moment. On March 26 Golitsyn came to Orenburg and was received with indescribable enthusiasm.

Bibikov had been waiting for this turning point with impatience. He had left Kazan in order to speed up the military operations, but he had got only as far as Bugulma when news of the complete victory over Pugachev reached him. He could not contain his joy. "What a weight off my mind," he wrote to his wife on March 26. "My army will enter Orenburg today; I am hurrying there, too, to be able to direct the operations more easily. The streak of gray, God is my witness, has increased in my beard, and my hairline has receded even more; but even so I go around without a wig in the freezing weather."

In the meanwhile Pugachev, eluding all the patrols that had been sent out, reached the village of Seitov on the 24th,[38] set it on fire, and advanced to Sakmara, collecting a new mob along the way. He evidently surmised that from Tatishchev Golitsyn would turn toward Iaitskii Gorodok with all his forces, and therefore he suddenly came back to reoccupy Berda, hoping also to take Orenburg by surprise. Golitsyn, however, was advised of this bold move by Colonel Khorvat, who had been on Pugachev's tracks ever since he had left Tatishchev. Reinforcing his troops with the infantry and Cossack detachments stationed in Orenburg—giving the Cossacks the last horses from under his own officers—Golitsyn set out against the pretender immediately, and made contact with him at Kargala. Pugachev, realizing he had miscalculated, beat a retreat, cleverly taking advantage of the topography of the area. He set up seven fieldpieces against Colonels Bibikov and Arshenevskii astride the narrow road and, under their protection, adroitly dashed off toward the Sakmara River. By now, however, Bibikov's fieldpieces had arrived too; his men took a hill and set up a battery. Khorvat, on his part, attacked the rebels in the last gorge through which the road passed, wrested their fieldpieces from them, routed them, and chased their hordes all the way to Sakmara, entering it close on their heels. Pugachev lost his last fieldpiece, 400 men killed, and 3,500 taken prisoner. His chief followers—Shigaev, Pochitalin, Padurov, and others—were among those captured. He fled with four factory serfs to Prechistenskaia, and from there to the Ural factories. The tired cavalry could not catch up with him. After this decisive victory, Golitsyn returned to Orenburg and detached Freymann to pacify Bashkiria, Arshenevskii to mop up along the New Moscow Road, and Mansurov to Iletsk to mop up that region and then proceed to liberate Simonov.

Mikhelson's maneuvers were just as successful. Having taken command of his detachment on March 18, he immediately set out for Ufa. Chika dispatched 2,000 men with four fieldpieces to block his advance. They waited for him in the village of Zhukovo. Leaving them at his rear, Mikhelson headed straight for Chesnokovka, where Chika stood with 10,000 rebels. On his way he scattered a few smaller rebel detachments, and at dawn on the 25th he arrived at the village of Trebikova (five versts from Chesnokovka). Here a band of rebels with two fieldpieces engaged him, but Major Kharin crushed and scattered them while the jaegers took possession of the fieldpieces. Mikhelson was able to move on. His supply train was protected by 100 men with one fieldpiece, who also served as a rear guard in case of attack. He encountered more rebels at dawn on the 26th, outside the village of Zubovo. Some of them sallied forth on skis or on horseback and, spreading out on either side of the highway, tried to encircle him, while a force of 3,000 men, supported by 10 fieldpieces, met him head-on. At the same time a battery inside the village opened fire. The battle lasted four hours. The rebels fought bravely. At last Mikhelson, seeing that a detachment of horsemen was arriving to reinforce the rebels, flung all his forces at their central corps and ordered his own cavalry, which had dismounted at the beginning of the engagement, to remount and rush to the charge with sabers. The first line of the enemy's defense took to flight, abandoning the fieldpieces. Kharin, hacking at them all the way to Chesnokovka, entered the village close on their heels. In the meanwhile the cavalry detachment coming to reinforce them at Zubovo had been repulsed; its members, too, began to flee to Chesnokovka, were met by Kharin, and were captured to a man. The skiers, who had managed to get around Mikhelson's main corps and cut off his supply train, were smashed by two platoons of grenadiers. They scattered into the woods. Three thousand rebels were taken prisoner. Serfs assigned to factory work and peasants under the jurisdiction of the College of the Management of Ecclesiastic Affairs were sent home to their villages.[39] Twenty-five fieldpieces and a large quantity of munitions were captured. Mikhelson hanged two leading insurgents: a Bashkir elder and the elected head of the village of Chesnokovka. The siege of Ufa was lifted. Mikhelson, without stopping, proceeded to Tabynsk, where Ulianov and Chika had escaped from Chesnokovka. There they were seized by some Cossacks and surrendered to the victor, who sent them to Ufa in fetters. Mikhelson detailed patrols in all directions and was able to restore order in most of the villages that had rebelled.

Iletskii Gorodok and the forts of Nizhne-Ozernaia and Rassypnaia, which had witnessed Pugachev's first successes, had by now been abandoned by the rebels. Their rebel commanders, Chuloshnikov and Kizilbashin, fled to Iaitskii Gorodok. The day they arrived, news of the pretender's defeat at Tatishchev reached them. Rebels fleeing from Khorvat's hussars galloped through the forts shouting, "Run for your lives, fellows, all is lost!" They hastily bandaged their wounds and hurried to Iaitskii Gorodok. The spring thaw set in, clearing the rivers of ice; the corpses of those killed at Tatishchev floated downstream, past the forts. Wives and mothers stood on the riverbanks, trying to identify their husbands or sons among the corpses. An old Cossack woman wandered along the Iaik by Nizhne-Ozernaia every day, drawing the floating corpses to the bank with a crooked stick and saying, "Is that you, my child? Is it you, my Stepushka? Are these your black curls, washed by the waves?" And when she saw an unfamiliar face she gently pushed the corpse away.[40]

On April 6–7 Mansurov occupied the abandoned forts and Iletskii Gorodok, where he found 14 cannon. On the 15th, as he was fording the swollen stream Bykovka under dangerous conditions, Ovchinnikov, Perfilev, and Degterev pounced on him. They were beaten back and scattered; Bedriaga and Borodin chased after them, but the bad condition of the roads saved the band's leaders.

The fortress at Iaitsk had been invested since the beginning of the year. Pugachev's absence had not cooled the rebels' fighting spirit. Crowbars and spades were forged at the smithies; new batteries were put up. The rebels assiduously continued their excavations, now breaking down the Chechora's levee, thereby cutting off communication between the two parts of the town, now digging trenches in order to block sorties. They were planning to dig a tunnel into the Staritsa's steep bank, all the way around under the fortress, in order to undermine the main church, the batteries, and the commandant's palace. The defenders found themselves in constant danger and were forced to dig counter-tunnels on all sides, working with great difficulty to break up ground that was frozen an *arshin* deep. They partitioned the inside of the fortress with a new wall and with barricades made of sacks filled with bricks from the blown-up bell tower.

At dawn on March 9, 250 regulars sallied out of the fortress with the aim of destroying a new battery that had been severely harassing them. They reached the town barricades, but there they encountered strong fire. Their ranks were broken. The rebels caught them in the narrow passages between the barricades and the houses to which they had intended to set fire; they slaughtered them, even those already wounded and falling; they chopped their heads off with axes. The soldiers beat a retreat. Some 30 were killed, and 80 wounded. Never had the garrison suffered so much loss from a sortie. All they had succeeded in doing was to burn down one battery, not the main one at that, and a few houses. The testimony they extracted from three rebels brought back as prisoners deepened the defenders' despondency, for the prisoners told them about the mines under the fortress and about Pugachev's expected arrival. The frightened Simonov gave orders to start new projects: they kept probing the ground around his house with augers and began digging a new trench. The men were exhausted, not only because of the hard work, but also because they got scarcely any sleep at night: half of the garrison always remained under arms, and the other half was only allowed to sleep sitting up. The hospital filled with invalids; the provisions left could not last more than 10 days. The soldiers' daily ration was reduced to a quarter of a pound of flour, one-tenth of their regular allowance. They ran out of both groats and salt. The soldiers would boil some water in a common cauldron, whiten it with a little flour, drink a cupful—and that was their daily meal. The women, unable to endure the hunger any longer, began asking for permission to leave the fort, and they were told they could go. A few debilitated and sick soldiers followed their lead. These men were not admitted into the town at all; but the women were kept under arrest for a night and then herded back to the fortress with the promise that they would be received and fed if the rebels' comrades kept in the fortress were released. Simonov, wary of increasing the enemy's numbers, could not agree to that condition. The hunger became more and more horrible every day. The horsemeat, which had been distributed by the pound, was all gone. Everyone began eating cats and dogs. Some dead horses thrown out on the ice at the beginning of the siege three months before were now remembered, and people eagerly gnawed at bones already stripped bare of their meat by the dogs. Finally even this supply ran out. New resources for sustenance were being invented. A kind of clay was found that was exceptionally soft and free of sand. People tried to cook it, making a kind of blancmange from it, and started eating it. The soldiers lost all their strength. Some could no longer walk. Infants of sick mothers wasted away. The women tried several times to touch the rebels' hearts, throwing themselves at their feet and begging to be allowed to stay in the town. They were chased back with the earlier demands. Only some Cossack women were admitted. The long-expected relief had not come. The defenders had to postpone their hopes from day to day, from week to week. The rebels shouted to the garrison that the government's troops had been crushed, that Orenburg, Ufa, and Kazan had already bowed down before the pretender, and that he would soon be coming to Iaitskii Gorodok, by which time there would be no mercy. On the other hand, they promised in his name that surrender would bring not only pardon but even rewards. They tried to impress the same on the minds of the poor women who were pleading to be allowed into the town. The commanders could not raise the hopes of the besieged by references to relief soon to come, because nobody would even listen to them without indignation: such despair had gripped them in their long futile waiting! What the commanders did try to do was to maintain the garrison's loyalty and obedience by emphasizing that no one could save his life by a disgraceful desertion, since the rebels, enraged by the garrison's long resistance, would not spare even those who broke their oaths. They tried to awaken in the souls of their unfortunate soldiers a trust in God, omnipotent and omniscient; and the sufferers, their spirits raised, would repeat that it was better to put one's fate into God's hands than to serve the impostor. Indeed no more than two or three men defected from the fortress during the whole time of the harrowing siege.

Passion Week came. The defenders had been eating nothing but clay for 15 days. None wanted to die of starvation. They decided that all of them (except those entirely incapacitated) would participate in a last sally. With no hope for victory (the rebels had erected such fortifications that they were unapproachable from the fortress on any side), they simply wanted to die the honorable death of soldiers.

On Tuesday, the day assigned for the sally, the sentries posted on the roof of the main church noticed that the rebels were running about town in confusion, saying good-bye to one another, congregating in large groups, and eventually riding out into the steppe. The Cossack women were going with them. The besieged suspected that something unusual was going on, and their hopes were raised once more. "All this buoyed our spirit so much," writes an eyewitness who had lived through all the horrors of the siege, "as if we had each eaten a piece of bread." But the confusion gradually abated, and everything seemed to have returned to normal. The defenders fell into even deeper despondency. In silence they fixed their gaze on the steppe, whence, only a short time before, they had expected their liberators to emerge... Then, suddenly, toward five o'clock in the afternoon, clouds of dust appeared in the distance, and whole legions could be seen galloping out in disarray one after another, from behind a wood. Everybody dashed to the gates, each to the one closest to his house. The besieged realized that the insurgents had been beaten and were on the run; but they still did not dare rejoice, fearing a last desperate assault. The townspeople ran up and down the streets as if the town were burning. Toward evening they rang the bells in the cathedral, gathered in a circle, and approached the fortress in one great throng. The defenders were getting ready to beat them back, but they noticed that the rebels were leading forward their leaders, Atamans Kargin and Tolkachev, tied up. The crowd came up close and loudly pleaded for mercy. Simonov admitted them, though he could hardly believe his deliverance. The garrison threw themselves on the loaves of bread brought by the townspeople. "There were still four days left until Easter Sunday," writes one eyewitness of these events, "but for us that day was already the holy day of resurrection." Even those who had been bound to their beds by weakness or disease recovered on the instant. The whole fortress was in an uproar, with everybody giving thanks to God and congratulating each other; that night no one slept a wink. The townspeople told the defenders about the lifting of the siege of Orenburg and Mansurov's impending arrival. On April 17 he did arrive. The gates of the fortress, which had been locked and obstructed since December 30, were opened. Mansurov assumed command of the city. The leaders of the rebellion, Kargin, Tolkachev, and Gorshkov, as well as the pretender's illegitimate wife Ustinia Kuznetsova, were taken to Orenburg under guard.

Such was the success that crowned the measures taken by an experienced, intelligent commander-in-chief. But Bibikov did not have the opportunity to complete what he had begun: tired out by work, worry, and troubles, taking little care of his already failing health, he developed a fever in Bugulma. Sensing that his end was approaching, he gave some last instructions. He sealed all his confidential papers, with instructions to have them delivered to the Empress, and handed the commandership over to his highest-ranking officer, Lieutenant General Shcherbatov. He still had time to send a report to the Empress about the liberation of Ufa, of which he had just received some oral reports, but soon after, on April 9 at 11 A.M., he died. He was in his forty-fourth year. His body had to remain on the bank of the Kama for several days, because it was impossible to cross the river at the time. The citizens of Kazan wanted to inter their deliverer in their cathedral, erecting a monument to him, but Bibikov's family wished to have his body brought to his village. A ribbon of the Order of St. Andrew, the title of senator, and the rank of Colonel of the Guards were too late to reach him alive. On his deathbed he had said: "I do not feel sorry to leave my wife and children, for the Empress will look after them; I feel sorry to part with my fatherland."

A rumor attributed his death to poisoning, supposedly by a Confederate. Derzhavin wrote a poem about his demise. Catherine wept over him and showered his family with favors. Petersburg and Moscow were seized with fear. Soon the whole of Russia was to realize what an irreparable loss had befallen her.

Chapter Six

Pugachev's new success.—Salavat, the Bashkir.—The taking of forts in Siberia.—The battle at Troitsk.—Pugachev's retreat.—His first encounter with Mikhelson.—In pursuit of Pugachev.—The inactivity of the government troops.—The taking of Osa.—Pugachev outside Kazan.

Pugachev, whose position seemed to be desperate, turned up at the Avziano-Petrovsk metalworks. Ovchinnikov and Perfilev, pursued by Major Shevich, rode across the Sakmara Line with 300 Iaik Cossacks and managed to join forces with Pugachev. The Stavropol and Orenburg Kalmyks wanted to follow suit, and advanced, with 600 covered wagons, toward Fort Sorochinsk. Retired Lieutenant Colonel Melkovich, an intelligent and resolute man, was in the fort at the time on a foraging mission. He assumed command of the garrison, attacked the Kalmyks, and forced them to return to their respective residences.

Pugachev moved quickly from one place to another. Mobs started to gather around him as before; the Bashkirs, who had been almost entirely pacified, rebelled again. The commandant of Fort Verkhne-Iaitsk, Colonel Stupishin, penetrated Bashkiriia and burned down some deserted villages; he caught one of the rebels, had his ears, nose, and right-hand fingers cut off, and let him go with the threat that he would do the same to all the other insurgents. But the Bashkirs did not relent. The old troublemaker Iulai, who had gone into hiding at the time of the executions of 1741, reappeared among them with his son Salavat. The whole of Bashkiriia rose up in arms, the conflagration spreading with even greater force than before. Freymann was supposed to pursue Pugachev while Mikhelson made every effort to cross his path, but the spring condition of the roads saved him. The highways were impassable; people were mired in bottomless mud; rivers swelled to widths of several versts; and streams became rivers. Freymann stopped in Sterlitamak. Mikhelson, who had managed to cross the Viatka while it was still iced over, and the Ufa in eight boats, continued his forward march despite all the impediments, and on March 5, near the Sim metalworks, caught up with a horde of Bashkirs under the command of the fierce Salavat. Mikhelson routed them, liberated the factory, and continued his advance the next day. Salavat took up position 18 versts from the metalworks, waiting for Beloborodov. They subsequently joined forces and took the field against Mikhelson with 2,000 rebels and eight fieldpieces. Mikhelson beat them once more, seizing their fieldpieces, slaying some 300 of their numbers on the spot, and scattering the rest. He then hurried on to the Uiskoe metalworks in the hope of catching up with Pugachev himself, but soon learned that the pretender was already at the Beloretsk plants.

Beyond the Iuriuzan River Mikhelson succeeded in crushing another rebel horde, pursuing them all the way to the Satkin works. Here he learned that Pugachev, having rallied some 6,000 Bashkirs and peasants, had advanced on Fort Magnitnaia. Mikhelson decided to move deeper into the Ural Mountains in the hope of joining forces with Freymann near the headwaters of the Iaik.

After plundering and burning down the Beloretsk metalworks, Pugachev quickly crossed the Ural Mountains, and on May 5 he set siege to Magnitnaia, even though he had no cannon with him. Captain Tikhanovskii defended the fort bravely. Pugachev himself took an arm wound from grapeshot and withdrew, having suffered considerable losses. It appeared as though the fort had been saved, but it soon became evident that there was a traitor within: one night the fort's powder magazine was blown up, after which the rebels stormed it, tore down the palisades, and rushed inside. Tikhanovskii and his wife were both hanged; the fort was plundered and burned down. The same day Beloborodov joined Pugachev with a mob of 4,000 rebels.

Lieutenant General Dekalong advanced from the recently liberated Cheliabinsk in the direction of Fort Verkhne-Iaitsk, hoping to catch Pugachev still at the Beloretsk works, but no sooner had he reached the Orenburg Line than he received a report from Colonel Stupishin, the commandant at Verkhne-Iaitsk, informing him that Pugachev was proceeding up the Line from one fort to another, just as he had done at the beginning of his dread career. Dekalong hurried on toward Verkhne-Iaitsk. As soon as he reached it, he heard of the taking of Magnitnaia. He set off toward Kizilskoe. He had already covered 15 versts when he learned from a captured Bashkir that Pugachev, having heard of the approach of government troops, was no longer heading for Kizilskoe but was taking a route straight across the Ural Mountains toward Karagaiskii. Dekalong turned around. Arriving at Karagaiskii, he saw only smoking ruins: Pugachev had left the day before. Dekalong hoped to catch up with him at Petropavlovka but missed him there, too. The fort was ravaged and burned, and its church had been plundered, the icons stripped of their frames and smashed to smithereens.

Dekalong left the Line and took a shortcut straight to Fort Uiskoe. He was down to his last day's supply of oats. He thought he might be able to catch up with Pugachev at Fort Stepnaia if not before; but he soon learned that even Stepnaia had already been taken; he rushed to Troitsk. On the way there, in Sanarka, he found a great many people who had escaped from the destroyed forts in the vicinity. Officers' wives and children, barefooted and in rags, were sobbing, not knowing where to seek refuge. Dekalong took them under his protection, entrusting them to the care of his officers. On the morning of May 21, after a forced march of 60 versts, he drew near Troitsk and at last set eyes on Pugachev, who had pitched camp outside the fort, which he had taken the day before. Dekalong attacked immediately. Pugachev had more than 10,000 troops and some 30 cannon. The engagement lasted four long hours. Pugachev lay in his tent through it all, suffering from the wound he had received at Magnitnaia. Beloborodov was in charge of operations. At last the rebels' ranks were broken. Pugachev, his arm in a sling, got on his horse and rushed from one place to another, trying to restore order, but his troops were all scattered and running. He got away with one fieldpiece and headed toward Cheliabinsk. It was impossible to pursue him; the cavalry was far too tired. Dekalong found some 3,000 people of both sexes, of all ages, from all walks of life, at the camp: they had been rounded up by the pretender and consigned to doom. The fort was saved from fire and pillage, but its commandant, Brigadier Freierwahr, had been killed in the previous day's assault, and his officers had been hanged.

Pugachev and Beloborodov, knowing that the exhaustion of Dekalong's troops and horses would not allow him to take advantage of his victory, reassembled their scattered hordes and began an orderly retreat, taking forts and mustering fresh forces along the way. Majors Gagrin and Zholobov, detached by Dekalong the day after the battle to pursue them, could not catch up with them.

Mikhelson in the meanwhile was advancing along little-known roads across the Ural Mountains. The Bashkir villages were deserted. It was impossible to obtain the necessary supplies. His detachment was in constant danger from the many bands of rebels swirling around it. On May 13 a group of Bashkirs, led by their seditious elder, fell on him. They fought so frantically that they would not surrender even when he had driven them back, into a swamp. All, except one who was forcibly saved, were slain together with their leader. Mikhelson lost one officer and 60 men killed or wounded.

The captive Bashkir, whom Mikhelson treated with kindness, told him about the taking of Magnitnaia and the movements of Dekalong. Mikhelson, finding these reports consistent with his own assumptions, left the mountains and advanced on Troitsk in the hope of either being able to liberate that fort or encountering Pugachev should he be retreating. He soon heard about Dekalong's victory and proceeded to Varlamovo with the intention of blocking Pugachev's way. And indeed, on the morning of May 22, as he approached Varlamovo, he ran into Pugachev's vanguard. Seeing an orderly troop, Mikhelson could not at first imagine this to be the remnant of the horde beaten just the other day, and he took it (as he says jokingly in his report) for the corps of Lieutenant General Cavalier Dekalong. He soon realized his mistake, however, and he stopped, retaining his advantageous position next to a forest that provided cover for his rear. Pugachev at first marched on him, but then suddenly turned off toward Fort Chebarkul. Mikhelson cut across the wood and intercepted Pugachev. This was the first time the pretender came face to face with the man who was to strike so many blows at him and was to put an end to his bloody enterprise. Pugachev immediately attacked his left flank, threw it into disarray, and wrested away two fieldpieces. But Mikhelson bore down on the rebels with the whole of his cavalry and managed to scatter them in one minute, taking back his fieldpieces along with the last cannon that had remained in Pugachev's possession after his defeat at Troitsk. Some 600 rebels lay slain on the field, 500 were taken prisoner, and the rest were pursued for several versts. Nightfall interrupted the chase. Mikhelson spent the night on the battlefield. In the next day's orders he severely reprimanded the platoon that had lost its fieldpieces, and he stripped the soldiers of their buttons and brassards until such time as they merited them again. Indeed the platoon soon made amends for its dishonorable conduct.

On the 23d Mikhelson marched on Fort Chebarkul. The Cossacks stationed there had mutinied, but Mikhelson administered a new oath to them, signing them into his own corps, and they gave him no reason thereafter not to be perfectly satisfied with them.

Zholobov and Gagrin operated slowly and indecisively. Having informed Mikhelson that Pugachev had rallied his scattered horde and was mustering new forces, Zholobov refused to march against the rebel under the pretext of flooding rivers and bad roads. Mikhelson complained to Dekalong. Although Dekalong promised to come forward to extirpate Pugachev's last remaining forces, he in fact remained in Cheliabinsk and, to make matters worse, ordered Zholobov and Gagrin to join him.

Thus the task of pursuing Pugachev was left to Mikhelson alone. Having heard of the presence of some Iaik Cossack rebels at the Zlatoust metalworks, he went there, but the rebels learned of his approach and escaped. The farther their traces led, the less distinct they became, and they finally disappeared altogether.

On May 27 Mikhelson arrived at the Satkin works. Salavat was ravaging the surrounding countryside with a fresh band. The Sim metalworks had already been plundered and burned by him. Hearing of Mikhelson, he crossed the Ai River and stayed in the mountains, where Pugachev, no longer pursued by Gagrin and Zholobov, managed to join him with a ragtag mob of 2,000.

At the Satkin works, which had been saved thanks to his celerity, Mikhelson took his first rest since his departure from Ufa. He set out against Pugachev and Salavat two days later and came to the bank of the Ai. The bridges had been dismantled. The rebels, seeing the small size of Mikhelson's detachment, felt safe on the other side of the river.

On the morning of the 30th, however, Mikhelson ordered 50 Cossacks to swim their horses across the river, each double riding with a jaeger behind him. The rebels were ready to fall on this group but were scattered by cannon fire from the other side. The jaegers and Cossacks held the bridgehead as best they could while Mikhelson forded the river with the rest of the detachment: the gunpowder was carried by the cavalry, and the fieldpieces were sunk to the bottom and dragged across by ropes. Mikhelson quickly attacked the enemy forces, crushed them, and pursued them for 20 versts, killing some 400 and taking a great many prisoners. Pugachev, Beloborodov, and Salavat—the last one wounded—just barely managed to escape.

The surrounding countryside was deserted. Mikhelson could find no one to tell him where the enemy had fled. He set out in a randomly chosen direction, and during the night of June 2 Captain Kartashev-skii, whom he had detached with a vanguard, found himself sur-rounded by Salavat's band. Mikhelson arrived at the location in the morning, in time to help. The rebels scattered and fled. Mikhelson pursued them with utmost caution: his infantry protected his supply train, and he himself rode at the head of the column, accompanied by some of the cavalry. This arrangement was what saved him. A large band of rebels suddenly surrounded his supply train and attacked his infantry. Pugachev himself led them: in a matter of six days he had gathered some 5,000 rebels around the Satkin works. Mikhelson gal-loped back to the supply train to help, and stayed there with the infan-try while Kharin went off to consolidate the cavalry. The rebels were beaten and took flight once more. Mikhelson learned from captives that Pugachev intended to march on Ufa. He rushed ahead to inter-cept him and on June 5 encountered him again. An engagement was inevitable. Mikhelson attacked quickly, defeating and driving away the enemy once more.

Despite all his success, Mikhelson saw that he needed to interrupt his pursuit of the enemy for a while. He had run out of both provi-sions and munition. Each man had only two cartridges left. Mikhel-son went to Ufa in order to stock up with everything he needed.

While Mikhelson, rushing this way and that, kept striking at the enemy, the other leaders of the army remained stationary. Dekalong stood at Cheliabinsk and, envying Mikhelson's success, deliberately avoided cooperating with him. Freymann, a physically courageous man but a timid, indecisive leader, stayed at Fort Kizilskoe, fretting about Timashev, who had gone off to Fort Zilair with his best cavalry. Stanislavskii had already distinguished himself by cowardice in all the proceedings, but when he heard that Pugachev had gathered a sig-nificant mob and was near Fort Verkhne-Iaitsk, he refused all further service and fled to Fort Orsk—his favorite hiding place. Colonels Iakubovich and Obernibesov, together with Major Duve, were near Ufa, but they allowed the rebellious Bashkirs to assemble all around them undisturbed. Birsk was burned down almost under their very eyes, but they just marched from one place to another, avoiding the remotest danger and not giving one thought to coordinating their actions. In obedience to Prince Shcherbatov's instructions, Golitsyn's troops remained in the vicinity of Orenburg and Iaitskii Gorodok, where they were entirely useless since these places were already out of danger, while the region where the conflagration was spreading again, was left defenseless.

Pugachev, driven away from Kungur by Major Popov, was about to advance on Ekaterinburg, but hearing of the troops stationed there, he turned off toward Krasnoufimsk.

The Kama region was left open, and Kazan exposed to danger. Von Brandt hurriedly dispatched Major Skrypitsyn with a garrison detachment and armed peasants to the town of Osa, and at the same time wrote to Prince Shcherbatov demanding immediate help. Shcherbatov, however, placed his hopes in Obernibesov and Duve, who were supposed to come to Major Skrypitsyn's assistance in case of danger, and he took no new measures.

On June 18 Pugachev appeared outside Osa. Skrypitsyn took the field against him, but on losing three cannon at the very beginning of the engagement, he hastily withdrew into the fort. Pugachev ordered his men to dismount and to storm the fort. They entered the town and burned it, but they were driven away from the fort itself by cannon fire.

The next day Pugachev and some of his chief associates rode over to the Kama, looking for a convenient place to cross it. He ordered his men to cover muddy stretches of the highway with logs and brushwood. On the 20th he stormed the fort once more, and was driven back once more. After this, Beloborodov advised him to encircle the fort with wagons full of hay, straw, and birch bark with which to set the wooden walls on fire. Fifteen wagons were drawn by horses to within a short distance of the fort, and then pushed forward by men who were safe behind them. At this juncture Skrypitsyn, who had already wavered somewhat, asked for a one-day truce, and on the following day he surrendered, receiving Pugachev on his knees, with icons and bread and salt. The pretender treated him kindly and allowed him to continue wearing his sword. The hapless major thought that in time he could justify himself, and he composed, together with Captain Smirnov and Lieutenant Mineev, a letter to the governor of Kazan, which he carried around with him, waiting for an opportunity to send it off secretly. Mineev told Pugachev about this. The letter was confiscated, Skrypitsyn and Smirnov were hanged, and the informer was promoted to colonel.

On June 23 Pugachev crossed the Kama and advanced on the Izhevsk and Votkinsk distilleries. The director, Wenzel, was tortured to death, the plants were plundered, and the workers were signed into the villainous horde. Mineev, who had earned Pugachev's trust by his treachery, advised him to march straight on Kazan. Familiar with the precautions the governor had taken, he offered to lead Pugachev, guaranteeing success. Pugachev did not vacillate for long: he marched on Kazan.

The news of the fall of Osa frightened Shcherbatov. He sent an order to Obernibesov to occupy the ferry at Shuni and dispatched Major Mellin to the one at Shurma.[41] Golitsyn was ordered to proceed to Ufa as fast as possible and to operate in that region according to his best judgment. Shcherbatov himself set out for Bugulma with a squadron of hussars and a platoon of grenadiers.

There were only 1,500 troops in Kazan, but 6,000 of the local citizenry were armed in haste. Von Brandt and the military commandant, Banner, prepared to defend the city. Major General Potemkin, the chairman of the secret commission created to investigate the Pugachev revolt, helped them in every way he could. Major General Larionov, on the other hand, did not wait for Pugachev's arrival: he and his men crossed the Volga and decamped for Nizhnii Novgorod.

Colonel Tolstoi, commander of the Kazan cavalry legion, took the field against Pugachev and on July 10 made contact with him 12 versts from the city. A battle ensued. The brave Tolstoi was killed, his troops scattered. The next day Pugachev appeared on the left bank of the Kazanka and pitched camp near the Troitsk mill. In the evening he rode out, in plain view of all the inhabitants, to inspect the city, then returned to his camp, postponing the assault until the next morning.

Chapter Seven

Pugachev in Kazan.—Catastrophe in the city.—Mikhelson's arrival.—Three battles.—The liberation of Kazan.—Pugachev meets his family.—Refutation of a libel.—Measures taken by Mikhelson.

At dawn on July 12 the rebels, under Pugachev's command, stretched their columns from the village of Tsaritsyn across Arskoe Field, pushing wagons loaded with hay and straw interspersed with fieldpieces. They quickly occupied the brick barns built close to the suburb, a coppice, and Kudriavtsev's suburban house; there they set up their batteries, sweeping aside the small detachment that guarded the highway. The detachment retreated in square formation, defending itself by using chevaux-de-frise.

The city's main battery was positioned directly opposite Arskoe field. Pugachev did not attack on that side, but sent a detachment of factory peasants from his right wing, under the command of the traitor Mineev, toward the suburb. This herd of riffraff, mostly unarmed and driven forward by the Cossacks' whips, nimbly ran from gully to gully and hollow to hollow, scrambling across ridges exposed to cannon fire, until it reached the ravines on the very edge of the suburb. This dangerous point was defended by grammar school students equipped with one cannon. Despite fire from this cannon, the rebels carried out to the letter the instructions Pugachev had given them: they clambered onto the promontory, chased the students away with their bare fists, took charge of the cannon, and occupied the governor's summer residence, which had a gate opening into the suburb; they placed the cannon in that gate, started firing into the streets, and burst into the suburb in packs. On the other side, Pugachev's left wing assaulted the Drapers' Quarter. The drapers (of different classes, but most of them skilled boxers) were encouraged by Archbishop Veniamin to arm themselves as best they could; they set up a cannon at Gorlov's tavern, and were ready to defend the area. The Bashkirs shot their arrows at them from Sharnaia Hill and charged into the streets. The drapers were about to counterattack with crowbars, spears, and sabers, but their cannon blew up, killing the cannoneer, the first time they tried to fire it. At the same time Pugachev set up his fieldpieces on Sharnaia Hill and fired grapeshot at both his own men and the drapers. The quarter caught fire. The drapers fled. The rebels swept away the guards and the chevaux-de-frise, and dashed into the streets of the city. Seeing the flames, the citizens and the garrison left the cannon behind and rushed inside the fortress—their last refuge. Pugachev entered the city. It became the rebels' prey. They rushed to plunder the houses and stores; burst into churches and monasteries, stripping the iconholders; and slew anybody in German clothes who fell into their hands. Pugachev set up his batteries in the tavern of the market hall, behind the churches by the triumphal gates, and opened fire on the fortress, especially on the Monastery of the Savior, whose ancient walls, barely holding together, formed its right-hand corner. On the other side, Mineev pulled up a cannon to the gates of the Kazan Monastery and another one to the portico of a church: from these positions he could hit the most sensitive areas inside the fortress. One of his cannon, however, was smashed by a ball from the fortress. The bandits decked themselves out in women's dresses and priests' surplices, and ran around the streets screaming, plundering, setting houses on fire. Those engaged in the siege of the fortress envied them, fearing to be left out of the booty... Suddenly Pugachev ordered them to withdraw. Setting fire to a few more houses, they returned to their camp. The wind rose. A sea of flames spread across the whole city. Sparks and charred pieces of wood were blown into the fortress and set several wooden roofs on fire. At this moment part of a wall collapsed with the boom of a thunderclap, crushing several people. The besieged, huddled in the fortress, sent up a wail, believing that the villain had burst in and their last hour had struck.

Those who had been captured were being herded out of the city, and the loot was being hauled away. Although Pugachev had strictly forbidden them to do this, the Bashkirs drove the people forward with whips and kept jabbing at the women and children who fell behind with pikes. A great many drowned while fording the Kazanka River. When the captives had at last been driven to the camp, they were lined up on their knees in front of cannon. The women burst into a howl. Then the whole crowd was told they had been pardoned. They all shouted "Hurrah!" and rushed to Pugachev's platform. Seated in an armchair, he was receiving gifts from the Kazan Tatars who had come to pay their respect to him. The question was put, "Who wishes to serve the Emperor Petr Fedorovich?"—Many were the volunteers.

During the entire siege, Archbishop Veniamin was inside the fortress, at the Cathedral of the Annunciation, praying on his knees with the citizenry for the deliverance of the faithful. The cannonade had hardly ceased when he raised the miracle-working icons and, defying the conflagration's unbearable heat and the falling pieces of wood, went all around inside the fortress, accompanied by all his clergy and all the citizenry, singing hymns. Toward evening the storm abated and the wind changed direction. Night set in—a night of horror for the citizens! Kazan, turned into heaps of burning charcoal, smoked and glowed in the dark. No one could sleep. At dawn the citizens hurried to the battlements and fixed their gaze on the side from which a new assault was expected. But instead of Pugachev's hordes they beheld, to their amazement, Mikhelson's hussars galloping toward the city under the command of an officer who had been sent with a report to the governor.

Nobody knew that Mikhelson had already fought a ferocious battle with Pugachev seven versts from the city and that the rebels had retreated in disorder.

Last time we mentioned Mikhelson he was doggedly pursuing Pugachev in his precipitate dash across the land. Subsequently, the colonel left his sick and wounded in Ufa, attached Major Duve to his own corps, and by June 21 arrived in Burnovo, a few versts from Birsk.

The rebels had put up a new bridge to replace the one Iakubovich had burned. About 1,000 rebels came out to counter Mikhelson, but he crushed them. He detached Duve against a band of Bashkirs gathered nearby: Duve scattered them. Mikhelson advanced toward Osa, and on June 27 he learned from a group of Bashkirs and Tatars whom he had subdued along the way that Pugachev had taken Osa and crossed the Kama. Mikhelson followed in his tracks. There were no bridges standing over the Kama, nor were there any boats available. The cavalry swam across, and the infantry made rafts. Mikhelson bypassed Pugachev on his right, heading straight for Kazan; by the evening of July 11 he was only 50 versts away.

His detachment moved closer during the night. In the morning, at a distance of 45 versts from Kazan, cannon fire was heard. By noon a thick crimson cloud of smoke announced the fate of the city.

The midday heat and the exhaustion of his troops forced Mikhelson to take an hour's rest. In the meanwhile he learned that there was a group of insurgents nearby. He attacked them and took 400 prisoners; the rest fled to Kazan and informed Pugachev of the enemy's approach. It was then that Pugachev, fearing a sudden assault, withdrew from the fortress and ordered his troops to vacate the city as soon as possible. He took up an advantageous position near Tsaritsyn, seven versts from Kazan.

Having received information about this, Mikhelson led his troops across the intervening woods in one column. When he came out into the field he was confronted by the rebels arrayed in battle formation.

Mikhelson sent Kharin against their left flank and Duve against the right, while he himself advanced directly on the enemy's main battery. Pugachev's men, buoyed by their victory and strengthened by the cannon they had captured, countered the attack with heavy fire. In front of the main battery there was a marsh: Mikhelson had to cross this, while Kharin and Duve tried to turn the enemy's flank on either side. Mikhelson overran the main battery, and Duve, too, was able to wrest away two cannon on the right flank. The rebels now divided into two groups. One advanced toward Kharin and, setting up batteries in a ditch inside a ravine, opened fire; the other tried to circle around to the rear of the government corps. Mikhelson left Duve to his own devices and went to reinforce Kharin, whose men were advancing across the ravine under enemy fire. At length, after five hours of stubborn fighting, Pugachev was beaten and put to flight, at a cost of 800 men killed and 180 captured. Mikhelson's losses were insignificant. The darkness of night and the exhaustion of his troops prevented him from pursuing Pugachev.

Having spent the night on the field of battle, Mikhelson proceeded to Kazan just before dawn. As he approached the city he kept coming across groups of looters, who had been carousing among the charred ruins of the city all night. They were slain or taken prisoner. As he arrived at Arskoe Field, Mikhelson caught sight of the enemy approaching: realizing how small Mikhelson's detachment was, Pugachev had hurried to prevent him from joining forces with the garrison. Mikhelson sent a report about this to the governor, then opened up his cannon on the mob charging toward him, yelling and shrieking; he forced them to retreat. Potemkin arrived with the garrison in good time. Crossing the Kazanka, Pugachev withdrew to the village of Sukhaia Reka, 15 versts from the city. Mikhelson was unable to pursue him, for he had fewer than 30 sound horses in his detachment.

Kazan was liberated. The citizens thronged to the battlements to take a look at their liberator's camp from a distance. Mikhelson stayed out, expecting a new assault. Indeed Pugachev, provoked by his failures, had his heart set on subduing Mikhelson at last. He rallied new mobs on all sides, gathered in his various detachments, and on the morning of July 15, after a reading of a manifesto to his troops in which he declared his intention to advance on Moscow, he charged at Mikhelson for the third time. His army was a ragtag band of 25,000. These multitudes advanced up the same highway along which they had twice fled. Clouds of dust, wild shrieks, clatter, and rumble announced their approach. Mikhelson took the field against them with 800 carabineers, hussars, and Chuguev Cossacks. He occupied the site of the earlier battle near Tsaritsyn, dividing his troops into three detachments though keeping them in close proximity. The rebels charged at him. The Iaik Cossacks brought up the rear, with orders from Pugachev to strike at anyone who turned back. But Mikhelson and Kharin mounted counterattacks on two sides, drove the rebels back, and chased them away. It was all accomplished in next to no time. In vain did Pugachev try to rally his scattered hordes, initially at his first campsite, then at the second. Kharin pursued him briskly, giving him no time to pause. At these camps there were kept some 10,000 Kazan citizens of both sexes, from all walks of life. They were now liberated. The Kazanka was dammed up with corpses; the victor took 5,000 prisoners and nine cannon. Up to 2,000 men, mostly Tatars and Bashkirs, were killed in the engagement. Mikhelson lost about 100 troops killed or wounded. He entered the city to the hails of its enraptured inhabitants—eyewitnesses of his victory. The governor, debilitated by an illness that was to kill him in another two weeks, met the victor at the gate of the fortress accompanied by the nobility and clergy. Mikhelson went straight to the cathedral, where Archbishop Veniamin celebrated a thanksgiving mass.

Kazan was in a terrible state: 2,057 of its 2,867 buildings had burned down. Twenty-five churches and three monasteries had also been destroyed in the conflagration. The market hall, and the houses, churches, and monasteries left standing, had all been robbed. Some 300 inhabitants were found either dead or wounded; about 500 were missing without a trace. Among those killed were the principal of the grammar school, Kanits; several teachers and students; and Colonel Rodionov. Major General Kudriavtsev, aged one hundred and ten, had not been willing to seek shelter in the fortress despite eloquent exhortations: he had gone to pray on his knees in the Kazan Convent, and when some pillagers burst in, he started admonishing them; the scoundrels butchered him on the portico of the church.

Thus had the poor convict celebrated his return to Kazan, whence he had escaped only a year before! The prison where he had been waiting for a sentence of lashes and forced labor had now been burned down by him, and the prisoners, his comrades of yore, had been released. The Cossack woman Sofia Pugacheva and her three children had been kept at a Kazan barracks for several months. The pretender is said to have burst into tears when he saw them, but he did not betray his identity. Some accounts claim that he gave orders to transfer them to his camp, saying "I know this woman: her husband has done me a great favor."

The traitor Mineev—the chief instigator of the sack of Kazan—was taken prisoner at the time of Pugachev's first defeat and sentenced by a military tribunal to run the gauntlet to his death.

The Kazan authorities took measures to lodge the inhabitants in the buildings left standing. The citizens were invited to the rebels' camp to sort out the booty captured from Pugachev and take back what belonged to them. They hastened to divide the goods as best they could, but some who had been rich became poor, and some who had been indigent ended up wealthy!

History must refute a libel that was irresponsibly bandied about in society: it was asserted that Mikhelson could have prevented the sack of Kazan but deliberately gave the rebels time to plunder the city so that he too could lay hands on a rich booty. As if he could prefer profit of any kind to the fame, honor, and imperial favors that were awaiting the liberator of Kazan and the pacifier of the revolt! We have seen how speedily and how persistently Mikhelson had been pursuing Pugachev. Had Potemkin and von Brandt done their duty and held the city for just a few more hours, Kazan would have been saved. Mikhelson's soldiers did of course lay their hands on some riches; but it would be a shame to level an unsubstantiated accusation at a venerable warrior, who had spent all his life on the field of honor and who was to die as the commander-in-chief of a whole Russian army.[42]

On July 14 Lieutenant Colonel Count Mellin arrived in Kazan and was detached by Mikhelson to pursue Pugachev. Mikhelson himself remained in the city in order to refresh his cavalry and reprovision. Other military leaders hastened to take some measures, knowing all too well by now that Pugachev, active and enterprising as he was, could still be dangerous despite his defeat. His movements were so fast and unpredictable that there was no way to pursue him; in any case the government cavalry was completely worn out. There were attempts to block his advance, but the troops, dispersed over large areas and unable to change direction speedily, could not get to the right places at the right time. It must also be stated that few of the military leaders of the time were capable of coping with Pugachev or even with his underlings.

Chapter Eight

Pugachev on the west side of the Volga.—A general uprising.—General Stupishin's letter.—Catherine's plans.—Count P. I. Panin.—The movement of the troops.—The taking of Penza.—Vsevolozhskii's death.—Derzhavin's dispute with Boshniak.—The taking of Saratov.—Pugachev at Tsaritsyn.—The demise of the astronomer Lowitz.—Pugachev's defeat.—Suvorov.—Pugachev is handed over to the authorities.—The conversation with Count Panin.—The trials of Pugachev and his followers.—The execution of the rebels.

Pugachev fled, periodically changing horses, along the highway toward Kokshaisk, in the company of 300 Iaik and Ilek Cossacks. At last they reached a forest. Kharin, who had been chasing after them for full 30 versts, was forced to stop. Pugachev spent the night in the forest. He had his family with him. There were two new faces among his followers. One of them was Pulaski, younger brother of the famous Confederate.[43] He had been living in Kazan as a prisoner of war and joined Pugachev's band out of hatred for Russia. The other one was a protestant pastor. He had been brought before Pugachev during the burning of Kazan, and the pretender recognized him as a person who had given him alms at the time he had been led about the streets of Kazan in fetters. The poor minister had been expecting his last hour, but Pugachev received him with kindness and appointed him a colonel. The colonel-minister was subsequently placed on a Bashkir horse, and accompanied Pugachev in his flight for several days, until at last he dropped behind and returned to Kazan.

For two days Pugachev wandered now in this, now in that direction, thereby misleading his pursuers. His mobs, scattering about, carried on their usual depredations. Beloborodov was caught on the outskirts of Kazan, flogged, and then conveyed to Moscow for execution. Several hundred fugitives joined Pugachev once more. On July 18 he suddenly rushed down to the Volga, to the Kokshaisk ferry, and crossed the river with 500 of his select troops.

Pugachev's appearance on the other side of the river caused a general commotion. The whole region west of the Volga rose up in arms and joined the pretender. The seignorial serfs rioted; non-Christians and new converts started killing Russian priests. Regional administrative officials began to flee from the cities, and landowners from their estates; the mob captured many of both groups and brought them before Pugachev. He guaranteed the people liberty, the extermination of the nobility, release from obligations, and the free distribution of salt. He marched on Tsivilsk, pillaged the town, and hanged the head of the regional administration. Dividing his band into two, he sent one division toward Alatyr and the other along the road to Nizhnii Novgorod, thereby cutting communication between that city and Kazan. The governor of Nizhnii Novgorod, Lieutenant General Stupishin, wrote to Prince Volkonskii that his city awaited the fate of Kazan, and that he could not even be sure of the safety of Moscow. All the military units stationed in Kazan and Orenburg *guberniias* were mobilized and dispatched against Pugachev. Shcherbatov from Bugulma and Prince Golitsyn from Menzelinsk each hurried to Kazan; Mellin crossed the Volga and on July 19 set out from Sviiazhsk; Mansurov advanced from Iaitskii Gorodok to Syzran; Muffel went to Simbirsk; and Mikhelson rushed from Cheboksary to Arzamas to block the way in case Pugachev should march on Moscow...

But Pugachev no longer had any intention of attacking the old capital. Surrounded by government troops on all sides and having no faith in his followers, he turned his attention to his own safety. His plan was to force his way either to the trans-Kuban region or to Persia. The chief rebels, on their part, could tell that their undertaking was doomed and were ready to strike a bargain for their leader's head. Perfilev, acting on behalf of all the culpable Cossacks, sent a secret emissary to St. Petersburg with a proposal to hand over the pretender. The government, which he had already deceived once, was disinclined to trust him, but nevertheless entered into negotiations. Pugachev was fleeing, but his flight seemed like an invasion. Never had his victories been more horrifying; never had the rebellion raged with greater force. The insurrection spread from village to village, from province to province. Only two or three villains had to appear on the scene, and whole regions revolted. Various bands of plunderers and rioters were formed, each having its own Pugachev...

The news of these sad events made a deep impression in St. Petersburg, overshadowing the joy there over the end of the Turkish war and the conclusion of the glorious Peace of Kuchuk Kainarji. The Empress, dissatisfied with Prince Shcherbatov's tarrying, had resolved as early as the beginning of July to recall him and to put Prince Golitsyn in command of the army. The courier conveying this order, however, was held up in Nizhnii Novgorod due to the hazardous conditions lying ahead. When the Empress subsequently learned of the fall of Kazan and the spread of the rebellion to the west of the Volga, she contemplated coming to this region of calamity and danger in order to lead the army in person. Count Nikita Ivanovich Panin managed to dissuade her. The Empress did not know whom to trust with the task of saving the homeland. At this time an aristocrat who was in disfavor and estranged from Court just like Bibikov volunteered to complete the noble deed left unfinished by his predecessor. This was Petr Ivanovich Panin. The Empress was grateful to see her noble subject's zeal, and Count Panin, just as he was setting out from his village to march against Pugachev at the head of his armed peasants and domestic serfs, received her order to assume command over the *guberniias* where the rebellion raged and over the troops sent there. Thus the conqueror of Bender was to wage war against the simple Cossack who had served under his command, unnoticed by him, four years previously.

On July 20 Pugachev's forces swam across the Sura below Kurmysh. The gentry and the government officials fled. The mob greeted the pretender on the bank of the river with icons and bread. A subversive manifesto was read to them. A troop of veterans was brought before Pugachev. Its commander, Major Iurlov, and a noncommissioned officer whose name, unfortunately, has not been recorded, were the only ones who refused to swear allegiance to the pretender and accused him of imposture to his face. They were hanged and, already dead, lashed with the whip. Iurlov's widow was saved by her domestics. Pugachev gave orders to distribute liquor among the Chuvash from the state warehouse; he hanged several noblemen who had been brought before him by their peasants; and he set out for Iadrin, leaving the town under the command of four Iaik Cossacks, assisted by 60 serfs who had joined the rebels. He also left behind a small band to slow down Count Mellin. Mikhelson, who was heading for Arzamas, sent a detachment under Kharin toward Iadrin—also the destination, as it turned out, of Count Mellin's troops. When Pugachev learned of this, he turned around toward Alatyr, but sent the small band on to Iadrin in order to secure his rear. This band was first beaten back by the head of the regional administration and the local citizenry; then it ran into Count Mellin and was finally dispersed. Mellin hurried on toward Alatyr, but first, on his way, he liberated Kurmysh, hanging several rebels and taking with him as an informant the Cossack whom they had called their commander. The officers of the troop of veterans who had sworn allegiance to the pretender justified themselves by claiming that their oath had *"not come from a sincere heart, but it served Her Imperial Majesty's best interests."* In their letter to Stupishin they wrote: "We repent as Christians of having broken our oath before God and Her Most Gracious Majesty, and of having sworn allegiance to that impostor; we beg with tears in our eyes to be forgiven for this involuntary sin, committed with no other motive than fear of death." Twenty people signed this shameful apology.

Pugachev dashed forward with exceptional speed, at the same time sending out bands in all directions. His pursuers could not tell which of these bands was his own. It was impossible to catch up with him, because he galloped along country roads, seizing fresh horses and leaving behind agitators who rode around the towns and the villages unopposed in groups of two, three, rarely more than five, and gathered new bands. Three such agitators turned up on the outskirts of Nizhnii Novgorod, but Demidov's peasants trussed them up and handed them over to Stupishin. He ordered them to be hanged on gallows erected on barges and left to float down the Volga, along the banks where the riots were taking place.

On July 27 Pugachev entered Saransk. He was received not only by the rabble, but also by the clergy and the merchants... Three hundred nobles of both sexes and of various ages were hanged by him here; peasants and house serfs flocked to him in droves. He left the town on the 30th. The next day Mellin reached Saransk; he arrested Ensign Shakhmametev, who had been appointed commander by the pretender, as well as a number of other traitors from among the clergy and nobility, and ordered the common people to be lashed beneath the gallows.

Mikhelson set out from Arzamas to race after Pugachev. Muffel hurried from Simbirsk to meet him head-on, with Mellin following in his tracks. Thus three detachments were encircling the pretender. Prince Shcherbatov, impatiently waiting for the arrival of troops from

Bashkiriia to reinforce the detachments already in action, intended to hurry after them himself; but on receiving the Empress's order of July 2, he handed over command to Golitsyn and left for Petersburg.

In the meanwhile Pugachev drew close to Penza. Vsevolozhskii, the regional administrator, managed to keep the rabble under control for a while, which gave the gentry an opportunity to escape. Pugachev appeared outside the city. The inhabitants came out to greet him with icons and bread, and knelt before him. He entered Penza. Vsevolozhskii, whose garrison had deserted, locked himself in his house with 12 noblemen, resolved to defend himself. The house was set on fire; the brave Vsevolozhskii and his comrades all perished; government buildings and noblemen's houses were plundered. Pugachev appointed a seignorial serf commander of the city and proceeded toward Saratov.

Hearing of the fall of Penza, the authorities at Saratov began taking measures.

Derzhavin was there at the time. As we have seen, he had been detached to the village of Malykovka in order to bar Pugachev's way in case he should flee toward the Irgiz. Having heard that Pugachev was negotiating with the Kirgiz Kaisaks, he set up a barrier between those peoples and the nomadic tribes roaming the region of the two Uzen rivers. Next he intended to liberate Iaitskii Gorodok, but General Mansurov anticipated him. At the end of July he arrived in Saratov, where his rank—Lieutenant of the Guards—his keen intelligence, and his ardent nature earned him considerable influence over public opinion.

On August 1 Derzhavin, together with the chief of the Board of Protection of Foreign Colonists, Lodyzhinskii, requested the military commander of Saratov, Boshniak, to hold consultations about measures to be taken under the circumstances. Derzhavin urged that the center of the city, around the state warehouses, be fortified and all government goods be transferred there; that the boats on the Volga be burned, batteries arrayed along the bank, and an offensive mounted against Pugachev. Boshniak would not hear of leaving his fortress, and proposed to hold out there, beyond the city. They argued, they raised their voices; Derzhavin, having lost his temper, proposed that the commander be put under arrest. Boshniak remained steadfast, repeating that he would not expose to plunder the fortress and holy churches of God entrusted to him. Derzhavin walked out and went to the city council, laying the motion before it that all the inhabitants to a man should report for digging at a place assigned by Lodyzhinskii. Boshniak complained, but no one listened to him. Derzhavin's vitriolic letter to the obstinate commander has been preserved as a memento of this dispute.

On August 4 word reached Saratov that Pugachev had set out from Penza and was approaching Petrovsk. Derzhavin requested a detachment of Don Cossacks, and rushed to Petrovsk to salvage government property, gunpowder, and cannon. As he drew close to the town, however, he heard bells ringing and saw the vanguard of the rebel forces marching into town, and the clergy coming out to greet the invaders with icons and bread. He rode on with a Cossack captain and two other Cossacks, but realizing there was nothing he could do, he galloped back toward Saratov with his three men. The rest of his detachment remained on the highway, waiting for Pugachev. The pretender, accompanied by his associates, rode up to the detachment. The Cossacks received him on their knees. Hearing them speak of an officer of the Guards, Pugachev immediately changed horses, seized a javelin, and chased after him with four Cossacks. He slew one of the Cossacks accompanying Derzhavin, but Derzhavin himself managed to get back to Saratov. The next day both he and Lodyzhinskii left the city, leaving its defense to the scorned Boshniak.

On August 5 Pugachev marched on Saratov. His army consisted of 300 Iaik Cossacks and 150 Don Cossacks—the latter having joined him the day before—as well as some 10,000 Kalmyks, Bashkirs, Tatar tributaries, seignorial peasants, serfs, and other riffraff. About 2,000 were armed somehow or other; the rest marched with axes, pitchforks, and clubs. They had 13 fieldpieces.

On the 6th Pugachev approached Saratov and stopped at a distance of three versts from the city.

Boshniak detached some of Saratov's Cossacks to take a prisoner who might provide some information, but they defected to Pugachev. In the meanwhile the citizenry sent a secret emissary, the merchant Kobiakov, to the pretender with seditious proposals. The rebels rode right up to the fortress, engaging the garrison in conversation. Boshniak gave orders to fire at them. At that time, however, the citizens led by Major Protopopov openly defied his authority and confronting him, demanded that there be no hostilities until Kobiakov's return. Boshniak asked them how they had dared enter into negotiations with the pretender without his, Boshniak's, knowledge. They continued to wrangle. In the meanwhile Kobiakov returned with a manifesto inciting the people to riot. Boshniak snatched it from the traitor's hand, tore it up and trampled on it, and gave orders for Kobiakov's arrest. The merchants, however, pressed him with pleas and threats, so much so that he was forced to yield, and to release Kobiakov. Nevertheless, he made preparations for the city's defense. In the interim Pugachev occupied Sokolov Hill, overlooking Saratov, set up a battery there, and opened fire on the city. The first shot sent the inhabitants and the Cossacks stationed in the fortress scurrying in all directions. Boshniak gave orders to fire the mortar, but the shell dropped to the ground only 50 *sazhens* away. Going around to inspect his troops, he found dejection everywhere, but he did not lose heart. The rebels stormed the fortress. Boshniak opened fire and had already succeeded in driving the rebels back when suddenly 300 of his gunners pulled the wedges from under their cannon, snatched up the fuses, and ran out of the fortress to surrender. At this point Pugachev himself led an attack on the fortress from the hill. Boshniak decided to cut his way through the rebel hordes with one garrison battalion. He ordered Major Salmanov to sally forth with the first half of the battalion, but noticing the man's fright and suspecting him of treason, he removed him from command. However, when Major Butyrin interceded on Salmanov's behalf, Boshniak, once again showing weakness, agreed to leave Salmanov in his post after all. Turning to the second half of the battalion, Boshniak gave orders to unfold the banners and march out from behind the fortifications. At this moment Salmanov surrendered, and Boshniak was left with 60 soldiers, including his officers. The brave man sallied out of the fortress with this handful of followers and spent full six hours fighting his way through innumerable rebel hordes. Nightfall put an end to the fighting. Boshniak reached the bank of the Volga. What state funds and chancery papers he had on him he sent to Astrakhan by boat, and he himself managed to reach Tsaritsyn by August 11.

As soon as the rebels captured Saratov, they liberated prisoners, opened up the grain and salt warehouses, broke into the taverns, and plundered the houses. Pugachev hanged all the noblemen who fell into his hands, and forbade their burial. He appointed a Cossack lieutenant, Ufimtsev, local commander, and at noon on August 9 set out from Saratov. Muffel arrived in the ravaged city on the 11th, Mikhelson on the 14th. Joining forces, they hastened after Pugachev.

The pretender followed the course of the Volga. The foreigners who had settled in this region, mostly vagabonds and scoundrels, all joined his forces at the instigation of a Polish Confederate (not identified by name; certainly not Pulaski because he had already left Pugachev, disgusted by his bestial atrocities). Pugachev formed them into a hussar regiment. The Volga Cossacks also came over to his side.

Thus Pugachev mustered greater and greater forces by the day. His army already consisted of 20,000 men. His bands spread over the *guberniias* of Nizhnii Novgorod, Voronezh, and Astrakhan. The fugitive serf Evstigneev, also calling himself Peter III, took Insar, Troitsk, Narovchat, and Kerensk, hanged the regional administrators and the gentry, and set up his own administration everywhere. The bandit Firska marched on Simbirsk, and in the fray killed Colonel Rychkov, the successor of Chernyshev, who had perished near Orenburg at the beginning of the uprising. The garrison defected, but Simbirsk was saved by the arrival of Colonel Obernibesov. Firska engulfed the outlying areas in murder and plunder. Verkhne-Lomov and Nizhne-Lomov were ravaged and burned by other villains. The state of this whole huge region was horrifying. The nobility was doomed to extinction. The bodies of landowners or their stewards hung on the gates of manor houses in every village. The rebels and the detachments pursuing them confiscated the peasants' horses, supplies, and last belongings. Law and order were suspended everywhere. The simple people did not know whom to obey. If asked, "To whom do you swear, Petr Fedorovich or Ekaterina Alekseevna?," peaceable people dared not answer, not knowing to which side their questioners belonged.

On August 13 Pugachev approached Dmitrievsk (Kamyshin). He was countered by Major Dietz at the head of a 500-strong garrison, 1,000 Don Cossacks, and 500 Kalmyks under the command of Princes Dundukov and Derbetev. An engagement ensued. The Kalmyks scattered at the first cannon shot. The Cossacks fought bravely and were pressing close to the cannon, but when they found themselves cut off they surrendered. Dietz was killed. The garrison and all the cannon were captured. Pugachev pitched camp for the night on the battlefield; the next day he took Dubovka and moved on toward Tsaritsyn.

That well-fortified city was under the command of Colonel Tsypletev. The brave Boshniak had joined him. On August 21 Pugachev laid siege to Tsaritsyn with his usual daring. He was driven back with losses, and retreated to a distance of eight versts from the fortress. Fifteen hundred Don Cossacks were sent out against him, but of these only 400 came back: the rest had defected to his side.

The next day Pugachev made a new assault on the city, this time from the Volga side, but he was again repulsed by Boshniak. He also received news of the approach of government troops and hurriedly backed off toward Sarepta.

Mikhelson, Muffel, and Mellin arrived at Dubovka on the 20th, and entered Tsaritsyn on the 22d.

Pugachev fled along the Volga. On the riverbank he chanced on the astronomer Lowitz and asked him who he was. Hearing that Lowitz observed the movement of heavenly bodies, he ordered him hanged "as close to the stars as they could pull him." Lowitz's adjunct Inokhodtsev managed to escape.

Pugachev rested in Sarepta a full 24 hours, secluded in his tent with two concubines. His family was also at the camp. Then he set out toward Chernyi Iar. Mikhelson was on his heels. At length, at dawn on the 25th he caught up with Pugachev 105 versts from Tsaritsyn.

The rebel forces occupied a hill between two roads. During the night Mikhelson went around them and positioned his troops facing them. In the morning Pugachev once again encountered his formidable pursuer, but he remained undaunted: he bravely fell on Mikhelson, throwing his pedestrian horde into combat against the Don and Chuguev Cossacks who had turned both his flanks. The engagement did not last long. A few cannon shots were enough to break the rebels' ranks. Mikhelson counterattacked. The rebels fled, leaving their cannon and the whole of their supply train behind. Pugachev, having crossed a bridge, tried to hold his men back, but all in vain: he had to flee with them. Mikhelson's troops butchered and pursued them for 40 versts. Pugachev lost some 4,000 men dead and 7,000 captured. The rest of his horde dispersed. Just above Chernyi Iar, 70 versts from the field of battle, he and his Cossacks, numbering no more than 30, crossed the Volga in four boats and entered the steppe. The cavalry chasing after them arrived a quarter of an hour late. Those of the fleeing rebels who had not managed to get into the boats plunged into the river, trying to swim across, but they drowned to a man.

This defeat was decisive and proved to be the last one. Count Panin, who had just arrived in Kerensk, was able to send the joyous news to Petersburg, paying full tribute in his report to Mikhelson for his speed, skill, and courage. In the meanwhile a new important personage appeared on the scene: Suvorov arrived in Tsaritsyn.

Bibikov was still alive when the State College, realizing the seriousness of the rebellion, had attempted to recall Suvorov, who was at the walls of Silistra at the time; but Count Rumiantsev refused to let him go, lest Europe attach too much significance to Russia's internal troubles. So great was Suvorov's fame! When the war came to an end, he received orders to proceed to Moscow immediately and report to Prince Volkonskii for further instructions. He joined Count Panin on his estate and reached Mikhelson's troops a few days after their last victory. He brought with him an order from Count Panin enjoining both the military leaders and the governors of the region to obey all his commands. He assumed command of Mikhelson's troops, mounted the infantry on the horses captured from Pugachev, and crossed the Volga at Tsaritsyn. In a village that had participated in the rebellion he confiscated 50 yoke of oxen as a punishment, and with this provision, plunged deep into the steppe, where neither wood nor water could be found, and where he had to orient himself by the sun during the day and by the stars at night.

Pugachev meandered about the same steppe. Troops were encircling him on all sides: Mellin and Muffel, who had also crossed the Volga, cut off the routes to the north; a light field detachment approached the rebel from the direction of Astrakhan; Prince Golitsyn and Mansurov barred the way to the Iaik; Dundukov was crisscrossing the steppe with his Kalmyks; patrol lines were set up from Gurev to Saratov and from Chernyi Iar to Krasnyi Iar. There was no way for Pugachev to slip through the net tightening around him. His followers, seeing inescapable doom on the one hand and hope for a pardon on the other, put their heads together and finally resolved to deliver him to the authorities.

Pugachev intended to head toward the Caspian Sea, hoping somehow to get through to the Kirgiz Kaisak steppes. The Cossacks pretended to agree, but, saying that they wished to take their wives and children with them, they drew him to the Uzen region—the usual refuge of criminals and fugitives. On September 14 they arrived at a settlement of Old Believers in that area. Here the Cossacks held their last council. Those not willing to surrender to the authorities dispersed; the others were to participate in delivering Pugachev.

Pugachev was sitting by himself, deep in thought. His weapons hung on the wall. Hearing the Cossacks enter, he raised his head and asked what they wanted. They started talking about their desperate situation, at the same time slowly moving closer in order to get between Pugachev and his weapons. Once more he tried to persuade them to go to Gurev. The Cossacks answered that they had been following him for a long time, and now it was time for him to follow them.

"What?" asked Pugachev. "Are you going to betray your Sovereign?"

"What else is there to do?" answered the Cossacks, throwing themselves on him. He managed to fight free. They drew back a few steps.

"I've been aware of your treason for a long time," said Pugachev. Then he called forth his favorite among them, the Ilek Cossack Tvorogov, and held his hands out to him: "Tie them!"

Tvorogov wanted to tie his arms behind his back, but Pugachev would not let him, asking angrily, "What am I? A bandit?" The Cossacks put him on a horse and led him to Iaitskii Gorodok. All along the way he threatened them with the Grand Duke's revenge. Once he managed to free his hands; he grabbed a sword and a pistol, wounded one of the Cossacks, and issued a command that the traitors be tied up. But nobody listened to him any more. The Cossacks rode up to Iaitskii Gorodok and sent word to the commandant. The Cossack Kharchev and Sergeant Bardovskii were dispatched to meet them; they took charge of Pugachev, put him in stocks, and had him carried into town, straight to Lieutenant Captain of the Guards Mavrin, who was a member of the investigating commission.

Mavrin interrogated the pretender. The latter revealed his true identity from the very beginning.

"It was God's will," he said, "to punish Russia through my devilry."

The citizens were ordered to gather in the town square, and all the rebels kept in irons were brought out; Mavrin led Pugachev forth and showed him to the people. Everyone recognized him; the rebels cast their eyes down. Pugachev started loudly implicating them, saying, "You were the ones who led me to ruin: you begged me for several days to assume the name of the late great Sovereign; I refused for a long time, and even after I agreed, I did everything according to your will and with your consent, while you often acted without my knowledge, and sometimes even against my will."

The rebels did not have one word to say.

In the interim Suvorov arrived in the Uzen region and learned from the hermits that Pugachev, tied up by his followers, had been carried off to Iaitskii Gorodok. Suvorov hurried after them. At night he lost his way and stumbled on the campfires that some Kirgiz freebooters had lit in the steppe. Suvorov set on them and chased them off, but not without losing some of his men, his adjutant Maksimovich among them. A few days later he arrived in Iaitskii Gorodok. Simonov handed Pugachev over to him. Suvorov questioned the famous rebel with curiosity about his military maneuvers and plans. He had him transported to Simbirsk, where Count Panin was due to arrive.

Pugachev sat in a wooden cage placed on a two-wheeled cart. A large detachment, supported by two pieces of artillery, surrounded him. Suvorov did not leave his side. In the village of Mosty (140 versts from Samara) a fire broke out close to the cottage where Pugachev was spending the night. He was taken out of the cage and tied to the cart, together with his son, a lively, bold little fellow. Suvorov himself guarded them all night. He crossed a choppy Volga on a stormy night from Samara to Kospore, and arrived in Simbirsk at the beginning of October.

The pretender was brought straight to the courtyard of the house occupied by Count Panin. The latter came out on the porch accompanied by his staff.

"Who are you?" he asked the pretender.

"Emelian Ivanov Pugachev" was the answer.

"How did you, jailbird, dare call yourself sovereign?"

"I'm no bird," responded Pugachev in an allegorical manner, which was customary with him. "I'm only a fledgling; the real bird is still flying about."[44]

It should be mentioned that the Iaik rebels, in order to refute hearsay, had spread the rumor that though there had indeed been a certain Pugachev among them, this person had nothing to do with the Emperor Peter III who was commanding their forces. Noticing that Pugachev's bold reply had struck a responsive chord in the common people crowding around the courtyard, Panin beat him in the face till he bled and tore out a tuft of his beard. Pugachev raised himself on his knees and asked for mercy. He was placed under heavy guard, with his hands and feet in fetters and an iron loop, chained to the wall, fastened around his waist. The academician Rychkov, father of the murdered commandant of Simbirsk, saw him and left a record of their encounter. Pugachev was eating fish soup from a wooden bowl. Seeing Rychkov enter, he greeted him and asked him if he would like to share his dinner. "This," writes Rychkov, "revealed to me his base mind." Rychkov asked him how he had dared commit such crimes. Pugachev answered, "I am guilty before God and Her Majesty, but I will try to make amends for all my sins." And he added an oath to his words for greater emphasis ("revealing his base nature," Rychkov remarks again). Speaking about his son, Rychkov could not refrain from tears; Pugachev, looking at him, also burst into tears.

At last Pugachev was dispatched to Moscow, where his fate was to be decided. He was conveyed in a covered wagon driven by horses hired locally at each stage. His escorts were Captains Galakhov and Povalo-Shveikovskii—the latter having been his prisoner a few months before. He was kept in irons. The soldiers fed him with their own hands, and kept telling the children who crowded around his wagon, "Remember, children, you have seen Pugachev." Old people still tell stories about how boldly he responded to the questions of gentlemen passing him on the road. He was cheerful and calm all along the way.

In Moscow he was met by a large crowd, which only recently had been impatiently awaiting his assault on the city and refrained from rebellion only because of the dreaded villain's arrest. He was kept at the Moscow Mint, where from morning till night, for two whole months, the curious could see the famous rebel, chained to the wall and still frightening even in his harmless state. It is said that many women fainted on meeting his fiery glance and hearing his menacing voice. Before the court, on the other hand, he betrayed an unexpected weakness of spirit. He had to be prepared gradually to hear his death sentence. He and Perfilev were condemned to be quartered; Chika to be beheaded; Shigaev, Padurov, and Tornov to be hanged; and another 18 men to be flogged and exiled into penal servitude. The execution of Pugachev and his followers took place in Moscow on January 10, 1775. From early morning an immense crowd stood gathered on the Boloto Square, where a tall scaffold had been erected. The executioners sat on the scaffold, drinking wine while they waited for their victims. Three gallows stood next to the scaffold. Infantry regiments were lined up on all sides. The officers wore fur coats because of the severe cold. The roofs of neighboring houses and stores were covered with people; the low-lying square and the adjacent streets were full of carriages and barouches. Suddenly a wave of stirring and clamor passed over the crowd; people shouted, "They're bringing him! They're bringing him!" Behind a detachment of cuirassiers came a sled with a tall platform where Pugachev sat, his head bare, facing a priest. An official of the secret commission also rode on the sled. As he was being driven along, Pugachev kept bowing to both sides. Some more cavalry followed; then came, in a group, the other convicted men. An eyewitness (then barely more than an adolescent, now a venerable old man, crowned with the fame of both poet and statesman) described the bloody spectacle in the following words:

> The sled halted before the steps leading up to the place of execution. Pugachev and his favorite Cossack Perfilev, accompanied by a priest and two officials, had hardly mounted the scaffold when the command "Present arms!" was heard, and one of the officials began reading the sentence. I could hear almost every word.
>
> When the official read the chief villain's name and full identification, including the name of the village where he had been born, the chief of police asked him in a loud voice:
>
> "Are you the Don Cossack Emelka Pugachev?"
>
> "Yes, sir, I am Emelka Pugachev, Don Cossack from the village of Zimoveiskaia," he answered in an equally loud voice.
>
> Afterwards, all through the reading of the sentence, he fixed his gaze on the cathedral and frequently crossed himself, while Perfilev, a man of con-

siderable height with stoop shoulders, a pockmarked face, and a fierce countenance, stood motionless, looking at the ground. When the reading of the sentence was over, the priest addressed a few words to them, blessed them, and descended from the scaffold. The official who had read the sentence followed suit. Pugachev, crossing himself, bowed to the ground facing the cathedral; then, with a hurried air, he turned to the crowd to say farewell, and bowed to all sides, uttering in a breaking voice:

"Farewell, Orthodox people: forgive me if I have trespassed against you; farewell, true believers!"

At this moment the executioner gave a signal, and the headsmen rushed on Pugachev to undress him: they pulled off his white sheepskin coat and started tearing at the sleeves of his crimson silk caftan. He clasped his hands and fell backwards, and a minute later a head dripping with blood was raised high.[45]

The executioner had received secret orders to cut short the suffering of the condemned. The headsmen cut off the corpse's arms and legs and carried them to the four corners of the scaffold; it was in fact only after this that they displayed the head, stuck on the end of a long stake. Perfilev, making a sign of the cross, prostrated himself on the floor and remained motionless. The headsmen lifted him up and executed him the same way as Pugachev. In the meanwhile Shigaev, Padurov, and Turnov were already in their last convulsions on the gallows. The jingle of a bell was heard: Chika was being driven to Ufa, where his execution was to take place. Then the lesser punishments were meted out and the crowd dispersed; only a small group of the curious remained around the post to which those sentenced to be flogged were being tied one after the other. The chief rebels' severed limbs were taken around to the city gates, and a few days later were burned together with their torsos. The executioners scattered the ashes to the winds. Those rebels who were granted pardon were lined up before the Granovitaia Palace the day after the executions. The amnesty was announced to them, and their shackles were taken off in front of the people.

Thus ended the rebellion that had begun at the instigation of a handful of disobedient Cossacks, had intensified due to the inexcusable negligence of the authorities, and had rocked the foundations of the state from Siberia to Moscow and from Kuban to the Murom Forest. Complete tranquility could not be restored for a long time. Panin and Suvorov stayed in the pacified *guberniias* a whole year, bolstering weakened local administrations, rebuilding cities and forts, and eradicating the last remnants of the subdued rebellion. At the end of 1775 a general amnesty was announced, and it was decreed that the whole matter should be consigned to eternal oblivion. Catherine, wishing to obliterate the memory of the terrible epoch, stripped of its ancient name the river whose banks had first witnessed the insurgence. The Iaik Cossacks were renamed Ural Cossacks, and their town became Uralsk. But the name of the dreaded rebel still resounds in the regions where he wrought havoc. People still clearly remember the bloody epoch that they aptly call Pugachevshchina.[46]

Appendixes

Omitted Chapter from 'The Captain's Daughter'
(1835–36)[1]

We were approaching the banks of the Volga. Our regiment entered the village of X. and stayed there for the night. The village elder told me that on the other side of the river all the villages had rioted, and Pugachev's bands were roaming everywhere. This news made me very anxious. We were supposed to cross the river the next morning. Impatience seized me. My father's village lay 30 versts away, on the other side of the river. I inquired if it would be possible to find a boatman who would take me across. All the peasants were fishermen: there were plenty of boats about. I went to Grinev to inform him of my intention.[2]

"Take care," he said to me. "It is dangerous to go by yourself. Wait until morning. Our detachment will be the first to cross, and we shall bring your parents 50 hussars as guests, just in case."

I insisted on going immediately. The boat was ready; I got into it with two oarsmen. They pushed the boat away from the bank and started rowing vigorously.

The sky was clear. The moon shone. The weather was calm. The Volga flowed smoothly and serenely. The boat, gently rocking, glided over the dark waves at a good pace. I gave myself over to the fancies of my mind. About half an hour passed. We had already reached the middle of the river... Suddenly the oarsmen began to whisper one to the other.

"What's the matter?" I asked, waking from my reveries.

"We can't tell, God knows," answered the oarsmen, glancing to the side.

I turned my eyes in the same direction and saw in the dark something floating down the Volga. The undiscernible object was coming closer to us. I ordered the boatmen to stop and wait for it. The moon went behind a cloud. The floating apparition became even more nebulous. It was already quite close to me, yet I still could not make it out.

"What could it be?" the oarsmen were saying. "Perhaps a sail, perhaps some masts, but there again, it's neither."

Suddenly the moon emerged from behind the cloud and lighted up a horrifying spectacle. What was floating toward us was a gallows fastened to a raft, with three bodies hanging from the transom. A morbid curiosity seized me. I wanted to look into the hanged men's faces.

On my orders, the oarsmen snagged the raft with the boat hook, and my boat knocked into the floating gallows. I jumped out and found myself in the midst of the horrifying posts. The bright moon lighted up the victims' disfigured faces. One of them was an old Chuvash; another one a Russian peasant, a robust, sturdy fellow of about twenty. But it was the third one that fairly startled me and made me cry out with pity as I looked at it: it was Vanka, my poor Vanka, who out of stupidity had joined Pugachev. A black board was nailed to the transom above the corpses on which was written in large white letters: "Brigands and rebels." The oarsmen looked on with equanimity and waited for me, holding the raft fast with the boat hook. I got back into the boat. The raft floated farther downstream. The gallows loomed dark in the night. At last it disappeared, and my boat came up to the high, steep bank...

I rewarded the oarsmen generously. One of them took me to the village near the ferry, to a man whom the villages had elected their chief. We entered the hut together. When the chief heard that I wanted horses, he at first received me rather rudely, but my guide whispered a few words to him, and the chief's surliness at once turned into bustling solicitude. A team of horses was ready in one minute; I sat down in the cart and ordered the driver to make for our village.

I galloped along the main highway, past sleeping villages. The one thing I feared was to be stopped on the road. If my nocturnal encounter on the Volga indicated the presence of rebels, it also served as a proof of strong countermeasures by the government. For any eventuality, I had in my pocket both the pass Pugachev had given me and the order Colonel Grinev had issued. But I did not run into anybody, and toward morning beheld the river and fir woods behind which our village was situated. The driver lashed the horses, and in a quarter of an hour I rode into the village of Y.

The manor house was at the other end of the village. The horses raced along at full speed. Suddenly, in the middle of a street, the driver pulled them up.

"What's the matter?" I asked impatiently.

"A barrier, sir," the driver answered, stopping his frenzied horses with difficulty.

Indeed I beheld a turnpike and a sentry with an oak staff. The peasant came up to me and, doffing his hat, asked for my passport.

"What is the meaning of this?" I asked him. "Why is there a turnpike here? And who are you guarding?"

"We're rebelling, so please Your Honor," he answered, scratching himself.

"And where are your masters?" I asked with a sinking heart...

"Our masters?" repeated the peasant. "Our masters are in the granary."

"Why in the granary?"

"Well, you see, Andriukha the notary put them in stocks and wants to take them to the Tsar Our Father."

"My God! Move that turnpike quickly, you idiot, what are you waiting for?"

The sentry hesitated. I jumped out of the cart and (I regret to confess) boxed him on the ear, then proceeded to move the turnpike aside myself. My peasant gazed at me in stupid bewilderment. I got back into the cart and ordered the driver to the manor house at a gallop. The granary was in the courtyard. At its locked door there stood two peasants, also with oak staffs. My cart stopped right in front of them. I jumped out and rushed up to them.

"Open the door!" I ordered them.

I must have looked frightening: at least they both dropped their staffs and ran away. I tried to knock off the lock and break down the door, but the door was made of oak and the enormous lock seemed to be indestructible. At this moment a well-built young peasant came out of the servants' quarters and asked me with a haughty air how I dared disturb the peace.

"Where is Andriushka the notary?" I shouted at him. "Call him to me at once."

"Me, I am Andrei Afanasevich—and not Andriushka," he answered proudly, with his hands on his hips. "What do you want?"

Instead of replying, I grabbed him by the collar and, dragging him to the granary door, ordered him to open it. The notary tried to be stubborn at first, but a *fatherly* chastisement had its effect on him, too. He pulled out the key and opened the granary. I dashed across the threshold and caught sight of my father and mother in a dark corner, feebly lighted through a narrow slit in the ceiling. Their hands were tied and their feet were in stocks. I rushed to embrace them, unable to utter a word. They both looked at me with astonishment: three years of military life had changed me so much that they could not recognize me. My dear mother cried out and burst into tears.

Suddenly a sweet familiar voice caught my ear.

"Petr Andreich! Is it you?"

I stood dumbfounded... When I looked around, I saw in the other corner Maria Ivanovna, also tied up.

My father looked at me in silence, not daring to believe his own eyes. His face beamed with joy. I hurried to cut through the knots of their ropes with my sword.

"Hello, hello, Petrusha," father said, pressing me to his heart. "Thank God, we've lived to see you."

"Petrusha, my dearest," said mother, "how did you get here? Are you all right?"

I hastened to lead them out of their captivity—but when I went to the door, I found it locked again.

"Andriushka," I shouted, "open up!"

"Not likely," answered the notary from behind the door. "Just please to sit in there yourself. We'll teach you to disturb the peace and rough up officials of the state!"

I went around inspecting the granary, looking for some way to break out.

"Don't trouble with it," said my father. "I'm not the kind of landowner who leaves holes in his granary for thieves to go in and out."

My dear mother, who had been momentarily cheered by my arrival, now fell into despair seeing that I was to perish with the rest of the family. But I felt more reassured now that I had joined them. I had a saber and two pistols with me: I was perfectly capable of warding off an assault. Grinev was bound to arrive by the evening and liberate us. I communicated all this to my parents and managed to calm mother down. They gave themselves over to the joy of reunion.

"Well, Petr," father said to me, "you've played some pretty pranks, and I was thoroughly annoyed with you. But there is no need to dwell on the past. By now, I hope, you've sown your wild oats and reformed. I know you have served as an honest officer should. I thank you for that. You have been a comfort to your old father. If I owe my liberation to you, life will be all the sweeter to me."

My eyes full of tears, I kissed his hand and glanced at Maria Ivanovna, who was so glad of my presence that she seemed entirely calm and cheerful.

Around noon we heard some unusual noise and shouts.

"What does this mean?" said father. "Could it be that your colonel's arrived?"

"It couldn't be," I answered. "He won't get here before evening."
The noise intensified. The alarm was sounded. People were galloping around the yard on horseback. At this moment the gray head of
Savelich appeared in a narrow opening cut in the wall, and my poor
attendant said in a mournful tone:

"Andrei Petrovich, Avdotia Vasilevna, young master Petr Andreich,
young mistress Maria Ivanovna, bad luck! The villains have entered
the village. And do you know, Petr Andreich, who's led them here?
Shvabrin, Aleksei Ivanych, the devil take him!"

Hearing that odious name, Maria Ivanovna clasped her hands and
remained motionless.

"Listen," I said to Savelich, "send somebody on horseback to the
ferry at Z. to meet the hussar regiment and inform the colonel of our
dangerous situation."

"Who could I send, sir? All the boys are rebelling, and all the horses
are taken. Gracious me! They're already in the yard. They're heading
for the granary."

At this time several voices could be heard from behind the door. I
signaled silently to mother and Maria Ivanovna to retire into a corner
and, baring my saber, hugged the wall by the door. Father took the
pistols, cocked them, and took up his position beside me. The lock
rattled, the door opened, and the notary's head appeared in it. I struck
it with my saber, and he fell down, blocking the entrance. At the same
time my father fired through the doorway. The crowd laying siege to
us pulled back with curses. I dragged the wounded man across the
threshold and locked the door on the inside with a latch. The yard was
full of armed people. Among them I recognized Shvabrin.

"Don't be afraid," I said to the women. "There is hope for us. And
you, father, don't shoot any more. Let's save the last cartridge."

My dear mother silently prayed to God; Maria Ivanovna stood by
her and awaited our fate with angelic calm. From behind the door
threats, abuse, and curses could be heard. I stood in my place, ready to
hack to pieces the first person bold enough to try to get in. Suddenly
the villains grew silent. The voice of Shvabrin, calling me by name,
caught my ear.

"I am here, what do you want?"

"Surrender, Bulanin, there is no point in struggling.[3] Take pity on
your old ones. You can't save yourself by obstinacy. I'll get you!"

"Try it, traitor!"

"I'm not going to waste my time trying to get in there, nor shall I
sacrifice my men. I'll give orders to set the granary on fire, and then
we'll see what you can do, Don Quixote of Belogorsk. Right now it's

time for dinner. In the meanwhile sit in there and give the matter some thought at leisure. Good-bye, Maria Ivanovna. I won't apologize to you; I'm sure you're having a fine time in the dark with your cavalier."

Shvabrin went away, leaving some guards at the granary. We were silent. We each kept our thoughts to ourselves, not daring to communicate them to the others. I imagined all the things that an enraged Shvabrin was capable of doing. About myself I hardly worried at all. Shall I confess it? Even the fate of my parents did not terrify me as much as the thought of what would become of Maria Ivanovna. I knew that all the peasants and house servants adored my mother; and my father, despite his strictness, was also well liked because he was fair and knew what the people under his authority truly needed. Their rebellion was an aberration, a temporary bout of drunkenness, and not an expression of resentment. For both of my parents, mercy was likely. But what about Maria Ivanovna? What fate was this corrupt and unscrupulous man preparing for her? I dared not dwell on this horrible question; God forgive me, I was ready to kill her rather than see her once more in the hands of her cruel enemy.

Another hour or so went by. The singing of the revelers could be heard around the village. Our guards envied them and, annoyed with us, heaped abuse on us, menacing us with torture and death. We awaited the sequel to Shvabrin's threats. At length a great commotion arose in the yard, and we heard Shvabrin's voice once more.

"Well, have you had time to think it over? Will you voluntarily place yourselves in my hands?"

Nobody answered him. Having waited a little, Shvabrin gave orders to bring some straw. In a few minutes a fire flared up, illuminating the dark granary; smoke began to seep through crevices under the threshold. At that moment Maria Ivanovna came up to me and, taking my hand, quietly said, "Enough, Petr Andreich! Don't destroy yourself as well as your parents. Let me out. Shvabrin will listen to me."

"Not for anything in the world!" I cried with fury. "Do you realize what would happen to you?"

"I will not survive having my honor trampled on," she answered calmly. "But perhaps I shall be able to save my deliverer and the family that has given such generous support to a poor orphan. Farewell, Andrei Petrovich. Farewell, Avdotia Vasilevna. You have been more than benefactors to me. Give me your blessing. And fare you well, too, Petr Andreich. You can be assured that... that..." With these words she burst into tears and covered her face with her hands. I thought I would lose my mind. My mother wept.

"Enough of that nonsense, Maria Ivanovna," said my father. "Who would let you go to the brigands by yourself! Sit here with us and be quiet. If we are to die, we'll die together. Listen, what's that they're saying now?"

"Will you surrender?" shouted Shvabrin. "Don't you understand? Within five minutes you will be roasted."

"We're not surrendering, villain!" my dear father replied in a firm tone.

His face, covered with wrinkles, was animated by amazing vigor, and his eyes flashed menacingly from under his white brows. Turning to me, he said, "Now is the time!"

He opened the door. The flames burst in and whirled upwards over logs caulked with dry moss. Father fired his pistol and stepped across the flaming threshold, shouting, "Follow me!" I seized Mother and Maria Ivanovna by the hand and quickly led them out into the open air. At the threshold lay Shvabrin, shot through by my father's feeble old hand; the crowd of brigands, which had fallen back from our sudden sally, soon gathered courage and began to surround us. I managed to deliver a few more blows, but a well-aimed brick caught me straight in the chest. I fell down and lost consciousness for a moment. When I came to my senses I saw Shvabrin sitting on the bloodied grass, and my whole family before him. I was lifted up by the arms. A crowd of peasants, Cossacks, and Bashkirs surrounded us. Shvabrin was terribly pale. He pressed one of his hands against his wounded side. Pain and anger were written on his face. He slowly raised his head, looked at me, and uttered in a weak, indistinct voice, "Hang him... Hang them all, except her..."

The crowd of villains immediately closed in on us and dragged us to the gate with shouts. But suddenly they let go of us and ran off: Grinev and behind him a whole squadron of hussars, with sabers bared, were riding through the gate.

The rebels took off in all directions; the hussars pursued them, hacking at them and capturing them. Grinev jumped off his horse, bowed to my father and mother, and warmly shook my hand.

"I've come just at the right time," he said to us. "Ah, here is your fiancée, too."

Maria Ivanovna blushed to her ears. My father went up to him and thanked him with a quiet though affectionate air. Mother embraced him, calling him our guardian angel.

"Please come in," father said to him, and led him into our house.

Passing by Shvabrin, Grinev stopped.

"Who is this?" he asked, looking at the wounded man.

"This is the chief, the leader of the gang himself," replied my father, not without a note of pride, betraying the old soldier in him. "God gave strength to my feeble old hand to punish the young villain and take revenge for my son's blood."

"It's Shvabrin," I said to Grinev.

"Shvabrin! I'm extremely glad. Hussars, take him! And tell our physician to bandage his wound and look after him like the apple of his eye. It is absolutely essential to hand him over to the Secret Commission in Kazan. He is one of the chief offenders, and his testimony must be important."

Shvabrin opened his weary eyes. The only thing you could read in his features was physical pain. The hussars carried him off in a cloak.

We entered the house. I looked around with emotion, remembering my childhood years. Nothing had changed in the house; everything was in its former place. Shvabrin had not allowed it to be plundered, preserving, even in his utter debasement, an instinctive revulsion from dishonest greed. The servants came into the entrance hall. They had not participated in the rebellion and were sincerely glad to see our deliverance. Savelich was triumphant. It must be mentioned that during the alarm caused by the brigands' attack he had run to the stables where Shvabrin's horse was standing, saddled it, surreptitiously led it out, and, thanks to the commotion, galloped off to the ferry unnoticed. He came across the regiment as it was resting on this side of the Volga. Grinev, learning of our danger from him, gave orders to mount and march forward—to march at a gallop—and, thank God, arrived in time.

The hussars returned from pursuing the rebels and brought back several captives. They were locked up in the same granary in which we had weathered the memorable siege.

Grinev insisted on displaying the notary's head on a pole by the alehouse for several hours.

We each retired to our respective rooms. My old ones needed rest. Having not slept all night, I threw myself on the bed and fell into a deep sleep. Grinev went out to give further orders.

In the evening we gathered in the drawing room by the samovar, merrily chatting about the danger that had passed us by. Maria Ivanovna was pouring the tea; I sat down by her and busied myself exclusively with her. It seemed to me that my parents were looking with favor on the tenderness of our relationship. That evening has remained fresh in my memory to this day. I was happy, completely happy; and how many such moments are granted in a man's paltry life?

The next day it was reported to my father that the peasants had come into the courtyard, repentant. Father went out on the porch to see them. When he appeared, the peasants knelt down.

"Well, fools," he said to them, "what made you rebel?"

"We're guilty, master," they answered in unison.

"Guilty, are you? I'll forgive you this time, out of joy, since it's been the Lord's will to reunite me with my son Petr Andreich."

"We're guilty! Indeed guilty!"

"Well, all right: it is not a valiant sword that strikes a repentant head. God gave us fine weather: it's time to gather in the hay; yet you, you fools, what have you been doing for three whole days? Elder! Order them into the hayfields, all of them to a man! And see to it, you redheaded devil, that all the hay is in stacks by Saint Ilia's day. Off with you."

The peasants bowed and went to do their corvée duty as if nothing had happened.

Shvabrin's wound turned out not to have been fatal. He was dispatched to Kazan under guard. I saw from the window how they placed him in a cart. Our eyes met: he lowered his head and I hastily left the window. I was loath to appear to be exulting in my enemy's misfortune and humiliation.

Grinev had to march on. I decided to go with him despite my desire to spend a few more days in the midst of my family. On the eve of our departure I went to my parents and, as was the custom in those days, bowed down to the ground before them, asking them to give their blessing to my union with Maria Ivanovna. They raised me up and gave their consent with joyous tears in their eyes. I brought Maria Ivanovna, pale and trembling, before them. They blessed us... What I felt, I will not attempt to describe. Those who have been in my position will understand me, and those who have not, I can only pity; I would advise them to fall in love and obtain parental blessing while there is still time.

The next day the regiment prepared to leave. Grinev said farewell to my family. We were all convinced that the military operations would soon come to an end; I hoped I would become a husband in another month. Maria Ivanovna, saying good-bye to me, kissed me in front of everybody. I mounted my horse. Savelich once more followed behind me, and the regiment set off.

For a long time I kept glancing back at the rural home that I was leaving again. A gloomy premonition tormented me. Something whispered in my ear that I had not yet escaped all misfortune. My heart felt the approach of a new storm.

I will not go into the details of our campaign and of the end of the Pugachev war. We passed through villages ravaged by Pugachev and, despite our best intentions, took away from the poor villagers whatever the brigands had left them.

They did not know whom to obey. Law and order were suspended everywhere. Landowners were hiding in the forests. Bands of brigands dealt destruction everywhere. The commanding officers of the various government troops sent in pursuit of Pugachev, who was at this time already fleeing toward Astrakhan, arbitrarily punished both the guilty and the innocent... Conditions were terrible in the whole vast region engulfed in the conflagration. May the Lord save us from another such senseless and ruthless Russian rebellion! Either those who conspire to bring about impracticable radical changes in our country are young and do not know our people or they are calloused men to whom neither another person's head nor their own necks are worth a kopeck.

Pugachev fled, pursued by Ivan Ivanovich Mikhelson. Soon we heard about his complete defeat. Finally, Grinev received news of the pretender's capture from his general, with orders not to proceed any farther. I could at last return home. I was in raptures; yet a strange premonition overshadowed my joy.

Minor Fictional Fragments

Nadenka
(1819)[1]

Several young men, mostly officers, were losing their fortunes to the Pole Jasuński, who was holding bank with a small sum just for amusement, surreptitiously replacing cards while cutting the pack with an important air. Aces, treys, tattered kings, and bent jacks were spread out like a fan, and dust clouds of erased chalk mingled with Turkish tobacco smoke.

"Is it really two in the morning? My God, we've kept at it!" said Viktor N. to his young comrades. "Isn't it time we quit?"

They all threw down their cards and got up from the table. While finishing their pipes, they each counted their own or someone else's win; they argued, settled the matter, and left.

"Would you like to have supper with me?" the wayward Velverov asked Viktor. "I'll introduce you to a very sweet little girl, you'll be grateful."

They both got into the droshki and went flying along Petersburg's sleeping streets.

In the Beginning of 1812
(1829)[2]

In the beginning of 1812 our regiment was stationed in a small town, a county seat, where we were having a very good time. Landowners from neighboring villages usually spent the winter there; we got together every day, and on Sundays danced at the house of the marshal of the nobility. All of us, i.e., all the twenty-year-old commissioned officers, were in love; many of my comrades met their future wives at those gatherings; and therefore it is not surprising that every trifling detail connected with that time is memorable and interesting to me.

Most frequently we visited the mayor's house. He took bribes and was a buffoon and a great host; his wife was a well-preserved and good-humored matron, very fond of playing whist; and the daughter, a slender, melancholy girl of seventeen, brought up on novels and blancmange...

Notes of a Young Man
(1829 or 1830)[3]

I was commissioned an officer on May 4, 1825, and on the 6th received an order to join a regiment in the small town of Vasilkov.[4] On the 9th I left Petersburg.

Only a few days ago I was still a cadet; only a few days ago they were still waking me at six o'clock in the morning, and I was still memorizing my German lesson in the midst of unceasing noise at the military school. Now I was an ensign, had 475 rubles in my satchel, could do what I liked, and was galloping along with relay horses to the small town of Vasilkov, where I would sleep till eight and would never utter one single word of German again.

My ears were still ringing with the noise and shouts of cadets playing and with the monotonous murmur of industrious students repeating the vocabulary lessons: "*le bluet, le bluet*—cornflower; *amarante*—amaranth—*amarante, amarante...*" Now the only noises disturbing the tranquil scene around me were the rumble of the cart and the tinkling of the bells... I still could not get used to this silence.

The thought of my freedom, of the pleasures of the journey, and of the adventures awaiting me filled me at first with a sense of inexpressible joy, approaching ecstasy. Calming down somewhat, I began to observe the motion of the front wheels and made some mathematical calculations. This occupation gradually tired me out, and the journey no longer seemed as pleasant as it had at the beginning.

Arriving at a wayside station, I handed my order for fresh horses to the one-eyed stationmaster and demanded to be served as soon as possible. But to my indescribable annoyance, I was told that there were no horses available. I looked at the station register: an official of the sixth class, traveling from the city of X. to Petersburg, had taken twelve horses for himself and for an unidentified future companion; the wife of General B. had taken eight; two teams of three had gone off with the mail; and the remaining two horses had been put at the disposal of an ensign like your humble servant. Only the team reserved for courier duty stood in the yard, and the stationmaster could not give that one to me. If a courier or special emissary should unexpectedly gallop up and find no horses, what would happen to the stationmaster? There would be a calamity: he might lose his position and have to go begging. I tried to bribe him, but he remained steadfast and resolutely rejected my twenty-kopeck piece. There was nothing I could do. I resigned myself to the unavoidable.

"Would you like some tea or coffee?" the stationmaster asked.

I thanked him and started looking at the pictures that adorned his humble dwelling. They depicted the parable of the Prodigal Son. In the first one, a venerable old man, in nightcap and dressing gown, was bidding farewell to a restless youth who was hastily accepting his blessing and a bag of money. The second one depicted the corrupt young man's lewd behavior in vivid colors: he was seated at a table, surrounded by false friends and shameless women. Farther on, the ruined youth, in a French robe and with a three-cornered hat on his head, was tending swine and sharing their meal. Deep sorrow and repentance were reflected in his features; he was remembering his father's house, where *how many hired servants*, etc.[5] At last his return to his father was shown. The warmhearted old man, in the same nightcap and dressing gown, was running forward to meet him. The Prodigal Son was kneeling; in the background the cook was killing the fatted calf, and the elder brother was asking the servants with annoyance about the cause of all the rejoicing. German verses were printed under each picture. I read them with enjoyment and copied them in order to translate them in some future hour of leisure.

The other pictures had no frames and were affixed to the wall with small nails. They depict the burying of the cat, a dispute between the red nose and the mighty frost, and the like—none deserving the attention of an educated man either from an ethical or from an artistic point of view.

I sat down by the window. There was nothing to look at: just a compact row of uniform cottages, one leaning against the other. One or two apple trees here and there, and one or two rowanberry bushes, surrounded by a decrepit fence. And a cart without horses, with my suitcase and hamper in it.

The day was hot. The drivers had gone off in various directions. In the street little boys with golden heads and smeared faces were playing knucklebones. Across the street an old woman sat hunched over before a cottage. Cocks crowed occasionally. Dogs rolled around in the sun or wandered about with tongues stuck out and tails hanging limp; piglets ran out from under a gate, squealing, and scurried off without any apparent cause.

What boredom! I went for a walk among the fields. A tumbledown
well. A shallow puddle beside it. Little yellow ducklings gamboling in
it under the eyes of a stupid-looking mother duck, like spoilt children
left in charge of a governess.

I set out along the main highway: there was a field of scrubby winter crop on the right; brushwood and a swamp on the left. A flat
expanse all around. Nothing but striped verst-posts ahead. A slow-
moving sun in the sky; a cloud here and there. What boredom! Having gone to the third verst-post and ascertained that it was twenty-
two more versts to the next station, I turned back.

Returning to the station I tried to have a chat with my driver, but
he, as though deliberately avoiding a decent conversation, would
answer my questions only with phrases like "I couldn't tell, Your
Honor," "God only knows," "that may be". . .

I sat down by the window once more and asked the fat serving
woman, who was continually running by me on her way either to the
back porch or to the storeroom, whether she could find something for
me to read. She brought out a few books. Delighted, I opened them
eagerly. But my joy vanished at once when I discovered a worn primer
and an arithmetic book published for elementary schools. The stationmaster's son, a nine-year-old little ruffian, used these books, as
the woman said, "to study all the sciences," and he had stubbornly
torn out each page he had memorized, for which, in accordance with a
natural law of retribution, he lost a corresponding amount of hair.

My Fate Is Sealed: I Am Getting Married
(1830)[6]
Translated from the French[7]

My fate is sealed: I am getting married...

She whom I have doted on for two whole years, whom my eyes
sought first wherever I went, and with whom a simple encounter
seemed to be bliss—she is, by God, almost mine.

Waiting for a decisive answer was one of the most painful experiences of my life. Watching for a long-expected card to turn up, suffering pangs of conscience, or sleeping before a duel are nothing compared with this experience.

Being rejected was not the only thing I was afraid of. One of my
friends used to say, "I don't understand how anybody can propose if he
knows for sure that there is no chance of rejection."

To get married—easy to say! Most people see in marriage no more than shawls bought on credit, a new carriage, and a pink dressing gown.

Others expect a dowry and a settled life...

Still others marry just to be doing it—since everybody else is doing it, and since they have reached the age of thirty. If you ask them what matrimony means, they will answer you with a banal epigram.

For me, marrying means sacrificing my independence—my carefree, whimsical independence—my extravagant habits, aimless wanderings, solitude, and inconstancy.

I am about to take on myself two lives, though even the one I have had has not been complete. I have never chased after happiness—I could do without it. Now I need it for two: where am I to get it?

While I am still not married, what are my obligations? I have an ailing uncle, whom I hardly ever see. If I come to visit him, he is pleased to see me; if I do not come, he excuses me: "The scapegrace is young, he has other things on his mind." I do not correspond with anybody, and I pay my bills every month. I get up when I like in the morning and receive whom I like. If I feel like going out, I have my clever and tame Jenny saddled, and ride down sidestreets, looking through windows of squat little houses; here a family is sitting around a samovar; there a servant is sweeping the rooms; behind still another window a little girl is learning to play the piano, with her drudge of a music teacher seated beside her. She turns her absent gaze on me, while her teacher scolds her; I slowly ride by... When I come back home, I sort out some books and papers, tidy up my dressing table, and dress either carelessly—if I am going visiting—or with painstaking care—if I am to dine at a restaurant, where I read a new novel or journals. If Walter Scott and Cooper have written nothing new, and if no criminal case is reported in the papers, I order a bottle of champagne on ice, watch the glass frost over, and drink slowly, rejoicing over the fact that the dinner is costing me seventeen rubles, and that I can afford such an extravagance. I go to the theater and seek out in some box a remarkable attire and black eyes; we trade glances, and this keeps me busy until it is time to leave. I spend the evening either in noisy society, where the whole town is crowding together, where I see everyone and everything, and where nobody takes any notice of me; or else in a cherished circle of the select, where I speak about myself and where they listen to me. I return home late; I fall asleep reading a good book. The next day I ride around on sidestreets again, past the house where the little girl played the piano. She is repeating yesterday's lesson. She looks on me as an acquaintance and laughs.—This is the life I lead as a bachelor...

If I were to be rejected, I thought, I would go abroad—and I was already imagining myself on board a steamer. Everybody around me is bustling, saying good-bye, carrying suitcases, looking at the clock. The steamer sets off: fresh sea air blows in my face; I look at the receding shore for a long time: *"My native land, adieu."*[8] A young woman standing close to me is beginning to feel nauseated, which lends her pale face an expression of languid tenderness... She asks me to bring her some water. Thank God, I shall have something to do until we reach Kronstadt...

At that moment a note was handed to me: it was an answer to my letter. My fiancée's father was amiably asking me to come over... Without any doubt, my proposal had been accepted. Nadenka, my angel—she is mine!... All my melancholy doubts disappeared at that heavenly thought. I throw myself into my carriage and go at a gallop; here is their house; I enter the anteroom; the bustling reception given me by the servants already shows that I am betrothed. This embarrasses me: these people see into my heart and talk about my love in their lowly tongue!

Her father and mother sat in the drawing room. The former met me with open arms. He drew a handerchief from his pocket and wanted to weep but could not; he decided to blow his nose instead. Her mother's eyes were red. Nadenka was sent for: she came in pale and ill at ease. Her father went out and brought in the icons of Nicholas the Miracle-Worker and the Kazan Mother of God. We were blessed. Nadenka gave me her cold, unresponsive hand. Her mother started speaking about the dowry, and her father about a village in the Saratov Guberniia: I was engaged.

And so, this is no longer the secret of two hearts. Today it is domestic news; tomorrow it will be broadcast through the streets.

In the same way a verse tale, conceived in solitude during summer nights in the moonlight, is later sold at the bookstore and is criticized in the journals by fools.

Everybody is glad of my happiness, everybody is congratulating me, all have grown fond of me. Each is offering his services: one would let me have his house, another would lend me money, and a third one recommends a Bukhara merchant who sells shawls. There is even a person who worries about the size of my future family and is offering me twelve dozen pairs of gloves with the image of Mlle. Sontag on them.[9]

Young men are beginning to stand on ceremony with me: they respect me as an adversary. The ladies, to my face, praise me for my choice, but behind my back they express their pity for my fiancée: "Poor thing! She's so young, so innocent, and he is such a wayward, unprincipled man..."

I must confess that all this is beginning to get on my nerves. I like the custom, prevalent in some ancient tribes, of the bridegroom secretly spiriting away his bride. The next day he could introduce her to the town tattlers as his wife. In our society preparations for family happiness involve printed announcements, gifts known to the whole city, formal letters, and visits—in other words, ostentation of all kinds...

A Fragment
(1830)[10]

Despite all the great advantages enjoyed by versifiers (it must be admitted that apart from the privilege of using the accusative instead of the genitive case after a negative verb and one or two other acts of so-called poetic license, we do not know of any particular advantages Russian versifiers could be said to enjoy)—however that may be, despite all their advantages these people are subject to a great deal of trouble and unpleasantness. There is no need to mention their usually low social prestige and poverty, which have become proverbial, or the envy and slander to which their own peers subject them if they attain fame, and the contempt and ridicule showered on them from all sides if their works are not liked; but I ask you what can be comparable to the misfortune none of them can avoid—I mean being judged by fools. Even this grief, however, great as it may be, is not the worst visited on them. The most bitter and intolerable bane of the poet is his title, his sobriquet, with which he is branded and of which he can never rid himself. The reading public look on him as though he were their property, and consider themselves entitled to hold him to account for the smallest step he takes. In their opinion, he was born for their pleasure and draws his breath solely in order to pick out rhymes. If his circumstances require him to spend some time in the country, when he returns the first person he runs into will ask him, "Have you brought with you something new for us?" If he visits the army in order to see friends and relatives, the public will inevitably demand that he write an epic about the latest victory, and the journalists will get angry with him for making them wait for it too long![11] If he is sunk in thought about his tangled finances, matrimonial inten-

tions, or the illness of someone close to his heart, this will immediately provoke the inane exclamation, accompanied by an inane
smile, "No doubt you are composing something!" Should he fall in
love, the lady of his heart will promptly buy an album and be ready to
receive an elegy. If he visits his neighbor on business or simply in order to be diverted from his work, the neighbor will call in his young
son, ordering him to recite *some* poetry, and the lad will treat the
poet, in the most doleful tones, to the latter's own verses with distortions. And these occasions are only what might be called his triumphs. What must the pains of his profession be like? I am not sure,
but it seems to me that they must be easier to bear. At least, one of
my young friends, a well-known poet, has confessed that all those salutations, inquiries, albums, and little boys have irritated him so
much that he has constantly had to be on his guard lest he make some
rude response, and has had to tell himself repeatedly that these good
people probably do not intend to exasperate him...

Although a poet, my friend was the simplest and most ordinary of
people. When he felt that nonsense approach (which was what he
called inspiration), he locked himself in his room and wrote lying in
bed from morning till late night; he would dress hastily in order to
dine at a restaurant, go out for about three hours, then, returning, get
back into bed and write until the cocks crowed. This would last about
two or three weeks, a month at the most, and occurred only once a
year, always in the fall. He assured me that he knew true happiness
only at such times. The rest of the time he led his dissipated life, reading little, writing nothing, and perpetually hearing the inevitable
question, "When will you present us with a new creation of your
pen?" The esteemed public would have had to wait for long periods at
a time before they received a new gift from my friend if it had not
been for the booksellers, who paid fairly high prices for his poetry.
Since he was always short of money, he published his works as he
wrote them, and then had the pleasure of reading critical judgments
of them in the press (as mentioned above), which he in his pithy par-
lance called "eavesdropping on the pothouse, to learn what the lackeys are saying about you."

My friend descended from one of our ancient noble families, a matter on which he prided himself with all the simplicity of his heart.[12]
Three lines of a chronicle mentioning one of his forebears were as
dear to him as three stars on the chest of an uncle are to a fashionable
gentleman of the bedchamber. Although he was poor—as is most of
our ancient nobility—he asserted, turning his nose up, that he would

sooner not marry than take a wife who was not a direct descendant of the princely line of Riurik. He even insisted he would take one of the Eletskii Princesses, whose fathers and brothers, as is well known, plow their own land nowadays and, meeting one another among the furrows, shake the mud off their plows with the words:

"Lord bless you, Prince Antip Kuzmich, how much has Your Highness plowed today?"

"I thank ye kindly, Prince Erema Avdeevich..."

Apart from this foible, which by the way we attribute to a wish to imitate Lord Byron, who also sold his poems very well, my friend was *un homme tout rond*, a perfectly well-rounded man as the French say, or a *homo quadratus*, a square person according to the Latin expression—that is, in plain Russian, a very decent man.

With very, very few exceptions, he did not like the company of his fellow men of letters. He thought they had too many pretensions, some to a sharp wit, others to a fiery imagination, still others to sensibility, melancholy, disillusionment, profundity, philanthropy, misanthropy, irony, and so on, and so forth. Some seemed to him tedious in their stupidity, others insufferable in tone, still others repulsive in their baseness or dangerous in their double line of business[13]—and all of them too vain, exclusively preoccupied with themselves and their own work. He preferred the company of women and of people belonging to high society, who, seeing him daily, no longer stood on ceremony with him and spared him conversations about literature as well as the famous question, "Have you written a new little something?"

We have expatiated on our friend for two reasons: first, because he is the only man of letters with whom we have had occasion to become closely acquainted, and second, because it was from him that we have heard the story herewith offered to the reader.

This fragment seems to have constituted a preface to a story that either has not been written or has been lost. We did not want to destroy it...

A Novel at a Caucasian Spa
(1831)[14]

On one of the first days of April 181.. there was a great commotion in the house of Katerina Petrovna Tomskaia. All the doors were wide open; the anteroom and the hall were piled high with trunks and suitcases; the drawers were pulled out of all the chests; the servants continually ran up and down the stairs; and the maids bustled and argued. The head of the household herself, a forty-five-year-old lady, sat in her bedroom, going over the accounts brought to her by her corpulent steward, who was now standing in front of her with his hands behind his back and with his right foot thrust forward. Katerina Petrovna pretended to be fully conversant with all the ins and outs of the management of her estate, but her questions and suggestions revealed the ignorance of a noblewoman about such affairs: they occasionally brought a barely perceptible smile to the steward's dignified face, though he nonetheless went into the details of all the required explanations with great indulgence. At this time a servant announced the arrival of Praskovia Ivanovna Povodova. Katerina Petrovna, glad to have an opportunity to interrupt her consultations, gave orders to have her guest shown in and dismissed her steward.

"Mercy on us, my dear," said an old lady, entering, "you're about to take the road! Where is it you needs must go?"

"To the Caucasus, my dear Praskovia Ivanovna."

"To the Caucasus! Marry, Moscow is saying the truth for the first time ever, and I didn't believe it. To the Caucasus! But that's frightfully far. What can possess you to go tramping heaven knows where and heaven knows why?"

"What else am I to do? The doctors have advised that my daughter Masha needs the mineral waters, and that my health requires hot baths. I've been suffering for a year and a half; mayhap the Caucasus will help."

"May God grant it. And how soon are you leaving?"

"In another four days or so; perhaps a week, no more. Everything is ready. My new carriage was delivered yesterday, and what a carriage! It's a toy, it's a beauty to behold; it's full of drawers and everything you could ask for: it has a bed, a dressing table, a provisions hamper, a medicine cabinet, a kitchen with crockery—do you want to see it?"

"Please, my dear."

Both ladies went out on the porch. The coachmen pulled the carriage out of the shed. Katerina Petrovna told them to open the doors; she got in and rummaged through everything, turning up all the cushions, pulling out all the drawers, revealing all the secrets and conveniences, letting up all the blinds, displaying all the mirrors, and turning all the pouches inside out—in other words, she acted very nimbly and energetically for a sick woman. Having admired the equipage, the two ladies returned to the drawing room, where they talked some more about the impending journey, about coming back to Moscow, and about plans for the following winter.

"I certainly hope to return in October," said Katerina Petrovna. "I shall be at home two evenings a week, and I hope, dear, that you will transfer your Boston parties to my house."

At this moment a girl of about eighteen, graceful and tall, with a beautiful pale complexion and fiery black eyes, entered the room quietly, kissed Katerina Petrovna's hand, and dropped a curtsy for Povodova.

"Did you sleep well, Masha?" asked Katerina Petrovna.

"Very well, mama; I've only just got up. You're probably surprised to hear about such laziness, Praskovia Ivanovna, but I can't help it. It's an invalid's privilege."

"Sleep, my dear, sleep, to your heart's content," Povodova replied. "But hark my word: come back from the Caucasus rosy-cheeked and healthy, and, God willing, married."

"What do you mean, married?" rejoined Katerina Petrovna, laughing. "Whom should she marry in the Caucasus? A Circassian Prince?"

"A Circassian! The Lord save her! All these Turks and Bukharans are infidels. They'd shave her head and lock her up."

"If God grant her good health," Katerina Petrovna said with a sigh, "suitors will be found. Masha, heaven be thanked, is still young, and she has a dowry. And if a good man grows fond of her, he'll take her even without a dowry."

"It's still better to have a dowry," said Praskovia Ivanovna, getting up. "Let us say good-bye, Katerina Ivanovna; I shan't see you before September: it's too far for me to drag myself all the way here, from Basmaniia to Arbat, and I will not ask you to visit me—I know you're busy just now. And good-bye to you, too, my beauty: don't forget my advice."

The ladies said farewell, and Praskovia Ivanovna left.[15]

I Have Often Thought
(ca. 1833)[16]

I have often thought about this horrifying family scene: I have imagined the pregnancy of the young wife, her horrifying situation, while her husband waited calmly, trustingly.

At last the hour of delivery arrives. The husband is present while the charming young sinner is in labor. He hears the newborn baby's first cry; he dashes to his child in ecstasy... and remains motionless...

A Russian Pelham
(1834 or 1835)[17]

I

I remember my life from very early childhood. Here is a scene that has remained fresh in my memory.

My nurse brings me into a large room, dimly lit by a candle under a shade. In the bed behind green curtains lies a woman dressed all in white; my father takes me by the hand. She kisses me and weeps. My father sobs aloud; I am frightened and begin to cry. Nurse leads me out of the room, saying:

"Mama wants to go beddy-bye."

I also remember a great commotion, a lot of guests, people running from room to room. The sun shines through all the windows and I feel exceedingly cheerful. A monk with a gold cross on his chest blesses me; a long red coffin is borne through the door. That is all the impression my mother's funeral has left in my heart. As I was to gather later from the stories of people who had not recognized her true worth, she had been a woman of exceptional intellect and sensitivity.

Past that scene my recollections become confused. I can give a clear account of myself beginning only with age eight. But first I must say a few words about my family.

My father was appointed sergeant when he was still in my grandmother's womb. He was raised at home up to age eighteen. His tutor, M. Décor, was a simple and warmhearted little old man, with an excellent knowledge of French orthography. It is not known whether my father was ever instructed by any other teacher, but it seems that he had no sound knowledge of any subject except French orthography. He married, against his parents' wishes, a girl several years his senior, and retired to live in Moscow that same year. Old Savelich, his valet, told me later that those first years of my father's marriage had been happy. My mother managed to bring about a reconciliation between her husband and his family, the latter having grown fond of her. But my father's frivolous and inconstant character did not allow her to enjoy tranquility and happiness. He formed a liaison with a woman well known in society for her beauty and amorous adventures. For his sake she divorced her husband, who was willing to relinquish her to my father for 10,000 rubles and who afterwards came to dine with us quite frequently. My mother was aware of everything but kept quiet. Her mental anguish undermined her health. She took to her bed, never to rise from it again.

My father had 5,000 male serfs. In other words, he was one of those noblemen whom the late Count Sheremetev used to call small-holders, sincerely amazed at how they could make ends meet! The point is that my father lived no worse than Count Sheremetev, though he was just about twenty times poorer. Muscovites still remember his dinners, his domestic theater and brass ensemble. A couple of years after my mother's death, Anna Petrovna Virlatskaia, the agent of her undoing, came to live in his house. She was what you might call a woman of striking appearance, though no longer in the first bloom of youth. A boy in a red shirt with cuffs was also brought into the house and introduced to me as my little brother. I stared at him wide-eyed. Mishenka scuffled his foot, first to the right, then to the left, and then wanted to play with my toy gun; I snatched it from his hands; he burst into tears; my father made me stand in the corner and gave my gun to my little brother as a present.

Such a beginning did not augur well for the future. And indeed I cannot recall one pleasant impression from my further sojourn under my father's roof. My father did, of course, love me, but he did not trouble himself about me, leaving me to the care of Frenchmen, who were perpetually being hired and dismissed. My first tutor turned out to be a drunkard; the second one, a man not without intelligence and knowledge, had such a violent temper that once he almost clubbed me to death for having spilled some ink on his waistcoat; and the third one, who lived in our house for almost a full year, was a madman, which was discovered only when he went to Anna Petrovna to complain against me and Mishenka for having allegedly incited all the bedbugs in the house to pester him, and for letting a demon build nests in his nightcap. The other Frenchmen could not get on with Anna Petrovna, who did not give them wine with dinner or let them have horses on Sundays; besides, their salaries were paid very irregularly. I ended up being blamed: Anna Petrovna declared that not one of my tutors was able to cope with such an impossible little boy. It is true, actually, that there was not one among them whom I had not turned into a domestic clown within two weeks after his arrival. I remember with particular pleasure a certain M. Grauget, a respectable fifty-year-old Genevan who, thanks to me, believed that Anna Petrovna was in love with him. It was quite something to behold his virtuous horror, mixed with an element of sly coquetry, when Anna Petrovna glanced at him askance at table, muttering under her breath, "What a glutton!"

I was naughty, lazy, and quick-tempered, but at the same time sensitive and ambitious; a kind person could have formed me any way he liked. Unfortunately, however, nobody could take me in hand, even though everybody tried to interfere with my education. As for my teachers, I laughed at them and played tricks on them; with Anna Petrovna fought tooth and nail; and with Mishenka constantly quarreled and exchanged blows. These affairs often led to stormy explanations with my father, which concluded with tears on both sides. At last Anna Petrovna persuaded him to send me off to a German university... I was fifteen years old at the time.

2

Of university life I have pleasant memories, even though, when you come to think of them, they relate to rather insignificant, and sometimes even unpleasant, events. Youth, however, is a great magician: I would pay dearly to be able to sit once more over a tankard of beer, amidst clouds of tobacco smoke, with staff in hand and a soiled velvet cap on my head. I would pay dearly for my room, always full of people—heaven only knows what assortment of them—for our Latin songs, schoolboyish duels, and altercations with the Philistines!

A liberal university education did me more good than the domestic lessons had, yet, all in all, the only subjects I thoroughly learned in the course of it were fencing and how to make rum punch. I received money from home at irregular intervals, which taught me to run up debts and live carelessly. Three years passed; then I received a command from Petersburg, from my father, to leave the university, return to Russia, and enter some kind of service. Some words of his about ruined affairs, extra expenses, and a changed way of life seemed strange to me, but I did not pay too much attention to them. I gave a farewell feast on the eve of my departure, during which I swore eternal fidelity to friendship and mankind, and vowed never to accept the position of a censor; and the next day set out with a headache and a heartburn.[18]

In 179.. I Was Returning
(ca. 1835)[19]

In 179.. I was returning to Livonia with the happy thought of embracing my old mother after a separation of four years. The closer I got to our country house, the more impatient I felt. I prodded my coachman, a phlegmatic compatriot of mine, and sincerely missed Russian drivers and reckless Russian rides. To make matters worse, my carriage broke down. I was forced to stop. Fortunately, there was a station not too far off.

I walked to the village to fetch some people for my feeble carriage. It was the end of the summer. The sun was setting. Plowed fields stretched out along one side of the road; meadows, overgrown with low shrubs, along the other. A young Estonian woman's melancholy song could be heard from a distance. Suddenly, in the midst of general stillness, a cannon shot boomed distinctly... and died away without an echo. I was surprised. There was not one fort in the neighborhood: how could a cannon shot be heard in this peaceful region? I came to the conclusion that there must be a camp nearby, and my imagination carried me back for a moment to the preoccupations of military life, which I had only just left behind.

Approaching the village, I saw a small gentry home on one side. Two ladies were sitting on the balcony. I bowed to them as I passed by, and went on to the post station.

I had scarcely settled things with the lazy blacksmiths when a little old man, a retired Russian soldier, came up to me and invited me in the name of his lady for a cup of tea. I accepted with pleasure and went back to the gentry house.

On the way there I learned from the soldier that the old lady was called Karolina Ivanovna, that she was a widow, that her daughter, Ekaterina Ivanovna, was of a marriageable age, that they were both such goodhearted ladies, and so forth...

In 179.. I was twenty-three years old, and the very thought of *a young lady* was enough to arouse my keen interest.

The old lady received me kindly and in a hospitable spirit. On hearing my name, she discovered we were related: I learned that she was the widow of von W., a distant relative and a valiant general, killed in 1772.[20]

While to all appearances I was attentively listening to the goodhearted Karolina Ivanovna's genealogical explorations, I was also casting some surreptitious glances at her charming daughter, who was pouring the tea and spreading fresh amber-colored butter on small slices of home-baked bread. Her eighteen years, round, rosy cheeks, dark, narrow eyebrows, small, fresh mouth, and blue eyes fully lived up to my expectations. We soon made friends, and by the third cup of tea I was treating her like a cousin. In the meanwhile my carriage was brought into the village, and Ivan came to report that it would not be ready before next morning at the earliest. This news did not distress me at all, and, accepting Karolina Ivanovna's invitation, I stayed for the night.

Outlines of Projected Works

Cards; Sold...
(1819)[1]

.... cards; sold; married—an attendant.
.... soldiering—becomes an officer...

A Devil in Love
(ca. 1821–23)[2]

Moscow in the year 1811.

An old woman, two daughters, one innocent, the other roman-tically inclined—two male friends visit them regularly. One is a prof-ligate; the other one is a Devil in love. The Devil in love loves the younger daughter and wishes to ruin the young man. He obtains money for him and takes him to all sorts of places. *Nastasia—a widow*, a she-devil. A night. A cabman. The young man. Quarrels with him—the elder daughter is losing her mind being in love with the Devil in love.

N. Chooses Nevskii Avenue as His Confidant
(early 1830's)

N. chooses Nevskii Avenue as his confidant—he confides all his domestic troubles and family grievances to it.—They pity him.—He is satisfied.

Outlines of a Story About a Strelets
(1833 or 1834)[3]

I

A Strelets, son of an old schismatic, sees Rzhevskaia through her window when her maid is helping her change; he sends a marriage proposal by his old nurse from the schismatic community; he receives a rejection.

A Strelets colonel carries great weight among his people; Sofiia wants to entice him into her camp. He tells her how he had learned of the conspiracy.

Sofiia: "What are you so sad about?"—"About a rejection."—"I am a matchmaker."—"But you must also be..." etc.

2

Sofiia at the palace.
Beggars, a jester.
The jester and an old schismatic.
The young Strelets. The conspiracy.

3

A Strelets falls in love with Rzhevskaia, sends a marriage proposal, receives a rejection. He is depressed. A friend initiates him into the secret of the conspiracy... He tells the Regent all about it. Sofiia receives him as a conspirator; an explanation. Sofiia is his matchmaker; a comedy at the boyar's house. The Strelets uprising; the boyar is saved by him; promises his daughter's hand to him.

Rzhevskaia married.

Her mother hastens to marry her off to a nobleman, a member of the boyar council.

4

A Strelets, in love with a boyar's daughter—rejection—comes to visit a friend who is a conspirator—joins the conspiracy.

5

The son of an executed Strelets is brought up by a widow together with her son and daughter; he joins the service in place of her son. On the Pruth River Peter entrusts him with a letter.

The widow's *steward* denounces his young master, and the latter, deprived of his property, is enlisted as a common soldier. The Strelets's son visits the family and intercedes with Peter to pardon the young nobleman.

Crispin Arrives in the Guberniia
(1833 or 1834)[4]

Crispin arrives in the *guberniia* to attend a fair—he is being taken for... The governor is an honest fool.—The governor's wife flirts with him.—Crispin asks for the daughter's hand.

Les Deux Danseuses
(1834 or 1835)[5]

Les deux danseuses. Un ballet de Didelot en 1819.[6] Zavadovsky. Un amant au paradis. Scène de coulisse—duel—Istomine est à la mode. Elle est entretenue, elle se marie.—Sa soeur est dans la détresse—elle épouse le souffleur. Istomine dans le monde. On ne l'y reçoit pas. Elle reçoit chez elle—dégoûts—elle va voir sa compagne.[7]

The Lonely Cottage on Vasilev Island
A Novella

(1828−29)[1]

Those who have had occasion to walk all around Vasilev Island have no doubt noticed that its opposite sides bear very little resemblance to one another. Take, for instance, the southern bank, lined with a magnificent row of huge stone buildings, and the northern one, which faces Petrov Island, with its long spit jutting out into the sleepy waters of the inlet. As we approach the extremity, the stone buildings thin out, yielding to wooden huts; among the huts vacant lots come in view; at last buildings disappear altogether, and you walk along a range of spacious vegetable gardens bordering on some woods on the left; these gardens lead you to the outermost elevation, adorned with one or two forlorn houses and a few trees; a ditch, overgrown with tall nettle and burdock, separates this elevation from the levee that serves as a bulwark against inundation; and beyond the levee stretches a meadow, muddy as a swamp, which constitutes the beach. These deserted places are melancholy even in the summer, and become much more so in the winter, when the meadow, the sea, and the woods lining the shores of Petrov Island on the opposite side are all buried under white snowdrifts as though in graves.

Some decades ago, when this region was even more lonely, there lived here, in a low-built but neat wooden cottage by the elevation we have mentioned, a little old lady, the widow of a civil servant who had served in I do not recall which collegium. On retiring from the service he had bought this cottage, together with a vegetable garden, and intended to do a little farming, but death prevented him from putting his plans into practice. His widow soon found herself forced to sell everything except the house and to live on the small capital her late husband had accumulated by his honest, or maybe at times not so honest, labors. The whole of her household consisted of one daughter and an ancient serving woman, the latter carrying out the duties of both chambermaid and cook. Far removed from the world, she led a quiet life, which, for all its monotony, might have seemed a happy one. Church on holidays; on weekdays chores in the morning; after dinner the mother would knit socks while the young Vera read to her from *The Lives of the Saints* and other holy books; or else the two together would tell fortunes by cards—an occupation widespread among women up to this day. Vera had long since reached the age when girls, as the expression goes, begin to worry about the future; but her chief character trait was a childlike simpleness of heart: she loved her mother, had grown fond of her daily occupations by dint of habit, and satisfied with the present, did not harbor in her heart any dark forebodings about the future. Her old mother, on the other hand, thought differently: she contemplated her own declining years with sadness, and looked with despair on the ripening beauty of her twenty-year-old daughter, who in their indigent solitude had no hope of ever finding a husband and protector. All this made the mother grieve at times and weep in secret. With other old women, for some reason, she did not readily associate; nor did other old women regard her with much favor. They claimed that toward the end she had not been getting on with her husband, that a suspicious male friend had kept coming to the house to comfort her, that her husband had died unexpectedly—and heaven knows what else, all inventions of evil tongues.

Some variety was brought into Vera's lonely life with her mother by the visits of a young man, a rather distant relation, who had come from his country home to Petersburg a few years before in order to enter the service. Let us call him Pavel. He referred to Vera as his little sister and loved her as any young man would a pretty and amiable girl; toward her mother he showed kindness, while she, as the expression goes, had her eye on him. But it was in vain to think of uniting him with Vera because he rarely found time to visit the family on Vasilev Island. It was neither business nor official duties that prevented him from coming more often: in fact he treated both of these rather carelessly and devoted his life to almost uninterrupted diversions. He was one of those moderate young men who cannot stand having excessive amounts of two things on their hands: time and money. As usually happens, he searched for and found obliging friends who willingly freed him of these totally unnecessary burdens and helped him, at his expense, to kill time. Card games, entertainments, and nocturnal outings were all resorted to in order to help with the enterprise; and Pavel was the happiest of mortals, for he did not notice how the days and months went by. It goes without saying that all this could not take place without some disagreeable occurrences: at times one's purse might be found empty; other times one's conscience might awaken with a sense of repentance or dark foreboding. In order to lift this new burden off his shoulders, he at first took up the habit of visiting Vera. But could he without pangs of conscience place himself on an equal footing with this innocent, virtuous young girl?

It was necessary to look for some other agent who would alleviate his feelings. He soon found one in a fellow pleasure-seeker with whom he became fast friends. This friend, whom Pavel knew by the name of Varfolomei, often taught him tricks that the simplehearted Pavel would never have thought of; on the other hand, Varfolomei also knew how to extricate him from the resulting dangerous situations. But Varfolomei's chief and undisputable claim to the title of friend lay in his ability to provide our young man, at times of need, with replenishments of that which is onerous to have in excess but even more onerous to have in short supply—that is, money. He obtained money with such ease and at such short notice on each occasion that Pavel began to suspect something strange. He resolved to get the secret out of Varfolomei, but each time he began his inquiries the latter stopped him with a single glance. "Indeed," Pavel said to himself, "why should I care how he obtains money? It's not I," he added muffling the voice of his conscience, "who will be sent to penal servitude... or to hell!" Besides, Varfolomei possessed the art of persuasion and the ability to please, though his occasional involuntary outbursts betrayed a cruel heart. I should also mention that he was never seen in an Orthodox church; but then Pavel himself was not exactly devout, and Varfolomei said he did not profess our faith. To make a long story short, our young man completely submitted at last to the influence of the friend he had chosen.

One Sunday morning, after a night spent in dissipation, Pavel woke up rather late. He was struck with a greater feeling of repentance and misgiving than he had felt for a long time. His first thought was to go to church, where he had not been for ages. But looking at his watch he realized he had overslept the service. The bright sun shone high in the hot summer sky. Involuntarily, he remembered Vasilev Island. "I've really been unkind to the old lady," he said to himself. "The last time I saw her the snow had still not melted. How cheerful it is at this time of the year in a lonely country cottage! Sweet Vera! She loves me, maybe she's upset that she hasn't seen me for so long, maybe..." He thought a little and decided to spend the day on Vasilev Island. When he had dressed and just left the house, however, Varfolomei appeared before him as if rising from the ground. Pavel was put off at the meeting but could not dodge it.

"I'm just coming to see you, friend!" shouted Varfolomei from a distance. "I wanted to ask if you'd like to come where we went the other day."

"Today I have no time," Pavel answered dryly.

"I like that: no time! You're not trying to tell me that you have some business? Nonsense! Let's go!"

"I'm telling you, I have no time: I must visit a certain relative," said Pavel, extricating his fingers from Varfolomei's cold hand.

"Oh, yes! I've almost forgotten about the witch you know on Vasilev Island. By the way, you've said your little sister is quite sweet: tell me, please, how old is she?"

"How would I know? I wasn't the one who baptized her."

"I've never baptized anyone either, yet I know your age and the age of every one of my cronies."

"Good for you; however..."

"However, that's not the point," interrupted Varfolomei. "I've been meaning to get a foot in that door for some time, with your help. Today the weather is wonderful: I'll enjoy a little walk. Take me with you."

"Upon my word, I can't," replied Pavel, annoyed. "They don't like strangers. Bye now, I mustn't lose any more time."

"Listen, Pavel," Varfolomei said, angrily barring Pavel's way with his arm and giving him one of those looks that had always had an irresistible effect on our weak young man, "I don't understand what's with you. Yesterday you were flying high like a crow; today you're puffing yourself up like a tom turkey. What does this mean? I've taken you, out of friendship, to more than one place, and therefore I have a right to demand the same from you."

"That's true," Pavel answered in embarrassment, "but right now I can't fulfill your request because... because I know it would be boring for you there."

"That's a poor excuse: if I want to go, that means I won't find it boring. Take me at once if you want to remain friends with me."

Pavel was at a loss; at last he said, plucking up his courage, "Listen, we are of course friends! But I know that in such matters nothing is holy to you. Vera is a good girl, pure as an angel, but her heart is simple. Will you give me your word of honor not to try to take advantage of her innocence?"

"You do think I'm an inveterate skirt-chaser, don't you?" interrupted Varfolomei with a diabolical laugh. "Don't worry: there are plenty of other girls in town. But why waste time blabbering? I'm not going to give you my word of honor: you must either trust me or quarrel with me. Take me with you, or else good-bye forever!"

Our young man looked at Varfolomei's menacing expression and remembered that both his honor and his prosperity were in this person's power, and a quarrel with him would be ruinous. His heart fluttered; he made a few more feeble objections—and finally agreed.

The old woman sincerely thanked Pavel for the introduction; she was very much impressed with his dignified, well-dressed friend; as was her habit, she looked on him as an advantageous suitor for her Vera. The impression Varfolomei made on Vera herself was not so favorable: she greeted him timidly when he bowed to her, and her normally rosy cheeks suddenly grew pale. His features were familiar to her. On two previous occasions, when she had left the temple of God with her soul full of humble, pious feelings, she had noticed him standing by a stone column on the church's portico, fixing on her a gaze that erased all pious thoughts and remained cut into her soul like a wound. That gaze captivated the poor girl, not with some amatory force, but with a sense of horror she could not explain. Varfolomei was a well-built man with regular features; but his face did not mirror his soul; it concealed its movements like a mask, and on his seemingly unperturbed forehead Gall would have discovered signs of arrogance—the vice of the outcast.[2]

Vera did, however, manage to hide her embarrassment, which was hardly noticed by anyone except Varfolomei himself. He initiated a general conversation and appeared politer and cleverer than ever before. The hours passed imperceptibly; after dinner a walk along the beach was proposed, after which all returned home, and the old lady settled down to her favorite evening occupation—telling fortunes by cards. Spread her cards as she might, however, nothing would come out. Varfolomei went over to her, leaving his friend to converse with Vera in another corner of the room. When he saw the old lady's vexation, he told her that by her method of laying out the cards one could not tell the future, and that the way they were just then arranged showed the past.

"Ah, my dear young man, I can see you're an expert: explain it to me, then, what they're showing," said the old lady, with a doubtful air.

"Here's what," he replied, and drawing up an armchair, he spoke for a long time in a quiet voice. What did he say? Heaven only knows, but she ended up hearing from him secrets about the life and death of her late husband that she had thought were known only to God and herself. Cold sweat appeared in the wrinkles of her face, her hair stood on end under her cap, and she crossed herself with a trembling hand. Varfolomei quickly left her and joined in the young people's conversation with his former ease. They would have talked till midnight if the two guests had not had to hurry off, fearing that the bridge would soon be drawn up and they might have to spend the night in the open.

We shall not describe in detail the numerous subsequent visits our friends paid Vasilev Island during the summer. It is enough for us to note that Varfolomei insinuated himself more and more into the widow's confidence, and that the warmhearted Vera, who was used to concurring blindly with her mother's feelings, forgot to some extent the unpleasant impression the stranger had originally made on her, though at the same time she openly showed her preference for Pavel. In truth, there was a good reason for such a preference; his frequent meetings with his young cousin had exercised a salutary influence on Pavel: he began to attend to his duties at the office with greater diligence and broke with several dissolute friends; in short, he tried to become a decent person. Also, his carefree nature readily submitted to the force of habit, and at times it seemed to him that he might be happy with a wife like Vera.

One might think that the charming girl's preference for his friend would have wounded Varfolomei's indomitable pride; in fact, however, he not only did not show any displeasure, but treated Pavel even more kindly and amicably than before. Pavel, reciprocating with sincere friendship, dismissed all his doubts with regard to Varfolomei's intentions, heeded his counsel, and let him in on all the secrets of his soul. On one occasion the two of them discussed their respective virtues and faults—which is quite natural when friends talk face to face.

"You know I'm not a flatterer," said Varfolomei, "but I must say that recently I've noticed quite a marked change for the better in you; and I'm not the only one who has. Several people have remarked that in the last six months you've matured more than others do in six years. The only improvement you need is to learn the ways of society. Don't laugh at the word: I myself have never been keen on society, and I realize it amounts to zero; yet a zero can increase the value of one tenfold. I forsee your objection: you're planning to marry Vera..." After these words Varfolomei stopped for a moment, as if lost in thought. "You are planning to marry her," he resumed, "and you have no wish to experience anything except domestic bliss and the love of your future wife. But that is just the point: you young people imagine that as soon as you're married the ball is over; in fact, however, that's only when it begins. Mark my word: having lived with your wife for a year, you will start thinking of other people again; but by then it will be more difficult to find your way around in society. At the same time it's necessary to know people, especially for a family man: in our country even truth cannot be obtained without protectors. Or maybe the big-sounding appellation 'high society' frightens you? Don't worry! Society is like a horse at the riding academy—it is really quite tame, only appears dangerous because it has its own habits to which one needs to get accustomed. But why am I wasting words on this? It'll be better if you test their truth in practice. The day after tomorrow there's a reception at Countess I.'s house: you have an opportunity to come. I visited her yesterday and talked to her about you; she said she would like to meet your priceless person."

These words, like some poison capable of turning one's internal organs inside out, altered all the young man's plans and wishes: having never been in high society, he decided to throw himself into that whirlwind, and on the agreed upon evening appeared in the Countess's drawing room. Her house was not in a street with a particularly high-sounding name, and on the outside did not appear distinguished, but inside the furnishings and the illumination were splendid. Varfolomei had already warned Pavel that one or two things might appear strange to him at first sight. For the Countess had just recently returned from foreign lands, was living according to foreign customs, and was receiving only a small circle—though that circle was the best in town. They found there several people of advanced age whose distinguishing features were that they wore tall perukes and enormously wide trousers, and did not take their gloves off all evening. This did not quite conform with the current fashions in Petersburg middle-class society, which was the only society Pavel was familiar with, but he had resolved not to be surprised by anything, and in any case, when would he have had time to notice such trifling details? All his attention was riveted on his hostess. Imagine a woman of striking appearance, in the luxuriant bloom of her youth, endowed with all the charms with which nature and art can adorn the female sex to the ruin of Adam's progeny; and add to all this that she had lost her husband and was in a position to allow herself the kind of liberty with men that the inexperienced among them can least resist. When juxtaposed to such seductive charms, could Vera's virginal image remain dominant in Pavel's inconstant heart? His passions flared up; he made every possible effort to win the beautiful woman's favor and, after several visits noticed that she did not look with disdain on his exertions. What a discovery for a fiery youth! Pavel no longer felt the ground under his feet; he was floating on clouds... But an unpleasant occurrence ruined the castles he had so boldly built in the air. Once, during a fairly crowded reception at the Countess's house, Pavel noticed that she was quietly talking with a man; with one, we must note, who always strutted around in the most foppish manner but who, all his efforts notwithstanding, could not hide his physical deformity, for which Pavel and Varfolomei had behind his back given him the nickname Pigeon-toed. Curiosity and jealousy drew Pavel nearer, and he overheard the man uttering his name and cracking jokes over his bad French accent, to which the Countess responded with pleasantries. Our young man was incensed and would have thrown himself on the joker to punish him there and then if he had not realized that such an act would expose him to even greater ridicule in front of the whole company. He left immediately and swore never to see the Countess again.

Distraught, he once more remembered his Vera whom he had abandoned, as a sinner remembers the path to salvation in the midst of an abyss of corruption. But this time he did not find the good cheer he longed for by the side of the charming girl: Varfolomei had taken over as if he were the master of the house, and received Pavel—the very man who had introduced him into the family a few months before—as though he were a casual visitor. The old woman was gravely ill. Vera seemed to be in a flurry and all distracted; she received Pavel with unusual coldness, and though she accorded him the attention required by civility, she did not stop preparing medications, running to fetch the serving woman, looking after the invalid—and often turning to Varfolomei for help. All this was of course strange and annoying to Pavel, on whom, as on Poor Makar, one failure after another seemed to be crashing down.[3] He thought of seeking an explanation, but was afraid of upsetting the sick old lady as well as Vera, who was already shaken by her mother's illness. There was only one thing he could do: have it out with Varfolomei. Having decided on this course of action, he said good-bye on the pretext of a headache soon after dinner. No one tried to hold him back, and he left, intimating to Varfolomei, with some sharpness of tone, that he wished to see him the next morning.

In order to imagine in what state the unfortunate Pavel awaited his former friend and current rival on the following day, we must comprehend all the passions that were battling in his soul, tearing their victim to pieces like birds of prey. He had sworn to forget the Countess forever, but his heart was aflame with passion for the false woman; his attachment to Vera was not as ardent, but he did love her with a brotherly love and was concerned about her good name, over which, he thought, he had lost his influence for a long time to come, if not forever. And who was to blame for all these misfortunes? The perfidious Varfolomei, this man whom he had at one time called friend and who had, in his opinion, cruelly betrayed his trust. With what impatience was Pavel waiting, and with what vexation was he looking out into the street, where a snowstorm, as fierce as the one in his own soul, was raging! "The knave is taking advantage of the bad weather," he thought, "and is going to escape my just vengeance; he is depriving me of my last joy—to tell him to his shameless face to what degree I hate him!"

But while Pavel was tormented by these fearful thoughts, the door opened and Varfolomei entered with the coolness of marble, just as the statue of the Commander would come to Don Juan for supper.[4] Soon, however, his face assumed a more human expression; he approached Pavel and said with an air of compassionate amity, "You're not yourself, my friend: what's the cause of your grief? Open your heart to me."

"I'm no friend of yours!" shouted Pavel, leaping away from him to the other end of the room, as if from a vicious snake. Trembling in every limb, with tears welling up in his bloodshot eyes, our young man wasted no time in giving vent to all his feelings, which were inflamed, perhaps, more than fairness warranted.

Varfolomei heard him out with an air of offended nonchalance and said at the end:

"Your language is impertinent and would deserve punishment, but I forgive you since you're young and don't yet know the value of either words or people. This wasn't how you spoke to me on past occasions when without my help you might as well have put your head in the noose. But all that is now forgotten because a cool reception by a girl has ruffled your petty, vain soul. It is his pleasure to vanish from sight for whole months, to play heaven knows what tricks with heaven knows whom, but I am expected to sit patiently and refrain from going where I like! No, sir: I will continue visiting the old lady, in order to annoy you if for no other reason. Besides, I have other reasons, which I will not hide from you: let me tell you that Vera is in love with me."

"You're lying, scoundrel!" cried Pavel in a frenzy. "Could an angel be in love with the devil?"

"It's understandable that you don't believe it," Varfolomei answered sarcastically, "for nature has not adorned me with your fetching features, with which you enchant distinguished ladies, and enchant them forever, inspiring fidelity and constancy."

This gibe was too much for Pavel to bear, especially since he had long suspected that Varfolomei had played some part in his friction with the Countess. He threw himself on his rival in a rage and wanted to murder him on the spot, but at that moment he felt a blow in the pit of his stomach that made him gasp for air, and without causing any pain, lose consciousness. When he came around he found himself at the opposite side of the room, behind closed doors. Varfolomei was not there, and Pavel could remember, as if through a dream, his parting words: "Careful, young man! You're not dealing with *one of your own kind!*"

Pavel trembled with fear and anger; a thousand thoughts raced through his mind. His first impulse was to find Varfolomei even if he had to go to the end of the world for him, and to crack his skull; then he wanted to go to the old lady and reveal to her and Vera all the traitor's previous misdeeds; then he remembered the enchanting Countess, wishing now to cut her throat, now to have an explanation with her, without, however, giving up his first wish—the two wishes being, of course, difficult to reconcile. He felt a tightness in his chest and, half-crazed, ran out into the courtyard, feeling symptoms of a feverish inflammation; pale and disheveled, he roamed the streets and would have no doubt found a solution to all his distress in the depths of the Neva if it had not, fortunately, wrapped itself for the season in its coat of ice.

We cannot say whether Fate had grown tired of persecuting Pavel or was preparing to wound him even more deeply while granting him a momentary respite from misfortune, but when he got home he found fulfilled what he most longed for. In the hallway the Countess I.'s elegantly dressed lackey was waiting for him with a note; Pavel unfolded it, trembling, and read the following words written in the Countess's all too familiar hand:

> Evil men wanted to create discord between us, but I can see through it all; if there is still a modicum of love left in your heart for me, or a modicum of compassion, come by at such and such hour this evening.
>
> Yours forever, I.

How stupid lovers are! No sooner had Pavel glanced through these magic lines than he had already forgotten both the friendship of Vera and the enmity of Varfolomei; as far as he was concerned, the whole of the present, past, and future crowded together in that slip of paper; he pressed it to his heart, kissed it, and brought it to the light to read it over and over.

"No!" he exclaimed in ecstasy, "this cannot be deception; I am indeed, indeed a happy man; no one would, no one could, write such a note but she. Or is she, the sly one, pressing her invitation on me only to fool me and mock me as before? No! I swear, that cannot be. 'Yours—yours forever'—let her show me in practice what these words mean. Otherwise... her reputation is in my hands."

At the appointed hour Pavel, well-combed and dressed up, is already on the Countess's broad front steps; he is shown into the drawing room unannounced; to his annoyance there are several visitors there; but at least the pigeon-toed one is not among them. The hostess greets him dryly, hardly speaking to him; but it cannot be for nothing that she fixes her large black eyes on him and then languidly casts them down; this is the arcane language of lovers, incomprehensible to the uninitiated. The guests sit down to a game; the hostess refuses to join in, claiming that she likes to take turns sitting next to each player in the hope of bringing luck to each. Everybody marvels at her exquisite delicacy.

"You haven't visited us for a long time," the Countess says a little later, turning to our youth. "Do you notice some changes in this room? Here, for instance, these drapes used to hang from under laurel garlands, but I thought it would be better to put them on arrow-shaped rods."

"Haven't you wounded enough hearts yet?" Pavel asks in a cool but civil tone.

"It's not just the drawing room that's got new furnishings," the Countess continues, rising from her armchair. "Would you like to see the parlor? We've hung there some recently imported Gobelins of exquisite design."

Pavel bowed and followed her. His heart fluttered with an indescribable sensation when he entered this enchanting room. It was a combination greenhouse and parlor. The myrtles arranged along the walls softened the bright light issuing from the candelabra. The plush sofas were shaded by the trees, but an even light illuminated the Gobelin tapestries, whose images, suggestive of sensuality, represented some mythical gods' amorous exploits. Across the room from the door there was a cheval glass, and next to it on the wall hung "The Abduction of Europa," demonstrating the power of beauty to turn just about anybody into a dumb beast.[5] The fateful love-confession began beside this cheval glass. Every enlightened person knows that an exchange between lovers always involves a huge amplification of details; for this reason I will repeat only its essence. The Countess assured Pavel that her jests about poor French pronunciation were aimed not at him, but at another man of the same name; that she had long been puzzled by his absence; that at last Varfolomei had explained it to her, and so on and so forth. Although it seemed strange that Varfolomei should possess information about an affair nobody had discussed with him, and that he should play a conciliatory role in it, Pavel nevertheless took the Countess's word for it all as a matter of course—not without pretending, however, to be incredulous.

"What other proof do you want?" asked the Countess at last, with tender impatience.

Pavel, as a gallant young man, fervently kissed her hand in answer; she grew stiff and shy and wanted to hasten back to her guests; he went down on his knees before her and, firmly holding her hands, threatened not only not to let her go, but also to shoot himself on the spot. This tactic achieved the desired effect, that is, a gentle, tremulous squeezing of his hand and the words softly whispered: "Tomorrow evening at eleven o'clock, on the back porch."

Though whispered, these words announced Pavel's triumph to him more loudly than cannon and powder could have.

It was a good thing the Countess returned to the drawing room when she did because two of the gamblers had almost gotten into a fight.

"Look here," said one of them to the Countess, puffing and panting with anger, "I'm losing several hundred serfs to him for no good reason, while he..."

"A few hundred rubles, you mean to say," she interrupted with a dignified air.

"Well, yes... sorry... I meant..." stammered the wrangler, glancing at our young man from the corner of his eye. The gamblers put a stop to the dispute, and the whole commotion subsided as if by magic. Pavel gave no ear to all this. He was so excited that he could not remain with the company for long; he hurried home to give himself up to rest, but he could not close his eyes for a long time; reality itself seemed to him like a sweet dream. The beautiful woman's large black dewy eyes incessantly haunted his inflamed imagination. They accompanied him through his dreams, too; but his dreams, either because of inmost forebodings or simply because of excitement rushing through his veins, all ended in a strange way. In one dream, he was walking through green grass; two flowers of wonderful colors sprang up before him; but as soon as he touched their stems to pick them, a black, black snake reared up and sprayed venom on them. In another dream, he was looking in the mirror of a transparent lake where, on the bottom, close to the shore, two goldfish were playing; but no sooner had he reached in with his hand toward them than a menacing amphibious monster woke him up. In still another dream, he was walking at night under a fragrant summer sky; two bright, inseparable little stars twinkled on high; but he had barely begun to feast his eyes on them when a black spot appeared in the dark west, grew into a long snake-cloud, and devoured the stars. Each time such dreams woke Pavel his anxious thoughts involuntarily fastened on Varfolomei; but after a while the Countess's black eyes prevailed again, until a new horror interrupted another enchanted dream. Despite all this, Pavel slept through the morning till noon and got up more cheerful than ever. The remaining eleven hours of the day, as might be expected, seemed like an eternity to him. It was not yet dark when he was already prowling about the Countess's house; no one was being received and no lamps were lit in the reception rooms; a weak light twinkled in one remote corner room alone. "That is where my charmer is waiting for me," thought Pavel, with his soul positively drowning in the anticipated bliss.

The clock on the Duma Tower slowly beat eleven o'clock,[6] and Pavel flew on the wings of love... But at this point I shall interrupt painting my picture and, following the example of the best classical and romantic writers of ancient, medieval, and modern times, will let you complete it from your own resources of imagination. To make a long story short: Pavel was about to savor bliss... when suddenly there is a quiet knock on the door of the Countess's study; she opens it in embarrassment; a trusted chambermaid comes in to report that there is somebody on the back porch who says he absolutely must see the young gentleman. Pavel, angry, sends word that he has no time; then thinks it over, and goes out in the hallway, where he is told that the man has just left. He returns to his beloved one.

"Nothing can take me away from you," he says passionately.

But there is a knock again, and the maid comes in with the same message.

"Tell the stranger to go to the devil," shouts Pavel, stamping his feet, "or else I'll kill him."

He goes out and hears that the stranger has just left; he runs down the stairs into the courtyard, but nothing stirs there, only the snow falls silently, in large flakes. Pavel scolds the servants, forbids them to let in anybody whomsoever, and returns to the perturbed Countess more ardent than ever; but only a few minutes pass before a third knock, louder and longer than the previous ones, is heard at the door.

"No, that's enough!" he cries, beside himself with rage. "I'm going to find out what sort of an apparition this is; it must be some practical joke."

Running into the hallway, he sees the hem of a cloak disappear behind the door just being closed; he hastily throws his coat over his shoulders, grabs his walking stick, and runs out into the courtyard, only to hear the gate slam behind someone.

"Stop, stop! Who are you?" he shouts after him and, springing out on the street, sees at a distance a tall man, who seems to stop and beckon with his finger, then disappears into a sidestreet. The impatient Pavel follows; it seems he is catching up with him; the other one stops again on the corner of a sidestreet, beckons, and disappears. This way our young man follows the stranger from one street to another, from one alley to another, until at last he finds himself trudging through knee-deep snow among low-built houses and coming to a crossroads that he has never seen before. The stranger has disappeared without a trace. Pavel stands rooted to the ground; and I must admit that nobody in his place, having run several versts, would enjoy finding himself in the snow, the devil knew where, in the dead of night. What is he to do? If he goes on, he might lose his way. Should he knock at someone's gate? He probably couldn't wake them. But, to his great joy, a sled appears unexpectedly.

"Vanka!" he shouts. "Take me home to such and such a street."

The obedient cabman drives him through unfamiliar places; the runners of the sled crunch the snow; a moon à la Zhukovskii lights the travelers' way obscurely, through shifting clouds.[7] They ride for a long, long time; they still do not reach any place that looks familiar; at last they ride out of town altogether. Pavel naturally recalls old tales about dead bodies found in Volkovo Pole, about cabdrivers cutting their passengers' throats, and so forth.[8]

"Where are you taking me?" he asked in a firm tone.

There was no answer. Pavel wanted to take a look, in the moonlight, at the cabdriver's tin license number, but discovered to his surprise that on the license plate neither the administrative region nor the police district was indicated; all there was on it was the number 666—the number of the Apocalypse as he was to recall later[9]—written in large figures of a strange shape and color. Confirmed in his suspicion that he had fallen into evil hands, our young man repeated his previous question even more loudly, and receiving no answer, swung his walking stick at the back of the driver with all his might. You can imagine his horror, however, when he realized that his blow had produced nothing but the clatter of bone against bone; when the supposed cabdriver, turning around, showed him the skull of a skeleton; and when this skull, frighteningly baring its jaws, said in a voice just barely audible, "Careful, young man, you're not dealing with *one of your own kind.*"

All the unfortunate young man had strength for was to make the sign of the cross, which his hand had not done for a long time. Then the sled turned over, wild, loud laughter could be heard, a terrible whirlwind rushed over the place; the carriage, the horse, and the driver were buried under the snow, and Pavel remained all by himself, half-dead with fright, outside the city gates.

The next day our young man lay exhausted on the bed in his room. Beside him stood his ancient good-hearted attendant who, holding his master's limp hand in one of his, often turned away in order to wipe with his other hand the tears that furtively welled up in his weak-sighted eyes.

"Dear, dear master," he kept saying, "it's not for nothing that I've been warning Your Honor against night outings. Where did you vanish to? What happened to you?"

Pavel did not hear him: he stared at the corner of the room with wild eyes for a while; then dozed off and, half-asleep, shuddered and laughed; then jumped up like a madman, calling some woman by name; and finally threw himself back on his bed and buried his face in the pillow.

"Poor Pavel Ivanovich!" the attendant said to himself. "The Lord have mercy on him, he's evidently gone out of his mind."

Following the impulse of his good heart, the servant ran off to fetch the doctor as soon as he could find a convenient moment. The doctor, seeing that the young man could not recognize those around him, and having taken the patient's feverish pulse, shook his head. The outward symptoms contradicted each other and revealed nothing about the nature of the illness; there was every reason to think that its cause lay deep in the soul, not in the body. The invalid could hardly recall anything about what had happened; his soul, it seemed, was wracked by some terrible presentiment. The doctor was persuaded by the faithful attendant that they should both stay by the young man's bedside all day. Toward evening the patient's condition became desperate: he tossed and turned, wept, wrung his hands, spoke about Vera and Vasilev Island, called for help to some unknown person, seized his cap and strained to get to the door with such force that the servant's and the doctor's united efforts could just barely hold him back. This frightful crisis continued till past midnight; then the patient suddenly grew calm and felt better; but his spiritual as well as his physical strength was completely exhausted by the struggle; he sank into a deep slumber, after which another, similar crisis occurred.

The attack held the young man in its grip for three full days, though with varying intensity. On the third morning, feeling a little stronger, he got up when he was told that the widow's old maidservant was waiting for him in the hallway. Her arrival did not foretoken anything good he felt as he went out; and the old woman was indeed sobbing.

"Yes! Still another misfortune!" said Pavel, approaching her. "Don't torment me, my dear: tell me all at once."

"The old mistress has passed away," said the maid, "and heaven only knows how long the young mistress will live."

"How come? Vera? What's with her?"

"Let's not waste words, master; the young mistress needs help. I've dragged myself here on foot; if you have mercy in your heart, let us ride to her in a carriage; she's at the priest's of the Church of Andrew the First Called." [10]

"At the priest's? Why?"

"For heaven's sake, get dressed; you'll learn about everything later."

Pavel wrapped himself in his coat and galloped to Vasilev Island.

When he had last seen Vera and her mother, the widow had already been afflicted for a long time with an ailment from which there was very little hope she could recover given her advanced age. Too poor to call a doctor, she had resorted exclusively to the advice of Varfolomei, who, in addition to his other accomplishments, boasted of some familiarity with medicine. He showed inexhaustible energy: he managed at one and the same time to comfort Vera, to look after the patient, to help the maid, and to fetch medicines, which he brought back at times with such speed that Vera wondered where he could have found a pharmacy so close by. The drugs he obtained did not necessarily cure the patient, but they always raised her spirits. It was strange that the closer she came to her grave, the more firmly her thoughts were riveted to matters of this world. She slept and dreamed about her recovery; about her children Vera and Varfolomei going to their wedding and beginning a happy, prosperous life; in which connection she worried whether her cottage would be too small for their future family and whether she would be able to find another one closer to town, etcetera, etcetera. A dim incomprehension of her approaching end was reflected in her eyes when she called the future young couple to her bedside and said with an unseemly smile, "Don't be shy, Vera, kiss your fiancé: I'm afraid I'll soon lose my sight, and then I shan't be able to see your happiness."

In the meanwhile the hand of death hung lower and lower over the old woman's head; her sight and memory grew dimmer by the hour. You could not see grief in Varfolomei's face: maybe all his efforts, his having to run about constantly, diverted his thoughts. Vera, on the other hand, was much troubled by reflections on her own fate, as well as her mother's. All brides are apprehensive before their wedding. She tried her best, however, to calm herself. "I am guilty before God," she thought, "for taking Varfolomei for a devil, for an evil person. He is in fact much better than Pavel: one only has to see what trouble he is taking over mother; the poor man never spares himself, therefore he must be good." But then her thoughts became confused. "He has an unyielding temper," she resumed her reflections. "When he doesn't want to do something and you say to him, 'Varfolomei, for God's sake, do it,' he starts trembling and grows pale. On the other hand," continued Vera, wiping a tear off her cheek with her little finger, "I'm not exactly an angel myself: each person has his own faults and his own cross to bear; I will improve him, and he will improve me."

Then some new doubts troubled her mind: "It seems to me he's rich. Did he obtain his money by honest means? I'll have to get this out of him: after all, he loves me." This was how the good-hearted, innocent Vera was trying to comfort herself; in the meanwhile the old lady's condition grew worse and worse. Vera communicated her anxiety to Varfolomei and even asked if he did not think it necessary to call a priest, but this irritated him, and he answered sternly, "That would be the best way to bring on your mother's death. Is that what you want? Her illness is dangerous, but her condition is not yet desperate. What keeps her alive? Her hope of recovering. If you call in a priest you'll take away her last hope."

The timid Vera agreed, muffling her soul's secret voice; but that same day—the very day, we must note, after Pavel's fateful meeting with the charming Countess—her prophetic heart all too clearly sensed the final approach of danger. She called Varfolomei aside and said in a firm tone, "I beseech you in the name of the Heavenly Father, don't let mother die without a confession; God only knows if she'll live till tomorrow." And she collapsed on a chair, shedding floods of tears.

What went on in Varfolomei's mind at that moment? His eyes were rolling; sweat appeared on his forehead; he tried to say something but could not.

"A young woman's faintheartedness," he muttered at last. "You don't have faith in anything... You, my dear young lady, do not trust my knowledge of medicine... Wait a little... I'm acquainted with a doctor who knows more than I do... Only, unfortunately, he lives rather far."

He seized the girl's hand and, drawing her quickly to the window, pointed at the sky, without, however, raising his eyes.

"Look, the first star will not have appeared up there before I get back: we'll decide then. Will you promise not to call a priest before I return?"

"I promise, I promise."

A prolonged moan could be heard from the bedroom just then.

"Do hurry," Vera cried, dashing toward the bedroom door, then turning back and casting one more glance, full of indescribable grief, at the man who stood rooted to the ground. "Hurry for my sake, for God's sake," she repeated, waving him on with her hand.

Varfolomei disappeared.

Clouds gradually gathered in the winter sky, while inside of the patient's body, life and decay fought their last, fatal duel. It began to snow; gusts of wind rattled the windows. Every time Vera heard the slightest crunch of snow, she ran to the window to see if it was Varfolomei; but the only things outside were a cat, mewing, some jackdaws on the gateposts, pecking at each other, and the garden gate, which the wind kept opening and slamming shut. Night spread out its dark shroud earlier than usual; there was neither a sign of Varfolomei nor the twinkle of a single star in the sky. Vera decided to send the old maidservant for the priest. The maid did not return for a long time, which was not surprising since the closest church was Andrew the First Called. The garden gate banged at last, but instead of the maid, Varfolomei appeared, pale and distraught.

"What? Is there no hope?" whispered Vera.

"Very little," he answered in a muffled voice. "I've been at the doctor's; he lives far away, knows a lot..."

"But what did he say, for God's sake?"

"What's the use?... We'd better send for the priest. Oh! I see you've already sent for him... Just as well," he said with a certain dryness, in which, however, a note of despair could be heard.

After a while, already into the middle of the night, the old maidservant crawled home, reporting that the priest was not in, but that as soon as he got back, he would be informed and would come. They decided to prepare the patient for the event.

"Are you out of your mind, children?" she said in a feeble voice. "Am I really that sick? Vera! What are you sniffling for? Take the lamp out: sleep will fortify me."

Vera kissed her mother's hand, while Varfolomei stood at some distance in silence, transfixing the patient with his eyes, which glowed like hot coals whenever the lamplight flickered on them.

Vera and the cook dropped to their knees, praying. Varfolomei wrung his hands and kept going out on the porch, complaining of a feverish feeling in the head. After half an hour he entered the bedroom, then ran out like a madman with the news: "All is over."

I will not try to describe what Vera felt at that moment. But the strength of her character was extraordinary.

"Lord, Thy will be done," she said, lifting her arms toward the sky; she wanted to move but her physical strength deserted her; she collapsed, half-dead, in an armchair, and the poor girl would have died altogether if a sudden flow of tears had not alleviated the tightness in her chest.

In the meanwhile the old woman, wailing, washed the dead body, placed a candle by the bed, and went to fetch an icon; but at that moment, whether from tiredness or for some other reason, she fell into an irresistible sleep. Varfolomei stepped up to Vera. She was so appealing in her grief that the sight of her would have touched even a fiend's heart.

"You don't love me," he cried fiercely. "With your mother I've lost the last support in your heart."

The girl was frightened by his despair.

"Yes, I do love you," she said timidly. He threw himself at her feet. "Swear," he said, "swear that you're mine, that you love me more than your very soul."

Vera had never suspected such passion in this cold person.

"Varfolomei, dear Varfolomei," she said to him with timid tenderness, "forget your sinful thoughts in this hour of horror; I will take a vow when mother is buried, when the priest blesses us in God's temple..."

Varfolomei did not hear her out but started gibbering frenzied nonsense, claiming that this was all just empty ritual, which loving hearts did not need; asking her to go with him to his remote homeland, where he would shower her with princely glitter; and embracing her knees, shedding tears. He spoke with such heat and passion that all the marvels he was describing seemed at that moment believable. Vera felt herself wavering, but the danger awakened her spiritual strength; she tore herself away and dashed for the door of the bedroom, where she hoped she could find the maid. Varfolomei barred her way and said, this time with pretended coldness but with a ferocious look in his eyes, "Listen, Vera, don't be obstinate: you cannot awaken either the maid or your mother: nothing can save you from my power."

"Here is the defender of the innocent," cried the poor girl, and in her despair she threw herself on her knees before the crucifix. Varfolomei froze; his face expressed impotent rage.

"In that case," he rejoined, biting his lips, "in that case... I can of course do nothing with you; but I'll make your mother force you to obey me."

"Is she then in your power?" asked the girl.

"Look," he replied, fixing his eyes on the bedroom's half-closed door.

It appeared to Vera as though two jets of fire shot out of his eyes, and as though the dead woman raised her head with indescribable pain in the burned-down candle's flickering light and signaled to Vera with her emaciated hand toward Varfolomei. At that moment Vera realized with whom she was dealing.

"May the Lord be resurrected, and may you vanish, Satan!" she cried, collecting all her spiritual strength, and collapsed unconscious.

At that moment the sleeping maid was awakened as though by a cannon shot. Coming to her senses, she saw to her horror that the door was wide open, the room was full of smoke, and a blue flame was engulfing the mirror and curtains that her late mistress had received as a gift from Varfolomei. Her first movement was to grab the pitcher of water standing in the corner and splash it on the flame; but the fire sizzled with doubled ferocity and singed the cook's gray hair. Beside herself with fright, she ran into the other room, shouting, "Fire! Fire!" Seeing her young mistress on the floor unconscious, she picked her up in her arms and, fright evidently lending strength to her decrepit body, dragged her out on the bridge past the gate. There was no habitation nearby; there was nowhere to turn for help; and by the time she finished rubbing the half-dead girl's temple with snow, flames were bursting forth from the windows and chimneys and above the roof. Seeing the glow of fire, a police brigade galloped up with buckets and pitchforks, for fire hoses were not yet in common use at that time. A crowd of onlookers gathered; among them the dean of Andrew the First Called, who had been on his way to the dying woman with the sacraments. He had not been on particularly good terms with the late widow, regarding her as an evil woman; but he loved Vera, about whom he had heard many good things from his daughter. Moved to compassion by the calamity, he promised to reward the firefighters if they managed to pull out the body, in order at least to give the dead woman a Christian funeral. But that could not be done. The fire, whipped by the snowstorm, rebuffed with contempt the effect of water and all human effort. A police corporal of a daring disposition tried to burst into the house in order to bring the corpse out, but after a minute ran out in horror. He related that he had managed to get as far as the bedroom, but when he tried to approach the dead woman's bed, Satan's ugly mug descended on him from above, part of the ceiling caved in with a horrendous crash, and he was able to get out in one piece owing only to the special grace of Nicholas the Miracle-Worker, for which he promised to place a half-ruble candle before his icon. The onlookers said among themselves that the man was a coward, and it was simply a falling beam that had seemed like the Devil to him; but the corporal remained firm in his conviction and was to preach in pothouses to the end of his days that he had once seen, face to face, the Evil One, fully incarnated, complete with tail, horns, and a large crooked nose, through which he fanned the fire as though with a blacksmith's bellows. "No, brothers, I tell you, God save you from facing the Evil One," was the eloquent admonition with which our genius usually concluded his story; and the landlord, in order to reward him for his courage and for the deep impression his story had made on his enlightened listeners, brought him a jugful of the finest vodka on the house.

Thus, despite all the efforts of the brigade, whose diligence in this case must be fully recognized by posterity, the lonely cottage on Vasilev Island burned to its foundations, and the lot on which it had stood has for some reason remained vacant to this day. The ancient maid, with the help of the dean and other clergymen of the parish, revived Vera and found shelter together with her in the house of the worthy pastor. The fire had started so unexpectedly and its circumstances were so strange that the police found it necessary to launch a detailed investigation of it. Since neither the old maidservant nor—still less—Vera could be suspected, it was assumed that the arsonist had to be Varfolomei. His description was taken down, and he was sought both openly and secretly, not only in every district of the city, but in the whole Petersburg region. All was in vain: not a trace of him was found, which was all the more surprising since no ships sailed in the winter, and consequently he could not have slipped out of the country on some foreign vessel. It is not known what a prolonged investigation would have led to; but the dean, who sincerely loved Vera and could not be certain just how close her ties with this man had been, wisely decided to make use of his connections to suppress the matter and avoid further publicity.

It was for these reasons that Pavel, who was sent for on the third day and learned from the old woman during their ride what she knew of the chain of unfortunate incidents, found his young cousin sick at Father Ioann's house. The priest's hospitable family invited him to stay with them until she should recover. Our flighty young man had in a short time received so many emotional shocks, and their hidden causes remained so terribly obscure to him, that all this left an indelible mark on his mind and character. He was reformed and often fell into deep thought. He began to forget both the mysterious Countess's charms and the wild escapades of his earlier days that had brought on such baleful consequences. His one prayer to heaven was that Vera recover and he be given the opportunity to serve as an exemplar of conjugal fidelity to her. Whenever they were left alone, he proposed this idea to her, but she, though in other ways showing a sisterly confidence in him, rejected it with invariable firmness.

"You're young, Pavel," she would say, "and I have already lost my bloom; the grave will be awaiting me shortly; and then, maybe, the merciful Lord will grant me pardon and peace."

Not an hour passed without her thinking about this: she was, it seems, tormented by the secret conviction that she in her weakness had allowed the evil man to bring about her mother's ruin in this world and—who knows?—maybe even in the world beyond. No medical treatment could restore her to cheerfulness and health. The freshness of her cheeks faded; but her heavenly eyes, though they had lost their former sparkle, were still enchanting, with their languid expression of the sorrow that was oppressing her beautiful soul. Spring had not yet adorned the fields with fresh verdure when this flower, which had promised such luxuriant growth, merged irretrievably back into all-accepting nature.

It may be surmised that Vera, before her death, confided not only to her father confessor, but also to Pavel, those circumstances of the last year of her life that had been known to her alone. When she died, our young man did not weep or show any outward sign of grief. But soon afterwards he left the capital and settled, with his ancient servant, on a remote ancestral estate. He soon acquired the reputation of an eccentric in that whole region, and indeed he betrayed some symptoms of madness. Past his first arrival, not only his neighbors but even his own peasants and servants were unable to set eyes on him. He grew a beard and long hair; did not leave his study for three months at a time; gave orders to his servants in writing; and it happened even that when a piece of paper was placed on his desk for him to sign he would not put his own name on it but return it with someone else's strange signature. He could not bear the sight of women; and if a tall, pale-complexioned man with gray eyes unexpectedly appeared before him, he would convulse with fury. Once, pacing up and down his room as was his wont, he came up to the door just at the time Lavrentii unexpectedly opened it in order to report something to him. Pavel trembled.

"It was you, not I, who drove her to death," he said abruptly, and a week later asked his old attendant to forgive him for pushing him out so violently that the old man almost broke his neck hitting a wall.

"Since that occasion," Lavrentii used to say, "I always knock first before I enter to report something to His Honor."

Pavel died long before reaching old age. His and Vera's conjoined story is known to a few middle-class people in Petersburg; I myself heard it related orally. But you, estimable reader, are actually in a better position to judge whether one can give credit to such a story and why the devils should have such a desire to meddle in human affairs when nobody has asked them to.

Notes

Notes

The Blackamoor of Peter the Great

1. The first six chapters of this unfinished historical novel were written in the summer of 1827 in Mikhailovskoe, and one more page—which is all that remains of Chap. 7—was added in the spring of 1828. Two fragments—from Chaps. 4 and 3, respectively—were published in *Severnye tsvety* (1829), pp. 111–24, and *Literaturnaia gazeta*, 13 (1830): 99–100. The assembled text of all the extant parts was published, with a few omissions, after Pushkin's death by the editors of the journal *Sovremennik* (6 [1837]: 97–145), who also gave it its title and distributed the epigraphs, all written together on the first page of the manuscript, among the various chapters.

2. From N. Iazykov's poem "Ala" (1824).

3. From Part 1 of I. I. Dmitriev's poem "NN.'s Journey to Paris and London" (1803).

4. The prototype for Ibrahim was Pushkin's maternal great-grandfather, Abram Hannibal, a black African who had been brought to Russia as a child during the reign of Peter I (b. 1672; r. 1682–1725). Pushkin's chief historical source on his ancestor, apart from oral family tradition, was a handwritten biography of Abram Hannibal in German, which Pushkin received from a great-uncle, Petr Hannibal. This source was not entirely reliable, but it served as an inspiration for several scenes of the projected novel. In his fictional account of his great-grandfather's life, Pushkin himself was not aiming at complete historical accuracy: for example, he makes Peter propose to the Rzhevskiis on Ibrahim's behalf, though the real Hannibal did not marry until well after Peter's death; and he makes Ibrahim's betrothed a member of the ancient Russian nobility, though the real Hannibal's wife was the daughter of a Greek sailor. Pushkin's chief sources for more general information about the life and times of Peter was I. I. Golikov's multivolume work, *The Deeds of Peter the Great* (1788–97), and a series of four sketches of life under Peter by A. O. Kornilovich, published in *Russkaia starina* (1824); reprinted in Kornilovich, *Sochineniia i pis'ma* (Moscow: Akademiia Nauk SSSR, 1957), pp. 149–203.

5. This is an error on the part of Pushkin, for the Ecole militaire by the Champ-de-Mars (today's Ecole supérieure de guerre) was not established until 1751. In fact Hannibal studied at a military school in La Fère.

6. The Anglo-French campaign of 1719–20 against Spain for alleged violations of the Peace of Utrecht (1713).

7. Philippe III, duc d'Orléans (1674–1723) became Regent of France in 1715, on the death of Louis XIV.

8. John Law (1671–1729), Scottish financier and speculator, founded in 1716 the Banque général, the first bank in France, which by issuing prodigious quantities of bank notes, brought the French economy to the brink of ruin by 1720.

9. Armand de la Porte, duc de Richelieu (1696–1788), a great-nephew of Cardinal Richelieu, bore the title of maréchal de France and played a prominent role at the courts of Louis XIV, the Regent, and Louis XV. Comparing him to the Athenian statesman Alcibiades (ca. 450–404 B.C.), Pushkin probably had in mind Alcibiades' dissipated life and expensive public displays, especially at the Olympian Games of 420 B.C., which led to his financial ruin.

10. From Voltaire's *La Pucelle* (1755), Canto 13. In Ernest Dowson's English translation it reads:

> The pleasant reign of license had its prime,
> As folly, tinkling loud her bells in hand,
> With lightsome step tripped over Gallia's land,
> Where to devotion not a soul was prone,
> And every act save penitence was known.

See *La Pucelle: The Maid of Orleans*, tr. E. Dowson, 2 (London: Lutetian Society, 1899): 246–47).

11. Arouet was Voltaire's original name, which he dropped in 1718. At the time described by Pushkin, the early 1720's, Voltaire (1694–1778) was in his twenties. Guillaume Amfrye, abbé de Chaulieu (1639–1720), was a lyric poet. Charles de Secondat, baron de Montesquieu (1689–1755), was just at this time publishing his *Lettres persanes* (1721). Bernard Le Boviet de Fontenelle (1657–1757) was the permanent secretary of the Académie française.

12. From G. A. Derzhavin's ode "On the Death of Prince Meshcherskii" (1779).

13. The son of a corporal or a groom, Prince Aleksandr Menshikov (1673–1729), who was once reportedly a pie vendor, began his career as the boy Peter's orderly in the Preobrazhenskii Regiment, eventually rising to be Generalissimus and Prince of Russia. He was several times investigated for corruption and suffered punishment at Peter's own hands, yet managed to maintain his position. Ia. F. Dolgorukii (1659–1720) was a senator and president of the Auditing Collegium. If, as other details indicate, Ibrahim returned to Russia in the early or mid-1720's, he could not have met with Dologorukii. Jacob Bruce (1670–1735), of Scottish background, was an outstanding military engineer. He had been born in Russia and belonged to the second generation of foreign settlers in Muscovy. The Raguzinskii famous for his role as a diplomat and close adviser to Peter was Count Savva Lukich (1670–1738), a descendant of the Bosnian princes Vladislavić; but he was already in his fifties at the time described by Pushkin, and therefore the reference may be to a member of his family.

14. Anthony de Vière (d. 1746), chief of police of the new Russian capital, had arrived in Russia as a cabin boy.

15. Protogen's words, in slightly altered form, from Act 3 of V. Kiukhel'beker's tragedy *Argiviane* (1823).

16. Field Marshal Count Boris Sheremetev (1652–1719) commanded the Russian army in several important campaigns during Peter's reign. Once

more, if indeed Ibrahim returned to Russia in the 1720's, he could not have met Sheremetev. I. M. Golovin (d. 1738), an ancestor of Pushkin's on his father's side, was the commander of the galley fleet under Peter.

17. A. B. Buturlin (1694–1767), a graduate of the newly established Naval Academy, served as a personal assistant to Peter. Feofan Prokopovich (1681–1736), archbishop of Novgorod, was an outstanding writer and ardent supporter of Peter's reforms; the Spiritual Reglament of 1721, outlining the new organization of the Church, was written mainly by him. Gavriil Buzhinskii (1680–1731), a learned monk, was put in charge of printing houses in 1721. I. F. Kopievich (d. 1706), a translator, had organized the Russian printing house in Amsterdam; as the date of his death shows, he could not have been at Peter's court during the time described by Pushkin.

18. This character, Ivan Evgrafovich Korsakov, is also based on a historical figure, V. Ia. Rimskii-Korsakov (1702–57), who had been sent to France in 1716 to study naval science and returned to Russia in 1724.

19. Natalia Kirilovna Naryshkina (d. 1694) was Tsar Alexis Mikhailovich's second wife and Peter I's mother. The years 1689–94, when she and her associates governed the country, witnessed the last flowering of Muscovite parochialism and suspicion of everything foreign; therefore her sable hat could be taken as a symbol of the old fashions Peter tried to discard. Likewise, the ladies' use of gowns resembling the sarafan, a long mantle, veil, or sleeveless cloak forming part of the national dress of Russian women, reflected an adherence to the old ways.

20. "What the hell is all that?"

21. From Canto 1 of Pushkin's own verse tale (1820). The wedding feast described is followed by the scene in which the sorcerer Chernomor snatches away Ruslan's bride before their marriage is consummated; taken in this context, the epigraph may be read as a foreshadowing of Ibrahim's unblessed matrimony.

22. Although the Russians were defeated in the Battle of Narva (1700), they scored several victories in Livonia and Estonia the following year, taking numerous prisoners. The reference later in the chapter to "the campaign of 1701" indicates that that was the time when the officer in question was taken prisoner.

23. The Russian term is *mestnichestvo*, meaning order of precedence both in appointments to public office and in seating at table on festive occasions. The precedence was based on ancient lineage and offices held by ancestors.

24. The Russian reads: *A dura-to vret, vret, da i pravdu sovret* (lit., "A fool gibbers and gibbers, and gibbers out the truth, too").

25. Ephesians 5: 22.

26. The Russian reads: *Skazal by slovechko, da volk nedalechko* (lit., "I would say a word, but the wolf is close by"). The allusion is to Peter's ubiquitous presence and dictatorial ways.

27. Menshikov.

28. In the fragment printed in *Severnye tsvety* there followed, at this point, an exclamation by Tatiana Afanasevna, expressing her fright at the blackamoor's appearance. This exclamation is missing from the manuscript.

29. Quotation, in somewhat altered form, from Act 1, Scene 4, of A. Ablesimov's comic opera *The Miller, the Wizard, the Cheat, and the Matchmaker* (1779).

30. Menshikov was reported to have once sold pancakes, or pies, in the streets of Moscow.

31. "Bova Korolevich" and "Eruslan Lazarevich" were romances imported in the first half of the 17th century and transformed into Russian fairy tales. "Bova" originated from the Carolingian romance "Bueves d'Anston" ("Bevis of Hampton" in English); and Eruslan is a distant descendant of the Persian Rustam.

32. The Streltsy, or musketeers, were soldiers of the first permanent regular regiments of the Russian army, organized by Ivan the Terrible around 1550. Some of the Streltsy regiments opposed Peter I in his struggle for the throne and were subsequently persecuted.

33. The reference is not certain, but Rzhevskii probably means the rebellion of 1682. In April of that year, the ten-year-old Peter was proclaimed Tsar, but because of his youth his mother became Regent, and her relatives, the Naryshkins, secured leading positions in the state. A month later, however, the so-called Miloslavskii party, led by Alexis Mikhailovich's daughter by his first wife (and therefore Peter's half-sister), Sofiia, inspired a rebellion of the regiments of the Streltsy. Leading members of the Naryshkin party were murdered, which would have been the occasion when a Strelets saved Rzhevskii's life. Evidently the Strelets later fell afoul of Peter, and Rzhevskii repaid him by sheltering his son.

34. The word fifteenth is missing from the manuscript; Pushkin left a blank space, evidently planning to enter the figure later. It has been provided by B. V. Tomashevskii, ed., *Polnoe sobranie sochinenii*, 10 vols. (Moscow: Akademiia Nauk SSSR, 1962–66), in consideration of the fact that Abram Hannibal was born in Abyssinia (Ethiopia).

35. "I'd ditch."

36. "A delicate little thing."

37. "Affected woman."

38. *Lastochka* means swallow (the bird).

39. No outline in Pushkin's own hand has survived to show how he intended to continue the novel. There is, however, an entry for September 16, 1827, in the diary of his friend A. Vul'f reporting how Pushkin had said he would continue the plot. The relevant sentence in Vul'f's diary reads: "The central intrigue in this novel, as Pushkin says, will be the infidelity of the blackamoor's wife, who will give birth to a white baby and will be banished to a convent for it." See V. E. Vatsuro et al., eds., *A. S. Pushkin v vospominaniiakh sovremennikov*, 1 (Moscow: Khudozhestvennaia literatura, 1974): 416.

The Guests Were Arriving at the Dacha

1. These fragments of a projected psychological novel were not prepared for publication by Pushkin and bore no title; they are known by the opening words of the first fragment. Fragments 1 and 2 were written in 1828, Fragment 3 in 1830. Although Fragment 3 was not juxtaposed to the first two fragments in Pushkin's manuscripts, it appears to be clearly connected with them, since the same Spaniard and Russian here seem to be resuming their conversation interrupted in Fragment 1. The three fragments have been assembled as a continuum only in Soviet editions.

2. A reference to N. I. Gnedich's idyll "Fishermen" (1821). Pushkin's character, however, in keeping with his flippant tone, changes Gnedich's expression *rusye lokon volny* ("blond waves of locks") to the much less poetic *belobrysaia* ("towheaded"). Gnedich's idyll is quoted at length in Pushkin's note 8 to *Eugene Onegin*.

3. "Began to sulk."

4. "He'll do nothing of the kind: he'll be all too glad to have the chance to compromise her."

5. At this point in the manuscript another sentence followed, which Pushkin subsequently crossed out: "I look on her as if she were a sleepwalker, asleep yet walking on the roof: one would like to wake her but dares not."

6. Hussein Pasha (1773?–1838) was the Dey of Algiers (1818–30).

7. At this point in the manuscript another phrase followed, which Pushkin subsequently crossed out: "because General-Adjutant Y. had resolutely declared at a court ball that Zinaida was the most beautiful woman in Petersburg and." In most editions, this phrase is not given, but it is reinstated in the Tomashevskii edition of Pushkin's collected works.

8. A novel by Pierre Choderlos de Laclos (1782).

9. Henri Jomini (1779–1869) was a soldier and military author of Swiss birth. He served in Napoleon's army during the Russian campaign, but switched sides in 1813 and became a high-ranking general and military adviser in the Russian army under both Alexander I and Nicholas I.

10. "And besides, he's a man of grand passions."

11. The Russian reads: *Tvoi sofizmy ne ubezhdaiut moikh podozrenii* (lit., "Your sophisms don't convince my suspicions"). An earlier version read, *Tvoi sofizmy ne ubezhdaiut menia* ("Your sophisms don't convince me"), which is much simpler and clearer; but evidently Pushkin was striving for an awkward, bookish effect.

12. Prince Riurik (d. 879) was one of the three Scandinavian brothers who, according to tradition, were invited to rule over feuding East Slavic tribes; he became ruler of Novgorod in 862. Vladimir Monomakh, Grand Prince of Kiev (r. 1113–25), made the last attempt to unite the petty Russian states before the Mongol invasion.

13. In referring to orderlies and pastry vendors Pushkin probably had in mind Prince Aleksandr Menshikov (see *The Blackamoor of Peter the Great*, note 13). Among Ukrainians who rose from obscurity to prominence in the 18th century, the best known are Prince A. A. Bezborodko (1747–99), a leading statesman during the reign of Catherine II and chancellor under Paul I; and Count A. G. Razumovskii (1709–71), son of a simple Cossack, who began his career as a chorister and eventually married the Empress Elizabeth in a secret ceremony in 1742. The target of Pushkin's allusion to sextons is less obvious, but he probably had in mind P. I. Iaguzhinskii (1683–1736), son of a poor Lithuanian sexton, who rose to the position of General of the Army. The Montmorency family gave France many distinguished statesmen, including Mathieu (d. 1160), high constable and co-Regent of France under Louis VII. The first Montmorency recorded in history was Bouchard I (d. 980); Pushkin's reference, however, is not especially to him, but to the title "premiers barons de France," which all members of the family bore until 1327. The Clermont-Tonnerres were another distinguished family, among whose members the best known are Count Stanislas Marie Adélaide (1757–92), a deputy

of the nobility in the States General who voted for the abolition of gentry privileges, and Cardinal Anne Antoine Jules (1749–1830), also a deputy in the States General.

14. The reference is to N. M. Karamzin's *History of the Russian State* (1815–24).

15. The following outlines for the projected novel have been preserved among Pushkin's papers (the original is partly in French, partly in Russian):

A man of high society courts a fashionable lady and seduces her, but marries another one out of calculation. His wife creates scenes. The other woman confesses everything to her husband; she comforts the wife, visits her. The man of high society is unhappy, ambitious.

A young woman is brought out in society.

Zélie loves a vain egotist; she is surrounded by the cold malevolence of high society; a complaisant husband; a lover who makes fun of her; a lady friend who forsakes her. She becomes frivolous, has a scandalous affair with a man she doesn't love. Her husband repudiates her; she is utterly miserable. Her lover, her husband...

1. A scene from the life of high society, at the dacha of Count L. The room is full, around the tea table. Zélie's arrival. She sought out with her eyes the man of high society and spends the whole evening with him.

2. A historical account of the seduction. The liaison. Her lover's indiscreet behavior.

3. A young provincial girl's arrival in high society. A scene of jealousy. High society's disapproval.

4. Rumors of marriage—Zélie's despair. She confesses everything to her husband. Her husband is complaisant. A visit during the wedding night. Zélie falls sick. She reappears in high society; men flirt with her, etc. etc.

In the Corner of a Small Square

1. This fragment, written sometime between November 1830 and March 1831, represents a new attempt on Pushkin's part to treat the same social and psychological theme as that of "The Guests Were Arriving at the Dacha." Chap. 1 was first published in V. A. Zhukovskii et al., eds., *Sochineniia Aleksandra Pushkina*, 11 (St. Petersburg: Tipografiia zagotovleniia gosudarstvennykh bumag, 1841): 143–47; and the second, fragmentary chapter first appeared in *Russkaia starina*, 7 (1884): 51–52.

2. From an unpublished correspondence: "Your heart is a sponge soaked with bile and vinegar."

3. The following exchange was crossed out of the manuscript:

"You mean the one who was at one time slapped on the face but refused to fight a duel?"

"No, not that one. This one just got a beating with a walking stick... Actually, this whole thing is a trick of his wife's: I didn't have the good luck to win her approval."

4. In the manuscript, the phrase originally read: "A fat, stupid, and insolent woman who takes bribes." It has been suggested in critical literature that

Pushkin might have been hinting at Countess M. D. Nesselrode, wife of the Minister of Foreign Affairs.

5. The original version read: "Confess, Valerian: the reason you're upset is not that some people you despise have scorned you, but that you've missed the opportunity to see some beautiful debutante."

6. "You write your 4-page letters faster than I can read them." Pushkin subsequently used a somewhat altered form of this epigraph for Chap. 3 of "The Queen of Spades."

7. From an elegant central location to an unglamorous district.

8. The following outline for the project (in Russian, but with a couple of French phrases) was preserved among Pushkin's papers:

Twilight in Kolomna. Vera is sick and affectionate. *He* lies. An evening party with a... A young girl brought out in society. He falls in love. A young man's morning. They will be giving balls until she marries. He is introduced. Scenes in Kolomna. He quarrels...

A Novel in Letters

1. This fragment, written in the fall of 1829, was first published, in part, by P. V. Annenkov in *Sochineniia Aleksandra Pushkina,* 7 (St. Petersburg: P. V. Annenkov, 1857): 125–38. The title *A Novel in Letters* was given to it by subsequent editors.

2. Alphonse de Lamartine's *Méditations poétiques* (1820) brought him great fame in both Western Europe and Russia. Translated into Russian in many different versions, his poetry was in vogue among Petersburg ladies, which is reflected in Liza's somewhat contemptuous "*your* Lamartine."

3. This was the name of an actual village, owned by P. I. Vul'f, in Tver' Guberniia. Pushkin was a guest on Vul'f's estate in late October and early November 1829, and it is evidently here that he worked on his epistolary novel. In the manuscript the first letter is dated Oct. 21, and the third one, "Nov. 1." Editors have generally assumed, from the context, that these dates do not belong to the fictional letters but indicate the time of their writing.

4. One of the Neva River islands in suburban St. Petersburg.

5. The heroine of Samuel Richardson's epistolary novel *Clarissa* (1747–48).

6. This description is lifted out at least partially from the fragment "In the Beginning of 1812" (see Appendix B) and is also used in "The Squire's Daughter."

7. The reference is to the Abbé Prévost's French translation of the novel, *Lettres angloises, ou Histoire de Miss Clarisse Harlowe.* Pushkin had the 1777 edition of this work.

8. The reference is to the French writer and politician Benjamin Constant's *Adolphe* (1816).

9. The name obviously comes from Edward Bulwer-Lytton's *Pelham, or Adventures of a Gentleman* (1828), which also inspired Pushkin's later fragment *A Russian Pelham* (see Appendix B).

10. Charlotte is a common enough name for heroines, but Pushkin seems to imply that Bellecour was also a typical name for fictional characters,

which is puzzling because it does not occur in any commonly known French novel of the 18th century. Pushkin might have been inspired by the name of the famous actor who went by that stage name: Jean Claude Gilles Colson (1725–78).

11. Prince P. A. Viazemskii (1792–1878), poet and literary critic, was a close friend of Pushkin's.

12. The former seminary student was N. I. Nadezhdin (1804–56), literary critic of the *European Herald*, who had accused Pushkin of impropriety in his review of *Count Nulin*. See *Vestnik Evropy*, 3 (1829): 215–30.

13. Fornarina was a Roman woman of great beauty, whose portrait Raphael painted. Sasha's reference to her is poignant, because she was the daughter of a simple baker (reflected in her nickname).

14. Kuzma Minin, nicknamed Sukhorukii (d. 1616), a Nizhnii Novgorod butcher, and Prince D. M. Pozharskii (1578–1642) commanded the Russian army that defeated the Polish king Sigismund III's forces and captured Moscow in 1612. The monument in memory of their victory stands in Red Square. "Privy councillor" translates *okol'nichii*, a dignitary close to the Tsar's court.

15. The reference is to D. P. Severin (1792–1865), an official of the Ministry of Foreign Affairs (subsequently Russian ambassador to Sweden), who had been a member of the Arzamas literary society with Pushkin but later snubbed the exiled poet in Odessa. He was the target of Pushkin's 1823 epigram "A Complaint."

16. "To affect scorn for one's birth is ridiculous in an upstart and dastardly in a gentleman." This is a literary mystification: scholars have not been able to find the quotation in La Bruyère.

17. Characters from D. I. Fonvizin's comedy *The Young Hopeful* (1782), who became symbols of brutal Russian feudalism.

18. An earlier version of the manuscript read: "I don't think I am in love with her, but I had begun to miss her."

19. Famusov's words from Act 2, Scene 5, of A. S. Griboedov's comedy *Woe from Wit* (1824). What Famusov says is that in Moscow young ladies run after officers because they are patriots.

20. "Indolent self-satisfaction."

21. "I am their most obedient servant." From Act 3 of Rossini's opera *The Barber of Seville* (1816).

22. "A fearless and flawless man / Who is not a king, nor a duke, nor even a count." It was the French knight Pierre Terrail, seigneur de Bayard (1473–1524), who was known in legend as *chevalier sans peur et sans reproche*. The second line of the quotation, however, refers to the Coucy, an ancient French family of Picardy, whose motto was "Roy ne suis, ne prince ne duc, ne comte aussy; je suis sire de Coucy."

23. At this point there is a gap in the manuscript.

24. The reference is to the hero of *Les Amours du chevalier de Faublas* (1787–89) by Jean Baptiste Louvet de Couvrai.

25. "With the servant of the Lord's servants," i.e., the Pope.

26. The reference is to the Scottish philosopher and economist Adam Smith (1723–90); the change in social attitudes described was a result of Nicholas I's suppression of the Decembrist uprising of 1825.

The Tales of the Late Ivan Petrovich Belkin

1. *The Tales of Belkin* was the first work of fiction completed and pub-lished by Pushkin. Although he had already jotted down the first draft of the Publisher's introduction to the tales in the fall of 1829, the bulk of the vol-ume was written a year later, during Pushkin's exceptionally productive so-journ at his family's estate at Boldino. He wrote the following dates of com-pletion on the manuscript of the five stories: "The Undertaker," Sept. 9, 1830; "The Stationmaster," Sept. 14; "The Squire's Daughter," Sept. 20; "The Shot," Oct. 14; and "The Blizzard," Oct. 20. This was the order in which he originally intended to publish them, but in the summer of 1831, when he was preparing the volume for publication and revising the Publisher's introduc-tion, he moved the last two tales to the front of the collection. The volume was published in October 1831. Originally Pushkin had planned to make it entirely pseudonymous, but eventually he decided to reveal his identity by placing his initials after the Publisher's introduction. His initials do not, however, accord with the Publisher's style, which is as parodic as that of the letter written by Belkin's neighbor. Indeed the *Tales'* original narrators (listed by the Publisher in a footnote); the collector of the tales, Belkin; the neighbor who provides Belkin's biography; and the Publisher himself are all tools of parody in Pushkin's hands.

2. From Act 4, Scene 8, of D. I. Fonvizin's comedy *The Young Hopeful* (1782), in which Prostakova tries to show off her son Mitrofan's learnedness in front of a number of guests, with little success. Seeing the boy's total igno-rance of grammar, one of the guests ironically suggests that Mitrofan must be equally strong in "history"—a word that Prostakova and her brother Skotinin proceed to interpret as "story" or "anecdote." The epigraph establishes a con-nection between the uncouth Mitrofan and Belkin. (Skotinin and his sister, it will be recalled, figured as examples of reactionary feudalists in *A Novel in Letters*.)

3. The principal obligations of the Russian serf under the feudal system were of two types: either corvée (*barshchina*), that is, field labor for the land-lord; or quitrent (*obrok*), that is, payment to the landlord, in kind or in money, from the yield of the serf's parcel of land.

4. It is assumed to be a deliberate joke on the part of Pushkin that Belkin's neighbor replies on Nov. 16 to a letter he received on Nov. 23 (as he indicates in the first paragraph of his reply).

5. The first epigraph is from the verse tale *The Ball* (1828) by E. A. Bar-atynskii. Its hero, Arsenii, an aloof, morose personality, feared for his sharp tongue, provokes a duel with a friend when his beloved Ol'ga seems to show a preference for the friend. "An Evening on Bivouac" (1823), the source of the second epigraph, is a short story by A. A. Bestuzhev-Marlinskii. Its hero, a young officer named Mechin, is wounded in a duel by an adversary who fires the first shot; when Mechin recovers he plans to claim his turn, but—thanks to the good offices of a friend—he is sent away by his superiors on an urgent mission. The reasons why Pushkin's hero does not fire his gun contrast iron-ically with the circumstances that prevent Mechin from shooting.

6. The description indicates that Silvio and his guests were playing faro, a betting game, with a banker holding the deal, as in blackjack, and several

punters, or players. When a winning punter turned down the corner of his card, he signaled that he intended to let his winnings ride on the next turn of the cards, thus doubling his stake. With several people punting against the banker simultaneously, it was customary to keep a written record of the stakes, as did Silvio and his guests. The use of a brush for erasing indicates that they were writing the score on the green felt cover of the card table. For details of the play of the game, which is central to Pushkin's "Queen of Spades," see note 3 to that story.

7. D. V. Davydov (1784–1839), who commanded a large Russian guerilla unit during Napoleon's invasion of Russia in 1812, was the celebrated poet of hussar life. Three of his poems (all written in 1804) were directly addressed to his irrepressible comrade A. P. Burtsov (d. 1813).

8. In his manuscript Pushkin put the date Oct. 12 after Chap. 1 and wrote: "The ending has been lost." Then he decided to proceed further, radically altering the meaning of the story by adding a new chapter. Chap. 2, as the final date indicates, was completed in another two days.

9. The Russian original contains an untranslatable play on the phrases *p'ianitsa s goria* (a drunkard from sorrow) and *gor'kii p'ianitsa* (inveterate drunkard).

10. Given in English in the Russian text.

11. Alexander Ypsilanti (1792–1828) had been an officer in the Russian Imperial Guard until he was elected head of the secret Greek revolutionary society Philike Hetairia ("Friendly Association") and made an attempt to liberate Greece by invading European Turkey from Bessarabia, in 1821. His attempt failed, partly because of Alexander I's refusal to aid him. One Hetairist division was defeated by the Turks in the region of Skuliany, on the Prut River, on June 17, 1821. The battle near Skuliany is described by Pushkin in some detail in his short story "Kirdzhali" (see below).

12. From V. A. Zhukovskii's verse tale *Svetlana* (1812). Zhukovskii's heroine, like Pushkin's, rides to a nightmarish wedding in a blizzard and wakes to a happy ending. But unlike Pushkin's heroine, she marries the man she originally intended to marry.

13. The Russian reads: *Suzhenogo konem ne ob''edesh'* (lit., "Even on horseback you cannot escape the man destined for you").

14. According to the outline Pushkin originally jotted down for the story, Masha would have lost both her father and her mother, and would have lived alone as an independent proprietress. The *guberniia* was the largest administrative unit in the Russian Empire; it was divided into *provintsii* (provinces) and *uezdy* (districts).

15. Artemesia (d. ca. 350 B.C.), bereft widow of Mausolus, King of Caria (d. ca. 353 B.C.), erected a tomb (Mausoleum) in his memory at Halicarnassus.

16. "Vive Henri Quatre" is a song from Charles Collé's comedy *La Partie de chasse de Henri IV* (1774). *Joconde*, staged in Paris in 1814, was a comic opera by Nicholas Isouard.

17. From Act 2, Scene 5, of A. S. Griboedov's comedy *Woe from Wit* (1824). In the comedy, Chatskii berates Russian women with these words for their stupidity in falling for uniforms. Belkin could only have heard this passage cited, or read it in manuscript, because it was not published until 1834.

18. "If this is not love, what is it?" From Petrarch's *Rerum Vulgarum Fragmenta*, no. 132.

19. A reference to Jean-Jacques Rousseau's *Julie, ou La Nouvelle Héloïse* (1761).

20. From G. R. Derzhavin's poem *Waterfall* (1794).

21. The manuscript version reads "attractive little coffin" instead of "chubby Cupid."

22. The references are to Act 4, Scene 1, of *Hamlet*, and to Chap. 24 of *The Bride of Lammermoor* (1819).

23. The reference is to a character in A. Pogorel'skii's (A. A. Perovskii) story "The Poppy-Seed-Cake Woman of the Lafertovo Quarter" (1825).

24. Napoleon's army.

25. From A. E. Izmailov's fable "The Fool Pakhomovna" (ca. 1814).

26. The Russian phrase is *Dolg platezhom krasen* (lit., "A debt is fine if repaid").

27. The manuscript version reads "sober and angry."

28. From P. A. Viazemskii's poem *The Station* (1828). The rank Viazemskii referred to was *gubernskii registrator*, which Pushkin changed to *kollezhskii registrator* (lit., "collegiate registrar"). The change was probably motivated by Pushkin's wish to give his character the 14th rank, the lowest on the official list of ranks in government service; it was equivalent to sublieutenant in the armed forces. A decree of 1808 awarded stationmasters this rank specifically in order to protect them, as civil servants, from physical abuse.

29. For the travels of low-ranking officials the State Treasury paid for only two horses (out of the usual team of three).

30. The original reads: *razdeliaet s nimi trapezu* (lit., "shares their table"). The word *trapeza* has an archaic Old Church Slavic flavor.

31. The description of these pictures first occurs in the earlier fragment "Notes of a Young Man" (see Appendix B). In that fragment they were accompanied by other pictures depicting "the burying of the cat, the dispute of the red nose with the mighty frost, and the like." Transferring the illustrations of the parable of the Prodigal Son to "The Stationmaster," Pushkin at first placed them in the company of "a portrait of General Kul'nev and a view of the Khutynskii Monastery," but eventually decided to make them the sole decoration of the stationmaster's wall.

32. Scholars have not tracked down the source of this line.

33. After these words we read the following in the manuscript version:

The reader knows that there are different kinds of love—sensual and Platonic love; love fueled by vanity; love in the fifteen-year-old heart; and so forth—but among them all the traveler's love is the most enjoyable. If you fall in love at one station, you hardly notice the journey to the next one (and sometimes even to the third one). Nothing can shorten a journey more: your imagination, not distracted by anything else, can fully indulge in its reveries. Carefree, lighthearted love! It strikes you vividly without wearying your heart; and it is extinguished as soon as you reach the first city tavern.

34. In the first edition the name of the stationmaster was given as Simeon Vyrin, but the mistake was immediately corrected in the list of printer's errors appended to the volume, showing that the original name, Samson, referring to the Biblical hero deprived of his power by a woman, was important to Pushkin.

35. The original reads: *Chto s vozu upalo, to propalo* (lit., "What's fallen off the cart is lost").

36. The Russian reads: *Chto sdelano, togo ne vorotish'* (lit., "What has been done you cannot turn back").

37. This scene of the stationmaster returning for his money was added to the manuscript later.

38. The Russian name of the church was Tserkov' Vsekh Skorbiashchikh.

39. The reference is to I. I. Dmitriev's humorous poem "A Caricature" (1791), which relates the return of a soldier to his homestead after 20 years of army service. He finds his house deserted, except for one old servant, Terent'ich, who tearfully tells him that his wife kept bad company, was arrested, and has not been heard of for five years. The soldier, seeing no point in grieving after his lost wife, remarries and lives happily ever after. The irony of the reference is that the narrator of "The Stationmaster" seems to have forgotten the context of Terent'ich's sorrow.

40. The outline Pushkin jotted down prior to writing this story is somewhat different from the eventual text. Since it sheds light on how the project took shape in Pushkin's mind, it is worth quoting in full:

A discourse on stationmasters. Unfortunate and warmhearted people as a rule. My friend, the widowed stationmaster. His daughter. That route has been abolished. I rode by it recently. I did not find the daughter. The story of the daughter. A clerk in love with her. The clerk goes after her to Petersburg. Sees her during holiday festivities. When he returns he finds the father dead. The grave outside the village. I ride by. The clerk is dead. The coach driver tells me about the daughter.

41. From Book 2 of I. Bogdanovich's narrative poem *Dushen'ka* (1783).

42. After the death of Catherine II in November 1796, her successor, Paul I, dismissed many of the people, especially officers of the Guards, who had surrounded her.

43. Given in English in the original.

44. From A. Shakhovskoi's satire "Molière, Your Incomparable Gift!" (1808).

45. Banks of the nobility had actually been granting loans to landowners, encumbering their estates, since 1754.

46. In the manuscript Pushkin at first wrote Moscow University, then University of Kharkov, then crossed them both out, and inserted this.

47. The mustache distinguished the military from the civilian in government service.

48. One manuscript version read: "Indeed he carried on a secret correspondence with the wife of one of his professors."

49. This description goes back to *A Novel in Letters* (see above, p. 52) and to the fragment "In the Beginning of 1812" (see Appendix B).

50. The manuscript version has "high society dolls" instead of "debutantes."

51. The quotation is from a French edition of the German writer J. P. F. Richter's works: *Pensées de Jean-Paul: Extraites de tous ses ouvrages*, tr. Augustin de Lagrange (Paris: F. Didot, 1829), p. 153. Pushkin had the book in his library.

52. "Our observation remains valid."

53. Samuel Richardson's novel (1740).
54. "Steady, Sbogar, to heel." The name comes from Charles Nodier's novel *Jean Sbogar* (1818). In the manuscript version the dog was called Lara, with a clear allusion to Byron's 1814 verse tale by that name.
55. In this sentence the Russian verbal forms indicate a masculine subject, though the narrator is supposed to be "the maiden K.I.T."
56. Given in English in the original.
57. Jeanne Antoinette Poisson, marquise de Pompadour (1721–64), was Louis XV's mistress.
58. A system of primary-school education, in which older students aided in teaching younger students. Named after the British educator Joseph Lancaster (1778–1838).
59. A story by N. M. Karamzin (1792).
60. From Act 2, Scene 3, of *The Young Hopeful*.
61. "Let me go, sir; are you out of your mind?"

A History of the Village of Goriukhino

1. This unfinished work, closely related to *The Tales of Belkin*, was written at the end of October 1830, right after Pushkin had completed the last of the Belkin tales. It was left in manuscript and was first published posthumously, with many omissions, in *Sovremennik*, 7 (1837): 197–200. The description of the village of Goriukhino is modeled on Boldino, the center of the Pushkins' estate in Nizhnii Novgorod Guberniia, where Pushkin stayed in the fall of 1830. He was no doubt aware of the fact that the peasants of this estate had participated in the Pugachev Rebellion of 1773–74. In several places in the manuscript the village is called Gorokhino, rather than Goriukhino. The former name has associations with the fairy-tale Tsar Gorokh (King Pea), under whose benign reign the villagers might have lived in the original "fabulous times." By contrast, the name Goriukhino, which Pushkin switched to in the course of writing the narrative, is derived from *gore* (sorrow). *A History of the Village of Goriukhino* is more than just a parody on historiography, but to the extent that it *is* a parody, its most probable targets are Vol. 1 of N. M. Karamzin's *History of the Russian State* (1815), and Vol. 1 of N. Polevoi's *History of the Russian People* (1829). The Belkin of *Goriukhino* is essentially the same person as the narrator of the *Tales*, though in his own account of his life in the introductory part he appears three years younger.
2. The *Handbook* (*pismovnik*) and its author were not Pushkin's inventions: N. G. Kurganov (d. 1796), a professor of the Naval Academy, had indeed published many editions of a composition handbook, which was still popular in Pushkin's time (first published, under a different title, in 1769; known as *Pismovnik* from the 4th, 1790, ed. on).
3. Barthold Georg Niebuhr was a German writer and statesman whose three-volume *Römische Geschichte* (1811–32) had a profound influence on the modern critical approach to the study of history.
4. Napoleon's army.
5. Later Pushkin partially transferred this scene to Vol. 1, Chap. 2, of *Dubrovskii*.
6. The manuscript version here reads instead, "the former cook, who had recently been working in the fields."

7. This seems to be a hint at the squire of Nenaradovo, who was to write Belkin's biographical sketch for the Publisher of the *Tales*.

8. A play by August Friedrich Ferdinand von Kotzebue (1789). The role of Amalia—a little girl—was usually played by pupils of drama schools.

9. *The Steadfast* (*Blagonamerennyi*) was a literary journal published in St. Petersburg between 1818 and 1826 and edited by the fabulist A. E. Izmailov; Pushkin himself published in it in the early period of his literary career. By *Hamburg Gazette* Pushkin probably means *Wochentliche gemeinnützige Nachrichten von und für Hamburg* (later the *Hamburger Nachrichten*), which had been published since 1792 and was widely read in foreign countries as one of the most highly respected newspapers of the time.

10. In the outline Pushkin jotted down before writing *Goriukhino* (see note 29), this scene is referred to as "Meeting with Bulg." The reference must have been to F. V. Bulgarin (1789–1859), a popular novelist and short story writer, the founder of *Northern Bee*, and a notorious police informer, one of Pushkin's chief adversaries in public life. The reference, however, is anachronistic, because in 1820 Bulgarin had only just arrived in St. Petersburg and was not yet known as an author.

11. The *Votary of Enlightenment and Beneficence* (*Sorevnovatel' prosveshcheniia i blagotvoreniia*), published in St. Petersburg between 1818 and 1825, was an organ of the Free Society of Lovers of Russian Literature, and as such voiced romantic literary opinions as well as political views close to the Decembrist movement.

12. See note 12 for "The Guests Were Arriving at the Dacha."

13. "The Dangerous Neighbor" (1811) was a humorous narrative poem by Pushkin's uncle V. L. Pushkin; the other two references are to anonymous satirical poems circulated in manuscript because of censorship conditions.

14. A reference to Claude François Xavier Millot's *Histoire générale ancienne et moderne* (1772–83).

15. V. N. Tatishchev (1686–1750) was the first scholarly historian of Russia; his five-volume *Russian History from Ancient Times* was published posthumously between 1768 and 1848. Both he and I. N. Boltin (1735–92) rendered great service to scholarship by publishing historical documents. I. I. Golikov was best known for his multivolume work *The Deeds of Peter the Great* (1788–97).

16. A reference to the pages describing the year 1787 in Edward Gibbon's *Memoirs of My Life and Writings* (1789; published posthumously), in which he recounts his feelings on concluding *The History of the Decline and Fall of the Roman Empire* (1776–88).

17. "Old Church Slavic abbreviations" translates the Russian term *titlo*, meaning a sign drawn above an abbreviated word or above a letter signifying a numeral. The discrepancy between 54 and 55 issues exists in the original.

18. Beating a servant "on account of the weather" is a later addition to the manuscript.

19. "Tradesman's script" translates *lavochnichii pocherk*.

20. A *desiatina* equals 2.7 acres. The section beginning with this sentence is placed here (as it is in standard Soviet editions) because this seems to be its most logical position; it should be noted, however, that in older editions the section entitled "Fabulous Times" preceded the general description of Goriukhino.

21. "Male serf" translates *dusha* (lit., "soul").

22. The names of the two villages are suggestive: *ukho*, "ear," is combined in the first name with the imperative of the verb *drat'* (to "pull" or "tear"), and in the second, with the syllable *perk*, which evokes associations with the noun *perka* ("drill") or with the verb *peret'* (to "push," "press," "drag").

23. "Strapping wench" translates *baba zdorovennaia.*

24. The Russian reads *nazyvaiutsia kopeishchitsami (ot slovenskogo slova kop'e)*, meaning "are called 'spear-women' (from the Slavic word 'spear')." The word *kopeishchitsa* also has associations with *kopeika* ("kopeck," "penny").

25. This type of marriage arrangement was designed to bring an adult, capable of hard work, into the household. In this paragraph Pushkin switches to the past tense, which reflects the great hesitation between the tenses observable in the manuscript. It has been suggested that he originally intended to put the whole description in the present tense but later began transferring some of it to the past in order to make it less offensive to a potential censor.

26. The double-headed eagle, the emblem of the Russian state, was displayed on the signs of taverns, for the selling of liquor was a state monopoly.

27. The lyrical poems (songs, eclogues, idylls, elegies) of A. P. Sumarokov (1717–77) were extremely popular in the middle of the 18th century but were considered old-fashioned by the beginning of the 19th.

28. The word citizens (for "they") was a later addition to the manuscript.

29. Pushkin jotted down an outline for *Goriukhino* that carries the story beyond the completed text:

My respect for the calling of writers
Especially of poets
Meeting with Bulg. and Milonov
Love
My experiments in different genres
with stories
with history
World history
Russian history
History of the *guberniia* capital
The county seat has no history
My arrival in the country
My genealogy, idea of writing its history
The calendars
Oral tradition
The priest's chronicle
Census registers with a characterization of peasants

A geographic survey of the village
Fabulous times
The rule of the elder Antip the Wise
The arrival of my great-grandfather, the tyrant Iv. V. T.
(A rebellion)—My grandfather manages the estate. A fire.
The neighbors. The epidemic. Church history.
The peasants are impoverished. My father. The elder. The steward.
Rebellion.

The steward

. . . corvée

There was a free wealthy village
It was ruined by tyranny
Was set right by strict measures
Fell into decline because of negligence.

Roslavlev

1. A fragment of this unfinished novel, written in 1831, was published by Pushkin in his journal *Sovremennik*, 3 (1836): 197–203; the remainder first appeared in print in V. A. Zhukovskii et al., eds., *Sochineniia Aleksandra Pushkina*, 11 (St. Petersburg: Tip. zagotovleniia gos. bumag, 1841): 115–19.

2. A reference to M. N. Zagoskin's *Roslavlev, or The Russians in 1812* (1831). Working on his own *Roslavlev* in June 1831, right after the publication of Zagoskin's novel, Pushkin told a friend that he found Zagoskin's heroine flat, and wished to show how to draw a richer character. Zagoskin claimed that he modeled his heroine on a real-life prototype; and indeed there were some unfavorable references in the Russian press, right after the Napoleonic invasion, to Russian women who had married French prisoners of war and subsequently deserted to the French side. Zagoskin's Polina does just that. In Paris before the war she falls in love with a Frenchman called Sénicour, but since he is already married she has no hope of ever being united with him. After her return to Russia she halfheartedly agrees to be engaged to the Russian officer Roslavlev but keeps postponing the wedding. During the French invasion of Russia, Sénicour, by this time widowed, is taken prisoner of war and is sent to live with Polina's family. She marries him, defects to the French side, and is eventually killed by a Russian grenade during the siege of Danzig (Gdansk). Since Pushkin's narrator says that she can recognize her old friend, by now dead, in Zagoskin's heroine, it is likely that he was going to follow, at least in broad outline, Zagoskin's plot; but he intended to elucidate and put a different interpretation on Polina's motives.

3. The key signified the rank of chamberlain, and the star was the highest decoration of the state.

4. Montesquieu is important to Polina's characterization, for knowing his works, especially *L'Esprit des lois* (1748), implied a high level of political awareness. The novelist Claude Crébillon (1707–77) also adds an interesting touch to Polina's characterization, for he was famous for his depictions of corruption in high society.

5. Familiarity with Rousseau's *Le Contrat social* (1762) would also imply a high level of political awareness on Polina's part; a fondness for *La Nouvelle Héloïse* (1761), on the other hand, might dispose her to view favorably a romance between a high-class heroine and a man of a lower station (in her case, a prisoner of war).

6. This comment reflects, as did the one in *A History of the Village of Goriukhino* (see p. 130 and note 27 to that work), the declining popularity of Sumarokov by the beginning of the 19th century.

7. *Iurii Miloslavskii* (1829) was another of Zagoskin's novels. The reference is evidently to the narrator's comments introducing the scene in Princess Radugina's salon in Part 1, Chap. 3, of *Roslavlev*. The words of Pushkin's

narrator are ironic, since Pushkin himself had claimed, in Chap. 3 of *Onegin,* that Russian women did not know their native tongue.

8. In the edition referred to, the translator is identified only by her initials. See *Youry Miloslawsky, ou la Russie en 1612,* roman hist. par Zagoskine, trad. du russe par M-me. S. C. née Ott., 4 vols. (Paris, 1831).

9. M. V. Lomonosov (1711–65), both an outstanding scientist and the founder of modern Russian literature, was most famous for his patriotic odes and for fixing the standards of the Russian literary language as well as those of prosody.

10. *History of the Russian State* (1815–24).

11. In addition to *Iurii Miloslavskii* and *Roslavlev,* Pushkin's narrator must be alluding to F. V. Bulgarin's novel *Ivan Vyzhigin* (1829). On Bulgarin, see note 10 to *Goriukhino.*

12. A fashionable shop versus the milliners of a provincial town.

13. It has been shown that Pushkin not only introduced Mme. de Staël as a character in his unfinished novel, but took some of his description of Moscow society life from her *Dix Années d'exil* (1821). Her novel *Corinne,* to which reference is made in the same paragraph, was published in 1807.

14. A reference to the resistance to the compulsory shaving of beards under Peter I.

15. Napoleon.

16. "My dear child, I am quite ill. It would be very kind of you if you would drop in to cheer me up. Try to obtain your mother's permission to do so, and please give her my best regards. Your friend, *de S.*"

17. A street in the center of Moscow where many French fashion shops were situated.

18. The formation of the Confederation of the Rhine (1806) put an end to the Holy Roman Empire and brought most of Germany under Napoleon Bonaparte's control.

19. In August 1812 F. V. Rastopchin (1763–1828), military governor of Moscow, had many posters displayed on the streets of Moscow with news (mostly falsified and written in a folksy style) about Russian resistance to the advancing French army.

20. See note 14 for *A Novel in Letters.*

21. An area of Moscow, not yet built up at the time, where people liked to walk; today it is the site of the Moscow Zoo.

22. Charlotte Corday d'Armont (1768–93) was the assassin of the French Terrorist Marat. Marfa Boretskaia (dates unknown), widow of the mayor of Novgorod, I. A. Boretskii, led the city's boyar party in its fight against Muscovite domination in the 1470's. Princess Ekaterina Dashkova (1743–1810) was a prominent political figure during the reign of Catherine II.

23. The Russian original, *palaty prenii,* contains an ironic allusion to French parliamentary debates ("les débats de la Chambre des députés").

24. M. A. Dmitriev-Mamonov (1788–1863) was chief procurator of the Sixth Department of the State Senate at the time Napoleon's army invaded Russia. He joined the Russian army and was decorated with the Golden Sword for courage. In April 1813 he was appointed major-general in charge of the regiment he had organized and equipped at his own expense. This regiment of untrained new recruits lacked discipline, however, and later that year, when it burned down a village already in the European phase of the war,

Dmitriev-Mamonov was reprimanded and resigned his commission. He was reinstated as a cavalry officer in 1816, but had to retire because of ill health in 1819; he was subsequently found mentally incompetent by an Imperial commission, and whatever estate he had left was placed under state trusteeship.

25. The idea referred to was the strategy of retreating into the interior of Russia, thereby stretching thin the French army's supply lines.

26. The manuscript has "Sinécour," which is clearly a slip of the pen.

27. This news would have been false, if Pushkin had indeed intended to follow Zagoskin's plot.

28. "Those barbarians" in the manuscript.

Dubrovskii

1. This is an unfinished novel based on some genuine court cases. The first inspiration for it originated with Pushkin's friend P. V. Nashchokin, who told him in September 1832 about the fate of an impoverished Belorussian nobleman by the name of Ostrovskii: having lost his land to a neighbor in a lawsuit, Ostrovskii became a robber, and eventually fell into the hands of authorities. In search of further information about dispossessed landowners, Pushkin managed to acquire the record of a similar court case, tried in Kozlov District Court in October 1832, bearing the title "On the adverse possession by Lieutenant Ivan Iakovlevich Muratov of the village Novopanskoe in Kozlov District of Tambov Guberniia, which properly belongs to Colonel of the Guards Semen Petrovich Kriukov." As the novel began to take shape, Pushkin inserted this court case, without even copying it over, into Chap. 2; all he changed were names and dates, but even some of those were left as they stood in the original.

The name Dubrovskii probably originated with an earlier historical incident. A serf of a certain Aprelev in Pskov Guberniia had escaped to Poland in 1737, allegedly with the aid of two serfs of a neighbor called Dubrovskii. Acting on Aprelev's complaint, the local authorities made several attempts to arrest Dubrovskii's two serfs, but their fellow villagers hid the culprits and put up strong resistance to the authorities, apparently with Dubrovskii's encouragement. Pushkin may have also known the case of another Dubrovskii, of Nizhnii Novgorod Guberniia, whose supposedly legitimate inheritance had been taken away through litigation by the wife of the *guberniia* prosecutor, Iudin, in 1802.

Inspired by all these real-life cases, Pushkin quickly wrote the first eight chapters (Vol. I) in late October and early November 1832. (Each chapter bears a date in the manuscript.) After Nov. 11 work on the novel stopped, to be taken up again on Dec. 14. From that date until Jan. 22, 1833, Pushkin persevered with the project; on Feb. 6 he added one more paragraph to the last chapter; but with that he abandoned his novel, never to show any further interest in it. The existing chapters were published posthumously, under the title *Dubrovskii* provided by the editors, in V. A. Zhukovskii et al., eds., *Sochineniia Aleksandra Pushkina*, 10 (St. Petersburg: Tip. zagotovleniia gos. bumag, 1841): 101–240.

2. In an earlier version, this sentence was preceded by the statement that "rare was the girl among the house servants who escaped the fifty-year-old satyr's amorous advances."

3. Most of this sentence, beginning with the words "yet they were devoted to him," was crossed out in the manuscript. It is carried in full in V. D. Bonch-Bruevich et al., eds., *Polnoe sobranie sochinenii*, 17 vols. (Moscow: Akademiia Nauk SSSR, 1937–59). B. V. Tomashevskii, ed., *Polnoe sobranie soshinenii*, 10 vols. (Moscow: Akademiia Nauk SSSR, 1962–66), leaves everything in except the phrase "yet they were devoted to him." In order to eliminate this inconsistency, I give the full manuscript version.

4. An earlier version read: "The glorious year of 1762 separated them for a long time. Troekurov, a relative of Princess Dashkova, rose rapidly in rank." The year 1762 was when Catherine II replaced her husband on the throne; Princess Ekaterina Dashkova (mentioned in *Roslavlev*, p. 140) was one of the engineers of the palace revolution. Pushkin evidently left the date out to avoid making Troekurov a very old man in the 1820's, when the novel's action takes place.

5. The Russian idiom is *gol kak sokol* (lit., "naked as a falcon").

6. The name Kistenevka (one of the villages on the Pushkins' estate in Nizhnii Novgorod Guberniia) was added to the document by Pushkin. The translation follows standard Soviet editions in correcting the names of the litigants where Pushkin neglected to do so, and in omitting numbers (of serfs, *desiatinas* of land, etc.) even where Pushkin left them in.

7. Lieutenant Muratov, whose actual case the document reflects, signed the court decision, reserving his exception, and only lost the case because he failed to appeal in time.

8. *Plet'iu obukha ne peresibesh'* (lit., "You cannot smash the blunt end of an ax with a whip"). Much of Anton's speech derives from popular sayings, which can be traced to collections of proverbs in Pushkin's library.

9. *Bylo by koryto, a svin'i-to budut* (lit., "As long as you have a trough, there will be no lack of swine").

10. *Na chuzhoi rot pugovitsy ne nash'esh'* (lit., "You cannot sew a button on another person's mouth").

11. Pushkin transferred this description, with some changes, from *A History of the Village of Goriukhino*.

12. From G. R. Derzhavin's poem "On the Death of Prince Meshcherskii" (1779).

13. Lyrics by Derzhavin set to music by O. A. Kozlovskii in celebration of the taking of Izmail in 1791.

14. The original reads, *Ia skoree soglashus', kazhetsia, laitat' na vladyku, chem koso vzglianut' na Kirila Petrovicha*, which is a paraphrase of the proverb *Sobaka i na vladyku laet* (lit., "A dog barks at a bishop, too," close to the English "A cat may look at a king").

15. From Ecclesiastes 2: 1.

16. From Psalms 34: 14.

17. The reference is to the Russo-Turkish war of 1787–91. This is one of the incongruities of the unfinished manuscript. Elsewhere it is indicated that the action took place in the 1820's, and that Vladimir was in his twenty-third year; yet his mother's letters refer to him as a child during the Turkish war.

18. Johann Kaspar Lavater's so-called science of physiognomy is set out in his four-volume *Physiognomische Fragmente zur Beförderung der Menschenkenntnis und Menschenliebe* (1775–78).

19. Maj. Gen. Ia. P. Kul'nev (1763–1812), killed in the war against Napoleon, was a popular hero; prints of his portrait were distributed widely.

20. The tales of the British novelist Ann Radcliffe (born Ann Ward, 1764–1823) were characterized by mystery plots, an atmosphere of terror, and poetically intense landscapes. They helped establish the vogue of the Gothic romance. Her most famous works in this genre include *The Romance of the Forest* (1791), *The Mysteries of Udolpho* (1794), and *The Italian* (1797).

21. Tsimlianskaia is a town on the Don River.

22. An earlier version read: "I'll dispatch twenty men under the command of my Frenchman."

23. Spitsyn's incorrect French phrase roughly means "I want to sleep in your room."

24. "With pleasure, monsieur. Make your arrangements accordingly."

25. The Russian verb *tushit'* means "to blow out." Trying to make it into a French verb, Spitsyn (prophetically) ends up saying "Why are you touching it?"

26. "I want to speak with you."

27. "What is this, monsieur, what is this?"

28. The transliteration of the Russian word for tutor into French is Pushkin's.

29. The hero of Christian August Vulpius's novel *Rinaldo Rinaldini, der Räuber-Hauptmann* (1798).

30. The Russian word for smack boats is *dushegubka*, which is also the feminine form of *dushegub*, meaning "murderer."

31. Amphitryon, the mythological Prince of Tiryns whose shape Zeus assumed in order to seduce his wife Alcmene, is shown in Molière's comedy by the same name (1668) as a generous host.

32. "All the efforts."

33. The reference is to Canto 5 of the Polish poet Adam Mickiewicz's narrative poem *Konrad Wallenrod* (1828).

34. An *arshin* equals 28 inches.

35. In an earlier version the red-haired boy would have received a thrashing yet would not have betrayed his chief.

36. In an earlier version the bullet would have only nicked Dubrovskii's ear.

37. This song is quoted in full in Chap. 8 of *The Captain's Daughter*; for its source, see note 49 to that story.

38. Five different plans for the novel, written down in Pushkin's hand, are extant. They give an idea of how the project developed and how he intended to continue it.

I

Ostrovskii, having been studying in Petersburg, returns after his father's death to his estate, which is being contested. All he finds is the manor house with some domestics, without land or peasants. His servants are hard put to feed him and themselves—the assessor comes, Ostrovskii's servants kill him out of revenge. An investigation begins. Court officials come to interview Ostrovskii. Ostrovskii stands up for his servants—he has the officials tied up and becomes a robber.

Indignant over his state of affairs, Ostrovskii decides to murder the landowner who had caused his misfortune. He prowls around the landowner's village, meets his daughter, and falls in love with her. He seeks an opportunity to become acquainted with her. He meets a French tutor on his way to the landowner, takes away his papers and passport, and presents himself to the landowner.

Festivities at the landowner's house. A neighbor is robbed. The little coffer. The tutor elopes with the young lady.

His wife delivers a baby. She is sick, he takes her to Moscow for cure—choosing from his band a few reliable people and dismissing the others. Ostrovskii leads a secluded life in Moscow, his postilion is arrested for rowdiness and he denounces Ostrovskii (with another member of Ostrovskii's band). The police chief.

2

Dubrovskii—1st chapter. The 2d, illness, the nurse's letter. An attempt at reconciliation, death, funeral; the young master's arrival, during the funeral feast he is busy sorting out papers. Thirst for revenge. Meeting with Troekurov's daughter.—His walk through the cemetery. The arrival of the court officials.—*Fire at night* (set by the servants, without Dubrovskii's participation). Arkhip murders the officials—Dubrovskii goes into hiding with his implicated servants.

3

a   Quarrel. Trial. Death.
Fire. The tutor. Festivities. Declaration.

b   Prince Vereiskii *visite*. 2 *visite*. Asking for her hand. A meeting. Letter intercepted. Wedding, departure. Detachment, battle. The band dismissed.

Maria Kirilovna's life. Prince Vereiskii's death. The widow. An Englishman. A meeting. Gamblers. The police chief. The denouement.

c   Separation, declaration, betrothal. The superintendent. The bridegroom. Prince Zh. Wedding. Kidnaping. Hut in the woods, detachment, battle. *Franc.* Madness. The band dismissed.

Moscow, the doctor, seclusion. The tavern, denunciation. Suspicions, the police chief.

The Queen of Spades

1. This short story was written in the fall of 1833 and published in *Biblioteka dlia chteniia*, 2. 3 (1834): 107–40. No manuscript copy has been preserved, but Pushkin made a few minor corrections in the version to be included in *Tales Published by Alexander Pushkin*, which came out later the same year. A revealing error in both of these early editions is that three times in Chap. 1 the old lady is referred to as Princess rather than Countess. This error confirms what Pushkin's friend P. V. Nashchokin was later to mention: that the old lady was at least partially modeled on Princess N. P. Golitsyna (1741–1838), who was present, like an indispensable ornament, at every Petersburg Court function in the early 1830's. According to Nashchokin, Golitsyna's grandson told Pushkin that once, having lost a large sum of money at

cards, he had asked his grandmother for help; the old lady did not give him any money but named three secret cards, with the aid of which the grandson did indeed recoup his losses. The title "The Queen of Spades" probably originates from the Swedish romantic writer Clas Johan Livijn's short novel *Spader Dame, en Berättelse i Bref, Funne på Danviken*, published under the pseudonym Hiarta in 1824 and translated into German by Friedrich Heinrich Karl, Baron de La Motte-Fouqué, under the title *Pique-Dame: Berichte aus dem Irrenhause in Briefen* (1826).

Some handwritten fragments representing early attempts at writing the story have been preserved. Of these the following two, both of which help to understand how the project took shape in Pushkin's mind, are the most important:

I

About four years ago a few of us young people, drawn together by circumstances, saw one another a good deal. We led a rather dissipated life. We dined at Andrieux's without appetite, drank without merriment, and paid visits to Sof'ia Astaf'evna only in order to make the poor old lady mad with our choosiness. We killed the time somehow during the day; in the evenings we took turns visiting one another.

2

And now allow me to acquaint you more intimately with Charlotte. In one of, etc.

Her father had been, in turn, a merchant of the second guild, an apothecary, the director of a boarding school, and finally a proofreader at a printing house. He died bequeathing to his wife a certain amount of debt and a wellnigh complete collection of butterflies and insects. He was a good man, who had at his fingertips much fundamental information, none of which, however, did him any good. His wife sold his manuscripts to the tobacconist, thereby settling the debts he had incurred at the tobacco shop; after which she and Charlotte began to earn their living by handiwork.

Hermann lived just across the courtyard from the widow; he and Charlotte met and fell in love so deeply as only Germans are capable of in our day and age.

One day, however, or to be exact, etc.

And when the charming young German drew aside her white curtain, Hermann did not appear at his window and did not greet her with the usual smile.

His father, a Russified German, had bequeathed a small capital to him, which Hermann left at the savings bank, not touching even the interest it earned, and living entirely on his salary.

Hermann was firmly, etc.

2. Pushkin's own poem, untitled and written in 1828.

3. The card game here, as in the *Belkin* tale "The Shot," is faro, which was imported to Russia from the Court of Louis XIV. It was strictly a gambling game, allowing very little, if any, latitude for skill and strategy. Each player (punter) picked a card of his own choice from his deck and put it on the table face down, placing his bet on it. The dealer (banker) shuffled the cards of another deck (an unused one if the stakes were high) and flipped up cards, plac-

ing them alternately on his right and on his left. If the card falling to the banker's right matched the punter's card in rank (the various suits making no difference), the banker won; if the card falling to his left matched the punter's card, the punter received a win equivalent to what he had put on his card. The punter, though he knew what he had picked, did not turn his card face up until he saw a matching one placed on the table by the banker. The term *mirandole* (derived, presumably, from the name of the Italian Mirandola family) denotes a cautious tactic in faro, consisting in small bets, with gains withdrawn rather than staked in a new round.

4. *Routé* meant that the punter wanted to double his bet and play the same card he had just won on.

5. *Paroli* meant that the punter, after a win, wanted to include his winnings in his new bet, thereby doubling the original stake. To indicate this, he bent down a corner of the new card he had just picked.

6. This is the same Richelieu, a great-nephew of the Cardinal, who is mentioned in *The Blackamoor of Peter the Great* (see note 9 to that story), though by the time he courted the Countess he would have been in his sixties or seventies.

7. An earlier name for faro; so called because one of the honor cards in the French pack of the 17th century bore the face of an Egyptian pharaoh.

8. This was evidently Louis-Philippe, duc d'Orléans (1725–85), grandson of the Regent mentioned in *The Blackamoor of Peter the Great.*

9. A famous adventurer (d. 1784).

10. The *Mémoires* of Giovanni Giacomo Casanova de Seingalt, another famous 18th-century adventurer, were being published posthumously in Pushkin's own time (12 vols., 1826–38). Pushkin derives his characterization of Saint-Germain largely from Casanova; but in Arthur Machen's complete English version of the memoirs, at least, Casanova never refers to the Count as a spy (for their three encounters, see Vol. 3, Chaps. 3, 10; and Vol. 5, Chap. 16).

11. "At the Queen's card party."

12. Winning *sonica* meant that the player won on the very first turn of the cards in a new deal.

13. The only way a punter could cheat in this simple game was to use a deck treated with sticky powder that would help him deface—and thereby alter the rank—of a card if he saw it was a loser.

14. S. G. Zorich (1745–99) was Catherine II's favorite in 1777–78.

15. Chaplitskii doubled his bet, a *paroli*, on his second card, and won. He then let all his gains ride, a *paroli-paix*, indicated by bending the card in the middle as if to make a bridge out of it.

16. "'It appears that monsieur definitely prefers waiting-maids.'—'How can I help it, madame? They are fresher'" This "conversation at a social gathering" was reported to Pushkin by the poet Denis Davydov (see note 7 for the *Belkin* tales); it first appears among Pushkin's papers in a draft version of *A Novel in Letters.*

17. From Canto 17 of *Paradiso*. Translation of Charles Eliot Norton (1902).

18. "You write me four-page letters faster, my angel, than I can read them." A variation of the epigraph used in Chap. 2 of "In the Corner of a Small Square."

19. Elisabeth Vigée-Lebrun (1755–1842) was a Parisian portrait painter. If the portrait of the woman described in the next sentence was of the Countess,

Vigée-Lebrun could hardly have painted it while the Countess was still young.

20. Julien Leroy (1686–1759) and his son Pierre (1717–85) were famous French watchmakers.

21. The brothers Joseph Michel Montgolfier (1740–1810) and Jacques Etienne Montgolfier (1745–99), of Annonay, France, launched the first hot-air balloon in 1783. Friedrich Anton Mesmer (1734–1815) was an Austrian physician who attributed induced somnambulism to a power similar to magnetism, which he called "animal magnetism."

22. The term galvanism is used in its original meaning, derived from the theories of Luigi Galvani (1737–98), a professor of anatomy at the University of Bologna: he attributed the twitching of a frog's leg when touched with a scalpel to electricity generated by the muscles and nerves of the animal.

23. The phrase is Pushkin's own: "A man without morals and without religion."

24. "Oblivion or regret." This was an invitation to dance. The man so approached had to choose one of the words without knowing which lady it stood for. The third lady mentioned was probably a chaperone.

25. This quotation has not been found in the works of the Swedish mystic Emanuel Swedenborg (Svedberg; 1688–1772) and is taken to be Pushkin's own playful invention in the spirit of anecdotes circulating about the adventures of the clairvoyant theologian.

26. A reference to the parable of the Wise and Foolish Virgins in Matthew 25: 1–13.

27. Punters used the peremptory French term *attendez* ("wait") to indicate to the banker that they wished to make or change a bet between actions. When pronounced with excited emphasis, this exclamation could sound like a rather rude command, offensive to the banker if he was a man of mature years and high rank. P. A. Viazemskii records in his *Old Notebook* that a certain Count Gudovich, having attained the rank of colonel, stopped taking the role of banker in faro games, explaining that "it is undignified to subject yourself to the demands of some greenhorn of a sublieutenant who, punting against you, almost peremptorily yells out: *attendez!*" See Viazemskii, *Staraia zapisnaia knizhka*, ed. L. Ginzburg (Leningrad: Izd. pisatelei, 1929), p. 135. It was probably this anecdote, current in St. Petersburg at the beginning of the 1830's, that inspired Pushkin's epigraph to the chapter.

28. That is, writing the amount on the green felt of the table.

29. The French word *simple* (in the sense of "single") was used to indicate the first card bet on by the punter in a given deal; since the practice was to keep doubling the stakes, it was unusual to place a large bet on a *simple*.

30. The Russian term for queen of spades is *pikovaia dama* (lit., "lady of spades"). "Lady" is easily associated with the Countess.

31. The crucial word is *obdernut'sia* ("to pull the wrong card"), which explains why Hermann lost despite the correct prediction by the Countess's ghost of three potentially winning cards. Intending to choose the ace, he apparently pulled the wrong card without noticing it, and was so sure of having an ace that he did not check its identity, even when the card was already face up, until his attention was drawn to the mistake.

Kirdzhali

1. This story was written in the fall of 1834 and published in *Biblioteka dlia chteniia,* 7.12 (1834): 197–204. It has been shown in scholarly literature that in Moldavia there was indeed a robber chief called Kirdzhali, who joined Alexander Ypsilanti's uprising with his band in 1821, escaped to Russia after the Hetairists' defeat near Skuliany, was arrested by the Russian authorities in 1823, and was handed over to the Turks. He escaped from prison that year, but was recaptured and hanged in 1824. Pushkin, who took some notes about leading Hetairists while living in Kishinev in the early 1820's, obviously heard about Kirdzhali's extradition to Turkey at the time it happened. The name first occurs in Pushkin's works in an 1823 lyrical fragment known as "A Civil Servant and a Poet"; and some lines jotted down by him in 1828 were intended for a verse tale entitled *Kirdzhali.*

Although this story is based largely on historical facts, its version of *how* the hero escaped from prison after his extradition is fictitious—a denouement that Pushkin probably took from a Moldavian ballad. Pushkin's failure to mention Kirdzhali's subsequent execution—although he obviously knew about it—also relates the story to a type of ballad for which the hero's triumph was an obligatory ending. For more on Ypsilanti, see note 11 for *Belkin.*

2. The Balkan Turkish word *kircali* means "marauder," "irregular soldier." It is derived from the name of a provincial center in southern Bulgaria, Kŭrdžali, so called after its founder Kirca Ali.

3. A reference to the Hetairists' defeat at Dragasani on June 19, 1821. Olympios (b. 1772) perished the same year. All personal names not annotated are unidentified and possibly fictitious.

4. The references are to the battles of Seku and Skuliany (on the Prut River), both of which took place in 1821.

5. Prince G. M. Kantakuzen (d. 1857) was a colonel in the Russian cavalry and a member of the Philike Hetairia.

6. There is a redundancy in the list of nationalities, for Arnaut is simply a Turkish name for Albanian.

7. A hospodar was a governor of Moldavia and Walachia under Turkish rule.

8. This person has been identified as S. G. Navrotskii, who had entered the service in 1767.

9. At the beginning of the 18th century, a group of Cossack Old Believers under the leadership of Ataman Ignat Nekrasa had fled from religious persecution to what is now Rumania.

10. Small Turkish silver coins.

11. This person was M. I. Leks (1793–1856), whom Pushkin knew during his sojourn in the south and met again in St. Petersburg in the 1830's. By that time Leks had risen to the post of director of the chancery at the Ministry of Internal Affairs.

12. This is an error on Pushkin's part; Kirdzhali was extradited in 1823.

13. Moldavian word for gold coins.

14. The Russian term is *kurgan*; ancient burial mounds were scattered all across the Ukrainian and Moldavian steppes.

A Tale of Roman Life

1. This fragment was first begun by Pushkin in 1833; he added the poems to the prose text in 1835. The extant autograph bears no title. First published in part by P. V. Annenkov in *Sochineniia Aleksandra Pushkina*, 1 (St. Petersburg: P. V. Annenkov, 1855): 397–400.

2. Gaius Petronius Arbiter (d. A.D. 66), to whom Pushkin is referring, was the author of *Satyricon* (ca. A.D. 60). Pushkin's source for the historical details is Tacitus's *Annales*, Book 16, Chaps. 18–20. The Caesar involved, as the text soon makes clear, is Nero (r. A.D. 54–68).

3. In Greek mythology, the Furies, or Erinyes; called the Eumenides for fear of offending them.

4. The original contains Pushkin's translation of Anacreon's Ode 56.

5. From Anacreon's Ode 61 (61 often figures as 60).

6. Pushkin's translation of Horace's Ode 7, Book 2.

7. From Horace's Ode 2, Book 3, Stanza 4. An outline preserved in Pushkin's hand suggests what seems to have been the main idea of the tale: Petronius, rather than awaiting a cruel fate at Nero's hands, decides to bleed himself to death; he lies in a warm bath, now opening his vein to let the blood flow, now bandaging it up to prolong his life a little more, while his friends entertain him with pleasant conversation. The outline reads:

> The first evening, such-and-such from among us were there; the Greek philosopher has disappeared—Petronius smiles—and recites an *ode* (an excerpt). (We find Petronius with his physician.—He continues his discussion of kinds of death, chooses a warm bath and blood), a description of the preparations. He bandages the wound, and the telling of anecdotes commences 1 / About Cleopatra; our discussions of the matter. 2d evening, Petronius gives orders to break a precious goblet, dictates Satyricon, discussions about the fall of man, the fall of god, the general lack of faith, and Nero's prejudices. A Christian slave...

The mention of Cleopatra seems to indicate that Pushkin might have planned to introduce here the theme of Cleopatra's nights—a theme that was to be placed in the center of both "We Were Spending the Evening at Princess D.'s Dacha" and *Egyptian Nights*.

We Were Spending the Evening at Princess D.'s Dacha

1. This fragment was probably written in 1835, prior to Pushkin's work on *Egyptian Nights*. The theme of Cleopatra's nights—central to both this fragment and *Egyptian Nights*—was first treated by Pushkin in his 1824 elegy "Cleopatra." The elegy was rewritten in 1828 with significant changes, and the incomplete version given in this fragment, half in prose, half in verse, represents the third major version of the poem. It is possible that somewhat earlier Pushkin had planned to treat the Cleopatra theme in "A Tale of Roman Life." (See note 7 for that work.) The extant manuscripts of "We Were Spending the Evening" consist of several fragments, some in first draft, some in clean copy. The text, as translated, represents a piecing together of these various segments. The work was first published, in part, by P. V. Annenkov in

Sochineniia Aleksandra Pushkina, 7 (St. Petersburg: P. V. Annenkov, 1857): 143–46.

2. The brothers Hamb were furniture dealers in St. Petersburg.

3. Françoise d'Aubigné, la marquise de Maintenon (1635–1719), was the mistress and eventually the wife of Louis XIV. Mme. Roland (b. 1754; Manon Philipon), celebrated for her salon, was a Girondist who was beheaded by the Montagnards in 1793.

4. "Who is being deceived here?"—a paraphrase of Don Bazile's words from Act 3, Scene 11, of *Le Barbier de Seville* (1775) by P.-A. Caron de Beaumarchais.

5. *Antony,* a melodrama by Alexandre Dumas Père, was written in 1831 and performed in St. Petersburg in 1832. Honoré de Balzac's *La Physiologie du mariage* was published in 1829.

6. The text of *Liber de Viris Illustribus Urbis Romae* has been preserved in several manuscripts, of which two types can be distinguished: (1) manuscripts that contain only *De Viris,* from which, however, the last nine lives, including that of Cleopatra, are missing, and (2) two manuscripts of the 15th century that contain *Origo Gentis Romanae* and *Aurelii Victoris Historiae Abbreviatae* (also known as *Liber de Caesaribus*) in addition to *De Viris;* this version contains the last nine chapters but lacks almost all of the first chapter. The full text, incorporating both manuscript traditions, can be found in Franciscus Pichlmayr's definitive edition, *Sexti Aurelii Victoris Liber de Caesaribus* (Leipzig: B. G. Teubner, 1911). Scholars generally agree that Sextus Aurelius was the author of *Liber de Caesaribus,* but not the author of the other two works contained in the corpus. The identity of the author of *De Viris* has not been established.

7. "She was so lustful that she often prostituted herself and so beautiful that many men paid with their lives for a night with her." In Pichlmayr's edition (see preceding note), this sentence is on p. 74.

8. A draft version reads, in part, as follows:

> Like Artemis, the hunting goddess,
> Drapes gathered up at loins and bodice,
> Through glades one sees her lithely dart,
> Bronzed like her sculptured counterpart;
> Or...   Nilus roaming,
> Prone in the sail's translucent gloaming,
> In her gilt vessel triple-tiered
> She glides, a Venus now; or, seared
> By torrid yearnings, she may rove
> Her pleasances and seek that grove
> Where, vigilant and sullen, dwells
> The gelded guardian of the cells
> Of handsome slaves, for her to choose,
> And bashfully impassioned youths.

Egyptian Nights

1. This fragment of a projected novel represents a new attempt at treating the Cleopatra theme (even entitled *Cleopatra* in a draft version). It was probably written in the fall of 1835, after Pushkin had put aside "We Were Spending

the Evening at Princess D.'s Dacha," and was first published in *Sovremennik*, 8 (1837): 5–24.

2. "What kind of a person is this man?"—"Oh, he possesses a great talent; he can make of his voice whatever he wants."—"Madam, he should make himself a pair of trousers from it." From *Almanach des calembours* (1771) by Georges Mareschal Bièvre.

3. The draft version reads: "His uncle, a tax-farmer in Saratov, had left him a handsome estate."

4. The direct source for this phrase—a catchword of neoclassical aesthetics—is N. M. Karamzin's poem "Gifts" (1796).

5. For an earlier treatment of this subject by Pushkin, see "A Fragment" in Appendix B.

6. Rezanov's was a confectionary shop in St. Petersburg.

7. "Sir, please excuse me if..."

8. "Sir, I thought... I believed... forgive me, Your Excellency."

9. From G. R. Derzhavin's ode "God" (1784).

10. The Italian's improvisation originated in Stanzas 12 and 13 of Pushkin's unfinished verse tale *Ezerskii* (1832–33). These stanzas, forestalling criticism of the poet's choice of his hero and defending the freedom of the poet's inspiration, were partially reworked in 1835, and another six lines, beginning with the words "Such is the poet: like the North," were added. These materials, in draft stage, were clearly intended for *Egyptian Nights*, though not included in the same manuscript.

11. The draft version reads: "This close tie between inspiration and external nature."

12. Angelica Catalani (1780–1849) was an Italian singer who performed in St. Petersburg in 1820.

13. An opera by Gioacchino Antonio Rossini, written in 1813 and performed in St. Petersburg during the 1834–35 season.

14. The manuscript shows that Pushkin originally intended to mention only one person—"a young diplomat who had just returned from Naples"—instead of a diplomat and an additional young man. This may be the reason for the discrepancy between the number of people suggesting themes (six) and the number of themes read aloud by the improvisatore (five).

15. "La famiglia dei Cenci" refers to the murder, in 1598 by his own family, of the wealthy Roman Francesco Cenci, which served as a basis for Adolphe Custine's tragedy *Beatrix Cenci* (1833). "L'ultimo giorno di Pompeïa" was the theme of a painting by K. P. Briullov exhibited in St. Petersburg in 1834. "La primavera veduta da una prigione" ("Spring comes to a prison") bears a relationship to Maroncelli's improvised hymn, which is mentioned in Chap. 87 of Silvio Pellico's *Le Mie Prigioni* (1832). (The text of the hymn itself is given by Pellico's fellow prisoner Maroncelli in an appendix.) "Il trionfo di Tasso" was a topical theme because of N. V. Kukol'nik's play *Torquato Tasso*, performed in St. Petersburg in 1833.

16. "Since the great Queen had a good many of them."

17. See notes 6 and 7 to "We Were Spending the Evening at Princess D.'s Dacha."

18. This poem, dating back to 1828, has traditionally been included in the text of *Egyptian Nights* in view of its thematic relevance, even though Pushkin did not attach it to the manuscript of the unfinished novel. Had he com-

pleted the novel, he would have no doubt revised the poem, but as it is, the 1828 version appears to be the closest available approximation to what Pushkin intended. The 1828 version represents the second major phase in Pushkin's treatment of the Cleopatra theme. The first version, dating back to 1824, is quite different from the second one; it is given here in translation in order to provide a more complete view of the development of the theme in Pushkin's oeuvre:

> Queen Cleopatra with her gazes
> And voice adorned her splendid feast.
> Exalting with a choir of praises
> The chosen idol of the East,
> Thronged to her throne the pleasure-seekers,
> When all at once she stooped, and so
> Fell still among the golden beakers,
> Her wondrous forehead drooping low.
> The rich assembly, never shifting,
> Stands silently as in a daze...
> Until the Queen announces, lifting
> Her brow again, with solemn gaze:
> "Hear me! This day it is my pleasure
> To make us equals in my sight.
> To you my love were highest blessing;
> But you may buy this bliss tonight.
> Behold the marketplace of passion!
> For sale I offer nights divine;
> Who dares to barter in this fashion
> His life against one night of mine?"
>
> Thus her decree. All breath abating,
> The strange and stirring challenge looms.
> Soon Cleopatra, coldly waiting,
> With calm audacity resumes:
> "Why are you silent? I am ready;
> Or shall I see you all take flight?
> Not few are here whose dreams were heady...
> Now purchase an enchanting night!"
>
> Her haughty glances scan the verges
> Of her admirers' silent throng...
> There! of a sudden one emerges,
> Two others follow soon along.
> Their step is bold, their gaze unclouded.
> The Queen arises in her pride.
> Three nights are bought: the couch is shrouded
> For deadly pleasures at her side.

Once more they heard the Queen's imperious voice resound:
"Let none remember now I was in purple crowned!
I shall ascend the couch but as a common whore,
To serve thee, Lady Love, as no one has before,

And vow my nights' reward a novel gift to thee.
O awesome deities of Hades, hearken me,
Ye melancholy Kings of nether realms forlorn!
Receive ye this my pledge: unto the languid dawn
I promise to obey my rulers' utmost wishes
With wondrous tenderness, strange arts, the deep delicious
Cup ever newly filled with love's entrancing wine...
But when into my chamber through the curtains shine
Young Eos' early rays—I swear by your grim shade
Their heads shall fall that morn beneath the headsman's blade!"

By holy augury each sanctified in turn,
The lots assigned the three now issue from the urn:
First Archilaios' lot, of Pompey's noble guard,
Gone gray in his campaigns, in combat hewn and scarred.
A woman's cold disdain resolved to bear no more,
He haughtily stepped forth, the somber son of war,
To heed the fateful lure, the last sweet test of mettle,
As earlier he had the glory-notes of battle.
Crito was second drawn, Crito the gentle sage
    Who, reared beneath the sky of Argolis,
Had glowing tribute paid, since barely come of age,
To Bacchus' fiery feasts, the Cyprid's fiery kiss.
The third one's name remains by annals unrecorded;
Unknown to all, unmarked, he would embrace his doom,
A downy youth as yet whose beard but faintly bordered
    His tender cheek with bashful bloom.
    With love's consuming fire his eyes now gleamed,
For Cleopatra meant his very life, it seemed;
And long and silently the Queen rejoiced in him.

A third, incomplete version, partly in prose and partly in verse, was written in 1835, and is included in the translation of "We Were Spending the Evening at Princess D.'s Dacha" in view of its clear relevance to that fragment. As for the arrangement of the 1828 version, included in *Egyptian Nights*, Walter Arndt and I have made two editorial decisions. First, since the position of Cleopatra's oath ("Thee, Holy Goddess of the Senses . . .") is ambiguous in the manuscript and has been placed differently in different editions, and since it seems to be Cleopatra's emotionally charged response to the three volunteers' stepping forward, we have placed it as Stanza 4 (essentially retaining the arrangement of the 1824 version). And second, we have included the last stanza, even though it comes from a different manuscript.

Maria Schoning

1. This unfinished novel is based on a supposedly genuine court case, "Enfanticide: Procès de Maria Schoning et d'Anna Harlin," recorded in *Causes célèbres étrangères, publiées en France pour la première fois et traduites de l'italien, de l'allemand etc. par une société de jurisconsultes et de gens de lettres*, 2 (Paris: C. L. F. Panckoucke, 1827): 200–213. Pushkin probably worked on the project in 1834 or 1835.

2. It is impossible to tell how closely Pushkin was planning to follow the court case, but a précis he made of it (in French) gives at least an approximate idea of the projected plot development:

Maria Schoning and Anna Harlin tried in Nuremberg in 1787
Maria Schoning, the daughter of a Nuremberg artisan, lost her father when she was seventeen years old. She had been looking after him by herself because poverty had forced them to dismiss their only maidservant, Anna Harlin.

When she returned from her father's funeral she found at her house two officials of the tax office, who demanded to see her late father's papers in order to ascertain whether he had been paying his taxes according to the size of his property. They concluded from their investigation that he had not been taxed in proportion to his worth, and they sealed his belongings. The young girl retired to a room stripped of its furnishings until such time as the directors of the treasury should decide the matter.

The tax officials returned with their superiors' decision and with an order for Maria Eleonora Schoning to vacate the house, which had passed into the possession of the treasury.

Schoning had been poor but economical. His illness of three years' duration exhausted all his savings. Maria went to see the commissioners. She wept, but the officials remained inflexible.

In the evening she went to the St. Jacob Cemetery... In the morning she left the cemetery, but later, faint with hunger, she once more found herself there.

The Nuremberg police pay an award of half a crown to nightwatchmen for the arrest of a woman after 10 P.M. Maria Schoning was taken to the guardhouse. Next morning they led her before a judge, who set her free but threatened to confine her to a correctional institution if she was caught a second time.

Maria wanted to throw herself into the Pegnitz... she heard someone call her name. She beheld Anna Harlin, her father's former maidservant, who had married a disabled soldier. Anna comforted her. "Life is short, my child," said she, "but heaven is eternal."

For a year Maria found shelter at the Harlins'. Her life with them was quite wretched. At the end of the year Anna fell sick. Winter set in; there was no work available; the price of food rose. They sold all their furniture piece by piece, except for the bed of the veteran, who died toward spring.

An indigent doctor had been giving free treatment to both husband and wife. He would sometimes bring them a bottle of wine, but he himself had no money. Anna recovered from her illness but became apathetic: there was absolutely no work available.

One evening early in March Maria suddenly went out...

She was arrested by a patrol. The corporal left her with the guards, saying she would be whipped in the morning. She cried out that she was guilty of infanticide... When led before the judge, she declared that she had given birth to a child with the assistance of a certain woman called Harlin, who had subsequently buried the child in the woods, in a place that she no longer remembered. Anna Harlin was immediately arrested and, after pleading innocent, was confronted with Maria—she denied everything.

Tools of torture were brought in. Terrified, Maria seized her alleged accomplice's tied-up hands and said to her: "Anna, confess what they are demanding of you. My dear Anna, everything will be over for us, and Frank and Nany will be placed in an orphanage."

Anna understood her, embraced her, and declared that the infant had been thrown into the Pegnitz.

The case was swiftly concluded. Both women were condemned to die. On the morning of the appointed day they were led to a church, where they prayed in preparation for death. In the cart Anna was calm, Maria agitated. Harlin mounted the scaffold and said to her: "In an instant we shall be there (in heaven). Take courage, one more minute, and we shall be before God."

Maria cried out: "She is innocent, I gave false testimony!" She threw herself at the feet of the executioner and the priest... She told them everything. The executioner stops in astonishment. Shouts are heard in the crowd... Questioned by the priest and the executioner, Anna Harlin says with distaste (simplicity): "She has, of course, told the truth. I am guilty of lying and having no faith in Providence."

A report is sent to the judges. The messenger returns in an hour with the order to proceed with the execution... The executioner fainted after decapitating Anna Harlin.—Maria was already dead.

The Captain's Daughter

1. The first outlines of what was to become *The Captain's Daughter* were jotted down as a result of a gift to Pushkin by Nicholas I in February 1832: the *Complete Collection of the Laws of the Russian Empire*, Vol. 20 of which contains the various sentences given to the participants in the Pugachev Rebellion (1773–74). Among those sentenced to exile was a young nobleman, Mikhail Shvanvich, who had been taken prisoner by Pugachev and had subsequently served the rebel cause. This traitor to the government was to be the central character of the projected novel. The first two outlines, referring to Shvanvich as the central character, were probably written late in the summer of that year; but in the fall Pushkin's interest was diverted by the story of another nobleman siding with rioting peasants, who was to become the hero of *Dubrovskii*. It was not until January 1833 that Pushkin turned once more to the projected novel about Pugachev's times, once more referring to the hero as Shvanvich. During the spring of that year, he gained access to archival materials relating to the rebellion, and the next two outlines for the novel, dating probably from March 1833, reflect his research. According to these outlines, the hero of the novel, this time named Basharin, was to save the life of a Bashkir during a blizzard; the Bashkir was subsequently to become a follower of Pugachev and ask the latter to pardon Basharin, captured by the rebels; Pugachev was to grant the request under the condition that the Bashkir answer for Basharin with his head; Basharin was to stay in the rebel camp for a while, participate in the siege of a fort, and save the life of an officer's daughter; later he was also to save his father's life, and eventually return to the government side after the Bashkir's death. These outlines were based on a document describing the case of a real-life Captain Basharin, whose life had been

spared by Pugachev at the request, not of a Bashkir, but of his soldiers. The marked change in these outlines in comparison with the earlier ones is that Basharin, unlike Shvanvich, is not an outright traitor, but only a temporary, involuntary participant in the rebel cause.

Another extant fragment, dated Aug. 5, 1833, demonstrates Pushkin's continued interest in the novel during the summer of that year. This fragment (not included in the final text) is the draft of an introduction to the novel, in which the narrator offers his memoirs to his grandson for his moral edification. After writing this fragment, however, Pushkin dropped his plans for the novel for a while, and concentrated his attention on a scholarly study of the same period, *A History of Pugachev*, which he published in 1834. Only after the publication of the *History* did he turn his attention to the novel once more, jotting down, sometime in late 1834 or early 1835, a final outline, with a central character named Valuev, that was quite close to the shape the novel was eventually to take. In the final stages of Pushkin's work on the project Pugachev himself emerged as a central character along with the hero, Grinev, while the original Shvanvich was relegated to a secondary role as the villain of the piece under the name of Shvabrin. The first draft of the actual text was probably written at the end of 1835 and during the first half of 1836. Of this first draft Pushkin preserved only one chapter, which he decided to omit from the final version (see note 75 and Appendix A), and the Publisher's concluding note claiming that Grinev's descendants had given the manuscript to him. The final, corrected manuscript, however, is extant (except for Chap. 7) and serves as the basis for the definitive text. The last chapters of the complete manuscript reached the censor on Oct. 24, 1836. The censor required a few minor changes (some of which are indicated in the notes), and the novel appeared, without the author's name, on Dec. 22 in Vol. 4 (1836) of the journal *Sovremennik*, edited by Pushkin.

2. From Act 3, Scene 6, of Ia. B. Kniazhnin's comedy *The Braggart* (1784–85). The first line is spoken by Verkholet in reference to his rival in love, Zamir. Pretending to be a rich, influential Count, Verkholet claims he could make Zamir a captain of the Guards if only Zamir was not so rude and inconsiderate. The person answering is Cheston, the wise old man of the comedy; what he implies is that serving in the active army would be better for a young man's character. Verkholet, who does not know that Cheston is Zamir's father, misunderstands Cheston's words and imagines that the old man is siding with him against Zamir.

3. Count Burkhard Christoph Münnich (1683–1767) came to Russia during the reign of Peter I and was appointed president of the War College by Empress Anne (r. 1730–40). He was exiled by her successor, Elizabeth, but rehabilitated by Peter III. After the palace revolution of 1762, in which Catherine II ousted her husband, Peter III, Münnich finally lost his influence at Court because he had remained loyal to the deposed Tsar.

4. In the manuscript Pushkin indicated the date of the elder Grinev's retirement as 1762. That date might have simply referred to Peter III's February 1762 edict exempting the nobility from obligatory state service. But if considered along with the elder Grinev's association with Münnich, the date 1762 would have suggested that he, too, had adhered to his oath of allegiance to Peter III, which would have lent greater poignancy to his son's friendly rela-

tions with Pugachev, who claimed to be Peter III. (The latter had actually been killed shortly after the palace coup in 1762, but rumors circulated that he was in hiding, and several impostors appeared on the scene, claiming to be Peter III.) The reason Pushkin removed the last two digits of the date 1762 from the final version was (as an extant fragment containing his calculation of the younger Grinev's age shows) that if his father had not married until after he retired in 1762, the young Petr could not have been eighteen in 1773, the year of the Pugachev Rebellion.

5. Such early registration was advantageous because, for purposes of advancement in rank, years of service were counted from the date of registration. The Semenovskii Regiment, established by Peter I in 1683 in the village of Semenovskoe, was one of the elite regiments of the Guards.

6. This distortion of *monsieur* reads *mus'iu* in Russian. For purposes of translation, it seemed most appropriate to borrow the distorted form the English novelist Elizabeth Gaskell used in Chap. 7 of *Cranford* (1853).

7. Pushkin's French transliteration of the Russian word for tutor.

8. A reference to Act 1, Scene 6, of D. I. Fonvizin's comedy *The Young Hopeful* (1782). In the scene referred to, Prostakova, an archetypal figure of uncouth provincial nobility, boasts that a foreign tutor, Adam Vralman, is teaching her adolescent son "French and all the sciences." Pushkin's Beaupré was a barber back in France; Fonvizin's Vralman turns out, at the end of the comedy, to have been a coachman in his native Germany. These and other allusions to *The Young Hopeful* enhance the comic nature of Pushkin's description of the Grinev family.

9. The Russian idiom in *Sem' bed, odin otvet* (lit., "Seven disasters, one solution").

10. The crosses of St. Andrew and Alexandr Nevskii, instituted in 1698 and 1725, respectively.

11. This maxim is a paraphrase of a passage from V. N. Tatishchev's *Testament* (1723; published posthumously 1777).

12. Each landowner was required periodically to surrender a specified number of serfs to the state for military service. These new recruits were brought from neighboring estates to regional centers, where their future commanding officers received them into their units. The procedure of recruitment at this time was governed by Catherine II's decree of Dec. 29, 1766.

13. A quotation from D. I. Fonvizin's verse epistle "A Letter to My Servants Shumilov, Vanka, and Petrushka" (1769).

14. An adaptation by Pushkin of a recruits' song published in the collection *Novoe i Polnoe sobranie rossiiskikh pesen*, ed. M. D. Chulkov, 6 vols. (Moscow: Universitetskaia tip. N. Novikova, 1780–81), 3, No. 68. Since folk songs of this kind do not lend themselves to verse translation, we have provided a literal rendering in prose.

15. The Russian reads: *Zashel k kume, da zasel v tiur'me* (lit., "Dropped in on the mother of your grandchild, ended up in jail").

16. The original reads: *Loshadi chuzhie, khomut ne svoi, pogoniai ne stoi* (lit., "The horses are someone else's, the harness is not your own, press forward and don't stop").

17. This dream episode was a later insertion.

18. From the region of the Iaik River, which was renamed Ural after the Pugachev Rebellion. The area of that rebellion, and many of the place names

mentioned in this novel in connection with it, are shown in the maps on pp. 369–70.

19. The events here referred to are described in Chap. 1 of *A History of Pugachev.*

20. That is, Empress Anne, who reigned from 1730 to 1740. Gen. Andrei Karlovich R. is modeled on I. A. Reinsdorp, military governor of Orenburg Guberniia from 1763 to 1782 (described in detail in *A History of Pugachev*), but in *The Captain's Daughter* Pushkin makes him considerably older than he actually was. In fact he had joined the Russian army only in 1746, and therefore could not have worn a uniform dating back to the reign of Empress Anne; nor could he have participated in Münnich's Prussian campaign (1733), to which the elder Grinev's letter, quoted in the next paragraph, refers.

21. The Russian expression is *Derzhat' v ezhovykh rukavitsakh* (lit., "To hold in hedgehog-hide gloves"). The German accent with which Andrei Karlovich comments on the elder Grinev's letter was introduced into the manuscript by Pushkin as a correction. He did not, however, make this change beyond the reading of the letter, and in the rest of the novel Andrei Karlovich speaks without an accent. Perhaps Pushkin felt that it would be tiresome to maintain an accent throughout the novel. The translation mirrors his practice.

22. Part of what is now Kazakhstan.

23. Probably Pushkin's own composition in imitation of soldier songs.

24. From Act 3, Scene 5, of Fonvizin's comedy.

25. The name Belogorsk is fictional; the location of the fort roughly corresponds to that of Fort Tatishchev.

26. The Prussian fort of Küstrin was besieged by the Russian army in 1758; Ochakov, on the Black Sea, was wrested from the Turks by Münnich in 1737.

27. According to the manuscript version, Prokhorov got into a scuffle, not with a woman, but with "the Cossack Petr Negulin."

28. The manuscript version has 500 serfs.

29. From Act 4, Scene 12, of Ia. B. Kniazhnin's comedy *Eccentrics* (1790). The scene cited is a comic duel between two servants.

30. The second half of this sentence, beginning with the words "even though," was cut out of the first edition by the censor.

31. Since Sumarokov, by the end of the 18th century, was considered the epitome of old-fashioned versifying (see note 27 for *A History of the Village of Goriukhino*), his praise for Grinev's poetry is of dubious value.

32. A somewhat revised version of a song in *Novoe i polnoe sobranie*, 1, No. 34.

33. V. K. Trediakovskii (1703–69) was best known for his 1730 translation of Paul Tallement's novel *Voyage à l'île d'amour* (1663), to which he appended a collection of his own poems. By the 1770's his poetry was considered old-fashioned.

34. The Russian reads: *Bran' na vorotu ne visnet* (lit., "A quarrel will not hang on your gatepost").

35. The Russian reads: *Khudoi mir luchshe dobroi ssory, a i nechesten, tak zdorov* (lit., "A bad peace is better than a good quarrel; you may be dishonored but you're healthy").

36. The quote is from the collection of songs *Sobranie narodnykh russkikh pesen*, ed. N. L'vov and I. Prach (St. Petersburg: Tip. Gornogo uchilishcha,

1790), p. 85. The manuscript contains two more lines from the song:

> When the morning sun broke free,
> Little Masha came to me.

37. From *Novoe i polnoe sobranie*, 1, Nos. 176 and 135, respectively. Both translations are literal renderings in prose.

38. The *vershok* is a measure of length equivalent to 1¾ inches.

39. From a song about the taking of Kazan by Ivan the Terrible, in *Novoe i polnoe sobranie*, 1, No. 125. A literal rendering in prose.

40. The original reads: *Gospod' ne vydast, svin'ia ne est* (lit., "The Lord will not forsake us, the swine will not eat us").

41. Alexander I abolished torture on Sept. 27, 1801.

42. "All right" in Tatar. (*Yahşi* in standard Turkish.)

43. The commandant of Nizhne-Ozernaia was Major Kharlov, whose attractive widow became Pugachev's concubine; she was eventually murdered by his associates. For details, see Chaps. 2 and 3 of *A History of Pugachev*. In the manuscript version of *The Captain's Daughter*, it is related that Masha became jealous of Kharlova on seeing her engaged in a long conversation with Grinev.

44. In the manuscript version these words were spoken by Ivan Kuzmich, rather than Grinev.

45. From *Novoe i polnoe sobranie*, 2, No. 130. A literal rendering in prose.

46. Pugach was Pugachev's nickname, bearing an association with the common noun *pugach*—meaning either "toy pistol" or "screech owl"—derived from the verb *pugat'* ("to frighten").

47. The *sarafan* is a Russian peasant woman's dress; Ivan Kuzmich is thus hoping that the rebels will spare his daughter if they take her for a peasant.

48. It has been suggested that this was probably I. N. Zarubin, nicknamed Chika (described in Chap. 3 of *A History of Pugachev*).

49. From *Novoe i polnoe sobranie*, 1, No. 131. A literal rendering in prose.

50. The Russian reads: *Nebo s ovchinku pokazalos'* (lit., "The sky looked as big as a sheepskin").

51. The Russian idiom is *udacha udalomu* (lit., "success to the bold").

52. The name of False Dmitrii, who succeeded Boris Godunov on the Russian throne in 1605 and was murdered after a reign of about a year.

53. The Russian reads: *Kaznit' tak kaznit', milovat' tak milovat'* (lit., "If to execute then execute, if to pardon then pardon").

54. From M. M. Kheraskov's lyrical poem "Separation" (1796; "Razluka," beginning with the line *Vid prelestnyi, mily vzory*).

55. Pushkin added this reference to the gallows, as well as the following description of Vasilisa Egorovna's body covered with a piece of matting, after the final draft had been copied.

56. Except for the last item, Savelich's list originates from an actual document Pushkin had come across: a petition that a certain Court Councillor Butkevich had submitted to the government in the hope of receiving compensation for the losses he had suffered during the rebellion.

57. This bowing down to the gallows is a later addition to the text by Pushkin.

58. The Russian reads: *S likhoi sobaki khot' shersti klok* (lit., "From a vicious dog you should be glad to get a flock of fur").

59. From Canto 11 of M. M. Kheraskov's *Rossiada* (1778), an epic poem about Ivan the Terrible's seizure of Kazan from the Tatars in 1552. Pushkin begins the quotation in the middle of a line, omitting the subject of the sentence—"the Russian Tsar"—because the parallel between a Tsar and Pugachev would have appeared offensive to the censors; but his readers, brought up on *Rossiada*, could immediately tell what was missing.

60. The censor struck out this sentence in the first edition.

61. The siege of Orenburg is described in Chaps. 3 and 4 of *A History of Pugachev*.

62. See note 43.

63. German for rascal.

64. In the manuscript "poor lad" was given in German at first (*"armer Kerl"*), then changed to Russian (*"bednyi malyi"*).

65. Written, in all probability, by Pushkin himself in imitation of A. P. Sumarokov's fables.

66. The manuscript shows that this passage underwent substantial change as Pushkin worked on it: according to the original version, Grinev would not have tried to ride by Berda but would have gone directly to Pugachev in order to ask for his help.

67. The Russian reads: *Bud' on semi piaden' vo lbu* (lit., "Be he seven spans broad in the forehead").

68. Iuzeeva was the village where Gen. Vasilii Kar, sent by the government to relieve Orenburg, encountered Pugachev; the rebels forced him to retreat with heavy losses. For a description of the battle, see Chap. 3 of *A History of Pugachev*.

69. The reference is to Frederick II (1712–86; r. 1740–86). The Russian army was instrumental in defeating him at Kunersdorf in 1759.

70. The Russian reads: *Ulitsa moia tesna* (lit., "My street is narrow").

71. The tale has not been traced to folklore sources; it is likely that Pushkin invented it.

72. A revised version of a folk song Pushkin himself had recorded. The translation is a literal rendering in prose.

73. A paraphrase of Matthew 6: 7. The original reads: *Nest' spaseniia vo mnogom glagolanii* (lit., "Much speaking will not be your saving").

74. Written by Pushkin in imitation of Kniazhnin.

75. See Chap. 5 of *A History of Pugachev*.

76. The "Omitted Chapter" followed this paragraph in the spring 1836 draft of the novel. For its full text, see Appendix A.

77. This sentence was crossed out of the first edition by the censor.

78. For details, see Chaps. 6 and 8 of *A History of Pugachev*.

79. Can be found in the collection of proverbs *Polnoe sobranie russkikh poslovits i pogovorok, raspolozhennoe po azbuchnomu poriadku* (St. Petersburg: Tip. Karla Kraia, 1822), p. 141, of which Pushkin owned a copy.

80. A. P. Volynskii and A. F. Khrushchev were both executed in 1740 for opposing Empress Anne's favorite, Ernst Johann Biren (1690–1722).

81. This is a chronological error on Pushkin's part, for the town of Sofia, in Petersburg Guberniia, was not established until 1785.

82. The reference is to the Kagul Obelisk, designed by Antonio Rinaldi and erected in 1771 to commemorate General Rumiantsev's campaign against Turkey in the summer of 1770, which culminated in the victory at Kagul.

83. This reflects Russian law under the Tsars, which allowed gentry estates to be divided among all the heirs. Pushkin commented in several writings that ancient families would not have fallen into decline if the law had made the eldest child the only heir.

84. For the "Omitted Chapter," which in the original manuscript came after the first half of present Chap. 13 (see notes 1 and 76), see Appendix A.

A History of Pugachev

1. From the summer of 1832 on, Pushkin was planning to write a historical novel about the time of the Pugachev Rebellion of 1773–74, which was eventually to become *The Captain's Daughter*. It is likely that in the spring of 1833, when he gained access to archival materials about the rebellion, he still had in mind no more than a historical introduction to his projected novel, but the deeper he delved into the source materials, the more he became attracted to the idea of writing a scholarly historical, rather than fictional, account of Pugachev's time. He completed the first draft of such a scholarly study by the end of May, continued researching the subject during the summer, and traveled to the Kazan-Orenburg region—the scene of the rebellion—in September. On his way back from that region, he stopped at his family's estate in Boldino to do some writing in solitude, and it was here that he completed the second draft of his *History* at the beginning of November. In December 1833 he asked for permission to publish his monograph, and Nicholas I—with a surprising gesture of leniency and generosity—not only gave him permission, but granted him a government loan to cover the cost of publication. Among the few changes Nicholas required was that the monograph should be called *A History of the Pugachev Rebellion*, for a villain like Pugachev, in Nicholas's opinion, could not have his own history. (The title was to be restored to *A History of Pugachev* in later editions.) Pushkin spent the better half of 1834 writing the notes, arranging the documents, and preparing the work for the printers. The *History* was published in December 1834. It consisted of two volumes, the first one representing the narrative part with annotations, and the second containing a number of source materials. Because the lengthy and often anecdotal notes to Vol. 1, as well as the documents included in Vol. 2, are of little interest to the general reader, the present translation contains only the narrative part of Vol. 1. Pushkin's notes are mentioned in the Translator's notes only when they are necessary for understanding the text. The narrative part will be of interest to the reader not only as a classic of historiography, but also as a background for *The Captain's Daughter*, which it anticipates in many passages.

2. In February 1833, in order to obtain more material on the Pugachev Rebellion, Pushkin requested from the Ministry of War several documents relating to the famous military leader Prince Aleksandr Suvorov (1730–1800), who had participated, albeit only in the final stages, in the suppression of the rebellion. Pushkin apparently had little interest in Suvorov, but he could not very well be refused access to archival materials on the famous generalissimo, and in creating the impression that he was working on Suvorov, he could lay his hands on some materials relating to Pugachev. The "larger project" is probably a reference to a broader study of Sovorov's times, which the authorities might have assumed he had been working on.

3. By far the most reliable of the foreign sources Pushkin was able to make use of was a French translation of an anonymous German essay, "Zuverlässige Nachrichten von dem Aufrührer Jemelian Pugatschew, und der von demselben angestifteten Empörung," *Magazin für die neue Historie und Geographie*, ed. A. F. Büsching, 18 (Halle: J. J. Curts Wittwe, 1784): 1–50. A French translation was published by Jean-Charles-Thibault Laveaux in *Histoire de Pierre III, Empereur de Russie* (Paris: Maison La Briffe, 1799), 2, 13: 255–360.

4. The most significant of the manuscripts Pushkin is referring to were P. I. Rychkov's eyewitness account of the siege of Orenburg; some 20 short biographies of various personages of the period, including Pugachev, made available to Pushkin by the archivist and historian D. N. Bantysh-Kamenskii, who was at this time preparing his multivolume *Dictionary of Noteworthy People of the Russian Land* (1836); and the poet I. I. Dmitriev's then-unpublished memoirs, containing an eyewitness account of Pugachev's execution. Among the important oral accounts of the events Pushkin heard were the fabulist I. A. Krylov's recollections of his father, Andrei Krylov, who had been among the defenders of the fortress at Iaitskii Gorodok. Most of this material, including Pushkin's notes of interviews with survivors of the rebellion in the Orenburg region, is included in Vol. 2 of the *History*. The question of how Pushkin used his sources is a complex one: sometimes he makes references to them in his notes; sometimes he assumes that the reader can trace them in Vol. 2; and sometimes he simply omits documentation, even though the sources used are not contained in Vol. 2 (which is not to say that he ever departed from verifiable facts). To trace the relationship between his voluminous sources and the narrative text is beyond the scope of annotations to a translation. The reader is referred to scholarly monographs on the subject, among which the following three stand out as most important: G. Blok, *Pushkin v rabote nad istoricheskimi istochnikami* (Moscow: Akademiia Nauk SSSR, 1949); R. V. Ovchinnikov, *Pushkin v rabote nad arkhivnymi dokumentami* ('*Istoriia Pugacheva*') (Leningrad: Nauka, 1969); and Anna Chkheidze, '*Istoriia Pugacheva*' *A. S. Pushkina* (Tbilisi: Izd. SSR Gruzii "Literatura i iskusstvo," 1963). Many of the sources that were available to Pushkin only in manuscript have been published since; moreover, much material not known to him has come to light since he published his *History*. For basic information, the reader is referred to N. Dubrovin, *Pugachev i ego soobshchniki*, 3 vols. (St. Petersburg: I. N. Skorokhodov, 1884); *Pugachevshchina*, 3 vols. (Moscow: Gos. izd., 1926–31); and V. V. Mavrodin et al., *Krest'ianskaia voina v 1773–1775 gg. Vosstanie Pugacheva*, 3 vols. (Leningrad: Leningradskii gos. univ., 1961–70). In English, a good account of the Pugachev Rebellion, based on the findings of modern scholarship, can be found in John T. Alexander, *Emperor of the Cossacks: Pugachev and the Frontier Jacquerie of 1773–1775* (Lawrence, Kan.: Coronado Press, 1973).

5. Pushkin received permission to open Pugachev's case only in the summer of 1835, after the publication of his monograph. Access to this material and new information from other sources prompted him to plan a second edition of *A History of Pugachev*, but he did not live to carry out this plan.

6. Voltaire's name was crossed out of the original edition by the censor.

7. Liubarskii (d. 1811) was the archimandrite of the Kazan Monastery of the Savior at the time of the Pugachev Rebellion, and his manuscript, entitled "A

Brief Account of the Villainous Acts of the Impostor Pugachev Against Kazan" (1774), was among Pushkin's archival sources.

8. The Kazak Kirghizes.

9. Mikhail Fedorovich is Tsar Michael (1596–1645; r. 1613–45), founder of the Romanov dynasty.

10. On the Strel'tsy, see note 32 to *The Blackamoor of Peter the Great* and note 3 to Appendix C.

11. Sten'ka Razin (d. 1671), a leader of the Don Cossacks, led a rebellion against the Tsar in 1670. Pushkin is in error here: in fact many Iaik Cossacks participated in Razin's rebellion.

12. Pushkin notes that at this time a field detachment consisted of 500 men, including infantry, cavalry, and artillery.

13. Later evidence gathered about Pugachev suggests that he was not a schismatic, though he associated with schismatics and at one time used a false passport, assuming the identity of an Old Believer from Poland.

14. After the famed Cossack Sech', or military settlement, on the Dnieper was abolished by Catherine II in 1775, some of its members emigrated to the Danube delta, then under Turkish rule, and established a new, so-called Zadunaiskaia Sech'. The descendants of these Cossack emigrés defected from the Turks at the beginning of the Russo-Turkish War of 1828–29.

15. The Grand Duke referred to is Catherine II's son, Paul (1754–1801), who was to reign briefly (1796–1801) after her death.

16. The Old Believers, opposed to the reforms initiated by Patriarch Nikon in the 1650's, adhered to making the sign of the cross with two, rather than three, fingers, and did not shave their beards.

17. Pushkin explains that the baptized Kalmyks living in Orenburg Guberniia came under the authority of the Stavropol chancery.

18. The Polish Confederates were participants in the Confederation of Bar of 1768, a Polish nationalist revolt against Russian domination that was soon suppressed by Catherine II.

19. This was a Cossack town; Pushkin mentions that normally up to 300 Cossacks were stationed there.

20. Pushkin lists the victims, including an old gardener who had at one time served in St. Petersburg and knew Peter III.

21. Pushkin's information is not quite accurate. In fact Khlopusha was sent with four letters addressed to particular individuals. He was recognized by one of Pugachev's men, brought before the pretender, and surrendered the letters under duress.

22. On the Belaia River.

23. Pushkin describes this barter court as a large center for trade with Asian countries.

24. The *ektenia* is a part of the Orthodox liturgy consisting of versicles and responses.

25. "Father" (*batiushka*) was a popular name for the Tsar.

26. The Samara Line, a string of forts and redoubts, stretched southeastward from Samara on the Volga to link up with the Orenburg Line at Fort Tatishchev.

27. The reference is to the Legislative Commission that Catherine II had conceived late in 1766 and convoked in 1767 for the purpose of considering reforms.

28. Korf, as Pushkin explains in a footnote, had attempted to entice Pugachev to the city gates under the pretext of negotiating the surrender of Orenburg.

29. A *sazhen* is approximately seven feet.

30. The second lieutenant of the Guards mentioned was the poet G. R. Derzhavin.

31. As Pushkin explains, this was Bibikov's grandmother, who had brought him up and later became a nun.

32. "It must be the Chevalier de Tott who is staging this farce; but we are not living in the age of Dmitrii, and the play that was successful two hundred years ago is hissed off the stage today." See Voltaire's letter of Feb. 2, 1774, in *Oeuvres complètes de Voltaire*, 70 vols. (Kehl: L'Imprimerie de la Société Littéraire-Typographique, 1784–89), 67: 289. The Chevalier de Tott (Ferenc Tóth, 1733–97) was a Hungarian engineer who served in the French army. He supervised the fortification of the Dardanelles in 1770, when the Russian fleet was threatening Constantinople. The other reference in the passage is to False Dmitrii, who claimed to be the son of Ivan IV and succeeded Boris Godunov on the Russian throne in 1605.

33. "Monsieur, it is only the newspapers that are making a lot of noise about this brigand Pugachev, who, incidentally, has no connection whatsoever, direct or indirect, with M. de Tott. The cannon cast by the one are as insignificant in my eyes as the undertakings of the other. There is one thing, though, that M. Pugachev and M. Tott have in common: that the one is daily weaving for himself a rope of hemp, while the other risks getting a silk cord at any moment." See Catherine's letter of March 4 [15], 1774, in *ibid.*, p. 291. Catherine was right in that despite his valuable services to the Sultan, Tott suffered a great deal of unpleasantness in Constantinople and could very well have expected strangulation by silk cord (which was the way the Sultan disposed of high-ranking officials who had displeased him). Tott, as it turned out, was not strangled, but he was forced to leave Turkey in 1776.

34. The reference is to Alexander I (r. 1801–25).

35. This was Iurii Bibikov; no relation to the general.

36. The reference is to the fabulist I. A. Krylov (1769–1844).

37. A *pood* is a unit of weight equal to about 36.11 pounds.

38. Pushkin mentions that the name Seitov, derived from the Tatar Seit-Khaialin, was sometimes used for Kargala.

39. The Russian historical term for these serfs is *ekonomicheskie krest'iane*, peasants who had belonged to the Church and monasteries until 1764, when they were put under the authority of the College (Kollegiia ekonomii dukhovnykh del).

40. Pushkin says in a footnote that the old woman's name was Razina. Nicholas I recognized in the passage a reference to Sten'ka Razin and forbade Pushkin to include it, calling it irrelevant to Pugachev.

41. Pushkin was in error in giving Mellin the rank of major here and that of lieutenant colonel on p. 424. In Pushkin's notes and in the documents he copied out, Count Mellin was clearly identified as a second major of the Tomsk Infantry Regiment—a rank equivalent to the later captain. Shurma is to the west of Izhevsk on the Viatka; off our map.

42. Mikhel'son was to command the Dnieper Army against Turkey in 1806; he died in Bucharest during the campaign.

43. Casimir Pulaski had taken part in the Confederation of Bar. After the suppression of the Confederation, he escaped to Turkey and eventually came to America to fight against the British in the American Revolution. His younger brother Antoni had been exiled to Kazan in 1772.

44. In the original the pun involves *vor* ("thief" or "impostor"), and *voron* ("raven") and *voronenok* ("raven fledgling").

45. The passage is an excerpt from I. I. Dmitriev's recollection of the execution; Pushkin gives its full text in a footnote.

46. Just after the two volumes of the *History* were published, Pushkin submitted them to Nicholas I with a set of notes intended for the Tsar alone. These notes, first published in *Bibliograficheskie zapiski*, 6 (1859): 179–81, *Poliarnaia zvezda*, 6 (1861): 128–31, and *Zaria*, 12 (1870): 418–22, contain some additional information that Pushkin must have thought would be of interest to Nicholas. They also include a final section entitled "General Remarks," which stands as Pushkin's conclusion about the events related in his *History*. These "General Remarks" read as follows:

All the common people were on the side of Pugachev. The clergy sympathized with him—not only the priests and monks, but even the archimandrites and archbishops. Only the nobility was openly on the government's side. Pugachev and his companions had tried at first to win over the nobles, too, but their interests conflicted too strongly with those of the nobles. (N.B. The class of managers and clerks was at that time still small in number and was definitely one with the common people. The same could be said about officers who had risen through the ranks. A good many of them could be found in Pugachev's bands. Shvanvich was the only one from a good noble family.)

All the *Germans* in the middle ranks—Mikhelson, Muffel, Mellin, Dietz, Demoran, Duve, etc.—performed their duty honorably, but all those having the rank of brigadier or general—Reinsdorp, von Brandt, Kar, Freymann, Korf, Wallenstern, Bülow, Dekalong, etc.—acted feebly, timidly, and without zeal.

If we analyze the measures taken by Pugachev and his companions, we must admit that the rebels chose the most reliable and effective means of achieving their goals. The government's actions, by contrast, were weak, slow, and ill-advised.

There is no cloud without a silver lining: the Pugachev Rebellion brought home to the government the need for many reforms, and in 1775 the *guberniias* were reorganized. Governmental control became centralized; the *guberniias*, which had been too vast, were divided up; communications among the various parts of the state became more expeditious; and so forth.

Appendix A

1. This chapter is the only one that Pushkin preserved from his first draft of the novel. In the original manuscript it fell halfway through Chap. 13.

2. Grinev here is the Zurin of the final version.

3. Bulanin here is the Grinev of the final version.

Appendix B

1. This fragment anticipates the introductory scene of "The Queen of Spades." It was first published by V. E. Iakushkin in *Russkaia starina*, 3 (1884): 654–55.

2. This fragment, written in the early fall of 1829, anticipates some passages in *A Novel in Letters*, "The Blizzard," and "The Squire's Daughter." It was first published by S. M. Bondi in Pushkin, *Polnoe sobranie sochinenii, Prilozhenie k zhurnalu Krasnaia niva*, 9 (Moscow: GIKhL, 1930): 504.

3. The description of the wayside station, especially of the pictures on the wall, anticipates "The Stationmaster," and the last paragraph, detailing the hero's attempt to find some reading matter, anticipates the introductory part of *A History of the Village of Goriukhino*. This fragment was first published, in part, by P. V. Annenkov is *Materialy dlia biografii Pushkina* (St. Petersburg: P. V. Annenkov, 1855), p. 273. The title has been given to the fragment by editors on the basis of a draft version of "The Stationmaster," where Pushkin indicated that the description of the pictures should be copied from "Notes of a Young Man." On the margin of the manuscript containing the fragment, the following partial outline is written:

The stationmaster, a walk, the courier.
A shower, a carriage, a *gentleman* [in English in the original],
   love.
Native region.

4. The original version of the manuscript, subsequently crossed out by Pushkin, read: "to join the Ch. Regiment in Kiev Guberniia"—a clear allusion to the Chernigov Regiment, stationed in Vasil'kov, which mutinied in December 1825, under the leadership of S. I. Murav'ev-Apostol, in sympathy with the uprising in Petersburg.

5. A reference to Luke 15: 17: "And when he came to himself, he said, How many hired servants of my father's have bread enough and to spare, and I perish with hunger!"

6. This fragment was written on May 12 and May 13, 1830, less than a week after Pushkin's engagement to Natal'ia Goncharova. It was first published by P. V. Annenkov in *Sochineniia Aleksandra Pushkina*, 7 (St. Petersburg: P. V. Annenkov, 1857): 139–42.

7. This note is just a mystification on Pushkin's part.

8. The quotation, given in English in the original, is a combination of the first and last lines of Childe Harold's song from Canto One of Byron's *Childe Harold's Pilgrimage* (1810–18).

9. Henrietta Sontag (1806–54) was a German opera singer who visited Russia in 1830.

10. The manuscript itself bears the title "A Fragment" and the date Oct. 26, 1830. It amounts to a preliminary sketch for the characterization of Charskii in Chap. 1 of *Egyptian Nights*, and was first published posthumously in *Sovremennik*, 8 (1837): 242–46.

11. An allusion to Pushkin's own journey to Arzrum to visit the army in 1829. A similar complaint against the journalists' treatment of his visit occurs in a draft version of his Preface to "A Journey to Arzrum." What hap-

pened was that Pushkin was still on the road when the military correspondent I. Radozhitskii expressed a hope that the poet would derive inspiration from his visit (see *Severnaia pchela*, 101, Aug. 22, 1829, col. 8); and Faddei Bulgarin subsequently censured Pushkin for his failure to do so (see Bulgarin's review of Chap. 7 of *Onegin* in *Severnaia pchela*, 35, March 22, 1830, cols. 1–6).

12. This discussion of ancient Russian nobility relates "A Fragment" to some other works of the same period, such as "The Guests Were Arriving at the Dacha" and *A Novel in Letters*.

13. An allusion to Faddei Bulgarin (1789–1859), who was both a writer and a police agent.

14. This fragment was written on Sept. 30, 1831, and was untitled. It was first published by P. I. Bartenev in *Russkii arkhiv*, 3 (1881): 466–68.

15. Pushkin left several outlines indicating how he might have continued the project. Since these outlines were obviously written only for his own use, he did not attempt to disguise the names of people he was using as prototypes. Most notably, it seems that the main plot-line was to be derived from the experiences of a Moscow lady, M. I. Rimskaia-Korsakova (1764–1832), who had been ambushed and robbed by natives when she had journeyed in a convoy from one Caucasian spa to another in the summer of 1828, and whose daughter Aleksandra had been the target of an attempted kidnaping. The villain of the piece, whom Pushkin implicates in the kidnaping, was modeled on A. I. Iakubovich (1792–1845), a notorious daredevil and scapegrace prior to his involvement in the Decembrist movement. (After 1825 he was exiled to Siberia.) The various pieces of Pushkin's notes and outlines (partially in French) have been arranged in standard Academy editions in the following way:

First version of the basic outline:
Caucasian watering places. A Russian family. Iakubovich arrives. He wants to get married. He gains admission into the family circle. The arrival of the actual lover. The women are enchanted with him. Evening rides in a Kalmyk carriage. The encounter. The explanation. The duel. Iakubovich will not fight. A condition. He disappears. Rumors, amusements, outings. Ambush by the Circassians, kidnaping. Moscow. Iakubovich's arrival in Moscow.

Further elaboration of the first version:
1   His brother, an invalid, is coming from Petersburg. He lets his convoy go with the paralytic and is attacked by the Circassians; he kills one, the others flee. Iakubovich is not there. He asks his sister whether she loves Iakubovich. Laughs at him.
   Iakubovich makes every effort to please him and asks for his sister's hand.
   The duel.

2   Iakubovich kidnaps Marie, who has been flirting with him.
   Her lover rescues her from the hands of the Circassians.
   A Circassian friend—a young man who admires her—spirits her away and returns her to her family.

Second version of the basic outline:
A season at the watering places; spring; who is staying in the Caucasus. An invalid, Major Kurisov, a womanish general, the wife of General Merlini, two physicians. The families get together. The N. family from Moscow. Father and daughter. The father forms a whist party: the invalid, a physician, and Kurisov. The daughter makes friends with a girl the General's wife has brought up. The girl is a sentimental procuress.

The poet, the brother, the lover, Iakubovich, over-ripe marriageable ladies, Iakubovich's gamblers (collaborators).

The day after the card game. All the ladies on the promenade are expecting Iakubovich. He arrives with the brother, who introduces him. They all try to captivate him. He falls in love with Maria. A cavalcade. The Beshtu [Besh-Tau]. Iakubovich asks for her hand through her brother Pelham. Refusal. *The duel.* Iakubovich's second is the poet; the brother's (since Kurisov refuses) is *the lover*, an officer wounded in the Caucasus, who had already been in love with her earlier and who had met Iakubovich in the mountains, had once been fleeced by him.

Iakubovich rides to the Circassian village to see a Prince at night.

At the time of the crossing from the hot waters to the cold waters.

Iakubovich kidnaps her. The other one rides out and rescues her with the aid of a Circassian friend.

Third version of the basic outline:

1   Today's situation in the Caucasus and earlier conditions.
Who were the inhabitants?
General Merlini with his wife. Major Kurilov, the commander of a detachment. A Cossack detachment.
A sick officer, two physicians (rivals, trying to get introduced first).
The arrival of a Moscow lady (her daughter, a companion, two maids, a coachman, a cook, two servants).
After her, Iakubovich's father and General Merlini with his wife. They are attacked by Circassians.

———————————

Moscow, the scene of departure or talk about departure.

———————————

Society at the watering places. Two physicians, Kurilov, an invalid, and an *officer*, who arrived earlier.

2   The old lady Korsakova and the old man Kubovich arrive at the post station. Korsakova proceeds farther, while he trudges back.
Granev, Kurilov, and Khokhlenko are seated by the sulfuric well. Kurilov tells about a Circassian raid. Korsakova is arriving. Schmidt lets Khokhlenko know about it beforehand. The paralyzed, decrepit old man arrives. Khokhlenko looks after him.
Alina flirts with an officer, who falls in love with her. Caucasian evenings. Kubovich's arrival. His father's death. A theatrical funeral. Alina begins to flirt with him. Kubovich is introduced into the Korsakovs' circle. They are enchanted with him. Granev begins to hate him. Iakubovich asks

for her hand; she refuses since she is in love with Granev. He helps the Circassians capture him.

He is let go (by a Cossack girl—a Circassian girl) and comes back to the watering place. Duel. Iakubovich is killed.

Preliminary notes for the third version:

1   Alina is kidnaped by Kubovich to a Circassian village and is rescued. Granev.

2   Iakubovich's Circassian friend, the captor of the officer, the Cossack girl's brother.

The arrival of Korsakova.

The last wayside station. The paralytic talks with Nik. and Korsakova. Society at the watering places.

The Prisoner of the Caucasus, the daughter flirts with him, she falls in love.

The arrival of the paralytic; his death in Konstantinogorsk. The arrival of the son with the Cossacks. The funeral. Everybody there. Flirtation.

The Prisoner's meeting with Iakubovich. An explanation.

A further development of the third version:

Khlapenko, a Ukrainian physician, a poet, a gambler, a soldier, an idler, an inquisitive person. He walks about with a Cossack officer or with a sick tax-farmer, who tells him stories.

A carriage with a Moscow lady drives by. *Khlapenko is late.*

A German takes his place. Where are you going, Adam Adamovich?

16. This fragment may indicate an attempt on Pushkin's part to take up the theme of *The Blackamoor of Peter the Great* once more. It may also be related to the outlines of "A Story About a Strelets" (see below). It has been published only in Soviet editions.

17. The title of this fragment, derived from the name of the hero and bestowed by posthumous editors, obviously refers to Edward Bulwer Lytton's *Pelham or Adventures of a Gentleman* (1828). It was first published in *Sochineniia Aleksandra Pushkina*, ed. V. A. Zhukovskii et al., 11 (1841): 135–41.

18. As for *A Novel at a Caucasian Spa*, Pushkin left several sets of outlines and notes for this project. And, as there, they involve real-life personages, most notably: V. A. Vsevolozhskii (1769–1836), who had conducted an affair with a certain Princess E. M. Khovanskaia and brought her, with her children, into his household after his wife's death, and whose son N. V. Vsevolozhskii (1799–1862) was a friend of Pushkin's; the notorious gambler and daredevil Fedor F. Orlov (1792–1835), whose eldest brother, Mikhail (1777–1842), was a Decembrist, and whose middle brother, Aleksei (1786–1861), helped suppress the Decembrist uprising but persuaded Nicholas I to give a

mild sentence to his brother Mikhail; several other Decembrists, including I. A. Dolgorukov (1796–1843), S. P. Trubetskoi (1779–1860), and N. M. Murav'ev (1796–1834); the Minister of Internal Affairs V. P. Kochubei (1768–1843, also referred to as Chukolei or Chokolei) and his daughter Natal'ia (1800–1855); a number of personalities from the world of the theater, including the dramatist A. A. Shakhovskoi (1777–1846), the actress E. I. Ezhova (1788–1836), and the ballet dancer E. I. Istomina (1799–1848); and finally some men—especially A. P. Zavadovskii (1794–1826) and the writer A. S. Griboedov (1790–1829)—who were involved in famous duels in the period preceding the 1825 uprising. The notes and outlines read as follows (the original partially in French):

I

A Russian Pelham, son of a nobleman, educated by Frenchmen. His father, frivolous after the Russian fashion. Pelham and his cousin, a mediocre *whippersnapper*. Pelham in society; the theater, men of letters, gamblers. He witnesses a young man's dishonorable behaviour. His friendship with Fedor Orlov. He helps him elope with his beloved one; refuses *to cheat at cards*. His brother receives a slap on the face during a card game; duel; the brother gets cold feet.

Orlov elopes with the girl. Her unfortunate situation. Poverty. Her husband's dissipation. She falls in love with Pelham. Her affair with him. The husband's suspicions. Fedor Orlov's death.

Pelham falls in love with a woman of the highest circle. Pelham in high society. Love in high society. His father dies. Pelham in the country. (An episode with F. Orlov's wife.) The neighbors. The life of the Russian landowner. Hears about his cousin's marriage. Goes to Petersburg. His brother becomes his enemy, discrediting him in government circles. He is banished from the city. (Fedor Orlov stoops to brigandage. Pelham is his confidant.) He witnesses an ambush. He is vindicated by F. Orlov himself.

II

Pelham enters high society and, getting bored with it, consorts with bad company.

In the company of actresses and men of letters he meets F. Orlov, becomes friendly with him, refuses to become a cardsharp, helps him elope with a girl.

Continues his dissipated life. His affair with a dancer, to Count Zavadovskii's annoyance.

Fedor Orlov's duel with Pelham's cousin.

The unhappy life of F. Orlov's wife; Orlov falls into poverty, stoops to brigandage.

Pelham learns of everything. Hides him at his house.

Pelham falls in love. His father dies. His transformation; quarrel with the dancer. He sends a marriage proposal. He is refused. He goes to the country.

A robbery. Denunciation. Trial. A secret enemy. A letter to brother, Tartuffe's answer. Learns of his brother's marriage. Despair.

He is freed due to the good offices of Aleksei Orlov; banished from the city.

Mental illness. Gossip in high society. A solitary life. F. Orlov is apprehended in a robbery, Pelham is vindicated, he receives permission to come
to Petersburg.

The dénouement.

Characters

Father and his mistress. A bastard. *Whippersnapper.* Fed. Orlov, Al. Orlov, Kochubei, his daughter; Prince Shakbovskoi, Ezhova, Istomina, Griboedov, Zavadovskii. The Vsevolozhskiis' house. Kotliarevskii. Mordvi-
nov and his associates. Khrushchev. The society of *the clever ones* (Il'ia
Dolgorukov, Sergei Trubetskoi, Nikita Murav'ev, etc.).

In the service; a cadet in the Guards, officer of the Guards, a German
commanding officer, *resignation,* debts, Neelov, Shishkin.

Father's funeral, etc. Extravagant habits. Dinners, men of letters. Iv.
Kozlov.

High society. The Pashkov family, etc.

Gamblers

Orlov, Pavlov.

III

The story of Fedor Orlov. A man-about-town, a kind of Zavadovskii, a
scapegrace, mistresses, debts. He falls in love with a penniless society girl
and elopes with her; the first years splendid, falls into poverty, seeks distraction with his earlier mistresses, becomes a crook and a duelist. Stoops
to brigandage, kills Shchepochkin; shoots himself (or disappears).

The story of Pelham. He meets F. Orlov in bad company, helps him elope
with the girl, refuses to become a cardsharp, serves as Orlov's second in a
duel. Learns from him about his killing of Shchepochkin, becomes the ex-
ecutor of Fed. Orlov's will, comes under suspicion (gives a pawn ticket).
Appeals to Al. Orlov from the fortress.

Episodes

The story of his brother. He buries himself at the chancery. He renounces
his mother, becomes Pelymov's enemy, makes a career, serves as Chukolei's secretary, secretly persecutes his brother, asks for the hand of his
brother's fiancée, marries her.

His mother (Princess Khovanskaia) spends Vsevolozhskii's money on
Porovoi, who is being fleeced by F. Orlov's gang and who receives a slap on
the face, etc.

Natal'ia Kochubei enters into correspondence with Pelymov, warning
him, etc.

A dancer. Pelymov becomes acquainted with her, finds Fed. Orlov at her
house.

Pelymov was brought up in his father's house by seven French, German,
Swiss, and English tutors. Father spends little time with him, though loves
him. They quarrel over Porovoi. His father gives him an allowance of 1,000
rubles a year and turns him out of the house. Dies in poverty. His son buries him.

Bask. translates vaudevilles to make a living. Shakhovskoi, Ezhova, etc., etc.

IV

I. Education. Mother's death. Princess Khovanskaia's arrival with Nigradskii, my altercations with him, his slanders. Tutors. Father's life: he frequents good male society and bad female society. I join the service and enter society.

II. Society life in Petersburg (I receive my mother's share), balls, the tedium of society life caused by the women's quarrelsome nature; following the example of other young men, he retires into male company; becomes friends with Zavadovskii (F. Orlov).

III. The company. Zavadovskii, parasites, actresses, his bad reputation; he falls in love. Pelymov is his confidant.

IV. The elopement. Pelymov becomes a scapegrace in the eyes of society. It is at this time that he enters into correspondence with Natalie. He receives her first letter just as he is leaving the house of Istomina, whom he had been comforting after Zavadovskii's marriage.

V. He is refused admission to Chokolei's house; he can only see her at the theater. He learns that his brother is Chokolei's secretary.

VI. Zavadovskii's luxurious life; he gives dinners and balls. Domestic difficulties. Creditors. Gambling.

VII. Porovoi and his duel.

VIII. A scene at father's house.

IX. An explanation with Zavadovskii.

X. Pelymov breaks with Zavadovskii.

I. A continuation of Pelymof's love affairs.

II. This chapter after the catastrophe. Zavadovskii's wife, F. Orlov becomes her husband. His new friends. Their exploits. They hold up Pelymof in the street. Fed. Orlov recognizes him and turns the matter into a joke.

III. The illness, loneliness, and death of Pelymof's father.

IV. The brother's situation.

V. A murder.

VI.

19. This fragment was first published posthumously in *Sovremennik*, 8 (1837): 247–49.

20. Presumably in Catherine the Great's First Turkish War, 1768–74.

Appendix C

1. In this fragment of an outline, written around November 1819, the beginning of each line is missing because the left top corner of the manuscript was torn off.

2. This outline, written sometime in the years 1821–23, anticipates "The Lonely Cottage on Vasil'ev Island" (see Appendix D).

3. These outlines may indicate that Pushkin was thinking of returning to the theme of *The Blackamoor of Peter the Great*, though the chronology of events referred to in the outlines does not quite mesh with that of the earlier

unfinished novel. The outlines may also have some connection with the fragment "I Have Often Thought." The Strel'tsy, or musketeers, were soldiers of the first permanent, regular regiments of the Russian army, organized by Ivan the Terrible around 1550. In 1682 they were instrumental in the victory of the so-called Miloslavskii party and in the appointment of Sofiia, the child Peter's half-sister, as Regent of Russia. They caused a great deal of trouble to Peter until at last, in 1698, he ruthlessly crushed their rebellion, executing more than a thousand of them. The "conspiracy" mentioned in the first four outlines evidently refers to one of the Strelets disturbances inspired by Sofiia against the Naryshkin party and the child Peter during her regency (1682–89). The fifth outline, which is not necessarily contiguous with the first four, refers to Peter's Prussian campaign of 1711.

4. This outline hints at a comic situation of mistaken identities that Gogol' was to adopt, at Pushkin's suggestion, for the plot of his comedy *The Government Inspector* (1836). Crispin was the conventional name of the wily servant in French and Italian comedies of the 17th and 18th centuries.

5. This outline may have been part of the broader design of *A Russian Pelham;* in any case it refers to some of the same real-life personalities.

6. Charles-Louis Didelot (1777–1837) was a French balletmaster and choreographer associated with the early development of the Russian ballet.

7. "The two dancers. A Didelot ballet in 1819. Zavadovskii. A lover from the gallery. A scene backstage—a duel—Istomina is in fashion. She becomes a mistress, she marries.—Her sister is in distress—she marries the prompter. Istomina in society. They do not receive her. She herself throws parties—disagreeable episodes—she goes to visit a fellow dancer."

Appendix D

1. The story was first published in A. A. Del'vig's almanac *Severnye tsvety,* 1829, pp. 147–217, under the pseudonym Tit Kosmokratov, which hid the identity of a budding young writer called V. P. Titov (1807–91). It was not associated with Pushkin's name until a letter of Titov's, dated 1879, was published in A. I. Del'vig, *Moi vospominaniia,* 1 (Moscow: Izd. Moskovskogo Publichnogo i Rumiantsevskogo muzeev, 1912): 157–58. In this letter Titov disclosed that he had heard the story from Pushkin at a social gathering in 1828, written it down afterwards from memory, shown it to Pushkin, and published it, incorporating some suggestions made by the poet. Other evidence, such as the closeness of the story to Pushkin's outline "The Devil in Love," corroborates Titov's testimony. But even if Pushkin did relate the story orally—as it seems he did—the written text cannot be regarded as genuinely his, and therefore in standard editions it is relegated to an appendix.

2. The German anatomist Franz Joseph Gall (1758–1828) believed that a relationship existed between the shape and size of the skull and mental faculties and character.

3. A reference to F. Bulgarin's story "Poor Makar, or He Who Stands Up for the Truth Is a Real Hero" (1824).

4. A reference to Molière's *Dom Juan* (1665), Act 4, Scene 12.

5. According to Greek mythology, Zeus fell in love with Europa, daughter of the Phoenician king Agenor, and assuming the guise of a beautiful chestnut-colored bull (a "dumb beast"—the Russian word is *skotina,* which

also means fool), he enticed her to climb onto his back, then sped away with her across the sea to the island of Crete. The abduction of Europa was the subject of many paintings during the Renaissance and Neo-Classic periods.

6. The tower of the city administration building on Nevskii Avenue.

7. Titov (or Pushkin) is probably alluding to Stanza 2 of *Svetlana* (1812), the best known of V. A. Zhukovskii's many references to a pale moon.

8. Volkovo Pole means Wolves' Field.

9. A reference to Revelations 13: 18.

10. Tserkov' Andreia Pervozvannogo today stands on the corner of Shestaia liniia and Bol'shoi prospekt on Vasil'ev Island.

PG
3347
.A15
1983

Pushkin

Alexander Pushkin, complete
prose fiction.

$27.95 pbk.

	DATE DUE		

**ERIE COMMUNITY COLLEGE/NORTH
LIBRARY RESOURCES CENTER
6205 MAIN STREET
WILLIAMSVILLE, NEW YORK 14221-7095**